Praise for *Eagle in Exile*

"[*Eagle in Exile*] has the pace and scope of a Michener or Uris epic. . . . Smale's action scenes slash across page after page, intense and bloody. . . . Grab your dagger and sword, for the battle continues."

—*Kirkus Reviews* (starred review)

"The highlight of *Eagle in Exile* is the world Smale built. It's familiar, yet foreign. . . . The depth of knowledge and detail here is usually reserved for more straight-laced historical fiction books—like Bernard Cornwell's *Saxon Stories*—but by infusing those same principles with elements of speculative fiction, Smale winds up carving out something unique for readers."

—*Tech Times*

"There is a lot of action, as well as twists and turns. . . . The thing I enjoyed the most in this story was the growth and expansion."

—*SFRevu*

Praise for *Clash of Eagles*

"*Clash of Eagles* is that rarest and best of alternative histories: the one you BELIEVE, the one that makes sense. Smale has a storyteller's flair for character, and presents an ensemble cast with a depth of detail that George R. R. Martin would approve of. *Clash of Eagles* is a triple threat: It works as a novel, as historical speculation, and as cultural extrapolation. But its real value is singular: It's a ripping good yarn, and one that will keep you reading long past your bedtime."

—MYKE COLE, award-winning author
of *Shadow Ops: Control Point*

EAGLE IN EXILE

BY ALAN SMALE

Clash of Eagles
Eagle in Exile

EAGLE IN EXILE

BOOK TWO OF THE CLASH OF EAGLES TRILOGY

ALAN SMALE

DEL REY • NEW YORK

2016 Del Rey Mass Market Edition

Copyright © 2016 by Alan Smale
Map copyright © 2015 by Simon M. Sullivan
Excerpt from *Eagle and Empire* by Alan Smale copyright © 2016 by Alan Smale

Published in the United States by Del Rey, an imprint of Random House, a division of Penguin Random House LLC, New York.

DEL REY and the HOUSE colophon are registered trademarks of Penguin Random House LLC.

Originally published in hardcover in the United States by Del Rey, an imprint of Random House, a division of Penguin Random House LLC, in 2016.

This book contains an excerpt from the forthcoming book *Eagle and Empire* by Alan Smale. This excerpt has been set for this edition only and may not reflect the final content of the forthcoming edition.

ISBN 978-1-101-88531-4
ebook ISBN 978-0-804-17725-2

Printed in the United States of America

randomhousebooks.com

9 8 7 6 5 4 3 2 1

Del Rey mass market edition: September 2016

For my parents, Peter and Jill Smale

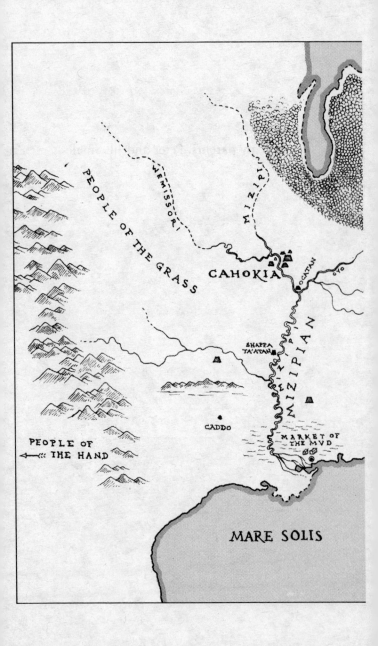

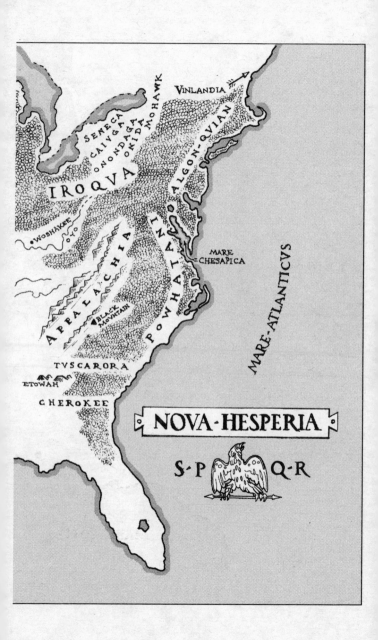

Contents

PART 1

HAUDENOSAUNEE

CHAPTER 1

YEAR THREE, THUNDER MOON

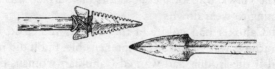

The sky was overcast, the air thick with humidity. The Iroqua captives sweated in their corral in the East Plaza, with the Great Mound and the Mound of the Smoke looming over them on either side. They had been imprisoned there for many weeks in all kinds of weather, with no shelter and minimal food. Water was provided twice daily from a single well-guarded jar. They could drink only as much as their cupped hands would hold.

Marcellinus had seen his fair share of suffering but rarely such extended neglect. Even the slave pens in the ports of Europa and Aethiopia had roofs and reasonably plentiful fodder, but slaves had resale value, and these braves had none.

Cahokian Wolf Warriors ringed the corral. There would be no breakouts or rescue attempts, and even if the gates were opened, the captives would be too weak to run.

These were Cahokia's sworn enemies, brought as low as men could get. This was the fate the rest of the Iroqua nation would face if Great Sun Man could bring it about.

Marcellinus had little sympathy for the prisoners. Any of these men would have delighted in butchering him and the people he cared about, hacking off their scalps to wear on their belts. On the basis of the atrocities committed by Iroqua war parties in the upland villages, he had no doubt that Cahokians in an Iroqua corral would fare even worse. But he did think it was a waste.

Absently, he fingered the golden amulet that Enopay had found for him. He had turned it over and over in his hands so often over the last several weeks that the image of the Hawk warrior incised on its flat surface was beginning to wear down.

If Cahokia had gold and the Iroqua wanted it, the Mourning War would be comprehensible. But it did not. And if the Iroqua had wanted Cahokian women, they would have taken them after the battle. They had taken a few, but it was obviously not the prime reason for their attack.

Revenge was the only motivation left. But really, revenge for what? Where could such unreasoning hatred have come from?

Marcellinus had been standing for some time before he noticed that he was not alone. Just a hundred feet away stood Pezi, who was also staring at the prisoners.

Deep in his own reverie, Pezi jumped when Marcellinus arrived at his side. Marcellinus had not seen the word slave from Etowah since the previous winter.

Embarrassingly, Pezi fell to his knees. "Wanageeska!"

Marcellinus had forgotten how abject a creature the boy was. "Gods' sakes, Pezi, stand up and pretend to be a man."

Pezi stood, eyes still downcast. He had grown an inch or two, and wisps of new hair adorned his chin and cheeks.

"Where were you during the battle, Pezi?"

"I fight for Cahokia," Pezi said.

Marcellinus regarded him calmly. "Who saw you fight?"

Pezi hesitated. "No. I hide down in a grain pit, under a house. I am not good to fight."

"Again?" Such a pit was where they originally had found Pezi, in the mound-builder town of Woshakee up the Oyo River.

Pezi was taller and probably stronger than Tahtay, who had valiantly tried to fight and had suffered a terrible injury to his leg in the attempt. Marcellinus swallowed. "What do they want, Pezi?"

"Who?"

Marcellinus waved at the prisoners.

Pezi shook his head. "To die quickly, I think."

"All the Iroqua. They want Cahokia destroyed, the Mizipian people scattered, scalped, or buried in the earth? Or do they want something else?"

"I do not know."

"Then let's ask them."

Grabbing the boy's arm, he began to walk forward. Pezi resisted, standing his ground. "No!"

"You still speak Iroqua?"

"Of course. But you will learn nothing from those men. Even if they have anything to tell, they will not tell you."

"You know the Iroqua," Marcellinus said bluntly. "You speak their language. And here they are, attacking Cahokia. But really, Pezi, why? For Cahokian land? Cahokian corn and women? Access to the Mizipi? Roman weapons? I don't think that's all of it. I really don't."

"I do not know."

Marcellinus loomed over the boy and held his gaze. "You understand your life belongs to me?"

"Yes."

"And you know I can have you put in there—" He indicated the corral. "—with just a single word?"

Pezi gave a little whimper.

"I've lost my legion and most of the friends I once had here. I have very little left to lose, Pezi. And you would not be the first translator I've killed for talking out of both sides of his mouth. So tell me the truth before I lose patience. What do you know?"

"The Iroqua fear Cahokia," said the boy. "There was war in the past. Many Iroqua raids and Cahokian raids. Now, with you here, the Iroqua fear that the People of the Mounds will come and kill them all. So they must strike first."

"Nonsense."

"Yes. Haudenosaunee lands and lakes are small, and the Cahokian and mound-builder rivers are long. And now Cahokia rules the air. What else can the Iroqua do?"

Just what Marcellinus had thought when he saw Sintikala's great map of Nova Hesperia. But hearing the words from Pezi's mouth made him resist the idea. "Cahokians do not want Iroqua lands. What threat is there to the Iroqua from mound builders? Will Cahokians force Iroqua to build mounds? No. What reason is that to attack mound-builder villages and towns and wage war on Cahokia itself?"

Pezi looked away. "As you say."

If Cahokia were Roma, the threat to neighboring lands would be obvious. But Great Sun Man was not an Imperator, and surely the Iroqua lands had nothing that Cahokia could possibly want.

"Pezi, how did the Mourning War start between Iroqua and Cahokia?"

"Because of you, making Cahokia stronger."

"No. Long before me. Generations ago. Was it because the Iroqua wanted Cahokian women?"

Pezi paused. "Long past, many lives ago, this city was not here."

"And before? Did the Iroqua live here?"

The boy laughed scornfully. "By this big greasy river that bursts its banks every spring? The Iroqua would not live here. But on the Oyo, the Iroqua were strong. Then came Cahokia, and then the Oyo belonged to the mound builders, too, and the Iroqua had only the lakes."

Marcellinus thought about it. "Pezi, the time may come when I will ask something of you. It will be just one thing, but you must do it. Afterward you will owe me nothing. Your life will be your own. But if you do not do what I ask, the whole of this land will not be big enough for you to hide from me. Do you understand?"

Pezi was already pale and shaking. "What must I do?"

Marcellinus released the boy. "When I am ready, I will tell you."

"I am looking for Wachiwi," Marcellinus said.

The warrior Takoda sat cross-legged on the ground. His left arm cradled Ciqala, his son of two winters; his right arm was splinted and heavily bandaged from the wounds he had received protecting Marcellinus in battle. From the other side of the fire his wife, Kangee, made a wordless grunt of disgust. Their newborn, whose name Marcellinus did not know, lay sleeping in a cradleboard on Kangee's back as she built the fire.

If it had been only Takoda, Marcellinus might have explained. But he did not really care what they thought, and especially he did not need to explain himself to Kangee, who had always loathed him.

"Is Wachiwi alive? Just tell me where she is."

"Ask Hanska," said Takoda.

Marcellinus was taken aback. He would not have thought that the fierce warrior woman Hanska and the gentle Wachiwi would know each other. "And where is Hanska?"

Takoda nodded to the southeast, then sighed. "The way is hard to describe. I will fetch Hanska here to you if you will bring us firewood and water."

"I would bring you firewood and water anyway if you asked," Marcellinus said.

Kangee spit into the fire. It fizzled. "We don't need his help."

"With two babies, and Ina like that?" said Takoda wearily, nodding toward the hut where his mother, Nahimana, lay. "And me with a smashed-up arm? If we don't need help, who does?"

Kangee stalked off without another word, squatting in front of a neighbor's fire and casting foul looks over her shoulder. Once she was safely out of earshot, Takoda said after her, "Hey, by the way, Marcellinus saved my life at Woshakee."

Takoda was referring back to a conversation many moons ago, a lie that Hanska had suggested he tell Kangee to make her warm to the Roman. Marcellinus smiled, grateful at even the pretense of humor on such a dour day. Shrugging sadly, Takoda put his son on his hip and walked away across the Great Plaza.

Marcellinus fetched a wheelbarrow and packed as much wood into it as he could. On his second trip he brought back four large jars of water. He also brought one of the new metal fire stands and a cooking pot that was the right size to fit it. By the time Takoda returned with Hanska by his side, bouncing Ciqala in her arms, Marcellinus had restarted the fire, heated water, and stepped down into their hut to bathe the still-comatose Nahimana.

Nahimana had survived the sack of Cahokia by the Iroqua with flying colors. She had worked without cease or sleep for the next two days looking after the wounded and then, quietly and with little fuss, had suffered a stroke. Now, two moons later, she still lay unconscious most hours of the day. The left side of her face hung piteously slack. Yet another casualty of war on Marcellinus's conscience.

Takoda looked sad. "Wanageeska, you don't have to do that."

"Yes, I do."

Hanska cleared her throat and handed Ciqala back to his father. "Need help, sir?"

It was the first time Hanska had ever called him "sir" as if she meant it.

"Yes. Help me turn her over. Wait outside, Takoda. No son should see his mother like this."

Gently and almost effortlessly, Hanska hefted the frail form of the elderly woman and rolled her onto her front. As for Hanska, long smears of the white salve on her legs and right shoulder were the only remaining signs of the wounds she had sustained fighting the Iroqua, though she seemed to favor her right side. "So you want Wachiwi?"

"Just to talk with her." Marcellinus rinsed his cloth in the pot of warm water.

"Talk only?"

"Yes. Believe it or not."

Hanska plucked the cloth from his hand. "This is woman's work. I am still a woman," she said, and took over the task of cleaning Nahimana, doing it more thoroughly than Marcellinus would have dared. Grateful, he looked away.

When they left the house, Kangee was back.

"Hey, little Kangee," Hanska said. "If the Wanageeska wants Wachiwi, he wants Wachiwi. Is it for you to sneer?"

"I did not speak of this to you, warrior," Kangee said.

"Well, I speak of it now. Answer me."

"It's all right, Hanska," said Marcellinus.

Hanska loomed over Kangee, and the shells braided into her hair rattled. "He's saved Cahokian lives. Made us strong. The Wanageeska has done more for Cahokia than you ever will. All *you* do is breed and spit."

Takoda stood. "Hanska. Please."

"Come on, then," she said to Marcellinus.

They walked a little west of south, past a flooded borrow pit toward an area of Cahokia where Marcellinus rarely went, the neighborhood of the cloth workers, leather tanners, and makers of moccasins. Despite lying on a line directly between the two main battles with the Iroqua, it appeared relatively unscathed.

Hanska strode beside him. Marcellinus had never been alone with her before. He wanted to thank her for keeping him alive, for standing over him and defending him as he lay stunned from the Huron's club, but he knew she would say something offhand and contemptuous if he dared mention it. After all, he would have done the same for her. They were warriors. "So you know Wachiwi?"

"Yes."

Marcellinus eyed her, uncertain. She looked irritated. "What? No. What you are thinking now? All men think that, because they are men. But Wachiwi and I have not been lovers. We were friends long ago, as children."

This was a surprise. "I would not have thought it. You are very different."

"You say so? Because I am not pretty like Wachiwi?"

Once again the ground was shifting under his feet. Marcellinus really was "no good chieftain of women," as Sintikala once had told him. "I did not mean—"

"We were different from other girls. She was Onida, taken from the Iroqua. And I was not girl-like."

Marcellinus remembered Tahtay's young friend Hurit, bloodied by bullies the previous year for being too interested in making bricks in Marcellinus's brickworks. "Yes, I see."

Hanska threw him another sharp look. *I see?* Yes, he had said the wrong thing again, implying an insult.

In fact, Marcellinus found Hanska spectacular. Well muscled, statuesque, but still strikingly female, she could have been cast in marble in the Roman Pantheon. But she was one of his warriors. It would not be proper to tell her that.

Futete. He would never lead the First Cahokian in battle again. But still she daunted him. He resorted to hand-talk. *You strong. Beautiful. I sorry.*

Hanska faltered and dropped her gaze. Perhaps she was regretting saving his life. But when he looked back, he found she was making hand-talk, too. *We know what it is to be different. That why you-I friends, too.*

Wachiwi, Hanska, Marcellinus. All outsiders. All very different. Marcellinus was embarrassed that he had never before thought of Hanska as a friend.

"I have bearberry tea," he said. "Let us drink some."

Finally he earned a grin. "You want to see Wachiwi."

"At another time, then. As friends." Her husband, Mikasi, he now remembered, was also an outsider, born far away in the grassy prairies across the Mizipi to the west of Cahokia. How ignorant he was about people that it took him so long to decode such obvious connections.

Hanska leaned in to him. "Maybe. But sir? This time, be more nice to Wachiwi. Or you and I will never drink tea."

A hot flush filled Marcellinus's cheeks. Naturally, Wachiwi would have spoken to Hanska of her brief physical relationship with him. All at once the warrior woman's habitual rudeness and overfamiliarity made sense.

"I mean Wachiwi no harm," he said. "If I hurt her, I did not mean to."

Hanska laughed. "Do not worry. Wachiwi is tougher than either of us."

They had walked past the last of the leatherworkers and were approaching a single house standing apart from the others, close to a low ridge mound. A small figure had seen them coming and was waiting outside.

Wachiwi and Hanska hugged. It was odd to see, the tall and muscular clasping the petite and shapely.

Wachiwi made no move to greet Marcellinus but regarded him neutrally, her arm still around Hanska's waist. He cleared his throat. "Hello, Wachiwi."

"It is all right?" Hanska said to Wachiwi in the tenderest tone he had ever heard from her.

Wachiwi nodded.

"Then I go. Wanageeska. Sir. If there is other help you need, come to me and Mikasi. Yes?"

Once more, breathing was hard. "Thank you, Hanska."

As she released Wachiwi, Marcellinus added, "In fact, Hanska? Rather soon I might need someone to watch my back."

"Again?" she said wryly, and strode away.

Wachiwi folded her arms around herself. She had been crying, Marcellinus now saw. "You are really all right? Not hurt?"

"Not hurt by Iroqua," she said.

"You have lost family?"

"What family? I have none. But many warriors I knew, men who were kind to me; they are dead now, from war. And others, too, who were not warriors."

"People who are not warriors should not die in war," Marcellinus said.

She gestured at the blanket that lay against the side of her hut, and, gratefully, he sat. Her hair was loose in mourning. He was used to seeing it like that only after lovemaking. It was appealing, and it distracted him.

"Gaius. Some say that all the death is your fault. But I do not think so."

Marcellinus grimaced. The unexpected support of Hanska and Wachiwi was almost as difficult to bear as the scorn of Enopay, Kangee, and Great Sun Man had been.

Wachiwi touched his arm. "Your Cahokian is very good."

"Thank you." It certainly felt odd to speak to her directly in Cahokian. The last time Marcellinus had seen her, his Cahokian had been rudimentary and they had communicated using simple Latin phrases, gestures, and touch.

She assessed him. "I will spend one night with you, Gaius. For comfort. But not more."

"That is not what I want." Sensitized by his clumsy words to Hanska, not wanting to give offense, he added, "You are beautiful, and I thank you. But that is not why I came."

"Then what?"

"I came to talk. I want us to be friends, Wachiwi."

"You have so few friends?" she said, unconvinced.

"Few now. And . . ." He took a deep breath. "You still speak Iroqua? You know of Iroqua things? Then I need your help."

Wachiwi put her hands up to her temples. "What?"

"Once you were Onida."

"I am of Cahokia!"

"But once—"

She shook her head violently. "The Onida are not my people."

"But still you can speak that tongue?"

She hand-talked: *No. No.*

"Wachiwi?"

"Look at this," she said. Her sweeping gesture encompassed the whole of Cahokia. "All of our hurt and death. That was Iroqua, all the Peoples of the Longhouse. Caiuga and Onondaga and Mohawk and Seneca . . . and Onida, Gaius. I remember their words, of course. But to speak them? I would die. The words would choke me."

"You don't know why I am asking," he said gently. "I need to understand. There are many things I need to know about . . ." He had been on the verge of saying "your people," but he let his words trail away.

"I do not care." Wachiwi was shaking. "They have hurt us and killed so many. Do not make me even speak of them, Wanageeska. You will not ask me."

Even in denial, her arms opened to him for comfort. He pulled her close, kissed her forehead, rubbed her shoulders. "All right, Wachiwi. Shhh."

"Do not ask me," she said. "I would die."

He had thought to get Wachiwi to help him interrogate the Iroqua captives to gain more recent intelligence of their customs, their language, their lands. He needed to understand. But the germ of the plan that had been forming in his mind was hopeless, anyway. It would probably never work, and he would just get more people killed.

Marcellinus gave it up and cared for Wachiwi instead.

CHAPTER 2

YEAR THREE, FALLING LEAF MOON

The autumn was a season of healing, a time for rebuilding burned houses and mourning the Cahokians who had died in battle. But it was also a time to replace the fallen Wakinyan and improve the Eagles, develop better throwing engines, and belatedly finish the palisade that enclosed the inner part of the city. Make more weapons. Teach more men and women to fight.

Marcellinus played his small part. He helped rebuild the brickworks and bring it up to full production again. When he could, he helped the steelworkers, but by now they were vastly more experienced than he was at forging metal.

The First Cahokian Cohort drilled without him under the command of Akecheta and sometimes directly under Great Sun Man. The Hawk craft of the Catanwakuwa clan trained almost constantly, flying up from the steel launching rail behind the Great Mound to loop and soar over the city.

Marcellinus was allowed to consult on the new, lighter siege engines. The Cahokians were building them two at a time, ballistas that threw huge bolts, like crossbows on wheels, as well as the more ungainly and unpredictable onagers. One afternoon he helped a special team strip a siege engine into its component parts, each of which could be carried by just one or two men, run the pieces up the Mound of the Flowers, and then rebuild it, using it to launch the Hawk warrior Demothi into the air over the great Mizipi River as an encore.

Marcellinus had lit a spark that would never be snuffed out.

The Cahokians were becoming a modern army before his eyes.

Great Sun Man no longer invited Marcellinus to the sweat lodge of the elders, although he was sometimes invited by Kanuna or Howahkan when Great Sun Man was not there. The war chief did not, however, exclude him from councils with the clan chiefs. There Marcellinus had learned that Sintikala and her Hawks were working at a feverish pace to bring back intelligence, map out the Iroqua lands, and help plan for the retaliatory strike the next year. Cahokian confidence was building.

The sick headaches from his terrible wounding in the battle persisted long into the fall and died away only gradually. Eventually Marcellinus could turn his head quickly without feeling dizzy, could even break into a trot without suffering an instant sick pain in his forehead and the back of his neck. There were still days when thinking was difficult and he lived in a fog and even had occasional black depressions that took until evening to shift. On those days he would walk endlessly around Cahokia, across Cahokia Creek to the northern farmlands, or paddle a dugout across the Mizipi and hike west into the grass, growing stronger in his body while he waited for his mind to clear.

His rekindled friendship with Wachiwi grew. He never pressed her to talk about her Onida childhood, but some evenings she brought it up herself. Once begun, her stories dredged up further memories. Some were pleasant recollections of her earliest years, others ugly, jagged images of the fighting between the Onida and the mound builders, the vivid terror of her abduction by Cahokian warriors, her first sight of the great city on the Mizipi, and the subsequent kindnesses of the Cahokian women in her adopted family. Her forced marriage to a Cahokian warrior and her abandonment once it became obvious that she could bear him no children.

It was a tale almost as distressing for Marcellinus to hear as for Wachiwi to tell. Many times he begged her to stop, but spilling her pent-up memories appeared to give her comfort. He, in turn, shared some of the horrors of his own past and his unease for the future, and obtained a measure of relief from that.

His three translator children, his first friends in Cahokia, he saw only rarely.

Enopay, the budding civil servant, had been absorbed into Great Sun Man's entourage. From what Marcellinus gathered from Kanuna, Great Sun Man had come to rely on the boy for accurate counts of the city's population, weapons, and food supply.

Now a full member of the Hawk clan, Kimimela was training intensively with Sintikala, Demothi, and the other pilots. She spent most days in the air or walking her wing home from some distant landing, and most evenings she was exhausted. As clan leaderships followed the maternal line, if all went well and she continued to grow in confidence and strength, Kimimela could expect to lead the Hawk clan one day.

As for Tahtay, the youth spent most of his time hiding from Dustu and Hurit and his shame, and limping on his twisted leg, using a stick as a crutch. One day Marcellinus saw him struggling up the steps of the tall Mound of the Sun, where Great Sun Man used to live before he moved back up onto the Master Mound, and hurried to talk to him.

"Oh, you," Tahtay said on seeing him.

At the boy's hostility, Marcellinus hesitated. "Can I help? Is there something I can fetch?"

"No."

They reached the first plateau. Marcellinus was breathing heavily. His head injury had left him unable to train properly, and despite the long walks, his physical fitness had ebbed away.

Grimly, Tahtay turned and began the long walk back down. Marcellinus watched for a moment, confused, then hurried to catch up with the boy.

"I do not need another shadow," Tahtay said. "The one I already have hurts me enough."

Marcellinus glanced left. It was true; Tahtay's long shadow magnified the ungainliness of his halting progress. It looked more like the shadow of Howahkan or Ojinjintka.

"All right. But now that I am here, I must go down, too. Will you sit with me at the bottom? I can get us tea or a pipe."

"A pipe?" Tahtay laughed bitterly. "You say so? I am not a man."

"You are a man, and one day you will be a great man." But as Tahtay's shadow hobbled beside them, Marcellinus faltered.

"Yes. I will be."

Even with the stick, Tahtay surely was putting too much strain on his injured leg. How could Marcellinus tell him that?

"I will walk again like a man. I will be a warrior again."

"Perhaps. But for that you must rest and heal."

"I am the son of Great Sun Man," Tahtay said.

Tahtay would never be able to earn the paramount chiefdom of Cahokia. "Of course you are," said Marcellinus.

"And I will walk again."

"Tahtay, you are walking now."

"No. I am not."

"Let us sit and talk."

"I will not sit. You can be no help to me. Go and make things for Cahokia. Kill Iroqua. But let me be."

"Tahtay. You were my first friend here, and you will always be my friend."

The boy stopped and leaned on his stick. "Please, Hotah. No more talk. I must walk alone."

"Tahtay . . ."

"Go away."

Marcellinus stepped past Tahtay and went home.

Smoke swirled above the sacrificial fires to the north, south, east, and west, and up high on the mound tops. It was midafternoon in the Great Plaza, and Cahokia had gathered for the rededication of the Mound of the Chiefs and the adjacent Mound of the Hawks that bounded the south side of the plaza. The ceremonial charnel houses at the peak of each mound had been rebuilt in crisp new wood and straw and shone golden in the sunlight.

Tonight would be a new moon again, meaning it was a full four months since the Night of Knives. To Marcellinus it felt like only days. His sense of time was still faulty; he would occasionally raise his head from what seemed a profound concentration and be unsure whether it was morning or evening around him and how much time had elapsed since he had last moved. His headaches had gone, but the confusion remained. He could only hope that he would eventually make a complete recovery with more rest, more quiet, more tea.

Here at the rededication of the mounds there was drumming and flute playing and many songs in the archaic version of the mound-builder tongue that Marcellinus generally heard only at festivals and feast days. Though the sun shone bright, this was the time of the shamans and the storytellers. Marcellinus's mind wandered.

Then the Wolf Warriors marched in the last of the Iroqua prisoners.

A season of hunger and deprivation had wrought havoc on the fearsome fighters of the Haudenosaunee. The light of life no longer glowed in their eyes. These were hopeless men, their hands bound with lengths of sinew. Blood leaked from their arms and legs, torsos and eyes, where battle wounds had long gone untreated. Nor had they even been permitted to bathe; a strong reek emanated from them, the stench of the latrine mingling with the sickly sweet aroma of gangrene.

Yet again, but as startling as if it were a new thought, Marcellinus realized how easily he could have ended his life like one of these unfortunates if Great Sun Man had not spared him. Marcellinus had been a novelty. He had owned value by virtue of his peculiarity, his incomprehensibility, the odd habits of the fighting force he led, his potential for providing information.

How well that had all worked out.

Time shuffled forward again, like a broken captive. Elders had stepped up and now stood by the Iroqua with knotted cords in their hands, waiting to dispatch the men. The prisoners were lined up in front of a deep trench in the Mound of the Chiefs, where they would be buried to serve Cahokia's former chiefs in the afterlife. Their blood would fertilize the new grass, and the Cahokian honored dead would sleep more easily in their burial mounds.

Marcellinus was among barbarians. He rubbed his eyes.

An Iroqua screamed briefly before the strangling cord choked off his last breath and he sagged. The prisoner was so light and weak after so many days of starvation that even Howahkan, the elder who held the cord in his hands, could support his weight. Leaning down, the elder sliced open the veins of the dying captive with an obsidian blade. Iroqua blood spilled.

By the Roman's count there were a dozen Iroqua sacrifices and only eight elders standing ready to slay them. Some of the grand old warriors of Cahokia would have to do double duty. He was grateful that Sintikala was not up there, or Anapetu or any of the other clan chiefs. Women as warriors, deadly and unforgiving in battle, Marcellinus had grown accustomed to. Women as executioners would be too much for him to bear, especially the calm, clever women he relied on to maintain his own precarious sense of reality.

The next prisoner was an Onondaga warrior who could not have been older than twenty winters. His braids were loose, and short hair had sprouted along the temples that previously had been shaved for battle. The fierce tattoos on his chest stood out in stark contrast to his weakened, abject state. He looked like he might throw up or faint at any moment.

No elder stood behind this prisoner. Great Sun Man strode along the line, a cord of death in his hand.

From the crowd, Tahtay hobbled forward onto the sacred mound.

Dead silence fell. Great Sun Man halted. Tahtay kept coming, climbing the Mound of the Chiefs with difficulty until he stood with the elders. The Onondaga brave on his knees squinted up at the boy.

Great Sun Man's eyes were ashen. "Tahtay?"

"It is my right," Tahtay said harshly, his voice carrying easily across the crowd. "I am still your son, *son of chieftain.* Will you tell me no?"

His people watched. Mute, Great Sun Man handed the hempen cord to his son and stood back.

"Me," said Marcellinus. "I will tell you no."

Tahtay's head swiveled, and his mouth dropped open. Around Marcellinus, people gasped. A man he did not know reached for his arm in warning.

As he walked from the crowd and ascended the mound, Marcellinus held the boy's eyes, not blinking. "I say no, not today."

"You say?" Tahtay pointed down at his leg. "See? See? And why?" He waved at the people around them, who murmured. Marcellinus did not know what they were saying, did not know if he was shaming Tahtay or profaning their sacred ceremony by interrupting it in this way. He did not care anymore. He was not a savage, and Tahtay of all people did not need to be one, either.

"Yes, Tahtay, we see that you are wounded. You are broken, and you are healing. And yes, it is because you were struck by a cowardly Iroqua in war."

Tahtay pointed at the Onondaga who knelt at the edge of the abyss. "And so his life is mine if I claim it. Why not? Because I am not deserving? Not my father's son? Who are you to say so?"

"No, none of that. But Tahtay, your first kill should not be a man in defeat on his knees and almost dead already. Your first kill should be as a warrior in battle."

"Huh."

The leading shaman, Youtin, stared at Marcellinus. The crowd was silent. Great Sun Man glared but said nothing. No one knew what to do about this.

"Tahtay, hear me. You will remember your first kill. Make it a kill for Cahokia, a kill you will boast of in the sweat lodge when you are old." Marcellinus raised his boot and shoved the Onondaga. The captive fell on his side, unresisting. "See? This man is already dead."

"You do not understand, because you are from another place." Tahtay raised his chin high. "This is the Mound of the Chiefs, and the death of this verpa makes it strong. This killing is good medicine, brave medicine for Cahokia."

"Verpa?"

A Roman curse on a Cahokian mound. Rites Marcellinus would not understand if he lived to be a hundred.

Marcellinus bowed to Great Sun Man, to Tahtay, and to the crowd. "If I act wrongly, if I intrude here, I mean no disrespect to you or the elders or your great chiefs of the past."

Great Sun Man nodded.

The Onondaga lay on the grass. Tahtay looked at the warrior and then up at Marcellinus, who held out his hand.

Tahtay laid the cord gently on his palm, but his tone was still rebellious. "Then why you?"

"Because I have killed many men. Because I have nothing left to lose."

The prisoners would all die today in any case. Why should their blood not stain Marcellinus's hands as well? As much as any man in Cahokia, Marcellinus deserved to share the task and the blame. Better even, quicker and more merciful to die at his experienced hands than at those which might be hesitant or ineffectual.

Marcellinus tugged the Onondaga upright. The warrior looked almost relieved that the talking was over and his ordeal was coming to a close.

Marcellinus wrapped the cord around the man's throat and yanked it tight. His pugio slashed a deep furrow in the Iroqua's neck, and the gush of blood warmed his fingers. When he was quite sure the man was dead, he pitched the body forward into the trench.

Even as he did it, Marcellinus felt another wound tear open in his soul. Killing Iroqua in war was one thing. But this, this . . .

Sweat stung his eyes, and his hands began to shake. He had lied. He had told Tahtay that this meant nothing to him, but it did. It meant something.

Marcellinus tried not to let that show on his face.

"For you," he said tersely to Tahtay. Handing the cord to Great Sun Man, he stepped down to take his place among the common people of Cahokia.

Sintikala landed on the first plateau of the Great Mound. Even watching from the West Plaza, several hundred yards away, Marcellinus could tell she was weary from the way she trotted to a halt. The wind against the tall Hawk wing on her shoulders nearly pushed her over.

She was in the air almost every day, out on scouting runs. Sometimes she was away for days, having failed to make it home before the warmth and the winds gave out, and then she had to sleep rough and walk back to Cahokia or wait on a ridge for the weather to cooperate.

Now Sintikala looked up the mound. From where she stood, she probably could not see the large new Longhouse of the Sun on its crest, on the opposite side of the top plateau from the Longhouse of the Wings, but she obviously had seen it many times from the air. With its copper-lined walls, the Longhouse of the Sun literally shone.

He could sense her reluctance as she began the walk up the final cedar steps to the top of the mound.

That evening after dark as Marcellinus cooked his

beans and cornmeal outside his hut, he heard approaching footsteps. His heart leaped, but it was just Kanuna. Marcellinus tried to conceal his disappointment.

Bundled in furs despite the remaining warmth of the day, the elder squatted by the fire. Perhaps one day Marcellinus's blood would run thin, too. He was not looking forward to being old in this village in the center of Nova Hesperia, where the winters seemed to last forever.

"Some food, Kanuna? Tea?"

"I do not like the new house of Great Sun Man." Kanuna rubbed his hands together.

Marcellinus raised his eyebrows ironically. "You come to tell me this?"

"The shaman Youtin, and the rest of the shamans, and Iniwa of Ocatan, they have all told Great Sun Man that he must live at the top of the Master Mound, where he will hear Ituha's voice and be strong."

"Yes." Marcellinus peered left. The permanent flame outside the new longhouse blazed in the night.

"Ituha lived up on the mound, you see."

"I know, I know." Marcellinus pulled the cooking pot away from the fire and tossed in some purslane, watercress, and sliced wild onions to season it. "Ituha lived up on the mound when he made one Cahokia out of three, but afterward he chose to come down and live with his people."

"And a little while after that, he lost his power over Cahokia."

"Because of bad harvests," Marcellinus said.

"No, because he stopped listening to the voices of the gods," said Kanuna, and grinned companionably to let Marcellinus know what he really thought.

"Ah, yes, of course." Marcellinus dipped a spoon into the pot, blew on it, and took a bite. Even after all this time he still missed salt. "Do we know what Huyana thinks of this?"

"Great Sun Man's wife agrees with the shamans." Kanuna shook his head.

"But Kanuna the elder, wise and well traveled, does not."

"Would I be here?"

Marcellinus got few visitors. He smiled at the elder. "Perhaps. I thought we were friends. Sit, Kanuna, and I will make us tea, and you can watch me eat corn and beans, and we will talk."

Kanuna remained squatting. Perhaps that was just as comfortable for him. "Do the gods live on high? Is Great Sun Man close to Ituha?"

"You ask me? I have not met your gods."

"But you know your own."

Marcellinus, about to reply, hesitated. Eventually he said, "I do not hear them. No gods, no ancestors."

"What does Sintikala say?"

"Sintikala does not speak to me either." He kept eating.

"Really?" Kanuna sighed. "I had hoped she did. But I suppose Sintikala is not often here. She flies around too much."

"She is here tonight. She came home in the late sun." By the way Kanuna turned and stared to the east of the Great Mound, where Sintikala's house lay, Marcellinus realized the elder had not known this. "Maybe you should go talk to her instead."

"Me?"

"You are the one with the questions."

"But you are the one she will not turn away."

"You are mistaken. I am not of the Hawk clan, and I have an uneasy treaty with its chief. If anyone, I was Great Sun Man's friend . . . but that was before."

"I do not think so. But either way, I think her tea is better than yours." Kanuna stood. "And I am safer when I can hide behind you. Well? Come."

Marcellinus grimaced.

"Wanageeska. I am a wise and well-traveled elder, and you are just a man. A boy, perhaps, since you have never been through the Cahokian coming of age and your hair is very short. I think you have to do as I say."

"A boy?" Marcellinus said in some amusement. "I see how it is, Kanuna."

Shaking his head, he got to his feet.

Over the last moon Marcellinus had not strayed far from the path between his house and Wachiwi's. Shunned by Great Sun Man and ignored by most of the other Cahokian high class, he had avoided the Master Mound and its environs altogether. The last time he had been in this area, Sintikala's house had been a smoking ruin, burned to the ground by the liquid flame of the Iroqua.

Her new house was a revelation. Twice as large as the old one, it extended over much of the earthen platform on which it rested. Its clay daub was so fresh that it glowed pale white in the starlight, and its trim palisade looked as stout—if nowhere near as high—as the one that surrounded Cahokia's central precinct. Great Sun Man was not the only one whose accommodations had taken a turn for the better.

Kanuna called up to Sintikala from the base of her mound, and Marcellinus almost curled up in embarrassment at the realization that she might not be by herself, that Demothi or some other strapping brave of the Hawk clan might be sharing her evening. But she was alone, stepping out to peer down at them over the palisade while still drying her face with a blanket and inadvertently repeating the words of Kanuna, but in a much more tuneful alto voice: "Well, come."

Inside, the house was less splendid. Built swiftly and hardly lived in since, it contained none of the elegant baskets or fine pots that had adorned the walls of Sintikala's previous home.

They sat while she built up the fire. Tiredness lined her eyes and she was obviously chilled to the bone, but at Marcellinus's offer of help she snapped at him to be still. Kanuna gave him a reproachful look for trying to impose on a woman's hearth, and they waited in silence.

Finally they had tea, which Sintikala slurped down as if she had spent the day sitting out on Mizipi River ice.

It must be colder, Marcellinus thought, up high in the air at this time of year.

"Well?"

Kanuna allowed Sintikala to pour him more tea and then explained his concerns: with the Longhouse of the Sun, Great Sun Man was creating a palace for himself high on the Master Mound, like a petty chieftain of a more primitive time; he was growing increasingly distant from his elders and his people, preoccupied with his gods and ancestors.

"Huh," said Sintikala. "And so now he is a bad war chief?"

"I do not know. The warriors—"

"And you want to be Great Sun Man yourself, Kanuna? Or put another man in his place?"

"No! No."

"Then what?"

"This does not worry you, then?" Marcellinus interjected. "I have known other great chiefs of their people—by which I mean my own people, of course—who considered themselves far above other men. It does not end well."

Sintikala did not respond, but loosened her braids and untangled her hair with her fingers. It was matted with sweat and twisted into knots by the wind. Marcellinus had never seen her with loose hair. It softened the lines of her face and made her look unexpectedly vulnerable. Once again, Marcellinus wished Kanuna had not brought him there.

She had been silent for many minutes. At last the knots were out of her hair, and she spoke. "Kanuna, Wanageeska. I agree that it may not be a good thing for Great Sun Man to build his new house. It might lead to jealousy and to him not feeling so easily the heart of his people. But hear me: I believe he feels that the defeat . . ." She paused and stared into the fire. "He feels that the suffering and hurt of Cahokia are his fault and that they arise from his failures as a man and as a chief. I would think that each of you would understand this, just a little . . . Wanageeska, are you all right?"

Marcellinus had put up both hands to his temples but had forgotten he was holding a cup. Warm goldenrod tea had splashed onto his neck and shoulder. "Yes. Sorry."

Certainly Marcellinus understood the idea of failing as a chief. He cleared his throat and pulled himself together.

Sintikala poured more tea into his cup without being asked. "It is nearly winter, with many moons until spring. I think that Great Sun Man will prepare us well and that in the spring he will lead Cahokia into battle with the Iroqua as no chief ever has before. I believe we will win a great triumph."

"You are young," Kanuna said bluntly. "I hope you are right, but perhaps you are not."

She grinned at him, not offended.

Marcellinus's frustration was rising. "That isn't the point. The point is that Great Sun Man is living up there to better hear the voices of his gods and his ancestors, which is all nonsense. And taking advice only from shamans . . . Such men are adept at telling you what you want to hear."

Sintikala shrugged. "Of course. I fly in the sky all day. If being up on the Great Mound helps you hear the voices of the gods, up in the clouds I should be deafened by them. But that is also not *the point*."

"Then what is?"

Her lack of concern was alarming. Marcellinus needed her to be as hard and contemptuous with Great Sun Man as she was with him. The Sintikala he had grown used to would have a clear view of the danger.

Ignoring the question, she turned to Kanuna. "I am tired and hungry. Why did you come? Did you want me to speak to Great Sun Man of this? I will. But Great Sun Man is Great Sun Man."

Kanuna's brow wrinkled. "In my life I have been far to the south and the east. I, like Gaius, have seen what chiefs can become when they seek fine things for themselves and the small group of men closest to them and do not live among their people. I would not wish that for Cahokia."

"It will not happen here."

Marcellinus said, "But when—"

Sintikala turned on him, and the steel was back in her expression, even under her wavy black hair with its echoes of intimacy and sorrow. "It will not happen! Not while I live. Yes?"

From his seated position, Marcellinus bowed.

She pushed her hair away from her face and appeared to relent. "Eat with me," she said. "Both."

"I . . ." Marcellinus thought of his dinner at home, and had already spent too much time in Sintikala's presence; between her power and the crackle of the fire, there was no breathable air left in the room. But Kanuna placed his hand on Marcellinus's arm to still him and replied for them both. "Yes. We thank you, daughter of chieftain, and we would be honored."

"Great Sun Man reclaims what is his right. Always before, since Cahokia was made, the greatest chief has lived on the greatest mound. And Great Sun Man sees any clan chief or elder who goes to bring him news or needs his counsel. At least now we always know where he is. He is much easier for us to find than when first you came to Cahokia, Gaius, or any time in the last ten winters." She looked thoughtful. "And it is easier to safeguard him there from those who might wish him ill."

Marcellinus spooned fish into his mouth. It was seasoned with a leaf he did not recognize. Sintikala was a better cook than he was, though he doubted she had to catch her own fish or harvest her own herbs.

He said, "How often has Great Sun Man been out of Cahokia?"

Sintikala eyed him. "His place is here."

"But?"

She took another mouthful of fish and bit at a hazel-

nut cake. "He has led many war parties deep into Iroqua land, and he has been to smoke a pipe in peace with
his brothers in Ocatan and in the river towns to the
north and also to the west. And to Woshakee. And many
chiefs have come here to visit."

"No farther?"

Sintikala raised her eyebrows. "It is far that he went,
especially to the north. And he has the wisdom of Ojinjintka and Kanuna and others who have traveled. And
he has my eyes and the eyes of the other Hawks."

"I see," said Marcellinus.

"Perhaps he is ignorant, then," she said ironically.
"With only the three of us to advise him, and all of the
other clan chiefs, and the rest of the elders, and Akecheta and Wahchintonka and his men of the Wolf Warriors, and Enopay and Tahtay."

Marcellinus fell silent.

"I trust Great Sun Man, and I will not make plans
against him. If that is what this is."

"We make no plots and schemes. We merely worry."
Kanuna grinned apologetically. "We are old men. Fretting is our job." Marcellinus winced at that designation.

"Then talk to the people and not just to each other,"
she said. "The people *want* more strength from Great
Sun Man. A war chief who walks among them, who is
only a leader when he needs to be, is no Great Sun Man;
he is just a man. Kanuna will remember that there was
much talk of it when Great Sun Man kept a house with
Nipekala, mother of Tahtay, down in the city. Now they
see where this common living has brought them. The
Iroqua have burned Cahokia and killed Cahokians."

"That is not Great Sun Man's fault," Marcellinus
said. "If it is any man's fault, it is mine."

She shook her head. "It is not yours. But many think
this is a time for a strong leader. They will be surprised
to hear that they are wrong."

"I agree," Marcellinus said, straight-faced. "Better to
sit at home in his big shining copper longhouse. And

perhaps you should also stay home here at the top of your mound in your nice new house."

"All this space." She shrugged. "It is too big. Too hard to keep warm. But all the clan chiefs have such a house now."

She had brushed it off, but it was enough for Marcellinus to know that she had understood him. He let it drop. "And where is Kimimela?"

Sintikala smiled at him quickly. "She did not know that I would return home today. She is with Luyu of the Wakinyan clan."

Marcellinus remembered Luyu. She was the granddaughter of Ojinjintka, a painfully skinny girl who was apprenticing on the Thunderbird flights. "Luyu is almost light enough to blow away into the air without needing a wing."

The mood lifted, and they gossiped for a while in a much more relaxed vein. But when Sintikala began to yawn, Kanuna immediately got to his feet.

"Thank you for seeing us," Marcellinus said. "It has been too long."

She looked at him quizzically.

"I mean too long since we have talked. Not that the evening has lasted too long. Um. Quite the opposite."

"The opposite of what? I think I am too tired to understand you."

Marcellinus smiled and stood. "I mean that I enjoyed speaking with you and the food was good."

He walked to the door with Kanuna.

"Gaius?"

He turned.

"You think that Great Sun Man *wants* to lead a giant war party against the Haudenosaunee? No. But he must, and Great Sun Man will do as he must until he dies. We must have our vengeance. The humiliation of Cahokia cannot stand. Iroqua blood must flow or they will attack us again. If there was a way to stop this . . ." She sighed. "There is not. Blood must have blood. He will lead us to victory. But for this he must prepare himself, and for that he cannot always be walking in the city preparing others. It is not so easy to be Great Sun Man."

"No," Marcellinus said.

"And you, Gaius? Your worry about Great Sun Man and your anger? I think perhaps you are not happy at being left out."

That rocked him. Was it true? Did he resent and mistrust the new elite merely because he was not a part of it?

"I will think about that," he said. "Sleep well, Sisika."

Sighing, she shook her head.

"I mean Sintikala."

"Good night, Kanuna, Gaius."

CHAPTER 3

YEAR THREE, LONG NIGHT MOON

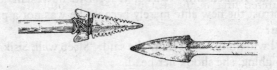

In the dead of winter, Marcellinus floated a thousand feet above Cahokia.

The Sky Lantern he rode in was tethered to a tall platform mound directly east of the Master Mound. The Raven clan now had the launches down to a straightforward routine.

In a few days everyone would be another year older. Tahtay would become fourteen winters. Kimimela would become eleven winters. Enopay? Marcellinus still didn't know. Despite his threats he had never asked Kanuna how old the boy was. Enopay's age was Enopay's business. His Raven clan chief, Anapetu, was right: Enopay was neither a child nor an adult but a new thing all his own.

And Marcellinus? He would be forty-four winters old, but preferred not to think about that. He was so cold up here, he could easily catch a chill and die before the Midwinter Feast anyway.

This feast would be a muted affair. A celebration would seem out of place after the carnage that had followed the Midsummer Feast. Canceling the feast would be disrespectful to the memory of the dead, but it was clear that no one's heart would be in it.

Of course, to calculate the exact day of midwinter, Youtin the shaman would need to see the sun at sunrise or sunset from the Circle of the Cedars and note where its path intersected the horizon. And nobody had seen the sun for many days.

The land was stark beneath him, the trees bare of leaves. The grasslands across the Mizipi looked more like tundra, flat and desolate. Soft glows of red from scattered fires in the distance were the only traces of color: hearth fires outside the tipis of the braves who lived out on the plains.

To the east was the floodplain with its clusters of houses and the frozen lakes in the borrow pits. Beyond them the river bluffs rose up, with homesteads on their lower slopes. The huts on the crest were far distant specks. Even farther away, Marcellinus saw wisps of smoke from the upland villages.

After their experiences that summer, nobody was about to take chances. An Iroqua raid in the middle of winter would be almost impossible. Ninety-nine guesses out of a hundred had the Five Tribes frozen tight in their lands near the Great Lakes, feasting and gloating in their longhouses and looking forward to springtime. But Great Sun Man would not rule it out, not after Enopay had sketched out a scenario for how it might be done. A series of corn stashes hidden in a line across the land, stealthily prepared; a fair estimate of what each brave could carry in baskets and litters; yes, with determination and ingenuity, it could work. And even a small Haudenosaunee raid in the dead of winter would be yet another terrible blow to Cahokian morale.

So despite the cold, the scouts were out on foot, the Hawks were in the air, and the Sky Lanterns were aloft daily to keep watch. Nobody had seen any sign of Iroqua yet, and Marcellinus saw none today. The land was just as frozen as the river.

Ohanzee perched on the opposite side of the Lantern's stout wooden frame, muffled in his buckskin and furs. By virtue of hard work and an almost suicidal courage, Ohanzee had become a leading member of the Sky Lantern teams. It was he who had devised the current launching method for the Lanterns, which was much less labor-intensive than the original scheme; it involved three fires in a line, a small bellows, and a steep—and, crucially, portable—wooden ramp to lay the bag on while it was being inflated. It was also Ohanzee who had been the first man to fly untethered. Ohanzee loved heights and had been known to stand up on the narrow frame and walk around on it, adjusting the ropes that held the frame to the bag while the Sky Lantern was careering across the landscape in full flight.

Although Marcellinus respected the broad-shouldered warrior and studied every detail of his operational mastery of the Lanterns, the two men rarely talked. From the very beginning Ohanzee had harbored a deep distrust of Marcellinus, a suspicion that had eased only marginally in the time since. He would never warm to the Roman now, and that was the second reason Marcellinus often chose him as a copilot: Ohanzee was unlikely to start a conversation. Aside from his determination to do his duty by Cahokia and take his turn at the very worst of jobs, Marcellinus went up in the Sky Lanterns for solitude.

The Master Mound looked strangely flat from overhead. The new Longhouse of the Sun had grown even since Marcellinus's last sentry flight. It was now almost the same area as the Longhouse of the Wings and much shinier. Marcellinus had never been inside, but from Sintikala and the elders he knew it contained many rooms, the cedar walls within lined with galena, hematite, and fine quartzes. In its main hall stood a birdman figure in exotic chert, greater than life size, and around the walls were other figurines, giant stone arrowheads, fire bowls, and ornate structures of shell. Great Sun Man himself was rarely out of his chiefly garb, with a new engraved copper gorget and lengths of mica and mussel-shell beads. Marcellinus shook his head.

No boats decorated the rivers, no dugouts or canoes. Winter was a time for sewing clothes and moccasins and making jewelry of shells, beads, and bone; for sharpening blades and tying arrows; for telling children the sacred stories that could be told only when no animals were around to spy on the humans and hear them. Also, since most people were indoors keeping warm, winter was also the smokiest time of the year. Even up here, Marcellinus could taste its acrid veneer on his tongue.

Marcellinus was wearing six pairs of Roman leggings, heavy fur-lined boots, and as many tunics and leathers and furs as he could put on himself and still be able to move his arms and legs. His face was covered aside from a narrow strip for the eyes. If he reached out a hand, he could feel the heat from the deep fire jar that kept the Lantern aloft, but the basket and rigging were designed to keep the heat flowing into the tall cotton bag that kept them aloft. Warming the crew was not a priority.

On the ground below, a few insects walked out to the creek for water. A few more clustered around the Big Warm Houses, waiting for their turn in the heat. Across the floodplain a plume of black smoke indicated that the metalsmiths were hard at work. It was not difficult to keep the steelworks staffed on a chilly winter's day like this.

And south of Cahokia, another dark square shape was marked out on the land. It was not a plaza, though it was as big as one. Even today in the harsh cold, braves walked its straight avenues, halting to bend and check, then walking again, as they made their systematic patrol. It was a sight Marcellinus had never before seen from above or had ever expected to see again from ground level until a Roman army returned to Nova Hesperia.

It was half formed and a little primitive, nowhere near as disciplined in its construction as Marcellinus would have liked, and currently almost unpopulated. But it was still very recognizable, as it would have been to any other Roman soldier if there had been one nearby to see it.

*   *   *

"Hello, young Enopay," Nahimana had said as the boy stepped down into the hut a few weeks earlier.

Enopay had almost jumped out of his skin. His mouth dropped open, and for a moment his blank expression resembled Nahimana's ancient face more than a little. "You speak?"

"I talk. I walk." Nahimana hobbled over and stoked the fire. "Again, I do all the work around here."

"She means that she complains and once more makes our lives a daily misery," said Takoda from the corner of the hut, where he was sewing extra flaps of hide onto a moccasin for warmth.

Nahimana lobbed a small piece of firewood at him, and he grinned. One side of her face remained slack and probably always would, but with the onset of the cooler weather and the patient help of Takoda, Kangee, Hanska, and Marcellinus, she had regained almost all her coordination. To everyone's surprise she had begun speaking again shortly after the first frost, and Marcellinus was gratified to see the same surprise mirrored on the boy's face now.

"That is good," said Enopay, still startled. "I had not thought."

"That I would get better? Ha."

"She will never die," Takoda said cheerfully.

"Tea?" Nahimana offered, and Marcellinus stood to pull the metal fire stand over the flame, for the old woman was still not strong enough to do that unaided.

Enopay looked sideways at Marcellinus.

"It's sassafras tea," he said quietly to the boy in Latin. "Nowhere near as awful as the clover slop she made before."

"Phew," Enopay said gratefully, and plopped himself down beside the fire.

"We have not seen you for a long time," Nahimana said.

"I have been busy," said Enopay, "for Cahokia."

"How is Great Sun Man's high temple to himself coming along?" said Marcellinus, which earned him a look of reproach. "Sorry, Enopay. He is just so different now."

"To plan a war is not an easy thing." Enopay leaned forward to help Nahimana scoop the dried flowers into the pot for the tea.

"So I am told," Marcellinus said wryly.

"There are things Great Sun Man wants to know." Enopay cocked his head at Marcellinus. "The Eyanosa is very ancient, but he may still be useful to Cahokia."

"'Eyanosa,'" Nahimana said, and cackled. "Big in all directions." It was a joke that never wore thin.

Marcellinus stared into the flames of the fire pit. "Great Sun Man told me I was no longer to lead the First Cahokian. Great Sun Man was angry with me for many things. And now he wants something from me?"

"You still eat Cahokian corn. He has not driven you from the city. And so you must work, too."

Enopay's face was kind, and he grinned in apology. He was only relaying the message he had been told to bring. Still, Marcellinus was irritated. "Every day I work for Cahokia. I help to make bricks and throwing engines. I train individually the few warriors who will still speak to me. I carry water and wood to families who need it. I do sentry duty by night and keep watch from the Sky Lantern by day. All of which Great Sun Man would know if he did not live always in his copper house at the top of his very large pile of earth."

"He does know this because I tell him so, and so does Sintikala and every other chief and elder. But he has indeed grown different, Eyanosa. Perhaps we all have."

"Not me," Nahimana said.

"No, because you are a nut that cannot possibly shrivel any more," Takoda said.

"Hush." The water in the pot was boiling, and the strong scent of the sassafras helped combat the reek of smoke in the small hut. "Enopay, I am happy to serve Cahokia. What does Great Sun Man ask of me?"

"With your Romans you made a strong camp every night. A camp like a plaza surrounded by a palisade of earth that you and your men could defend against attack. We want that."

"Castra," Marcellinus said. He remembered a conversation in the sweat lodge nearly two years earlier during which he had confidently believed that the Cahokians would never build such a thing in his lifetime. Times certainly had changed. "A castra is not such a simple thing to build. It requires—"

"Later." Enopay sipped his tea. "Tell Great Sun Man and the warriors who will build it. We will try it and see if Cahokians can use a Roman camp to march on the Iroqua."

Marcellinus thought about that.

"Do not make such a face," Enopay said. "We have all winter to practice and prepare."

"The Roman tents are probably full of mold and holes," Marcellinus said, but the boy was shaking his head and smiling.

"I had the tents unloaded from your Roman wagons long ago. We have hung many from the rafters in the Longhouse of the Thunderbirds and smoked them. Our castra will be smaller, and we need only half your tents to be usable. It will work."

Marcellinus should have known that Enopay would not have come to him until he had an opportunity to be smug about his own cleverness. "Even so—"

"If we can make mounds and throwing engines and wheelbarrows and palisades and steel and Sky Lanterns, we can make castra," said the boy reasonably enough. "Can I have more tea?"

Marcellinus had not thought to look upon a castra again until the Romans returned. Then again, he had not thought to see another longship until the Vikings came back, either.

For now, the earthen ramparts were marked out rather than being as deeply dug as they would have been by legionaries. The winter ground was much too hard for the sustained digging of trenches. However, the perimeter of the camp was the least of their worries. No one doubted that Cahokians could build long piles of earth.

The castra was complete now, the tents being aired out and treated against the damp, new tent poles being hewn where needed. They were leaving it up so that the Wolf Warriors could get familiar with it; the regimented lines and relative confinement were not initially comfortable for them. But to maintain the safety and ease of so many warriors behind so small and defensible a perimeter, a castra it would have to be.

Bathhouse, castra, siege engines. Roman army formations. Marcellinus had hoped this would begin to feel comfortable to him, too, one day. It did not. With every day that went by, he felt a larger mass of foreboding at the changes he had wrought here.

And when his headaches began to return, Marcellinus knew for a fact that this was not how things should be in Nova Hesperia.

He could think of only one solution, and it was still as half baked an idea as it had been when he'd first thought of it.

The line of the tether binding them to the earth had begun to bend into a deeper arc, showing that the Sky Lantern was gradually losing height. Ohanzee threw more wood and charcoal into the fire jar. As the new fuel caught, both men felt the tug as the Lantern drifted higher into the winter skies.

Marcellinus surveyed the horizon. He was up there to watch for enemy incursions, not to sightsee and think his gloomy thoughts. He was too far along his path to deviate now. He could not turn back the calendar. He had been trained in Stoicism. Right now, a little more of it might serve him well.

No invaders would come. Ice would keep the armies of the Haudenosaunee at bay and the warriors of Cahokia at home. His new people would have the winter to themselves to lick their wounds and heal as best they could.

This winter was only half done, by definition, but for the first time Marcellinus did not look forward to spring.

Tahtay walked across the Great Plaza, alone as always. He carried no stick and was not exactly limping, but the steps he took on his right leg were visibly shorter than the strides on his left. Nonetheless, Marcellinus had not thought that the boy—a young man, really, in terms of age—could have come even that far.

Off to the left a group of Turtle clan warriors were playing chunkey, rolling a carved stone disk across the ground and flinging spears after it. Their cheerful shouts and banter touched Tahtay not at all. He did not look at the warriors or even glance to either side as he walked.

Marcellinus had seen that hopeless look on many men's faces. He had felt it on his own.

He thought of Hanska, Mikasi, Wachiwi, himself. Tahtay had been born to a great family but had now become an outsider, partly by fate but also partly by choice.

It would not do.

Marcellinus ducked into his hut and came out again carrying two swords. Striding into the plaza, he threw one of them at Tahtay's feet.

"What is this?" Tahtay asked. His voice had deepened and he had grown taller over the last couple of moons. Or perhaps he just no longer stooped as he had after the battle.

"You see what it is. Pick it up."

Tahtay looked at him warily. "Why?"

"We are going to fight."

"Fight?"

Marcellinus grinned. "Not to the death, Tahtay. I am not as foolish as that. But it is time for you to start your warrior training again."

"You say so?" Tahtay looked around him for the first time. Nobody was paying them any heed, for which Marcellinus was grateful. He had no wish to humiliate the boy. But neither had he any intention of letting Tahtay leave the plaza without picking up the gladius.

"Yes. Today we will work on the positions of the sword. Tomorrow we will bring in Mahkah and Hanska and practice with sword against spear, one man against two or three. Gladius, spear, pugio, shield. Fists, too. Because you have a lot to learn, and you are not learning it now, hobbling around the city pretending to be dead."

Tahtay regarded him sadly. "I know what you try to do, Wanageeska."

"Pick up the sword."

"You try to make yourself feel better about—" He gestured down at his leg. "About bringing this to me. Not getting to me in time. You do not need to. It was war."

"Cahokia needs warriors. I want you to fight at my side."

"They say you will not fight again," said Tahtay. "They say you are broken."

"They are saying you are broken, too," Marcellinus said brutally. "Who is right? Are the cowards right who talk behind their hands about us? Or do you and I decide whether we are broken men?"

"I am not a man."

"No," Marcellinus said. "And if you walk away from that gladius, you never will be. And you and I will be all-done."

Tahtay paused. "Good. Perhaps it is past time."

"Pick up the sword or limp away. Fight or hide. Choose."

The moments stretched out. The wind picked up, and Tahtay shivered. A Hawk flew up from the top of the Master Mound and looped around quickly to land again on its first terrace. After a round of arguing that came perilously close to a brawl, the chunkey game began again. Spears glided through the air not far away. Still Tahtay stood, and Marcellinus waited.

Tahtay nudged the gladius with his moccasin. "It is not because we are friends. It is because you owe me.

You do. Not for the battle but for all the time I wasted guiding you around Cahokia and learning your useless Roman-talk."

"I never asked you to."

Tahtay bent and picked up the sword.

Marcellinus swung at him immediately, but Tahtay expected that. Their blades met, then Tahtay dipped his shoulder as he came out of the parry and swung at Marcellinus's unprotected thigh. The Roman jumped back, but the move had unbalanced the boy and he dropped forward onto his good knee with a grunt.

Marcellinus did not help him up. He raised his sword high and whipped it down, pulling the strike at the last second. But Tahtay's gladius was up to parry anyway, in the fifth position of the sword. Once again the plaza echoed with the ring of steel.

Marcellinus stepped back. The young Turtle warriors had stopped their game and stood watching them, open-mouthed.

"You are too slow," said Tahtay. "Weak. Out of practice."

"You say so? Stand up."

And for the first time in months, Tahtay smiled.

CHAPTER 4

YEAR FOUR, GRASS MOON

Cahokia was whole again. No scars from the burning and pillage remained. At least none that were visible to the eye.

Great Sun Man came down from his high mound. He seemed as bluff and good-natured as ever, but the new lines by his eyes betrayed him. He and Enopay strode the streets and neighborhoods of Cahokia, the boy sometimes adding a skip to his step to keep up with his chief. Wherever Enopay went, his bag went with him, and in the bag were strips of deerskin parchment and slabs of bark, neatly indexed on their edges with shells and beads in a code that only Enopay understood. If Great Sun Man needed a fact or a figure, Enopay could produce it. He would have looked for all the world like a shorter version of a Greek adjutant who had served Marcellinus in his campaign against the Khwarezmian Sultanate if the Greek had worn braids.

These days Tahtay was more often with Marcellinus than with his own father. Marcellinus's military cadre had shrunk to a mere handful: Mahkah, Takoda, Hanska, Mikasi, and Tahtay. Sometimes Kimimela would come to visit; it was she—over all his protests—who kept his tunics and moccasins wearable, for Marcellinus was the master of a sword but a complete dunce with a needle, whether of bone or steel. Kimimela claimed she needed the practice, as it was part of her duties to sew and repair the fabric of the wings she flew daily, and he welcomed her company and her endless stories of flying. She was growing like a beanpole and her arm muscles were becoming substantial, but she still giggled like a little girl when she got carried away with the simple joys of her tales.

Sintikala, Marcellinus saw rarely. How she could fly so high or so far in winter and early springtime with so little assistance from heat rising off the ground was a mystery to him. Certainly no other Hawk could match her in the air. Kimimela—lightly, as if it were a joke—claimed that her mother was kept aloft by rage. And when Sintikala was not flying, she was in the Longhouse of the Sun in consultation with Great Sun Man or on the mound tops training other Hawk pilots.

All in all, Marcellinus was growing increasingly irrelevant. He had infected Cahokia with his ideas, and now the contagion was spreading by itself. He suspected that if he died tomorrow, it would make little difference to the eventual course of the war.

Unless . . .

He folded the thought away. After all these months, it was still barely a plan. If he mentioned it to anyone else, they would think it either treachery or lunacy and suspect he had not truly recovered from his blow to the head.

So be it.

Marcellinus went to look for Wachiwi—and beer.

In the fading days of the Grass Moon hundreds of warriors from Shappa Ta'atan and the other downriver towns and villages arrived to help Cahokia in its war. Rather than enter the strong palisade that now surrounded Cahokia, they were shown straight to the castra. This had moved around by several hundred yards in each direction as the Cahokian warriors practiced striking and rebuilding it but was now situated largely where it first had been erected, surrounded by high earthen embankments and with firing platforms at each corner.

As Marcellinus watched glumly from the Northgate of the castra, a voice came from behind him. "Ah, you are here."

Marcellinus turned and stood up straighter. "Great Sun Man."

The war chief wore his customary kilt and feathered cloak, copper gorget and beads, but had left the heavy mace of office behind. He looked somber, and his hands hung by his sides. "Wanageeska. How are you?"

"I am recovering. My head aches more rarely. And you?"

Great Sun Man shrugged and looked past him at the Shappa Ta'atani exploring the tents. "War."

"Yes."

The chief waved at the camp. "This is good, Wanageeska. Easier to protect from Iroqua attack." He glanced sideways at Marcellinus. "Castra is why we could not slay you by night as you marched with your legion."

Marcellinus grinned. "Well, then. A good thing we always had one."

Great Sun Man examined the sky, looked behind him, and seemed to come to a decision. "Wanageeska, what you did on the mound . . ."

Marcellinus shook his head. "Which mound?"

"With my son. With Tahtay. Killing for him instead of letting him kill. And then afterward, much after, with the sword. I have been told of that." Great Sun Man looked uncomfortable. "And so I must say to you: after the battle, on the Mound of the Sun, my words to you may have been . . . raw. Angry. Not just."

Marcellinus swallowed, not trusting himself to speak.

"Wanageeska. Thank you for bringing my son back to life."

Marcellinus looked away. "You are most welcome, Great Sun Man."

"Welcome?"

"I mean, I thank you."

"Good. And so you will come to war with us?"

"To war? With the Iroqua?"

"Of course."

The trees were budding. New green decorated the crowns; new white blossoms were on the dogwoods. And once again it was time for war.

"I don't know," Marcellinus said. "You told me I would not command."

"I said that. Now I unsay it. I will give you back the First Cahokian." Great Sun Man peered at him, perhaps trying to read his expression. "The hundred-and-hundred warriors who still trust you and can do clever tricks other warriors cannot."

Marcellinus stared at the ranks of Roman and Cahokian tents.

"Wanageeska? Gaius?"

"All right," he said. "Thank you."

It was all Marcellinus could say. He had to agree to be useful to Cahokia so that he would be allowed to stay.

"You are . . . welcome," said the war chief.

But after Great Sun Man walked into the castra and Marcellinus stood a few moments longer, he realized that he had already made his decision.

He would not be going to war. And he would not be living in Cahokia much longer.

"Ohanzee will be here soon," Marcellinus said, and the three Raven clan braves nodded. Above him the Sky Lantern bag swelled and billowed like a living thing, struggling to rise off its ramp. The young Cahokian maintaining the second launching fire goosed it with a small pot of liquid flame, and despite himself Marcellinus jumped at the controlled explosion. The glow warmed his cheeks in the breezy chill of the dawn.

He tied his bag onto the wooden slat and loosened the cords on his deerskin cloak. Chogan, the warrior preparing the fire jar, looked disdainfully at the fur lining; spring was well advanced, and most braves had put their furs away. "Yes, yes, I'm getting old," Marcellinus grumbled. "You sit up there in the wind for half the day dressed as you are now and then we'll talk."

The Lantern bag soon stood vertical, an undulating tower of cotton. The wooden frame stirred and scraped a few feet across the ground before the tether halted it. Smoke bloomed out of the top of the fire jar. Marcellinus walked around the Lantern, scrutinizing it professionally, and Chogan did the same thing. The others were looking around for Ohanzee. It was not like him to oversleep.

Marcellinus took his place on the Sky Lantern frame next to his bag and tested the balance. Much of the wood and charcoal and the ranked pots of liquid flame were to his right and left. He got off the frame again to adjust the position of one of the piles of wood and then climbed back aboard. Better.

Chogan pointed to the young brave tending the second launching fire. The brave muttered and went to get his bag and buckskin. If Ohanzee did not show up, he was the one doomed to spend most of the day in the air above Cahokia with Marcellinus, staring out over the fields and grasslands at nothing. Without exception the men loved free flying and hated the tethered sentry duty. Once the original excitement of being high in the air with Cahokia spread out beneath them had worn off, it was drudgery at best, cold and dangerous at worst; that was why they were happy for Marcellinus to go up so often in their stead.

That left two braves with Marcellinus. The Lantern strained, more than ready to be off.

"I'm sorry," Marcellinus said.

"What?" said Chogan.

"Tell Great Sun Man that Wanageeska did this of his own will."

The men looked at each other.

"Tell him I am loyal to Cahokia. But tell him we must have peace." Marcellinus grinned. "And tell Ohanzee I am sorry I misled him about who would fly today."

Realization dawned. Chogan darted forward, but it

was too late. Marcellinus had released the iron bolt that held the tether to the frame.

Already straining at the leash, which was weighted for two passengers but carrying just one, the Sky Lantern used its buoyancy to hurl itself aloft. As it surged out of the lee of the Master Mound, the wind caught it, knocking the bag sideways at a steep angle and spinning the frame. Marcellinus clung on for dear life.

He had never been aboard a Sky Lantern in free flight. His excursions had been limited to tame controlled ascents for guard duty, with the tether being paid out gradually until the Lantern swung at its sentry altitude of about a thousand feet. Now it was only moments before his Lantern surpassed that height and kept on going up, up, up. People on the ground soon became almost invisible, and the Great Mound and Great Plaza shrank to the size of a pebble and a small square of cloth. Never had Marcellinus been this high, not in Lantern or Hawk, Thunderbird or Eagle.

Peering far behind, he saw a Hawk leap up from the Master Mound but quickly lost sight of it. It could never catch him. Perhaps even Sintikala could not fly at the height he was now approaching, and still he was rising. And Sintikala and Kimimela were away from Cahokia today. That, along with the wind strength and direction, had been his necessary condition for making his escape.

He hurtled northeast with the wind, past the ridge mound that marked the edge of the city. Already he was much higher than the river bluffs that bounded Cahokia to the east. As he crossed them, the land changed color and became fields.

He was *cold*. His hands were already losing feeling. Forcing himself to release his hold on the Lantern frame, he shuffled leftward to throw a large chunk of wood into the fire jar, then a second piece. The third piece gave him a splinter so tenacious that it plucked blood from his thumb, the red drop flying into space and disappearing. "Futete."

As he was flying with the wind, the air around him

had become misleadingly calm. Below him was only farmland, the scattered homesteads almost imperceptible.

With no warning—he was looking down, not up—he flew into a cloud. He shouted aloud as white wetness shrouded him. How would the cloud affect the Lantern? Not at all, it appeared; he quickly popped out above it, its diffuse puffy white top replacing the ground beneath him.

So high, so out of control. To distract himself Marcellinus threw in more wood, rationalizing that the more fuel he burned, the faster and farther the Lantern would go, the lighter the platform would be . . . and then he stopped. If he went too high, he might freeze to death despite the extra clothing he had brought. And although it might be his imagination, it already seemed harder to breathe, as it had on some of the high mountain passes he had led a legion over in the Himalaya ten winters before.

He settled for burying his face in his furs and clinging on like grim death.

Time went by. He soared through more clouds. Between them he could see that he was over forests. Breathing had become easier, which meant that he was losing height. He threw in layers of wood and charcoal and eventually refreshed the fire jar with two small pots of liquid flame. The second pot sent a stabbing jet of flame upward into the cotton bag, and Marcellinus held his breath. If he had not seen Ohanzee and others do the same thing, he might have succumbed to panic. But the bag did not catch fire, and the Sky Lantern again soared up through the clouds.

His next problem was that the frame was becoming seriously unbalanced. On taking off, Marcellinus's side of the platform had been heavier; on a normal day the weight of Ohanzee across from him would have balanced it. Throwing in wood had restored the balance and more. Now Marcellinus sat on the upper side, facing slightly downward and with his back to the direction in which the Lantern was flying. Soon he would have to work his way around to the other side of the frame and throw in fuel from that side.

But not yet. To rest his cramping fingers, he looped his arms around the frame and clasped his wrists instead. Once more he closed his eyes.

To his astonishment, he slept and had no idea for how long. He jolted awake in alarm, convinced he was falling. He was not. The sun was well past the meridian, and by his best guess he was still being swept to the northeast. The Sky Lantern was back down below the clouds; he flew over a small river and a few scrubby hand-cultivated fields. From the style of the homesteads and the continued presence of small earthworks he knew he was still over mound-builder territory.

Somehow, his dozing had alleviated his fear. Brazenly Marcellinus shuffled around the frame, careless of the way it rocked beneath him. Into the fire jar went wood and charcoal, in went the liquid flame. But the Lantern was dropping, and all the fuel he could toss into the fire jar merely limited his losses instead of throwing him higher into the sky.

He looked at the bag. Was something wrong with it? No. It appeared to be some quality of the air itself.

Ah. He was much warmer now. Sky Lanterns had the most lift in winter or at dawn, when the contrast between the heat of the air in the bag and the heat of the air outside was at its maximum. He was losing out to daylight. It was the exact reverse of the situation with the Hawk wings, which flew better in the heat of the day.

Nonetheless, he must already be many weeks' walk from Cahokia.

He threw in fuel with abandon, to coax as many more miles out of the Lantern as possible, and then another thought struck him.

Landing. Never his strong point.

Marcellinus peered at the terrain below. Ideally, as he came down to his inevitable reacquaintance with the ground, he would avoid rivers, trees, and, above all, mountains.

Well, at least there were no mountains.

He allowed the Sky Lantern to sink to within a thousand feet of the ground. Beneath him were trees and clearings. It looked very much like the landscape of endless forest and meadow that his 33rd Legion had marched through for weeks on end.

If it was tricky figuring out how far above the treetops he was flying, assessing his rate of descent was almost impossible. He flung in more wood, trying to avoid the crowns of the tall oaks and come down in a clearing, then sailed on right over the clearing at which he had aimed. Obviously he was still much higher than he had thought. The Raven clan had developed a method of deflecting the hot air from the neck of the jar so that less of it flowed into the bag; he had watched Ohanzee do it many times to help bring them gently to ground. But Marcellinus was afraid to try it. If he got it wrong and the Lantern dropped like a stone, he could easily break his legs or his back when he crashed down to earth. Or worse.

Back over a shimmering carpet of trees, he threw in one of the last pots of liquid flame. The *whomph* of its ignition made only a small difference; just minutes later the first twig scraped the base of the fire jar, which was the lowest-hanging part of the Sky Lantern assembly. Instead, Marcellinus cut all the remaining wood adrift and watched it fall into the trees. Freed of its weight, the Lantern carried him over a stand of hemlock and a small stream, but then he drifted down again. The treetops were above him now. He was coming down *fast*. He scooted across the frame to his right. "Shit, shit, shit . . ."

He hit, but not the ground. A gust of freshening wind blew the Lantern into a tall oak. The corner of the frame opposite Marcellinus slammed into the oak's trunk first, skipped, and seemed to try to dodge around its girth. But above him, a branch snagged the bag. The Sky Lantern skewed sideways, curtsyed, spun dizzily, and dropped again.

It came down on another branch from above, knocking the fire jar to one side. Ashes and hot embers cascaded into space, dusting the trunk of the oak. The platform took another hit, and Marcellinus threw his weight to the side, hoping to swing the frame around between him and the tree trunk.

The loss of so much ash and wood carried the Sky Lantern up a few feet, just enough to free it from the grasp of the oak, but its buoyancy was at an end. Snapping through some tree limbs and bouncing off others, the Lantern slumped toward the forest floor, arrested only when the bag got irretrievably hooked over a broad limb.

Marcellinus dangled on a splintered plank of what little remained of the Lantern's frame. Punctured and torn, the bag gave up the last of its hot air. The fire jar bonked into the tree trunk. The wrecked assembly finally came to rest with Marcellinus about twenty feet above the ground.

In the circumstances, he counted that as a success.

Sky Lanterns were equipped with extra lengths of hempen rope that people on the ground could pull on to bring it down. Marcellinus dropped a coil over the side. Watching it spiral down to the forest floor, he revised his estimate; all right, he was thirty feet up.

He untied his bag of food and clothes and hooked it over his shoulder. Hand over hand, he climbed down the rope.

His feet were on the earth again. He was jolted and aching but had no broken bones. It felt like he'd been flying for a week, but in reality it was not even far into the afternoon. Not knowing how strongly the winds had been blowing at altitude made it impossible to know how far he had come. But that hardly mattered, since even with perfect knowledge of his journey so far, he still could not know how many miles lay ahead.

Hoisting his pack onto his back, Marcellinus set off to walk.

He slept under a tree when night fell, and the next morning he was up before the dawn. He was walking through an endless forest that did not appear to be maintained. Nobody had burned away the brush, and several times he startled a deer close by, but he had no bow and arrow. He ate berries from the bushes and pemmican cakes and nuts from his pack. He made tea when his legs were so weary that he could go no farther, despite the smoke that drifted up through the trees. Not caring who saw him gave him a reckless feeling of freedom. He walked on through the trees alone.

In three days of hiking he saw nothing and nobody. He had discovered a true no-man's-land. That evening he killed a browsing rabbit with his sling and ate well, with enough left over for the next day.

The following noon Marcellinus stood up from his lunch and stretched his weary limbs, getting ready to throw earth over his small fire. Then instinct kicked in, and he dropped back down into a crouch without knowing why.

He looked up and around. His hand was on the hilt of his gladius, but he did not draw it because of the sound it would make or the light that might glint off it. Either would draw attention to his position.

The Catanwakuwa looped around for another pass. Marcellinus stayed absolutely still as it swooped by, barely above the treetops. The Hawk wing banked and swung back up, regaining height almost effortlessly.

Marcellinus stood. There was no mistaking that particular style of flying, the almost magical way the Hawk's pilot had detected an invisible rising air current and ridden it back up into the sky.

She had located him with her usual uncanny skill. He assumed that she would fly home and report his whereabouts to Great Sun Man. She had not called down to him, so obviously she had brought no message.

Instead the Hawk weaved in between the tree trunks, fluttering back and forth like the butterfly after which she had named her daughter.

Sintikala alighted on the forest floor at a run, tilting her wings even as she landed to scamper in a curve and avoid a dense stand of silver birch. She came to a halt, panting, and pushed up her falcon mask.

She surveyed Marcellinus in his Roman helmet with its plume, his breastplate, shoulder greaves, tunic, ring buckle belt, and sandals. The forked pattern painted around her eyes emphasized her glare. "Huh. Who are you today?"

"I am Gaius Publius Marcellinus. As I have always been."

"Now you dress like a Roman?"

"Yes."

A short silence. "I do not like it."

"It's important," Marcellinus said. "I'm here to bring peace. As a Roman."

Sintikala snorted. "Now it is Roman to bring peace?"

At the point of a sword or without one. "Roma always brings peace." Eventually.

Sintikala knelt, lifted the frame of the Hawk wing from her shoulders, and started to dismantle it. "You wear those things to not look Cahokian. You want to look like someone else. This will not fool the Iroqua."

"Of course not," said Marcellinus. "Nonetheless."

"Means what?"

"It means that even though you speak truly, today I will dress like a Roman."

Marcellinus was impressed at how quickly Sintikala broke the Hawk wing down into its component parts. Even during this short conversation it was becoming a collection of unremarkable skins and wooden rods. Anyone coming across it in its deconstructed form might assume it was a tent or a hide for hunting birds. Left out in the open, it would rot away to nothing in a year, leaving no evidence a flying craft had ever existed.

"It was foolish to land," he said. "You should have stayed aloft. You'll have a long walk back."

"Back? Gaius is going on."

"But Sintikala is not."

She shoved the remains of the wing under a bush. Rising, she brushed twigs and scraps of sinewy thread off her fingers. "Huh."

"Sisika, go back to Cahokia."

"While you walk to the Iroqua?"

"Yes."

"You go to kill them all, perhaps? By yourself?"

"No."

"Then the Iroqua will kill you."

"Once I get near the Iroqua powwow, I will hide my weapons and go unarmed. Then I will be safe. Protected. Right?"

"In that helmet?" she said skeptically.

"Just a traveler. A man who would speak with them."

"Gaius, you are not a Mizipi merchant. You are Roman. You are important to Cahokia. Just a few moons ago, Iroqua warriors killed many Cahokians who held no weapons. The Iroqua will use you or kill you."

"If so, maybe I deserve it."

"After all you have done, the Iroqua may take a long time over it."

After an awful pause, Marcellinus blinked. "Let them."

He checked the sun's position and began to walk. She watched with amazement as he strode off into the trees.

Presently he heard her jogging after him. Catching up, she eyed him shrewdly. "Why?"

"Because this is all my fault. Ever since I came to you . . ." In his emotion, his spoken Cahokian weakened. The only words he could recall were simple and direct. "I come to the land, to Cahokia, and bring weapons and smoke and heat. I bring Iroqua to attack you. All I bring is war."

"Your head is big," Sintikala said with scorn. "This is

all you? What of us? Cahokians work and fight. What of the Iroqua? Fighting is their life; fighting is all they do. Did you make the Iroqua? Did you make Cahokia? Did you make the Mourning War?"

"I made it worse. Wherever I go, death follows me. However much I try to help. Just more death." He shook his head. "So. No more."

"Long ago, you promised me you would not go to the Iroqua."

Marcellinus considered. "No, I promised I would not help the Iroqua against Cahokia."

Sintikala stepped in front of him. Marcellinus had to halt abruptly or barge into her. When he moved left to go around her, she grabbed his chin so roughly that his jaw snapped closed, catching his tongue between his teeth.

He knocked her hand away. She shoved him back against a tree trunk.

Marcellinus raised his fist again but let it fall by his side. Sintikala tugged his head down, trying to skewer him with her gaze, but he pulled back and stared past her, up into the treetops. "No. Today you do not get to see my soul."

But Sintikala had seen enough. "You do not just go to die."

"No."

Her voice was low and dangerous, and she flexed her fingers as if she was already squeezing his neck.

"The Iroqua want." She tapped his forehead with her knuckles. "They want what is in you, in here. They want you to help them. Against us. As I said long ago. And you will do it."

"I will never help the Iroqua. I swore that to you. Sisika, I'm of no use to them. Before, yes. Now Cahokia has everything I have to give, and the Iroqua have already taken what they need through their traders and spies."

"So instead they will kill you slowly, over a fire. And Cahokia will not have you."

"You don't need me anymore."

"But we do," she said.

Her hand was still on his steel breastplate, pushing at him. Gently, he moved her arm away.

She studied him. "Whatever you intend to do, it will not work."

"You're probably right."

"Yet still you go."

"Yes."

"I should kill you now rather than let the Iroqua get you."

Marcellinus pointed northeast. "Sintikala, kill me or let me walk, but I go that way." He waited.

She stood aside, and he walked by her.

Marcellinus hiked another ten miles before the darkness and the growing chill stopped him. He wrapped himself in a blanket at the foot of a tree. His hand never left his sword hilt.

Sintikala arrived. Without a word she sat barely two feet away from him and curled herself up in her blanket. She was small enough that it almost covered her.

Settling herself for sleep, she pushed up against him, so close that he could taste her on the air. He knew it was not a physical advance or even a gesture of friendship. Sharing warmth was the warriors' way, and as he knew she did not want him, it had little effect on him.

He did not understand what she hoped to gain, why she was still there at all, but he was too exhausted to think about it. It was her business, just as what Marcellinus was doing was his.

Marcellinus had one job now and one alone.

In the dawn they lay entwined at the base of the tree. Somehow in the night his arms had gone around her and her arms around him.

Carefully, Marcellinus disengaged. Sintikala lay like a tiger. Even in repose she was muscular and dangerous. She smelled of sweat, war, and the forest.

He went on, leaving her asleep on the forest floor. It

took half an hour to work the stiffness out of his muscles, and he ate only the berries and fruits that were close enough to pick as he walked by.

By midmorning she had caught up to him. Now she walked by his side.

"You did not tell me you would leave Cahokia. You did not tell Kimimela."

"No."

The wind rustled the leaves at the crowns of the trees. "You know how she fears the Iroqua will kill you. You did not have the courage to say good-bye."

It had never occurred to Marcellinus to do so. "It was not lack of courage. I had to leave secretly."

"Kimimela would not have given you away."

Marcellinus laughed.

"She would not. Even to me."

He shook his head. Sintikala shrugged. "Believe me or not, she—Gaius, your sword. You still have it."

"Yes."

"You should not. Put it down here, quickly. Leave it behind. We are now in Iroqua land."

"Already?" Marcellinus looked around him as if expecting warriors to erupt out of the trees. Now he saw the marks of the controlled burns, the traces of soot near the tree roots. How could he have been so lost in his thoughts that he had missed them?

He touched the egg-shaped pommel of the gladius. He had no attachment to this particular sword, having left his favorite blade in Cahokia, but it still went against his instincts to relinquish it and proceed unarmed. "Wachiwi said there were bears in Iroqua territory."

"There are. They do not carry swords, either." She paused. "Keep it and you are a warrior. The Iroqua will cut you down where you stand. You know this."

"Yesterday you said that they would kill me anyway."

"Without it you at least have a chance."

It had to be done. Marcellinus unbuckled the sword and laid it behind a bush, scraping soil and leaves over it. Sintikala watched quizzically. "You will come back for it?"

"You want an Iroqua brave to use it to kill a Cahokian?"

She raised her eyebrows. Despite Marcellinus's obsessive caution about the Cahokians trading away gladii or perhaps because of it, the Roman swords had not caught on with the Iroqua. During the whole assault on Cahokia, Marcellinus had never once seen a gladius in an Iroqua hand. "Nonetheless," he said.

"When you have no answer, it is always 'Nonetheless.' You have another weapon in the bag? Your small knife you can keep to cut food. If you have a sling, you can keep that, too. Nothing else."

"Just the gladius. I am now unarmed."

Unarmed and in Iroqua territory.

"And not happy about it," he added.

Sintikala grinned thinly. "Let us walk on."

"Wait." Marcellinus had made another connection, again very belatedly. "That's why you first came to my legion with no weapon. You believed you would be safe if you were unarmed. Because it is the custom of your people, you believed it would be the custom everywhere."

Her mouth twisted. "I learned fast."

For Marcellinus, learning always seemed a long, drawn-out process. "Yes. Let's walk."

Sintikala said: "Tell me more of what you think you will do when you arrive at powwow. The Iroqua will not stop fighting us just because they have captured you. You understand this?"

"Of course."

"Then what do you hope to do?"

"I'm going to try to talk them out of fighting."

"What?"

"Sintikala, did you never wonder how five ruthless warrior tribes made peace among themselves in the first place? How they put aside their animosities and allied?"

"They had a strong leader. A strong man. An *Iroqua* strong man."

"That's right, but even a strong man was not enough to bring them to make a treaty."

"What, then?"

"Necessity."

She shook her head. "They will listen to you? No. Gaius, you will die."

"And you care?"

"My daughter has been sad once. I do not want to see her sad again."

"Huh."

If Sintikala did not understand him yet, she never would. Marcellinus walked on.

"I think perhaps you are mad," she said.

"Do you mean angry? Or insane?"

"Angry."

"It is not hatred that I feel," he said. "It is guilt."

Sintikala looked even more frustrated. "Guilt again? For helping us to make war?"

Where to start? He turned on her. "Do you remember Fuscus? The day you and I first met, the Powhatani . . . the *slave* whom I used as a translator?"

She grimaced. "I remember him."

"I murdered him. Killed him when he had no weapon."

"He attacked you?"

"No. He lied to me. Gave me bad information. I was angry, and so I killed him. I slit his throat, and I watched his life bleed out into the dirt."

Sintikala did not look as horrified as he had expected. "You have killed many people. Why does Fuscus matter?"

"Killing in war is different. Fuscus, well . . . it was not right."

She shrugged, not caring. "You did bad things to us and also to the Iroqua. Cahokians killed many of your people. That is all war, too."

"There is more. So much more. Other things that were not war."

"Gaius, we are in Iroqua land. Tomorrow, or soon, we may be dead ourselves. This matters now? What you are almost crying like a little boy to say?"

"Yes. Now of all times."

"This is not a good time to make me hate you again," she said matter-of-factly. "I have killed people, too. I have killed Romans. In the night, in the day, as you walk west with your legion. Your men die, yes? One here, two there, three here, when away from your marching line or your castra, hunting deer or shitting in the woods like dogs? Who do you think killed them? Powhatani? No."

Marcellinus stopped. "Don't tell me that."

"You want to know how many Romans I killed? Would you stop talking about Fuscus then?"

His fingers itched, but he had no sword, no weapon beyond a pugio. "Sintikala killed them."

"Gaius, you are a fool. Sisika and Sintikala? I am only one person."

Marcellinus closed his eyes. "Not to me."

"Do you want to kill me yet?"

He took a deep breath. "No. And now I will try very hard to forget that you told me this."

"So let us make treaty, Gaius. I will shut up if you will shut up."

Marcellinus started walking again. "I agree. You have your treaty."

In the middle of the afternoon his left sandal broke. Gratefully Marcellinus eased himself down onto a rock by the side of the path and brought out his pugio and sandal tacks to mend it. He had been pushing a strong pace to work out his pain and frustration, but the break was welcome. His stomach growled, but he would not stop to eat until nightfall.

He and Sintikala had not spoken further. Now she took advantage of the halt to disappear into the bushes and then to seek out water.

Marcellinus hammered the sandal with the pommel of the dagger, resisting the urge to swear. He had not thought to bring spare sandals. He had Cahokian moc-casins in his pack but did not want to wear them. To think like a Roman again he needed to wear Roman clothes. No matter how uncomfortable or, apparently, breakable they were.

Sintikala returned and perched on a rock beside him. "Gaius. You were a great leader of your people. Big clever."

"Yes. So?"

"So you are not foolish enough to leave on a journey without knowing the trail ahead."

Marcellinus kept his expression neutral. "And?"

"And I know that Pezi is no longer in Cahokia."

That surprised him.

"Cahokians are not as stupid as you think, Gaius. When will you learn this?"

"All people here in the land," he said. "The Iroqua, with the longships and throwing engines? It is not just your people who have surprised me. And I am hoping they can surprise me again."

Sintikala would not be distracted. "So where is Pezi?"

"I think you already know."

"Gaius."

Relenting, he told her.

CHAPTER 5

YEAR FOUR, PLANTING MOON

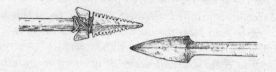

I know you can get a message to the Haudenosaunee, Marcellinus had said, and Pezi had begun to quiver. Convinced that the boy would flee at any moment or fall to his knees and beg, Marcellinus had shoved him down into the snow.

Standing over the shivering boy, Marcellinus had continued. *I know you betrayed Cahokia. If Great Sun Man and the others were not so distracted by grief, they would have realized long ago. And you would die in agony. Those Iroqua prisoners? Those were simple deaths. It would go much harder than that for you.*

So what do you want? Pezi had asked, and it had taken all Marcellinus's strength not to kill him there and then for his calculating determination to live at any cost. Even now, the boy's devious mind had not stopped working. Pezi knew that if Marcellinus had intended to kill him or yield him up to Great Sun Man, he would have done so already.

I want you to run, Marcellinus had said. *Run to your Iroqua brothers in the north. Tell them Gaius Publius Marcellinus will come to speak to the chiefs of the Haudenosaunee when they next meet for powwow.*

Pezi stared up at him, wide-eyed. *The Haudenosaunee Council?*

Remember, Pezi, I own you. And if you do not do as I

say, one day I will find you, and that will be the first day of a year of suffering for you, and at the end of that year you will be broken and torn, and maybe then I will let you die.

Pezi shook his head. *I could run far. The land is big. Would you follow me to the Market of the Mud? No. Tell me the other reason why I will do this.*

Marcellinus grinned. *Because you, too, want this war to be over. And I am the only man who can stop it.*

And why do I want the war to be over?

Because then you will never again need to hide in a grain pit. And there will be important work for a man who can speak both tongues, whom the Cahokian and Iroqua chiefs both trust.

Trust? Pezi put his head on one side.

Why not? Marcellinus said. *I am trusting you now. With my life.*

He let the boy up. Pezi stood, shivering, brushing the snow from his skin. *And that is all I tell them? That you are coming?*

Tell them that I have brought war but that now I will bring peace.

"If I could possibly have told you, I would." Was that true? Perhaps.

Sintikala pondered it. "And so you sent Pezi to the Iroqua?"

"He was easy to convince. Pezi *is* Iroqua."

That stopped her in her tracks. "Yes?"

"Yes. Oh, he speaks Cahokian like a native, but he learned it from captives. He has never been to Etowah as he claimed. He grew up Onondaga."

Hatred flooded her face. Sintikala finally understood. "You knew he could get a message to the Haudenosaunee because he has done it before."

He nodded. "Pezi was one of the spies who betrayed Cahokia to the Iroqua. He sent information back to them with the traders. Probably even the whereabouts of our clan chiefs' houses. Including yours."

Prowling back and forth, rage shimmering from her, Sintikala almost shouted, "And still you let him live?"

"I told you. I am done with killing in cold blood. Whatever the reason."

"That was not your decision to make!"

"I think it was."

She blew out a long breath, trying to calm herself, but her expression was still grim. "You forgive easily."

"No. It's the hardest—" The words stuck in his throat, and he turned away suddenly. "Don't ever talk to me about forgiveness being easy."

"But you forgive often."

"I've had a lot of practice. And Sisika? Once I spared a woman from certain death to send her on an errand no less foolish."

She snorted. "And so you think the Iroqua know you are coming?"

"Yes, with luck."

"And that is why you walk without hiding."

"Yes."

"And Great Sun Man knows as well?"

Marcellinus put his sandal on and stood. The repair had stretched the leather tight across his foot, but it would ease up with a few miles of walking.

"Great Sun Man sent you?" she persisted.

"No."

Sintikala looked unconvinced. "You would not do this without asking your chief. It is not who you are."

Always Marcellinus had been the Imperator's man. But he was impressed that she realized this. She had not even needed to look into his eyes.

"Gaius. Do not play games. Great Sun Man knows you are here."

"That," said Marcellinus carefully, "might depend on who asked him."

Once again Marcellinus had stormed the Master Mound, this time with Anapetu and Kanuna flanking him to get him past the guards at the great gate in the palisade. He had climbed up the mound to its crest, and there, in shock, he had halted.

The new Longhouse of the Sun had grown even larger. Its resemblance to the longhouse on Ocatan's Temple Mound was now unmistakable. And as it was heavily guarded by Wolf Warriors, it had taken Anapetu and Marcellinus half an hour just to persuade them to take a message to Great Sun Man.

After that, though, Great Sun Man had come out immediately. Galena dots sparkled on his robe, and shell beads clattered as he walked. He wore feathers of eagle and falcon and ear spools of bright copper and was every inch a chieftain. Nonetheless, he listened to them.

Great Sun Man, I beg you. This war must stop. For Cahokia's sons. Its daughters.

It can never be stopped.

The war chief's expression was bleak. Marcellinus looked away, at the wood smoke rising over Cahokia, the canoes on the river, the clouds lining the horizon. *And if it could?*

It cannot.

But . . . if it could?

"If I succeed, Great Sun Man will accept the peace. If I fail, he knows nothing of my plan."

But Sintikala's mind had moved on already. "Anapetu knows of this, too? *Anapetu?*"

"Anapetu is my clan chief. I had to—"

"And *Kanuna?*"

"We tried to talk to you, Sintikala. I had not yet talked of this to Kanuna the night we came to your hut, but—"

"And Great Sun Man, too, but still you did not think to tell *me?*"

She was shouting again. Marcellinus eased himself a little farther away. "I did not know that I could trust you."

"Trust?" she said in disbelief. "Trust, Gaius?"

"How could I know? Perhaps I would have come to you saying, 'Sintikala, I would make peace with the Iroqua,' and you would say, 'They killed my husband and destroyed my city, and there will never be peace,' and then where would I be?"

"Dead," she said. "Or still in Cahokia. But I would not have said that thing. Never."

"I didn't know that."

Sintikala frowned. "What else do I not know? Why do you think they will listen to you? What will you say to the Iroqua?"

Marcellinus shrugged.

"I think you know," she said. "But you will not tell me because you are still afraid I will kill you."

She stopped. Marcellinus walked on. The skin on his back prickled. It could come at any moment. He did not think Sintikala would stab him from behind. But even now, how little he knew her . . .

"Gaius. In my hut, before I showed you the map, you told me I was the one person in Cahokia who had always been honest with you."

Now he turned. "And I'll never lie to you again, Sisika. But I have no more to say."

Their eyes met. Quickly he looked away, but the damage was done. Sintikala's jaw dropped, and now she spoke so quietly that he could barely hear. "So you have told me everything. You have no plan yet. You do not know what you will say to the Iroqua."

"Some. Not all. It depends what manner of men they are." Wryly, Marcellinus added, "And we still have a long way to walk. Plenty of time to think."

She rubbed her temples and stepped forward. "All right, Gaius. I will come with you. But the instant you do anything that is against Cahokia, I will kill you with my bare hands. The same instant. Be ready."

Sintikala alone might have gotten farther before being noticed. Plenty of lone women and men walked the trail they now traveled, wearing much the same clothing as she. By herself, Sintikala might have made it all the way to the powwow without being detected as one of the hated mound builders.

Marcellinus was a different story. Even if he was garbed like a Hesperian, his skin color would have marked him out. His olive Mediterranean complexion differed from the tawnier hue of the Haudenosaunee, and even at a distance his very short hair marked him as an interloper. In Roman armor and helmet, he was unmistakably alien and recognizable. As they walked up through the mountains, Iroqua stared openmouthed and Iroqua Hawks circled overhead, but no one tried to detain him.

The terrain was hard, but Marcellinus welcomed the exercise of the harsh slopes. He was steadily regaining his fitness. As for his head, despite the uncertainty that lay before him, it did not ache at all.

Sintikala had left him in the night; when Marcellinus awoke under a sprawling oak tree, she was not there. The nearby brook chuckled at his unease.

He waited by the brook for a while, but she did not reappear, and so he waded across it and kept walking, head down into the wilderness, waiting for his legs and tunic to dry and for something to happen.

"They are here," she said.

Her voice came from his left, away in the bushes. He could not see her. "Who?"

Closer than he had imagined, Sintikala stood. "Iroqua warriors are all around us."

An invisible hand clutched at his heart. Suddenly Marcellinus was deathly afraid. Not for himself but for Sintikala. He wished by all the gods she had not come. "You should have gone back."

"I go where you go." She walked out of the undergrowth to stand by his side.

Marcellinus turned in a slow circle, studying the bushes, and spoke out loud and clear: "Haudenosaunee, step forward. I am Gaius Publius Marcellinus of Roma and Cahokia, and I claim safe conduct. I have come to powwow."

Sintikala gasped, for Marcellinus had spoken the words in the Iroqua tongue.

They came out of the bushes, two war parties of six apiece, Caiuga and Seneca. The Haudenosaunee warriors carried tomahawks and clubs studded with stone; it was not Cahokian chert but a blacker, more sinister-looking rock. Their heads were shaved aside from their long war braids.

Sintikala stood absolutely still with her arms by her sides. "You speak Iroqua now? Yet more truth you did not tell me?"

"Go, Sintikala. Back to Cahokia. Maybe they will let you leave. It's me they came for."

"I do not need your protection." She said some words to the Caiuga leader, and he nodded.

"Sisika," Marcellinus said slowly.

"What?"

"You just told him your name was Sisika."

"Why do you think that I do not like you to call me that?" Sintikala hissed bitterly. "It is because that is what *they* call me!"

Of course the Iroqua knew of her: she was the Cahokian clan chief who had warned them about the Romans and told them to let the invaders through. Marcellinus felt a huge relief. Sintikala might be safer in Iroqua hands than he was.

The Seneca and Caiuga braves watched them with interest. The tension that crackled between Marcellinus and Sintikala must be apparent even if they were not able to understand the Cahokian they spoke to each other.

"Then I'm happy to have your company," Marcellinus said with just a trace of irony.

"Perhaps I will kill Wachiwi," Sintikala said.

"You will not. But why?"

"It is Wachiwi who teaches you Iroqua tongue."

"Yes. The words I would need. Just enough to keep me alive." He grinned at her sideways. "Maybe."

"Even *Wachiwi* knew you planned to come here?"

"Yes," he said.

She shook her head, stunned. The Iroqua formed an escort around them, and they set off again into the mountains of the east.

They walked for days. Nova Hesperia was a *large* land. Marcellinus and Sintikala set the pace, and their Iroqua honor guard set the direction. The Caiuga point man walked thirty feet ahead, guiding them along paths in the woods that were almost invisible to Marcellinus. The rest of the Caiuga and Seneca braves walked in a loose group surrounding them, sometimes so far off to the left and right that they disappeared into the brush, with the leader bringing up the rear. At night they slept in the same ring around Marcellinus and Sintikala, waited for them to be ready to leave in the morning, then again fell into position guiding, flanking, and guarding.

The Iroqua rarely spoke, rarely even came within speaking distance. Marcellinus's questions about how much farther they had to march went unanswered. Sintikala they treated with quiet deference, allowing her privacy for her ablutions but not answering her questions, either.

Every day on the trail they saw more of the Iroqua people going in the same direction: warriors, women, families, even war bands that scowled when they saw Marcellinus's Roman steel and Sintikala's tattoos. Their honor guard grouped around them even more closely at such times, keeping the curious away.

"And so," she said, "you decided it was time to go and *talk* with the Iroqua."

"Yes."

"Why? Really?"

Marcellinus took a deep breath. "I asked Wachiwi where she lived when she was taken from the Onida as a child. She told me that she grew up on the banks of the Oyo River. The Onida lived on the Oyo then, Sintikala. Closer to Cahokia than Woshakee is now."

"Yes, until my father drove them back. What of it?"

"Exactly."

Baffled, she said, " 'Exactly' what?"

"Sintikala, when the Cahokians went to war on the Oyo a life and a half ago, were you with them?"

She looked offended. "Of course not. I was perhaps ten winters. I am only five winters older than Wachiwi."

"What do you know of it?"

"That the Iroqua had been spreading down the Oyo for many lives. That they were raiding Cahokian villages and homesteads. That my father led war parties against them on land and by canoe. That it was the last big fight between the Iroqua and Cahokia until now."

"And also war parties by air. Your father's war party carried Hawks and Thunderbirds and launched them from the hills and river bluffs. The Cahokians had built the first Wakinyan only recently. It was the first time they were used against the Iroqua."

"I know," she said impatiently.

"Hundreds of Iroqua died," he said. "Brutally. In the dawn. With no warning."

Sintikala was mute, her eyes large.

Marcellinus swallowed, picturing it: Wakinyan drifting down silently from the hilltops in the half-light, unloading liquid flame onto the unsuspecting villages of the Onida and Onondaga. The screams, the fiery devastation. And then the Cahokian warriors racing down the hillside into the river villages to finish the job of slaughter. "They burned them and slew those who remained. Nobody was spared except for the girls and boys they stole to adopt. Then they hiked up the Oyo to the next Iroqua village, and they did it again, and again."

Sintikala cleared her throat. "Wachiwi told you this?"

"Yes."

"She was just a child then, Gaius. And what a child remembers is not—"

"Kanuna was there," he said. "Matoshka. Howah-kan. They do not like to tell of it. It takes a lot of really good beer to loosen their tongues."

She paused. "If it was done, then it had to be done. My father was a good man."

Great Sun Man had given the order to use the same combination of Thunderbirds and liquid flame to slaughter thousands of Romans of the Fighting 33rd. Marcellinus had turned a blind eye to the slaughter of Iroqua captives by the same Romans. And to many other things over his long military career.

"I do not judge your father," he said quietly.

Others might. Marcellinus could not.

With steel in her voice, Sintikala persisted. "My father won a great victory for Cahokia!"

"Yes, he did. And then, beaten back to the Great Lakes, the five Iroqua tribes that used to fight one another as often as they fought the mound builders came together to form the Haudenosaunee League. They raided and stole Cahokian Hawks and learned to make flying craft of their own—"

"Not like Cahokia's."

"And licked their wounds and bided their time and grew strong." Marcellinus shook his head. "And when I brought the throwing engines to Cahokia, the Iroqua took that idea, too."

"We're at war!" she said. "*At war.*"

"So what comes next? A greater slaughter of Iroqua, to be avenged in the next lifetime, and around and again forever?"

She struck him on the chest, eyes blazing, bringing him to a halt. "You pity the *Iroqua*?"

Marcellinus eyed her steadily. "I pity anyone who is burned by fire from a Wakinyan."

"The Oyo did not belong to the Iroqua! Did the drunken, tearful old men in the smoke lodge also tell you of the wars before my father's war? The killings by the Iroqua?"

"Yes, a little—"

"Of Ituha uniting the three Cahokias into one city, ending the bloodshed between mound builders? And of how the Iroqua fell upon us and slaughtered us while we were weak after those battles with ourselves, and put our heads on poles, and stole our women?"

"Great Sun Man told me long ago."

"Because of *that*, Cahokia was weak! It was because of *that* that the Iroqua thought the Oyo was theirs!"

Marcellinus felt very tired. "Yes. And why did the Iroqua fall upon Cahokia back then?"

"How should I know?"

"Perhaps because two hundred winters ago, Cahokia did not even exist as the Great City it is now? I think that it was when Cahokia was founded that the Iroqua were first pushed back. I think that the Oyo was originally Iroqua."

"You cannot know that!" she said derisively. "You, who have been here just a few winters."

That was true enough. For this idea Marcellinus had only Pezi's intimations, and the boy could hardly be trusted on history. But the point remained. "And that is why it has to stop, Sisika. Because *you don't know* and nobody else remembers, either, not Ojinjintka, not Ogleesha, not Kanuna. No one. It's lost. The hatred lives on. What really happened all those years ago, nobody knows."

"Things that happened so long ago do not matter," she said. "What matters is *now*!"

Marcellinus looked at her.

"What?" she demanded.

"At last we agree."

But of course they did not. Sintikala spit on the ground at his feet. "And you think that if you talk to the Iroqua of this, they will stop fighting? You will tell them your long, sad tales of the past, and because of that they will bury the ax and we will have peace?"

"Someone must try."

"Wanageeska, when *you* looked at the map in my old house and saw where the Iroqua were, *you* were the one who said we must push them back even farther. That even where they live now, the Iroqua are too close to us!"

"I did say that. But I was wrong. And I also told you a thing that I had only just then realized, that the Iroqua see *Cahokia* as the giant destabilizing threat. And about that I was right."

He had lapsed into Latin for "giant destabilizing threat," but it hardly mattered. Sintikala had already pulled her knife from its sheath.

"You will not kill me today," Marcellinus said.

"You say so? You order me?"

"Yes."

Marcellinus kept walking, his eyes on the almost invisible trail ahead. The Caiuga and Seneca braves watched with interest, none moving to interfere. Sintikala stood staring after him, the knife still in her hand.

Perhaps an hour later she appeared beside him again.

Marcellinus had hoped she had gone for good, had finally decided to go back to Cahokia. "Still can't shake you, can I?"

She grabbed his arm and pulled him to a standstill. "Enough. Gaius? Are you really ready to die? When this long walk ends, at powwow?"

Her sudden intensity took him aback. "Of course I am."

"And if they kill you, do you know *how* you will die? Wachiwi told you that?"

"No." Marcellinus had not forgotten the mutilated corpse of his Norse scout and friend Thorkell Sigurdsson, with its burned legs and missing heart. It still appeared in his dreams, its dead eyes staring in reproach. "I do not dwell on it."

"You must."

Their Iroqua escort waited patiently, faces blank. As always they were a little too far away to hear the conversation, though Marcellinus did not think any of them spoke Cahokian, anyway.

She persisted. "Gaius, you must know. You must be ready."

"I prefer to think positively."

"What?"

"It means don't tell me. I cannot be distracted by fear."

Marcellinus strode away. He heard her footsteps as she hurried to catch up to him and then her voice. "First, they will make you run between two rows of warriors."

Running the gauntlet. "Shut up."

"Warriors with sticks and clubs will strike you. You must run fast. If at the end you are still running, if you can dodge and defeat every threat and get up whenever you fall, then you may be freed. That does not happen often. Very few can do this. So after running you may be dead already, or if not they will tie you up high on a frame—"

"Be quiet!" Marcellinus turned on her. "I cannot hear this! Don't you understand? Such knowledge puts fear into me, robs me of my confidence."

The Caiuga chief appeared at Sintikala's side, club held high, glaring at Marcellinus with a face already made ferocious by red and black war paint.

An Iroqua was protecting Sintikala from him.

Appalled, Marcellinus took a step back.

She muttered words in the Iroqua tongue that Marcellinus did not know. Still wary, the Caiuga lowered his club but stayed by her side.

"You must know of this," Sintikala said remorselessly. "You must be ready. Hear me. They will tie you up high on a platform. They will slice away your fingers. They will cut and burn you. They may take your scalp, cut your stomach, and pull out your guts. As they do so, you must mock them."

Fear struck Marcellinus like a fist. Gone were the days when he could sneer at the prospect of pain. "Mock them?"

"It may take many days for you to die, but you must be brave. You must sing your war song. You must laugh at the Iroqua and never show pain. You must not be broken. Only that way will they eat your heart."

"Eat my heart?"

"Always sing your war song." Her eyes drilled into him. "Always mock. Then, when you are dead, they will know you for a great warrior, and they will eat your heart to gain some of your courage. They will remember you. And, just as important for you, they will fear other warriors like you when they come. I mean the Romans."

The wind caught the leaves around them. The trees shivered.

"Choose your song now," Sintikala said. "When the knives cut you, you will not be able to think. You must be ready. Do as I say."

No moisture remained in Marcellinus's mouth. He swallowed painfully. "We should walk on."

"I will be there when you die," she said, her voice catching at last. "Make me proud. Make Cahokia proud."

She raised her hand toward him. He did not know if she meant to seize his chin and pull his face down to meet her gaze or merely touch his arm in support, but he hastily stepped away.

Marcellinus did not need to see into Sintikala's soul, and he hardly wanted her to see into his. Terror had hold of him. His stomach churned, and his heart was icy.

He began to shake. Had she crushed his resolve and sapped his confidence beyond all recovery? If so, she had already condemned him to the agonizing death she had described so eloquently.

Again she reached out. He knocked her hand away. "Damn you," he said. "Now that you've told me, be quiet. Do not speak again."

Without conversation, the days stretched into an endless walk. Marcellinus strode on as late into the evening as his Iroqua guards would allow, regardless of the blisters on his feet. Deep in his thoughts, he rejected Sintikala's attempts at reconciliation, and after a day the Hawk clan leader walked instead with the Caiuga war party's chief.

Gradually the heavy forests of oak and basswood pine gave way to lighter woodland of beech and birch. Marcellinus saw more signs of husbandry again, the low brush cleared or carefully burned, the fruits of the forest nurtured under Hesperian care.

They came to the edge of a great lake and walked along its shore for several days. Fishing boats dotted the lake's surface, mostly coracles and canoes, but once Marcellinus saw a broad-beamed vessel that looked like a Norse knarr, one of the oceangoing trading ships that had accompanied them across the Atlantic, being sailed by Iroqua braves.

After an eternity of hills and forests occupied by only the occasional tipi, they passed a succession of stout Iroqua villages that lined the lakeshore. These were a far cry from the hardscrabble Iroqua homesteads Marcellinus had marched through and over during the 33rd Legion's westward trek years earlier. They appeared fine and well kept, with hundreds of healthy-looking inhabitants in each one.

The first village they came through was palisaded, and Marcellinus could not see within it easily. The people came out to see him, though, especially the children. None had the air of warriors, and none ever could have been mistaken for Cahokians. The women wore wraparound skirts of a kind he had not seen before in Nova Hesperia or even what appeared to be buckskin dresses laced together with cords of sinew. The men wore britches or red leggings, again corded together, and ornate geometric tattoos. He saw an astonishing variety of colored beadwork in belts and braids and pouch trimmings, much more than he was used to from the Mizipians. The lakes Iroqua were a proud people.

The children were eager to see the pale stranger and came running. Just as in Cahokia after the first battle, the Hesperians did not keep their young ones away from

Marcellinus. There seemed to be no thought that he might pose a danger to them. Nor did he, of course.

However, it was the Iroqua matrons, the senior members of the community, who showed the most interest. They studied him intently with that keen Hesperian female gaze that always seemed to pass right into his brain. They did not seem hostile, but at least from the older female perspective he was clearly a man to be evaluated and understood.

Despite the scrutiny, there was a festive air about the villages. The people were preparing for powwow. Children were excited. The healthy babble of voices had a calming effect on Marcellinus, and the lake breeze refreshed him. He tugged off his helmet and let the air cool his damp brow.

"You will smile at the Iroqua but not at me?" said Sintikala. "Me you hate, for preparing you for what you might face here?"

Her words were harsh, but her face betrayed her hurt. Marcellinus gave in. "I feared that the knowledge would weaken me. It has not. It has merely made me more focused."

"Focused?"

"I am thinking more. Concentrating."

"Shall I tell you how much longer till we arrive at powwow? Or will you hate me again for that?"

He raised his hand to touch her shoulder but dropped it back to his side before he made contact. Being even this close to her made his thoughts flow more slowly.

"I have never hated you," he said. "I cannot hate you. I'm glad you're here."

Sintikala cut him off with a hand gesture, but gently. Perhaps she was worried about what he might say next. "Three days more, Gaius. Then powwow and the Council of the Haudenosaunee. There not everyone will smile."

Marcellinus nodded. "Good. We need to speak of serious matters."

He expected Sintikala to probe him yet again about

how he intended to handle this. She did not, and he was glad, for he knew now and had no intention of telling her.

After all, there were still three more days in which she could kill him.

The next village they passed had no palisade. Marcellinus saw four longhouses in a row alongside a small plaza surrounded by neat gardens of corn, beans, and berries.

The Iroqua residential longhouses were neither as huge nor as square-cut as the Longhouses of the Wings, Thunderbirds, and Sun that Marcellinus knew from Cahokia, yet they seemed sturdier and better established. They stood fifty feet long and twenty feet wide and were only a single story high. Roughly rectangular in floor plan, they had rounded corners and curved roofs formed by bending branches across in arcs and binding them. The longhouses had doors and curving porches at each end and were walled and roofed with shingles of elm bark. Up to five chimneys along each roof's center gave evidence of the many hearths that must line the spine of each longhouse.

"Many families live in each," Sintikala said. "Inside the houses are separate rooms. Two families live in every room and share the fire in the center."

It seemed entirely too snug an arrangement to Marcellinus, and he said so.

"Winters are harsh here," she said. "Do you think Cahokia is cold? Spend a winter here. Then you would *want* to be in such a house with your neighbors close."

"Have you? Wintered somewhere like this?"

Sintikala nodded. "Not with the Iroqua, of course, but along the Mizipi in our upriver towns where the weather is the same. There, even mound builders build houses like these to survive the winter."

"At least we won't still be here when winter comes," said Marcellinus, and immediately regretted it. The truth was that he might well be still here, dead and buried in the frozen soil.

Seeing his expression, Sintikala stepped in quickly. "Longhouses have five hearths and five chimneys. Each of them. You see?"

"Yes, five. So?"

"Five chimneys. Five tribes of the Iroqua. The number is important." Raising a hand, she spread her fingers. "Five. In their own tongue, the Iroqua are the Haudenosaunee, which means 'the People of the Longhouse.' See the real houses here? Always they are set northeast to southwest, just like the tribes. From northeast to southwest the five tribes are the Mohawk, named for the river that flows through their homeland, then the Onida, Onondaga, and Caiuga, each named after the lake where they live, or perhaps the lake is named after the tribe. Farthest west are the Seneca, and I do not know what they are named for."

"Yes," said Marcellinus, who already knew most of this.

"The council is like the longhouse," Sintikala persisted. "This is why I tell you of it. The Mohawks are called the Keepers of the Eastern Door. The Seneca are the Keepers of the Western Door, and the Onondaga are the Keepers of the Central Fire. This is why the high chief of the council must always be of the Onondaga tribe."

"All right."

"And the remaining two tribes, the Onida and Caiuga, are called the Younger Brothers. But when you see the sachems in the Council of the Haudenosaunee, the Older Brother chiefs sit together, so the Mohawk and Seneca on one side, and Younger Brothers sit together on the other, and the Onondaga sit always in the center. The Onondaga high chief of all the Haudenosaunee is always called the Tadodaho no matter what his real name is. When you are presented to them, you must find and address the Tadodaho first, then the Older Brothers, then the Younger Brothers, but show respect to all."

This was new. Kidnapped by the Cahokians at a young age, Wachiwi had been able to tell him little of the council. Marcellinus nodded. "How do they reach decisions?"

"Decisions must be unanimous among all the sachems and are then binding on all the tribes. Any chief can say no."

"All five sachems must agree?" That was worrying.

Sintikala stared at him. "Five? The Council of the Haudenosaunee is fifty sachems. Fourteen chiefs from the Onondaga, ten Caiuga, nine of the . . . Gaius, you did not know this?"

He had not.

Marcellinus had to convince fifty Iroqua war chiefs of his sincerity. All must agree. Any could veto.

"Well, that makes it easy," he said.

She looked at him, baffled.

"I'm joking. Roman sarcasm."

"Do not joke," Sintikala said severely. "*Focus.*"

They spent the next day again walking along the lakeshore, mostly in silence. The villages they passed now were mostly empty, their residents already at powwow. Behind them and in front of them, a steady stream of Haudenosaunee hiked the same lakeshore trail on their way to the big meeting. The sheer volume of Iroqua surprised Marcellinus, along with the hatred on the faces of the men dressed and painted as warriors. The dozen braves of the Seneca and Caiuga who formed their escort could easily have been overpowered, but they showed no fears for their own safety.

That night, an hour after they had made camp on the shore of the lake and finished a dinner of beans and fresh fish, Sintikala came to him. "Gaius?"

Marcellinus was staring out over the darkening lake. Their escort formed a loose semicircle behind them; the nearest was a score or more paces away. No other Iroqua were near. "What?"

"You still speak little to me."

He had been thinking of his youth, his early campaigns. His wife, Julia, Vestilia's mother. Bad decisions made, now regretted. Thoughts, he realized, more appropriate for a man on his deathbed than for a legate with a job of diplomacy ahead of him.

"Do you hate me?"

Marcellinus did not know why she harped on this. "Sintikala, not all my thoughts are about you."

"Have you chosen your song?"

His death song. "Yes. Do not ask me what it is."

Marcellinus had tried not to think about it, but once Sintikala had set him the task, it had eaten away at him till he had come to a decision. He had, in fact, chosen two: a drinking song from his Sindh campaign, with words simple and profane enough that he felt confident of remembering them under duress, and a lullaby he had sung to Vestilia when she was very little, which would serve as his lament. War song be damned: if it really came to this, let his Iroqua tormenters share his sorrow as well as his rage.

"I do not hate you," he said. "But perhaps I should."

She sat down by his side, holding a knife with an obsidian blade that he had not seen before.

"You've decided," he said.

For an instant, he found himself looking around for a weapon, checking the ground underfoot, preparing for the battle to come. And then he realized he could never cause her harm. A fight to the death with Sintikala was unthinkable.

For himself, he had no regrets. Death at her hand would surely be kinder than torture at the hands of the Iroqua. Nevertheless, he regretted the lost opportunity.

"It's a mistake," he said. "You should let me try. But as you wish."

"No," she said almost tenderly. "What we shall do now, we cannot do as enemies."

"You are not my enemy."

"No. And for what we must do at powwow, we must be more than friends."

The blade glinted in the early starlight. Marcellinus suppressed a shiver. "I don't understand."

"You gave me a choice. You said I must kill you or ally with you. Either we must be enemies and fight until we die or bury the ax and walk the trail ahead with peace between us."

"We cannot forget the past," he said. "And you are holding a knife. So you have decided."

"Yes," she said.

She bent forward and sliced gently into her own forearm.

"Sisika!"

She held out the knife to him. Its blade dripped. "I will be your sister in blood."

Light dawned. "Blood brothers? You and I?"

She nodded. "When we face the Council of the Haudenosaunee, I need to know the blood of Cahokia beats in your heart."

"But that means that my blood would also beat in yours," he said.

On the rocky beach of a great lake far from home, Sintikala stared into his soul.

"My Roman blood," he added, as if this could have slipped her mind.

"Yes, Gaius."

Her deep brown eyes were hooded in the growing dusk, her body strong and clean. Blood still welled from the wound on her arm. Sintikala shook the blade, urging him to take it.

Instead, he offered her his arm. "You do it."

Their eyes locked. She moved forward, kneeling close against him, and took hold of his wrist. She braced herself, her hip against his ribs. Her braided hair brushed his shoulder.

The cold obsidian touched his forearm. As furtive as a caress, Sintikala drew the blade along his flesh.

The pain was immediate and ferocious. Marcellinus jerked, and his blood splashed her.

It was a small cut but deep. Blood surged out of it and

flowed in rivulets. Sintikala lifted his wrist, and the blood spilled down his arm and pooled in the crook of his elbow.

Their wounds touched. Their blood mingled. Sintikala looped a braided cord around their wrists, pulling it taut. Their arms formed a cross, tied together.

Sintikala leaned forward until their foreheads touched; brothers in breath as well as in blood. The sting of the gash in his arm dwindled, replaced by the rush of an emotion that had no name. It was a bond of an intimacy closer than any he had experienced.

Sintikala was breathing hard. Marcellinus twisted his arm a little, smearing his blood against hers. She clutched him.

Minutes went by. Marcellinus felt their breathing synchronize. He imagined that their hearts did, too. In that moment, he seemed to be flying.

This was not a meeting of souls. More visceral than that, it was a meeting of blood, of true warriors.

Sintikala raised her other hand, fingers extended. He clutched it with his own free hand, palm to palm, fingers to fingers.

"Nothing is the same now," he said.

She sighed, not her usual impatience but something deeper. "Always change. With Wanageeska, always there is change."

"And always, too, with Sintikala."

"For you," she said, "I am Sisika."

Marcellinus opened his eyes. She stared at him from less than an inch away. Her intensity made his heart skip. He straightened, and their foreheads parted.

He let go of her hand, put his arm around her. Sintikala let him hold her for a moment, her head resting against his shoulder. Then she unlooped the cord that bound them. "It is done."

Marcellinus was still overwhelmed. Perhaps blood was magical, after all. "Sisika. Wait."

"It is done. We are blood."

He could find no words.

Sintikala sat up and tenderly disengaged. Their arms slipped apart, and he felt cool air on the wound. Their conjoined blood had already begun to dry.

All business now, she produced a white salve from her deerskin bag and dressed his wound. Then her own.

"All right. Gaius?"

He brushed at his eyes. "Yes?"

"Lie down, Gaius. We sleep now."

"Yes."

"And then, maybe tomorrow, we go to die."

"No," he said. "We go to live."

CHAPTER 6

YEAR FOUR, PLANTING MOON

Two days later they arrived at powwow.

Their Iroqua escort had ushered them away from the shore and back into the birchwood forest. They had passed a small field of corn and a pleasant homestead of two longhouses with cheerful families that had, as always, come out to watch the strangers go by. Then they had started climbing a hillside on an almost invisible trail, heading back into the wilderness. The path grew rocky as they gained height.

Appearances were deceptive. All at once they walked out of the forest and into a bustling crowd. Their Caiuga and Seneca escort hastily moved in close around them, for this was no longer a festival crowd. These were not ordinary people of the Iroqua tribes but warriors, their faces painted a fearsome black and red, a few wearing full-face wooden masks of even more terrifying aspect with bulging eyes and tongues, horns, or the features of animals. The men held no weapons, but their martial bearing was clear, as was the way they naturally grouped into sixes and tens, the smallest units of Iroqua war parties.

They knew who Marcellinus was. They jostled the Caiuga on either side of him, knocking them into him. Behind Marcellinus, Sintikala swore as she was bumped and almost tripped.

Most uncanny: her curses and their footfalls were almost the only sound. The mass of Iroqua warriors that surrounded them had fallen eerily silent.

They had come out into a large natural amphitheater. Low mountains surrounded them, with the great lake now forming the far boundary of the bowl down in the valley.

The hillsides were full of people, Iroqua beyond counting.

They marched him downhill. Grudgingly, the crowd parted to let the Iroqua honor guard through. Now Marcellinus saw more regular people: farmers and weavers and others.

"Catanwakuwa," he said. Above them Iroqua Hawks looped, dived, and soared, men and women launched from the crags that bounded the natural amphitheater.

"Not Catanwakuwa," said Sintikala. "We do not use the Cahokian name for the Hawks of our enemies." She said a long word in Iroqua that he didn't catch.

They walked uphill again, ascending toward a wide wooden stage. From that stage several dozen men in bright ceremonial garb and tall headdresses watched them approach.

The Council of the Haudenosaunee.

To their right, well beyond the edge of the stage, stood two high wooden frames. The bodies of four men hung limp from those frames, their legs twisted and burned, their arms and chests caked with blood, their eyes dark. Marcellinus's pulse raced. His fists clenched.

"They are not Cahokians," Sintikala said from behind him. He squinted. She was right; the men wore the tattoos of Mohawk and Onondaga. Local criminals, then, not mound-builder captives.

His breath still caught in his throat. After long weeks of journeying, it was suddenly all happening too fast.

A shaman halted them before the stage. His face was covered with a black mask with obscene red lips, his fringed and beaded tunic draped with amulets and feathers, shiny stones, and jagged shapes in copper and shells.

In his right hand he brandished a rattle made from a turtle's shell. Marcellinus eyed the man warily.

The shaman spoke harsh words in Iroqua far too quickly for Marcellinus to catch them.

The Caiuga leader of the war party that had escorted them for so long turned to Marcellinus and hand-talked, *Query, what name, you?*

Sintikala stepped forward past him. "I am Sintikala, also called Sisika, chief of the Catanwakuwa clan. We have come to powwow."

As she spoke, the Iroqua shaman flinched, his movement exaggerated by the heavy mask he wore, and whisked at her with his free hand as if trying to drive her away. Sintikala's body was taut, and hatred blazed out of her. Marcellinus understood. She was no longer among the ordinary people. These were the shamans and leaders of the Iroqua who had directed the war that had killed her husband, and it looked as if it would take only the slightest provocation for her to lash out and attack, dealing death with her bare hands.

"Gently, Sisika," he said.

Above them, at center stage, a tall Onondaga moved forward.

"Tadodaho," said the Caiuga, and fell on his knees, his forehead almost touching the earth.

Marcellinus half bowed, lowering his eyes for the first time that day, and then raised them to stare boldly at the leading sachem of the Haudenosaunee. He saw a broad-chested man, surprisingly young, easily the equal of Great Sun Man in strength and charisma.

"You are from Cahokia," said the Tadodaho of the Haudenosaunee in Cahokian.

"Yes," said Sintikala.

"No," Marcellinus said loudly.

All eyes swiveled to look at him.

"Sintikala is chieftain, daughter of chieftain, and mighty in the ranks of Cahokia. I am Gaius Publius Marcellinus of Roma, formerly Praetor of the 33rd Legion, now disbanded. I am the legate of Hadrianus III, Imperator of Roma."

Almost none of this was comprehensible to the Haudenosaunee. The Onondaga chief blinked. Sintikala eyed him coldly.

"But you speak for Cahokia?" the Onondaga prompted.

"Sintikala speaks for Cahokia. I speak for Roma."

The chief shook his head. "Roma?"

"It will not help us," Sintikala said sotto voce, "if they decide that you are mad."

"Roma is a great nation," said Marcellinus, and pointed eastward. "Far away, over the great sea. I came here first with my army. We marched through your lands. You know of this and of the harm that we caused to your people. Now I live in Cahokia, but I am still a Roman. I will live and die a Roman."

Sintikala shot him a worried look and raised her chin to speak again. "We come to powwow to speak to your great council. We hope to end the long Mourning War between our peoples."

The Tadodaho shook his head. Her words were apparently beyond the Onondaga chief's grasp of Cahokian. She began again in halting Iroqua, but his warriors were already converging on Marcellinus and Sintikala, hustling them away.

"Wait," Marcellinus said. "We must speak with you. Tadodaho?"

It was no use. Warriors clutched his forearms, shoved at his shoulders. A broad doorskin was pulled aside in front of him, and he was ushered through it, underneath the stage.

"No!" came the voice of Sintikala. "Stop! I go with him! Take me with him!"

Warriors hustled her past. The curtain fell behind Marcellinus.

They were separated.

From above and all around came a din of chanting and stamping. Marcellinus heard one voice and then thousands, and heard them again: a call and response between a man on the stage above his head and the mass of Iroqua assembled in the valley.

Marcellinus sat. Few useful thoughts crossed his mind. But he was still alive, had not been taken away any farther than the stage. Perhaps in the evening, once the day's ceremonies were done, he would get the chance to speak to one of the sachems, maybe even plead his case for being allowed to speak to the Tadodaho and others of the council.

Or perhaps tonight he would run the gauntlet, and when the next dawn came he would be suspended high on one of the Iroqua torture frames, trying to remember his war song. Trying to die with honor.

A high scream pierced the air, and he knew it for Sintikala's. Marcellinus was up on his feet in an instant, bulling his way to the doorskin, but his Iroqua guards swarmed him and knocked him to the well-trodden soil, yanking his arms behind his back. Marcellinus struggled and roared, but it was no use.

They dragged him backward and bound him to one of the posts that supported the stage.

Marcellinus stopped resisting. He was listening. More screams came, but this time they were male voices raised in pain. Two, perhaps three different men were suffering the agonies of Iroqua torture just a few yards away from him.

After what seemed like an hour, the screams weakened and bubbled and a merciful silence descended.

The stomping began again, and he heard flutes and a thousand voices raised in a coarse, high song.

"What's happening?" he said to his guards, but they either did not understand him or pretended not to, and with his hands bound behind him he could not make hand-talk.

Sisika. The shaman had whisked her away with that dismissive shooing motion, and the Tadodaho had not heeded her. And then a single scream and nothing more?

Night fell more slowly than on any other night of his

life. Many hours after dark, the throbbing dance of powwow at last fell silent. No longer did the stage creak above him. His captors took turns sleeping, the wakeful ones surrounding him, two of them always sitting behind him where they could see the bonds that tied him to the pole by the light of the lanterns that the women had brought in.

Marcellinus was bound so tightly that he verged on losing all feeling in his hands. Desperation knitted his brow so that his face felt almost as tight as the cords on his wrists. He wandered in and out of a heavy sleep and eventually awoke to find gray dawn light spilling in past the doorskin and through the cracks in the wooden stage covering. In front of him, a face stared intently.

Marcellinus's throat was dried to a husk, and when he spoke, it was almost a croak.

"Pezi."

"And so I owe you my life," Pezi said ironically. "You say so?"

He spoke without blinking, no smile on his face.

"Yes," said Marcellinus. "Bring me water and have them free my wrists."

Now Pezi smiled.

"What will happen, Pezi? Will the chiefs hear me?"

"Does the council confide in me?" Pezi said. "No, they do not."

"But you told them I was coming."

"Of course I did."

Memory was rekindled as Marcellinus came fully awake. "Sintikala! Where is she? Did they harm her?"

Pezi studied his face. "You think I am Cahokian? That I care what happens to either of you?"

"No," said Marcellinus. "But I think you do not like war."

Pezi shrugged. "I do not like to fight. But war?"

"You have someone's ear. You are here instead of . . ." He had intended to say *running away.* "Instead of watching from a distance. So why are you here?"

"I am a speaker of words. I am here to speak yours."

"To the Tadodaho and the sachems of the Haudenosaunee? My words and Sintikala's?"

Pezi grinned. "You think to trick me to telling you what will happen next and also whether the angry Hawk chief still lives. You forget that I hate you."

"This must be a happy day for you, then," Marcellinus said.

"I was sent here to ask you questions. How far is the giant Cahokian war party? When will they arrive? How fast can they travel?"

Marcellinus stared him down. "What war party?"

"We know that they have left Cahokia. We do not know the way they will come. By river? No, they are not on the river. By the main trail? No, they are not on the main trail. So they must be coming by a clever path, up and then across from the north, perhaps, or directly through the forests, or eastward and then north. We have not yet found them. Soon we must, for a war party of that size that makes a Roman camp every night cannot stay hidden for long."

Once again Pezi leaned in close. "They cannot come by the Oyo. We control the upper river now with our giant longships. We have scouts out looking for them. But you can tell us, and that will be quicker."

"I—" Marcellinus was about to say *I don't know.* He had no idea when the Cahokians had left or which way they would take. Truly it had been easy to avoid learning details of the Cahokian war plan, because he had not been in the councils of the chiefs and elders.

But it would be poor strategy to emphasize his uselessness.

"How many of them? And how many warriors remain in Cahokia? Is the palisade completed? Are there traps inside? So many questions the sachems have for you."

"Then let them ask me."

"Perhaps the Haudenosaunee will string you up on their frames of death. Then you will speak."

Marcellinus grinned without mirth. "You say so?"

Pezi's fingertips touched his chest. Marcellinus tried not to recoil. The boy studied him, reached around his arm, and prodded the white salve that protected the cut where he had become blood kin to a Cahokian clan chief.

"You should tell me. It would spare Sintikala much suffering."

Marcellinus shook his head. "Take me to the council, Pezi."

Pezi's thumbnail bit into the scab over the wound the obsidian blade had inscribed in Marcellinus's flesh. Marcellinus tried to pull away, but he could move only an inch.

"They will not speak to you," Pezi said. "By the end of powwow you will be a dead man. Today Sintikala is already half dead. She will tell the council what they need to know of the Cahokian war party if you will not. And then many more things will happen to her before she completes her journey into death."

Marcellinus had heard only one scream from Sintikala's lips, and surely the torture of a high-ranking Cahokian would be an extended event. Hope surged within him. "You lie, Pezi. You always lie."

"Do I?" Pezi scratched himself contemplatively. "You, of all men, should be used to the sound of women screaming. But the Hawk chief, screaming? I think I will enjoy watching your face as she suffers."

Marcellinus closed his eyes and then opened them again. He would not allow Pezi to see him in pain. If anything could make him sing his war song into death and beyond, it would be to frustrate this evil boy and rob him of his pleasure.

And after all, it was true. "Yes, Pezi, I am used to the sound of screams. I'm glad you're here. I will enjoy listening to yours."

"You had better get used to the sound of your own," Pezi said. "No words for me? Well. It is early yet. I must get something to eat." Grinning, he left.

*   *   *

They fed Marcellinus from a bowl of a simple mash of corn and beans, put a chamber pot under him, and wiped him coarsely when they removed it. Otherwise Marcellinus was left to hang in his bonds, well guarded but otherwise ignored. As morning turned to afternoon, the speeches began above him, the debates, the call and response.

As dusk fell on the second day, Marcellinus again heard a single scream that could only have come from the throat of Sintikala. His guards watched him carefully, but this time Marcellinus did not move, did not visibly react at all.

Tonight there was no torture of other men. The music began and the dancing. Above him, many feet stamped in time. He was living inside a drum. His head ached remorselessly. He missed Sintikala every moment of every hour of the day. And Pezi had not returned, nor anyone else to question him. All thoughts of strategy left his mind. From now on, he must merely concentrate on survival.

On the third morning they unbound his hands, took him outside to a spot far to the left of the great stage, and allowed him to wash as best he could using a small bowl of cold water. They fed him corn. They returned to him his greaves and breastplate and even his helmet. He did not see Sintikala or Pezi or anyone he recognized, only the ever-present warriors.

Even as Marcellinus grimly strapped his Roman armor to his body, he could see the gauntlet of Iroqua warriors forming in two long lines between him and the stage.

Mud smeared the steel of his breastplate, and Marcellinus cleaned it with his hand and the sleeve of his tunic. No one hurried him. They merely watched in fascination as he prepared himself for his last battle.

He had no weapons, of course. Perhaps he could take the metal strips of the apron that hung to guard his groin and wrap them around his fist as a primitive knuckle-duster. If he used his helmet as a club, a blow struck with its sharp crown might have some effect. But it seemed too late for such measures.

Marcellinus was not a young man anymore. He had lived much longer than he had expected. He had fought and flown; he had loved and seen many wonders. Sometimes he had even been happy. He would not cling to life when all hope was gone.

He had come to speak to the Haudenosaunee, but they did not want to speak to him. Perhaps they had already located the Cahokian army. Perhaps Sintikala had broken and told them everything they needed to know. Either way, Marcellinus was obviously of no further use to them except as a public spectacle.

The platform was loaded with several dozen warriors in full regalia. The Council of the Haudenosaunee had assembled to watch this. Standing in front of the Seneca chiefs was Pezi, dressed in a plain tunic.

Marcellinus stood. The sun of midmorning sparkled from the steel that garbed him. He placed the helmet on his head and strapped it tight beneath his chin.

Taking a deep breath, he walked forward to the mouth of the gauntlet. The two lines stood a scant eight feet apart.

This was powwow, so the weapons of the warriors were simple. Marcellinus saw no bows, spears, or tomahawks, not even a blade. Each man carried a straightforward wooden club, a large rock, or a pot. But these were still fearsome warriors, the cream of the Iroqua crop. Their cheeks were daubed heavily in red and black, their chests and faces scarified and tattooed with clan battle markings. Men like these could kill him with their bare hands and feet before he had passed a dozen of them, and hundreds stood between him and the stage at the other end. Most grinned unpleasantly, shifting their weapons from hand to hand.

There was no ceremony, no proclamation from the high stage. So far the assembly had been quiet and calm, almost patient. Now a slow murmur began from the massed crowd and built until it became a steady roar. Everywhere he saw mouths moving, shouting at him. Abuse was hurled that he could not understand. Still Marcellinus stood at the mouth of the gauntlet.

On the stage, a central figure who had to be the Tadodaho had risen to his feet. Raising his hands, he tried to calm the crowd, but this had passed beyond his control.

The warriors in the gauntlet bounced up and down on the balls of their feet, waving their clubs, menacing him with the rocks they held. Taunting him. Daring him to make his run. The men farther away were challenging him to make it even that far.

Marcellinus, too, raised his hands and then presented them palm first. The Iroqua mob howled.

To hell with them all.

He looked at his hands and saw not the faintest tremor in them. Good.

Marcellinus undid the straps of his helmet again and cast it aside. He pulled the greaves from his shoulders and then unbuckled the heavy chest plate and left it lying on the ground with the rest of his armor.

Wearing only his Roman tunic, belt, and sandals, Marcellinus stepped into the howling gauntlet.

Spittle landed on him from the left and right. The deafening roar continued unabated, but Marcellinus no longer heard it. He took another step.

A rock grazed his forehead and pounded into the dirt in front of his feet. Marcellinus tried not to flinch. He stepped over the rock and kept going.

A whirled club cracked into his right calf. The pain was sudden, immediate, and deadening. His leg gave way, and he dropped heavily onto his knee.

Breathing was difficult. He closed his eyes for a moment and felt the thrum of another missile pass inches from his head. Someone kicked him in the ribs on his left side; he flailed his arms to keep his balance and managed not to fall. More wetness on his head and cheeks; saliva carried on voices of rage.

Still he waited for the blow to his skull that would end

it all. His temples throbbed in anticipation. He sucked in another breath and felt a wheeze begin in his chest. His right foot felt dead from the blow to his shin.

Marcellinus stood. Raising his head, he looked around him.

The raucous noise continued, but it no longer came from the warriors to his immediate right and left. Instead they watched him keenly as if he were a new breed of animal.

"Kill me or let me walk." His voice was gravelly, but still it carried. Nobody understood him. "I am Gaius Publius Marcellinus. Kill me or let me walk!" He took another step.

Someone shoved the backs of his knees, and he stumbled forward again. This time his hands touched the ground. He ducked his head forward. No blow came.

"Gods' sakes," said Marcellinus.

Again he stood. Iroqua warriors studied him. Some glanced back and forth between him and the stage. Screwing up his eyes Marcellinus peered up at the high platform, but nobody was giving any orders from up there. The Tadodaho watched, arms folded. The rest of the chieftains sat as calmly as if they were watching a dance.

Resisting the dizzy urge to wave, Marcellinus took another step.

He was on the ground again before he knew what had hit him. He felt no pain, just dizziness and a nonspecific ache in his spine. A blow to his shoulders or the back of his neck? He had no idea, but he still was not dead, could still move.

He shoved himself back up onto his feet. He had walked maybe twenty feet into the hundred-yard gauntlet of warriors.

Setting aside his armor had been his attempt to hasten the final blow. Marcellinus wanted nothing more than a quick end to this: a sudden dazzling strike, the bright final explosion. In the Iroqua assault on Cahokia he had experienced serious injury and did not wish that on himself again. Better death than mutilation, much better.

Hence he had relinquished all protection and was walking. No sense in making a futile run when he would merely be tripped and smashed to the ground in seconds. Instead, he would die with dignitas.

He raised his head high. How much of a target did he need to make it?

But the men in the gauntlet were stepping back. No club was raised against him. No pots or rocks flew by his head. Nothing smashed sickeningly into his skull or his back or his legs.

Marcellinus took ten more paces and then stopped, bemused. He saw stones raised again, clubs brought up, but they were only readying to defend themselves should *he* attack *them*. Their bloodlust had drained away into the ground. The Roman welcomed death? Nobody here was going to grant it to him. The Roman did not fight? Then nobody here was going to cast a blow. Where was the honor in that?

Every Iroqua warrior in the gauntlet was standing down.

As he hobbled painfully but with head raised high and defiant, easing his weight onto and off his damaged right shin, it seemed to take Marcellinus the other half of the morning to complete his walk the length of the Iroqua gauntlet.

At its very end a Mohawk warrior blocked his way. From the man's feathered headdress and beaded tunic Marcellinus guessed he must be a man of high standing, perhaps even one of the sachems. The Mohawk held a mace in his hand.

Marcellinus halted, regarding the warrior without rancor. "Now, then? Are you to be my executioner?"

The Mohawk shook his head in incomprehension. From the platform came Pezi's voice as he translated.

Time stood still for a moment. Above him on the stage he heard voices talking, speaking over one another, interrupting. Then one voice rang out from the others, and all fell silent.

Marcellinus swallowed. "Well?"

The Mohawk chief spoke a single word. It was an Iroqua word that even Marcellinus understood.

"Come."

No steps led up onto the broad wooden platform. A crude ladder of extended cross-posts jutted from the side, and the Mohawk climbed it quickly, hand over hand.

Marcellinus could hardly feel his right foot, and his breath still wheezed. "No," he said in Iroqua, and they ushered him around the long way, to where the natural slope of the hill made it simple to step across onto the boards. He tried not to look up at the torture frames, where three new bodies hung, bloody and torn.

The Mohawk chief waited for him at the platform's edge. Marcellinus glanced at the sun and understood. The platform was oriented northeast to southwest, and he would step onto it at its eastward end. The Mohawks were the Keepers of the Eastern Door; thus, their chief must consent to allow him passage.

Marcellinus bowed. The Mohawk let him pass.

There they sat, the sachems of the Haudenosaunee, young and old, broad and lean, all in their finest regalia for powwow. All had gained their status through being great fighters, and every face and chest was adorned with finely crafted geometric tattoos. Each wore a headdress, some of deer antlers or eagle feathers, others of wolfskin or bearskin or the pelt of a panther. Armbands and ankle bands of fur were common. Their raiment was much more vivid than the ceremonial garb of the Mizipians. Beneath the furs Marcellinus saw breeches of red as well as brown and even a lemon-yellow color brighter than the light tan of the Cahokian hand-woven cloth that was dyed with white oak galls and goldenrod.

The fifty chiefs of the Haudenosaunee viewed him curiously in return, eyeing him up and down the way a

Roman farmer might study a horse. And a fine sight Marcellinus made in the simple ragged tunic he had worn under his armor. He still limped from the blow to his calf; glancing down, he saw blood, and the black of bruising had already spread. He was lucky the bone had not been smashed.

His ribs ached. Breathing required effort.

He looked up again, and Sintikala was there, at the far end of the platform beyond the sachems. She was bound at the wrists and flanked by two Seneca of the Western Door. Her face was bruised and her tunic was dirty, but she was not bleeding and did not seem to be in pain. She looked very alive and very annoyed.

Marcellinus's heart leaped. While they both lived, there was hope. He glanced at Pezi and was gratified that the boy looked as startled to see Sintikala as he was himself.

At a word from the Tadodaho, the braves cut the sinews that bound her and pushed her forward.

The crowd murmured as Sintikala walked over to Marcellinus. She pulled a cloth from her pouch; briskly, in front of the massed Haudenosaunee, she rubbed it across his head and shoulders. Marcellinus remembered the spitting of the warriors in the gauntlet and was grateful. He had not planned to face the Council of the Haudenosaunee battered, bruised, and soiled. He tried to stand erect and compose his features while the chief of the Hawk clan smoothed sweat, dirt, and worse from him.

"You screamed," he said. "What did they do to you?"

Her lips pursed. "Nothing. An Iroqua ritual to test my courage. I shouted out only so that you would hear and know that I still lived."

"Sisika, what did they do?"

"I told you. Nothing."

He eyed her uncertainly, but she was walking and talking and did not seem harmed. "They did not torture you?"

"Torture? Let them try."

Marcellinus glanced accusingly at Pezi. "He lied to me. Tried to bluff me, to find out where the Cahokian army was."

"Huh. I told them already. Why not? The sooner we go to war, the less far the Cahokians have to walk." She tugged his tunic straight, centered his belt. "You look very bad."

"Thanks."

From his other side Pezi spoke, translating their words to the Iroqua chiefs so that there could be no deceit.

Marcellinus's helmet landed at his feet, lobbed up by one of the Iroqua warriors. A moment later his steel breastplate sailed up onto the platform with a clang. His greaves and metal apron followed in short order. The steel no longer gleamed, and the high red plume of the helmet looked distinctly battered.

"Leave all that," said Sintikala.

She was right. His sorry armor would not help him. Any sense of presence or authority would have to come from Marcellinus himself.

Everyone was waiting. Marcellinus pulled himself together. "I may address the Tadodaho now? The council?"

Sintikala shook her head. "Not the council, Gaius."

The Mohawk chief barked a command. Sintikala nodded formally to Marcellinus, the Tadodaho, and the council, and stepped away.

Marcellinus bowed to the Tadodaho, who continued to regard him without discernible emotion.

The Mohawk escorted Marcellinus and Sintikala to the center of the tall platform. The Tadodaho spoke, indicating Pezi. Marcellinus looked back and forth between them, but the boy shuffled his feet and did not translate.

The Onondaga chief grunted and hand-talked instead. *The boy. He is yours?*

Marcellinus hand-talked back. *I save his life, at Woshakee. Send him here, tell you I come here.*

Boy is good with speak. Iroqua, Cahokia.

He speaks good. But he hates me. May not speak true, Marcellinus signed, blocking his hand-talk with his body so that Pezi could not see. But the massed crowds could, and a smattering of laughter came from the men and women nearest the stage.

Marcellinus looked back over his shoulder. "Pezi, speak my words faithfully or I will come back to haunt you at night and you will never sleep again."

"I will follow his words as best I can," Sintikala said. "Others here, too, speak some words in both tongues and can watch for treachery." Piercing Pezi with her glare, she said something contemptuous in Iroqua, and now many of the chiefs smiled.

The Mohawk nodded to Marcellinus and walked back to take his seat with the other Older Brothers at the Eastern Door.

The Tadodaho said something.

" 'Speak,' " Pezi translated. " 'Speak, Wanageeska, to the people of the Haudenosaunee.' "

"The people?"

" 'We are Haudenosaunee. This is powwow. Here the people decide.' "

Marcellinus looked out over a vast sea of faces. The Five Tribes spread out before him, almost silent, their expressions stark.

The people? *These* people? Then it was as good as over. He might as well have died in the gauntlet.

"Merda," Marcellinus said under his breath.

He had traveled all this way hoping to speak with a few key war chiefs. A back-and-forth discussion like the councils of Great Sun Man in Cahokia. Instead, the Council of the Haudenosaunee was half a hundred men, and he would give a speech to thousands.

If he had known this would happen, he might have spent more time rehearsing what to say.

His golden Roman lares were still in their small pouch at his belt, along with the Hesperian birdman amulet. Marcellinus touched the small, heavy lump once and then let his hands drop down by his sides.

Marcellinus straightened his back, relaxed his shoulders, and began to address the Iroqua nations.

"My name is Gaius Publius Marcellinus. I come from the Roman Imperium, a great nation across the sea. Three winters ago I came to this land as the war chief of an army of mighty warriors, men of the Eagle clan, the greatest fighters of Roma."

Only those who sat within a few hundred feet could hear his words as translated by Pezi. The braves beyond followed along with the hand-talk that was passed back through the crowd, all the way down to the lakeshore. The reactions spread in a slow wave. It was distracting.

"When the Eagle clan came ashore onto the land of the Powhatani at Chesapica, we brought great suffering and death. When we passed through Iroqua lands, we fought many battles with you. And then at last we came to Cahokia, to the peoples who build their mounds along the banks of the Mizipi. There my Roman army was destroyed by the Cahokians and by the Catanwakuwa of Sintikala and the enormous Wakinyan that flew above us and blocked out the sun, dropping fire and death among us. That day the Cahokians destroyed my clan, the great army of Roma."

Marcellinus paused and swallowed while Pezi caught up. There was no lump in his throat, but his mouth was dry. He felt calm and unemotional, but the people before him were not. Many men looked somber. Women had their hands to their mouths. Whether they knew of the Cahokian Thunderbirds from firsthand experience and had suffered losses to their own families and clans from their fiery aerial bombardment, Marcellinus could not tell. All he knew was that perhaps they felt a moment of sympathy for him for losing his entire clan at a stroke.

Either way, it was of no importance as long as they kept listening. For Marcellinus's own sufferings were not the point, not at all.

"But Haudenosaunee, hear me. The Roman army I brought with me is but one among many. My army's name was the 33rd Legion. That is thirty-three. This many," and he hand-talked the number so that there could be no mistake.

"Some of you saw the 33rd Legion. Perhaps some of you even fought against it. So think upon this: for every warrior in my army, Roma has forty more in the armies that have not yet come here."

A murmur spread through the crowd. He waited for it to propagate out before he spoke anew. Not all would come to Nova Hesperia, of course, but this was not the time for semantics. "Hear this: one day another Roman army will arrive on your shores.

"Roma *will* come. Tomorrow, next moon, or five winters from today; I cannot say. But I *do* know that *they will come.*"

He swallowed again. He was about to step beyond the pale. In this moment, Gaius Publius Marcellinus willingly walked into that gray area between being a faithful servant of the Imperator and being a traitor to Roma.

It had to be done. After all, Hesperian blood beat in his veins now, too.

"And when the army of the Imperium comes, the Haudenosaunee League must not be weak."

Sintikala twitched. Her hands closed into fists and opened again.

The Iroqua had fallen utterly silent. A feeling of unreality threatened to unbalance him.

"On the day the Romans arrive, you must not be worn down by years of war with the mound builders. The best of your warriors must not lie in charnel houses or burial mounds. You must not be turned inward, fighting among yourselves. And you must not be far from home. You must be here, in your homelands, and ready to stand with your brothers. Your brothers, the Cahokians."

In an instant, that uncanny quiet dissolved into deafening fury.

Braves stood and shouted at him. Thus encouraged, others stood to add their voices. Men and women from farther back stood also, reacting late to the delayed hand-talk. All Marcellinus heard was a broad bellowing in a language he did not speak. He waited.

Pezi shrank back at the din, trying to make himself as small as possible. Marcellinus's head began to pound. "Stand up, coward," he snarled at Pezi. "Must all translators be craven?"

The fifty chiefs of the Haudenosaunee League were on their feet, hand-talking to their tribes in broad gestures, calling for calm. The Tadodaho raised his hands high, but the hubbub continued. He sat back down for a few moments and then stood and raised his hands once more. This time the din of the crowd faded. The council sat.

Again Marcellinus faced the thousands-strong crowd. His heart beat faster, in time with the throbbing in his head. He had lost his focus. What had he been saying?

As if sleepwalking, Sintikala came toward him. Her expression was severe, and for a moment he thought she might strike him. Then she turned outward to face the crowd. She was so close that her arm almost touched his. He could feel her heat and her immense calm, and she anchored him.

" 'Be ready to stand with your brothers,' Gaius," she said quietly. " 'Your brothers, the Cahokians.' "

"I thought you were coming to kill me."

"I still might. I do not know what you are doing."

"You wanted me to think of something. All I could think of was to tell the truth."

Because Sintikala had been right. The past was dead. All that mattered now was the future.

The Five Tribes of the Haudenosaunee were waiting. Marcellinus raised his voice and spoke again to the crowd. "I do not know what will happen when the Romans arrive. That will depend on the war chiefs who stand at the head of those mighty legions of the Eagle. But this I swear to you in blood, today and for all days: I swear to you that I will powwow with the Romans, and powwow with the Haudenosaunee, and powwow with the Cahokians, and I will do my best to prevent another war. For I am tired of war, and you, too, should be tired of war."

Again the murmur of the crowd rose to become a frenzy. Beside him on the stage, a warrior stood. From his regalia he had to be the paramount chief of the Caiuga tribe, and he held a knife. He did not look like a man tired of war.

"I have more to say before you kill me, sir," Marcellinus said. "Not much more. Just a little."

Pezi translated. The Caiuga sachem shook his head. He handed the knife to Marcellinus hilt first.

Marcellinus took it and looked to Sintikala for guidance.

"You just swore a blood oath," she said. "But you did not seal it with blood."

"What must I do?"

"Hold your arm high and cut into it with the blade. But please, Gaius, for me: not your arm that I cut when we became blood kin."

Turning to the crowd, Marcellinus raised his hands for quiet. Transferring the knife to his right hand, he slashed his left forearm.

Blood spurted. He had struck deeper than he intended, but unlike the last time, he felt almost nothing.

He raised his bleeding arm high. Blood gushed down onto his shoulder and soaked his tunic. "I swear to the Haudenosaunee on the blood I have spilled that I will do all in my power to prevent war between Roma and the great nations of this land.

"You all, Haudenosaunee and mound builder, must be strong. If you are strong, the Romans will want to make trade more than they want to make war.

"And again I will speak the truth to you, People of the Longhouse: the Romans may demand much. Food for their armies. Passage through Iroqua lands. They may create damage and disturbance. They may take without asking. It may not be easy. But it will be easier than a war that would destroy so many of your people and mine."

His head still pounded, and the smell of his own blood made him nauseous. He lowered his arm and struggled on.

"I have learned many things here in the land, and the lessons have been brutally hard. I have shed much of my own blood, much blood of brave warriors and of peaceful people, but I have come to learn that it is better to talk than fight. Better to have peace and trade than war and death."

In front of him in the broad grassy amphitheater, Iroqua warriors howled again. Behind him, the war chiefs muttered.

Marcellinus raised his hands for calm. "I say it again. If you are strong, they will want to make a treaty with you. They will want to go to market with you and make trade. They will want to pass through your lands and go west, toward the evening. You should make them buy that right. Not fight for it, as my army did, but barter for it.

"Understand, Haudenosaunee, that I am no traitor to my people. Roma will gain, too, if the Iroqua and the mound builders are strong. The Imperium will gain a powerful ally and strong neighbors, and they will gain in goods and in skills. Because when you steal goods in war, the spoils are only for that day. When you make trade, you can trade again tomorrow. Am I not right?"

Nausea threatened him. Marcellinus forced himself to stay erect. "Do not think me weak for seeking peace. I am not weak. I will fight today, tomorrow, always. I have fought you before, and I will stand with my brothers in Cahokia and fight you again if I must.

"But I say that the time for war is over. I say that you have lost enough of your men, enough of your women, enough of your children. I say that Cahokia has lost enough of its men, enough of its women, enough of its . . ."

He faltered. Sudden nightmare images flashed before his eyes: Tahtay smashed to the ground by an Iroqua club, Enopay spitted on a spear, Kimimela maybe being carried away by Iroqua warriors just as Wachiwi once had been stolen by Cahokians.

Marcellinus gritted his teeth. "Enough of its children."

He drew himself up to his full height. The pounding in his head faded, and all of a sudden he felt very calm. "People of the Longhouse: when I lost my war with Cahokia, I did not kill myself as a Roman should. But if I lose the peace today, then my life has no purpose. I will leave here in peace, or I offer you my life. Command me so, and I will end it here, in front of you."

Sintikala gasped. Pezi hesitated before the translation. "Yes? You say this?"

"Yes, I say this. Tell them."

"Translate his words," Sintikala said. Pezi did so.

Marcellinus turned back to the massed Iroqua and raised his voice in oration for the final moments. "I will have peace in this land or I will have death. I have made my choice, and now you, too, must choose.

"That is all I have to say. I am Gaius Publius Marcellinus, and I have spoken."

He lowered his head, the knife still in his hand.

It was a long time before silence descended again over the great valley.

The paramount chief of the Onondaga stood. "Sintikala. You speak for Cahokia? What do you say?"

Sintikala plucked the knife from Marcellinus's grasp and stepped forward. Her voice rang out clear across the crowd.

"I am Sintikala of Cahokia, known to some of you as Sisika, and I speak for Great Sun Man, the war chief of Cahokia, my cousin by blood. I am daughter to the previous Cahokian war chief, and I am the chief of the Hawk clan.

"I say that Cahokia will have peace with the nations of the Haudenosaunee. And I say that if you do not choose peace, I will stand with this man, this Roman from far beyond our land, and I will die here with him."

She cut deeply into her arm, and her blood dripped down onto Marcellinus's feet.

"Among the Haudenosaunee, as in Cahokia, women lead the clans. Women choose the war chiefs. And now, when I ask for peace, I ask the women to help make it so."

In the front row, a Caiuga woman turned her head and spit on the ground.

"We will have peace or we will die. I am Sintikala and also Sisika, and I have spoken."

As Pezi finished his translation, Sintikala stepped back to stand shoulder to shoulder with Marcellinus once more.

The terrible roar of the crowd began anew. Marcellinus let it flow over him like water, like rain, aware only of the smell of his own sweat and Sintikala's blood, and of her shoulder resting against his, solid and strong.

Sintikala had stood by him. In the end she had chosen Marcellinus and the hope of peace.

As they stood waiting, the bloody pools at their feet began to merge.

The noise did not abate, but eventually Onondaga warriors stepped forward to get Marcellinus's attention and turn him around to face the sachems. The Tadodaho gestured in hand-talk, for words could not have been heard: *We speak more of this.*

Marcellinus's eyes met Sintikala's, and for an instant they stared deeply into each other's souls. Then the warriors grabbed his arms and hustled him away, and two muscular tattooed female warriors came forward to pull Sintikala off in the opposite direction.

Bound at wrist and ankle with heavy sinew, lying at the foot of a pole just inside a palisade, Marcellinus had come full circle.

Here, as on his first morning in Cahokia long before, an elderly woman came to feed him, but she sat him upright and spooned broth or corn mash into his mouth and left without comment when the bowl was empty.

She did not understand his words, and tied as he was, he could not do the hand-talk.

His outdoor incarceration lasted eleven days. During that time he saw only the old woman who brought him food morning and evening, roughly smeared salve on his battered leg and the cut on his arm, and three times a day pulled his breechcloth aside and sat him on a chamber pot. On the fourth morning and again on the fifth afternoon it rained; on both occasions the woman eventually showed up to tie an animal skin over him and protect him from the worst of the downpour, but by then the ground beneath him had turned to mud. The woman refused even to meet his eye, which considering that she had to deal with his bodily functions was perhaps all to the good.

Marcellinus endured the indignities as best he could. He was faring better at the hands of the Iroqua than many of them had fared at his. And he was still alive, which meant that Sintikala was probably still alive somewhere, too. In the distance he occasionally heard the sounds of the call and response and the dancing in the evenings. Clearly, powwow was not yet over.

On the twelfth day of his bondage the old woman brought him a savory deer-meat stew. After the food Marcellinus had survived on until then, the smell of it made his mouth water so much that he almost drooled.

Placing the bowl next to him on the ground, she produced a rough wooden spoon and an unhealthily large chert knife.

Marcellinus lifted his wrists. Surely she had not brought herself lunch to eat over his steaming corpse. And he was right: the sinews binding his arms fell away under the sharply honed stone blade.

Suddenly freed, his flesh stung. The woman rubbed his wrists until the feeling came back into them.

"Thank you," he said, unable to do the hand-talk, and she handed him the spoon and smiled.

* * *

" 'The rope,' " said Sintikala. " 'The pole . . . Holding you captive. It had to be, while the elders and chiefs . . . and people of the Five Tribes of the Longhouse . . . smoked? Yes? Smoked and talked. I hope you understand. I hope you will, um, will overlook it.' "

With some difficulty, Sintikala was translating the words of Otetiani, the paramount chief of the Onondaga, known also as the Tadodaho. Behind him in the longhouse sat a dozen or more of the other council members, representing their tribes. Marcellinus had been allowed to bathe and change his clothes before this audience, and apparently so had Sintikala. Her long black hair was still wet and hung loose and unbraided as if she were in mourning. She looked as tired and wretched as Marcellinus felt.

"I understand," Marcellinus said. He didn't, not entirely, but there was little else he could say.

"All must agree," she said. "The Five Tribes . . . They have to talk and smoke until they decide. There was much arguing, many men of loud voices. It takes time."

"They couldn't have just voted?" Marcellinus said a little ironically. Sintikala shot him a warning look, and he shut his mouth.

Again the Onondaga spoke. Sintikala said, " 'Now you will go.' " She glanced at Marcellinus. "He means both of us."

Marcellinus shook his head. "What did they decide?"

"He has not told me."

Sintikala turned back to Otetiani, who spoke for a long time. Marcellinus tried to control his impatience.

Sintikala looked skeptical and spoke again. Otetiani responded. Marcellinus could tell she was having difficulty with the Iroqua words. He would have been almost glad to see Pezi appear.

She asked another chief a question and another. Her eyes widened.

Finally, Marcellinus could no longer stand it. "Well? Sisika?"

But it was Sintikala of Cahokia who turned to face

him then, and she spoke the words of Otetiani, Keeper of the Hearth, the Tadodaho and paramount chief of the Five Tribes of the Haudenosaunee.

" 'By land and water, my warriors will guide you to Woshakee. From there you will go on alone, for it is not safe for the Haudenosaunee to go farther until the news of the peace has spread and all cities of the mound builders agree that the war is over.' "

Marcellinus sagged. "Holy Jove."

" 'In the full of the Falling Leaf Moon, I will come by the Oyo River and the Mizipi River to Cahokia in one of the great canoes that is like a house, in the full light of day. With me will come two other chiefs of the Older Brothers and only a few warriors. We will leave our weapons behind in the great canoe. I will bring a pipe to smoke with your Great Sun Man and your chiefs and elders of Cahokia, and we will talk, and we will bury the ax. I will do this if you—' He means again the two of us, Gaius. '—if you will come forward to greet us when we arrive and stand with us unarmed to guarantee the safety of my chiefs and my warriors.' "

Tears were trickling down Sintikala's face. The paramount chief of the Onondaga and all the Haudenosaunee stared straight ahead, politely disregarding her emotion. Marcellinus slumped forward, his head in his hands.

"I gave him our answer," she said. "I spoke for Cahokia. We will wait for his longship on the banks of the Mizipi at Cahokia by day, when the Falling Leaf Moon is full. And I will bring my daughter for him to meet."

Abruptly she sat down on the blanket and blinked at Marcellinus, more like an owl than a hawk.

His mouth was dry. "Terms?"

"They will want the freedom to travel the Oyo and live on its banks. Beyond Woshakee and perhaps even nearer Cahokia, but they will leave our existing towns in peace."

"Great Sun Man will accept that? And the elders?"

"Will Great Sun Man smoke a pipe with Otetiani

rather than lead a thousand warriors a thousand miles? Yes. He will. And the clan chiefs will accept it if the terms are fair. That talk is for them to make. But if our towns are not threatened and theirs may grow . . ."

Marcellinus struggled to think. "Pezi told me the Cahokian army was already on the march. Is it? Does Otetiani know where they are?"

"He knows only what I told him. They are still far. But we will send runners and canoes south to the Algon-Quian, and they will send the news by smoke signal, west across the land to Cahokia, to halt it. This will work. Demothi will know where the army is and fly to them to take the news."

Still she looked up at him wide-eyed. Marcellinus felt dizzy. "I must think. I must rest."

He swayed, and Sintikala stood quickly and steadied him. "Come."

Marcellinus bowed to the Tadodaho and to the silent chiefs of the Haudenosaunee. Otetiani bent at the waist, bowing awkwardly back. And so the Roman bow traveled one nation farther into Nova Hesperia.

Conversation broke out again. The measured syllables of spoken Iroqua washed over him, guttural but no longer hostile, but Marcellinus had stopped listening.

It was done. They were alive. And the Mourning War was over.

CHAPTER 7

YEAR FOUR, FLOWER MOON

The dragon prow of the Iroqua longship loomed over the oily waters of the Oyo River. Behind Marcellinus and Sintikala the broad black and yellow mainsail flapped loosely. As dusk approached, the prevailing easterly wind had dropped, and the longship was beginning to drift and skew toward the right bank.

Though competent, the Onondaga sailors were no Norsemen in their command of the shallow-draft ship. Terse commands flew, and from Sintikala's amused expression Marcellinus guessed they included a fair selection of Iroqua curses. Rivermen were the same everywhere.

The helmsman steered back into the current while half a dozen Iroqua hauled on hempen lines to reef the sail. Behind Marcellinus and Sintikala, working around their fellows, other braves lifted squares of pine decking to bring the remainder of the long oars out for later, when the wind dropped completely.

Here the Oyo was several hundred yards broad and healthily deep, and they had no fear of running aground. The banks were wooded, and the terrain was gently rolling to the south and mostly flat to the north. They would not need to pull ashore until the light was almost gone. Soon the longship would be rowing into the sunset.

"Sintikala, all of this that you call the land, from Chesapica through to Cahokia? Everything on the big map you showed me? The Romans call this Nova Hesperia, New Land of the Evening. And that's how it feels to me: fresh and new, just made."

Never before had Marcellinus told a Hesperian what the Romans called their continent. It would have seemed presumptuous. But Sintikala knew the land more thoroughly than anyone. He felt that it was important for her to know.

"Just made?" Sintikala shook her head. "It was here always."

"But new to me." Marcellinus met her eye. "New and wonderful."

"Hesperia." She tried out the word. It sounded exotic on her tongue and full of promise. "It is a good word."

"And the land is good. But it is a shame that your map of it was destroyed."

"Destroyed?"

His mouth dropped open at her expression. "Your big map? It didn't burn up when the Iroqua burned your house?"

"I keep it hidden under the floor. In my grain store. I took it out that day so I could show you. The fire did not burn it."

Marcellinus smiled. She still had the map. It was a good omen. "Nova Hesperia," he said again.

She grinned wryly back at him. "But no more Mourning War. No revenge for what Cahokia suffered. No revenge for the Iroqua digging up the Mounds of the Chiefs and the Hawks. Many will not like it. Some may even want to kill you."

"They'll have to stand in line. Chogan and Ohanzee will want to kill me even more. Perhaps even Tahtay." That thought made him sad.

"Not Kimimela, though. Not the farmers and ordinary people, not most of the women. And Cahokia is a great city with great warriors. Those warriors will need to be great enough to put aside their revenge and live with not fighting Iroqua."

"To the Haudenosaunee, what they did to Cahokia *was* revenge," Marcellinus reminded her. "Iroqua revenge for what Cahokians did to their people here along the Oyo."

"So long ago," she said. "What they did to us, that was *now*."

Marcellinus thought of Roma's long history and the lines of hurt that still extended across Europa and eastward from wars fought centuries before. "Two generations. Twenty. Sometimes nations have long memories. But it will work? The peace will hold?"

She waggled her fingers, the hand-talk for uncertainty. "Not for all. Some will always raid. Some Mohawk bands, most of all, and their Huron brothers. Some Seneca. Some of our Wolf Warriors and men from Ocatan. The mound-builder cities that are not Cahokia may want more Iroqua scalps before they rest. But those who fight now break the law of Cahokia as well as of the Haudenosaunee League, and Great Sun Man will stop it. There will be no more big fight. No more complete war."

Marcellinus grunted. For now, Cahokian hegemony had a limited reach. But the spread of writing would help, along with speedier communications once they could install Eagle launchers up and down the Mizipi and fly the three-person birds regularly, with envoys, gifts, and expertise.

And then it would be time for a Cahokian League.

No, greater than that, much greater. A Hesperian League.

"Cahokia should talk more with the western tribes and the southern peoples. I meant what I said to the Haudenosaunee. All of Nova Hesperia needs to stand together, not just the Cahokians and the Iroqua. The Five Tribes already know they are stronger when they are allied than when they make war on one another. If the other peoples of the land can learn this, too, maybe we will make a true confederation of Nova Hesperia."

Over a millennium before, Parthia had been the equal

of Roma. The attempt to shatter Parthian power had left the Roman Imperium so weak that it had almost foundered. That and the civil war between the sons of Septimius Severus that had almost destroyed the Imperium from within were the biggest crises in Roma's history.

Eventually Roma had ground the Parthian Empire into the sand. Geta had crucified his mad brother Caracalla in the Roman Forum, and the Severan Dynasty had unified the Imperium again. After that, Roma had gone from strength to strength for a thousand years.

Surely Hadrianus would not risk any such crisis again.

"If Nova Hesperia is strong enough, Roma will not attempt to annex it. Not with a war in the east against Chinggis Khan to be fought. If Nova Hesperia is developed enough, it can trade with the Imperium without further Romanization—with no further changes beyond those which the people want. There will be no benefit to Hadrianus in conducting a war over such an extended area and every benefit in establishing trading links."

Marcellinus looked at her. "Are you understanding?"

"Some. And I understand you try to convince yourself, not me."

He looked out over the river.

"And you still believe you can march with Roma and dance with Cahokia?"

"I have to."

"Huh."

"I can't fight my own people. When the Romans come again, I won't take up arms against them. I would die first."

Sintikala nodded soberly.

"And so there must be peace," he said.

"If we can make peace with the Iroqua, and you and I with each other . . ." She did not complete the sentence but smiled and leaned so that her shoulder bumped his arm.

Marcellinus could feel the warmth that radiated from her in the evening sun. His heart ached. Her blood now flowed in his veins, but that was not enough, could never be enough. "Sisika . . ."

She raised her hand and shook her head slightly. "What you are about to ask me, Gaius. It is still no."

Three short steps brought Marcellinus to the port gunwale of the longship. He grasped it, looking out over the southern bank of the Oyo and the rolling hills beyond.

"Not yet," she added.

She had spoken so softly that Marcellinus barely heard her. He turned abruptly.

Sintikala's hand was still up. "Perhaps never. You understand? But certainly not yet." She stared deep into his eyes, her gaze steadfast, and for a moment he glimpsed her soul. "Because the past is not forgotten, and we are still broken. Brothers in war, brothers in peace. But not more. It is enough?"

The splash of Viking oars in the waters of the Oyo, the birds on the riverbank, the soughing of the breeze across the bow of the ship; Marcellinus was aware of every sound, clear and crisp, and still gliding above them all in the air, the memory of those words. *Not yet.*

But maybe sometime.

"Yes," he said. "It is more than enough. Thank you."

Her gaze was too penetrating, his own soul too fragile. He had to look away.

"Thank you," he said again.

Sintikala sighed almost sadly. She stepped back to his side. "And one more thing."

Marcellinus was afraid now, more afraid than he had been when he had faced the Council of the Haudenosaunee. Another thing? What else could there possibly be? All of a sudden he stood on the brink of a precipice. "Please. I am old and broken. Speak carefully."

"You are not old. We are different by, what, ten winters?" She peered into his face, trying to catch his eye again. "Gaius, you should listen. I have something else for you."

"Something else?"

"Kimimela," she said simply. "Now she is your daughter as well. She is the daughter of Gaius as well as the daughter of Sisika. If that is what you want."

He could barely comprehend what she had just said. The blood rushed in his ears, roaring like a waterfall or like the flame from the fire jar that kept a Sky Lantern aloft.

His voice shook. "Sisika, I need to understand. Please tell me again."

"It will be three winters or more before Kimimela comes into her moon time and becomes a woman. Until then, she should have a father. So if you will take Kimimela as your daughter, too, I would, it would—"

She turned her face away.

Marcellinus reached for her, not as a lover now but as a friend. "Sisika?"

Tears streaked her cheeks, though she made no sound. "It would be a good thing, I think. For us all."

His arms went around her. His heart was bursting, trying to escape. "I would be very, deeply happy. I would be honored. But Sisika . . . this must be Kimimela's choice. Not mine, not even yours."

"Kimimela has chosen," Sintikala said. "She told me so, very long ago."

The tears came then. Marcellinus did not even try to hide them. Emotion racked his whole body.

He had been dead for so long. Now, all of a sudden, he lived again.

"Thank you," he said at last.

And he kept his hold, chastely clutching Sintikala to him in the cool of the Hesperian evening.

Now they paddled a Woshakee canoe, guests of the Iroqua no longer. The clan chiefs of Woshakee remembered Marcellinus well, of course, from when he had helped liberate their town from the Iroqua. They had offered Marcellinus and Sintikala a warrior escort the rest of the way down the Oyo. But Woshakee still lay close to the frontier of mound-builder territory, and Marcellinus did not want to deprive them of their few men of fighting age, not till he knew the peace would hold. He and Sintikala traveled on alone.

They turned at Ocatan without stopping there and headed north. Here they were paddling against the Mizipi current, but Marcellinus welcomed the honest toil. The closer they drew to Cahokia, the more concerned he grew about the reception that might await them.

He was startled out of his thoughts by a delighted yelp from overhead as a Hawk wing buzzed their canoe. "Sintikala!"

Marcellinus raised his hand to wave, but Demothi had already sped past, back toward the Great Plaza, to announce their approach.

"Well," Marcellinus said. "At least Cahokia has not forgotten how to guard its borders."

Even in that there was sorrow. The Great City would never return to the pastoral complacency it had known during his first months there. "Cahokia does not forget a lesson," said Sintikala.

"Nor do I."

Sintikala looked away. "Really?"

All of a sudden, after all these days alone together, they didn't have much time. Marcellinus could not help himself.

"Sisika? Not soon, not this winter or the next, maybe, or even five winters. But think on it sometimes. Ask yourself whether the good match is Gaius and Sisika."

"Do not think it," she said sadly. "Claim your victory of the treaty. Accept your new daughter. Enjoy them. Do not think of anything more. Do not always be waiting."

Marcellinus met her eye. "It's very hard."

She shrugged, feigning dismissiveness. But her eyes were tender until she looked away.

Already a gaggle of excited Cahokians were running down the riverbank toward them. As Marcellinus stepped ashore, he braced himself, almost dreading it.

Hanska arrived at a dead run, with Takoda and Mahkah a few yards behind. Panting too hard to greet him, the three of them took up formation behind him. Hands on the hilts of their gladii, they eyed the crowd.

"That bad?" Marcellinus said to Hanska.

"Yes," she panted. "Sir."

Sintikala threw Marcellinus a complicated look. He shook his head, bemused.

Others were joining them on the riverbank, the common folk of Cahokia. Many cheered; some would always be pleased to see Sintikala or Marcellinus, and others openly celebrated the peace. But skulking silently all around them Marcellinus saw Cahokian braves he didn't know, many of them Wolf Warriors capable of killing him in an instant.

Wachiwi strode past the Mound of the Flowers with Enopay half walking, half running by her side. She did not greet Marcellinus either but passed him to stand by Hanska.

"Come to the Great Mound," said Enopay. "No delay."

"Not here to welcome me home, then?" he said for something to say.

Wachiwi nodded at Hanska. "She is here to watch your back. I am here to watch hers. She already nearly died for you once."

Enopay pulled at Marcellinus to make him start walking. "Cahokia is close to war. Not with Iroqua now. A war of Cahokia with Cahokia. Many are angry. For today, Great Sun Man is still chief, but many would prefer him gone. Warriors. Shamans."

"Kimimela?" Sintikala asked Enopay.

The boy nodded. "Kimimela is well. Waiting at the Great Mound."

Marcellinus broke in. "But the Cahokian army is back? Great Sun Man welcomes the peace?"

"Of course." Enopay's eyes still darted around the crowd. "That is why you are not already dead."

"The First Cahokian come," said Sintikala.

A few dozen of his men marched—in step, for once—

from the outskirts of western Cahokia with Akecheta at their head. At their approach the circling Wolf Warriors ducked their heads, looking everywhere except at Marcellinus or the cohort.

Amid the First Cahokian, Marcellinus saw Dustu and, next to him, Tahtay, still with a slight limp but managing to keep up. His heart leaped, but Tahtay did not meet his eye.

Akecheta arrived by Marcellinus's side.

"Welcome, sir," said the centurion. "You robbed us of a war."

"Yes, I did."

"And now not all in Cahokia are your friends."

"But you are."

His centurion grinned tightly. "Until I am ordered not to be, sir. Come."

Marcellinus balked. "If Cahokia is on the verge of rebellion, I cannot—must not—walk into Cahokia at the head of the cohort. It would look—"

"Then walk behind us," Akecheta said. "But hurry."

Once again, Marcellinus and Sintikala traveled with an armed escort.

They faced no challenge as they walked through western Cahokia. The Cahokians who rejoiced outnumbered those who scowled, and once the members of the Hawk clan joined the procession, they held the threat at bay. Still, Marcellinus was unsettled. Now accustomed to being accepted in Cahokia and after all he had been through, he grieved that there were men and women here who hated him again.

As they passed the Circle of the Cedars, Marcellinus looked sideways at Sisika. Except that she was Sintikala now, haughty and imperious, seeking out Wolf Warriors with her eyes and glowering at them. "You're all right?"

"They should be dead," she hissed. "Opposing the will of Great Sun Man in this? They should all be dead."

Marcellinus grinned.

They entered the Great Plaza. Atop the Master

Mound, the Longhouse of the Sun gleamed even more brightly. In front of it on the top plateau stood Great Sun Man. Even from this distance there was no mistaking his stance.

"A hero's welcome," Marcellinus murmured.

"Shut up."

As they entered the palisade that surrounded the mound, the warriors closed the gates behind them. Once again, Marcellinus climbed the Great Mound in silence.

"Well done," said Great Sun Man a little ironically. "On the peace? Well done. And can you now bring peace to Cahokia?"

The paramount chief wore his full regalia of office and held his mace in his hands. Beside him stood several of his handpicked warriors. Some paces behind them were Tahtay and Kimimela.

Marcellinus was hot, tired, and bug-bitten. All he wanted was to dip his face in the cool water of Cahokia Creek, brew some bearberry tea over a low fire, and drink it with Sintikala and Kimimela.

As so often happened in Nova Hesperia, what he wanted was not what he was getting.

By Great Sun Man's side, Wahchintonka gripped his spear so tightly that his knuckles were white. Sintikala glared at him. "Your Wolf Warriors must observe the peace. All of them. You have not told them so?"

"Of course he has told them," Great Sun Man said. "And they obey."

Wahchintonka eyed them balefully. "And what will our warriors do now? Sharpen spears they will not use? Polish swords to admire their reflections? How will our young men prove themselves if not by fighting Iroqua?"

Sintikala looked at Great Sun Man. Great Sun Man looked at Marcellinus. Marcellinus was momentarily speechless.

Sintikala said, "A man can prove he is quick and strong without killing another man."

Wahchintonka ignored her. "And what of those who

died here in Cahokia last year? Will we have no revenge? The Iroqua laugh at us now. This is not peace. This is defeat."

Marcellinus was not prepared to face such anger from Wahchintonka. Somehow he had not anticipated it. He respected Wahchintonka as a fine warrior; on that terrible day when Cahokia had been sacked, only Wahchintonka's quick thinking and tactical skills had saved the Master Mound from falling to the Iroqua.

But if Marcellinus had learned anything in a lifetime of campaigning and especially over the last few years, it was that even a fragile peace with honor was better than a war.

He had spoken truly to the Iroqua. The Hesperians could not afford the Mourning War, that constant cycle of raiding and revenge. Not anymore. That was their old world. A new world had come to them now. Marcellinus had brought it, and other Romans would follow; he could not hold it back, and he needed to help the Hesperians understand that.

"There may be other battles ahead," Marcellinus said. "And . . . there is honor in other things."

Marcellinus did not have the words within him right then to explain it to this angry young man. And so he held Wahchintonka's gaze steadily, not blinking, and said no more.

Great Sun Man had been watching soberly. Now he raised his hand and stepped forward. "Enough. These are words we have spoken many times already and will speak again. Even the elders argue about it. But I am Great Sun Man, and I say we will have peace. Peace with the Iroqua, peace in Cahokia, and especially peace here on the mound. We are not two Cahokias. Wahchintonka?"

Marcellinus looked away at the heat haze rippling over the Great City. Eventually, out of the corner of his eye, he saw Wahchintonka nod.

"And now we must talk," Great Sun Man said. "I must hear what you learned of the Iroqua. And tonight the Wanageeska must tell it again to the elders in the Mound of the Smoke."

"Yes." Sintikala glanced around the warriors. "But before you talk with us, I would ask for some time in private with Kimimela."

Great Sun Man nodded and waved the girl forward. "Come," he said to Marcellinus, and ushered him toward the door of the Longhouse of the Sun.

"With Kimimela *and* Gaius," Sintikala said.

Kimimela's eyes widened. She gave a little squeak, and her hand went to her mouth.

Nonplussed, Great Sun Man looked from the girl to Marcellinus and back to Sintikala. "*And* Gaius?"

"Yes," said Sintikala. "It is . . . a family matter."

Part 2

Mizipi

CHAPTER 8

YEAR FOUR, HEAT MOON

Kimimela had grown even in the few short months Marcellinus had been away, and some of her baby fat had turned to muscle. Flying almost every day had given her confidence. "Hello, Gaius."

They stood in the Longhouse of the Wings. Above them, Catanwakuwa hung from the rafters. Sintikala had greeted her daughter almost formally and then had walked out of the longhouse without another word, leaving the two of them together.

In the presence of Great Sun Man, Kimimela had stood still and calm with her chin up. Now Marcellinus could sense the restless energy that bubbled inside her.

Now that it had come to the moment, Marcellinus felt tongue-tied and unaccountably shy. "Hello, Kimimela."

Her face was more angular. He saw more of Sintikala in her now. If he had been meeting Kimimela today for the first time, it would have been much easier to guess who her mother was.

Kimimela was assessing him in return. He hoped she was not too displeased with what she saw. He, too, had turned some winter fat into muscle during his long trek to Iroqua country and back.

She spoke. "And so now you are my father?"

"Your mother said . . ." Marcellinus swallowed,

ducked his head awkwardly, and began again. "If you are willing, Kimimela, I would be honored."

"Have you been a father before?"

"Yes, I had a daughter back in Roma. Her name was Vestilia. But I was not good at it."

Kimimela shrugged. "I am used to that. Sintikala does not know how to be a mother, either. How old is Vestilia? What happened?"

"She is a grown woman now, of . . ." Marcellinus thought briefly. "Twenty winters. Or twenty-one. I was never there for her. Always away at war, and we grew apart."

She eyed him shrewdly. "You will not want to go home to her?"

"No; that bridge burned long ago." He thought about it and said with some wonder: "There is nothing for me across the Atlanticus anymore."

Besides, if he ever did go back to Roma, he would probably be in chains.

But he did not wish to speak of Vestilia or Roma now. "What must I do, Kimi?"

"Many men are fathers. You should ask them. And then let me do whatever I want." She gave him the same quick half grin that he occasionally saw from Sintikala.

She was obviously enjoying his discomfort. This was absurd. "Kimimela, please, tell me what you are thinking."

"I am thinking . . ." Kimimela stepped forward and bowed. "I am thinking that if you are willing to be my father for a while, Gaius, then I would be honored."

"For a while?"

"Well," she said playfully, "you might not like it." And now she smiled, a deep and happy smile.

Marcellinus had often seen Cahokian men hug their daughters. Yet in the three years he had known Kimimela he had never touched her except to guide her when she was making finger-talk on bark with charcoal. The moment called for some kind of emotional resolution, but how to bring it about was quite beyond him. He blinked, and finally Kimimela took pity on him and reached out her hands, palms down.

As he took them, a great weight sloughed off his shoulders. He felt almost light-headed. "You never know. I might like it a great deal."

Kimimela nodded. "Then welcome home, Father."

"Thank you. Daughter."

All at once her face straightened and became stern again. "But."

He resisted the urge to step away. "But what?"

"You left without telling me. You stole a Sky Lantern that was Cahokia's more than it was yours, and you ran off. I am very angry with you."

"I had to," he said. "And I did not *run*."

"You did not trust me. You should have trusted me."

"So Sisika says." He flinched at the look in her eye. "Perhaps I should have. Yes."

"I am glad you made peace with the Iroqua. But if you ever go away again without telling me? And more than that, you went without telling my mother, and that hurt her more than she will say. And if that happens again, then you are not my father, and I will not speak to you again until I die or until you do."

Marcellinus nodded, not trusting himself to speak.

"But at least you came back alive."

"Yes," he said, and then belatedly: "I'm sorry."

Kimimela bowed again. "And so, what would you like me to do now, Father?"

Her face was demure, an expression Marcellinus had never before seen on Kimimela, though the mischievous twinkle in her eye spoiled the effect. "I don't know."

She squeezed his hands and then released them. "I think you should talk to Great Sun Man. And after that, come home, and I will make you tea."

In the early evening Marcellinus stood outside Sinti-kala's house atop the Mound of the Hawk Chief. Sinti-kala was firing a pot, and her kiln radiated heat in the already warm and muggy evening. Kimimela sat cross-legged at the mound's northern edge, adjusting the tension in the sinews that held her Hawk wing taut. From time to time she donned the wing and ran off the mound, glided down to ground level, then climbed up again and worked on the wing some more. She wore a look of utter concentration, and well she might since her life and limbs depended on her handiwork.

Marcellinus and Sintikala had spent most of the day on the Great Mound. Great Sun Man had wanted to know all about their journey, everything they could tell him about the geography of the lakes and the natural arena where the powwow had taken place, the nuances of the Council of the Haudenosaunee and their speeches to the Iroqua nations, and every last detail about the Tadodaho. Later on, Sintikala had left to talk to her clan and Anapetu had arrived. Kanuna, Matoshka, Howahkan, and other high-ranking Cahokians had come to ask questions of their own, and so Marcellinus often had to repeat himself. Once they had dismissed him in the late afternoon, he had found Enopay waiting for him on the first plateau of the Great Mound and had told the story once more. He was hoarse and tired and just as happy to be ignored by his new family for a while as the sun set behind the Great Mound. After all, soon enough he would have to go to the Mound of the Smoke and repeat it all yet again.

"The city is stormy," Sintikala said. "It is not only the Wolf Warriors of Wahchintonka who do not like the peace. Even some of your First Cahokian and my Hawks. They ask where their glory is if they cannot fight. How they measure themselves as warriors if they cannot revenge their dead, bring home scalps, even count coup. Are they men at all?"

Marcellinus thought of Hanska, and of Hurit's lightning-fast gladius work. "Some of them aren't men."

"Most are." Sintikala shook her head. "Most in Cahokia believe the Romans will never come again. The speech you gave to the Haudenosaunee would not work here."

"Really? And what do you think?"

She met his eye. "I think that Roma cannot come quickly enough."

He snorted in disbelief. "You must be joking."

"I think you have used Roma as a threat for long enough. Sometimes when you know a bear is there, it is good to see the bear. People do not believe in what they cannot see."

"Tell that to Youtin."

"You know what I mean. In some ways the Iroqua saw more of Roman power than Cahokia did."

Marcellinus shook his head.

"Anyway. Everything is different again. You cannot live now in the hut we gave you before. You must live here."

Marcellinus glanced behind him at Sintikala's house, his mouth suddenly dry. He almost stammered. "Here?"

"I do not mean always in our house. I mean close by, on one of these high mounds where we can guard you."

Sintikala lived on the northernmost of a line of three platform mounds. They were intended for the senior clan chiefs, but the heads of Thunderbird and Deer were too frail to make the climb and the other clan chiefs chose to live with their families, and so two of the elders lived on them instead.

"Tonight, yes, you must sleep here. But tomorrow Howahkan will move down from his mound, and then you will live there, next to us." Sintikala pointed to the house on the next mound.

"And what does Howahkan think of that?"

"Howahkan has already agreed. Better for his pride to grant a favor for your sake than admit that he wheezes and gasps for an hour after he climbs up to his own house. And that way your mound is flanked by mine and Kanuna's and overlooked by the Great Mound." She looked at him sideways, eyes twinkling. "You can bring Wachiwi there if you like."

"We are not lovers. You know that."

"Very well. But someone must be with you to watch and guard. Another pair of eyes on you."

Marcellinus's face was hot. All day long he had chafed at the almost constant presence of Hanska, Mahkah, and Akecheta in his peripheral vision, and even now he knew that several members of the First Cahokian were skulking around the bottom of Sintikala's mound, keeping watch. "I'll take my chances."

She shook her head. "What does that mean?"

"I want no guards. If any of these hotheads want to kill me, let them try. My friends already hover around me like . . . dragonflies."

Sintikala's mouth quirked at the image. "I am not the one who decides. You are the man who made the peace. If the Iroqua come and we have killed you, what will they say? If Great Sun Man lets you die, what does it say of his leadership? So it is for Cahokia and for Great Sun Man that we must keep you safe on a mound."

She broke the seal on the kiln. Taking up a wooden ladle, she reached inside. The pot glowed a baleful orange as she slid it out and scrutinized it.

Marcellinus had to admit that her logic was unassailable. He was no longer his own man. He had responsibilities. Preparations to make. A daughter, even. He squatted to admire the pot even as it radiated the kiln heat up at him. "All right. But—"

"So this is the Wanageeska, mighty warrior of Roma?"

The new voice was loud and haughty. An even deeper baritone than Great Sun Man's but with an edge of arrogance and derision Marcellinus had never heard from the war chief.

Sintikala had risen to her feet immediately, and Kimimela hurried to her side. But the voice had come from some twenty feet away, probably at the edge of the mound, and so Marcellinus took his time about finishing his examination of the bowl before he looked up.

Striding toward them was a tall muscular brave, his skin covered in battle tattoos and brutally etched in scarifications of whorls and lightning. His braids glistened with fat and clinked with the animal teeth he had woven into them, and around his neck he wore a necklace of bear claws. Marcellinus got to his feet, his hands hanging loosely by his sides.

Mahkah and Yahto flanked the brave warily as he approached. Behind them at the edge of the mound stood the Raven warrior Ohanzee and the young shaman Kiche.

"And who are you?" said Marcellinus.

The warrior ignored the question and instead addressed Sintikala. "This is the outlander you walked with to the snakes of the Iroqua to make Mapiya's secret peace?"

"Avenaka," Sintikala said icily. She picked up the wooden ladle again and held it out before her.

Avenaka laughed. "You think I am here to fight you? I am not. Not today. Nor do you need to protect your old Roman from me." Again he appraised Marcellinus and repeated, "Not today."

"Then why do you approach my house uninvited? If you oppose Great Sun Man, you oppose me. You will leave."

"In good time." Avenaka eyed Marcellinus from top to toe. Stalked around him, making a big show of studying him.

Marcellinus did not turn his head to keep the warrior in his sight. Avenaka was testing his mettle, and Marcellinus had no intention of showing fear. If the tall brave made a move against him, his friends would react, and then Avenaka might find that Marcellinus was not as old as he thought. It would not be the first time someone had fatally misjudged him.

Avenaka came back around and stood contemptuously almost nose to nose with him. Now Marcellinus could smell his sweat and the rancid bear fat that streaked his hair. Like the elder Matoshka, Avenaka was a warrior of the Bear clan. The brave was perhaps two inches taller than he was. Marcellinus held Avenaka's gaze but did not tilt his head back.

"And so, soon the snakes of the longhouse will come and tread Cahokian soil, *invited* by this creature of Roma."

"To bury the hatchet with Great Sun Man and to smoke the pipe of peace with your elders," said Marcellinus.

"To accept our surrender. To gloat upon our cowardice."

"Cahokia has not surrendered," Marcellinus said. "Cahokia has made a treaty."

Still addressing Sintikala, Avenaka said, "This man reeks of lies. He is an outlander and a coward, and he does not speak for *me*."

"And now that you have satisfied your curiosity," Marcellinus said, "you will leave the Hawk chief's mound. Immediately."

Avenaka put his head to one side. "The Roman challenges me?"

Marcellinus stared into his eyes. "Go away, verpa, as the Hawk chief commanded."

Sintikala said, "Avenaka, you will not make trouble when the chiefs of the Haudenosaunee come. Do you hear my words?"

"Trouble?" Avenaka spread his arms. "I, make trouble? Stoop to kill lazy old Iroqua sachems? That is not where honor lies. Let them bring their long pipe and their tabaco. And let Mapiya shower them with his gifts and abase himself before the men who burned his city, just as he smiled upon *this* Roman enemy who would also have burned it had we not burned his soldiers first. Let the people of Cahokia watch Mapiya kiss his enemy's feet. Again. And then we will see."

"What will we see, Avenaka?" Marcellinus demanded. "Tell us."

Once again the warrior looked down his nose at Marcellinus and did not deign to reply. Turning his back, he stalked away. Kiche made the usual whisking motion that shamans made whenever they saw Marcellinus, as if they were trying to flick away dirt or a bad smell, and he and Ohanzee followed Avenaka off the mound top.

"Merda." Kimimela blew out a breath.

"They grow bolder," Sintikala said.

Marcellinus raised his eyebrows. "And who is Avenaka?"

"Brother to Huyana. Once a friend and lieutenant to Great Sun Man. No more, it seems."

"Avenaka owns western Cahokia," Kimimela said grimly.

Sintikala frowned. "He does not. But yes, many who oppose Great Sun Man live there."

Shaking his head, Marcellinus sat and studied the pot again. "Don't worry about him, Kimi. He was just posturing."

"Posturing?"

"Measuring himself against me. Men like Avenaka like to shout and bluster, to show their strength and courage. It's mostly an act. Truly strong men don't need to boast."

It was the quiet ones Marcellinus worried about, the men who faded into the background but who might stab you in the back or poison your food.

Somehow he doubted Kimimela would find this reassuring. He smiled. "Well, so much for that. And now the sun is sinking, and I must go and smoke with the elders."

"There, too, tread carefully," Sintikala said, still dour.

"Have they gone?" Kimimela called, and from the mound's edge Mahkah and Yahto nodded. "And must you go?" she said to Marcellinus.

"Of course he must," said Sintikala.

"You'd have me hide from a man like that? Never." Marcellinus reached out a hand, and Kimimela grasped it, a moment later leaning back to pull him up onto his feet.

He took a deep breath. More talking. Would the day ever end?

"Be careful," Kimimela said.

Marcellinus forced another smile. "Always."

"And so Cahokia gets no revenge on the Iroqua for all those who died," Tahtay said the next afternoon.

"We get peace," Marcellinus said patiently.

Howahkan's house—now Marcellinus's house—had a low brick wall around its yard rather than the wooden palisade that surrounded Sintikala's. Kimimela sat on the wall swinging her legs, staring wistfully at the Great Mound that overshadowed them. A few minutes earlier Sintikala and Demothi had been hurled off it along the giant steel rail, and now they were sparring in the air above. Kimimela's flying had improved markedly in Marcellinus's absence, but she hadn't yet been catapulted off the mound top herself. It might be a long time before Sintikala gave her blessing for *that*.

Now Kimimela looked over at the three of them: Marcellinus, Tahtay, and Enopay. "And how many more of us would die taking our revenge? How many of them could we kill? How many of us would they then kill later to take *their* revenge? And revenge and revenge and revenge? It's stupid."

Tahtay stood, leaning on his left leg. The bend in his right leg was still visible. "And so they get away with *this*?"

Kimimela shook her head. "Tahtay, we killed and injured their boys, too."

"Fine words for you to say," Tahtay said. "Where were you in the battle? Hiding away on that mound."

Marcellinus frowned. "Tahtay . . ."

The leg swinging stopped. Kimimela's voice frosted. "Only because I was too young."

"And who would ever let you fight in battle? Sintikala? *Him*? No."

At "him," Tahtay had jerked his thumb at Marcellinus. Kimimela slid off the wall onto her feet. "Gaius is only my father. He does not tell me who I can fight and who I cannot fight."

"He tells everyone else who they can fight."

"Futete," said Kimimela. "If I fight *you,* he will not stop me."

"No, he would stop *me.* Stop me smacking your head till you beg for mercy."

Marcellinus, who had been on the verge of breaking this up and telling Tahtay to apologize, saw the trap looming before him and closed his mouth.

"Listen again, verpa," Kimimela said, advancing on Tahtay, and for the first time Marcellinus heard the chill tone of Sintikala in her voice. "The Mourning War has gone on for*ever.* People die and die. And it's stupid. I lost one father already. Do I have to lose another? And a mother? And how many more of my friends have to die or, or be . . . hurt, like you? Well, I'll tell you. None. Because now Cahokia has peace. But if you call me a coward, you basket of shit, you and I *will* fight. Right now."

Tahtay was a full head taller than Kimimela. Yet he did not smile but eyed her balefully. "You say so?"

"Stop!" said Enopay. "Please, just stop. Or a hundred hundred winters from now your many-times-great-grandchildren will be sending armies to burn one another's cities."

Everyone's head swiveled to look at him.

"Huh," said Tahtay.

Now Marcellinus spoke. "Are we enemies over this, Tahtay? Enemies over peace? You and I?"

"If you're the Wanageeska's enemy, you're my enemy, too," Kimimela said to Tahtay, still angry.

"You're not helping, Kimi," Enopay said. "Look, the reason you are angry and Tahtay is angry is the same reason *I* am angry, which is not because Eyanosa made peace with the Iroqua but because he ran away and did not tell us where he was going, and we did not know where he was for months."

"Shut up, shrimp," Kimimela said in exasperation.

"Don't call him—" Tahtay sighed. "Kimimela, this is

stupid. I am nobody's enemy, and we should not be shouting at each other."

"At last!" Enopay said.

Kimimela breathed out and looked up into the sky, where Sintikala and Demothi were still flying past each other in the summer-white sky, back and forth in their odd drill.

Eventually she nodded. "All right, then. What *should* we be doing?"

"We should be talking about how to keep Eyanosa alive," Enopay said.

They all stared at him again.

Tahtay cleared his throat. "Well, *I* am going to walk and run. I am going to practice with the sword and the bow, for Cahokia, so I am ready to fight the Iroqua when they break the treaty and the Romans when they come to our land again."

Kimimela snorted. Marcellinus glared, afraid she was about to mock Tahtay further, but she said: "Then *I* am going to fly. For Cahokia." She jumped to her feet and jogged to the mound's edge and down the stairs.

Tahtay shook his head. "Watch your back, Hotah."

Enopay looked quizzical. It had sounded almost like a threat, but Marcellinus understood. "I will, Tahtay."

Tahtay left. He did not walk to the cedar steps but headed directly south, over the edge of the Mound of the Roman and down its grassy bank.

Marcellinus blew out a long breath. "Those two will be the death of each other. Maybe Tahtay should watch his own back." He turned to find the boy already leafing calmly through his books. "Enopay?"

"Do not worry. Kimimela must do that. Much better for Tahtay to be angry than go back to moping, unhappy."

"She's provoking him deliberately?"

"Of course. She cares for Tahtay, and he for her. If they did not, they would not shout at each other so much."

Marcellinus looked at the boy uncertainly. "You say so?"

Enopay shrugged. "Or maybe she is just doing it because she is her mother's daughter and a pain in everyone's side. Did you really *want* to become her father?"

"Yes," said Marcellinus, "more than anything," and then bit his tongue. Enopay, he remembered belatedly, had no father and no mother either.

Enopay tucked his books into his pouch and stood. "Do not worry. I need no father. It is enough that you are my friend. Come, we should walk. Cahokia must get used to seeing you walking around. Once they get used to you again, they will forget they are supposed to be angry with you."

They crossed the Great Plaza. Marcellinus did not have to look around to know that Hanska and Mikasi were coincidentally strolling in a similar direction and that others of the First Cahokian loitered nearby. He shook his head.

"And so you did not take me to see the Iroqua," said Enopay.

"You're joking. Aren't you?"

"Of course. They would just have stolen me and tried to make me a warrior. I did not want to go there with you. But I did not want *you* to go there either."

"Someone had to go. It couldn't be Great Sun Man."

"And now Great Sun Man plays a dangerous game," Enopay said. "He plays chunkey with himself as the rolling target when everyone else holds spears. He hopes that Cahokia's desire for peace and life, and the trust the people have in him, will be stronger than our need for revenge."

"And is it?"

"It cannot be," Enopay said soberly. "For it is the fiercest warriors and the most stupid and violent of our people who are against him, and the peaceful men and women who like to make their pots and grind their corn and bounce their babies on their laps who are for him."

"Oh," said Marcellinus. It was well put.

"Great Sun Man can only win by being stronger and more forceful than the most warlike of his warriors, while also talking of peace. That is a hard thing to do, even for Great Sun Man."

"But there can be no army unless Great Sun Man says so."

Enopay nodded.

"How many soldiers did we have, Enopay?"

"Which we? Cahokia?"

"Mound-builder warriors. Friends from Shappa Ta'atan and other cities along the river. When you began to march to war against the Iroqua, how many were there?"

"How would I know?"

Marcellinus pointed at Enopay's satchel. "Don't mess around, Enopay. You know how many to the man."

Enopay nodded. "Four thousands and six hundreds and a few more who spoke tall but would probably have found an excuse to drop out before we got there. But some of them should not have gone. They were not good enough fighters, and they would have died when the first axes fell." Enopay shook his head. "Some olds would have been lucky just to survive the walk."

"Juno." Marcellinus was impressed. He had deliberately avoided learning how big the Cahokian army was to be or any other useful information that the Iroqua could have tortured out of him.

The number was higher than he had expected, although from what he had seen at the powwow, the Cahokians still would have been outnumbered by the Iroqua.

"How many Romans were in your legion?"

"My legion was understrength," Marcellinus told him. "It had only eight cohorts, where most legions have ten. Each cohort is six centuries. And my centuries had only seventy men. The goal is a hundred per century, although some have only eighty."

"So you had three thousands and, oh, nearly four

hundreds. But other legions can have five thousands or even six?"

Marcellinus looked at the boy sideways. "If you were any sharper, you'd cut yourself."

Enopay frowned. "Praise? Insult?"

"Both."

"So my numbers were right?"

"No, you miscalculated."

The boy grinned. "I did not."

"And how many died when Cahokia fell to the Iroqua?"

Enopay's smile vanished.

"Don't pretend you don't know that, either, Enopay."

Enopay looked out over the shimmering streets of Cahokia, at the men and women carrying jars of water back from the creek. Above them Sintikala and Demothi were no longer visible. Either they had landed while Marcellinus had not been looking or they were above the clouds.

"Enopay?"

"That number I will not tell you."

"Why?"

"Because I do not want you to know," Enopay said. "Because you will add that number to the three thousands and four hundreds of your men, and carry them in the ledger in your heart as the people whose deaths you are responsible for. And I will not help you hurt yourself."

Marcellinus stopped walking. Thirty feet behind them, Hanska and Mikasi stopped, too.

Enopay turned to face him. "You cannot do arithmetic with people. You are not to blame for everything. Just stop."

"What do you suggest I do instead?" Marcellinus asked. "Gardening?"

" 'Gardening' is making a garden, growing corn and askutasquash by your hut? No, not that. That would be a waste of you as well."

Marcellinus took a long look around him. Ahead of

him were the Mounds of the Chiefs and Hawks, marking the southern boundary of the Great Plaza. Ambling around within a hundred yards were even more of the First than he had expected. And beyond them, sitting outside their houses or walking in the streets, were other men. Wolf Warriors. As aware of Marcellinus as he was of them.

"This is absurd," he said.

"What is?"

"My very presence in Cahokia serves as a colossal irritant, doesn't it?"

"What? An irritant is an itch?"

Some still blamed him for the sack of Cahokia by the Iroqua. Others for the peace. Marcellinus had done his best, but he would forever be alien here. He did not have the power to make them love him.

"I should leave," he said.

Enopay paused. "Go? Leave Cahokia again? You have only just returned."

"Yes."

The boy looked away. "Very well. But this time do not forget to tell us when you walk away."

Marcellinus stared, taken aback at the edge in Enopay's voice. "I did not just *walk away* to the Iroqua, and I would not just be walking away now."

He had said nothing yet to Enopay of his plan for a Hesperian League, of building a confederation of Hesperian allies to stand against Roma. Here in the bright open air of Cahokia's main square it might sound like a fever dream. And of all the people in Cahokia, Enopay's scorn might be the hardest to bear.

Marcellinus temporized and said what was also true: "By being here I make things harder for Great Sun Man. Cahokia needs time to accept the peace. Perhaps it will take less time if I am not here."

Enopay nodded. "The Wanageeska. The outsider. The man Great Sun Man listens to instead of listening to his own elders."

"People really say that? Ordinary people, not just Matoshka and Avenaka?"

"Of course."

Marcellinus blew out a long breath. Again he looked around the plaza.

He had spent most of his life traveling. And just last year he had ached to break away from Cahokia and explore, see more of the Mizipi. See the Wemissori, and the lands of grass that went on forever, and the great buffalo herds.

Right at this moment, all he wanted was to stay in Cahokia and live in peace.

But such peace was an illusion with the Wolf Warriors glowering at him from the shadows, Cahokia racked with discontent, and the eternal shadow of Roma looming just over the horizon.

Cahokia's chances of peace were greater if Marcellinus was not in it. And Nova Hesperia's only hope of peace was a strong confederation against Roma.

Marcellinus had a great deal more to do before he could rest. "Damn it."

Enopay was studying him closely. "Eyanosa? You have really decided? To be *not-here*?"

"Yes, Enopay."

Unexpectedly, the boy's lips quirked into a smile. "Then how about building a boat?"

Marcellinus took a cautious step closer to the crumbling edge of the riverbank and peered again into the hull of the Viking—Iroqua—longship. It was a hundred feet long, twelve feet wide at its widest point, yet only three or four feet deep. Marcellinus had always been perturbed by the shallow draft of the Norse longships; they had never seemed deep enough to him, especially in a heavy ocean swell. It was, of course, the keel beneath that kept it stable. The keel that was in this case rammed hard into the river mud below the bank.

In addition, the longship was mired in a cat's cradle of branches and bore the dark scorch marks at the starboard bow where it had been seared by Cahokian liquid flame. But the thwarts and gunwales seemed sound enough. The tall prow, carved into a serpent's body with a gaping mouth, still reached imperiously above the wooden tangle that held the boat firm.

This longship was a drekar, one of the three dragon ships that had assaulted Cahokia on the day of the Iroqua invasion. For a moment Marcellinus felt a chill at the memory of his first sight of them sailing up the Great River: their blood-red sails, the swarms of Iroqua on their decks, the ballistas that had fired on Great Sun Man's position atop the Mound of the Flowers and punched a Thunderbird out of the sky.

"So what do you say?" Enopay asked a little anxiously. "What do you say, Eyanosa?"

Marcellinus said nothing, because he was counting the circular holes for the oars that ran in a line under the shield rack. He counted thirty on each side, yet there were only half a dozen long oars strewn in the bottom of the hull. He wondered if any more remained in the storage area under the pine decking.

Originally the ship had had an iron anchor larger than Enopay and considerably heavier, but it was nowhere to be seen. The bailer and buckets were gone. The copper cauldron that had served as a water cask had been ripped from the hull, with the harsh splinters of torn wood still visible. Marcellinus had seen the glint from such a cauldron in at least one of the drekars as the Iroqua had sailed upriver during the sack of Cahokia, and so he knew they had not removed them. Some enterprising Cahokians undoubtedly had performed some salvage of their own.

Yet the oaken rudder was still there, attached to the starboard side by a tough pleated leather band, and the Norse shields still lined the gunwales in their pine batten racks.

The mast was gone, splintered into shreds about a man's height above the deck. The linen sail, probably one of the few immediately useful things in the boat, presumably also had been carried away and cut into pieces for clothes or bags. Mounted toward the rear of the boat was a horizontal cylinder with a handle; Marcellinus blinked at it for a few moments, thinking vaguely of a wringer for laundry, before realizing it must be a windlass to help raise the yard and sail . . . unless it was for raising the anchor.

He shook his head. "I don't know anything about rigging, Enopay. I mean the ropes that used to hoist the sails." Stays, shrouds; Marcellinus had heard the words but had no real idea how a ship worked, how sailing was achieved.

"The holes for the ropes are still there. If the Iroqua can make it work, we can, too."

Marcellinus experienced another moment of disorientation and nostalgia. Once this bold vessel had been crewed by Vikings. On the long voyage across the Atlanticus, while Marcellinus had occupied a master's cabin aboard one of the mighty troop vessels, this dragon ship had traveled either ahead of or behind him. It had sailed past Graenlandia, down the coast of Nova Hesperia to Vinlandia, and on to the Chesapica.

Then, after all that, an Iroqua crew had captured it and presumably taken it up the great river that flowed into the Chesapica. Somewhere in Iroqua territory they had portaged the boat across the hills and into the Oyo River watershed. They had crewed it and sailed it down the Oyo and up the Mizipi to attack Cahokia, where Marcellinus and Great Sun Man's army had surrounded it with burning trees and done their level best to sink it.

Abandoned by the Iroqua, the longship had beached on a sandbar. Then, when the Mizipi had burst its banks the next spring, the drekar had been swept farther downstream to be dumped ignominiously here in the mud. And here it lay, some ten miles south of Cahokia.

Quite the saga, and a sad end for a craft born in the forests and fjords of Scand that had come a quarter of the way around the world.

If, indeed, this was the end.

"Eyanosa? Gaius?" Enopay shook his head, not understanding Marcellinus's silence. Farther back on the bank stood Akecheta and Mahkah, Mikasi and Hanska, and a dozen other warriors of the First. Few of them looked particularly impressed with the longship; most, in fact, were scanning the river and the copses of trees on the land.

Guarding Marcellinus. And not from Iroqua but from angry Cahokians who might want to pick a fight with him.

"Once you wanted to see the Mizipi," Enopay said. "And the Wemissori, the great plains, the grass and the buffalo. I want to see them, too. Perhaps we can go in this."

"It would take a huge effort to make it riverworthy again. And once mended, a lot of rowing to get it anywhere."

"Rowing?"

"Paddling. While facing backward."

"Why backward?" Enopay shook his head. "Anyway. If the Iroqua have these, Cahokia should have them, too."

"We're at peace with the Iroqua, Enopay."

"The Mizipi is our river," Enopay said obstinately. "We must have these. And we must make more."

Marcellinus laughed. "A longship is not like a siege engine. Building a boat like this is a skill that takes generations to master, passed down from man to boy, father to son." A man had to practice for years even to split a plank with an ax and wedges competently. Marcellinus himself had always been poor at it.

"The pole in the middle will be easy. Cahokian and Ocatani woodmen make such poles all the time. And to make paddles like these will be easy, too."

That, at least, was true, if they could persuade the local woodturners to have any interest in the project. "Say 'mast' for the pole in the middle. 'Oars' for those."

"Great Sun Man will want us to do this," Enopay

said. "He will. And the people of Cahokia will want to see that there is nothing the Iroqua have that we do not have."

Cahokia had cotton to make a sail. Cahokian ropes could be pressed into service. But . . . "Enopay, honestly, I have no idea how to sail a ship like this. I'm a complete landlubber. And we don't have any Norsemen."

On the bank, Mahkah scratched himself. "How much longer here, Hotah? There are many bugs."

Enopay persisted. "Let us at least find men to help us cut the branches away and take it back to Cahokia and out of the water so it does not rot away into nothing."

Hanska stepped down beside Marcellinus. "The boy is right. We should try. We can make a Longhouse of the Big Canoe near the creek to put it in, and you can hide in there away from the warriors of Avenaka who want to kill you."

Enopay nodded. "When your Iroqua friends arrive in their longship to smoke the pipe of peace with Great Sun Man, it would be a nice gesture if we had one, too."

"A nice gesture," said Hanska, at the same time making a crass hand-talk sign. Enopay laughed. Marcellinus winced.

He couldn't resist a jibe at Enopay. "Isn't this another 'clever new thing we do not need in Cahokia'?"

"Yes, but *this* one looks like fun and will not get anyone killed."

"You hope."

But Enopay was right. Cahokia had an army. No reason why they couldn't have a navy as well. And the dragon ship was still a thing of beauty.

Marcellinus gave in. "All right, Enopay. If you can persuade Great Sun Man to be interested, we'll cut it out of the bank and see what we can do with it."

Marcellinus hated his new house. He rattled around in it. It was bigger than his Praetorium tent of the 33rd had been yet had almost no furniture. He was embarrassed by its size, embarrassed that he—the outlander who had brought so much grief to Cahokia—now lived in accommodations intended for a chief or an elder, and embarrassed above all to be constantly guarded.

Whenever he walked out of his front door, someone's head turned. Whether it was Kanuna or one of his warrior friends who just happened to be visiting on the mound south of him; Sintikala, Kimimela, and other Hawks on the mound to the north; Great Sun Man's sentries on the peak of the Great Mound that loomed over him to the west and cut off the sun in the early evening; or even two warriors in a Sky Lantern far above him, there was always someone.

Marcellinus never called for an escort—would never have done such a thing—but somehow it was rare for him to walk across the Great Plaza without seeing Takoda, Mahkah, and others of his First Cahokian in the area and rare for him to approach Wachiwi's hut without seeing Hanska or Mikasi in the vicinity, and he never once headed off across the broad empty space between the Great Mound and the new Longhouse of the Ship without several of his woodturners and warriors arriving at his side to walk him the rest of the way to Cahokia Creek.

He complained to Great Sun Man and Sintikala. Both denied having him watched, and perhaps it was true; Marcellinus was more inclined to blame Kanuna, Akecheta, or Hanska. Or perhaps it was just one of those spontaneous acts of organization that happened from time to time in Cahokia.

Anyway, as the heat of summer gave way to the fall and the leaves turned golden, the threat appeared to recede. Many in Cahokia embraced the peace. The rest, still being whipped up by Avenaka and the shamans, had become convinced that all they needed to do was wait until springtime, when their eternal enemies would break the treaty of their own accord and start raiding again. Then even Great Sun Man would have to accept that all deals were off, and Cahokia again could storm forth and take Iroqua scalps.

Marcellinus doubted it. His own distaste for the Iroqua had evaporated almost completely. If so many Iroqua sachems had agreed, he was confident of their good intentions. But he didn't know it for a fact and had to admit that he had been wrong many times before.

CHAPTER 9

YEAR FIVE, GRASS MOON

Thanks to strenuous efforts by Great Sun Man, Sinti-kala, and Marcellinus himself, the Haudenosaunee peace-making visit in the autumn went off smoothly. The arrival of the Iroqua longship, flanked by an escort of Ocatani canoes, coincided with the peak of the harvest, when many Cahokians were out in the fields anyway or were already exhausted from the heavy work of bringing in the corn. The elders and clan leaders moved around the city enforcing the calm, and Great Sun Man impressed upon the Wolf Warriors that anyone acting against the Iroqua sachems would suffer a long and painful death. Even the intemperate Avenaka stood back, repeating that there was no honor in assaulting an unarmed group of Haudenosaunee bearing a pipe of peace, and ordered his followers to stay away.

And so most Cahokians retreated to their homes and neighborhoods rather than witness the procession of the Tadodaho and his strangely dressed contingent through the streets of Cahokia to the Mound of the Sun. Their visit lasted only a few stilted hours, after which the Iroqua retreated to their longship and set sail again imme-diately.

The peace sealing was followed by an unusually harsh winter, with heavy snowfalls and many weeks in which the temperature plummeted far below freezing and stayed there. Naturally, Youtin and the other shamans declared this the vengeance of the gods on Cahokia for its cowardice, but it did have the useful effect of keeping people off the streets and tucked up in their homes, huddling over their hearths. Marcellinus, who cared little what the Cahokian gods said, worked with the brickworks gang to improve the air and water flow in the Big Warm House and otherwise kept to himself.

He was rarely invited to the Mound of the Smoke. His presence would only have aggravated the situation. From Kanuna, Howahkan, and others he was well aware of the continuing bitter divisions among the elders. Matoshka and Ogleesha were the most vocal critics of peace, but they were not alone. The councils of the elders often broke down in acrimony, with one or another party storming off the mound. And if Great Sun Man could not keep the peace among his elders, it was even worse in his own household; it was widely known that his wife, Huyana, had left the Longhouse of the Sun and gone back to western Cahokia to live with her clan. These days she was seen only in the company of shamans, the hood of her cloak up over her head, or surrounded by Avenaka's warriors, her expression sour. And in the springtime when the snow melted and the river flooded, the flames of dissent lit up the streets once again.

Marcellinus kept his head down. He could not resolve Cahokia's discontent. He had a boat to rebuild, places to go, a league to forge.

"Upriver or down?" Enopay asked for the fiftieth time, and turned it into a chant, marching back and forth along the bank beside the drekar. "Up or down? Up or down? Up or down?"

The woodworkers laughed. Marcellinus sat up in the bow, wiped the rain from his neck, and brandished his adze at the boy. "I don't know, Enopay. Shut up!"

From the stern of the *Concordia,* Kimimela shouted, "Enopay! Merda, do something useful."

"I am doing something useful," Enopay said. "I am stopping you all from dying of boredom. Or melting and draining away in this never-ending rain."

"Go to Ocatan and bring us the rest of the oars," said Mahkah. "*That* would be useful."

Rain cascaded down on the roof of the Longhouse of the Ship and dripped between its planks onto Marcellinus and the carpenters as they worked. The longhouse had no real walls, being a temporary structure that overhung the creek to give the drekar some measure of protection from the elements and prevent it from filling with snow during the winter months. Whenever the wind gusted, Marcellinus and the shipbuilding crew were showered with even more water. Obviously, the weather gods had not finished punishing them for their sins yet.

Nonetheless, the mood in the longhouse was cheerful. Enopay, tireless enthusiast of all things nautical, was joking with the carpenters and woodturners. Those not entertained by him were being charmed by Kimimela. Spring was here, most of the ice was off the river, and a trip was in the air. The boat was almost finished, its hull caulked and watertight. The decking and thwarts were mostly in place, and today Wapi was leading the work on the broken sea chests and shield racks. A new mast of red cedar lay alongside the ship, ready to be installed, and the wood carvers of Ocatan had delivered about three-quarters of the oars the ship would need. Over the winter Anapetu and the Raven clan had sewn Marcellinus a thick yellow sail from cotton leftover from the Sky Lanterns. The dragon prow of the ship had even been cleaned and daubed with war paint, making it an odd hybrid of Norse and Cahokian artwork.

They had a great deal of hemp rope for rigging that they did not yet know what to do with, largely as a result of the efforts of the two men they called the Rope Twins, a pair of middle-aged rope makers who were unrelated but so similar in manner that no one could tell them apart. With their help, Marcellinus had hoisted the sail on the mast once between the many showers of Aprilis to check that it would fit and had tied some of the ropes to it to keep it taut. But it would be another month before he would be ready to guide the longship laboriously along the sinuous creek to the Mizipi and experiment with sailing it.

Upriver or down? Shappa Ta'atan was downriver, along with several other medium-size mound-builder towns whose support Marcellinus wanted to acquire. But the Mizipian communities upriver were Cahokia's buffer with the Iroqua and Huron lands and were perhaps more likely to be directly in Roma's line of march. And then there was the Wemissori River, which led to the tribes of the People of the Grass. Ideally, Marcellinus wanted to talk to them all and enlist them in his league.

Upriver would be harder and thus safer. With the river in spate with the winter melt, rowing or sailing against its current would be difficult work, but at least they knew that current would carry them back to Cahokia when they were done. If they sailed downriver, the return would be a battle every inch of the way, and it would be hard to know how much time to leave for it before winter came.

Then again, the golden birdman amulet that Enopay had given Marcellinus had come from downriver. If there was gold in Nova Hesperia, it came from the south, and Marcellinus wanted to find it.

The decision was not Marcellinus's alone. Great Sun Man would have to agree, and the war chief had other matters on his mind.

Marcellinus stood and stretched and walked the hundred-foot length of the longship, back to Kimimela. "Thank you."

She tugged at the rudder, and the stern of the drekar swayed slightly in response. "Done, I think."

Kimimela had been strengthening the pleating around the band that attached the rudder to the boat. Most of Kimimela's time was spent in the Longhouse of the Wings with her mother or in leaping off the Great

Mound to practice her flying, but knowing her skill with close work, Marcellinus had begged her to come and ensure that the rudder was fastened to the boat adequately enough to withstand anything short of a collision. Kimimela sewed her Catanwakuwa wings with heavy sinew every day, and Marcellinus had blanched at the idea of asking Anapetu or Hurit to do yet more sewing for him. Besides, Kimi could not fly today in this rain, and Sintikala had departed four days earlier, flying east, and had yet to return.

Now Kimimela pulled her feet under her to sit cross-legged, looking down the spine of the longship. "Upriver, and I might even come with you. Down, too many bugs—"

"Hotah." Mahkah stood. Four other men did likewise. The boat rocked.

Mahkah was pointing up at the Great Mound just south of them. Marcellinus turned.

The Longhouse of the Sun was in flames. Great Sun Man's "high temple to himself," as Marcellinus had sardonically called it, was burning. Even in the steady rain, fire shot upward from its roof.

"The Sacred Flame?" Marcellinus asked, but Mahkah shook his head. "That flame is not sacred, I think."

"Shit!" Kimi leaped up. "If those flames reach the Longhouse of the Wings . . ." She vaulted over the gunwale, almost catching her foot on the shield rack, and sprinted off. The palisade wall ran parallel to the creek fifty feet away, but they had placed ladders against it; Kimimela was up and over a ladder in no time and running for the base of the Great Mound.

Still eyeing the blaze, Mahkah dropped the hammer he had been holding and strapped on his belt and gladius. His expression was grim. The other six members of the First Cahokian who were helping that day stepped up beside him, looking to him for guidance. Wapi and the other Cahokian craftsmen looked nervous, clutching their tools.

"Mahkah, what do you see?"

Mahkah's eyes were keener than most, but he shook his head. "Nothing. That is why I fear." He climbed ashore.

Marcellinus's own sword was in the bow of the *Concordia*. He also kept a full breastplate, helmet, and greaves there in case of attack, but there was no time to don them now. He ran to snatch the gladius and clamber over the side of the ship, joining the warriors on the bank.

Kimimela had already passed the Longhouse of the Thunderbirds. Others of the Wakinyan clan had streamed out of their longhouse and were running with her up the slope beside the steel launching rail.

"You should not have let her go," Mahkah said.

Marcellinus wiped the cold rain out of his eyes. The fire on the mound top was sputtering out by itself, yielding to the downpour, and the Longhouse of the Wings had not caught fire. Still he saw no one on the top of the Great Mound. Mahkah was right: a fire like that, and nobody fighting it? Chill foreboding wormed up his spine. "Come on."

They jogged to the palisade wall and climbed over it. The grass was slick, and Marcellinus slid as he ran. Fearing a twisted ankle, he fell behind Mahkah and the others before they reached the mound. By then Kimimela and about thirty members of the Wakinyan clan were about halfway up. The northern face of the Great Mound was the steepest and had no plateau, and in the rain even the young and fit were finding it hard going.

All of a sudden the top of the mound erupted into violent activity. Even over the rain Marcellinus heard the clash of weapons, shouts, and more than a few screams. As they stared upward, a man came running off it. He tumbled, rolling and bouncing and bumping uncontrollably.

Following him over the edge of the mound, almost falling himself but managing to keep his legs under him in an ungainly, asymmetrical run, came Tahtay with a gladius in his hand.

"Juno!" Fear lent Marcellinus speed, and he hurried up the steep incline after Mahkah and the others.

Warriors fought on the mound's edge, many others falling over it to skate and slide on the wet ground. In the gray light, Marcellinus saw the darkness of blood.

Around the base of the mound came more people. Some were warriors, running in their strange lope with axes and spears at the ready, others the ordinary towns-folk of Cahokia.

The first man who had tumbled off the crest of the mound came to a halt in the wet grass. He rose to a knee, grimacing in pain, looking back at the mass of people above him.

He wore a kilt in a blocky pattern, and his short feath-ered cloak was drenched and torn.

Tahtay arrived at Great Sun Man's side in his painful half-limping run, grabbing at tufts of grass to stop him-self. He had been waving the gladius as he ran to help keep his balance, almost as if he were attacking Great Sun Man himself, but now he pushed the hair away from Great Sun Man's eyes, talked to him urgently, tried to force the sword into his father's hand.

Great Sun Man was bleeding from the head, neck, and stomach. He looked up at Tahtay, dazed.

On the slope above Marcellinus, Kimimela screamed in fury and sprinted out ahead of the members of the Wakinyan clan. With a sick fear, Marcellinus saw that she was unarmed except for a pugio she had pulled from her belt.

Huyana appeared at the mound's crest, rain streaming off her hair. She held her head high, looking down at her wounded husband with no sign of emotion.

Beside her was the tall figure of Avenaka, who strode off the mound top and down toward the kneeling figure of Great Sun Man. In one hand he held an ax; in the other, Great Sun Man's massive chert mace of office.

Tahtay was on Great Sun Man's right. Kimimela ran in from the left and knelt by his side.

Wolf Warriors lined the top of the mound now. The

members of the Wakinyan clan had stopped, frozen in fear.

Avenaka stomped down to Great Sun Man, death in his eyes. A dozen of his warriors followed him.

Tahtay stopped trying to push the gladius into his father's hand and stood to face Avenaka. But Kimimela was talking to Great Sun Man, her face close to his, and now she lifted his hand and placed it on her shoulder.

Great Sun Man shoved himself upright, seized the sword from his son, and, with a howl more animal than human, hurled himself up the slope at Avenaka.

Chert mace met Roman steel. The mass of the mace knocked Great Sun Man's gladius aside, but with his last vestiges of agility the war chief whipped it around and thrust upward at Avenaka's gut, roaring in pain.

Avenaka dodged back from the blade and kicked out. His boot met Great Sun Man's ribs just above the wound in his stomach. The war chief fell and rolled.

Marcellinus, gasping but near them now, found some breath to shout. "Kimi! Tahtay! Bring him *down*!"

They heard him, leaping to Great Sun Man's side and pushing him farther down the hill, away from Avenaka.

Marcellinus ran at Avenaka. The muscled warrior barged into him, shoving him aside, intent on pursuing the injured Great Sun Man as Tahtay and Kimimela half pushed, half pulled the war chief down the side of the mound.

The warriors of Avenaka and Mahkah had clashed now and were fighting, gladius against ax. The high ground benefited the Wolf Warriors, but the footing was treacherous, and more than one warrior swung a blow only to slide and crash to the ground.

Marcellinus threw himself after Avenaka and swung his sword. Avenaka ducked and lashed out. Marcellinus felt the slash of the warrior's ax in his calf even as Avenaka's boot met his sword arm; the impact took Marcellinus off his feet and onto his back, and he skated helplessly for several feet.

A Wolf Warrior landed untidily on top of him, and

Marcellinus grabbed at the brave's war braid to yank his head back and deliberately lurched outward to let gravity help him. They rolled another ten feet, and Marcellinus at last managed to get his gladius around.

The Wolf Warrior kicked at him again, but Marcellinus slashed him in the face, opening his skin from mouth to ear, and dragged the sword across the man's stomach. Struggling free and pushing himself up to his knees, he drove the gladius home for the kill.

Now below him on the mound, Avenaka had caught up to Great Sun Man once more. Marcellinus sat on the mound, dizzied but determined, and slid down toward the two men.

Hands grabbed his arms and shoulders. He saw Mahkah bowled head over heels down the mound. Many of the other warriors of the First Cahokian were bloodied and fallen.

Great Sun Man struggled to get to his feet, and the tall warrior allowed it, waiting for his opponent.

The war chief lunged, and Avenaka swung the terrible mace.

The crack it made as it met Great Sun Man's neck was audible all the way up and down the mound. Great Sun Man's head twisted at an uncanny angle, blood spraying into the air, and he slumped to the ground.

Everything went still. Clutching the mace, Avenaka looked down at the body of Great Sun Man as if he could not believe it himself. Tahtay was a statue, mouth wide, gaping at the fallen body of his father. Kimimela looked from Avenaka, to Tahtay, to Great Sun Man, to the dagger in her own hand and then, finally, at Marcellinus.

From the mound top Huyana gazed down, her face still expressionless.

Mahkah held up his hands, palms forward. The Wolf Warriors' arms fell to their sides. Where men were still fighting, their comrades waded in and pulled them apart. Everyone knew the battle was over.

Avenaka took a step toward Great Sun Man's body,

and that drew Tahtay out of his funk. Climbing upward on hands and feet, he plucked the sword out of his father's hand and stood facing Avenaka.

"Tahtay, no!" Kimimela shouted.

Marcellinus held his breath. Tahtay and Kimimela were both within Avenaka's reach, and no one else was anywhere near them.

Marcellinus was a good twenty feet above them on the mound and off to one side. He recognized the two Wolf Warriors who held him from the fight against the Iroqua on the slopes of the Mound of the Flowers the previous year; perhaps this was why they had chosen not to slay him. "Let go of me," he said, and as they did, he clamped his hands on the wound in his calf and tried to stand.

Below him, Avenaka stared at Kimimela and Tahtay. For a moment he did not seem to know what to do.

"Step away," said Avenaka, and then seemed to pull himself together. Drawing himself up to his full height, he repeated it in his resounding and imperious baritone. "Tahtay and Kimimela, step back. And tell your Roman to stay where he is."

Moving as if in a dream, Tahtay moved to stand over his father's body, sword still in hand. Marcellinus, too, ignored the command, limping painfully down the slope until he arrived by Kimimela's side.

Great Sun Man was dead, his neck broken. Blood still leaked from his other wounds. It was too late to help the paramount chief who had spared Marcellinus so many years before. But if Avenaka made a move against Tahtay, Marcellinus was utterly willing to yield his life to defend him.

Otherwise, attacking Avenaka would be suicide. Avenaka had the greater weight and the longer reach, and Marcellinus stood literally on a slippery slope.

At the top of the mound, Youtin lifted his head. "The gods have spoken. The people have heard them and have acted. Mapiya has been called to the gods, and is no longer a chief of Cahokia."

More townsfolk were coming now, drawn by the hubbub, streaming around the base of the Great Mound to either side.

Avenaka spoke. It was the voice of command, Marcellinus realized: the loud and deep baritone, similar to Great Sun Man's, that the people associated with their leaders. They would listen to what Avenaka had to say, this bastard who had just slain their war chief.

Marcellinus felt sick, the delayed reaction of Great Sun Man's death now sinking into his soul. He reached for Kimimela, who grabbed him to steady him. Tahtay was looking down at his father's face. His expression was solemn, and there were no tears in his eyes. The fight had drained out of him, replaced by sorrow and desolation.

Marcellinus forced himself to listen to what Avenaka was saying.

". . . south and east of Cahokia, killed the men of our village, and took the women. Our women, fifteen women of the Mizipi, of Cahokia, stolen by filthy Iroqua raiders just yesterday.

"And so we went to the coward Mapiya and demanded that he send out a war party after them. The elders spoke, and the shamans, and his warriors, and even his wife, Huyana, and his lieutenant, Wahchintonka. Mapiya stood firm against us all."

Avenaka looked around again. Everyone was listening. He nodded and hit his stride. "We demanded our vengeance on the Iroqua. Mapiya refused us. We again demanded that he send war parties after our stolen women. Mapiya became angry, said that it was a lie, that the raids were a trick. He accused us of plots against him. It was wild talk, foolish. Had we killed our own men, abducted our own women? No. But so Mapiya said. Mapiya told us that the Iroqua would not break his secret treaty, the alliance he made using this snake of Roma as his tool. Mapiya said we could not have blood for blood, that he would merely send a runner to the Tadodaho and beg for—"

"You lie," said Tahtay. "The raiders who took our women were of the Tuscarora, from the east and south, not of the Five Tribes. Our braves saw their Tuscarora tattoos with their eyes and told Great Sun Man of this with their mouths, and these are the truths—"

Avenaka paused, looking down on Tahtay in contempt as the rain poured down his face and off his nose. Now he broke in. "Many of you cannot hear his feeble little voice, but Mapiya's crippled spawn tells me that I lie, that I am a dog and not a man, and that the raiders of yesterday were some other Iroqua tribe and not the tribes his lying, treacherous father begged for mercy. This is not so. I have spoken, and if my words are not enough, then hear Huyana, his wife, or Matoshka the elder, or Wahchintonka, his first lieutenant, or any of a hundred warriors who were on top of this mound this day, seeing with their eyes and hearing with their ears, and they will tell you the same."

Tahtay shook his head and knelt. Gently he forced his father's head back in line with the rest of his body and then straightened his arms and legs, the cloak around his shoulders. Placed his hand on his father's breast and closed his eyes.

Avenaka nodded in satisfaction. "And so Mapiya ordered his warriors against me. Instead, they stood back. The rest you see before you."

On the mound top the Wolf Warriors moved aside. In their places the other elders and clan chiefs had arrived. Mute, they gazed down at the scene before them: Avenaka speaking, Great Sun Man dead in Tahtay's arms, Kimimela and Marcellinus standing close by, the townspeople at the base of the slope.

Avenaka looked up at them, trying to catch each eye in turn.

More movement now as the rest of the First Cahokian walked around the base of the Great Mound from the right, not in marching formation but as a group of men and women, walking with Akecheta at their head. They formed up in three ranks. In a military formation but with few weapons, and those held down by their sides.

Marcellinus understood. They were not preparing for battle. They were honoring the fallen.

Hanska stepped forward from the First and began to climb the mound, head bowed. With her came Enopay.

Avenaka looked up at the assembled elders and clan chiefs again. "Mapiya is dead, and I live. And so I say that I am now war chief of Cahokia."

And there it was. With a simple declaration, the world had changed. Again.

Marcellinus braced himself. "Over my dead body."

Avenaka inclined his head, a smile on his lips. "Very well."

From the top of the mound came Huyana's voice. Marcellinus had never heard her address a crowd before, but she sounded firm and calm as she said: "Spill no more blood today. There is no cause."

Avenaka waited, still holding Marcellinus's eye.

Huyana continued. "I was Mapiya's wife. But Mapiya stood against the gods and against Cahokia. My brother Avenaka speaks the truth, and now my brother takes Mapiya's place. It is done. I have spoken."

The clan chiefs looked at one another, except for Anapetu, who was worriedly trying to catch Marcellinus's eye. Marcellinus resolutely ignored her. "And so, Avenaka, you will make war on the Iroqua again?"

Avenaka regarded him and spoke to him directly for the first time. "We will send a war party after our stolen women. We will stand ready to avenge ourselves. But first we will clean out the rot in Cahokia, the festering stink that has polluted it."

Well, the man couldn't possibly have been any clearer than that.

With Great Sun Man dead, Marcellinus was as good as dead, too. He held no power in Cahokia anymore, had been spared in the first place only through Great Sun Man's protection. Now, with a war chief in power who hated him, Marcellinus knew his prospects were bleak indeed.

Marcellinus raised his gladius.

Tahtay caught the movement and quickly got to his feet. Kimimela raised a hand as if to seize Marcellinus's arm but realized the foolishness of impeding him and instead stepped aside.

Behind Avenaka, Wahchintonka and Matoshka were walking down the slope toward them.

And beside Marcellinus appeared Hanska and Enopay.

"Get away," Marcellinus said. "No need for you to—"

"Shut up," Hanska said quietly. "Do not do this. Sir."

"I offer you mercy, Roman," Avenaka said. "But I offer it only once. Refuse it and you are a dead man." He turned his head. "And you, son of Mapiya, the same. Only once."

Avenaka raised his voice. "You there below, who call yourselves the First Cahokian and use Roman weapons and take orders from this man: I offer you mercy, but only once. Brave warriors of Cahokia, if you will be a friend to Avenaka and an enemy to the Iroqua, join me now. Swear allegiance to Avenaka and be welcome. Refuse and you are banished, never to return to the Great City or any town or village that bears fealty to Cahokia."

Avenaka half smiled. "Even you, Mapiya's crippled spawn, and you, Roman. Swear allegiance to—"

"Never," said Marcellinus.

"Avenaka will die," Tahtay said venomously. "And all who serve him. Heads smashed. Scalps taken. Throats slit. Bodies burned in the fire. I am Tahtay, I am the son of Great Sun Man, and I have spoken."

Avenaka glowered at him. "Then you are banished, Tahtay, gone from the Great City as if you had never lived. And you, Wanageeska, who betrayed us: you also are banished, and you will go today and never return to Cahokia, on pain of death. And do not think to go to Ocatan or any other Mizipian town or village nearby. Those, too, you shall not enter.

"You others, brave warriors of Cahokia, swear allegiance to me and be welcome."

"Eat your own shit," said Hanska.

Avenaka stared at her in disbelief.

"I go with the Wanageeska. Someone has to keep him alive."

"Hanska . . ."

"Not just me," she said.

She gestured down to where the First Cahokian Cohort was dividing into two groups. Most were already turning and walking back into Cahokia. Marcellinus saw Takoda among them, along with many other family men. The second group, by far the smaller, was marshaling under Akecheta. He saw Yahto, Napayshni, and—to his surprise—Chumanee.

Marcellinus blinked. "They can't do that. They can't give up their homes, their—"

"That is for them to choose. Come. Tahtay, you, too."

Tahtay shook his head, his gaze still fixed on Avenaka.

"Tahtay . . ." Wahchintonka looked at Avenaka and back to the boy. "We will take the body of Great Sun Man and lay it in the house of the dead. He will be buried in the Mound of the Chiefs, with honor." Wahchintonka looked at Avenaka. "Is it not so, war chief?"

Avenaka paused, then conceded. "It is so."

Marcellinus was counting the men. It was difficult until Akecheta marshaled them back into ranks, and then he knew. Three ranks of twelve. Thirty-six warriors and Chumanee, plus Hanska and Mahkah, who stood beside him. The men and women who were giving up everything for him and for Tahtay, for Akecheta and Mahkah, and for one another.

Marcellinus did the arithmetic again and raised his eyes to look out at the Longhouse of the Ship.

"No," Avenaka said. "The big canoe belongs to Cahokia. You will walk."

Marcellinus lifted his gladius. "That longship was built by my people. We will take it."

Avenaka shook his head. "You are banished, and you

will walk. Be grateful I let you take the clothes you wear and the sword in your hand and do not cut you down like a dog."

Marcellinus looked at the *Concordia* again. With the drekar they might have a chance. Without it, how far could they possibly get?

His fingers tightened around the hilt of his sword. But when he turned back to face Avenaka, he saw Enopay walking away from him, up the hillside toward Avenaka.

"Let them take it," Enopay said. "It is a stupid canoe, anyway, and slow. What use is it to Cahokia?"

Avenaka looked at Enopay in surprise and some suspicion as the boy came to stand by his side. "You say so?"

"I say so," Enopay said. "And of everyone here, I should know. It is another stupid Roman thing we do not need. Let the banished take it. Let us clear every useless Roman thing out of our Great City as the shamans have said. Let us mend Cahokia."

Enopay put his hand over his satchel and looked up at the new war chief. Avenaka eyed the boy shrewdly. "And you will swear allegiance to me?"

"Of course," Enopay said. "I serve Cahokia, and now Avenaka is Cahokia."

"I will kill you, shrimp," Tahtay said thickly. "I will take your stupid young scalp and wear it on my belt."

Enopay shook his head. "I do not think so. I think you will leave Cahokia in the big canoe with your pitiful collection of banished friends, and we shall not see you again."

He met Marcellinus's eye once and then looked away.

Avenaka looked up at Youtin.

At last the rain was stopping. Youtin smiled and raised his hands. The shaman said nothing, but his meaning was clear: Avenaka ruled, and the gods were happy. Marcellinus resisted the urge to spit.

"Then go," Avenaka said. "I give you your lives. But go now, immediately, and never return."

Even now, Marcellinus paused. Backing away and leaving this man to his victory stuck in his craw. Leaving Great Sun Man, fallen in the wet grass.

But there was no sane alternative. They were hopelessly outnumbered. Avenaka's Wolf Warriors still lined the top of the mound, and most of the First Cahokian had gone. The townsfolk and the men and women of the Wakinyan clan were drifting away in silence.

The day was lost. Marcellinus had to swallow his pride and retreat. Even with that, it would be a miracle if they survived to see another dawn.

"Gaius?" Kimimela looked up at him, close to panic. "What do I do?"

"Go with the Wakinyan clan. They will protect you until Sintikala returns. Stay with them. Be safe."

"But you and Tahtay . . ."

Marcellinus closed his eyes briefly. "Stay. Serve Cahokia. Forget us."

An edge entered her voice. "That is the stupidest thing—"

"Stay with your mother, damn it." Marcellinus pulled her closer and kissed her on the forehead. "Good-bye, Kimimela."

And without another word Marcellinus turned his back on the new war chief of Cahokia and hobbled down the mound toward the palisade and the Longhouse of the Ship beyond.

"Mahkah, get the shields into the shield racks wherever they'll fit. Stack the others under the deck. Then get the decking down and in place. You men, put the tools into the chests. Oars into the holes. Clear all the wood away from underfoot—no, Wapi, inside the ship, under the decking; we're taking it. Then bring the mast aboard and lay it down the center of the hull. Chumanee, are you sure?"

Her eyes were red and her face streaked with tears, but her voice was strong and clear. "Of course. Live under the shamans? No." She spit.

"Thank you," he said awkwardly.

"Great Sun Man brought me to Cahokia," said Chumanee. "He gave me my life. Avenaka . . . ?" Words escaped her. She shook her head and went to help Mahkah with the shields.

Marcellinus took stock. Shit, they had almost nothing. A few swords. Two water jars. No bows or arrows. No food at all. He hoped someone had a flint in his pouch to make a fire.

This was madness.

But the men around him were relying on him. He had to try.

He looked again. Yes, aside from Chumanee they were all men. Hanska was not there. But she had sworn to stay with him, had stood up to Avenaka. Had she changed her mind? Had someone gotten to her? "Juno . . ."

In the bow of the drekar Tahtay huddled in a blanket, staring into space, still in shock. The woodturners were wide-eyed, the Rope Twins on the edge of panic. The warriors of the First Cahokian were more methodical, with Akecheta and Mahkah helping to direct everyone, getting ready to go. Three dozen warriors plus fifteen craftsmen: just over fifty people in all in a Norse longship designed to be rowed by sixty at a time and crewed by a hundred.

Well, at least they had oars for everyone. And they weren't under attack. Yet.

Mahkah pointed. "Two more coming."

A boy and a girl had come around the corner of the palisade and were running toward the boat. For a moment Marcellinus's heart leaped into his mouth, thinking of Kimimela, but this girl was taller.

"Dustu. Hurit." Mahkah nodded and went back to stacking shields.

Of course, those two would never abandon Tahtay. They clattered on board, Hurit with a sword and Dustu carrying six spears. Marcellinus wished they'd had the presence of mind to bring food.

Hurit hurried to Tahtay's side and tried to put her arms around him, but he flinched and fought her off.

"Tahtay?" she said, hurt.

"Go back, idiots!" Tahtay shouted. "There's no need for us *all* to die. Go back!" He shoved Hurit again, and she fell onto the pine decking.

"Hey!" Dustu pushed Tahtay back. "Hey, shithead, respect her!"

"Stop!" said Marcellinus. "Now. All of you. Dustu, leave three spears in the front and put the others in the stern. Yes, in the stern, go. Hurit, let Tahtay be until we're away from here. Get ready to cast off the ropes. Everyone else grab an oar except, uh, you two men; go to the bow and fend off the bank if we get too close. Akecheta, you'll take the helm."

They shoved off. Too close to the bank to row, they poled themselves clear with the oars so energetically that they careered across and rammed the bank on the other side. Cahokia Creek was only thirty feet wide. It was a mercy that the creek was high from the spring thaw and that Norse ships had such a shallow draft.

"Gods' sakes," Marcellinus said. "All row together. Keep to the center. One . . . two. Come on, all pull at once when I say. Akecheta, you need to anticipate when you're steering. The ship doesn't respond immediately. Think ahead. One . . . two."

They started to get it. Marcellinus spared a glance for the top of the Great Mound and the Wolf Warriors who still watched them. He was absolutely sure that if the crew of the *Concordia* tried to come ashore again, Avenaka's warriors would use it as an excuse to attack.

On they went. It was a nerve-racking journey. The way Cahokia Creek twisted and turned, it had to be a full six miles to the river. After they went aground for the second time, Marcellinus sent Hurit into the bow to prod with one of Dustu's spears and shout back to Akecheta where the deepest part of the channel might be.

Painfully slowly, over the next two hours the longship wound back and forth toward the Mizipi. The rain had stopped, but a cool wind still blew. Everyone was simultaneously sweating and shivering, and Marcellinus had to shout at them constantly to keep them rowing in time. He half expected them to throw down the oars and storm off the longship, but since they were facing backward, they could all see the war parties of Wolf Warriors who watched contemptuously from onshore, axes and spears in their hands. There was no going back now.

They passed the Circle of the Cedars. Now western Cahokia was on the port bow, the part of the city where most of the Wolf Warriors lived. Still no one attacked them. In fact, a celebration seemed to be going on in the West Plaza. In the bow Tahtay put his hands over his ears and buried himself even deeper into his blanket.

Marcellinus knew how Tahtay felt. The death of Great Sun Man still weighed heavily on him.

And he had lost Kimimela. Would never have the chance to say good-bye to Sintikala, who was presumably still far from Cahokia and had no idea what she would fly into when she returned.

Enopay. Hanska. Kanuna. Takoda. Howahkan. Marcellinus was leaving behind almost everyone he knew. Of all his original Cahokian friends, only Tahtay, Akecheta, and Mahkah remained to him. And Tahtay was broken physically and perhaps now in his mind as well.

Up ahead he saw the Mound of the Flowers. Gods, at last they were coming to the Mizipi.

And two more people were heading for them, running. Warriors, and armed . . .

Hanska and Mikasi. Each carrying six unstrung bows, several quivers of arrows, and a deerskin bag full of swords. And each, thank the gods, clutched a bag of what looked like food, although that surely would not go far with four dozen mouths to feed.

"Sorry," Hanska said as they climbed aboard. "Couldn't leave without my man, could I?"

Marcellinus felt touched and overwhelmed. "Thank you, Hanska, Mikasi . . ."

Mikasi dug into his pouch. "Fishhooks and lines. Nets. Flints. Pugios to trade if we must. Some dried deer meat." He grinned. "And tea and hazelnut cakes from Nahimana. She says to tell you that you are a headstrong fool and will be dead in days. And your toy people, who Wachiwi says are important to you." He handed Marcellinus his small golden lares, representing his household gods.

Hanska unwrapped the swords. "Below your toys in your little shrine was a fine gladius, and we brought that, too. Is it good?"

Lost for words and in danger of losing his composure completely, Marcellinus could only nod. It was the gladius with the ornate hilt he'd had specially made before going to war with the Khwarezmian Sultanate just after being promoted to tribune, the sword that he had thought lost after his legion perished but that Great Sun Man had returned to him before the battle of Woshakee. This sword and his golden lares were the only pieces of his former life that remained aside from the Aquila of the 33rd itself. He was oddly overcome to be holding them again, and they gave him strength.

Although he had to admit that the fishhooks would probably be much more useful. He resisted the urge to hug Hanska and Mikasi for their quick thinking. "It is all very good, and I am grateful and very happy you are both with me," he managed eventually, and sat down.

As the First Cahokian rowed the longship into the Mizipi, the current took it, forcing the bow around. They swung helplessly, spinning broadside as they were thrust downriver. Then Marcellinus got them all rowing again, and Akecheta steered the ship's nose into the current.

The Mizipi had them in its grip. It was good that Marcellinus had not set his heart on going north.

"Well, Enopay, I guess we're going downriver," Marcellinus muttered under his breath as they passed the Mound of the River and picked up even more speed.

It was all he could do by way of a good-bye. In all likelihood he would never see the boy again.

Marcellinus took a deep breath. He was leaving Cahokia, after all, a moon earlier than he had anticipated, with a meager crew, few weapons, and little food, in a half-finished boat they had yet to learn how to sail.

Staying alive; now, *that* would be the challenge.

"Enopay," Tahtay said dully. "How could he?"

Marcellinus had been sitting at the bow with Tahtay. Not talking, because the boy merely sat morosely staring into the boards of the hull. But Marcellinus wanted Tahtay to know he was there and have company of a sort. And now he had spoken.

Marcellinus's heart ached. "He had to. Enopay holds the trade numbers, counts the corn, counts the warriors. Avenaka would never have let him go, and even if he had, Kanuna would have died before he let Enopay be banished. Enopay knew all that. So instead of defying Avenaka, he helped us. Said the words that would make it easier for Avenaka to let us go."

"He swore allegiance to Avenaka! He swore!"

"Yes, and he was lying."

"How can you know that?"

"Because he also said the longship was stupid."

"It *is* stupid," Tahtay said. "And we will all die in it. What can we do? How can we live?"

"Hunting. Fishing. Trading."

Tahtay snorted. "Trade with what? Once the spare pugios are all gone?"

Looking up, Marcellinus saw that a good half of the *Concordia*'s crew were within earshot and looking somber. It was an important question.

And so he forced a laugh that was much more cheerful than he felt. "Pugios? We have a lot more than that."

He waited for someone to bite, and naturally it was Hanska who called out. "What? A lot of what?"

"Expertise," he said promptly. "Hurit, Dustu, Tahtay: you understand brickmaking and bricklaying like no

one else in Cahokia. You can make fine kilns and granaries. I know about smelting iron and steel, and a few
others of you have worked in the steelworks. And I
know some blacksmithing."

He stood up and paced down the center of the longship by the mast. It was critical to raise their confidence,
make them a team. "I brought wheelbarrows, nails, and
bronze to Cahokia; I can bring them to other towns.
And all of you here? Either fine warriors who can teach
men to fight or excellent craftsmen—woodturners, rope
makers, with steel tools of a quality no one else on the
Mizipi can match. Wapi and the others can make more
spears and arrows as we travel. We aren't just going to
survive, Tahtay. We're going to thrive."

"Thrive?" Tahtay laughed painfully, almost gasping.
"You are a fool. We have lost Cahokia, and we are too
few to protect ourselves, and we are dead."

A brittle silence descended over the boat. Men lowered their heads.

Nobody, including Marcellinus, wanted to argue with
a boy who had just seen his father murdered before his
eyes. And in truth Marcellinus had given up much less
than had the Cahokians around him who had abandoned family and clan. So he merely said, "We'll see.
But if we stand together now as we have stood together
before—"

"Catanwakuwa," Dustu said suddenly. "Hawks coming."

Mahkah stopped rowing and leaned back, shading his
eyes. "Three of them. No, five. And one's an Eagle."

Marcellinus peered upward. He could see three of the
wings; he'd have to trust Mahkah about the other two.

He might have known it had been too easy.

"Bows," he said tersely. "Dustu, Hurit, pass bows to
Mahkah and Yahto . . . String them, nock arrows, be
ready. Remember to fire well ahead of them. Akecheta,
hold us steady in the main current. Everyone else, stop
rowing and grab shields."

They pulled the round Norse shields out of the shield

racks. Marcellinus took a wooden shield for himself—
they had more shields than people—and walked forward down the center of the ship.

"Fighting," Dustu said in amazement.

It was true. The birdmen were ducking and weaving
in the sky, a thousand feet up.

One of the Catanwakuwa swooped in hard over the
Eagle craft, which spilled air and slid to the right to
avoid it and then banked hard. On its other side another
Hawk reared up as if in defense of it, almost stalling,
then dived again.

"Slings," said Mahkah. "Slings and rocks. The one
above has a bow. Oh . . ."

The Eagle craft had seen the longship. It arced around
into a dive and headed straight for them.

Marcellinus exhaled and picked up one of Dustu's
spears.

Two of the Hawks followed the Eagle down. They
saw the larger craft shudder as rocks hit it and bounced
off the taut wing material.

As the Eagle craft loomed, a broad white ribbon unfurled behind it.

"Holy Jove," Marcellinus said.

"Shit," said Hanska. "She's going to—"

Akecheta hit the deck as the Eagle roared over his
head and then spilled air. The Hawks came after it.
Rocks and a couple of arrows smacked into the hull of
the *Concordia*.

The Eagle belly flopped into the water between the
Concordia and the bank. One of the Hawk pilots hurled
rocks while the other sent arrows into the wing. The
other two Hawks were dueling above the ship, wheeling
back and forth. More arrows flew.

Mahkah and two other men shot at the same time.
Only one of their arrows found its mark, burying itself
in the chest of the Hawk pilot who was even now banking above them and hurling rocks into the boat.

Several hundred feet above them one of the Hawks
shattered, its right wing appearing to crumple. The craft

flipped and then fell out of the air, spiraling hard into the Mizipi with an immense splash. The surviving Hawk headed for the bank.

"Demothi, that," Mahkah said laconically. "Do not shoot him."

The single remaining Hawk streaked north away from the *Concordia*. But still Marcellinus could see no movement from beneath the Eagle craft. "Akecheta, get us over there, damn it."

As one, Dustu and Hurit dived over the side of the longship and swam splashily over to the wrecked Eagle.

A head broke the surface, spit, and then ducked under again. Dustu kicked hard, sending himself underwater while Hurit grabbed the wing and started ripping at it, breaking spars, shoving debris aside.

Kimimela's head appeared. Hurit pulled up another figure.

The *Concordia* had floated downstream of the Eagle, and in the chaos of the moment its crew were all rowing against one another. Oars collided, and the longship swung around. From the bank Demothi watched, shaking his head, hands on his hips and the broad Hawk wing resting on his back.

Sintikala and Kimimela broke surface and swam free of the Eagle. Hurit and Dustu unbuckled the third pilot and dragged her away from the cords and spars. All five swam for the shore and pulled themselves out of the water, panting.

Belatedly, the *Concordia* arrived at the riverbank, and Napayshni jumped out to moor it.

Ignoring everyone else, Sintikala stepped into the longship and strode to the bow, where Tahtay sat. She perched beside the boy and began talking to him quietly. Tahtay, startled out of his funk for once, looked up at her, shook his head, then nodded at whatever she was saying to him.

The third Eagle pilot looked familiar, but Marcellinus couldn't place her. She and Demothi began to strip the Hawk down, loosening its sinews, unhooking its wings, and folding them so that they would fit in the confines of the longship.

Shivering and dripping, Kimimela stared up at Marcellinus. "You really thought we'd stay in Cahokia?"

"You banished yourselves?" Stunned, Marcellinus looked again at Sintikala in the bow.

Kimi shrugged. "You did tell me to stay with my mother."

"Not us," said the third pilot. "Demothi and I return to Cahokia. I am Chenoa."

Demothi gave Marcellinus a wry look and walked forward to say good-bye to Sintikala. The Hawk deputy clan chief had never really taken to Marcellinus.

Now Marcellinus understood the plan. Kimimela was not yet proficient enough to fly a Hawk the distance needed to catch up to the *Concordia,* and so Sintikala and Chenoa had brought her on an Eagle. But Sintikala would need a Hawk, and so Demothi had brought one for her. And now Chenoa and Demothi would return to Cahokia on foot.

"You will be safe there?" he said to Chenoa. "After helping Sintikala escape?"

By her look of scorn he recognized her now: Chenoa was the pilot of the Eagle who had flown him to the Mizipi during the battle for Cahokia, who had swooped down over the longships so that Marcellinus could see into them and know that they were fighting Iroqua, not Norsemen or Romans. She looked young and tough and no fonder of him than Demothi was. "We will tell him Sintikala threatened us and gave us no choice. If Avenaka wants his clans to fly, he will not slaughter their best pilots."

"You will swear allegiance to Avenaka?"

Chenoa's eyes narrowed. "Of course. We have family."

Marcellinus nodded.

Sintikala rested her hand on Tahtay's shoulder, then walked back down the drekar. She nodded to Marcellinus as if they had just met in the Great Plaza and set about stowing the Hawk for the voyage.

Demothi and Chenoa raced into the trees, and the *Concordia* put out into the river again. Marcellinus stood with Akecheta in the stern, talking to the crew in as encouraging a way as he could manage. He pointed out how well the dragon ship rowed, how sound it was, how they already had enough planks and nails on board for any repairs.

Eventually Marcellinus walked between the rowers to where Sintikala stood in the bow, almost as rigid as the wooden dragon head at the prow.

"You banished yourself." The magnitude of what Sintikala had done overwhelmed him. She had left her city and her clan, perhaps forever.

"Serve the man who murdered Great Sun Man? You could not. How can you think that I could?"

That logic was unassailable. "Yes. Sorry. Will they pursue us? Try to get us back?"

She hand-talked, *No.* "Avenaka has Cahokia. We are gone."

"And Great Sun Man is dead."

"Yes."

Marcellinus looked south into the sun. "I hardly even know Avenaka."

"You have never favored shamans and those who put their faith in them."

"And our treaty with the Iroqua?"

"If the Iroqua raid again, Avenaka will strike hard. Blood will be met with blood. And if Avenaka and the shamans want war, they will always find an excuse or make one."

"Then it was all for nothing? The Mourning War begins again?"

"Perhaps."

"And will they really be safe? Demothi, Chenoa, after helping the two of you to escape?"

"Avenaka kills Chenoa and Demothi at his peril. They

are popular. If he wants anyone to lead the Hawks and fly Eagles now that I am gone, he will accept the allegiance they swear."

Marcellinus nodded. They had made their choice, and there was nothing he could do to help them, anyway.

Instead, they were heading rapidly away and could never return. Every day they sailed downriver with the current would take them three, or four, or five days farther away from their old lives. "And so we go south."

"Yes. Now we are birds that fly south for the winter." She pursed her lips. "Maybe you will find some gold."

"Ha." His renewed obsession now seemed as foolish as it had the first time around. Hold off the Romans with gold?

Roma was a task for tomorrow. Today it might be all they could do to stay alive.

"We'll need fresh water," he said. "There's little enough left in the jars. And a strong place to sleep where we can hide the longship behind some overhanging trees or up a creek. Behind a sandbar, perhaps. Four watches of three men each. We'll need to stay alert. And keep the crew busy so they don't brood."

Sintikala nodded, but Marcellinus had never seen her look so tired and broken.

"Thank you for standing with us," he said quietly.

Her face was a mask. "I had no choice. Kimimela stood with you. Tahtay stood alone. And you and I, we swore a blood oath."

"You regret the oath?" The words were out of his mouth before he could stop them.

Sintikala stared out over the waters as if she had not heard. "I have lost Cahokia. My father was war chief. Now his daughter is banished. And when Great Sun Man needed me, I was not there."

"You can hardly blame yourself for that."

She turned on him, eyes flaring. "Can I not? You do not remember what I told you? When my husband was killed, when he needed me most, I was not with him, I was not there. Today-now, once again I was in the wrong place. *Not there*. It is my life, to *never be there*. To fail. And then men die. Men die."

Marcellinus did not know what to say. Bitter memories of his own failures came flooding back.

He reached out. He wanted to comfort her, somehow, or perhaps to comfort himself. But she stood like iron, and he let his hand fall back by his side.

"We will keep an eye out for a creek, then," he said. "For fresh water."

Once more Sintikala nodded, her expression forlorn, as their somber crew rowed the *Concordia* down the endless river.

CHAPTER 10

YEAR FIVE, PLANTING MOON

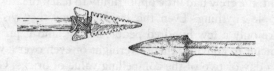

South they went, day after day.

They passed Ocatan at speed early on the third day and kept going. The blue waters of the Oyo, still swollen by snowmelt, entwined with the greenish murk of the Mizipi to produce a broader river with water of a deep golden brown. Relatively straight as it passed the hills and forests north of the confluence, the Mizipi now twisted sinuously through an endless procession of broad curves and oxbows, arcs of water that almost looped back on themselves. Sailing was difficult on a river that could not stay remotely straight for even a few miles at a time, and they relied on the oars to keep them in the deepest part of the channel, where the current could carry them; left to its own devices, the *Concordia* would spin off into eddies and end up in the shallow waters on the outer edges of the curves. The crew also had to stay constantly alert for floating tree trunks, submerged snags, and the endless sandbars that would rise beneath them and threaten to ground them even when they were far from the bank. The Mizipi was not a tame river.

They passed mound-builder towns, villages, hamlets. Most nights they stopped and made camp on the bank, sleeping either ashore or on the longship. After two weeks they judged themselves safely clear of Cahokian hegemony and cautiously began to make contact with the communities along the river. Occasionally they stayed as guests in the huts of a riverside homestead. Always they were welcomed; always those mound-builder communities already knew who Marcellinus was. Word had clearly spread far and wide.

But even in his grief and cynicism, Tahtay had been right: the crew had little opportunity to teach the townspeople anything. Even the largest towns they visited were only a few hundred people strong, and it proved difficult to convince them overnight or even over a visit of a day or two of the compelling value of bricks. Gifts of Cahokian iron and Roman steel were greeted enthusiastically enough, but the townsfolk did not jump at the opportunity to learn how to smelt and forge such items themselves. Mostly their interest was in the Wanageeska, with his unusual skin tone and curly hair, his odd bearing, and his quirky way of speaking their language. He was a curiosity and a local celebrity, and they were pleased to meet him.

What the villagers valued above all else were Marcellinus's traveler's tales: of the Iroqua lands, of making peace, of the Roman Imperium and the lands across the ocean from Nova Hesperia. Marcellinus had not anticipated that one of his most useful talents would be as a storyteller, but this happy discovery played nicely into his desire to warn people of the dangers of Roma and to build his Hesperian alliance piece by fragile piece.

As for their own status, it was a tricky balancing act. In most villages they chose not to mention their banishment at all. By now they were traveling well ahead of the news that Great Sun Man was dead, and raising that issue would only have created complications. Fortunately, at this far remove from the Great City, none of the men and women they met knew Great Sun Man personally or asked after him. Sintikala merely declared herself the chief of Cahokia's Hawk clan, and that was that.

As for Marcellinus, he was being educated at breakneck speed in the ways of the mound builders. Each village and town was different from the one before. He saw a huge variety of building styles, customs, and standards of dress. The farther south they traveled, the more the townsfolk lived in pole-and-thatch houses that were round instead of square, and after pitching in one day to help build one, Marcellinus saw that this might be a more effective building technique.

Most villages used dugout canoes or round hide-covered coracles braced with wood rather than the sleek birch- or elm-bark vessels of the Cahokians and Iroqua. Everyone harvested fish from the river, but in different ways. The larger towns used broad nets of hemp with rocks for weights and dried goldenrod galls as floats. The villagers fished from coracles or from the bank, using smaller nets, hooks and lines, or even spears. Apparently only Cahokia used the fish weirs, static traps with wooden stakes and webbing of vegetable fiber that used the Mizipi current to funnel the fish into big nets that took a dozen men to haul to shore.

Many towns and villages specialized in certain crafts or trades, such as carving and firing exotically glazed and ornamented cups and pots. One town was totally devoted to the carving of arrowheads, which they traded to Cahokia for the other items they needed. All, however, farmed and built mounds; in many towns the chieftain or head shaman would live atop the largest platform mound, staring regally out over his domain like a feudal lord of pagan Europa. Other villages might have no building at all on the principal mound, merely a carved cedar pole.

But all Mizipians buried their honored dead in the conical or rectangular mounds. After a while Marcellinus grew adept at estimating the population of each new town from the river, based on the number of mounds he counted as they paddled closer; all he needed to do was multiply by forty.

Naturally gregarious, most of the crew helped Marcellinus considerably in entertaining the villagers and being good guests. Sintikala and Kimimela, though, were prone to moodiness and often stayed in the longship to guard it. As for Tahtay, he had no interest in talking to anyone and frequently disappeared onshore for hours at a time, following the boat unseen and wandering into their camp again late at night.

The first time he stayed away overnight, Sintikala walked out to a hill large enough to launch herself from and took to the air to look for him.

It was fortunately a day of sufficient warmth to keep her aloft. Meanwhile, as the dense forests had given way to relatively open country, Kimimela, Hurit, and Dustu were jogging along the riverbank. Some distance behind them came a group of a half dozen Cahokian warriors, among them Hanska and Mikasi, Yahto and Napa-yshni, who also chafed at sitting still on the *Concordia* the entire day. The novelty of the river journey was beginning to wear off for all of them.

Sintikala reappeared from the east, flew across to the far side of the river, and looped up, swinging around. Sometimes when a suitable hill or crag offered itself and the wind was right, she would launch herself and fly ahead of the boat to look for a good mooring place for the night and land there to await the ship. Today the strength of the southerly wind would limit how far she could go, meaning that they'd need to pull over to the bank to pick her up.

Akecheta helmed the longship. The wind was blowing against them and the sails were stowed, but the waters were capricious, and the First Cahokian centurion was finding it tough to keep the *Concordia*'s nose straight and not be pushed out into the slow eddies on either side of the main current. Now he glanced up and behind him in some alarm as Sintikala swooped down and came in low over the water toward them. "Merda!"

"Oh, gods," said Marcellinus, scrambling to his feet and running forward, bumping into Mahkah and Chu-manee, who also were making all haste away from the rear of the dragon ship.

Spilling air from her wing, Sintikala passed over the

raised stern with inches to spare and thumped down hard into the hull of the *Concordia*. The drekar pitched with the force of her landing and then yawed hard to the left as Akecheta lost his grip on the rudder altogether and tumbled forward onto his hands and knees.

Sintikala was safely aboard with her feet beneath her but was now in danger of being pulled over the side by the wind. She dropped to one knee, yanking at her straps and pointing the nose of the Hawk downward, as two of the woodturners jumped up and grabbed the edges of the wing. On the nearby shore, Kimimela and the warriors stood stock-still, mouths agape. The *Concordia* swung broadside to the current, and some of the men in the bow dug deep with their oars. Akecheta got to his feet, muttering and shaking his head, and grabbed the rudder again.

The two men lifted the wing off Sintikala, and she began to break it down. His heart still pounding, Marcellinus stepped back toward her. "You should have warned us you were going to try that."

Sintikala grinned. "More fun this way."

"You might have gotten wet," he said. "Or worse."

"Someone is following us," she said quietly. "Not Tahtay. Someone else. Watching us from the far bank. Staying under cover. You've seen?"

"Yes, of course," Marcellinus said shortly. "I'm not blind." He moved in closer. No sense in spooking the crew with this.

"For three days now. Sometimes we leave him behind when the waters and winds are with us, but always he is back again the next day."

"Not Enopay, I presume." Marcellinus was only half joking. "I only catch a glimpse now and then."

"A grown man. A warrior by the way he moves. If there are others, they are clever enough to not be seen."

"Might Avenaka have sent a runner to check that we keep heading south?"

Sintikala shrugged. Who knew?

"And you didn't see Tahtay?"

She shook her head.

Now that they were farther from Cahokia, they moored the *Concordia* in defensible locations when they could, sometimes on islands or sandbars in the middle of the river, to deter thieves or any roving bands of Tuscarora. They already assigned watches through the nights. There was little else they could do but remain vigilant. "And how far to Shappa Ta'atan?"

She shrugged again. "This is farther south than I have been before on the river. From high in the air it all looks different."

They saw nothing more for the rest of the day, nothing but the twists and turns of the Mizipi. By now Marcellinus could tell the difference between the natural eddies in the water and the ripples that showed where the underwater snags were. Like Akecheta and Mahkah, he was learning to read the river.

It was just as well. They might be on it for a long time.

When they stopped to fill the jars with water that afternoon, Tahtay appeared as if he had never been away, stepping into the longship and retreating to his place in the bow. Hurit and Kimimela went to speak to him, but he ignored them both, curled up, and apparently went straight to sleep.

Back on the river, Dustu and Hurit approached Marcellinus in the stern. "Wanageeska? Tahtay can't go on like this."

"You're telling me?"

"You need to fix him again."

Marcellinus shook his head. "I may have managed it once, but then his only problem was a leg wound."

Hurit looked worried. "If he keeps wandering around by himself, a bear will eat him."

"Eat Tahtay?" Dustu snorted. "Tahtay is so bitter that the bear would spit him right out again."

"Dustu, Tahtay's father was killed. Right in front of him." Marcellinus took a breath. "Tahtay was proud of Great Sun Man. And now he feels . . . shamed as well as grief-stricken."

Even for Marcellinus it was hard to speak of this. He shook his head again. "Breaking things is easier than mending them. Give him time. Gods know, we have enough of that."

It seemed that Marcellinus had only just put his head down on his kit bag when something touched his knee, and he was awake again in an instant. Hanska's silhouette was there before him in the dark of night, her fingers over her mouth in the hand-talk that meant *Be silent.*

Nodding, Marcellinus sat up cautiously. It was the early days of the Flower Moon, and the crescent moon would not rise until just before dawn. The Mizipian constellation known as the Spread Hand was directly overhead, meaning it was just past the middle of the night.

Following his warrior's lead, Marcellinus carefully picked up his sheathed gladius and crawled to the gunwale of the longship.

They had tied up to the trees at the river's edge. The ground nearby had been too marshy and damp to sleep ashore. Starlight glistened in muddy pools across the reeds.

Aside from that he saw nothing, no one. But again came Hanska's hand on his arm, stilling him and warning him to keep silent.

Marcellinus stole a glance down the longship. Around them everyone slept except Sintikala, who watched them unblinking from near the bow. The Hawk chief reached out and touched Kimimela on the shoulder, and the girl, too, came awake. She reached up to rub her eyes, but her mother pushed her hand down. Understanding immediately, Kimimela reached for her dagger.

Marcellinus and Hanska lay side by side like statues. The shoreline was in shadow. A breeze grazed the top of the waters, and the reeds rustled. Marcellinus felt his hair prickle.

Hanska exploded into motion in an instant, leaping

onto the gunwale and hurling herself out onto the river-bank. The longship lurched and rolled in reaction, and its crew awoke and scrabbled for weapons. All at once the night was alive.

Marcellinus stood and flicked his gladius. The sheath flew away and clattered down between the thwarts, baring cold steel. He vaulted over the side of the ship, but his toes caught on one of the shields and he almost tumbled into the shallows of the Mizipi that lapped against the hull. Recovering his balance, he began to run.

Hanska was thirty feet away, pounding into the reeds. She had thrown her sword aside and was reaching out.

A man scrambled to his feet and turned to run. He had left it much too late. Hanska crashed into him and took him down in an almighty splash.

Marcellinus was close behind but could no longer see them in the murk. He expected enemies to rise up around them at any moment. Behind him, Akecheta shouted, "Bows! Nock arrows! Wait for the order!"

As Hanska dragged her man to his feet, Marcellinus passed her and skidded to a halt to cover her, blinking into the night, gladius up and ready for any assault.

Again he scanned the bushes. No one else came at them. Could the man really have been planning to attack them alone? Marcellinus looked up the bank, down it.

"Just this one." Hanska wasn't even breathing hard. "And he's not armed."

"Bows down!" Akecheta called from the *Concordia*. "Stand easy."

Marcellinus was not so sure and spent a few more moments staring into the darkness before he would lower his blade.

A sneak thief, then?

"All clear," Hanska said. "Really. Uh, Wanageeska?"

Marcellinus nodded and exhaled. "All right."

He turned.

Hanska had wrestled the man's arms behind his back,

but he was not struggling. He stood peaceably enough, streaked with mud, watching Marcellinus.

Marcellinus blinked. The man had a mustache. The first mustache, he thought dazedly, he had seen in years.

"Hello, sir," the man said in Latin.

Marcellinus took an involuntary step back and rubbed his eyes. The man before him did not vanish; rather, Aelfric smiled tentatively and had the good manners to look a little sheepish.

"Gods above," Marcellinus said in awe. "How is it that you live?"

Aelfric shook his head. Marcellinus had spoken in Cahokian.

A feeling of unreality rocked Marcellinus like a strong wind. Was he still asleep and dreaming?

From behind them Kimimela translated Marcellinus's words into Latin, and now it was Aelfric's turn to look startled.

Marcellinus made a grand effort to pull himself together. "What happened to you? Where have you been all this time? How could you possibly—"

"Bind him." Sintikala strode up to them, sinew coiled in her hand. She tossed it to Kimimela.

"Wait," Marcellinus said. "This man . . ."

"Bind him."

Kimimela looped the sinew around Aelfric's wrists and knotted it while Hanska held him firmly.

"I know him," said Marcellinus.

"Talk to him, then," Sintikala said. "Ask why he creeps around in the night. Ask why we should not kill him."

Kimimela translated the questions for Aelfric. Aelfric cocked an eye at Marcellinus. "A word, Praetor?"

"Ask him if there are others near," Sintikala said. "Other *Romans*."

Kimimela did so.

"Well, are there?" Marcellinus asked. "Who else lived? Don't tell me you're the only one. That would beggar belief."

"None nearby," said Aelfric. "Up the Wemissori, a couple of dozen, living with the People of the Grass. About fifty more headed northeast two years back, hoping to make it through to Vinlandia. I didn't fancy their chances, frankly. Instead, I came looking for you. Isleifur Bjarnason is with me, but he went on ahead, downriver a ways, in his canoe." Aelfric grinned. "There's scouts for you. Always have to be out in front."

Kimimela shook her head in frustration. "You talk funny."

"He's a Briton," said Marcellinus, also in Latin. "They all talk funny. His name is Aelfric."

A long silence fell as everyone looked at everyone else, and then Kimimela shook her head and said to Sintikala in Cahokian, "No other Romans around here," and Akecheta at last sheathed his gladius.

"What do you want with us, Aelfric?" Kimimela asked.

Aelfric looked at her. "With you, pet? Nothing."

Hanska yawned. "Can I kill him yet? Or at least gag him till dawn?"

"Why come by night?" Marcellinus demanded.

"I've been following you downriver by land," said Aelfric. "Watching. Waiting to get you by yourself so we could talk without me getting—" He quirked his mouth wryly. "—captured or killed. Last two nights in the middle of the night you've left your bed to take a piss, but I've been too far away. I hoped you'd come ashore again tonight, and maybe I could get your attention after, and we could talk. Quietlike. *Can* we talk?"

Kimimela turned to Sintikala. "He wants to talk. In case you couldn't tell. It seems to be what he does best."

Marcellinus sighed. "Back to bed, everyone. Sintikala, Akecheta, this man saved my life once. Let me speak with him and find out what he knows."

Gratefully, Akecheta and the warriors clambered back into the longship. Sintikala still frowned. "Hanska and Kimimela stay with you. And *he* stays tied up."

"Me?" Hanska said indignantly. "I caught him and *I* get to suffer?"

Sintikala turned away. "Just keep him quiet and keep everyone safe."

"After the battle? We ran hard and fast into the north. Swam across the Mizipi after we had an ill meeting with an Iroqua war band and went on westward across the grasslands. There we'd probably have died if Isleifur Bjarnason hadn't caught up with us. He took us north to the other big river, the Wemissori, and then along that for a month or two. And that bloody grass goes on forever and has some strange beasts browsing on it. It's not just the buffalo. Have you seen the horns on the wild sheep? And out there we stayed with the People of the Grass, and some of the men took native women to wife and decided things weren't so bad. But others were burning to get home if it was the last thing they did."

"Talk slower," Kimimela said.

Aelfric grinned. "All right, lass. Sorry."

It was so long since he'd heard such a torrent of Latin that Marcellinus could barely keep up, either.

Aelfric was muscled and long-haired. He wore a tunic in the style of the tribes of the plains and torn and well-worn moccasins. Not a trace of Roman clothing remained on the man, yet somehow he still held himself erect like the tribune he'd once been. Marcellinus tried to sit up straighter. "And was it?"

"Was what?"

"Was it the last thing they did?"

"Don't know. Perhaps. It's a devil's long way, Vinlandia, according to Isleifur. Far out beyond the lakes, right on the other side of Iroqua country. There's the biggest of the lakes, and that spills out into a river and leads you there, but the river is locked down hard by the Iroqua and the Hurons and the Ojibwa, and there's no canoeing along it, not if you want to keep your heart inside your chest. They own the water, and they own the land." Aelfric shrugged. "I wasn't up for that, but a bunch of the men would do anything for the chance to get themselves out of Nova Hesperia and home, and I'm not saying they were wrong. Off they went."

"How long ago?"

"This was in the second summer."

Marcellinus worked the numbers in his head. "And the rest stayed, but you came south?"

"Yes. I missed trees."

Kimimela screwed up her face. "Trees?"

He grinned. "Up there? Pretty much grass, grass, grass to the horizon. I wanted to see honest woods again. If you ever go up there, you'll understand. And as for the others, they remembered what the summers were like down here." Aelfric fidgeted, twisting his arms to try to keep the blood flowing. "And then I heard about the Wanageeska. Making war. Making peace. Generally making a nuisance of himself."

Marcellinus rubbed his eyes. Dawn was still three hours distant, but he might not get any more sleep tonight. Tomorrow would be a long day.

"My turn to ask something," Aelfric said. "Where are you going?"

"South."

"Well, I see that."

Marcellinus saw no reason not to tell him. "We're banished from Cahokia. Exiled, forbidden to return. Now heading for Shappa Ta'atan, another Mizipian city." He paused. "Shappa Ta'atan may have gold."

"Gold?" Aelfric stared.

Marcellinus dug into his pouch and held up the bird-man talisman. "Yes, I'm afraid so."

Aelfric exhaled. "Damn."

"Yes."

Kimimela looked from Marcellinus to Aelfric and back again. "What's that? What is gold?"

Her bafflement broke the tension. The Briton grinned at her. "What's gold? You're a cute one."

"Stop flirting with my daughter," Marcellinus said, provoking a double take from Aelfric. He pointed to the talisman Enopay had given him and continued, "And 'damn' is right. Kimimela, this is gold, and my lares are gold, and the Romans will do *anything* for gold."

She looked at the shiny object carefully and handed it back. "Including send more legions?"

"Especially send more legions," Aelfric said.

"But *do* they know?"

"Once they realize I lost a legion here, they'll be back, anyway. But one of the reasons the 33rd was sent here in the first place was to search for gold. If Roma found out it was here, they'd be back double-quick. They would fly here."

"Fly?"

"Not literally. But they would come very fast."

"And your Romans might find out from the men who went to . . . Vinlandia?"

"Or from any survivors from our garrison at Chesapica who managed to escape the Iroqua."

"Oh, they know," Aelfric said. "I'd bet you a good sword—or you a fine coney for dinner, young lady—that the Imperator knows the fate of the 33rd by now. Even if none of them made it back, Hadrianus will have sent out ships to sniff around and see what became of us. They know. I feel it in my water."

"In your *what*?" Kimimela gaped.

"And on that fine note, we should get some sleep." Marcellinus looked over his shoulder at the dark outline of the dragon ship, trying to remember which warriors he was supposed to wake up to take the last watch of the night.

Aelfric raised his wrists. "Marcellinus, man. You're really going to keep me tied up? Can I at least go and get my pack and my gladius from over yonder?"

Marcellinus grinned. "We'll ask Sintikala in the morning."

"She's the fierce one?"

Kimimela laughed, and Marcellinus nodded. Aelfric eyed the sleeping Hanska; unable to follow the conversation, she had nodded off some time earlier, sword still in her hand. "And women rule the roost in this tribe? Where does that leave you?"

"Alive," said Marcellinus. "At least for now."

Dawn saw the longship back out on the river and Aelfric freed; even Sintikala saw no need to bind a man who could row, especially a man surrounded by Cahokian warriors. From the look in her eye Marcellinus suspected she would not be particularly sorry if Aelfric jumped over the side and swam away again, but that seemed remarkably unlikely; after he had been alone for so long, it was as much as they could do to stop the Briton from talking even as he rowed. It was only when the crew's unease at hearing so much spoken Latin became apparent that Kimimela persuaded him to shut up for a while and give them all some peace.

"Well, you landed on your feet, and no mistake," Aelfric said quietly much later on. "Lucky bugger."

They were sitting in the bow. The current was so strong on this stretch of the river that rowing was almost superfluous, and most of the oarsmen were taking a break. Marcellinus stared. "You're joking. Nomads, living from day to day?"

Aelfric grinned. "We're all living from day to day. But you really like these people. And they like you."

"This wasn't how it was with you? You didn't make friends up the Wemissori?"

"Some of the tribes upriver are decent enough. The Hidatsa took us in and fed us. Made us work for it, of course, and wanted a gift or two from our pockets. But they could have slit our throats on the first night, and I'm rather glad they didn't." Aelfric looked out over the Mizipi. "The Grass People reminded me more than a little of the Picts, truth be told. But I can't say I made any real friends up there, and I doubt that any of 'em mourn my absence. Your friends here are a little keener. Better organized. The difference between city folk and country folk, I'm guessing."

"I wish you'd seen Cahokia," Marcellinus said.

Aelfric shivered. "I did. It was nearly the death of me."

"I meant really seen it."

"I'm sure it's lovely this time of year." Aelfric sobered. "But what happens when they come again?"

"Roma?"

"Who else?"

Marcellinus shook his head and stared out across the fetid waters.

"All right," said Aelfric. "But I'll only ask you again tomorrow and the day after."

"I hope it doesn't have to be war," Marcellinus said. "I hope there's a way to avoid fighting."

"Aye, there is, if the Cahokians lay down arms and agree to become a Roman province and pay taxes and all. Simple."

Marcellinus laughed. The look on Aelfric's face acknowledged that that would be anything but simple. "Another way."

"And which side will you fight with when it comes to that?"

Britons were very direct. Marcellinus had been hoping to dance around that topic a while longer. "Not with Roma."

He glanced into Aelfric's eyes for his reaction but saw nothing.

"Interesting," Aelfric said.

"And not against Roma either."

Aelfric weighed it. "You really think you can do that? Not pick a side? Stand aloof? You're dreaming."

"I could never fight my own people. Kill Romans in battle? I'd let them cut me down first."

"Easy for you to say now. You'll change your tune when some lad runs at you waving a gladius."

"No," said Marcellinus.

"You killed Corbulo, right enough."

"That was different."

Aelfric laughed. "Because he was a friend of yours? That's comforting."

"I killed Fuscus right enough, too. Doesn't mean I'd do it again now."

"All right." Aelfric shrugged. "None of my business anyway."

"And you?"

"I don't want to live and die in this godforsaken country," said Aelfric. "I really do not, and that's a fact. I want to go home. Trouble is, when the next Romans march into Nova Hesperia, they aren't exactly going to welcome me back with open arms. Being a deserter and running from the battlefield and all."

"You don't have to put it quite like that," Marcellinus said.

"Yes, I really do. I cut and run, Praetor. Didn't stop for my men. Didn't stop for anything. I tossed away my helmet and my breastplate so I could run faster, and I took off like the wind. Got clear by a miracle of God and hid in a borrow pit until nightfall. Right under the water with only my nose showing. Oh, I abandoned my duty, all right. What do you think of that?"

Marcellinus hesitated. "I don't think anything."

"As Praetor you'd have had me killed for less," Aelfric said bluntly. "An example to others. Discipline."

"Things change. Now I'm just glad you're alive."

"Huh," said Aelfric. "We'll see."

"I'm hardly the man to judge you."

"Plenty of others will. Anyhow, that's why I didn't try for Vinlandia with the rest of 'em. Okay for the foot soldiers. But a fine tribune like me?" Aelfric shook his head. "And you, too. All this talk of who we'll fight for is grand. But the truth of it is that when the Romans come for us, we're dead men. And so I don't know where that leaves me. Whose side am I on? I'm on my side. Living for today."

"It's not as easy as that."

"Certainly it is. And if you're half as smart as you

should be, that'll be your answer, too. As for *him*, he'll just disappear into the woods like magic."

"Him?"

Aelfric pointed. And there, standing on a spit of land at the next bend, was Isleifur Bjarnason.

The Norseman lifted his canoe into the longship, stepped aboard with a nod to Marcellinus as if he had seen his Praetor just last week, and went straight to Sintikala and Akecheta in the stern, bowing to each and saying a few words in Cahokian that were so fast and accented that even Marcellinus couldn't catch them. Sintikala blinked in surprise, and Akecheta smiled. Isleifur bowed again and worked his way forward, greeting everyone in turn with a grin and a comment, clasping hands and punching shoulders. Even Tahtay sat up and stared and nodded in acknowledgment when Isleifur spoke to him.

Aelfric shook his head. "I'm guessing nobody is going to tie *that* bugger up."

"Told you you should have come by daylight," Marcellinus said, although that obviously wasn't all there was to it. Isleifur's shoulder-length hair was combed and his beard was full and he wore no tattoos, but aside from that he easily could have passed for Hesperian in his appearance, demeanor, and—if the crew's reactions were anything to go by—speech.

At last Isleifur arrived at the bow, where Marcellinus and Aelfric stood. Akecheta had given the order to cast off again, and the *Concordia* was already nosing back into the current while they tried to catch the wind.

"Still alive, then?" Marcellinus asked for want of anything better to say.

Isleifur shrugged casually as if to say, *Who'd have thought it?* "Nice ship, sir. You've made a sorry mess of the rigging, though. Makes my teeth itch."

Marcellinus felt unaccountably embarrassed. "We were guessing."

"We'll fix it before you have to fight your way back upriver," said the Norseman. "There's fresh water around the next bend if you need it, and deer three bends on if you want to send hunters ahead. Um . . . excuse me." And Bjarnason strode back down the boat to talk to Akecheta.

Sintikala and Kimimela were already back at work on their wing as if nothing had happened. Aelfric was grinning.

Marcellinus shook his head and went to talk to Mahkah about supplies.

CHAPTER 11

YEAR FIVE, FLOWER MOON

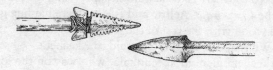

"Up, lazy thing," Kimimela said with scorn, and Marcellinus came awake in a moment, grabbing for the pugio under the spare tunic that served as his pillow.

"Planning to murder me for waking you?" she said.

"Sorry. I was dreaming." These days Marcellinus's dreams were often bloody. In light of the store that Cahokians set by dreams, he did not tell them this.

He sat up with some difficulty, blinking into bright sunlight. Beside him was their dead fire, and nearby the macabre sight of the bones of the three deer they had feasted on over the last two days. Beyond, the warriors were already piling weapons and pouches into the longship. Yahto was stacking the spare firewood under the deck planking to save foraging time in the evening.

"So easy it is for you to sleep," his daughter said with a touch of spite.

Marcellinus grunted. In fact he had been wide awake and worrying for the first half of the night. "One of the benefits of a clear conscience."

She frowned. "Humor?"

"Sarcasm." He scanned the crew again. "Tahtay?"

"No."

Tahtay had disappeared into the woods again as soon as they had landed, and they had not seen him since.

Marcellinus stood, stuffing the spare tunic into his

pouch and looking around for Sintikala. "But we're leaving anyway?"

Kimimela scowled and spoke in a deeper register in a passable imitation of her mother: " 'The men are fat and restless. We sail.' "

Shaking the stiffness out of his legs, Marcellinus walked to where Akecheta stood supervising the loading of the *Concordia*. Aelfric and Isleifur were hauling gear and wood with the rest of the warriors.

"What about Tahtay?" he said to Akecheta.

Akecheta glanced at Sintikala, who was on the longship standing guard over her Hawk wing as the men loaded. Warriors tended to be clumsy and overenthusiastic, and the boat often rocked unexpectedly, and her concern was always that someone would stumble into the wing and damage it. "Tahtay will catch up."

"He'll catch *up*?"

"We don't travel that fast. Especially today." True enough; there wasn't a breath of wind, and the strength of the Mizipi current was slackening as they slid into summer. The men would be rowing.

Tahtay often walked the bank alongside the longship anyway, which was just as well; when he was aboard or in camp, his black mood made him almost impossible to be around. "Yes, but . . ."

"He has to learn not to be such a pain in our hides," Kimimela said viciously.

Hurit and Dustu were loading the boat, eyes downcast. Kimimela followed where he was looking. "Oh, they lost patience with him days ago as well."

Marcellinus had already lost this battle while he slept. "Very well. We sail."

"Glad you agree," Kimimela said, and stalked off to board the drekar and stand by her mother.

By then, two months after fleeing Cahokia, the crew of the *Concordia* had divided into two groups.

By and large, the warriors of the First Cahokian were on an adventure. Of course it was the men with the greatest thirst for novelty who had joined the First Cahokian in the first place, and the unattached men among them who had stuck with Marcellinus and Tahtay to come on this voyage. As far as Marcellinus knew, none of the men on the boat had wives at home, at least not wives they cared about.

Ultimately, his crew had options. Many were confident they'd be able to go back to Cahokia once all the fuss had died down. Or Shappa Ta'atan. Or another mound-builder village. Some liked the idea of Woshakee, where good men would always be welcomed with open arms.

Others were happy to see where the river would take them. None of them had been this far from home before. And when their good cheer lagged, when the work of navigating the endless river became drudgery, Akecheta was there to buck them up, along with Hanska, Mikasi, and Chumanee. And also Aelfric and Isleifur, who had taken it upon themselves to be relentlessly cheerful at all times and defy anyone else to be grumpy.

Remaining aloof from any hint of good cheer was the much smaller group of Sintikala and Kimimela and of course Tahtay, when he was there at all. Marcellinus, Aelfric, and Akecheta did their best to chivvy them along, Aelfric in atrocious Cahokian and hand-talk, but Sintikala in particular was still morose at the loss of Great Sun Man and Cahokia, and Kimimela took her cue from her mother.

Now they floated downriver in the middle of the current. The air was too still to sail, and by the afternoon it was too hot to row in more than a desultory way. Isleifur was at the rudder, keeping the ship's nose straight; in truth, he was a better scout than seaman and despite his caustic comments knew little more about the ropes and rigging than anyone else, but he did seem to be better at steering than most.

In the bow Marcellinus kept his eyes peeled for any sign of Tahtay onshore. Chumanee and Aelfric moved among the men with a cheerful word or two before arriving by his side, where they flopped down, sweating.

"Thank you, Aelfric," Marcellinus said in Latin.

"For?"

"Keeping spirits up."

Aelfric mimed an exaggerated look of confusion. "Eh? We Britons are always cheerful."

"No, you really aren't."

Chumanee curled up in the hull at their feet and fell asleep immediately. Marcellinus blinked. "That's a talent."

"She's a talented lass," Aelfric said, deadpan. "But don't tell the other boys."

Marcellinus shook his head, bemused. "You are an utter rascal, Aelfric."

"Well, you can be sure I'm not doing all this for *you,* you grumpy old bugger. And anyway, this?" Aelfric waved his hand, the gesture including the *Concordia,* the Mizipi, even the sky. "This is the best time I've had in this benighted land, and that's a fact. These are good people. You lucked out with this crew."

"Some of it may not be luck."

"Aye. But your trouble is you spend too much time worrying. Food, water, Iroqua, and Romans, Romans, Romans. You know what? Screw the Romans. They'll come when they come, and there's not a damned thing we can do about it anymore."

Marcellinus thought about that. Aelfric punched him on the arm. "Gaius, man. Stop it. Didn't I just say there was nothing we could do?"

"I don't have to be happy about it."

"You surely do or we'll throw you overboard. Three sourpusses per ship is all that's allowed."

Marcellinus looked at Sintikala or, rather, at the back of her head.

"She'll get over it," Aelfric said. "And she likes you. A great deal. God help her."

"Nonsense."

"I'll cheer up the riffraff if you cheer up the nobility,"

Aelfric said. "The boy has lost his father, fair enough. But what about *her*?"

"Sintikala has lost her people. Lost her whole city."

Aelfric cleared his throat. "I didn't mean *that* her. I meant your *daughter*."

"Oh."

"You're neglecting her. That's why she's being such a pain in the arse. If she's really your daughter, act like it."

"I do," said Marcellinus, surprised.

"You used to talk a good game," Aelfric said. " 'Vestilia this, Vestilia that, oh dear me, I ignored her so much she went away and hated me, oh futete, what a bad and evil father I am.' "

Marcellinus stared. "Eh?"

"Kimimela came to stand by you. Did she need to? No. Did her mother need to? Doubly no. So . . . don't fuck it up again."

"Are you done?"

Aelfric glanced down. "Are you?"

Marcellinus unclenched his fists and blew out a long breath. "Yes. It's far too hot for this conversation."

"Then go astern and start another," Aelfric said. "Talk to them. Both of them, but especially Kimimela."

Marcellinus hesitated.

"Get on with it, man," Aelfric said. "And that's an order."

"There." Isleifur's arm was out straight, pointing to the right bank. "Tahtay."

Marcellinus shook his head; he could not see the boy. They had just completed a large meandering loop to the left and were heading into another rightward curve. After a while the endless slow looping back and forth became monotonous, and he found himself staring ahead of the boat, hardly blinking.

Today the *Concordia* was under sail, more for practice than anything else, as the longship was in the center of the channel and the current was pulling them along briskly enough without it. If they had been heading upstream, they would have had to stay in the shallows to keep out of such a current, perhaps even haul the drekar upriver from the bank like a barge. Marcellinus was not looking forward to that.

The shoreline was marshy on both sides. On the outside of the bend the current had eroded away the bank, which had partially collapsed into the water, trees lying horizontally, branches jutting into the air. On the inside curve where Isleifur was pointing, the silt had piled up in the shallows.

Kimimela arrived at his side. "Yes, I see him."

Marcellinus took their word for it. "Can we even get the ship in there?"

The Norseman wrinkled his nose. "In, maybe. But if we stick hard in that mud, it'll take us all day to get free."

"Ah." Now Marcellinus could see Tahtay, standing still in the shadow of a tree, well back from the bank's edge. The Norseman had good eyes.

"Decide quickly," Isleifur said, "or we'll be past and have to beach downstream and send a party back."

"That won't be easy either," Aelfric said, and he was right. The shores were overgrown here, and such a trek would be a long chore.

"I will fetch the idiot," Kimimela said. She picked up one end of Isleifur's canoe, which lay in the stern of the *Concordia*. "Aelfric, help me with this."

Aelfric stood and looked at Marcellinus, who nodded. "I'll come with you."

Hurit was already strapping a gladius to her belt and hurrying back to them. She bent to lift the other end of the canoe. "Let's go."

"Not without me." Dustu leaped up from where he'd been pulling on an oar.

"You two will stay aboard." Sintikala strode back along the spine of the dragon ship. "We are far from the last mound village. There may be hidden hunters here who might not be friendly. Hanska, Mikasi, Mahkah: come here and launch the canoe. Take Gaius and Kimimela. Aelfric, too, if you want him. Take swords and bows and be watchful. Get Tahtay and come after us. We will slow down to keep you in sight. Isleifur, get us out of this current."

Hurit set her chin. "Sintikala, let me—"

Sintikala clapped her hands impatiently. "I have spoken. Go!"

The canoe pitched and swung in the turbulence of the drekar's wake, and it took several minutes of intense effort to steer out of the deep main channel and head in toward the bank. By then they had passed Tahtay and had to push back against the current and pick their way between the shallow mud banks and barely submerged tree trunks to the shore.

By the time the canoe kissed the bank and Mahkah stepped out holding the rope, Tahtay had backed away toward the thicket. Hanska, silent for once, nocked an arrow onto her bowstring and stood on the bank, scanning the underbrush.

After they had spent most of the day aboard ship, the ground felt as if it were still moving beneath Marcellinus's feet as he and Kimimela walked toward Tahtay. "Where the hell did you go? It's been three days now."

"To be alone." Tahtay shook his head. "I came here to watch you sail by one last time. You have nothing for me anymore. None of you."

Kimimela frowned, hands on her hips. "You're *leaving*? Sintikala stood by you, and this is how you repay her?"

"Me? She stood with *him*." Tahtay looked at Marcellinus. "But it is good that you came ashore. I have one last thing to say."

The *Concordia* was already half a mile downriver. Akecheta and Dustu had lowered the sail, but Isleifur had steered back into the channel again, perhaps to avoid snags or grounding on the treacherous mud on the sides of the river. "Say it while we paddle, Tahtay."

Tahtay shook his head. "Do you not hear me, Hotah? I am not coming."

"Of course you are."

"Huh." Tahtay took a single step forward, his hand on the haft of the ax that swung from a strap over his shoulder. "Always you know best. You are right to teach the weapons and the Roman way of fighting even if people die. You are right to make peace with the Iroqua even if it means shame and destruction for Cahokia. Nothing you say is wrong. You break everything, but still they all do as you say. And now my father is dead."

"Tahtay . . ."

"You stole my father's glory. His chance to be the greatest war chief Cahokia has ever known. Instead he will be remembered as the coward who hung back when he should have run forward to fight. Who took gifts from our enemies instead of taking their scalps. Who listened to a stranger not of our land and threw away Cahokia."

Despite the warmth of the day, Marcellinus felt chilled. "Tahtay, Great Sun Man will be remembered as the man who brought peace—"

Tahtay spit. "Better to die than that."

"You are wrong, Tahtay," Kimimela said softly.

"You say so?" Tahtay eyed her. "I am a man without a father. And if you call this man *your* father, then you are not my friend."

Kimimela's hand went to her pugio.

"Stop, stop." Marcellinus glanced back at the riverbank, where his Cahokian warriors stood vigilant. "Tahtay—"

Tahtay shook his head. "Say nothing more. Leave me. We are all-done."

"Yes." Kimimela surged forward. "Stay out of this, Gaius. Go back to the others."

Tahtay watched her warily. "I have nothing more to say to you, Kimi."

"You think so?" Kimimela said. "Come with me." She grabbed him, shoved him back, walked on. Tahtay raised his hand to hit her, then dropped it by his side and strode after her.

Now Aelfric's hand was on Marcellinus's arm. "Come away, man. Let them talk."

"Talk?" Marcellinus said, for Kimimela had turned to remonstrate with Tahtay, arms waving, her face inches from his, so close that she must have been spitting on him. Tahtay glared down at her.

"This is crazy," said Marcellinus.

"So is being this far away from the *Concordia*."

The longship was curving around the next bend, almost out of sight. For a moment Marcellinus had the mad thought that Sintikala and Akecheta had taken this opportunity to be rid of them all, that he would never see them again. The humidity closed in around him, and flies buzzed. "Shit."

The sound of a slap echoed back to them, and they turned. Kimimela and Tahtay were fighting now, throwing punches, trading blow for blow. Kimimela landed a punch on Tahtay's nose. He grabbed her arms, and they went down, rolling over and over in the mud.

Marcellinus surged forward, but Aelfric was holding him firmly, calling for Hanska.

Tahtay and Kimimela were on their feet again. Kimimela aimed a kick at Tahtay's groin, but Tahtay punched downward, knocking her calf away with his fist. She stumbled and fell again.

Tahtay looked at Marcellinus. Their eyes met for the briefest of instants, and then the boy turned and sprinted into the underbrush.

When they reached Kimimela, she was squatting in pain, panting and wiping blood from her lip. "Let the verpa go. We will not see him again."

Marcellinus turned to Hanska. "Go after him. Please, get him back."

"Run after a boy who wishes to leave?" said Hanska. "And what then? Tie him up?"

"You tied *me* up," Aelfric said.

"*You* deserved it."

"Tahtay will not be caught." Kimimela was already limping toward the canoe, rubbing her shoulder, her eyes clouded. "He has made his choice. He is gone. And we do not need him anyway."

"Kimimela . . ."

"Do not talk to me."

Hanska and Mikasi hurried after her. Marcellinus still had not moved. "Futete."

"He'll be fine," Aelfric said.

"Fine? Tahtay's not a woodsman. He grew up in the Great City!"

Aelfric shook his head. "Tahtay looks like he knows the woods well enough. He's good with a sling, and he makes fire well. He won't starve."

"All alone out there?" Marcellinus walked to the bank's edge and watched the greasy water lapping at his feet, his thoughts an unhappy blur.

"Come," said Mahkah. "Hotah? Come to the canoe. We have a longship to chase."

The others were already aboard. Only Mahkah stood on the shore, waiting. Kimimela sat in the prow, staring downriver, still holding her shoulder. The *Concordia* was out of sight.

Marcellinus looked once more into the deep undergrowth and went to board the canoe.

CHAPTER 12

YEAR FIVE, HEAT MOON

"Catanwakuwa," Yahto said from the bow.

"Shappa Ta'atan," said Sintikala.

After the grace of Sintikala and the other pilots of the Hawk clan, the wing that buzzed them now seemed clumsily flown. Wobbling, it quickly lost height and came to ground on the west bank a few hundred yards away. Its pilot shucked the wing, waved cheerfully at the Cahokian longship, and shot an arrow into the air. To Marcellinus's surprise, the arrow exploded with a sharp bang on achieving the highest point in its arc. Glowing debris shards cascaded down, and wisps of purple-black smoke drifted higher into the sky.

"A signal?" Marcellinus asked, leaning into the rudder to correct their course. The warriors had shipped their oars to pull on their tunics, and the longship was slewing with the current.

"Shappa Ta'atan takes care" was Akecheta's reply, but the skin around his eyes grew tight.

"I did not hear that their walls were so large," said Sintikala.

Marcellinus looked at Akecheta. "Centurion? Speak."

"Shappa Ta'atan is used to war."

"War with Iroqua?"

"Yes, there are Iroqua-friendly tribes to the east. But

also war with other peoples." Akecheta gestured vaguely toward the southwest.

"Other peoples?"

"Far peoples. The People of the Hand. And, long ago, many winters, two lives ago, they were at war with us."

Marcellinus looked at Sintikala. "Perhaps someone should have mentioned this before we got here."

She shook her head. Clearly, she had not known.

"The People of the Hand do not come here now anyway," Mahkah added, though Marcellinus did not know how he could be so sure.

A contingent from Shappa Ta'atan met them at the riverside, smiling and gracious and, despite the heat and humidity, well dressed. Marcellinus was disoriented by the extensiveness of their tattoos; he was familiar enough with Cahokian clan and battle tattoos, but those of other cities were crafted differently. Here many of the warriors had faces completely covered in tattoos and scarifications, a far cry from the more subtle adornment of most of the Cahokians. The unfamiliar whorls, figures, and jagged crosses on the locals' skin added to his anxiety.

At the front of the reception committee stood the war chief of Shappa Ta'atan. He was heavyset but muscular, and wore the impressive woven and dyed kilt, copper gorget, and headdress of a Mizipian chieftain. With the images of Great Sun Man's death at Avenaka's hand so vivid in Marcellinus's memory, the spiked chert mace the chieftain held seemed threatening rather than reassuring. Nonetheless, the war chief stepped forward with a friendly smile to clutch Marcellinus's forearm in the Roman style. Clearly he had been better briefed than the other chiefs Marcellinus had met along the river.

The war chief spoke incomprehensibly. Marcellinus couldn't follow the man's words, and didn't want to break eye contact to see if anyone else in his party could. "It is an honor to meet you," he replied in Cahokian, and when the chief released his arm, he repeated the sentiment in hand-talk.

Sintikala began to speak, but the war chief cut her off. "Ah!" he said, and hand-talked back to Marcellinus. *We hear of the Wanageeska. Welcome. Query, food?*

Marcellinus nodded politely and said, "I am Gaius. Here is Sintikala, Hawk clan chief from Cahokia. Here is Akecheta, mighty fighter." He hand-talked as he spoke, but the chief was watching his face, and Marcellinus was sure the man understood him. "And I thank you, but we are happy to eat when you do, at your time."

Our walls, signed the chief. *Query, they are strong, no?*

It was almost the same question Iniwa had asked when greeting Marcellinus on his first trip to Ocatan. Clearly, Cahokia's allies all took pride in their towns' defenses.

And indeed, the palisade of Shappa Ta'atan was solid enough to give any attacker pause, tall and robust, with raised and covered platforms for archers every thirty feet and a complicated structure around the main gate. Marcellinus could not see over the palisade to count the mounds, but it was clear that Shappa Ta'atan was bigger than any other city they had visited along the Mizipi.

Marcellinus made a show of admiring the bastions of wood and hardened clay, but his unease was growing. Normally, when they arrived at a new village or town, Sintikala took care of the formalities. And as a rule the formalities were not quite this formal. No other chief had greeted him in ceremonial garb or ignored his fellow travelers so completely. He glanced over at Sintikala, but her face was impassive.

You will enter? signed the chief.

Sintikala stepped forward again. "We come from Cahokia, but we do not speak for it. We have left the Great City. I must tell you now that Great Sun Man is dead, struck down. His wife's brother, Avenaka, now rules as paramount chief, and we are no friends to Avenaka."

Marcellinus held his breath. In most of the villages along the Mizipi they had been accepted as travelers and only rarely had been asked for their bona fides. Here, in what might be the second largest city on the whole river, its ruler naturally would assume they came as envoys. Here they could not dissemble, could not evade the topic.

However, Marcellinus had planned to take a much softer approach to relaying this news.

The chieftain was pondering it. Now he turned and raised his arm in a complicated hand-talk symbol that might have meant *Word speak*.

A lithe girl Hurit's age ran forward from the rear of the Shappan contingent. The chieftain addressed her imperiously, and she turned to Marcellinus. "'Our great chief, Son of the Sun, asks you: You prefer your own company to Avenaka's?'"

Obviously the conversation had become too delicate for hand-talk and pidgin Cahokian. "We do," said Marcellinus.

The translator cocked her head on one side and studied him. "'You are banished? And is there now peace in the city of Cahokia?'"

"We are not there, and so we do not know. We hope so." This was true enough. For the sake of Enopay and Kanuna, Nahimana and Takoda, Anapetu and his many other friends who had remained behind, Marcellinus fervently hoped the city was at peace.

Son of the Sun spoke. His word slave translated. "'I have not met Avenaka. But if he rules in Cahokia, then he should be my brother. You ask my help against him? For my warriors to make war parties against him?'"

"We do not," Sintikala said, and looked at Marcellinus.

Marcellinus said: "That is not why we are here. We seek no help, make no case. We ask for nothing except hospitality and understanding. And perhaps there are ways we can serve you, knowledge that we can bring, to repay you for such hospitality."

"'Offering you hospitality might make my new brother unhappy.'"

To Marcellinus's surprise, Sintikala shrugged and smiled. "All families argue. We are still Cahokians. We hope that one day we will be welcome there again. Until then, we travel."

"And there are other matters we would discuss with you," Marcellinus said. "Matters of even greater importance to the land than who sits upon the Great Mound in Cahokia."

Son of the Sun looked intrigued, then nodded and gestured. *Welcome, travelers. Enter, peace.*

"'You are welcome here,'" said the word slave. "'Enter the great walls of Shappa Ta'atan in peace.'"

Sintikala smiled again. "We enter as your guests, under your hospitality. We are under your protection, great chief."

Marcellinus almost expected the chief to ask them to relinquish their weapons, but he did not. And to his relief, now that the party was on the move into Shappa Ta'atan, some of the pomp dissipated. The elders and leading warriors of Shappa Ta'atan came forward with smiles to greet the warriors of Cahokia, and two older women whom Marcellinus took for clan chiefs hurried to greet and honor Sintikala.

The entryway to the city was an L-shaped alley guarded by high firing platforms on either side. Marcellinus strode forward, concentrating on his conversation with his host, but as they walked into the city, he heard Sintikala laugh behind him at something one of the women said.

It was a higher-pitched laugh than her usual quiet alto chuckle. Sintikala felt no calmer than Marcellinus about passing through the robust defenses of Shappa Ta'atan.

Aelfric and Isleifur had stayed back while the formalities were observed, but now Aelfric appeared at Marcellinus's shoulder. "Well, this is quite a place."

"It is."

"If Cahokia had looked like this, we might've hung back a bit."

"We might."

Aelfric grunted. "And we know what we're doing, do we, going in?"

"Of course."

For once, Marcellinus would not leave the sarcasm to his former tribune.

They walked through the gates and into the walled city.

In Cahokia the plazas and the tallest mounds were carefully arranged and oriented, but that was the extent of the city planning. Not so here; Shappa Ta'atan was laid out on a grid pattern almost as organized as the newer suburbs of Roma. Where Cahokia was a relaxed sprawl, Shappa Ta'atan was regimented; where Cahokia was informal, with the location of the winding major thoroughfares mostly a matter of evolution and group consensus, Shappa Ta'atan possessed a rigidity that gave Marcellinus pause. Every red cedar pole looked new. The mounds were more scrupulously landscaped, their clay sides freshly shaped and tended. Most were platform mounds, presumably bearing the homes of ranking Shappa Ta'atani, with few of the more ceremonial conical mounds or sprawling decorative ovals seen upriver.

With his military background, Marcellinus might have felt more at home in this more orderly environment. He did not.

Nonetheless, few danger signs presented themselves. The Cahokians were soon at their ease and swapping stories with their local counterparts, who apparently did speak a dialect similar to Cahokian, after all. The elders who were talking with Marcellinus now, marveling how far he had come across ocean and land and river over the years to be with them today, also spoke heavily accented Cahokian. The only person who did not was the war chief, and that gave Marcellinus the confidence to ask him about it.

"I speak," the chief responded in Cahokian. "Not well. I—" He waved his hands. "—shamed at poor Cahokia speak."

"I, too," Marcellinus said with a smile. "And the language you do speak?"

"Caddo." The chief pointed south and a little west. "Those words."

Very helpful. But how could a native speaker of a southern tongue become paramount chief of Shappa Ta'atan? No answer was forthcoming, and it seemed impertinent to probe further. Marcellinus smiled and nodded and allowed himself to be guided deeper into the city.

He was startled to encounter another stockade even taller and stouter than the first. Above it he could see the upper part of a giant mound of black clay, small in area compared with the Master Mound at Cahokia but still a good seventy feet high and broad enough to have required many years of effort to construct. The longhouse that crowned the mound had a curious appearance. As he attended to the small talk of his hosts, it took Marcellinus a moment to notice that the longhouse was fortified. It had ramparts, with warriors patrolling them.

" 'Here-inside is our Sacred Center,' " said the girl who was translating. " 'Our place of good and of chiefs.' "

"Your place of medicine, of your fathers and many-fathers?" Marcellinus prompted.

She seemed surprised that Marcellinus knew those words. "Yes, it is so."

"Here, too, the walls of Shappa Ta'atan are great," Marcellinus said. He looked around casually for Sinti-kala, but she had been swallowed by a gaggle of admiring women; as for Chumanee, from the way she and the younger women were passing flowers and tied bunches of greenery back and forth, it looked as if an impromptu herbalists' market had broken out.

The paramount chief spoke. " 'Now we will show you the houses where you will rest before the feast,' " said the translator.

The chief said something else and then signed, *Feast, great, sunset.*

"We are honored, and you are most generous," Marcellinus said.

The chief bowed. Then he and most of the elders of Shappa Ta'atan left them, striding off into the city. The remaining elders and the translator guided Marcellinus and the others to a small plaza bounded by large round houses that were neatly kept up and without the usual millstones outside their doors for grinding corn or lean-to gardens against their walls. These were obviously the guest quarters.

Around him the Cahokians were already exploring their accommodations. Marcellinus surveyed the area for a few moments more. Beyond the guest complex the ordinary folk of Shappa Ta'atan went about their daily errands, but Marcellinus suspected that an attempt to walk over and strike up a conversation might be frowned upon. He ducked into his hut and stripped off his tunic, digging into his travel pouch for something a little fresher.

Bare-chested, he stood in his hut's doorway and looked out. Before him was the plaza that separated their accommodations from the organized rows of houses where the people of Shappa Ta'atan lived. From where he stood, he was overlooked by several rectangular platform mounds, many with houses and even small palisades of their own. Behind his house was the stockade that surrounded their Sacred Center, fully fifteen feet tall. He had seen no gates into the inner compound other than the heavily guarded entryway.

A couple of hundred yards away two women were showing Sintikala and Kimimela into their hut at a discreet distance from the rest of the group. This, too, was not unprecedented, though Marcellinus often found the separation inconvenient. Before Sintikala entered her hut, she straightened and caught sight of him. She was too far away for him to see her expression, but her posture was relaxed enough, and her quickly hand-talked gesture of *All is well* seemed genuine.

And truth be told, these days Cahokia itself might

present a forbidding face to a visiting stranger with its size and military bearing, the increasing number of brick buildings, and the gouts of black smoke from the brick-works and foundry. But in the pit of Marcellinus's stomach his instincts were cautioning him to stay alert here in a way they never had in the other towns and villages along the way.

Marcellinus finished his ablutions. He slid his pugio up under his tunic, held in by his belt where it could not be seen. Then he went to talk to the others.

Aelfric and Isleifur were as disconcerted as Marcellinus, but Akecheta shared few of their forebodings; though impressed by the fortifications, he had received no unfavorable impression at their first meeting with the Shappa Ta'atani. Marcellinus's own misgivings faded over the next few days as they were feasted and feted by their hosts.

The paramount chief, Son of the Sun, certainly had not exaggerated about the food. Out on the river the Cahokians had eaten sparingly from their provisions, supplemented with what they could forage as they traveled. Most of the towns they had passed through had provided sustenance no grander than their daily fare back home, mostly corn, beans, squash, and fish. Here in Shappa Ta'atan they dined well every night on waterfowl or fish rich with aromatic spices with which even Chumanee was unfamiliar.

Their conversations with the local elders and warriors established to Marcellinus's satisfaction that although Shappa Ta'atan was still keen to be considered an ally of Cahokia, they were even more keen to share in the peace with the Iroqua that Marcellinus and Sintikala had brokered. Even so far south, Shappa Ta'atan had suffered Iroqua incursions and predations from the east on a regular basis; the previous year nearby homesteads had been raided, many men slain, women purloined. Marcellinus sat grim-faced at the news, which was conveyed to him by Son of the Sun with a calm matter-of-factness that he could not imagine from Great Sun Man. But if the Iroqua would keep the peace, Shappa Ta'atan would do likewise.

And indeed, the people of Shappa Ta'atan were eager to learn from Marcellinus, especially about iron and steel. He was cheered to discover that they already smelted iron in aboveground furnaces and so were one step ahead of where the Cahokians had been on his arrival. He spent many happy days with their metalsmiths, discussing the colors of superheated metal and the exact moments to quench, and picked up a trick or two in return about techniques for heating and hammering iron that he hoped to experiment with someday.

Nowhere, however, did they see any gold.

"Ceremonial dress?" Marcellinus repeated. A little worried, he looked over at Sintikala.

"Wear your helmet?" Kimimela said. "Breastplate, Roman-soldier clothes?"

His envy obvious, Akecheta said, "It is a great honor they give you, to be invited to feast in the Sacred Center with the chiefs. This is a corn ceremony of the air as well as the soil. The priestesses of Shappa Ta'atan will fly for you."

"I've already feasted out here." Marcellinus patted his growing stomach. He badly needed more exercise beyond the few minutes of swordplay he insisted on each morning before breakfast with Akecheta, Hanska, and Mahkah. And for the last two days, during the Green Corn Ceremony, he had not managed even that.

The Green Corn Ceremony was held once the corn out in the fields was ripe enough to fill its husk but still retain its green hue. This generally happened late in the Thunder Moon. Before the ceremony, nobody was permitted even to taste the corn; during the festival, everybody did.

In Cahokia the Green Corn Ceremony was largely a family celebration. On the first day at noon all the fires would be extinguished and then relit, and then the first corn would be cooked: boiled into soup or roasted on the cob. The aroma of burned corn wafted over Cahokia like a benediction, and families and clans gathered for private thanksgivings in their own individual ways. Inevitably drumming and dancing would break out in the evening, but Great Sun Man gave no speeches and the shamans gave no blessings. The full harvest, the final gathering in of the corn, was the real celebration.

In Shappa Ta'atan, they celebrated the early harvest much more emphatically with a four-day festival. The previous day they had snuffed all their fires at noon all at once, and a respectful silence had fallen over the entire city as the last smoke drained away into the skies. Shamans had intoned long prayers of thanksgiving for the bounty of the sun, the Son of the Sun, and the Corn Mother (in that order, as far as Marcellinus could tell). With a crackle of flint and tinder the fires were relit, and a citywide party broke out immediately.

Marcellinus ate moderately, drank almost nothing, and certainly did not sing or dance, but by the end of the evening he was exhausted. The din of the hourlong event known as the Stomp Dance was particularly wearing.

The party went on without him for most of the night, with the howling of flutes and the banging of the drums keeping him awake till almost dawn.

According to Mahkah's weary but cheerful report the next day, it had been quite a night. The second morning had been quiet, but once the sun reached the zenith, gods help them all, exactly the same thing began again— the death of all the fires, followed by an excess of reverent prayer and the birth of the new flames, and out came the green corncobs and the corn soup and the corn beer, and the thump and tootle of the musicians, and the games of chunkey and the southern ball game, which was almost a war, played with long sticks with nets mounted on the end, where the players practically murdered one another for custody of a small ball of deerskin stuffed with corn silk. By late afternoon of this festive onslaught even Mahkah was forced to beat a retreat and rest his head, leaving Marcellinus and Sintikala and Aelfric and the others to watch from the sidelines, bemused. Would this really go on for another two and a half days?

"Food for the chiefs in the Sacred Center, much better," said the Shappan runner who had just brought word of the invitation.

"Sintikala is not invited? Akecheta?"

"She is not a man, and he is not a chief. Just Son of the Sun, the chiefs, and you." The messenger pointed at the sky, his arm at an angle. "Be ready when the sun is there."

Marcellinus surveyed the stockade that surrounded the Sacred Center. Alone behind that, separated from his crew? He certainly would wear all the "ceremonial" armor he could.

At his expression, the messenger looked worried. "You must go. You cannot refuse. No harm will come to you."

Across the table Akecheta nodded in agreement. Marcellinus eyed the runner sourly. "I am not concerned about *harm*."

"Flying priestesses?" Sintikala said sardonically. "I am surprised that you hesitate."

She switched to her shaky Latin. "Not be foolish. They honor you. Boy is right. You cannot say no. They will not kill you in there." She cocked an eye at him. "At least, the men will not."

"Sisika . . ."

Across the courtyard the women elders beckoned and giggled. Sintikala sighed. "In truth? Women here may be the death of me, too. They talk and talk. And talk. And talk."

"They honor you," Marcellinus said straight-faced. "You cannot refuse."

Sintikala flashed an entirely unconvincing smile at the women and stood. "Feast well. Make sure your breastplate is shiny."

"Tell Son of the Sun I will be honored," Marcellinus

said to the messenger. As the boy sprinted away, Marcellinus grinned wryly at Kimimela. "All right. Time to eat, drink, make merry. Whether we like it or not."

Marcellinus had not expected a procession, never having seen one in Cahokia. Now he and Son of the Sun walked together at the head of a column of chiefs. Drummers drummed and flautists trilled as they marched through a corridor of smiling townsfolk who all looked so clean and well appointed that Marcellinus suspected they had been chosen specially.

Son of the Sun was decked out in his full regalia of kilt and headdress, augmented with a copper gorget, armbands and ankle bands, and the heavy earrings of the Long-Nosed God. Only his chert mace of office had been left behind. Marcellinus wore steel shoulder greaves as well as his helmet and breastplate and the apron of metal strips that protected his groin in battle; tonight he looked more of a Roman soldier than he had since walking to the Haudenosaunee powwow, an association of ideas he did not find comforting.

As they approached the gate to the Sacred Center, the faux-adoring crowd dropped away. Only the chiefs marched now, along with the cordon of tough-looking braves that flanked them. Marcellinus swallowed, trying to control his disquiet.

Like the main city gateway, this entranceway was L-shaped, with tall log gates at either end and bastions to the left and right. Warrior guards looked down on them from the battlements. None of the Shappa Ta'atani chiefs appeared to find this alarming.

The outer gate closed behind them. The inner gate in front of them had not opened yet. Marcellinus looked around, playing the tourist but alert to his surroundings, and only now noticed a tall painted gourd, a set of carved shell drinking cups, and a wide trench in the corner of the L.

Son of the Sun spoke, and some of the chiefs laughed. The younger men looked apprehensive. Marcellinus caught the eye of one—the chief of the Beaver clan, judging by the tails that swung at his belt—and raised his eyebrows. "Asi," said the man as the cups were passed around. *Black drink,* he signed, and when Son of the Sun was not looking, he made a face.

It was the vilest concoction Marcellinus had ever swallowed. At the first sip, his stomach roiled. Around him the chiefs were gulping it down as if in self-defense. Marcellinus stared in shock at the beautiful conch that he was drinking this abhorrent liquid out of and tried again. The second swallow seared his throat. As he began to panic, his only rational thought was, *This is no drink, and it's not even black.*

Nausea rose in him, and he staggered, desperately trying to keep the liquid down. Son of the Sun took another long draft out of the fine conch he held and smiled at Marcellinus. Then the paramount chief of Shappa Ta'atan bent over the trough.

Marcellinus's stomach convulsed, and his body took over. Folding at the waist, he gave himself over to nature. Around him the other chiefs were vomiting, too.

Eventually the purging abated. Marcellinus sat on the ground, his eyes streaming, his breastplate and tunic befouled. He had spun away from the other men and hurled his conch cup at the wall; it now lay on the ground in a dozen pieces.

The Shappa Ta'atani were getting to their feet. Son of the Sun stood serenely over the trough surrounded by the wreckage of his chiefs. Mercifully, Marcellinus was not the only one to have disgraced himself in the purification ritual; the Beaver chief was still facedown and groaning.

The second jar held water. The youngest chief, of the Snake clan, served it out to them in wooden cups. His hands still shook.

Marcellinus flushed out his mouth but still could not swallow. His throat was too raw. His head pounded, his stomach ached. Now he was supposed to feast?

The inner gate swung wide. Around him, the chiefs began to disrobe.

Naked, they walked into the Sacred Center. Women had already taken their stained ceremonial clothing away to be cleaned, including Marcellinus's breastplate and helmet. So much for his plan to spend the evening armored.

Son of the Sun's chest was surprisingly muscular, his torso and legs lined with scarifications and battle tattoos. He was almost as impressive unclothed as he was when garbed as a paramount chief. By contrast Marcellinus's skin seemed clean and almost babyish even to himself, though the younger chiefs nodded in respect at his many scars.

The Sacred Center was not larger in area than the Great Plaza in Cahokia but was so empty that it appeared enormous. It was bounded by the tall stockade and carpeted with a flat expanse of pure green grass, a lawn the likes of which Marcellinus had not seen since leaving Roma. Clearly, few were permitted to walk on it.

Throughout the space Marcellinus saw several elegant platform mounds with what he knew must be mausoleums or charnel houses at their crests, along with low conical mounds apparently scattered at random. At the exact center rose the Temple Mound of Shappa Ta'atan. It dwarfed all others in its height and area, and the longhouse that spanned its peak put the others to shame.

People began to spill from some of the doorways of the "mausoleums," men from some, women from others. Not charnel houses, then; every assumption Marcellinus made here seemed doomed to be shattered. These must be the priests and priestesses, and the houses on the low mounds were where they lived.

As they hurried across the grass toward him, Marcellinus controlled a heavy sigh. The women were beautiful, and the men were eunuchs. Some things were the same the world over.

Here came an oaken chair for Son of the Sun so finely carved that it looked gilded, suspended between two long carrying poles. Behind it was a series of less ornate yoked litters for the chiefs. Marcellinus, who had been forced to endure a litter only once before in his life, at the behest of his least favorite Imperator, Vespasianus II, gritted his teeth and climbed aboard. Four eunuchs shouldered the wooden poles to hoist him high, and off they went across the massive lawn of the Sacred Center.

Giant moths fluttered at the edges of his vision. While Marcellinus had been boarding his litter, the air above him had filled with wings. He looked up at the Temple Mound, and this time he registered the audible twang as a winged priestess was shot into the air above it, quickly followed by another.

The wings were multicolored; the women who flew them were not warriors but entertainers. The wings ducked and wheeled thrillingly enough, but without the deft control of Sintikala and her clan, and these fliers lacked their ability to ride the currents of the air to gain height. Grace, elegance, and beauty were the point here, not martial skill. They came to earth quickly, scattered iridescent across the grass.

His bearers turned his litter sideways to carry him up the broad cedar stairs of the Temple Mound. Marcellinus could feel every footfall as they gingerly nursed the litter higher. The swaying played havoc with his still-sensitive stomach. He would rather have walked.

The walls around the Sacred Center were so tall that even now, halfway up the mound, he could see nothing of the world beyond. The determinedly calm faces of the priests and priestesses that surrounded him unsettled more than they reassured. Separated from the main city of Shappa Ta'atan by no more than a thousand yards, Marcellinus felt out of his depth.

At the top of the broad plateau, under the heavy ramparts of the fortified temple, they were permitted to disembark. As his bare feet touched the grass, a priest handed Marcellinus a clean tunic of some sheer material. "Cotton," Marcellinus said, and the eunuch smiled politely. The other chiefs were already pulling the shifts over their heads to cover their nakedness, and with relief Marcellinus did the same.

Women still flitted above them, launched into the air with slings of some elastic material, perhaps the same one the Iroqua had used at Woshakee. Son of the Sun and the other chiefs watched appreciatively as the aerial priestesses soared and dipped, flattening out to land at the base of the Temple Mound and then scampering to climb the mound and be launched again.

Watching them run, Marcellinus saw only now that the women were entirely naked, their breasts bouncing, their broad smudges of pubic hair clearly apparent.

Marcellinus was embarrassed for them and just as embarrassed by the fascination of the Shappa Ta'atani around him. For them the aerial nymphs were clearly a rare treat, a high point of their feast days and holidays.

From the backstreets of Subura to the courts of Imperators and sultans, Marcellinus had seen his fair share of dancing girls. But after several years in Cahokia this felt like a perversion. Perhaps because of the matrilineal clan system, Cahokian women were never treated as mere entertainment for men, and for Cahokians flying was an athletically functional skill. Marcellinus could not imagine Matoshka or Kanuna or any of the other Cahokian elders relishing such a display.

Well, maybe Howahkan.

Naturally, this being Nova Hesperia and a feast day, there were speeches and invocations to be endured before they went in to eat. The rites were performed by Son of the Sun and spoken in a mixture of Caddoan and archaic Shappan, and Marcellinus could not follow them at all.

Son of the Sun raised his hands high to the golden orb of the setting sun. Shamans shook their tortoiseshell rattles. Around them, priestesses knelt. Behind them, a priest played a haunting tune on a short flute. For a fertility ritual the mood was oddly mournful.

Marcellinus looked out over the city of Shappa Ta'atan and beyond, up and down the Mizipi. The floodplain was very flat here. Visible from everywhere in the city, the top of the Temple Mound was an excellent vantage point. Quite likely, lookouts here had spotted the signal flare sent up by the Shappan Hawk on the Cahokians' arrival.

At last the sun set. Ceremonies over, the eunuchs ushered the chiefs toward the longhouse. The entrance was flanked with tall figures carved in chert: a birdman to the left, masked and broad-winged, and on the other side a plump matronly figure holding a corncob, and with corn tassels in place of braids, who could only be the Corn Mother.

Within the building, an avenue of small fire bowls marked the way. Marcellinus followed the chiefs down a darkened passageway with alcoves and small rooms to either side, almost like the side chapels in a temple to the Christ-Risen.

The hallway opened out into a tall, broad feasting room. At its far end a ceremonial fire roared into life; from the walls, its light reflected off ornately carved and decorated shields of burnished copper. Marcellinus looked again with care, but it was definitely copper and not gold.

There were lush blankets and furs and a broad table. In the center of the table was a bowl. Around it the places were marked with drinking cups.

They directed Marcellinus to a seat that appeared to be the pride of place, directly opposite the large bowl from Son of the Sun. To either side the clan chiefs of Shappa Ta'atan flopped down in cheerful disarray, no respecters of the finery that surrounded them.

Even now Marcellinus could not remember the chiefs' names, but he had learned long before that the tattoos they wore identified the clans they led. To his left was Panther, with Turtle beyond, and to his right sat Deer and Snake. Facing him and flanking Son of the Sun were the chiefs of the Beaver and the Crow clans. A serving girl moved among them, splashing water from her gourd into the conch-shell drinking bowls. As the girl passed by Turtle, he lunged for her ankle and Marcellinus recoiled, but the clan chief was only shoving the lower hem of the serving girl's billowing shift away from one of the fire bowls.

Flammable, of course, unless treated. Marcellinus tucked his own cotton shift underneath him with care.

Men drank now, and Marcellinus lifted his conch gratefully to his lips, his mouth still dry from the fiery emetic he had swallowed at the gate.

His nose alerted him. This was not water. He sipped it carefully. Corn beer, naturally; it smelled much more potent than the Cahokian brand that had been prevalent on his arrival and was not the slightest bit more palatable.

The other men raised their conches high in salute and then drained them, and Marcellinus did likewise once he saw that other chiefs were calling for water—real water—to slake their thirsts. The beer brought a quick wave of dizziness and a gurgling protest from his long-suffering stomach, and he knew that even to save face he could drink little more of it this night.

Food was coming, platters and bowls in the hands of more of the cotton-clad priests and priestesses. Beneath the ubiquitous odor of burned corn Marcellinus smelled a heavy, more pungent richness. His meals so far in Shappa Ta'atan had been mostly fish and fowl, but on this special night it appeared they would eat meat.

With the food came Son of the Sun's word slave, Taianita, also garbed in the long cotton dress of a priestess. Clearly she had two roles tonight: to translate and to transfer Son of the Sun's food from the bowl to his mouth.

"'Here we can speak of matters we cannot speak of outside,'" she said, relaying Son of the Sun's words. "'And here we can do as we wish, guided by the sacred corn.'"

A mild cheer greeted this pronouncement, and many chiefs toasted it with beer. Conversation broke out among them, though Taianita continued to speak, looking at Marcellinus.

"'We are here to honor the Corn Mother through her priests and priestesses. To give thanks for the fertility of the soil. To rejoice for another year of plenty and to sow the seed for next year.'"

The translator dropped her eyes.

"Yes," Marcellinus said, equally uncomfortable at the implications.

He could not identify the meat immediately. It was delicious, tender and full of flavor. It was the closest thing to beef he had tasted since he had left Europa.

"This is what?" he said to the leader of the Deer clan, who sat cross-legged on the blankets next to him, stuffing meat into his mouth. "Not deer, I think."

The chief chewed busily, apparently taking Marcellinus's words as neither quip nor insult. Next to him the Snake leader lowed at him, moving his head ponderously back and forth in imitation of something large.

"Oxen?" Marcellinus asked, hope surging. He had seen no beasts of burden since his arrival in Nova Hesperia. It was the only resource this giant continent lacked, aside from gold. "Four legs? You milk the she-oxen? It can pull a cart?"

This caused some confusion, and it took Taianita, the two other chiefs, and a great deal of miming to convey that the animal in question was the large buffalo apparently common on the western plains that Marcellinus had heard so much about in Cahokia. Like cattle, the buffalo traveled in herds, and like oxen, they had a pronounced hump, but there the resemblance ended; the beasts they ate had hides useful for rugs and robes but were too stupid and aggressive to carry or pull anything.

"At least they taste good," Marcellinus said.

"We give you skin," said Son of the Sun, for once bypassing his translator. "As gift, for winter, for wear."

Taianita stuck her tongue out at Marcellinus, and the men laughed. "This is tongue," said Turtle, clarifying. "Meat you eat now is buffalo tongue, best of buffalo."

The girl nodded, and Son of the Sun played with her hair as she fed him another slice of buffalo tongue.

Marcellinus preferred the larger buffalo steaks that followed, from the haunch of the animal. Along with the steaks the priests brought deer hearts and freshwater mussels and clams, the finest delicacies of the Mizipi. If you were a chief, Marcellinus mused, it was not all corn at the Green Corn Festival.

At least it was now clear how Son of the Sun kept his chieftaincy. He bought it with bread and circuses for the masses and women and buffalo for the higher classes. How he had acquired the chieftaincy in the first place was still unknown to Marcellinus. For form's sake, Marcellinus took another tiny sip of the corn beer.

" 'How is it that you are not the master of Cahokia?' "

Taianita had spoken Son of the Sun's words. Taken aback, Marcellinus replied, "I would not wish to be. I have responsibilities enough."

She put her head on one side. "Responsibilities?"

"Duties. Things I must do." He resorted to hand-talk, not wanting to risk being misunderstood or mistranslated. *Cahokia had fine chief: Great Sun Man. I was happy to serve him. Now, travel.*

Although his meaning was clear, the girl translated it into Caddo anyway. Through her, Son of the Sun replied, " 'But is it not better to rule than to serve?' "

"Sometimes." Marcellinus applied himself anew to his buffalo steak.

Son of the Sun studied him as he ate. Taianita waited. Once it was clear that Marcellinus had nothing to add, he said, " 'I think that you did not bring your warriors west to serve Cahokia. Your Roman warriors.' "

"No. I came with my legion to blaze a trail—find a road—to the west."

Even as Taianita translated, Son of the Sun smiled. Both men, along with the chiefs seated around them, knew this for an evasion. Silence fell as each man devoted himself to the remaining food as best he could.

" 'And now we will smoke,' " said Son of the Sun.

The pipes were being brought already, not the squat flint clay pipes of Cahokia and the north but long flute-like pipes of wood decorated with feathers like the ones the Iroqua favored. There was a pipe for every two chiefs, and Marcellinus would share his with Son of the Sun.

By this time of the night there was little deference to authority. The chiefs did not wait for Son of the Sun to smoke first but eagerly pulled the pipes close and sucked the smoke into their lungs.

As the air around them grew acrid, the paramount chief of the Shappa Ta'atani took a long drag of his pipe and passed it over the bowl to Marcellinus.

Proficient in the Hesperian custom after his many nights on the Mound of the Smoke in Cahokia, Marcellinus took a deep pull. The draw on this pipe was long, and it required a big breath to take the smoke and keep the weed alight.

The taste was sweeter than he had anticipated. The flame in the bowl burned bright. His mouth filled with saliva, and his eyes stung. As he exhaled a wreathing cloud of smoke, his head seemed to lift and expand.

He managed not to cough, but his eyes widened. What on earth was stuffed into the bowl of this pipe?

" 'How can I help you?' " the girl asked.

Marcellinus screwed up his eyes to inspect her and then Son of the Sun. Ah, yes. He passed the pipe back and fought to concentrate. To Son of the Sun he said, "You have been a gracious host to me and my traveling companions. I ask nothing more."

" 'But we should talk of this further. Of Cahokia.' "

A priestess refilled his conch to the brim with corn beer, but Marcellinus left it where it was. He was now sure that the pipe held something wilder and more unruly than the tabaco of Cahokia. Everything around him was shinier than it had been just moments before, and his head sang.

Nonetheless, he still had his wits about him. He nodded in a noncommittal way and waited to see where the conversation would go.

" 'You did not ask for my help. But perhaps, if you wished to rule in Cahokia, we could come to an agreement. We would be brothers. And you would have the alliance you seek.' "

Invade Cahokia again at the head of another conquering army, this time of Shappa Ta'atani? Marcellinus could not imagine it. He kept his features serene. "You would lend me warriors after all? A war party to topple Avenaka?"

" 'Perhaps. There would need to be much talk between us about this. You have friends in Cahokia? There could be a quiet attack, perhaps? One that could succeed before the warriors of Avenaka could rally?' "

A quiet attack? A coup by night?

Marcellinus could not imagine allying with Son of the Sun on such a dishonorable venture. He was sure Sintikala would not be able to imagine it either.

Nor, even if such a coup could be successful, would they be able to trust Son of the Sun afterward.

Marcellinus met the chief's eye. "Myself, an outlander, as ruler of Cahokia? Tell me how such a thing would be possible. You, for example, Son of the Sun? How is it that you rule here, you who are from outside and do not speak the language of Shappa Ta'atan?"

Son of the Sun smiled. " 'I bring peace to Shappa Ta'atan. Peace through power, through strength against our enemies.' "

Marcellinus nodded, and the smoke that still seethed in his lungs made him say, "And reward for those who help you." He gestured around them at the other chiefs.

" 'Of course. A good chief shares what he owns with his friends.' "

Great Sun Man would have said, *A good chief gives away everything he owns to his people.* Marcellinus nodded again. "And who are your enemies?"

" 'I keep the people of Shappa Ta'atan safe. I protect the lands and villages around from the Iroqua, from the

People of the Hand. Even from Cahokia if I must. We are a rich city, a city of great bounty. Always there are enemies.'"

Some of Marcellinus's natural caution had evaporated. "And still you have not told me how you came to rule here."

Kneeling at his feet, Taianita translated. Son of the Sun had been playing with her braids; now he absently stroked her cheek. The girl flushed, but still her translation came from her lips clear and strong. "'Shappa Ta'atan's defenses were broken by war with the People of the Hand, its chiefs killed or fled, its warriors weak. Its elders sent scouts to my town to beg me. There I am mighty leader of men, mighty fighter. With me I bring strong warriors to Shappa Ta'atan to help fight the People of the Hand and later the People of the Longhouse. If I leave, Shappa Ta'atan would fall to the Iroqua.'"

"But we are at peace with the Iroqua." Marcellinus looked to his right and left.

"For now," Panther said ominously. Other men grinned.

"And for how long have you been here, Son of the Sun?"

"'Many winters. A year of winters.'"

Marcellinus knew the slang phrase: to Nova Hesperians "a year of winters" meant as many winters as there were moons in a year. The clan chiefs around him were young, and many would have come to their manhood under Son of the Sun's rule. Interesting.

"'With my strength, with this house and my chiefs and elders and my priests and priestesses, I make the corn grow. This pleases the Corn Mother and brings bounty to my people.'"

Again the chiefs nodded.

Not merely a war leader, then, but a god. A petty monarch and a tin-pot god.

Marcellinus worked hard to keep his expression neutral, but his mind still hummed. He leaned forward.

"Son of the Sun, is this a wise claim? If the corn fails, do you really want to bear the blame?"

Taianita's eyes widened. Marcellinus had addressed his question directly to her rather than to Son of the Sun because he could hardly stand to meet the man's eye.

Son of the Sun spoke. The girl translated. "'The corn does not fail, nor the maygrass or the little barley. The birds, the fish, the buffalo and deer. They all come to me.'"

"I see."

Marcellinus sat back. Statements like these made Son of the Sun vulnerable. If even Ituha could be brought down by a bad harvest, to threaten Son of the Sun's reign Marcellinus would need only to attack his corn.

For a moment, wreathed in the clouds of pipe smoke, this seemed like an insight of great wisdom. Then his logical mind caught up, and he remembered that this had been exactly the Haudenosaunee strategy in burning the Cahokian granaries; in addition to weakening the people, it had potentially weakened the leadership.

But Marcellinus would surely like to see the birds and the buffalo come to Son of the Sun. He smiled. "So, you . . ."

Taianita was staring at him intently. The tension in her neck was clear. Her face remained blank, but her body language sent him a clear warning.

Rightly so. Marcellinus pulled himself together. For Son of the Sun's guest to mock his words would be unspeakably bad manners as well as poor strategy.

"So you must tell me more about the People of the Hand," he said.

The People of the Hand were savage warriors of the desert who carved their temples and homes into mountainsides and made sacrifices to strange gods. But the Shappans' tales of this arid and slightly crazy civilization paled next to their stories of the People of the Sun. This southern tribe apparently built pyramids of stone even larger than the Temple Mound of Shappa Ta'atan to commemorate blood sacrifices atop them: hearts were ripped out of living bodies in such multitudes that the steps of the pyramids flowed with blood.

For once, Son of the Sun sat back and let his chiefs talk. Energized by the beer and the smoke, the chiefs vied with one another to tell the rawest tale of the savagery of the nations to the south. Marcellinus, who had traveled across Asia to the Himalaya and back, knew that the fiercest tribe was always just over the next hill or across the closest sea and took it all with a pinch of salt and a puff of smoke.

" 'And even on the great plains,' " said Son of the Sun through his translator, instantly stilling the voices of the chiefs. " 'Closer to Cahokia by far, the tribe of the Pawnee will sacrifice a girl to the Morning Star. A girl the same age as you . . .' " Taianita cleared her throat. "He says, as old as I am."

"Yes, I understand."

" 'A girl captured in a raid on a neighboring tribe, an innocent girl. For many moons the Pawnee hurt this girl and submit her to much tortures. Then they tie her high on a scaffold of elm, of elder, and of willow, and they complete the sacrifice to the Morning Star.' "

Son of the Sun watched Taianita carefully as she spoke, aware of every drop of sweat on her forehead, but he continued, unrelenting, and so the girl did, too. " 'They . . . burn her in the dawn, alive, and then only at the last they . . . shoot her in the heart with an arrow, and her blood falls into a pit of feathers, and then the other warriors—' "

"Stop," Marcellinus broke in harshly. "You will say no more. I have spoken."

Sudden silence bathed the room. Taianita flashed Marcellinus a look that mingled gratitude and alarm. The chiefs looked away.

Son of the Sun regarded him coolly, his expression impossible to read. Then he smiled. "More pipe?"

Priestesses appeared around them, pouring liquid into conches and cups.

Marcellinus pulled himself together. "Thank you."

The paramount chief spoke again. The girl said, " 'As you see, we are not as these people. Shappa Ta'atan is a great city, as is Cahokia. A city of peace, protecting all around it.' "

Fumbling for words, Marcellinus replied, "The great cities of the Mizipi are indeed beacons of peace to all who live near."

Son of the Sun nodded. Marcellinus drained the corn beer from his conch, after all.

The evening was degenerating. Several conversations were going on at once, and Marcellinus had trouble following them. The Beaver chief was asking him about Roma, beside him Panther and Snake were talking of buffalo and other more unlikely-sounding creatures, and the chiefs on his other side were noisily comparing the charms of the serving women.

The smoke in his head blew his thoughts sideways. He was at the same time very alert, very soporific, and almost dazzled by the light from the fire bowls.

This calmness was a danger. In Cahokia, Marcellinus was capable of social blunders at the best of times. If he let his guard down here in Shappa Ta'atan, the perils would be multiplied tenfold.

" 'If you want to stay in Shappa Ta'atan, you would be welcome,' " Taianita said and, leaning toward him, repeated the notion a little more loudly. " 'You would be welcome in Shappa Ta'atan if you want to stay.' "

Marcellinus took a long pull at the pipe and squinted through the smoke at her earnest, unsmiling face. She nodded to her left; Son of the Sun was there in the gloom of the banqueting room, a comely priestess now leaning on his shoulder. His words, of course.

"Thank you, but we have taken enough of your hospitality and time. We must leave soon, I think."

Taianita reached forward to move his conch cup away from his knee; in twisting to talk to her, Marcellinus had nearly knocked it over. She was very pretty but very serious. He supposed she did not have a great deal to be cheerful about.

" 'Or if you would rule in Cahokia, you would have our help,' " she said next. " 'Cahokia is far, but we would welcome a strong ally who thinks as we do. You and I, ruling the big-river Mizipi together as brothers.' "

Marcellinus eyed her. Time to nip this in the bud once and for all. "I do not seek to rule in Cahokia."

" 'But once you did.' "

"Once, many things were different." His Cahokian was failing him. He resorted to hand-talk. *A different season. A different year.* Excuses and platitudes common enough to have succinct gestures.

" 'Yes, and once Cahokia was different, too.' "

Marcellinus shook his head. "Meaning?"

" 'Once, the Haudenosaunee think the Oyo is theirs.' "

"Yes, I know."

The translator listened carefully to her chief and spoke again. " 'A life and a half ago, the Oyo belonged to the Iroqua. Then men of Shappa Ta'atan helped Cahokia fight the Iroqua. Then the Oyo was owned by mound builders, by Cahokia. Now, by the treaty, it is shared. Today-now, Shappa Ta'atan belongs to Shappa Ta'atan. But in a life and a half?' "

Marcellinus thought he understood. "I doubt that you need fear Avenaka. Cahokia has no war with Shappa Ta'atan."

" 'Less fear if you ruled there.' "

"Never," Marcellinus said bluntly. "Do not speak to me of this again."

" 'And when your people return?' "

He breathed deeply and frowned. "You talk now of the Romans? They will come, Son of the Sun. Sooner or later."

" 'Shappa Ta'atan would be a friend to the Romans. Shappa Ta'atan wants no war with an army from over the sea.' "

"I bet you don't," Marcellinus said in Latin. "I just bet."

"What?"

Marcellinus pulled himself together. "And that is why you must stand shoulder to shoulder with your brothers in the land, with Cahokia and with the Iroqua, if you can. To be strong together in a league of the land against Roma. So that Roma will want to make trade with you rather than making war."

"'Or perhaps, when your Roman chiefs come from across the sea, Shappa Ta'atan would be willing to ally with them.'"

Marcellinus blinked. "Ally *with* Roma?"

Son of the Sun watched him carefully. The words sounded so pleasant and cooperative when spoken by Taianita. Marcellinus had to keep reminding himself that they came from the mind of Son of the Sun, whose body language conveyed quite a different message.

Marcellinus met his eye. "Maybe I misunderstand. You speak of forging an alliance with Roma *against* other mound builders along the Great River and against the Iroqua and the People of the Hand and any other enemies? If your help would be useful to Roma?"

"'Roma is strong. We do not have Cahokia's defenses, its Wakinyan. And perhaps we cannot trust Cahokia. As for the Iroqua and the People of the Hand . . .'" Son of the Sun shook his head while Taianita spoke his words.

Slowly, Marcellinus said: "You believe you could use the power of Roma to help you settle old scores?"

"'Scores? No. But perhaps we would cooperate to keep the peace. To help the other towns to understand Roma. And you, perhaps you could help the Romans to understand Shappa Ta'atan?'"

Marcellinus tried to swallow his repulsion. This candid talk of protection rackets, as brazen as that of any crook in Subura, turned his stomach far more than Son of the Sun's fairy stories of atrocities out on the plains.

Divide et impera. Divide and rule. For centuries it had been the key to Roman domination of foreign lands occupied by tribes and petty warlords. Exploiting local factionalism, permitting—or actively enabling—the settling of old animosities. Pitting groups and tribes one against another.

Just the tactic a Praetor of any new legion might employ.

Marcellinus had no stomach for this. After this evening's combination of purging, heavy food, potent and acidic drink, and intoxicating smoke, he felt that almost literally. Even with Cahokia in Avenaka's hands he would not double-deal against the Great City or pretend a friendship he did not feel that might somehow set the groundwork for any future double-dealing. Even for the sake of his proposed Hesperian confederation, Marcellinus could never be beholden to a man like this. And as for Son of the Sun's talk of allying with Roma, betraying his own Mizipian people . . .

Well, this was obviously no time to confess that Marcellinus himself might be swiftly put in chains or executed by a new Roman force.

"When the Romans arrive," Marcellinus said, "when the iron fist of Roma comes again to Nova . . . to the land, Son of the Sun, you might find them a hard people to ally with."

As the willowy translator relayed his words, Marcellinus wondered if that had sounded like a threat.

If so, then so be it.

His eyes opened. He felt that he had closed them only for an instant, but many of the priestesses were now naked except for the scantiest breechcloths. They were young, their skin flawless.

Some were prepubescent, not even women yet. Bile came to his throat at the unwilling image of Kimimela or Hurit subjected to such indignities. He looked around quickly, but Taianita was still clothed, still at Son of the Sun's feet, her eyes downcast.

Others of the temple women—Marcellinus could no longer think of them as priestesses, even ironically— were sitting in the other chiefs' laps now, fondling their arms and brows, feeding them sweetmeats. The night air was growing light with laughter and musk. If Marcellinus had not been present, the evening might already have degenerated into an orgy.

A woman leaned over him. Like the others she wore only a breechcloth almost too skimpy to warrant the name, and she smelled beguilingly female. Running her fingers through the hair above his ear, she began to ease herself into his lap.

"No," Marcellinus told her. "Thank you, no."

Take her, Panther signed. *You will cause no offense. It is expected.* The priestess smiled, and her hand dropped onto his knee.

"I shouldn't," he said. "It's against my, uh. I would not wish to cause problems."

Snake shook his head, not understanding. Panther looked scornful.

Marcellinus disengaged the priestess's hand, but then, of course, she started caressing his fingers. With some difficulty, since hand-talk had been rendered impossible, he got her to stop. She pouted and moved away, pretending to tidy the bowls and conch beakers in front of him.

No? the Panther chief signed with derision. *Is the great Wanageeska a man at all?*

Marcellinus bridled, but this was not the place to cause a scene. *It is not my custom,* he signed.

It was impossible to hand-talk quietly, of course; everyone within eyeshot could see what he was saying.

Son of the Sun spoke. " 'Someone older? Younger? A boy, perhaps?' "

Marcellinus shook his head.

" 'This one, who can speak sweet words to you?' "

Son of the Sun gave Taianita a shove, sending the girl sprawling onto Marcellinus. He saw sudden shock on her face, pain in her eyes, creases that should not have been there in one so young.

Bizarre that this girl should have to translate the words of her own humiliation. To Son of the Sun she was a chattel, less than human.

Marcellinus helped the girl sit up again, bowed his head to her respectfully, then swiveled his gaze back to Son of the Sun and allowed a steelier tone to enter his voice. "No."

Son of the Sun spoke. Taianita gulped. " 'You do not approve.' "

Marcellinus struggled to find the right words. "This medicine is not my medicine."

The Snake chief cocked his head on one side and signed. *Our women are not pretty enough?*

Marcellinus did not want to cause offense or lose face. Especially for his pride and his strength in negotiations, he did not want these young strapping chiefs to think he was too old. The first thing that came into his head was, *Sintikala would not like it.*

Sintikala is your woman? signed the Beaver chief.

From the frying pan to the fire; again Marcellinus was stuck for a good answer. He merely shook his head and smiled.

They didn't care anymore. With priestesses in their laps, they were losing interest in their guest, and with good reason. Marcellinus stopped talking and let them forget he was there.

Yet he could not stand and leave. He could tread neither the soil of the Temple Mound nor the grass of the sacred precinct below, and he did not want to make a scene. He would just have to wait until he could be carried out with the others.

By his side Taianita knelt stock-still, as if trying to be invisible.

Marcellinus took another drink, faked another deep pull at the smoldering drug pipe, and allowed himself to slide into feigned unconsciousness.

At dawn the Shappan messenger was waiting for him at the gate. The boy seemed tired and a little resentful. "You enjoyed it?"

Marcellinus stifled the impulse to be honest. Around them, sleepy chiefs staggered back into the city. Son of the Sun had stayed behind in the Temple Mound, but anything Marcellinus said would obviously go straight to the paramount chief's ear. "It was amazing. Eye-opening."

"Tell me of the birdwomen," said the boy.

"You have not seen them?"

"Only in the air, from long away. The priestesses of the Sacred Center are not for me."

"They are beautiful," Marcellinus conceded. "And they fly well. But as you say, it is a shame that they are caged and cannot fly free."

"I did not say that," said the boy in alarm, looking around him.

"Nevertheless," Marcellinus said.

The boy shook his head. "Is there anything else you need, great chief? I received word that you might not yet be ready to sleep." The youth met his eye brazenly, with a slight tilt to his hip. "Anything?"

Would it never end?

"Nothing at all," Marcellinus said. "Nothing at all."

CHAPTER 13

YEAR FIVE, THUNDER MOON

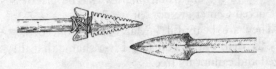

They did not see Son of the Sun again until after the fourth and final night of the Green Corn Festival. By then Marcellinus would have been quite happy never to see an ear of corn or hear a drum again.

Even in the chief's absence the sudden increase in attentiveness of the Shappa Ta'atani had become very obvious. In the last two days Marcellinus had rarely been left alone for a moment. At least one of the chiefs or warrior lieutenants was with him at all times, ostensibly to ensure that he had everything he needed. Sintikala was now never without her own cadre of women who watched her every move and never left her to her own devices either. The elite warriors of Shappa Ta'atan carefully mingled with their Cahokian counterparts.

When Marcellinus sent Isleifur and a half dozen other men on an errand to the dragon ship, most were turned back politely at the gate. Only a single man, Mahkah, was permitted to go to the ship.

Obviously Marcellinus had made a tactical error in spurning Son of the Sun's offers of alliance. The nature of Shappan hospitality had changed significantly as a result.

At dinner the first night after the festival, Marcellinus found himself separated from Akecheta by several Shappan warriors. He couldn't even see Hanska, Mahkah, or

Aelfric. As always, Sintikala was off to the side, surrounded by women.

Marcellinus rose and proposed a lavishly complimentary toast to Son of the Sun.

Toasting in this way was new to the people of Shappa Ta'atan, but they had become an appreciative audience for it; after all, it enabled them to drain their cups and ask for more. Afterward, with all eyes on him, Marcellinus said: "You have been most kind, but we should soon pack up your generous gifts and fare you well."

"What?" said Beaver.

Marcellinus simplified. "I say that we must leave in a day or so."

The chief of the Deer clan applied himself to his fish with renewed vigor. Beaver took a swig from his cup. Graciously, Son of the Sun nodded.

Each man had reacted much too casually to the suggestion.

From twenty feet to his left, Akecheta said, "My chief speaks true. We must paddle farther south, perhaps even to the Market of the Mud, and make ourselves a long camp for the winter."

Son of the Sun laughed politely, and even Marcellinus grinned. "Winter?" They were all sweating even in the relative cool of the evening. It was unarguably still summer in Shappa Ta'atan.

"There are few of us. It will take time."

"You might winter here."

"We thank you," Marcellinus said. "But it is time for us to move on and seek adventure elsewhere." He sat before anyone could respond.

Marcellinus had finished his meal long before, and so had Son of the Sun. The chiefs were served first, and the elders ate more slowly and chewed longer, but by now only the Deer clan elder was still eating. Son of the Sun called for tabaco, and a young brave came running to bring him an already lit long clay pipe. Once again Marcellinus could not stop himself from thinking that back in Cahokia, Great Sun Man had lit his own pipe.

" 'We are honored by your presence, and there is much to learn,' " said Son of the Sun through Taianita. " 'We must be brothers, you and we.' "

"Of course," Marcellinus said politely. Taking the proffered pipe, he pulled a long draw and managed not to cough at the pungency of the smoke from the combination of leaves, barks, and weeds that burned in the bowl. At least there was none of the disorienting drug he had experienced on the Temple Mound. Eyes watering, he passed the pipe to his left.

Son of the Sun spoke again. " 'Tomorrow I show you the fire arrows you asked of. And we shall talk about the stone, for house?' " He mimed.

"Bricks," Marcellinus said. He had offered to show the Shappa Ta'atani how to make bricks when they had arrived, but at that time the chiefs had shown no interest. He nodded comfortably.

" 'Perhaps you stay ten nights more,' " said the chief.

Akecheta shook his head. "Ten is too many."

Marcellinus leaned forward to take the pipe again, aware of the hilt of his pugio pressing lightly into his stomach beneath his tunic. How much of a fuss should he make about this now? He glanced casually across at Sintikala, but she was giving every appearance of being engrossed in her conversation with the women.

He would not want to push this any harder before consulting Sintikala. Marcellinus decided to let it go for the evening and forced himself to relax.

Marcellinus came awake all at once, mouth still dry from the pipe, nerves jangling. The darkness pressed in on him.

Keeping his breathing even and his head still, he searched around with his eyes.

He felt it again: the merest of air movements, a faint rustle, and grabbing the pugio from under his pillow, he rolled off the bed and leaped forward.

He slammed into someone smaller and lighter than himself, who spun away with a yip of pain. Marcellinus barely registered the high-pitched sound before he snatched back his outstretched pugio lest it cut her.

He had bowled her over. He could see her silhouette now as she pushed herself up onto her hands and knees, sucking air back into her lungs.

Cautiously, he whispered: "Taianita?"

"Yes," she croaked. "Please . . . do not kill me."

Marcellinus stayed where he was. Anyone could bear a poisoned blade. "Why are you here?"

"Because Son of the Sun wishes to give you up to Avenaka," she whispered.

"What?" He glanced at the door, which Taianita had eased shut behind her. Were men coming or outside already? Damn these Hesperian huts for having no windows.

Taianita sat up. "Not yet. Not here in Shappa. But he has sent runners north."

Marcellinus rubbed his eyes. She was not an assassin. If Son of the Sun wanted Marcellinus dead, he would have sent the warriors first, probably several, to make sure the job was done quickly and quietly. "Did anyone see you come here?"

"I do not know. I tried to be a shadow."

"Gods." His mind whirled. "I'm sorry I hurt you. Come here, sit. Tell me what you know. Quietly."

She perched beside him on the bed, still shivering in shock and fear. He draped his blanket over her shoulders. "Tell me."

"Avenaka of Cahokia sent men here, envoys, soon after he defeated Great Sun Man in single combat."

"Single combat? He . . ." Marcellinus swallowed. It didn't matter. "Go on."

"The envoys left only days before you arrived. They told Son of the Sun that Avenaka wants him as a brother so that they may rule the Mizipi together and be strong against the Iroqua. And also the envoys warned him about you, you exiles in your big canoe.

"Avenaka repents of his generosity to you. He is angered at the loss of his Hawk chief and the stories of the

Wanageeska and Sintikala seeking alliances as they go downriver, forming a league against him. He says these are not the actions of people banished, never to return."

"A league to resist the Romans," Marcellinus said. "I sought no alliance with Son of the Sun against Avenaka. You know this."

"Of course," she said simply. "I am here."

Marcellinus still was not thinking straight. Obviously Taianita believed him. "Anyway. So Son of the Sun was expecting us. But . . . then he offered to ally with me against Avenaka."

"Yes. On the Temple Mound, Son of the Sun's questions to you . . . He was wondering whether to be the brother of Avenaka or the brother of Wanageeska. Avenaka's words to him were haughty, as of an older brother to a younger. But now that Son of the Sun knows you will not ally with him, he has decided to hold you here, delay you until the Cahokians arrive, and make a gift of you to curry favor with Avenaka."

Marcellinus nodded.

"You knew of this?"

"No."

"But it does not surprise you?"

"No."

"Son of the Sun does not know Avenaka, but . . . in you he saw a man he might ally with to take Cahokia. Increase his rule over the Mizipi, become an even greater chief. Shappa Ta'atan is his, but Cahokia? Great City of the Mizipi? And so he measured you as a friend and ally, but you pushed him away, and so now . . . Now he will instead build faith with his Cahokian brother by delivering you to him. That is why he tempts you to stay, offers you hospitality for the winter. So that Avenaka can send warriors for you."

The Great River twisted and turned, but a single runner could go straight on the trail. Still, it would take time. How long? Marcellinus did not know.

"Why not just . . ." He stopped. Bitter memories of

the Iroqua captives in their corral flashed through his mind. Perhaps better not to say the words.

Taianita's silhouette nodded. "You are liked," she said simply.

"Liked?"

"By the people of Shappa Ta'atan. You and your men and women. You have made friends here, and they will be sad to see you leave. And you have been granted Shappan hospitality; you are here under Son of the Sun's protection. And so he cannot just slay you or put you in a pit until the warriors of Avenaka come for you."

A pit. Marcellinus almost felt the ground shifting beneath him even now. "And why are you telling me this?" he asked, although he already suspected.

"So you will escape and take me with you," she said.

"Taianita, we are fugitives. Wanderers on the river with no home. We may die tomorrow. I would rather leave you here to live than take you with us to die."

"And I would rather live free on a big canoe and die in a year than live my whole life as the slave of Son of the Sun." Taianita leaned forward, and her hand found his. "Wanageeska. I beg you. I beg you."

His face felt hot. "I . . . Please. You do not need to beg. I will see what I can do. But you should go now. Be a shadow again."

"Of course." She touched him once on the arm, very lightly. "I am a shadow. And now I go."

They assembled into ranks outside the guest huts at dawn, weapons and possessions in hand. Akecheta moved up and down the line, pushing men into place, asserting his authority. For a dissonant moment Marcellinus felt pride at their discipline until he remembered the extraordinary odds they faced.

It was clear they could not fight their way out of Shappa Ta'atan. From the plaza where they lived and feasted and worked with the local warriors and metalsmiths it was a good half mile to the riverbank, and they would have to pass through the narrow guarded passageways that were the only breaks in the palisade. To have any real chance of escape they had to be outside the city to begin with. So they would have to try to start with persuasion . . .

Right on cue, here came Son of the Sun, with Taianita walking submissively five steps behind him.

The chief was alone, with no warriors nearby. If Marcellinus seized him now and put a knife to his throat . . .

Son of the Sun hand-talked: *You leave?*

"Yes," Marcellinus said. "Once again we thank you for your hospitality, but it is time for us to go."

Shappan warriors were appearing now, forming up between them and the gates. Marcellinus frowned. "Inside your walls we are under Shappa Ta'atani protection. Is it not so?" He signaled *Speak words* to Taianita, but Son of the Sun was already nodding and speaking his response in Caddoan.

Taianita came forward. "'It is so. And I would have you remain within our walls so that we may protect you further.'"

"We will leave," Marcellinus said. "Today. Do you bar your gates against us?"

Son of the Sun spoke. A look of surprise crossed Taianita's face. She cleared her throat and, almost stammering, translated. "'Warriors come from Cahokia . . . Avenaka wants you dead, Wanageeska, and your head on a spear. The same for Sintikala if she will not pledge allegiance. Your men slain and scalped. Your women he has offered to me as my slaves. And to all of this, I said no. And why? Because I am a fair and honest ruler, and you entered Shappa Ta'atan under my hospitality, and that cannot be betrayed.'"

Sintikala grinned, with no humor in it. "And so you would protect us from Avenaka?"

"'For as long as you are within Shappan walls.'"

"Then we must go now, no delay." Sintikala stepped forward, Marcellinus by her side. Kimimela fell in behind her.

Akecheta snapped out a command, and the First Cahokian came to attention.

Son of the Sun nodded and stood aside.

His warriors, too, divided and formed an honor guard.

A clear path to the great gates of Shappa Ta'atan was hardly what Marcellinus had anticipated. He glanced again at Taianita, but her eyes were downcast, her face carefully formal.

And now Son of the Sun was warning him about Avenaka? Had Taianita been trying to trick him? Had it all been a lie in hopes that Marcellinus would free her from Son of the Sun?

Or was there still more to this than met the eye?

"By the left, march," he said to Akecheta in Latin. "And be ready for anything."

As the Cahokians moved forward, more warriors and townspeople came to line their path, but none tried to stop them.

The First Cahokian paraded out of Shappa Ta'atan. Unusually, most of them were even marching in step.

The warriors of Shappa Ta'atan watched them go. Many looked wistful. Whether it was envy of the Roman weaponry, disappointment that they wouldn't get to have a crack at facing the Cahokians in combat, or genuine sadness that the visit had come to such an abrupt end, Marcellinus could not tell and did not care. All that mattered now was getting his crew as far from Shappa Ta'atan as possible and selling their lives dearly if it came to a fight.

Akecheta led the column, and Marcellinus brought up the rear, with Sintikala by his side. They had put Kimimela and the artisans into the middle of the column for their protection in case any fighting started.

They passed through the L-shaped main gate, watched from above by the warriors of Shappa Ta'atan. Marcellinus's hand rested on his gladius, as if a sword could have helped him so many yards beneath the walkway. It was a tense moment, but they walked through without incident.

A cool northerly breeze sent ripples across the Mizipi. The skies were blue. Aside from a handful of fishing dugouts and a fur trader who had passed southward a few minutes before, the waters were free of boats.

And there was the *Concordia* on the bank, waiting for them. No warriors stood between the Cahokians and their ship. Son of the Sun was smiling, every inch the dutiful host.

Now Marcellinus felt the prickle of true fear. This was too easy. This was not right at all.

"Check the boat," he said tersely to Mahkah. "Have the men check everything, look everywhere. Is the hull sound? Are there traps? Hurry."

As his crew went aboard, Marcellinus turned back.

A large crowd of Shappa Ta'atani had filed out of the city to watch them leave. Hundreds of ordinary men and women would bear witness that the Cahokians had left their city safely and in peace, the sanctity of Shappan hospitality preserved.

Standing in front of his honor guard and his chiefs, Son of the Sun watched the First Cahokian prepare for departure with a flinty look in his eye and a smile on his lips. Behind him, Taianita was sweating and terrified, on the verge of panic. And when Son of the Sun glanced back at her and grinned, his cruel joy at his word slave's torment was readily apparent.

Marcellinus nodded. It was clear that Son of the Sun knew Taianita had betrayed him. There was no point in any further pretense.

His anger barely in check, Marcellinus stepped closer to the chief. Son of the Sun's guards looked wary, but Marcellinus kept his hand away from his gladius. Instead, he reached out and clasped the chief's forearm.

"I know you planned to give my head to Avenaka yourself," he said quietly. "My head and my ship."

Taianita's mouth dropped open, and Son of the Sun's arm twitched. Marcellinus held him firmly, digging his fingernails into the war chief's skin almost deeply enough to draw blood. With his other hand he slapped the chief on the shoulder in a way that looked nothing but comradely, although the knock contained a bite.

Son of the Sun held his gaze.

"So what now? We sail away from Shappa Ta'atan safe and sound? I don't think so."

"All is well with the longship," Kimimela called from behind him in Latin. "Gaius? Nothing is wrong."

Marcellinus nodded, and to Son of the Sun he said, "Who waits for us downriver? How far?" He looked over the chieftain's shoulder at his clan chiefs. He saw the clan chiefs of Beaver, Snake, Deer, Crow . . . "Where is Panther?"

Son of the Sun began to speak. White-faced and quivering, Taianita translated. " 'You . . . you have been my honored guest. I look forward to the . . . the day when I see you again.' "

"Oh, you shall. And I will make a count, and for any man or woman of mine who dies today, that will be one extra day I keep you alive, Son of the Sun, before I send you to your many-fathers. Then I will put your head on a spear, and I will wear your scalp on my belt. I have spoken."

Son of the Sun laughed derisively. Marcellinus released him and backed away.

"Take me with you," Taianita said. "Wanageeska? He knows we spoke. Take me or Son of the Sun will tie me to a frame and kill me slowly just as soon as you are gone."

Son of the Sun seized the girl's wrist. His other hand held his spiked chert mace of office. At his waist he wore a wide obsidian blade. And behind Son of the Sun stood half a dozen warriors with spears.

Son of the Sun smiled. "You like girl? You take girl. If I take—" He pointed. "—that girl. Or that girl."

Hurit. Kimimela. The chieftain of the Shappa Ta'atani was offering him Taianita in exchange for one of his own people.

From the bank, Sintikala cast a worried glance back toward Marcellinus. The Cahokians were all at the water's edge, the greasy Mizipi licking at their ankles. Only the Roman was still back amid the warriors of Shappa Ta'atan.

"Please," Taianita whispered in desperation.

"My crew is mine," Marcellinus said. "And this girl wishes to leave Shappa Ta'atan. You say she cannot?"

"Yes, I say she stay unless . . ." The chief pointed at Kimimela, who flinched even though she was thirty feet away.

"Gaius?" Sintikala called from the dragon ship. "Problem?"

Marcellinus held Son of the Sun's gaze. "Once you offered me Taianita. Now I will take her."

The Shappan chief spoke. Taianita translated, blushing. " 'I offered her to warm your bed. Not as a slave to take forever.' "

Marcellinus put his hand on the hilt of his gladius.

Out of the corner of his eye he saw Kimimela start back toward him, saw Akecheta grab her and hold her back. None of them could hear the exchange, but Marcellinus was not coming to them and an ugly mood was spreading through the crowd of warriors of Shappa Ta'atan. Hands were going to spears, maces, and clubs, and braves were looking at one another and spreading their feet for a surer balance if they had to leap into the fray. In an instant the Cahokians were scrabbling for weapons, too, snatching them up from the longship.

Roman steel glinted. Arrows were swept onto bowstrings.

Marcellinus gritted his teeth. "I will fight you for her. You and I, Son of the Sun of the Shappa Ta'atani and Gaius Publius Marcellinus of Roma and Cahokia. Fist to fist and foot to foot. Here on this shore. Or if you prefer, we can fight with steel and stone. Either way, I will leave with this girl."

Son of the Sun had not moved. Now he smiled faintly

and raised his arms in hand-talk. *You want fight? Then we all fight.*

Every man and woman there saw the hand-talk and understood it. On the riverbank Mahkah and Yahto looked at each other, nonplussed. Their commander was squabbling with the chief of Shappa Ta'atan, risking their lives over a girl?

A wave of consternation spread out over the crowd. Quite definitely, the ordinary townspeople did not wish them to fight.

Marcellinus looked again at Taianita's terrified face and into Son of the Sun's eyes.

He could not leave her.

There had to be another solution to this.

He became aware of his hand, firmly clutching his sword hilt. He was wearing the gladius that Great Sun Man had returned to him at Woshakee, that Hanska had brought for him from Cahokia. He had owned it most of his fighting life. With it, Marcellinus had killed Germans and Magyars and Sindhs and, more recently, Iroqua.

It was ornate but well balanced. He knew the weight of it. This gladius was almost a part of his arm.

But with this blade he had also killed Cahokians.

With this blade he had killed Fuscus in cold blood.

"We make trade," he said. "For the girl, this fine sword."

Marcellinus stepped back and drew the gladius with finger and thumb, his other hand outstretched to pat the air and make his intentions crystal clear to the Shappan braves. He handed the sword to Son of the Sun hilt first.

The chief set his mace down and grasped the sword, looking into Marcellinus's eyes. He did not release the translator.

Marcellinus saw clearly that the chief would prefer to fight. To provoke a battle, take Marcellinus's head here and now.

But the crowd was restive, men and women shouting out, urging Son of the Sun to make the trade.

You are liked, Taianita had said.

For once Marcellinus saw the virtues of diplomacy, of smiling at strangers.

Son of the Sun looked around him and looked again at the gladius. Finally he nodded and said, "I take sword," and in a high-pitched and rather desperate voice, Taianita repeated it for all to hear. "Son of the Sun says he makes the trade!"

Marcellinus released his hold on the sword, stepped back, bowed respectfully to the Shappan crowd. "Come," he said to Taianita.

Turning his back, he walked toward the *Concordia*.

No chieftain worth his salt could strike down a guest in cold blood in front of his own people rather than honor a trade. Son of the Sun's loss of face would be immeasurable. Nonetheless, Marcellinus watched Akecheta and Kimimela. At the merest signs of alarm, her mouth dropping open or his hand beginning to rise in warning, Marcellinus would whirl to defend himself.

He did not need to. Taianita ran past him and clambered into the dragon ship, shaking like a leaf.

The rest of the Cahokians got into the drekar, the word slave still swinging her head around wild-eyed as if she expected a rain of arrows and spears. But behind them now were only warriors standing at ease and a chief raising a Roman gladius in a slightly menacing salute of farewell.

Marcellinus saluted back curtly. "Let's go. Hurit, Kimimela, cast off. Akecheta, to the helm. To oars, everyone else."

"Push off!" Akecheta repeated. "Row! One, two . . ."

Taianita sat in the gunwale, staring at the tall walls of Shappa Ta'atan. "Thank you and thank you and thank you . . ."

Sintikala pointed at the girl. "What is this?"

"Fuscus," Marcellinus said, and looked at Aelfric.

The Hawk chief shook her head. "What?"

Marcellinus's brain clouded. He reached over the side

of the dragon ship for a handful of river water and dashed it into his face. "Paying a debt. More than one."

Aelfric nodded.

As the drekar swung into the current, the Cahokians put their backs into the rowing. They headed into the bend, and Shappa Ta'atan slowly disappeared from view. Marcellinus eyed the banks, but so close to the city there were few trees. They would not be attacked yet. It would be too suspicious.

"Well," said Aelfric. "Thank God that's over."

Marcellinus just shook his head.

The Briton frowned. "Not over?"

"Hasn't even begun." And in Cahokian he said, "Stay vigilant. Watch the river, watch the banks."

There was a brittle silence. Eventually Mahkah said in disbelief, "They will come after her?"

"They will come after *us*." Marcellinus stood so that they all could hear him. "Son of the Sun has sent a war party ahead of us, led by the chief of the Panther clan. They will attack us today on the river or tonight onshore. Son of the Sun wants our heads to send to Avenaka and seal their brotherhood as warlords of the Mizipi."

The dragon ship swung in the water. "One, two," Akecheta called mundanely to bring them all back to rowing in time.

"Futete," Kimimela said. In the bow of the ship Sintikala shook her head and turned to stare downriver.

Marcellinus looked at Taianita. "Enjoy your freedom. You may not have it long."

"Shit," said Aelfric. "For this I gave up comfort, easy women, and all the buffalo I could eat?"

"Look on the bright side," Marcellinus said. "Trees everywhere."

Since the wind was favorable, Marcellinus had them raise the sail; he wanted to put as many river miles behind them as possible, but not at the cost of tiring out his crew.

He put Mahkah and three other men on lookout duty in the bow and stern, port and starboard. They cleared the sea chests to the sides and readied the shields in case waves of arrows came from the trees on the riverbank. They quickly stocked up with fresh water at a small creek with no trees nearby and long sight lines.

Despite those precautions, Marcellinus did not think the Shappa Ta'atani would attack them on the open water. The First Cahokian would see them coming literally a mile away. The *Concordia* could smash through any canoe in its path, and boarding the dragon ship from canoes in midriver would be fraught with difficulty unless Panther's warriors had overwhelming force. It would be much easier to wait for the Cahokians to land, then assault them by night.

"Napayshni, Dustu: make a weapons inventory. Count swords, spears, bows, arrows. But quietly, so no one onshore would notice."

Marcellinus looked at his carpenters and rope makers, who immediately looked nervous, as they always did when he paid attention to them. "Whatever the numbers, we'll need more. Wapi, you others: look at our stores of wood. How many sharpened stakes can you make by nightfall? Do we have sinew?"

He scanned the terrain onshore: meadows and copses, irritatingly flat as always.

"Wanageeska?"

"What is it, Taianita?"

"What can I do? I want to help. To repay you."

"You don't need to repay me." He appraised her. "Can you fight? Are you willing to kill braves of your own people, even men you may know?"

She met his eye. "I am not a warrior. But I will kill. Especially men who try to kill you and your people."

"Very well. Tell me everything you know about Panther."

"The animal?"

"The clan chief. I don't know his real name." Marcellinus's mind churned. How would he handle this if he had a whole legion of soldiers under his command? Or even a cohort? How could he scale that down for his meager force of only a few dozen warriors?

He eyed the word slave again. "Can you run fast?"

Taianita looked at him uncertainly, but Marcellinus was already studying the sky and beckoning to Isleifur and Yahto. "And who recalls how high the moon was just after sundown last night?"

They had swords. Twenty spears. A dozen bows. More arrows than a dozen bows could shoot in the duration of any reasonable skirmish. A few clubs and axes.

What they could have used above all else was Roman shields, the rectangular steel-rimmed scuta forty inches tall that they had used in the testudo when they had besieged Woshakee many years before, but those were all back in Cahokia. They did not have a single one.

They would just have to improvise.

By noon Marcellinus had explained his plan to everyone. And by midafternoon his crew was giving a convincing impression of being drunk, with a great deal of laughter and tuneless singing. Isleifur took the helm and cheerfully steered the boat in a series of broad curves to the left and right, sometimes taking them completely out of the current to spin in the shallows or scraping them along the branches of a sunken tree. Toward dusk they struck the sail and allowed the boat to drift for a while, lying back and talking noisily of the joys of the Green Corn Ceremony.

As night fell, they pulled themselves ashore at a meadow on the western side of the Mizipi surrounded by trees and sloppily moored the boat. The adults roved into the nearby copses to pull together some dried wood for a big bonfire while the younger members of the crew ran around in a rambunctious mock fight.

After a light meal at dusk, they set about preparing their bedrolls for the night.

* * *

The scar from the calf wound Marcellinus had received on the Great Mound of Cahokia had chosen this night to itch unbearably. Marcellinus tried to welcome its help in keeping him awake. He could not move to scratch it.

Like Sintikala beside him and the others around them, he lay still, breathing regularly. The fire had burned down an hour earlier, with pots of water sitting forgotten on rocks in the hot embers and unburned sticks still jutting from it.

On Marcellinus's right, the supine Mahkah faked a brief half snore. A signal. He had seen something.

Marcellinus's hand closed around the hilt of his second-best sword under the blanket next to him. In the dimness of the moon he saw Sintikala's eyebrow move once and knew that she was still awake.

He was damned if he could tell which direction the Shappan warriors were coming from. They should have arranged a more comprehensive set of signals . . .

Then came the first scream, which sounded like Hurit's, followed by another that could only be from Taianita.

Marcellinus threw aside his blanket and rolled up onto his feet, then hopped. His left leg had chosen the most inopportune time possible to fall asleep. Beside him Sintikala sprang up, jumping closer to the fire to seize a long stout branch with a glowing tip. Mahkah was already up and running.

In the pale glow from the setting first-quarter moon, Marcellinus saw two Shappan war parties converging on them. The larger group came from the south, but the smaller group from the north was nearer. They were so close that it was a good thing he had been lying under his blankets fully armored in his breastplate, greaves, and helmet.

Seeing they had lost the element of surprise, the Shappans whooped, raising themselves from their half crouch and running full tilt into the camp of the Cahokians.

The first attackers tripped over the stretched-out sinews that the Cahokians had prepared, tied between low sticks, and half a dozen Shappan braves screamed in pain as they landed on the line of low sharpened stakes that the carpenters had prepared on the boat that afternoon and crawled around jamming into the ground shortly after sunset. The warriors behind leaped over them and began to spear the Cahokian bodies that lay closest to them, shadowy forms that had not moved yet.

Swearing sounded much coarser in the Shappa Ta'atani accent. There were no sleeping bodies under the bedrolls the Shappans were attacking. Closer to the fire Cahokians were still rising to their feet, clubs and fire-heated spears in hand, preparing to counter the Shappan attack.

From the southern group Marcellinus heard Panther snapping out orders but could not tell which shadowy figure the voice came from or what he was saying. Panther was using warrior speech, the language of the Shappan secret societies. Around Marcellinus to the south of the bonfire a dozen Cahokians were forming up, ready for the assault. From off to the west came more screams as the Cahokian girls and women ran pell-mell out of the camp.

Marcellinus allowed himself a wry smile. The screams came from Hurit, Kimimela, Chumanee, Taianita, and Hanska, fleeing westward into the night. He pitied any Shappan braves who were fool enough to chase them.

But a hundred yards to the south he saw at least eight Shappan war parties in their groups of six. These warriors had slowed their charge and were picking their way deliberately across the ground that separated them from the warriors of Cahokia, alert for further traps.

Now they found them: dozens of iron nails in the dirt, twisted and bent so that they would rest on a triangular base with their sharp points upward. Under cover of their earlier games, the younger Cahokians had scattered the caltrops, and now they effortlessly pierced the Shappan moccasins. Some of the men screeched and hopped, pulling out the treacherous nails from the soles of their feet and flinging them away.

Other Shappans raised their bows.

As the arrows began to fly, Marcellinus and Sintikala lifted up the flat square panels of pine decking they had brought ashore from the *Concordia* and knelt behind them. To their left and right the other Cahokians were doing the same thing. Shappan arrows thwacked harmlessly into the decking.

"Forward!" Marcellinus shouted, and the Cahokians began to advance slowly behind their wooden shields.

His Cahokians, including Sintikala, were all nearby; Marcellinus had not needed to issue his order in such a loud tone for them to hear it. But the order had been a signal to another Cahokian force farther away, and now the battle was joined. From the right a wave of arrows flew into the Shappan flank, and then a second wave. Akecheta and the twelve best archers on the boat, including Dustu and Wapi, had emerged from the copse of trees to the north and were piling arrows into the exposed Shappan flank, their targets well illuminated by the moon.

The screams of the women and girls had ceased abruptly, and now they heard cries in a very different timbre and the clash of weapons. Hanska, Hurit, and the others had turned to face their attackers head on, and at the same time Marcellinus's second reserve of a half dozen warriors, led by Aelfric and including Napayshni and Isleifur, also had burst out of the trees to attack them from the rear.

Marcellinus almost felt sorry for them. But the largest group of Shappa Ta'atani, led by the Panther clan chief, were almost upon him.

Panther was commanding his men to jump past the nails. The chief was no fool. He had realized the iron caltrops were limited to a dark band of earth that ran to the south of the camp, near the stream. Marcellinus's people would need to know where they were as well, and placing them in the grass would have reduced their effectiveness.

More arrows came from Akecheta's archers, and some

of Panther's turned to shoot back at them. But by now Panther had recognized Marcellinus and Sintikala. He roared, and the rest of the Shappa Ta'atani threw aside their bows and charged.

Turning, reaching back, Marcellinus and five other men snatched up pots from the fire and threw them. The water in them was no longer boiling but was hot enough to startle and scald; Panther's men might instinctively fear it was liquid flame, and indeed several of the nearest Shappan warriors dropped to the ground and rolled, crying out. The others kept coming.

Three Shappan war parties—eighteen warriors in all— had peeled off and were running at Akecheta's archers, heads down behind their shields, ululating, furious. The five war parties that remained came for Marcellinus and Sintikala.

As Marcellinus and his men had been throwing water, Sintikala and the others had been bracing the deck planking with stout wooden poles. Now the mob of at least thirty Shappan warriors crashed into them. Expecting them to be held up by men and not braced with the weight of the world behind them, several of the Shappan warriors bounced back. If they'd planned to bull the Cahokians backward into their own bonfire by brute force, they were sadly disappointed.

The squares of planking had become field fortifications: four of them side by side, with four crew members behind each one. Two Cahokians held firm and aimed blows over the top of each makeshift shield while the other two stood in the gaps, hacking at the attacking Shappans. Beside Marcellinus, Sintikala was fighting with her ax in one hand and her stout fire-hardened branch in the other; Marcellinus was half aware of the screams of the Shappan warriors as she jabbed the smoldering tip into their stomachs and abdomens below the wooden armor that each warrior wore and then clouted them in the neck and shoulders with the ax.

This was the first time Marcellinus had seen Sintikala fight in earnest. Her strength and anger were impressive.

In the moments he had left for conscious thought, he was grateful he had never had to fight her himself.

Those rational moments were few and far between now as the battle rage swept him, as it always did in moments of extremity. Banished by Avenaka? Betrayed by Son of the Sun and now attacked in a night ambush by a much larger force? He let the fury fill him, that almost berserker strength, let it drive him forward and guide his arm.

As if the rage had sharpened his senses, he now saw Panther clearly, twenty feet to his left. The warrior chief had taken position at the edge of his battle formation as centurions and other field leaders often did and was in bitter hand-to-hand combat with—who was it, Yahto?

Men were running in behind Marcellinus now; with a fractured glance he saw with relief that they were Cahokians who had polished off the smaller Shappan group that had come in from the north. The trip wires and sharpened stakes on that side of the camp had done their work well. Six men, seven . . .

No time to calculate the odds, but the Cahokians were still outnumbered. Only the surprise assaults by Akecheta's archers, the distraction of the fleeing women, and the use of the deck planking as a makeshift defense had kept them alive this long.

Cahokians were falling now, overwhelmed by the superior odds. Marcellinus had to go for the Shappan leader. He had to take Panther out and hope that the resulting loss of morale would turn the tide in his favor.

He crashed through two Shappan warriors, sending them sprawling. Yahto was fighting valiantly but being pushed back by Panther's greater weight and reach. Now he slipped, almost tumbling into the fire. Panther leaped forward and swung a vicious blow with his club. Yahto spun in the air and crashed heavily to the ground.

Marcellinus almost managed to slay Panther then and there, roaring in from the Shappan warrior's left. Panther leaped and swung again, his chert-studded club rising toward Marcellinus's crotch.

The Roman jumped left and kicked at the campfire. Sparks and embers sprayed into the air around Panther.

It did not stop him. The Shappan clan chief was fast, whirling and snarling like his namesake.

Marcellinus had no time to raise his sword in a parry, and Panther's long club would have smashed it away anyhow. He had to drop, fall sideways away from it, roll on the ground. It was about the most dangerous thing he could have done, but the alternative was to accept a crushing blow or fall into the glowing fire.

Panther lunged. Marcellinus swung. The club glanced painfully off Marcellinus's shoulder. His gladius slammed into solid wood and stuck fast. Marcellinus had crashed into the upright deck planking.

The planking was held up by a pilum. Marcellinus reached around behind him, pulling a muscle in his shoulder, and his forearm met the spear. Rising to his knees, he shoved at the deck planking, and it fell away.

He grasped the heavy spear and yanked it out of the soil with both hands. He barely had time to raise it quarterstaff style before Panther's brutal club swung down again.

Parrying the blow almost wrenched Marcellinus's shoulders from their sockets. The pilum bent in the middle. Before Panther could pull the club away, Marcellinus twisted, pushing up with his stronger right leg, forcing the club to the left.

If the chief had released his hold on the club immediately and barreled into Marcellinus, he might have won the day. But instead he stepped back, jerking at the club to free it, and Marcellinus rushed forward in a barely controlled attack.

Marcellinus's helmet slammed into Panther's jaw. Releasing the bent pilum, Marcellinus reached for the chief's throat, but his hands slipped on the man's sweat, and instead he went for Panther's eyes.

Panther dropped the club, swung his fists, missed. Marcellinus grabbed the chief's hair with one hand and forced the other fist back under Panther's chin.

It was the first time he had ever tried to break a man's neck with his bare hands. It was harder than he had expected. Meanwhile Panther was kneeing him and reaching for the dagger in his belt.

If Panther got that dagger, Marcellinus would be gutted like a fish. He tugged backward with all his weight, pulling the other warrior off balance.

They landed in the fire, kicking up ash and smoldering sticks. Marcellinus still clung to Panther, twisting and squeezing with all the strength he could muster.

When Panther went limp, Marcellinus took it for a trick, banging his helmeted head into the man's forearm to force the dagger away from him. But it was no ruse. Panther was dazed either from lack of air or from loss of blood to the head.

Marcellinus shoved Panther down once more, grabbed a sharpened stick, and drove it into the warrior's throat.

Panting, he became aware that the skin on his arms was singed and that someone was right behind him.

He roared again and rolled, but Sintikala seized his burning tunic and hauled him up and out of the fire. Without a word, she turned away and launched herself back into the fray.

Marcellinus glanced down again to make sure Panther was dead and then picked up the warrior's club. It was heavier than it looked, and his arms ached horribly. Could he even wield it?

He would find out soon. A Shappan warrior was lumbering toward him.

Men and women were running back into camp, shouting "Cahokia!" Marcellinus recognized Aelfric's voice, Hanska's, Dustu's; it was strange to hear Aelfric invoking the name of the city where he'd nearly died as a battle cry. They were running in behind the Shappans now to cut off their retreat.

The tide had turned. The spirit was knocked out of the remaining warriors of Shappa Ta'atan. Even as they fought they were backing up, glancing left and right, looking for a way to flee. But the paths back to their canoes were blocked.

Four men turned and ran. "Arrows!" Akecheta called.

Marcellinus was still locked in combat with the bulky Shappan brave. He had dealt the man severe blows in the stomach and leg, but this brave still wouldn't go down; he was panicking, fighting for his life. Had the warrior thrown his weapon aside and dived flat in surrender, Marcellinus might have spared him.

Hurit trotted calmly up and drove her sword into the man's kidney. With a gut-wrenching scream he fell thrashing to the ground, and she finished him off with a slash to the head.

Marcellinus swung right and left, looking for another threat. There was none. The warriors of Shappa Ta'atan were all down now. Those who still groaned and rolled on the torn-up and blood-smeared grass were being dispatched by Sintikala, Dustu, Hanska, and the others.

It was over. Marcellinus sucked in a long breath, exhaled. "Stop. Let them live or die in their own time."

Sintikala did not spare him a glance. "Kill them all," she said tersely. "We need nothing from them and need not allow news of this to return to Son of the Sun. Let him wonder what happened here."

Mahkah hesitated. Dustu and Hurit looked at each other. "Kill them all," Sintikala said again, and slammed her ax into the side of a man's head as he crawled away from the fire, already gut-struck.

Napayshni and three other men were moving around the outskirts of the battlefield, strangling the surviving Shappans with sinew. On the other side of the fire, Wapi the carpenter was messily carving his first scalp. The dying Shappan warrior's gray skull glowed eerily in the moonlight for a few moments and then seemed to vanish as a cloud crossed the moon.

Marcellinus squatted on his heels. His rage had drained away as soon as Akecheta's archers had shot arrows into the backs of the four fleeing Shappans. He had no taste for slaughter after a battle.

Looking around him, he saw Akecheta stretching, working the kinks out of his arms. Aelfric and Isleifur were collecting the Shappan weapons and piling them by the fire. Other Cahokians were turning to scalping now. The stench of blood surrounded them.

Taianita stood off by herself in the clearing, half sobbing and half laughing with relief, blood dripping from her hands. She sounded unhinged. One of the Cahokian artisans knelt and rocked back and forth with his eyes closed. Whether he was praying or trying to hold his sanity together, Marcellinus had no idea.

Marcellinus recalled his first kill as a foot soldier in Galicia-Volhynia, one of the feuding Rus's principalities. A full Roman charge into a massed mob with pilum and gladius. Hacking. Destroying. He remembered vividly the crash of arms, the smell of death, the open mouth and bulging eyes of the Slav he had spitted on the end of his heavy spear. It seemed a very long time ago.

Marcellinus was tiring of blood.

"Gaius?" Sintikala stared down at him.

"I'm all right."

"Panther was too confident. He expected us drunk and unready, easy deaths." She looked solemn. "We lost Yahto and two other warriors. And the Rope Twins and six other artisans not used to fighting. Napayshni limps. Many other men are wounded, another woodturner out cold from a blow. But . . . we live."

Yahto dead. Marcellinus's heart was heavy. He had liked the boastful young brave, always keen to prove himself. And Mahkah would miss Yahto, too; the two men often had sparred and joked together.

Perhaps he should instead try to be grateful that almost all of them had survived.

"We'll bury them tomorrow before we sail. We'll do it properly." Marcellinus stood. "For now I'll check the river in case there's a second attack coming."

It seemed unlikely. But Marcellinus needed to be alone for a while.

CHAPTER 14

YEAR FIVE, FALLING LEAF MOON

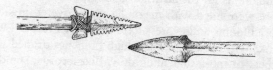

They smelled the Market of the Mud long before they saw it. First came the aromas of smoke and roasting meat, then the sharp scents of freshly cut wood. And after that the deeper, darker smells on the air: the sour odor of the corn soak used by the tanners of deer and buffalo hides, the reek of warm people in large numbers, and finally the wafting bass notes of a fetid river used as a lavatory by thousands of men and women.

It was not the smell of Roma or even of Cahokia, which had shocked Marcellinus with its filth when he first had arrived but now seemed positively fastidious by comparison with the odors of the Market of the Mud. It was certainly the smell of a large and sprawling city.

By now it was all that Marcellinus and Sintikala, Akecheta and Hanska, could do to keep the crew together. The warriors' early elation had worn off, and Sintikala's depression had deepened. Despite their losses, the dragon ship that had seemed so huge when they'd left Cahokia now felt so cramped that it was only a matter of time before someone in the crew turned around and knifed his neighbor.

By now they were far beyond the reach of Cahokian influence and rarely visited the villages at the river's edge. The towns and villages here were still built around mounds, but their inhabitants spoke no language that anyone aboard the *Concordia* could understand. And the Mizipi itself had changed. It still wound interminably back and forth as if conspiring to hold them back, but now it ran shallow and broad and its waters were a sickly green, its shores sprinkled with ferns and lilies. Few now were the oaks that had been their constant companions for the last thousand miles. The forests onshore were filled with magnolia trees covered in sickly white blooms and cypress trees a hundred feet tall with trunks ten feet across, their high branches draped with carpets of moss that hung down like beards, standing guard over silent, stagnant lagoons.

As they moved into the Mizipi Delta, the river got ever broader, ever muddier, the flies thicker. Yet the water levels had sunk to their fall lows, and Akecheta and Isleifur had to navigate the *Concordia* with some care between mud flats and sandbars that constantly threatened to ground the longship and hold it firm.

After many months of being largely alone on the river with only floating branches and sometimes whole trees for company, they saw canoes and dugouts passing them frequently. Some swerved around the longship to hurry south; others paddled north through the shallows to avoid the worst of the current. These were traders, men whose boats were loaded with furs and baskets and jars, men who did not travel armed as warriors and therefore felt they had nothing to fear. Many took the presence of the longship oddly in stride, while others gaped at its size. One even ran aground on a sandbar in his surprise and had to start digging himself a new canal to extricate himself as the *Concordia* sailed serenely by.

As for Marcellinus, he was trying to live from day to day as Aelfric had advised. It was not easy. In Cahokia he had built a life again against all odds. The peace he had forged with the Haudenosaunee had at last given him a glimmer of hope for the future, the chance that he might atone for some of his errors and failures before he died. Now that peace was at the mercy of Cahokian shamans and an aggressive new war chief, and Marcellinus was a nomad exiled on a longship a thousand miles away from the Great City, drifting through unknown territory, struggling to preserve a fragile accord with the few dozen men and women with whom he shared the voyage.

They were outcasts, broken and lost and quite literally approaching the end of their road. What would come after that?

Well, first they had to overwinter. Travel, or even survival, would be impossible higher up the Mizipi in the winter months. The previous winter the river had frozen with ice two feet thick to well south of Ocatan. Best to stay here in the warmer south, rest up, kill animals and dry their meat, mend the longship, and make more weapons.

And make friends. Ally with local tribes. Warn them of Roma even if the armies would probably pass far north of them.

After winter was over? Although Marcellinus had spoken of it to no one yet, he was considering a run up the east coast of Nova Hesperia. If they could pilot the dragon ship by sea, they could attempt to ally with the various Algon-Quian tribes, perhaps even the Iroqua-speaking Tuscarora and the peoples of the more southerly coasts of the Atlanticus. Those might be the first towns and villages to suffer a new Roman incursion. Any Hesperian League would have to include them.

They would need to improve their sailing, particularly their tacking against the wind, before they faced the open ocean. And of course the Algon-Quian had no reason to love Marcellinus since his own legion had enslaved so many of them. But he had to try.

Better not to air that possibility yet, though. Let his fractured crew rest up from the ardors of the Mizipi before he raised anything new with them.

Dustu feinted and threw his weight to the left. Marcellinus stepped back to parry the new strike, but Dustu's gladius clashed with his, knocking it from his hands. At the same time Hurit ran in low and hard from Marcellinus's other side and slammed into him, bowling him over. He tried to roll back up onto his feet again, but Hurit and Dustu were quicker. When Aelfric stepped into the clearing, he found his erstwhile Praetor disarmed and flat on his back, with his two young opponents holding their blades to his neck and Hanska laughing from the sidelines.

"Are you allowed to be that cheerful?" Aelfric asked.

"Do not tell the others," said Hurit, "but some of us refuse to live the rest of our lives with long faces."

Marcellinus gently pushed the gladius points away and sat up, still breathing hard. "Your turn next?"

Aelfric looked at Dustu and Hurit and mock shuddered. "Not likely. Oh, and the scouts are back."

At the riverbank Marcellinus discovered that Aelfric had exaggerated; Mahkah and Isleifur Bjarnason were in sight but still paddling Isleifur's canoe back toward the bank where the *Concordia* was moored. Most of the crew was sprawled on the ground resting. Some were doing maintenance on moccasins, tunics, bows. Chumanee was frowning at her supply of herbs and looking blankly at a piece of bark covered with charcoal scrawl; apparently Aelfric had been helping her make a shopping list, which she couldn't read. Sintikala, hard at work whittling a replacement wooden rod for her Hawk wing, did not even look up.

"How is the market?" Marcellinus asked once they arrived.

"Large." Isleifur wiped away sweat. "Bright. Busy."

By his side Mahkah blew out a long breath, still winded from paddling. "People from far. A big crowd. Some of them . . . odd. Even some People of the Sun."

"Is it safe?"

Isleifur grunted. "Is anywhere? They want it to be. Guards on the high mounds, alert for trouble. The Chitimachans want to keep the trade flowing."

"Chitimachans?"

"Local tribe who run the place."

Marcellinus nodded. "And does the market have what we need?"

The Norseman glanced at Sintikala, who at last looked up from her work. "They throw wings in the air from the mounds, aye, and in the market there are men who make and sell them. And weapons, baskets and pots, herbalists. Food. Beer. Furs and skins. Merchants everywhere, though to my eye it's really more of a fair than a market."

"All right." The sun was getting low. "We'll go in at dawn and take a look."

"And no, I didn't see any gold. Or silver. A few freshwater pearls, nothing of real value."

Aelfric scratched. The mosquitoes were intolerable today, and they found the Briton particularly appetizing. "We go in how? Sail the ship right in or moor and walk?"

Isleifur laughed. "Good luck trying it on foot. It's on a series of broad islands in the middle of a cypress swamp. Market . . . of the Mud? Yes?"

"Yes, all right; no need to be a smart-arse," said Aelfric.

"And no point trying to hide the *Concordia* now. Their chiefs are already paying attention. We got a few questions."

Marcellinus didn't like the sound of that, but he supposed it was difficult to remain incognito in a hundred-foot warship.

"Besides," Mahkah said, "we *might* not have the biggest boat there."

Marcellinus strolled through the Market of the Mud, trying to look everywhere at once while maintaining a calm smile. His demeanor was relaxed, but his hand rested on the hilt of his pugio, and he wished with all his heart that it was a gladius.

Marcellinus and the Cahokians were not the only visitors suffering culture shock. Half the men and women walking the market seemed quite at home, but the other half looked anything from mystified to terrified.

Bjarnason's calling the market busy was an understatement. It was frenetic. Despite the heat, Chitimachan boys and girls scampered back and forth, shouting at the tops of their voices. Men babbled, and women laughed. Everyone was shouting. The atmosphere was a cross between the Forum in Roma and one of the markets in Sindh, though a lot more spread out and chaotic than either and with a bewildering assortment of tipis, wigwams, wattle-and-daub huts, and simple merchants' blankets in place of marble buildings and wooden stalls. Marcellinus could have bought just about anything from the vendors around him if he could only figure out how.

The Market of the Mud made the Cahokian seasonal markets look hopelessly provincial.

Nova Hesperia had no currency, and so all markets ran on barter, but instead of the straight two- or three-way exchanges Marcellinus was familiar with, here at the market there appeared to be an extended barter network run by a gaggle of youths and urchins who ran around the tents and blankets at full tilt. Those sharp-eyed boys and girls served as middlemen, helping to cut deals on behalf of anyone and everyone, and were tipped for their efforts with anything from scraps of food, to feathers, to shell beads, coils of sinew, and old moccasins.

"We need Enopay," Kimimela said. "He would understand."

"Maybe," said Marcellinus, and did another slow scan around to see where everyone else had gotten to.

Just under half the crew had accompanied Marcellinus on this first foray, and to his surprise, he had found no shortage of volunteers to stay aboard the longship. Just sailing the *Concordia* up to the rough wooden wharf where the canoes and other boats moored had been daunting enough what with the size of the crowds that thronged the planked causeway over the mud to the market area and the size of some of the traders' dugouts, constructed from the great cypress trees. And that was before they saw the alligators swimming in the bayous and heard the din of the morning drums that announced the market was open for business. Also, it was *hot*, humid, and almost unbearably sweaty even an hour after dawn.

"Watch her," Sintikala had said. "All the time. Kimimela has never been to a place like this."

"Have you?" Marcellinus asked.

"There is a market upriver from Cahokia where the Hurons and Ojibwa, the People of the Grass, and the mound builders all meet and trade."

"Like this?"

"No. Not really."

They spoke quietly at the prow of the *Concordia* while the men stowed the oars under the decking and Hanska and Bjarnason tied up the boat. Kimimela and Hurit were already ashore, trying to look casually brave but not straying far from where Akecheta and Mahkah stood and leaned on their spears.

"We all stay together," said Marcellinus.

"Yes. But if anything happens and you have to decide quickly, stay by her, leave me. And even if nothing goes wrong, do not let her be stupid."

"All right." Marcellinus looked at Sintikala's taut features and would have said, *We'll be all right, it'll be fine*, if he hadn't been afraid of getting his head bitten off, and if he'd been absolutely sure of that.

Mahkah and Isleifur would take them into the market. Akecheta would stay and captain the *Concordia*, with Hanska to keep him vigilant. A dozen of the First Cahokian would come with Marcellinus; the rest would happily remain aboard the longship.

Sintikala glanced into the boat. "Aelfric stays?"

"Yes. He guards Chumanee. It might be as well for our healer to not go ashore in the first group. They can go for herbs once we know it's safe."

"Pity," she said. "Now I have to watch your back as well as my own."

"I thought I was watching yours," Marcellinus said straight-faced.

Sintikala did not smile. She picked up a second pugio and slid it into her belt. "Huh. Well, then. Let us buy a wing."

New Hawk wings were the most important things they needed to acquire at the Market of the Mud. In Cahokia the Hawks were stored in the Longhouse of the Wings atop the Great Mound, and even so they needed regular repair to keep them safe and flyable. On the river Sintikala was fighting a constant rearguard action against the elements: the rain, heat, and humidity wrought havoc on the deerskin material of her wing, and the wooden struts and sinew were aging and becoming fragile.

With only one Hawk wing they were one flight or bad landing from disaster. And ideally they'd also have a wing for Kimimela.

So, they needed wings or the materials used to make them: deerskins scraped parchment-thin; long cords of thick sinew from bear, moose, or buffalo; and straight spars of a wood that was light enough to fly yet stout enough to withstand the stress of launch. There was no mystery to the making of wings, but it took weeks or months to do from scratch; whole neighborhoods of western Cahokia under Ojinjintka's control were devoted to turning out the extensive materials needed for Cahokia's fleet of Hawks and Thunderbirds.

In addition, Marcellinus wanted to build a throwing engine. The flatness of the landscape around the Mizipi was a source of perpetual frustration to Sintikala, who now demanded to be dropped off onshore whenever she saw even a low river bluff.

In principle a throwing engine was much easier to construct than a Catanwakuwa. They needed a solid oak base, a throwing arm, a twisted rope of hemp and sinew, a simple windlass arrangement to crank it tight, and that was it. They had woodworkers, one remaining rope maker, and all the tools they needed, and Akecheta and several others on the *Concordia* had served on the original ten-man onager teams in Cahokia. The Iroqua had mounted onagers on their dragon ships, perhaps even on this one, and so there was no reason Marcellinus could not do the same thing. It was just a matter of acquiring materials of the necessary quality.

Without Hawks they were blind, reliant for scouting information on Isleifur and Mahkah, who could barely travel faster than the dragon ship itself. And in an emergency, launching Sintikala might be the key to their defense.

Perhaps most crucial, if Sintikala remained unable to fly whenever she wanted, there was the distinct possibility that she might go mad or drive everyone else on the longship crazy.

To continue as river nomads they also needed other things. New jars to transport fresh water, without which they had to constantly hunt for streams. More rope for the days when towing the longship upriver from the bank would be more effective than rowing. Food that was easy to keep and transport for times when they could not hunt or forage: pemmican, dried meat and berries, nut cakes. Baskets, to keep it all in. Isleifur Bjarnason wanted scrapers, preferably of antler horn, to clean the *Concordia*'s hull. And the warriors wanted beer, although if it was half as bad as the mess of brewed grain and fermented sap that the Cahokians used to make, Marcellinus would happily give it a miss.

And it certainly wouldn't hurt to have more weapons.

Marcellinus was familiar with the markets of Cahokia and other towns of the upper Mizipi, which were already surprisingly rich in goods for a land of such huge distances with no beasts of burden and no wheeled carts other than the ones Marcellinus had introduced. Cahokia produced baskets, pots and jars of clay, bowls and beakers carved of wood, many fine skins and furs and feathers for clothing, hoes and adzes of chert, arrowheads and ax heads, bows and spears, chunkey stones made of sandstone or quartzite, tabaco and herbs, and, lately, various new items of iron and steel. The rivers and forest trails of Nova Hesperia brought in more exotic goods from farther afield: seashells from the coasts, copper from the lakes area, mica from Appalachia, obsidian and galena and crystals and bears' teeth and beads of various kinds from who knew where.

The Market of the Mud was in a different category entirely. There was a much wider array of trade goods, from tiny beads to canoes and wings. Turquoise, jade, and lapis lazuli; much more copper; many more crystals and semiprecious stones; high-quality flints. Conch shells and sharks' teeth, many more extravagant shells, engraved marine-shell cups. Alligator heads and the skulls of animals and fish with which Marcellinus was unfamiliar. Foods of all kinds and a bewildering array of plants and herbs that cast heady scents across the market.

And above all, more finished goods. Buffalo-skin cloaks. Ornate beadwork already sewn into belts and sashes and moccasins and made up into fine necklaces. Carved figurines of flint clay. The range of items and the high levels of artistry and workmanship were astonishing. And live animals: deer, rabbits, and birds, especially the parrots of a kind he had never seen before, some a bright red, others blue-winged and orange-breasted, and yet more of a vivid green, but all with similarly long tails and dangerous-looking hooked beaks.

Marcellinus was less happy to encounter an array of goods that had come across the Atlanticus with the 33rd Hesperian. Shields and breastplates, gladii and pugios, helmets, and a variety of other items such as heavy sagum cloaks and tin dishes, Roman scarves and belts and kit bags. He found a Roman tack hammer, a stylus and wax tablet, and what looked very much like a set of padded woolen undergarments that once had supported Roman armor and prevented it from chafing the wearer. The abandoned Roman wagons had been plundered for their booty, and some of that booty had traveled far indeed. Marcellinus would hardly have been surprised to have turned a corner and come face-to-face with one of the legion's lost horses.

Some things he didn't recognize at all, including a composite reflex bow of a sophistication he had not known existed in Nova Hesperia and a well-cast iron tube with a bitter aroma whose use he could not fathom. Something about this item caught his curiosity, and so he traded a bent pugio for it.

Occasionally they came across a stall that sold Hawk wings, but Sintikala gave them short shrift and even Marcellinus could tell at a glance that they were no-where near the high standard of the Cahokian Catan-wakuwa. The likelihood of the Hawk chief going aloft with an inferior wing was remote. Instead, she sought out raw materials: spars of pine and cedar, sinews of the right tensile strength and suppleness. Even after half an hour, Marcellinus could see that her main problem would be acquiring the deerskin for the wing material itself. Wapi and the others hunting for hemp and hard-woods for the throwing engine were having a much easier time of it.

Kimimela raised her hand to touch a scarlet-breasted parrot, which eyed her disdainfully and with a loud squawk stepped sideways on its perch to avoid her. The elderly woman standing at the stall smiled and handed her a long blue feather.

"People are looking at us," Hurit said.

Kimimela sniffed. "You always think men are looking at you."

Hurit sighed patiently. "*People,* and not just me. All of us. *Him.*"

Marcellinus nodded. Even though he was surrounded by Hesperians of a wide range of types and skin tones and was wearing a Cahokian tunic and moccasins, his hair and bearing would always mark him as different. "Well, stay alert. Especially if anyone starts following us."

"Merda, it's hot." Mahkah wiped his brow. "Have you seen any beer yet?"

"When can we go back to the longship?" Hurit asked.

"Holy Juno." Marcellinus froze in shock.

Aelfric sat on the causeway with his legs dangling over the edge, sewing a moccasin. He looked terrible. "How was it? You didn't come back with much."

"They'll bring us the wood by raft. What on earth happened to you?"

The Briton looked unconvincingly innocent. "Me? Nothing."

"Your mustache just melted in the heat?"

"Ah, that." The Briton grinned, which made his upper lip seem even more shockingly bare. "Chumanee insisted. Hey, we all have to make sacrifices."

"So I see."

"Much cooler, though. How was the infamous Market of the Mud?"

"Hot. Crazy." Gratefully, Marcellinus sat down beside Aelfric while Kimimela went to the water jars to bring them all wooden beakers of water, still goggling at Aelfric. "Difficult. The Chitimachans desperately need to invent money."

"You could invent it for them."

Marcellinus paused. "Not this time. You had no trouble here?"

"All quiet. Some Cherokees came to talk with us. Seemed friendly enough."

"Some what?"

Aelfric waved vaguely eastward and then to the northeast. "I don't know. Warriors from a ways away, but not armed. Fascinated by the boat. Wondered where they could get one."

Marcellinus laughed. "Not from us, that's certain."

Kimimela stopped dead, looking downriver past them. "Merda."

"Ah," said Isleifur. "The Yokot'an Maya."

"The People of the Sun," Mahkah said. "I told you their boats were big."

Three longboats of the Yokot'an Maya sailed toward them in a V formation. Almost identical, they were close to eighty feet long with a raised prow and stern and a crew of around fifty men apiece. The sails appeared to be of reed matting, suspended between wooden spars above and below. Simple shrouds held their masts in place, and each craft was steered by a broad rudder in the stern. Oddly, amidships on each longboat stood a small hut thatched with reeds. Aside from that, their resemblance to Norse longships was remarkable.

A command rang out from the leading Yokot'an longboat. Its captain had seen the *Concordia*, and now the boat's path through the water curved to the left toward them. The other two ships matched its course.

As the flotilla of the People of the Sun sailed by, the crews studied one another. Akecheta and Kimimela raised their hands to wave. Not wanting to just stand and stare, Marcellinus saluted the captain of the lead vessel.

He did not salute back. The Maya watched them impassively as their ships went by.

"Well, well," said Aelfric. "Glad I don't row for *them*."

On the *Concordia*, Marcellinus, Sintikala, and Akecheta wore clothes indistinguishable from those of their crew. Not so on the Yokot'an ships. On them, the working crew wore only breechcloths, showing how much darker their skins were than those of the more northern Hesperians. With a shock Marcellinus saw that many were tied to their oars with long cords of sinew; they looked dirty and unspeakably tired. Others looked strong and healthy and had the eyes and bearing of warriors despite their place at the ship's oars.

By contrast with the rowers, the ship's captain was dressed magnificently. He wore a blue kilt woven in rich patterns, of a cloth more sumptuous than Marcellinus had seen anywhere else in Nova Hesperia. On his broad, bare chest hung a heavy necklace of carved jade, and draped over his shoulders was a cape made from the whole skin of a big spotted cat, a leopard or a similar majestic feline. Most striking of all was his headdress, constructed of blue-green feathers each a good two feet long.

"I'll not be arguing with that gentleman," Aelfric said softly. "Even if he does have a funny head."

"Hmmm." Now that Marcellinus had dragged his gaze down from the magnificent plumage of the headdress, he saw that the captain's forehead was unnaturally flattened and elongated. The warriors' heads were all similarly shaped. Those of the slaves manning the oars were not. "They must do that in the crib."

"Hope it doesn't catch on with the other Hesperians," said Aelfric.

Marcellinus shook his head. "Doubt it."

The captain's ear spools were also of jade, and around his wrists and ankles he wore bands of metal that gleamed in the sun. "Damn," Marcellinus said. "That's not copper."

Aelfric sighed. "If only Hadrianus knew. Stupid duffer sent us to the wrong place."

"You . . ." Even now Marcellinus had been about to chide his tribune for his disrespect. He closed his mouth and watched the Yokot'an ships.

Once past the *Concordia*, the most gaudily dressed of the People of the Sun walked into their huts, and the doorskins dropped. The officers of lower status shouted orders in a terse but lyrical language as the slaves worked to bring down the sail, and the longboats coasted in to dock at the wharf a safe two hundred yards beyond the Cahokian dragon ship.

"Later, send someone to talk to them," Sintikala said to Akecheta. "One or two of your warriors, young. Let them be impressed by the Yokot'an boats, let them smile a lot. We need to know more about these People of the Sun."

Akecheta nodded and looked at the crew of the *Concordia*.

"Not Hanska, not Hurit. Send men. No weapons and long before dark. We would not want them to misunderstand."

"I will go," Mahkah said.

"Do they know hand-talk?" Sintikala asked Isleifur.

"No idea," said the Norseman. "Just now was the closest I've been to them."

"They must bargain somehow," said Kimimela. "Perhaps they have a tame Pezi."

"I'll go with Mahkah," Marcellinus said. "I want to see those boats up close and take the measure of their commanders."

"No," Sintikala said. "Not you, not yet. You're too different. You stay away from them. And now I need two strong men to carry iron to the market to trade and help me carry back skins for wings. Taianita, come with us to speak words."

Aelfric looked back down the footpath from the market. "Well, that's peculiar."

Sintikala and the others had emerged from the crowd on the causeway and were approaching the longship. Marcellinus whistled softly. "Should we be worried?"

They had not seen such a spring in Sintikala's step for months. The frown she had worn since Shappa Ta'atan was gone, and by her side Kimimela was practically skipping. The braves carried a heavy mass of what looked like rolled deerskins suspended from a pole. Sintikala and Taianita carried a roll of something else. Marcellinus could not imagine what it might be. Clothing fabric?

"Good buying trip?" was all he could think of to say as they arrived.

For the first time in an age, Sintikala's eyes sparkled. "You will like this. With this, you will throw us in the river."

"Really?" Marcellinus reached out and tugged at a

loose corner of the material. He leaned back to stretch it taut, and when he released it, it snapped back against Sintikala's hand. She mock glared, Taianita giggled, and everyone else looked puzzled.

Marcellinus had seen this twice before in Nova Hesperia, first at Woshakee, where the Mohawk Iroqua had used it to launch Hawks from the hills over the town, and then at the Temple Mound of Shappa Ta'atan, where it was used to launch the priestesses. "Ah, yes. We can experiment with using this for launches until the throwing engine is ready."

Sintikala nodded. "We will try it first without a wing, until we understand it."

"How is it made? Where does it come from?"

"A tree. Far south. Beyond even the People of the Sun."

"A tree? You're sure?" It did not seem likely.

"Me first," said Kimimela.

Sintikala frowned. "Why?"

"You may fly higher," her daughter said rather smugly. "But I swim better."

That was true, though Marcellinus blanched at the idea of flinging Kimimela into the air using such material. "It might be difficult to . . . aim." Time to change the subject. "You bought this from the Maya? What language do they speak?"

Kimimela gestured, *Hand-talk.* "Some of them know it, anyway. When they speak, it sounds like . . ." She made a face and shook her head. Obviously nothing like the regular Hesperian languages they were familiar with, and the Maya traders had not learned a local language.

Aelfric was still looking at Sintikala's roll of material. "We might use small bits of this to throw stones. Could be handy at close quarters, places where you can't carry a bow and arrow. Make yourself a belt of it and you'd always be able to whip it off and use it to snap a rock into someone's eye. Like a sling but better."

"Good, yes." They could experiment with small pieces before throwing anyone anywhere.

"Heads up," Isleifur said, and everyone looked around at hearing the tone in his voice.

Over a dozen Hesperians were approaching along the causeway. They were laughing loudly, and some weaved back and forth at some risk of toppling into the bayou.

Aelfric squinted. "It's the Cherokees. Bit the worse for wear by the look of it."

"No," said Hanska, and climbed aboard the longship, casually standing by a thwart next to her gladius. Her eyes were alert.

Marcellinus looked over the canoes and dugouts plying the river, at the longboats of the People of the Sun. The Yokot'an Maya were paying attention, too. "Hanska's right. I don't believe it, either." He glanced toward the *Concordia*'s prow, where Akecheta was trying to catch his eye. Most of the other men were looking to see where the nearest weapon was.

"Put the skins under the boards," Sintikala said, and the braves hurried to stow the precious wing material away from harm.

Akecheta stepped ashore to stand by their side. "Something is happening."

"You don't have to tell us that," Aelfric said. "Chumanee, Taianita, into the ship. You too, Kimimela. Go to the bow." For once, Kimimela did not argue.

They waited as the Cherokee approached.

"Damn them," Aelfric muttered. "I *liked* them the first time. Uh oh. Look left."

Marcellinus looked around. Ten more men were approaching from the other side. Their shoulders drooped and they looked tired, but they were walking a little too fast on legs that did not seem weary. "I see them."

"Up, all," said Sintikala, and everyone on the longship stood, reaching for bows, swords, clubs, axes. Kimimela picked up a sling. Chumanee tossed a club to Mahkah. On the wharf, Marcellinus, Aelfric, and Akecheta stepped into close order, shoulder to shoulder, gladii drawn, and Hanska and Mikasi joined them.

A movement caught Marcellinus's eye. Across the

harbor the Yokot'an Maya were getting up, too. "Shit. Kimi, keep an eye on the People of the Sun. Sing out if—"

Two long dugouts slammed into the longship. Armed men sprang out from beneath what had appeared to be piles of furs and leaped aboard the Cahokian vessel. The dugout paddlers, not simple traders after all, raised bows with arrows nocked. Behind Marcellinus the *Concordia* rocked sharply, throwing many of the First Cahokian off their feet. Sintikala and others lashed out, but their attackers were fast and well trained.

A few of the First Cahokian swung their weapons, but the men of the assaulting force were already on them, knocking swords from their hands and stabbing upward with daggers of Roman steel. Too close for a melee, it quickly became a brawl.

But Marcellinus had no time to look, for in front of them the Cherokee had dropped all pretenses and were charging. Badly outnumbered, Marcellinus and his four warriors nonetheless stepped forward to meet them.

Marcellinus was no knife fighter and no bar brawler, either, and barely missed being eviscerated in the first moment of battle. In twisting away from the Cherokee who assailed him, he stepped backward, tripped, and crashed painfully back over the port shield wall into the hull of the longship. The warrior jumped onto the thwart beside him and kicked at his head; Marcellinus caught the blow on his forearm.

A stone flew into the Cherokee's cheek: Kimimela, defending her father from a distance. Then, of all things, an arrow flashed past a few inches in front of Marcellinus's face and buried itself in the man's thigh.

Marcellinus jumped up. One of the attackers had his hands around Isleifur Bjarnason's throat but quickly released the Norseman when Marcellinus swung a punch at him. Marcellinus brought the hilt of his gladius down and broke the man's nose, then dropped the sword altogether to grab his assailant and shove him into the Cherokee behind him. Both went over the side of the ship into the water.

A fast glimpse told Marcellinus that the Cahokians had the edge in the fight but also that the lead vessel of the People of the Sun had cast off and was headed across the narrow channel toward them.

Two more arrows in quick succession from Sintikala took care of two more attackers. For a woman who typically shot her enemies while piloting a Hawk, finding her target on a swaying longship was clearly child's play. Beside her Kimimela was slinging stones into the fray with more enthusiasm than accuracy. Aelfric and Mahkah, fighting side by side, were battering men with a ferocity Marcellinus had rarely seen in them.

Now he saw why. Hurit was down and bleeding, and Dustu had been rammed back into the decking with a man on top of him—a man whose deerskin hood had been knocked aside to show that he wore no braids, and no tattoos either.

Marcellinus gaped in astonishment, blinking as the shock of it hit him.

Then he grabbed up an oar from the deck beside him and threw it like a javelin. It twisted in the air but struck the man a hard blow on the shoulder. Taking advantage of the distraction, Akecheta slammed his fist into the man's temple, and he crashed down into the hull.

In his best Praetor voice, the one that had boomed over many battlefields, Marcellinus shouted in Latin: "Romans! Surrender or die!"

CHAPTER 15

YEAR FIVE, FALLING LEAF MOON

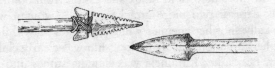

"Centurion! Order your men to stand down. First Cahokian! Any Roman who surrenders is not to be harmed further."

Marcellinus strode down the center of the longship, gladius in hand, shouting his orders again in Cahokian, but already his effect on the fight was clear. Heads turned. Men stood, raising their hands cautiously. Cahokians stepped back.

One of the attackers—not, in fact, the one Marcellinus had taken for their leader but a broad-shouldered man who shoved his hood aside to reveal equally close-cropped hair—rapped out orders in a terse Hispanian accent. "Century! Break for orders. Weapons *down*, hands *down, now*! Damnation, Unega; tell the Cherokees to give it up."

One of the Cherokee snapped out an order in a brisk soprano. Marcellinus did a double take. He had thought all the Cherokee warriors were men. The other braves froze in place as she spoke.

"Every man not on his knees on the count of three is dead," Marcellinus said. "Yes, Unega, you, too. And centurion, order your allies to stand clear. One. Two."

Half the attackers were already down. Unega called out again, and the Cherokee knelt with bad grace.

"Allies?" The centurion looked behind him. The

Yokot'an Maya had stopped rowing now, and their ship was coasting up to the *Concordia*, not twenty feet distant. "Them? The Sunners are no friends of ours."

The leader in the tall headdress at the prow of the Maya ship was hand-talking. Marcellinus did not take his eye off the centurion.

"They ask if we need help," said Chumanee. "They come to assist us against the outlanders. They would be happy to take them and . . . kill them for us."

All Cahokian eyes swiveled to look at the Romans.

"Make friends easily, do you?" Aelfric asked.

"Thank them and tell them we have it under control," Marcellinus said.

Isleifur cleared his throat. "Offer them some beer tomorrow night? We seafaring types should stick together. A good chance to talk with them."

Marcellinus looked at Sintikala. "Yes," she said, and began making the hand-talk herself. The Maya officers nodded, and the Yokot'an longboat began to turn away.

"Name and legion, soldier," Marcellinus said crisply. "Quickly now."

The man faced forward at attention. "Centurion Manius Ifer, Third Century, Fifth Cohort, Legio VI Ferrata, Praetor Calidius Verus commanding. Sir."

Marcellinus tried to keep his expression rigid, but inside his thoughts were churning.

He had imagined this moment countless times over the last five years. He had not envisaged anything like this.

Romans, not at Chesapica or Vinlandia, not marching in from the east, but here in the far south of the Mizipi Delta. Not a crisp steel-armored legion in battle order but a stealthy squad of pirates in Hesperian disguise.

Marcellinus did not know Calidius Verus, but every Roman soldier had heard of the Sixth Ironclads. "Where are you stationed?"

"Not here." Ifer looked around him, and a cloud crossed his face. Ten of his Romans and eight Cherokee were dead. "Some help for my wounded, sir? And yours?"

"There could be more of them," Isleifur said in Cahokian. "Ifer could be playing for time. We need to move, get away from shore, *now*. Let's go."

Sintikala gave curt orders to the crew. The Romans watched her nervously. They might not understand her brisk Cahokian, but her authoritative tone left no doubt that she was one of the leaders on the longship.

"You men sit nice and still now," said Aelfric, "and we'll do our level best to stop her from killing you."

Half of Akecheta's men had been scanning the shore with bows raised ever since Ifer's Romans had stood down in defeat. Marcellinus doubted such a small group would have ambushed them in such a way if they'd had more men available; it would have been much easier to overrun them with the weight of numbers. Nonetheless, the altercation had drawn attention from the market folk. A little distance could not hurt, and night was not so far away. He looked at Ifer and said in Latin: "We'll head out to one of the islands for some privacy. Your men can row us there."

They ran the *Concordia* aground on a sandbank two miles upriver and split the Roman soldiers and Cherokee warriors into manageable groups to guard them. Four Cahokians were dead, members of the First Cahokian whom Marcellinus did not know well. Hurit, still bleeding from a cut to her head, was sitting in the bow with Dustu holding her. Chumanee had patched up the wounds sustained by the Cahokians and was working on the Romans. Two had broken arms, which she bound up as best she could. Three more had Sintikala's arrows in their legs and shoulders, and several were unconscious. Hanska and Mikasi appointed themselves Chumanee's honor guard to make sure no one tried to grab her and hold her hostage, but it was clear that no Roman had anything other than cooperation in mind now.

Ifer sat cross-legged on the sandbank with his hands bound. Akecheta stood over him with a gladius. Sintikala squatted nearby, her face furious, with Kimimela beside her to translate.

Ideally Marcellinus would have talked to the centurion alone, Roman to Roman, but it was clear Sintikala could not be excluded. "Why did you attack us?"

Ifer gestured at the *Concordia*. "Roman property, isn't it? A dragon ship in native hands? Best take it back, we thought. Ideally we'd have waited for a better time, but for all we knew you might head out immediately. We couldn't take the chance."

Marcellinus nodded. "You were about to tell me where the Legio VI Ferrata was stationed."

The centurion considered. "Am I addressing the Praetor of the lost 33rd Hesperian?"

"You are. I am Gaius Publius Marcellinus."

"A pleasure to meet you, sir," said Ifer, grim-faced. "And who else?"

Marcellinus couldn't think of a reason not to answer. "Sintikala, chieftain and daughter of chieftain of Cahokia. Aelfric, formerly a tribune of the 33rd. Isleifur Bjarnason, scout. Akecheta . . . warrior of Cahokia."

Aelfric smirked at that, but Marcellinus was not about to complicate things by announcing that as far as he was concerned, Akecheta also held the rank of centurion.

Marcellinus sat. "Ifer, I'll be candid with you if you will do me the same honor."

"And what of my men, sir?" Ifer said bluntly. "Why tell you anything if you'll just slit their throats and drop them in the river anyway?"

"We will slit nobody's throat," Marcellinus said.

"So you'll free us?"

Sintikala shot Marcellinus a vicious look, but he was hardly about to slay a few dozen men in cold blood just to placate her. "We will not harm you further if you cooperate. Whether we release you is still to be decided."

"Are there more of you? Of the 33rd?"

Marcellinus grinned. He could see something of Pollius Scapax in the gritty resolve of this centurion, and in that moment he missed Roma and the tough, no-nononsense men of his legion. "We'll discuss that later. Now, where is the Sixth Ferrata?"

Ifer stared hard into his eyes and then shrugged. "All over the place."

"Come on, Ifer. Tell me or I'll walk away and leave you to Sintikala."

Ifer did not have to think about it for long. He began to draw in the sand with a finger. "This is north. Here's us, where the big river spills into the sea. Here's the eastern coast of Nova Hesperia." He paused. "You know the lay of the land around these parts already, yes?"

"Assume I don't."

"Very well, sir. The coast continues downward in a long spit of land many days' sail long, a gigantic . . . peninsula, I suppose, marking the eastward edge of the big gulf we're on the edge of now. The coast does something like this. The gulf curves around, and the Sunners are from way down here, on the southern side of it."

Marcellinus affected a confident lack of interest, but he was experiencing the same feeling he'd had when Sintikala had shown him her giant map of northeastern Nova Hesperia. Such a huge continent. And now, against all expectations, the Romans were opening up the southeast.

"And the Sixth?"

"The Sixth Ironclads have established two fortresses. Our first is here, at the end of the peninsula. The main one is halfway around the coastline between there and where we sit now."

"Gods," Marcellinus said involuntarily.

Aelfric's eyes narrowed. "Really? News *does* travel in this land, soldier. Why isn't this the talk of the market?"

"Roma can travel softly if it pleases. We set up in sparsely populated areas. Didn't take slaves. Longships and quinqueremes have been up and down the east coast for the past couple of years. The Norsemen helped us make friends with the Cherokee, and they've been invaluable. In return, we may have helped them settle a local dispute or two with their neighbors."

"Exploratory forces," said Marcellinus. "Small, stealthy groups, blending in. No fuss."

Aelfric grunted and stretched out his legs. "Hadrianus has gotten smarter since our day."

"You made him smarter," Ifer said. "Losing a legion so completely that it takes him a year or more to even find out how, that'll get Hadrianus's attention every time."

There was an uncomfortable silence, broken only by Kimimela quietly translating for Sintikala and Akecheta. Marcellinus looked down at the sand.

"I meant no disrespect," said Ifer. "This country's a hard nut to crack. I know it. Praetor Verus knows it. Hadrianus, too. Pity we had to find out the way we did."

"And how long have you been here?"

"Me personally? Over a year," Ifer said.

Marcellinus's jaw dropped. He glanced over at Aelfric, who looked as startled as he did.

He stood and stretched, wiping sweat from his forehead. "All right. Let's go back five years and begin again from there."

Hadrianus had gotten off to a quicker start than Marcellinus had dared imagine. A few dozen survivors from Marcellinus's garrison at the Chesapica had escaped the Iroqua assault in a single longship and had made it as far as Vinlandia before the winter closed in and made sea travel too dangerous. The next spring they had sailed on to Graenlandia and then to the coast of Caledonia, where they had made contact with the Legio XVI Flavia and been whisked south to Roma.

By the end of the second year, while Marcellinus had been traveling to Ocatan and developing the Sky Lantern, Hadrianus had already suspected the loss of the 33rd Hesperian and had dispatched a small fleet of Norse ships to probe the eastern seaboard of Nova Hesperia further to gather more intelligence. From traders and scouts they had confirmed the destruction of the 33rd. During the third year the Norse had mapped the coast, the southern peninsula, and the great gulf beyond.

Meanwhile, the Legio VI Ferrata had been pulled back from peacekeeping duties in Syria and Arabia to train for their new mission. Hadrianus had chosen wisely this time: the Sixth Ironclads were fierce and battle-hardened, having been dealing with insurrection from the shahs and mullahs for some time. And there, too, as Marcellinus now remembered, separate cohorts and smaller units of the Sixth were well known for their ability to act independently.

The first half of the Sixth had sailed for Nova Hesperia in the middle of the third year, the summer Cahokia had been sacked by the Iroqua. Well before Marcellinus had set off on his trip to make peace with the Haudenosaunee, a crack Roman legion had been setting stakes and building its fortress among the tribes of the Calusa at the foot of the Hesperian peninsula, far to the south.

It was a sobering thought. And all Marcellinus's careful preparations—the lines of signal fires, the letters in Latin for the Powhatani and other Algon-Quian tribes of the coast—appeared to have been circumvented quite by chance.

Ifer had arrived with the second half of the Sixth and helped construct the second fortress. Even before that fortress was finished, Calidius Verus had begun sending out his forces to explore the territory.

"And what ships does the Sixth Ferrata have?"

"Big transports, quinqueremes, longships. Little Norse knarrs to ferry cargo around."

"How many quinqueremes?"

"Couldn't say, sir." Ifer held his gaze.

Marcellinus nodded. Fair enough. He wouldn't have answered a question from Ifer about the details of Cahokian military strength, either.

"But you came equipped for river travel," Aelfric said. "Because those quinqueremes must roll like a bear on the open Atlanticus, and you wouldn't have brought 'em here otherwise."

"I suppose," said Ifer. "I came on a big transport myself, and *those* things roll like holy Hades."

"I remember," Marcellinus said.

Through the inland travel of small expeditions like Ifer's over the last year, the Sixth Ironclads of Calidius Verus—and thus Roma—had learned that the occasional trinkets of Hesperian gold came by way of the Yokot'an Maya and their sister peoples. They knew that the mighty Mizipi River that spilled out into the gulf was a thousand miles long or longer and reached up through the heart of the mound-builder culture. And because cities like Cahokia and Shappa Ta'atan were renowned all up and down the Great River, the Romans knew of them, too.

They knew that Cahokia was the mound-builder city that had annihilated the 33rd Hesperian. And they knew that the Cahokians had done it with flying machines and liquid fire.

What Calidius Verus did not know, at least as far as Ifer was aware, was that Marcellinus himself had survived.

Sintikala paced, anger still darkening her face. Kimimela came and stood by Marcellinus, staring at Manius Ifer with a troubled expression she did not try to hide. Ifer glanced at her and Marcellinus and back at the *Concordia,* where the Cahokians and his Romans sat patiently in the late sun with their hands on their heads, guarded by the First Cahokian with swords drawn. "Well? Have I said enough to buy my men's lives?"

"You have," said Marcellinus.

"And what of your story, Praetor?" Ifer asked idly. "A tale for a tale. How did you live? How did you manage to get yourself in so good with these Cahokians?"

"No." Sintikala strode forward, evidently understanding enough Latin to follow the conversation. "That story we will not tell."

Ifer looked at Kimimela, but she did not translate for him.

"We kill him," Sintikala said. "We kill this man and all the rest of them. We leave them here dead on the sand, and we sail for Cahokia. Today."

Marcellinus looked at Ifer and then at Sintikala. Keeping his face straight and speaking Cahokian, he said, "Kill them? Why?"

"You heard him. His chieftain does not yet know that you live. In time, the Romans will come to revenge themselves on Cahokia for your lost legion. For now, they are more interested in the gold of the People of the Sun. But once they know you are alive, they will stop at nothing to get you."

"Divert a whole legion on my account?"

"Once they learn you are in Cahokia, they will set out tomorrow with no delay."

Aelfric shook his head. "They might send an envoy. Not an army."

"They'll find out anyway," Marcellinus said. "I'm not invisible. It's surprising they haven't heard already. They just need to hear the right story, ask the right question."

"But the later they know it, the better. We must prepare."

Marcellinus looked around him. "Anybody else want to massacre a few dozen unarmed men?"

Sintikala looked venomous. "You were happy enough to slay Shappans. You would spare Romans just because they are like you?"

Marcellinus bit back a curse. "You say so? Once the battle with Panther was over, I tried to stop you from killing the Shappan survivors. I did not wish them dead, and I don't want these men to die now." He took a deep breath. "Besides, I need Ifer to take me to the Roman fortress."

Sintikala's jaw dropped.

"No," Kimimela said. "What, now, already? What? No!"

"Shit," Aelfric murmured.

Sintikala drew her knife. "You would go back to the Romans? You say so?"

"Not *back* to them. But I have to talk to them. Sintikala, I lost my legion. I must go to Calidius Verus and tell him what happened. I need to explain."

"Explain?"

Marcellinus shook his head, angry and baffled. "We spoke of this in Cahokia long ago. This was always the plan. I must talk to the Romans, tell them what we have done in Cahokia. Find out what they want. Try to avoid war. As I promised."

Sintikala surged forward, her eyes furious. "We know what the Romans want! Everything we own. Our city, our corn, our people as slaves . . . I told you so when first we met in Cahokia. And so nothing that has happened since has mattered. Nothing."

She raised her arm, and Marcellinus glimpsed the faint scar from where they had become blood kin.

"You will go back to Roma. Already with these two, Aelfric and the Norseman, you have moved halfway back to Roma. I see it in your voice, in how you stand. *That* is what has changed."

"That's ridiculous," Marcellinus said. "Sintikala, we need to talk."

"Talk? Why do we *talk* to these men who tried to kill us, who you are so anxious to free?"

"Whoa," said Aelfric. "Slow down now, everyone. It's too hot, and this is getting—"

Sintikala lunged. Ifer rolled onto his side away from her dagger, but Akecheta jumped in to parry and Sintikala's blade rang against his sword.

Marcellinus strode forward. "Stop! Drop it! Now!"

Sintikala's eyes flared, and she lashed out again, but Kimimela was faster, throwing herself between her mother and the Roman centurion. Akecheta stood firm, eyes narrowed. Marcellinus grabbed Sintikala's shoulders, shoving her away.

Her dagger came up, and Marcellinus jumped back, drawing his pugio in reflex. She stabbed out at his torso, but he punched at her arm with his free hand, deflecting her aim, and swung across and down with his blade, forcing her to dodge away from him.

They squared off face-to-face, knife to knife, three feet apart, Sintikala breathing hard, Marcellinus hardly daring to breathe at all. Both rocked on the balls of their feet, ready to react instantly. Their eyes met.

A soft wind soughed across the surface of the Mizipi. Behind Marcellinus the murmur of conversation from the *Concordia* had stopped. Nobody was talking now. No one even moved.

The brittle moment extended. Very quietly, from the sand behind Marcellinus's feet, Kimimela said, "Please stop."

The moment stretched. Akecheta said something that Marcellinus did not hear. Ifer lay on his side, perfectly still, Kimimela crouching next to him. Sintikala's eyes flicked down to her daughter, then back up to Marcellinus.

Akecheta stuck the tip of his sword into the sand and walked forward to Sintikala, his hands patting the air, gesturing for calm, making the hand-talk for *step back*. Aelfric moved, too, reaching out to push Marcellinus's arm and usher him away from the Hawk chief. "Move off. Both of you."

Sintikala lowered her dagger. Marcellinus bowed his head. His heart still pounded.

Akecheta pointed at Marcellinus, and gestured toward the western edge of the narrow sandbar. "You. Over there."

Marcellinus looked at him in disbelief.

"Stand away. I have spoken, Wanageeska. Sintikala, come with me."

Sintikala thrust her dagger back into its sheath and strode ahead of Akecheta until the waters of the Mizipi lapped against her feet. She stared out across the waters, her expression bleak.

"You heard the man," Aelfric said. "Come along."

As they moved away, Kimimela ran past them both

along the sandbar to slump at its northern tip, her head in her hands.

"Well, that would be a pretty pickle," said Aelfric. "Our two valiant leaders slaughtering each other. The Romans would piss themselves laughing."

Fifty feet away Akecheta and Sintikala argued in a low tone, glowering, both gesturing. Marcellinus glanced back at Manius Ifer, who was sitting alone on the sand. The centurion did not look amused. "She would kill that man and all the others. In cold blood."

"She might not be wrong," Aelfric said. "What? I'll just say that if the Romans attack Cahokia, more than this scrappy bunch of foot soldiers are going to get themselves killed. Come on, man."

"That would be war," Marcellinus said tightly. "This is not. Ifer has been square with us."

"Aye, square enough since we stopped them from murdering us for the *Concordia*."

"They wouldn't have killed us. They were going for the capture."

"You know that, do you?"

"Yes."

Marcellinus looked again at Akecheta and Sintikala. He took a deep breath, held it, let it out. "And Aelfric? Perhaps we should go with them."

Aelfric stood very still. "With *them*?"

"We need to try to negotiate with Roma. Here, Calidius Verus is Roma."

The Briton's eyes narrowed. "Just because you argued with your girlfriend, there's no need to fall on your sword."

"She's not . . ." Marcellinus shook his head. "Aelfric, be serious. A Roman legion is here. The *Sixth Ironclads* are here, for gods' sakes."

"I know the fucking Romans are here!" Aelfric snapped. "I can see them. I can certainly smell them. And if we give 'em the chance, they'll kill you and me a lot quicker than they'll kill the Cahokians. Better to walk onto Sintikala's blade than into Verus's fortress. You know that as well as I do."

"It's our duty."

"Well, I have a rather more relaxed idea of our *duty*," said Aelfric. "And if we let them go, what's to stop them from whistling up another couple of centuries and coming right back after us?"

"Perhaps Ifer would be good enough to grant us a head start," said Marcellinus.

"Now who's joking?" Aelfric snorted.

"Maybe. But even if he'd bring the whole Sixth to us in days, I can't cut his throat."

Aelfric looked thoughtful.

"Or let you or Sintikala do it, either," Marcellinus added.

About to say more, Aelfric caught sight of the expression on Marcellinus's face and thought better of it. "Ah, well, just have to hope for the best, then, won't we? Hullo, they're done."

Akecheta had moved away from Sintikala and was beckoning. Marcellinus took a step forward, but Akecheta shook his head and hand-talked, *Stop. Aelfric, come here.*

Aelfric nodded. "Stay put, sir. Time for the grown-ups to have a little chat."

Marcellinus looked the other way. Alone at the end of the sandy spit Kimimela was crying quietly, her arms up around her head. "Can I at least go and comfort my daughter?"

"I'll ask." Aelfric began to make hand-talk gestures to Akecheta.

"Don't bother. That wasn't really a question." Marcellinus shoved Aelfric aside and strode across the sand to sit by Kimimela.

"You swore an oath to me."

Marcellinus looked up. Sintikala, alone and unarmed, stood just behind them. Kimimela kept her eyes lowered.

Sintikala stepped forward and sat on Kimimela's other side, not looking at either of them. "You swore, Gaius. Do you remember?"

Marcellinus did not know whether she meant his oath not to return to the Romans or the oath of blood kin that he had sworn to her on the way to powwow, but either way his answer was the same. "Yes. And I will keep my vow."

"Swear me now again that you will not go back to the Romans."

"We must talk with them," Marcellinus said wearily. "I will not fight for them."

"You will go only when I say so." At last she turned to look at him over Kimimela's head. "Gaius. If you go to them now, you are lost. And we cannot lose you."

Marcellinus raised an eyebrow. "'We?'"

"Cahokia. And Kimimela." Her voice trailed off.

He nodded, looked away. "Of course."

"And me," she said.

Kimimela's eyes widened. Marcellinus swallowed.

"And so we must return to Cahokia, and you must come with us."

"To Avenaka's Cahokia?"

Sintikala's expression was grim. "To *our* Cahokia. And so you will swear to me now that you will not go to the Romans until we both agree that the time is right."

"Gaius will swear this," Kimimela said, "if *you* swear to him that you will never kill or hurt Romans in cold blood. Never bound and helpless. Only in battle."

They both looked at her. "I never said such a thing," Marcellinus said.

Kimimela stared ahead with red-rimmed eyes. "And you will *both* swear to never fight each other again. Never. Never. You will swear that to *me*. Right now."

Sintikala and Marcellinus both looked away.

"You will swear all of these things or I will stay here."

"Here?" said Marcellinus, and almost grinned, but Sintikala caught his eye and shook her head in warning.

"Here on this sand," Kimimela said. "Because if you two fight, my life is over."

Ducks flew low over the river, and clouds drifted by overhead. It was very hot.

To Sintikala, Marcellinus said, "These Romans will live. We will set them free today. Whatever the consequences."

Sintikala nodded. "And we will return to Cahokia. You. Me. Kimimela."

"To do what? We're banished."

"We must warn them about the Romans." Sintikala held out her hand. "How? That, we will decide together. All of us. As a family."

Marcellinus's heart skipped a beat. He reached out and grasped Sintikala's hand. "All right. I swear."

"And you two will never fight again," Kimimela said. "Swear it to me. Please."

Marcellinus looked at Sintikala. She looked at his hand enfolding hers.

"I will never again fight with Gaius," she said softly.

He nodded. "We will not fight again."

Only then did Kimimela's hand, smaller and gentler but still callused from the oars, reach up to touch theirs.

PART 3

CAHOKIA

CHAPTER 16

YEAR SIX, CROW MOON

They rowed steadily north past Shappa Ta'atan in the mists of dawn with their oar blades muffled. From their lookout positions at the bow and stern of the *Concordia*, Sintikala and Marcellinus watched carefully. Even if the sentries on the ramparts of the walled Mizipian city studied them just as intently in return, none challenged them, and no alarm was raised.

No Cahokian warrior held a weapon, but all had them ready to hand. If the Shappa Ta'atani attacked, the *Concordia* would try to outrun them, and if that was impossible, they would fight to the last man; this they had sworn at their winter camp several hundred miles downriver. If they could not go north to Cahokia and beyond, their lives meant nothing, anyway.

Such desperate measures had proved unnecessary. Shappa Ta'atan faded from view behind them. They would not fight today.

Aelfric was taking his turn at the oar, and his eyes briefly met Marcellinus's. On this return journey the two Romans had spent little time together, Marcellinus strategically favoring the company of his family and his old friends of the First Cahokian, Aelfric that of Chumanee and the younger warriors.

Alongside Aelfric, Kimimela and Hurit rowed, too. At thirteen and sixteen winters, respectively, neither had the reach or strength of an adult, but they were shooting up like beanpoles and insisted on pulling their weight. There were no passengers on the *Concordia;* Marcellinus, Sintikala, and even Chumanee and Taianita took their turns as readily as anyone else.

As far as they knew, the Romans of the Legio VI Ferrata were not following them upriver. If they had chosen to, it would not have been hard. The *Concordia* was making poor time against the early spring current. By Marcellinus's best guess they were averaging less than ten miles a day, and those were river miles. The way the Mizipi snaked and bent, a squad of determined men on foot would have no difficulty keeping up with them even through undergrowth and swamps. As for the quinqueremes of the Sixth, they would make shorter work of riverine travel. Since a quinquereme might be crewed by three hundred oarsmen and a couple of hundred marines, a single warship would easily be sufficient to overhaul, engage, and defeat the *Concordia.*

They kept a watch as best they were able. When Isleifur Bjarnason and Mahkah were not scouting ahead, they often paddled downriver as far as a day or two behind, alert for pursuers or for any intelligence they might gather. Few traders were abroad at this time of year, most having returned to their homes for the winter, and so their main source of news had dried up.

The land was huge. They were several months north of the Market of the Mud and still well over a month from Cahokia. But Marcellinus somehow had managed to heed Aelfric's advice and had grown comfortable with the knowledge that on any given day, anything at all might await them around the next bend and anyone might come up on them from behind, and to be at peace with that.

Even though in all likelihood nothing at all would happen for weeks except for the tedious, grinding haul up the Mizipi.

*   *   *

"Is that a boat?"

Aelfric squinted. "A coracle? Someone fishing?"

Marcellinus might have called it a bull boat. Made of animal hide stretched over a light wooden frame, perhaps willow, it looked small and ungainly and difficult to steer and appeared to be crewed by a dwarf, although it was still several hundred yards away and the western sun was in their eyes.

"He's not fishing; that's for sure."

"Seems to be trying to get across to us—"

Beside them Kimimela shrieked and dived over the gunwale into the Mizipi. With a smooth but splashing stroke, she propelled herself through the cold, muddy water toward the little boat.

"What the hell?" said Aelfric.

As her daughter went overboard, Sintikala grabbed her bow, but then she put it down. Marcellinus was laughing with joy and relief. "It's all right. It's Enopay. Bjarnason, steer for the bull boat!"

Aelfric looked again and shook his head. "Who's Enopay?"

Over the last year Enopay had grown more barrel-chested but not a great deal taller. His head was shaved at the sides in the warrior style, but he wore no tattoos. Always popular with the First Cahokian, he was practically passed up and down the longship by men greeting him, thumping him on the back, and hugging him before Marcellinus managed to rescue the boy and sit him down with a beaker of water. "Still alive, then, thank Juno."

"And you, too, Eyanosa, which is much more of a surprise."

Aelfric scanned the shores, his eyes dark. "You're alone, laddie?"

"Of course. Who are you?"

"And you're from Cahokia?"

"Where else would he be from?" Kimimela said, shivering and rubbing her wet hair with a blanket. "Enopay, how did you know we were here?"

"News travels even faster than *my* longship," Enopay said.

Marcellinus grinned. "I am glad you are safe, Enopay. You took a big risk, pretending to stand with Avenaka, persuading him to let us take the *Concordia*. I worried about you every single day."

"So Avenaka knows we're coming?" Sintikala broke in impatiently.

"Not from me," said the boy. "Iniwa has runners out in all the Mizipian towns awaiting you, and so I learned from him, but who is to know whether Avenaka has runners, too?"

"Iniwa is the chief at Ocatan, the town south of Cahokia," Marcellinus explained to Aelfric, and then said to Enopay, "Avenaka still rules in Cahokia?"

"Yes, and badly, because he listens to the shamans and to Huyana. And so men vanish in the night, those who speak out against Avenaka. The warriors of western Cahokia are arrogant now and take people's food from them without asking and strut around more than they ever did under Great Sun Man, with none to keep them in check. They have stolen women, too, from the People of the Grass and even from some of the Iroqua-friendly tribes to our east. They plan to send war parties up the Oyo to take back what they think is theirs, caring nothing for the peace you made with the Iroqua. And they are confident, because the shamans tell them this is their right."

"Gods," said Marcellinus. "Does the Tadodaho of the Haudenosaunee know of this? Has the peace with the Iroqua held so far?"

"Yes, mostly, but that is not . . ." Enopay shook his head. "Eyanosa, I have a hundred things to tell you, and many of them are not good. I must tell you in the right order, and probably . . ." He looked uncertainly at Aelfric and down the boat at the First Cahokian. "Probably ashore and quietly, just us. Can we stop and—"

Enopay broke off and looked up and down the ship again in alarm. "Where is Tahtay? He is not with you? What did you do with him?"

"Tahtay left us, Enopay," Kimimela said gently. "He ran away. I had hoped you would have heard news of him."

Enopay's eyes narrowed. "Hurit chose Dustu over Tahtay?"

Marcellinus looked at Kimimela, who said, "Not really. Not till long after Tahtay had gone. Enopay, we don't know where he went. We thought perhaps he tried to return to Cahokia."

Enopay shook his head. "If he had come, even in secret, he would have found a way to talk to me. I know it."

Marcellinus nodded. Enopay was right, of course.

Enopay lowered his voice and leaned in. "We must find him."

"I'm open to suggestions," Marcellinus said.

"You do not understand. Cahokia needs a leader to stand up against Avenaka, a reasonable man, a man they will not fear. A chief to rally behind, someone everybody likes. Who other than Tahtay? You, Akecheta? You, Eyanosa? No."

Kimimela bridled. "Sintikala, of course! You think Cahokia would rally behind *Tahtay*? Tahtay is an idiot."

Enopay looked surprised. "Not the Tahtay I know. And Sintikala cannot be war chief."

"You say so? Her father—"

"*I* say so," Sintikala said. "Enopay is right."

Marcellinus shook his head. "Then what—"

"Ashore," said Enopay. "I will say no more until we are ashore. Nothing. Take me ashore. Come on."

Kimimela eyed him, irritated. "Can you swim yet?"

He looked at her uncertainly and dropped his hands to hold on to the thwart.

"Down, Kimi," Marcellinus said.

"Head for shore!" Sintikala called to Isleifur. "Today we will camp early and plan for what comes next."

The rowers looked cheerful, and Enopay relieved, but Marcellinus knew from the strain at the corners of the boy's eyes that he would not enjoy what Enopay had to tell them, news that was so important that the rest of the crew could not hear it.

"You trust this man?"

They had made camp and quickly assembled a series of fires from the underbrush in the nearby trees; the farther north they went, the sooner the evenings became uncomfortably cool. Now Enopay sat warming his hands with Sintikala, Kimimela, Akecheta, Marcellinus, and Aelfric, and it was Aelfric whom Enopay asked about.

"He is a Roman?"

"Pleased to meet you, too," said Aelfric.

"He was one of my tribunes. I had no idea he had survived until he found us, and Isleifur Bjarnason, too."

"From your legion? But you trust him with anything I might say? You are sure?"

"Yes. I'd be dead if not for Aelfric."

"That is not an answer," the boy said. "You would be dead if not for a lot of us."

Marcellinus laughed. "Enopay, you can tell Aelfric anything you would tell me."

"Very well. Now, again: What happened to Tahtay?"

Kimimela looked at Marcellinus. With some reluctance, Marcellinus said, "Tahtay took Great Sun Man's death badly. And his shame at being mocked by Avenaka. He became . . . difficult."

"Angry," said Sintikala. "Broken."

"Then you will have to mend him again," Enopay said. "Cahokia loved Great Sun Man. And though young, his son threw himself into battle for Cahokia and nearly died for it."

"Many Cahokians fought," Kimimela pointed out, still grumpy with him.

"Yes, but Tahtay's is the name everybody knows. I have spent a year talking about Tahtay and making everyone remember him and love him and long for his return. The young hero who fought for Cahokia in the front line and took a great wound in its defense, who lost his father in a cowardly murder. The great hope of Cahokia, who is banished. The last descendant of a noble line of chiefs that goes back to Ituha and beyond. Great Sun Man's family and Sintikala's family have provided the war chiefs in Cahokia for as long as there has *been* a Cahokia. Eyanosa, I cannot believe you just *lost* him."

"I didn't . . ." Marcellinus gave it up.

Kimimela made an explosive, wordless sound of frustration and walked away, but Sintikala nodded slowly.

"See?" Enopay called out at Kimimela's retreating back. "Your mother understands!"

Marcellinus put his hand on the boy's arm. "Give her time, Enopay. This has not been easy."

"Easy? This is not about *easy*. We *have* no time, Eyanosa. We must find Tahtay, and very soon. Because . . ."

"Yes?"

Enopay met his eye. "Because the Romans are back."

"Yes, we met some of them at the Market of the Mud. Enopay, what?"

Enopay's mouth had dropped open. "At the market, too?"

A chill started at the base of Marcellinus's spine. "What do you mean?"

"I mean, they are *here*, Gaius. They landed at your old garrison at Chesapica six moons ago. We received the smoke signals from the Powhatani, and our fleetest paddlers and runners have gone to see, and Demothi has flown to gaze down on their armies and returned to tell us."

Marcellinus stared. Sintikala shook her head. "Chesapica? Demothi cannot fly so far. Only me."

"He did not need to. The Romans march along your roads, building giant wooden castra as they go. Keeping up their, how do you say it, Eyanosa? *Supply chain.*

They made it to Appalachia before the snows came down, and there they winter."

"Another legion." Marcellinus sat back and looked at Aelfric in shock.

Ifer had not told them. But perhaps he had not known.

Enopay shook his head. "Two legions."

"*Two?*"

Aelfric found his tongue. "And how do you know that?"

"I am sure. If full strength can be five thousands, like you told me, there are probably twice that many. Usually the army builds two castras instead of one, on adjacent hills, because they are so many."

Aelfric frowned. "And someone's counted them all, lad? One by one?"

To Marcellinus, Enopay said, "Tell your hairy warrior I am not a fool. The Romans have between nine thousands and ten thousands of men in two legions. I have seen them myself, and I have spoken."

"Seen them yourself?"

"Avenaka sent me with the runners. I was—" Enopay frowned in embarrassment. "—sometimes carried. Avenaka trusts my numbering. He wanted to be sure."

"You work for Avenaka?" Aelfric's voice dripped scorn.

"Avenaka thinks I do. But I work for Cahokia. Gaius? Please?"

Marcellinus was rubbing his temples, still mulling it over. Now he saw the pain in the boy's eyes and said, "Aelfric, Enopay is one of the most brilliant people I have ever met, adult or child. Quick-thinking, too; we only escaped Cahokia because of his words when he pretended to align himself with Avenaka. Please trust what he says and respect him."

" 'Brilliant' is good?" Enopay asked.

"Not always," Aelfric said darkly.

"It means 'big clever.' "

Enopay nodded. "Also, the Romans have brought the four-legs you told me of, horses, many horses that they ride or that carry bags for them. I have seen those, too. They are much bigger than I expected."

"How many?"

"That was harder to make a count. Many more than a thousand."

Two legions from the east, plus cavalry. And the Sixth Ferrata to their south. "On which side of Appalachia are they camped?"

"They overwinter on the east side, closer to their, uh, supply chain. But they have established a path across the Appalachia and cleared out many Iroqua there. When I saw them, they were at castra on the west side."

"Oh, dear God," said Aelfric. "Over the mountains in a single season?"

"*Damn* it." Marcellinus looked at Enopay. "Any other good news?"

"Good? Not really. How big is the legion in the south?"

"We don't know. They were sending out small expeditionary groups to explore. They have many big ships they can row or sail up the Mizipi if they choose. Much bigger than your longship."

Enopay looked at Marcellinus shrewdly. "And you did not go to them? Give yourself up? Try to talk with them?"

"Hmm," Aelfric said to nobody in particular. "Perhaps he *is* clever, after all."

"I wanted to. Sintikala talked me out of it."

Enopay smiled at Sintikala, who, much to Marcellinus's surprise, grinned back.

"So what is happening in Cahokia? How is Avenaka preparing for Roma?"

Immediately, Enopay sobered again. "Avenaka marshals an army. And builds Wakinyan."

Marcellinus shook his head. "Aerial bombing cannot hold back such a massive Roman force. We must assume the Praetors of the new legions know what happened last time. The Powhatani know what happened to the 33rd, and so by now the Romans must know, too. They won't be caught the same way twice, and besides, there are at least three times as many of them as there were of the 33rd. If it comes to another battle, the Wakinyan will kill many Romans, but Cahokia will fall."

"Yes, of course," said Enopay.

"And you've told Avenaka this?"

"Avenaka knows he can win. Youtin and the other shamans have told him so, and so Avenaka has heard it straight from the gods. Cahokia beat the Romans once, so Cahokia can beat the Romans again. It is clear to him. I could speak and speak until my throat was dry and cracked and Avenaka would not believe me. Instead I tell my grandfather Kanuna, and Howahkan the elder, and Ojinjintka and Anapetu, and they all tell him, and he ignores them instead. Cahokia is strong, he says: Cahokia will destroy the Romans and eat their hearts, then take their weapons and their horses and march on the Iroqua, and we will have our revenge on them, too, and then Avenaka will be the greatest war chief Cahokia has ever known, second only to Ituha, who united the three Cahokias."

Sintikala looked perplexed. "And Cahokia swallows this wild tale?"

"Some days I think Cahokia will believe anyone who stands on the Great Mound and speaks in a loud voice." Enopay shook his head. "And now Cahokia has a fine palisade and Roman weapons and throwing engines. And in our past fights with the Romans and the Iroqua, the fight with the Romans was easier. Cahokia has been told to believe the second war with Roma will be won easily."

Aelfric muttered something under his breath in his Celtic native tongue. It sounded profane.

"That war must not come," said Marcellinus, and at the same time Aelfric said, "If it comes to that, we are all dead and our souls forever damned."

"Yes, and so Cahokia needs you," Enopay said. "All of you . . . and Tahtay. If we are to remake Cahokia as the city it must be, a city without fear, we must have

Tahtay. And so, Sintikala, you and Akecheta must defeat Avenaka and his Wolf Warriors. Tahtay, son of Great Sun Man and of Ituha's blood, must stand on the Great Mound. And then you, Gaius, and, uh, maybe you, Aelfric: you must help stop the Romans."

Aelfric stared. "You don't ask much, do you, boy?"

Enopay met his gaze, unblinking. "Tell me another way. There is none."

"The other way is that I run like hell and don't look back," Aelfric said.

"Ah," said Enopay, and nodded as if he had been expecting Aelfric to say that very thing.

"Take back Cahokia from Avenaka?" Sintikala said slowly. "That is really possible?"

"Perhaps," Enopay said. "After the war with the Iroqua, the people were unhappy with the peace. They were unhappy with the Wanageeska and you and with Great Sun Man. But now that Great Sun Man is dead and they have seen how Avenaka rules in his place, they are unhappier still." Enopay looked up at Sintikala. "The truth is that Great Sun Man and you were the father and mother of Cahokia, and now you are both gone. Now the father and mother are Avenaka and Huyana, and many are—" He stopped. "I have spoken badly?"

Sintikala was lost for words. Kimimela leaned forward and mock whispered, "Sintikala does not think of herself as a mother, Enopay."

Sintikala glared at her. Enopay looked away hurriedly. "Oh. Well. Anyway . . . the stories have grown of your loyalty to Great Sun Man and to his son Tahtay, and also of the Wanageeska who stood between us and destruction at the hands of the Iroqua, and of his First Cahokian that turned around the great battle with the Iroqua and saved Cahokia, and then saved it again with your peace. Many speak of it around their fires."

Marcellinus almost choked. "But that's not true!"

"Is it not?"

Marcellinus remembered Enopay standing among the dead on the battlefield the morning after the sack of Cahokia. "And it is not what you said after the battle. You told me that the things I had done for Cahokia had brought only death."

"The other thing can be true, too. The shamans tell people pretty stories. Why can't I?"

Marcellinus thought about it. Stories could grow to become real. Stories had made the Iroqua the enemy for wanting to reclaim the Oyo lands that had been stolen from them in the first place. Rumors of imaginary beasts had run through his 33rd Legion like wildfire. Maybe it could work.

"You say that many speak of this," said Sintikala. "*How* many? Enough?"

"That, we will not know until you march into Cahokia."

The fire crackled. Everyone looked at everyone else. "Not me," Aelfric said under his breath.

"No, of course not you," said Enopay. "Cahokia knows the Wanageeska, but if they see an unknown Roman with him, it will just complicate things."

Eventually Marcellinus said, "Three dozen of us? Against Wahchintonka's thousand Wolf Warriors? You're just hoping the rest of Cahokia decides to fall in behind us?"

Enopay grinned. "I have only one more thing left to say, and then I am done with everything I floated down-river to tell you."

Marcellinus shook his head. He could not imagine what that might be.

"But you all look tired, and perhaps I will wait and tell you tomorrow."

Marcellinus controlled his impatience. Enopay would have his jokes even when talking of matters of critical importance.

"Tell us now, shrimp, or we will smack you silly," Kimimela told him.

Enopay idly played with a charred stick that had fallen from the fire, then looked at each of them in turn in the flickering light. "The last thing is also the first thing.

What was the first thing I said on the longship? Well? None of you?"

"Enopay . . ."

"Iniwa," said Aelfric.

"Yes," Enopay said in surprise. "Very good, hairy warrior."

"So?"

"So, Wanageeska, Sintikala, Akecheta: What if I could deliver you the warriors of Ocatan?"

Marcellinus shook his head. "Iniwa did not like me or trust me. I wasted a week or more in Ocatan doing nothing."

"You? Iniwa loved Great Sun Man much more than he distrusted you. And he trusts Avenaka less. Too many good men have disappeared since Avenaka took power. Iniwa does not want to make war again on the Iroqua. Iniwa spoke out when Great Sun Man was killed. Now there is bad blood between Cahokia and Ocatan. Ocatan bows to Cahokia, but Avenaka and Iniwa are not brothers; they are far from brothers."

Sintikala was staring up into the night, apparently studying the stars. Then she blinked once. "Who leads the Hawk clan now?"

"Demothi," Enopay said.

"He cannot. He is a man."

"Yes, but no woman of the clan will do it. I have spoken to Demothi. He does not want to lead either, but it is best to have a Hawk clan chief that people are unhappy about. Then when you return, the people will welcome you all the more."

"You're swallowing all this?" Aelfric said. "Gaius? Really? I mean, come on. How old is this kid?"

Enopay barely spared him a glance. "Old enough."

Kimimela turned to Aelfric. In Latin she said, "You should shut up now. Everyone here trusts Enopay. If he says something, it's true."

"Except when he's lying? Like he did to Avenaka?"

Marcellinus put his hand on the Briton's arm. "Later, Aelfric. All right?"

"You're all barking mad," said Aelfric, but subsided.

Enopay leaned forward and looked into Kimimela's eyes. "And so where is Tahtay?"

"She doesn't know, Enopay!" Marcellinus said with growing frustration. "None of us do."

Enopay continued to stare until Kimimela blew out a long breath. "All right. Wait here."

Marcellinus turned in shock. "You *do* know?"

"Of course she does," Enopay said.

Kimimela stood up. "No. And yes. Wait here. I will be back in a moment."

CHAPTER 17

YEAR SIX, CROW MOON

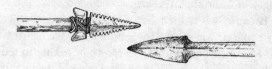

"Here they come."

Marcellinus turned. Kimimela was practically marching Hurit toward them, and Hurit was not happy about it. Behind them trailed Dustu, looking worried.

"Well?" Marcellinus said.

"Hurit needs to tell you something."

Hurit shook off Kimimela's hand. "I told you in secret. You promised!"

"And that is why you will tell the Wanageeska and I will not," Kimimela said sweetly.

Marcellinus looked from one girl to the other. "Yes?"

Hurit sighed.

"She knows where Tahtay is," Dustu said.

Hurit turned on him. "I do not know where he is. I know where he *went*. It is not the same!"

"He's alive?" Marcellinus said.

"How would I know?"

"Juno's sake, Hurit! Do you know something or don't you?"

"He is not dead," Hurit said in a quiet voice. "If Tahtay was dead, I would know it."

Dustu grinned wryly. "So would I. He would be haunting me, letting me have no rest. Tahtay lives."

Marcellinus shook his head. Superstition was worth

nothing to him. "So where did he go? If not to Cahokia, where? The hill villages?"

"No, north and west along the Wemissori to look for his mother, Nipekala." Hurit looked around in the sudden silence. "What? Where *else* would he go?"

"How could you possibly know that Nipekala is no longer in Cahokia? And where she is now?"

"Because we helped her, Dustu and me, before we came to join you on the longship. When we heard Great Sun Man had been killed, we ran to Nipekala to tell her to flee, and we ran with her to the edge of the city. If she had stayed, Huyana would have killed her."

"I thought . . ." Marcellinus had assumed that Great Sun Man's wives were friends. Obviously not. "But where is she now?"

"Wanageeska, Nipekala was not born in Cahokia. She was born among the People of the Grass, to the tribe of the Blackfoot. You did not notice the black moccasins she always wore?"

Marcellinus was in way over his head. "No, of course not."

"And so she will have gone back to her people, and that is where Tahtay must have gone, too."

"Up the Wemissori?"

"Of course."

Marcellinus turned to Aelfric. "Blackfoot?"

"Yes," Aelfric said. "Because of the moccasins."

"I mean, you know where to find these people?"

"Well, not really. They're all over the place. Nomads and hunters. They follow the buffalo."

"They're not the tribe you were with?"

"Isleifur and I were with the Hidatsa. They farm and grow things. The Blackfoot tribe was very different, a rough lot. Hard, warlike. If Tahtay has gone to them . . ."

Marcellinus met Enopay's eye. "Is it possible? That we could go to find him?"

"Yes," Enopay said.

"But the Romans . . . Is there time? To get up the

Wemissori . . ." And back to Cahokia. He shook his head.

"We will have to make time," Sintikala said slowly.

Marcellinus's thoughts were racing. He looked at Sintikala, Aelfric, Enopay, Hurit, and Dustu.

Sintikala was looking at him. "We must think on it, Gaius. And talk tomorrow. Now we must sleep. Unless?" She looked at Enopay.

"I have nothing else to tell you. Sleep is good."

"Thank God," Aelfric said. "You people would talk the hind leg off a donkey. What?"

Enopay was shaking his head. "Talk a leg off? You are a very strange man, hairy warrior. Very strange."

"So you're planning to put all our lives into a boy's hands?" Aelfric shook his head in frustration. "And he . . . How the hell old is he, anyway?"

It was the next morning, and they were packing up the longship in light rain. The showers had broken out around midnight and drenched them all; in the afternoon they would need to spread out their sleeping blankets to dry. Everyone was grumpy and on edge, Aelfric more than most.

"Nobody knows," Marcellinus said. "He seemed very young five years ago. Now he just *looks* young."

"I'm willing to believe he's clever. But what if he's lying? What if this is Avenaka's trap to lure you and Sintikala to Cahokia and get rid of you once and for all?"

"There are simpler ways. I trust Enopay."

"You'd trust him with my life?" Aelfric asked.

Marcellinus grinned. "Much more than that."

"Fantastic," Aelfric grumbled. "And now here comes your girlfriend."

Sintikala was approaching, her face and hair wet where she had recently dunked her head in a stream to wash. Unlike everyone else, she seemed cheerful. Her eyes glinted. "Time to talk, Gaius. Let the others row awhile. Walk with me."

* * *

Unfortunately, it was not a rowing day. The pace of the river that morning and the shape of the currents against its shores made that impossible. This was a day for hauling the boat up the river from the bank at the end of a long rope while Bjarnason stood at the rudder and a few other men sat on board to fend off the bank and the inevitable trees, branches, and bloated buffalo carcasses that came floating downriver toward them. It would be a slow day with few miles gained, and even more strenuous than rowing.

Yet Sintikala's mood was bright. Marcellinus had rarely seen her this happy. No longer merely a wanderer on the waters, she had a purpose now and a challenge ahead. Whatever the outcome, Sintikala was going home. She had a restless excitement, an attractive energy, and Marcellinus could hardly take his eyes off her.

They walked together into the wilderness. Ahead the Mizipi curved in a long oxbow, hooking to the west, and by cutting across and meeting the river again later they could shorten their journey.

It was the first time Marcellinus had been alone with Sintikala for any length of time since they had escaped from Shappa Ta'atan heading south, and for a while they avoided discussing Tahtay, Cahokia, and Roma. Instead they talked of Kimimela, of supplies and the weather, which of the crew were the strongest and most trustworthy, and which were the mischief makers and complainers who caused trouble.

Finally she said, "And so, Gaius, your Romans are coming. How long?"

Marcellinus had given this a lot of thought. He answered quickly. "They won't be able to start again over the mountains of Appalachia until the snows have melted and the ground dried. It could be Maius—the Planting Moon—and then after that another two months to Cahokia. Four or five months from now . . . or longer."

"Why longer?"

"There are many things to take into account. I pushed my legion hard, with few rest days, because we needed to find food. A legion that travels too slowly loses its morale. But fast travel puts stress on them. They make mistakes. And this one . . . A larger army takes much longer to move than a smaller one. If Enopay is right, they are building sturdier castras, so that takes longer and they stay longer. They're maintaining a supply line that they can't afford to outpace. And also there are the animals, the four-legs."

"The horses?"

Marcellinus nodded. "Although some may be pack mules. Enopay says that the supply train contains almost no wagons and that the horses the men ride are bigger than the ones that carry provisions. Mules are half horse, half . . ." He hesitated, reluctant to get sidetracked into equine breeding. "Mules are smaller than horses but stronger. They carry more than a horse but eat less and handle rough ground more easily than a wagon can. And they're why these Romans don't need to take slaves. But four-legs eat grass, and a lot of it, so the Romans will need to rest them regularly and graze them on pastureland, which will slow them down still further."

Sintikala pondered it. "If you were Praetor of these legions, what would you do?"

"I'd split up the legions. Divide my forces. I'd know I wouldn't face a large army until Cahokia, so I'd gain nothing but logistic difficulties by keeping them together. I'd send the first legion on ahead to clear the way and build fortresses. I'd use our old castra sites where possible—the campsites of the 33rd—to save energy. I'd rest my men and animals every third day and switch the legions' order every ten or twenty days so the first legion could rest while the second took over spearheading the trail. But that may not be what this Praetor decides to do. Especially if he has as much trouble with the Iroqua as we did."

"The Iroqua." Sintikala nodded.

"It must take several cohorts just to protect the supply train. They probably need a mule for every three or four men in the army. Enopay may be right about the sizes of the legions, but there must be even more men than he saw. There must be hundreds, maybe even a couple of thousand more soldiers, just guarding the mule train." He grinned. "It's a pretty problem. Praetors worry much more about food than about fighting."

She frowned. "We only have until summer?"

"They're being very methodical. This is a systematic invasion. This time, they're here to stay." Marcellinus considered. "I think they'll take their time and aim to arrive rested and in fighting form in the Hunting Moon or even the Falling Leaf Moon. Given the choice, they'll want to fight after the heat of summer has broken and after Cahokia has taken in the fall harvest. They have nothing to gain by arriving sooner than that. And it may even take them longer."

"Later would give Cahokia longer to prepare."

"They don't care how long they give Cahokia to prepare," Marcellinus said. "They know they can beat you."

Sintikala paused. " 'You'?" she said sadly.

"I will not be fighting them, Sintikala. You do remember that? I cannot lead a Cahokian army against my own people. And an all-out war would be a disaster. That cannot be what happens. We must find another way."

"And what way is that?"

"I don't know yet."

"You knew you could beat us, too," she said. "And look what happened."

"But their army is three times larger than mine. They have more solders than Cahokia has men of any age, and cavalry besides. And they will not helpfully bunch up into a normal Roman triplex acies line like the 33rd did so you can bomb them with liquid fire."

She shook her head, not understanding.

"I mean they will not group together, and the Cahokian liquid flame will be much less effective, because they will have prepared for it. For all I know they may even have designed armor against it or have coated their skin with, oh, something, to reduce its burning. I would certainly experiment with such ideas."

"I think you are right," she said unexpectedly. "They will not be rushed into fighting. They will wait until the autumn when the leaves are falling."

Marcellinus smiled at her, and she grinned quickly back. The rain had stopped now, and they were reaching the top of a hill, although the trees surrounded them, giving them little view of the land ahead.

He took a deep breath. So far, despite the seriousness of the conversation, their mood with each other had been light and friendly. Marcellinus felt very close to her. For a moment they were at peace, they were a team again, whatever the future might bring. In another world this might signal the beginning of a deepening relationship between them, a more permanent bond.

But he had the feeling that what he was about to say might shatter that completely.

"They may have read my letter. Remember, we prepared letters and sent them to the leaders of the Powhatani and Nanticoke peoples on the coast. If they were delivered, then the eastern legions know that I am alive and that we are willing to talk.

"And so, Sisika, *this* time I must go and talk to the Romans. While the rest of you go to Cahokia or look for Tahtay, I must go east to meet the legions. Give myself up, take whatever comes. Attempt to negotiate, try to put off this war. And I don't yet know how, because a lot will depend on who I find in command when I walk into their fortress."

She kept walking, apparently lost in thought. Marcellinus peered at her. "You *do* understand that I must do this?"

"You have a name for this land," she said.

"Yes," he said, surprised. "You know that Romans call it Nova Hesperia."

Sintikala nodded. "And that is how you think of it. You have named it, and so it is yours. It is Roman. The Praetor of those two giant war bands of Roma who sits now in his big fortress of wood on the eastern lees of Appalachia waiting for the thaw, he thinks the land is already his. He can do whatever he wishes with it, because he is strong and he has many men. He thinks the land is Nova Hesperia."

"Yes."

"And he thinks it is new, just as you do. You said this when first we met, when you held me captive in the castra of the 33rd. Again you said it as we traveled home after the powwow with the Haudenosaunee. Fresh, you said. Our land is fresh and new, just made. But it is not new, Gaius. It is our old land, not your new Roman land."

"Yes," Marcellinus said again. It could hardly be denied.

"And you will go to this man, this Praetor, and negotiate."

Now Marcellinus saw the trap she had led him into.

"I can speak his language," he said. "I will know how he thinks. I can speak in a way he will understand."

"Yes, that is true," Sintikala said. "And I agree that you will go to speak with him, but you will go as part of a Cahokian parley, and not yet."

Marcellinus looked around him and saw a fallen tree trunk. "Let us sit and talk more of this."

Sintikala remained standing. "Once we have retaken Cahokia, once we truly speak for Cahokia and not just for ourselves, you and I will go to the Romans and speak with them. I and perhaps Kanuna, perhaps Akecheta, and Tahtay if we can find him: the people who are strong and can lead. And you will come with us to help us speak with the Roman Praetor. We cannot do it without you, Gaius. But you will not do it without us."

Marcellinus thought about that.

She sighed. "And now you are thinking that I cannot stop you, that if you choose to go alone, you may. You flew away once before to speak for us, and you can go again. You do not believe I will kill you to stop you."

He glanced up, but she had no weapon in her hand.

"You are right," she said. "You can go where you please. But I do not think you will. I think you will see that my way is the best way. Yes?"

"I'm still thinking," he said.

"Because you are not Cahokian and you never will be, but despite that Cahokia is your friend, and you and I are sworn blood kin and family. And so we will do this together or we cannot do it at all."

Marcellinus looked into her deep brown eyes, and his breath caught.

She met his gaze calmly. "And besides all of this, you swore to your daughter that you would not leave again."

His chest tightened. But it was not just his heart that knew. It was his head, as well.

He nodded. "You're right."

"Do not answer quickly. Take time to think. And know that if you walk away again, I will not follow you a second time. Walk away from me again, from this family again . . . and we are all-done."

The moment lingered in the air. Marcellinus cleared his throat. "Sisika, I want to help. I want to save Cahokia from war. And I do not want Roma to rule Cahokia. I want Cahokia to rule itself as a strong friend to Roma. If that is at all possible, I will do whatever it takes. I swore this to the Haudenosaunee, and I swore it to you. Do you believe me? Do you understand?"

"I think so." She looked up at the sun. "Let us go on. I do not like to be out of sight of Kimimela and the ship for too long."

They began picking their way down the hill.

"You liked the word 'Hesperia,'" he said a little defensively.

"Hesperia is a nice word. Evening is a pleasant time. But not *Nova* Hesperia. Not new."

"All right. Just 'Hesperia,' then. And a Hesperian League."

He had talked little about it to her on their journey south down the Mizipi. It would have seemed absurd to dwell on it then, traveling as outcasts and with Sintikala mourning the loss of Great Sun Man and her city.

It was clear that she thought it barely less absurd now. She gave him a wry look. "Your League of all the Land? Standing together against Roma?"

"Yes."

"Even now, when Cahokia cannot stand with itself?"

"We will mend that," he said. "With Tahtay or without. We must. And then forge our league, not just of the mound builders and the Iroqua but also of the Powhatani, of the People of the Grass, and others in the south and north. As many as we can find."

"And Shappa Ta'atan? And those of the Market of the Mud? And . . . I think the Powhatani have no reason to be your friends."

"But every reason to be Cahokia's with Roma again on the march through their lands," he pointed out.

Sintikala shook her head slowly, wide-eyed, feigning being dazed. "I think perhaps we should think of one thing at a time, Gaius. And that one thing is Cahokia."

Marcellinus assumed a solemn expression. "I think we should consider everything all at once."

"You think very big."

"We both must," he countered immediately.

She grinned and shrugged. "Very well. And so I will go to Cahokia and think big there, and perhaps also to Ocatan to speak big words with Iniwa in the quiet of the night, and meanwhile you must go deeper into Hesperia to find Tahtay."

Marcellinus sobered. He had reluctantly been coming to the same conclusion, but still he fought it. "I have no idea where Tahtay is. I don't know the country. It might be a wild goose chase." He took a deep breath. "I want to stay with you, Sintikala. Help you."

"You help us all by bringing us Tahtay. Enopay is right. And now that Great Sun Man is gone, you are the closest thing Tahtay has to a father. You are a man

Tahtay will listen to, perhaps the only man. He has listened to you before . . . Do not make that face. After he was injured, he hobbled around Cahokia like a dead man for months. Did he listen to Great Sun Man, who he adored and looked up to? To the mother he loves? To the friend of his soul, Dustu, or to Hurit, who would have gladly been his wife if he had only been a man and claimed her? No, he did not. He picked up a sword only when you told him to. He smiled again because you gave him a reason."

"And then he ran away without telling me."

"Because his father was dead. His heart was broken, and he went after his mother. I will not say he was wrong to do that. When my husband was killed, I—"

Marcellinus jumped. Sintikala had reached out and seized his arm. He glanced around the trees, his right hand going to his gladius, but he saw no enemy. "What?"

Then he looked at Sintikala and saw sudden tears in her eyes, blind tears that ran down her nose and dripped to the forest floor. He reached for her then, and his arms went around her before he even knew what he was doing.

He held her to his chest as she cried quietly. He breathed her in, his heart pounding, and stared over her head into the forest.

She broke away and strode on along the path ahead of him, wiping her face.

"Are you all right?" he said stupidly.

Sintikala cleared her throat. "When my husband was . . . killed, I did many things, Gaius. I ran from Cahokia. I killed men, some of them my friends. I was . . ." She hit herself lightly on the side of the head with the palm of her hand. "The shamans said I was on a bad spirit journey. I was not. I was just not in my mind, not inside myself. Do you understand? But in the end I came home." She turned back to him. "You must find Tahtay now. You must bring him home."

Her face broke again, and she reached out, and he grabbed her and clasped her to him again as she cried.

* * *

"So we are returning to Cahokia?" Kimimela said. "How will we do it?"

"*You* are not," Sintikala said. "*You* will go with Gaius. Cahokia is too dangerous."

"I go where you go!"

"Not this time."

Kimimela looked at Marcellinus. "I don't want her to go either," he said. "And how will you do it, anyway?"

"Quietly. I can walk into Cahokia unnoticed."

Marcellinus looked at her doubtfully.

"Yes. Without the Hawk paint at my eyes, I am different. I can put ash in my hair to be older. It will still be early in the year and cold, and I can bundle in furs and wear a hood. Stones in my moccasins will change my walk."

"Even with all that I would still know you," Marcellinus said.

Her mouth twitched. "You would know me anywhere, and so would Kimimela. But you will not be there. I have not been seen in Cahokia for a year. No one will expect me, and I will stay far from the Great Mound and the Wolf Warriors."

"And when you reveal yourself to Demothi or Kanuna, the news will spread like wildfire."

"Demothi would never risk my life. Or Kanuna. Anyone I would speak to and show myself to, any of them would die for me."

Kimimela broke in impatiently. "But why must you do this at all?"

Sintikala stared at her. "In Shappa Ta'atan we saw a glimpse of what Cahokia will become under Avenaka. You want that?"

Enopay reached over to touch Kimimela's arm. "I know many who will gladly take Sintikala. Hide her, help her, feed her."

"But, the longship?" said Aelfric. "If someone notices it going by, Avenaka will be on the lookout for any of us."

"I will be in Cahokia long before you," Sintikala said.

Marcellinus laughed in disbelief. "Your new Hawk is not complete yet, and the new throwing engine still does not throw straight. And even if they were ready, you would fly to Cahokia and expect to remain unnoticed?"

Sintikala looked up into the air above them. "I will finish my new Hawk soon. At this time of year I will be lucky to make it halfway. Even for that, the day will have to be warm and the winds helpful. But once I land I can still run."

That, Marcellinus knew. Sintikala ran every day they were ashore.

"I will arrive in Cahokia on foot and quietly. And after Cahokia, I will fly to the Iroqua or send a runner, a man we trust. The Iroqua must slow down the Romans, harry them, buy us time. Blockade the rivers they must cross. Attack the supply train. Be always ahead of Roma and always behind them."

Marcellinus nodded. "But before that, start a rumor in Cahokia. Have it spoken around the campfires that we are all dead, the *Concordia* burned and sunk." He thought a little more. "Not by the Romans. That's too complicated. The Caddo?"

"The Tuscarora," Enopay said. "The Wolf Warriors will be happy to spread a story of you being killed by allies of the Iroqua."

"No, that plays into Avenaka's hands. Many Cahokians who are friends to the crew will then hate the Iroqua more."

"Why say anything?" Kimimela demanded. "Why make our friends grieve?"

"So that Avenaka will lower his guard. We still have to sneak the *Concordia* past Cahokia to get to the Wemissori."

"Oh. Yes. The Caddo, then."

Sintikala half smiled. She obviously had understood right away. "Enopay must go back to Cahokia as soon as he can. Avenaka believes he is in Ocatan, but we do not want him to grow suspicious. Enopay must be back in Cahokia by the time the river floods so that people do not know he went so far from home. Isleifur and Mahkah, will you take him?"

Mahkah looked almost relieved. "By canoe? I would be happy."

Enopay frowned. "You do not like my longship?"

"I love the longship," Mahkah said quickly. "With all my heart."

"We'll take you," Isleifur said.

Enopay ran his fingers over the thwarts and the shield next to him on the shield rack. "Well, *I* will miss the *Concordia* even if none of you do."

"Enopay . . ." Unexpectedly, Marcellinus's breath caught in his throat. "Be very careful. Do not let Avenaka know the game you are playing."

"Oh, I am not playing a game," Enopay said. "I have not been so serious my whole life."

Marcellinus believed him.

"And I must go and look for Tahtay?" Kimimela shook her head and gave out a long, deep sigh.

"No, you have to come and stop me from getting into trouble," Marcellinus said.

The look she gave him was priceless. For once, even Kimimela was lost for words.

A mere two weeks later the spring meltwater was flowing down the Mizipi in earnest. It was as if the greasy river were conspiring with Avenaka and the shamans, constantly pushing them away. Already Marcellinus felt as if they had been on the river for years rather than months. The Great River was a long nightmare, and now it wasn't even going to end at Cahokia.

Because he had to go past it and up another river he knew even less about. He had to find Tahtay.

They were a quiet, somber boat. Like Marcellinus, they all had thought they were going home to Cahokia, but now they were not; they were going up the Wemissori. And upriver was very similar to uphill: long, hard drudgery day after day.

Eventually Sintikala was ready. Marcellinus was not. "You really want us to throw you in an untested wing?"

Even as they talked, Sintikala was still sewing the front peak of the wing with sinew, doubling its strength. "You know that I make and adjust my own Hawk wings in Cahokia. That I do this always."

"Yes, but you test those by jumping off the mound."

"Then I must be thrown on the rail. And the wing must unfold. That is much worse than being tossed into the air over a river."

Marcellinus looked at Kimimela. His daughter nodded. "But still. Would it not be better to take you to a hill and use the springy material from the market? Isn't that why you bought it?"

Sintikala just pointed west. The hills on the horizon were several days' walk away. "That will take too long. I will *fly* to the hills."

"Perhaps."

"Yes, perhaps, and perhaps not." She lay down inside the Hawk wing, and Kimimela folded it around her. "Hmm. Open." Kimimela let her out, and she set to work easing the tension on one of the sinews on the right wing. "The wind is strong and in a good direction. It is warmer than last week. I can make it to the hills and then . . ." She gestured spiraling upward, soaring on the updraft from the hills. "Or, if you are right, I will land short. Then I will either walk to the hills and try, or walk back to the boat and try again, and you will be right and I will be wrong. Now, the throwing engine?"

Marcellinus looked at Kimimela helplessly. She grinned back and stood. "Akecheta, Wapi! Have your men prepare the throwing engine. Isleifur! We will need to steer into the wind when we throw her. Dustu and Hurit, can you clear that rope out of the way so we can move the engine forward? Chumanee, can you pack her some food? Nuts, cakes. All small and light."

Aelfric looked amused. Kimimela's growing confidence with ordering people about was also new, and he was obviously enjoying Marcellinus's discomfort.

Sintikala opened the sea chest where she kept her flying tunic and pulled it down over her head and shoulders. She took out her falcon mask and stared at it a moment.

Marcellinus went to stand with her, feeling helpless. "Be careful. Very careful."

She smiled briefly. "Look after our daughter. Do not worry about me."

"Impossible," he said. "I mean the not worrying. I will certainly look after Kimimela."

She put her hand on his. He looked down, surprised, and then up at her face as she said, "I will be careful, Gaius. And you, be wary of the Blackfoot. They are not an easy tribe. The People of the Grass you have met in Cahokia are gentle and quiet; they are traders. The Blackfoot are not like this. They are loud and bold and ruthless, more like the Iroqua."

"Great."

"Gaius, stay safe. Stay alive."

"I will." His eyes roamed her face, drinking in her strength and beauty while he still could. "I have every reason to."

"Yes," she said. "Every reason."

They had often launched Sintikala from such a throwing engine, but that had been many moons in the past. Today it took Akecheta's men an hour or more to move the engine forward into a position where it could be fired, check it thoroughly, do a test firing, and then crank the throwing arm back again.

When they threw Sintikala, the longship rocked so hard that several men grabbed the gunwale. The Hawk veered sideways as it opened, and even Kimimela gasped as Sintikala yanked it back on course. Then the wind caught her, and she ducked and looped and somehow gained height from that, and then she was weaving upward, and farther upward, and steering west across the grasslands.

"I don't know how the hell she does that," Marcellinus said once he regained the power of speech.

"It looked easy enough," said Kimimela, and then, "Hey!" as Marcellinus poked her.

Sintikala was streaking toward the hills at uncanny speed. Marcellinus knew that she was on her way and that in all likelihood he would not see her again for many months.

If, that was, they both survived their coming ordeals.

His heart ached already.

CHAPTER 18

YEAR SIX, THUNDER MOON

"Well," said Aelfric, "it was a damned sight easier coming *down* this river, and no mistake."

Even with their extensive experience fighting the Mizipi, the strength of the Wemissori current had come as a shock. At the confluence of the rivers the Wemissori flowed out with such force that it spewed mud halfway across the Mizipi. And the farther they got up the Wemissori, the more the landscape folded and grew around them, its rocky valleys channeling the waters against them.

Now, far to the northwest of the Great City, they had left the forests behind. Plains of endless grass surrounded them, hilly grasslands that stretched far into the distance. From atop one of those hills Marcellinus at last had seen his first herd of living buffalo, an immense swarm of giant beasts that covered the land like a stain. The bellow of their mating carried clear across the plains and made the girls giggle. And at the other end of the size scale, the mosquitoes had grown so fierce that many members of the crew were a mass of welts.

Aelfric leaned forward. "Am I talking to myself?"

Marcellinus grunted, distracted. "The Romans are marching toward Cahokia, and we're going in the opposite direction. That's marvelous."

"Seems entirely sane to me."

"But it's taking too long." Marcellinus studied him. "After we find Tahtay, you're leaving us, aren't you? Staying here or going on?"

Aelfric grinned. "You'll just have to wait and see, won't you?"

"But you've decided?"

"No, I haven't. And that's a fact." Aelfric looked at him askance. "You Romans, you plan ahead obsessively. Not all of us are like that."

Marcellinus chose to say nothing.

The *Concordia* limped upriver, clumsily tacking, making slow headway. They could have made faster progress using the oars, but everyone was weary and aching from rowing.

On the bank Kimimela and Akecheta were having little difficulty keeping up with the boat's progress at a casual stroll, even stopping now and then to look at a rock or a plant. Kimi's occasional laughter was not improving Marcellinus's mood.

Happily, passing Cahokia had been anticlimactic. Mahkah and Isleifur Bjarnason had rejoined them just south of Ocatan with the news that Sintikala and Enopay were safe and well in Cahokia. Enopay was working openly with Avenaka once again, and Sintikala was lying low in the houses of Demothi, Anapetu, and other Cahokians loyal to the memory of Great Sun Man and opposed to Avenaka's leadership. The power of the shamans was growing more oppressive, and doubts were growing about the ease with which Cahokia might win its impending wars.

The *Concordia* had rowed quietly past Ocatan by night. The next few days were jittery for the crew as they traveled between Ocatan and Cahokia, moving mostly after dark and hiding beneath the undergrowth along the shores or in tributaries as best they could by day. They had passed Cahokia two hours before dawn on the fourth morning, at a time when the sentries on watch had been hand selected from the Raven clan by Anapetu for their loyalty to both her and Marcellinus, their clan brother. They had muffled the oars of the longship with hides, had passed by close to the western bank with almost half a mile of river between them and Cahokia proper, and by sheer luck had chosen a foggy night. They had passed Cahokia in a matter of minutes and then rowed hard for the Wemissori.

For the whole next day the mood on the boat had been surly. Aside from Aelfric and Isleifur, everyone aboard was homesick for Cahokia and worried about friends and family.

As for Marcellinus, his need to see Sintikala again had grown unbearable. He still fretted that a careless word might expose her, but there was nothing he could do about that. And Kimimela had curled up in the bottom of the boat and refused even to look toward Cahokia as they rowed by, and was curt and snappy with everyone for a week afterward.

Marcellinus suspected that Kimimela thought this trip up the Wemissori was a forlorn hope. The land was huge, the Wemissori was long, and oddly, the people among the crew who knew it best were not the Hesperians but Aelfric and Isleifur.

"So you love my mother."

Marcellinus laughed. It was now his turn to accompany his daughter along the bank. Ahead of them on the river the Cahokians rowed relatively easily; the Wemissori mercifully had broadened for a while, and they had to keep up a stiff pace to avoid being left behind. It felt good to exercise his legs for a change.

Kimimela peered up at him mischievously. "So you do *not* love my mother?"

"Your mother does not love me, so it hardly matters."

"Have you told her you love her?"

Despite her bantering tone, Marcellinus knew she was serious. "Not in those words. But she can see my eyes, and I have told her that I think that we are . . . the good match."

Kimimela snorted. "The good match? *That* was how you tried to win Sintikala?"

Marcellinus was out of his depth. "It was not an easy conversation. And I don't believe anyone could actually *win* your mother."

"And she said what to 'the good match'?"

"Kimimela, that is between me and Sintikala."

She studied him with that penetrating expression that was common to mother and daughter. "Obviously she did not say yes. But now I think she did not say no, either."

Marcellinus kept walking. Kimimela stepped into his path and put her hand on his chest. "Gaius, what did she say?"

He looked down at her hand. "That's exactly how Sintikala stopped me when we were walking in the Iroqua forests. But in her case she was threatening to kill me."

"And you think I am not? Gaius, this matters as much to me as to you."

From her eyes he saw it was true. "You want Sintikala and me to be together."

"More than anything," she said.

Marcellinus blinked and stared.

"Gaius, I know it is hard for you to trust people, but you can trust me always, forever. Tell me what my mother said to you."

"You think I don't trust people?"

Kimimela drew her dagger. Her eyes twinkled as she held it up to his neck. "Is this what she did?"

"Not exactly."

"Never mind. Tell me right now or you are dead, dead, dead."

"You're certainly your mother's daughter—"

Very gently, she poked the end of the dagger into the skin at his collarbone and smiled. "Then you understand your life hangs in the balance. Now, think of her as Sisika and not Sintikala and *tell me*."

He grinned back at her and took a deep breath. "She said . . . she said: 'Not yet.' "

"Aha." Kimimela took the knife away from his throat.

"But that was on the way back from the Haudenosaunee powwow. Since then—"

"Yes, I know what has happened since then."

"I think that now, perhaps . . . too much has happened. She and I, we are too . . ."

"Similar." Kimimela nodded.

"Different. We are too different, Kimi."

"Well. I will see what I can do." She pursed her lips. "Once we have found Tahtay and taken him back to Cahokia, of course."

"Oh, of course," said Marcellinus.

"In the meantime," she said, idly playing with her hair, "since my mother is not here, perhaps you could do something for me."

They tried to launch Kimimela with the springy material from the Market of the Mud, but it was too hard to control, and even she declared it too unpredictable and dangerous. Next they tried to fly her like a kite, attaching a rope to the cleat on the front of her wing and running along the bank, but even in a brisk wind that proved ineffective. Kimimela managed to glide a few feet above the ground, but she quickly came down again once they released the rope. Eventually even Marcellinus was forced to agree that the throwing engine was the only way to get her airborne.

The first time they tossed Kimimela from the throwing engine it was at half tension, and she barely had time to open the wing before splashing into the muddy river. It was an ignominious plunge, and Marcellinus expected his daughter's temper to erupt, but she took the embarrassment in stride. Perhaps she was not quite as blasé about this as she pretended. Later her confidence grew, as did Marcellinus's faith that she would not kill herself, and by the fifth launch they were hurling her into the air with the full torsion power of the engine and she was staying aloft for several minutes and making controlled landings back on the bank.

She still could not attain sufficient height to scout ahead and return on the wing effectively, but it would have been remarkable if she had. Sintikala's skills had taken a lifetime of learning, and even with such dedication there was still something uncanny about the Hawk chief's ability that could never be taught or learned, something innate, perhaps magical. But Kimimela showed utter dedication and good cheer, and the crew was happy to help her.

Launching Kimimela was a welcome distraction. Overall, the Wemissori River was even harder going than the Mizipi. On the days they were blessed with a strong following wind, they could make headway against the current and make some miles. Other days, when they had to row, were less easy. The Wemissori currents were capricious, and often they would be making good progress only to be caught by a freshening of the current as the river shallowed beneath them, and the *Concordia* might be slewed sideways or even shoved backward as if by a firm hand. Isleifur, who had learned to handle the longship on the Mizipi with some skill, claimed he had to relearn everything for the Wemissori.

Once they exchanged the forest for the prairies and firewood grew scarce, they resorted to burning dried buffalo dung. The warriors among the crew did not care to touch it, but ever contrary, Hurit took it as her cheerful duty to go collect it from the grasslands; she found a short walk and a light load preferable to the duties of unloading and cleaning the ship or to cooking later. The buffalo chips burned well, smelled surprisingly floral, and even flew well when skimmed through the air like a discus.

In addition to the buffalo they saw herds of elk, antelopes with prong-shaped horns, and above their heads the occasional gigantic flock of pigeons that might take hours to pass. And there were bears, too, not the medium-size brown bears of Marcellinus's acquaintance but larger, grayer, and more grizzled-looking creatures. They gave the appearance of viciousness but fortunately took themselves off promptly whenever the crew came across them.

"Hawk," said Isleifur, and everyone on the longship leaped at once as if struck by lightning.

Rather unusually the afternoon wind was strong and stable, and the *Concordia* was proceeding upriver under full sail. Men who had rowed earlier in the morning were taking the opportunity to nap. Up here in unknown territory in the dark of the Thunder Moon, no one was sleeping well, anyway. The river here was narrow, and rarely did they find a suitable island or sandbar where they could moor. The shores were hilly, and the chances of a night ambush were too high for anyone to feel comfortable.

As far as any of them knew, the Blackfoot tribe did not possess Hawks. But here came one low and fast, its dark wings swept back and predatory.

"Bows up, arrows ready," said Akecheta, too late, as most of the warriors already had their bows raised. Marcellinus always feared Greek fire, the Hesperian liquid flame, even in small pots; out there they were sitting ducks.

Isleifur shaded his eyes against the sun. "Oh. Stand down." Mahkah was already sitting and picking up the whetstone and sunflower oil he had been using to sharpen his gladius.

"Sintikala?" Marcellinus looked at Kimimela, but her radiant smile was all the confirmation he needed.

The dark Hawk waggled its wings and shot over their heads toward the far bank, and as he glimpsed Sintikala lying prone beneath it, Marcellinus felt his heart lift to join it.

"Everyone mind the boom," Isleifur said a little irritably, trying to balance the boat. "I suppose we'd better pull ashore and pick her up."

* * *

"Avenaka's shamans did not know it was me," said Sintikala, "but they knew something new had happened. They searched, they asked, but they did not find me."

She sat in the stern with Marcellinus, Kimimela, and Akecheta, wiping the sweat from her eyes, her muscles still shaking from the long flight. Isleifur pulled at the rudder, trying to steer the *Concordia* back into the best of the wind. Sintikala's Hawk lay beside her, sleek and strong, and Kimimela kept eyeing it enviously and reaching out to touch the taut parchment-thin leather. Some of the crew had their ears pricked for news of home; most of the rest had nodded without surprise at Sintikala's arrival, stowed their weapons, and gone straight back to sleep.

"And Enopay?" Marcellinus would have liked to talk to her alone, but it might be some time before he got the opportunity.

"Safe. He is often in Avenaka's company. I saw him rarely. The Hawks hid me, and I spoke most often with Kanuna."

"And the mood of the city?"

She drank deep from a skin of water and shrugged. "It is Cahokia."

Kimimela stroked the spars of the Hawk again and then looked up at the sail and at the lush grasses onshore rippling in the wind. It was clear that she would rather be aloft than having this conversation. "Do the people love Tahtay as much as Enopay says?"

"They certainly do not love Avenaka. Tahtay is remembered fondly, and his father and many-fathers are still honored. But remember, I spoke only to the Hawks I trust and to Kanuna and Enopay and their friends. It is not as if the people sing songs of Tahtay every night around their campfires. As for the warriors, they will serve the man who promises them war."

"What does Kanuna think? Demothi? Others who you spoke to? Can we depose Avenaka?"

"They do not know if this will work even if we find Tahtay," Sintikala said bluntly.

"But they love *you*," Kimimela said. "Everyone does."

Sintikala smiled and shivered. "Everyone does not. I am not the answer. We need Tahtay, and I need to rest. We will talk more tonight."

Marcellinus cleared his throat. "And what about the other Romans, the legions in the east? What news of them?"

"They have battled the Iroqua and tightened their grip on the lands they have taken," she said. "They are supplied now by river as well as land. I sent word to the Tadodaho to do his best to harry them and cut the Roman supply line. He tries, but it is hard. The Romans are strong. They own the Oyo now, from the Appalachia to Woshakee and beyond."

Later they camped on a low hill with a good view over the plains so that they could see anyone who approached. With the rest of the crew carrying bags ashore, Hurit on her walk for fuel, and Kimimela bossing everyone around as usual, Marcellinus stepped back into the longship for a quiet word with Sintikala. "Aelfric and Isleifur are beginning to recognize the scenery."

"And?"

"Hidatsa territory. We are close."

"Good."

"And so you came back to us. I did not know that you would."

"Did you not?"

"I am very glad you did," he said.

Sintikala took in a breath to say something, then stopped and shook her head. She had the expression of a woman trying to bring to mind a word she couldn't quite recall.

He took her hand and squeezed it. "Hello."

She looked down. "I was glad to see Cahokia again. But I had to come back."

"Did you?" he said.

"Yes. You know already that when my first husband died, I was not there. Perhaps I could have saved him.

And you know that when Great Sun Man died, also I was not there. Here . . . Kimimela may be threatened. If ever I am *not there* for Kimimela and something happens, then that is the end of my life."

Marcellinus nodded. "Kimimela, yes."

And then said, "First husband? There was another?".

"No." She looked away. "No other. I spoke poorly."

"I see." Marcellinus found a lump in his throat.

Kimimela saved them then, bounding across the shield wall and bouncing off the thwarts to crash into them both. "All together again! I love it!"

Sintikala looked quizzical at her exuberance. Marcellinus laughed and messed up Kimimela's hair.

"Sorry to break in," she said. "But this is where I needed to be." She hugged them both and in the process pushed them closer, and for a moment Sintikala rested her head on Marcellinus's chest and exhaled long and hard.

They saw the smoke from their fires first and then the tipis, a dozen grubby-looking cones of skin draped over wooden frames twice as tall as a man, all clustered around an open area. Marcellinus had never been inside a tipi or even seen one up close. Neither the Mizipians nor the Iroqua used them; both nations looked down on them as being old-fashioned, inelegant, fit only for the nomadic hunter tribes. Even the Algon-Quian in the east made huts or earth lodges. Not that there was a huge amount of wood in this area to make huts out of.

As the longship approached them, the Hidatsa came in ones and twos from out of the tipis and from the fields beyond. They looked unspeakably nervous, and with reason: in all likelihood they had never seen a vessel as large as the *Concordia*. Spears in hand, the men looked uncertainly back and forth between the longship and their women.

"Will they attack us?"

"More likely to run like hell," said Isleifur.

Marcellinus took off his breastplate and put his gladius aside. "See anyone you recognize?"

"Hardly. We were much farther upriver."

Aelfric said something in a garbled, hiccupping kind of speech. Everyone except the Norseman looked at him blankly. "None of you speak Hidatsa, then?"

"Ha," said Kimimela. "At last you're useful for something."

"Oh, thank you."

Sintikala clapped her hands. "Hurit, Kimimela, Chumanee, Taianita? Be ready."

Isleifur nodded. Aelfric grinned. "You're going to charm 'em to death? Nice."

"Yes," Aelfric said. "They saw him. Tahtay was here."

"Told you," Hurit muttered.

"Gods!" Kimimela put her hands up to her mouth, her eyes wide. She took a few restless steps away, then hurried back. The Hidatsa youths watched her with interest. "Gods, really? Really Tahtay?"

Sintikala frowned. "Hush, all of you. Aelfric, you are sure they are not just telling you what you want to hear?"

"A tall thin boy with a limp who spoke to them in Cahokian, looking for a Blackfoot woman? I'm sure."

They stood on the bank with five Hidatsa. The two youths still carried their spears, but the three elders now held Cahokian adzes and Roman pugios as their price for talking to Aelfric, and nobody expected any trouble. Meanwhile Isleifur had ambled past the welcoming committee, waved at an old woman who sat tending a fire outside her tipi, and squatted down to talk with her.

Marcellinus felt a huge weight lift from his shoulders. This was the very first Hidatsa village they had come across and obviously also would have been the first Tahtay would have arrived at as well. This was hardly coincidence or blind luck. Nevertheless, he was greatly relieved. "Where is Tahtay now?"

"I'm working on it." Aelfric chatted to the Hidatsa for what seemed an inordinately long time and then turned back to them. "They liked Tahtay. He spoke well."

"We know he speaks *well*," Hurit said, almost stamping her foot in impatience.

Aelfric grinned at her. "He came last year, long before winter. The Hidatsa here sent a runner to the Blackfoot, and eventually a Blackfoot war party brought his mother over to pick him up."

"Don't hold anything back," Marcellinus said, studying his face.

"All right. These boys here? They didn't fancy Tahtay's chances. The warriors who came for him were Fire Hearts. Tough as nails, the Blackfoot are, and the Fire Hearts are the fiercest and scariest of them all. And Tahtay with that wounded leg?"

"They said all that?"

"Well, in different words. Anyway, the Fire Hearts took him, and these folks haven't seen him since."

"And where are the Blackfoot?"

"Anywhere and everywhere," said Aelfric, and in the sudden silence he shook his head and added, "What? You expected them to know where Tahtay is *now*? At least we know he made it this far."

"Ask how long it took the runner to bring the war party," Kimimela said.

"They say half a moon, but I bet that means they don't remember. Doesn't matter anyway. The Blackfoot people are nomadic; they won't still be where they were last year."

Belatedly, Isleifur strolled back to them.

"Any luck?" Aelfric asked, and Isleifur grinned.

Marcellinus's heart leaped. "*You* know where the Fire Hearts are?"

"Nope," said the Norseman. "But I know how to find the winter buffalo hunt."

*   *   *

Eight days later they found the second band of Hidatsa, who were setting up their winter camp in a shallow valley. Although their tipis currently were grouped in a circle near the stream, their older braves and women were busy clearing the underbrush from a nearby cottonwood grove before moving the lodges into the trees for better shelter against the winter winds and snows. Here the Hidatsa would stay until the geese flew north, until the first thunder. Then they would pack up again and follow the buffalo herds out onto the open grasslands.

They were a small band, barely twenty lodges in total and mostly related by blood or marriage. Their tipis looked small and inadequate against the crushing weight of the winter that would soon descend on them.

Marcellinus was already perpetually cold, and the first snows had yet to arrive. Months earlier he had been worried about Cahokia and the new Roman invasions from the south and east. More recently he had worried about finding Tahtay. These last days, all he could think of was getting off the high plains and scurrying downriver before the ice came to the Wemissori and trapped them in this desolate hell for the next five moons.

The Hidatsa would remain, though, hunkered down in this valley as they had every winter for time immemorial, eking out a living.

"And they really don't eat fish?" he said again. "With the Wemissori just over there, half a mile away?"

Aelfric shook his head. "No fish, no fowl. They're unclean; everyone knows that. Buffalo, that's the thing. Tasty, nutritious buffalo meat, dawn, noon, and night. And they need more if they're to make it through the winter. Time to go fetch it."

"But if it snows now—"

"They'd still go to join the Blackfoot and other Hidatsa in the last hunt. Whatever the weather. They have no choice."

Marcellinus glanced inland and shivered.

"Oh, don't worry," Aelfric said. "You're not going on the hunt, and neither am I. We'd be bad luck. *Him* they might make an exception for, because he's half willow himself."

"Half willow?" Marcellinus looked across at Isleifur Bjarnason, who was sitting next to Akecheta and Mahkah, smoking a pipe with the Hidatsa band chief outside his lodge. The Norseman was more stocky than willowy.

Aelfric shrugged. "Don't ask me. I just know it's a Hidatsa compliment."

Marcellinus looked up the valley again to the plains. Despite his lack of enthusiasm for hiking into the wilderness, chilling his heels here while Isleifur and the Cahokians went would be even worse. "What will it cost?"

"Gifts?" Sintikala walked up to them, shaking her head. "You cannot buy passage to the hunt with an ax or a spear."

"No?" Marcellinus said drily. Too many times already on the Wemissori they had handed over precious iron or weapons as the price for the privilege of coming ashore. Just getting access to the headman of the Hidatsa whom Isleifur was now smoking with had cost them one of their best water jars, three fine steel ax heads, and almost half a day of tactful diplomacy on the part of Aelfric, Akecheta, Mahkah, and Isleifur. The *Concordia* had brought stone adzes and bronze ax heads, the typical Cahokian gifts, but word had spread and the tribes of the Wemissori demanded iron and steel.

These were poor people, barely surviving. Marcellinus would have been happy to give them gifts as friends, but needing to buy their favor irked him.

"No," Sintikala said. "We will find Tahtay if he is there and bring him out to you."

"And if he won't come?"

"If Tahtay will not come for us, he will not come for you."

"Enopay would not agree," said Kimimela. "And neither do I. The Wanageeska should go to Tahtay in case Tahtay will not come to the Wanageeska."

Sintikala shook her head. "He cannot. It would show disrespect to the buffalo."

"They have to agree to be killed, you see," Aelfric said.

"The buffalo have to agree?"

"Of course," said the Briton. "How long have you been in Nova Hesperia?"

Marcellinus eyed the clouds gathering above them. "When is the hunt?"

"Oh, the Blackfoot started a week ago," Aelfric told him. "It takes a while to set it up. They have to wait this late for the big summer herds to break up into smaller groups as the grass dies back. And then they have to find one of those smaller herds in the right place or move one there."

"And where is the right place?"

"Over there." Aelfric pointed southwest into the grasslands.

"Yes, but how far?"

"They won't say."

Marcellinus shook his head. "Marvelous. So it could be over already, and the Blackfoot scattered to the four winds, before Isleifur finishes his pipe?"

But now Akecheta was rising to his feet, and the Norseman and Mahkah, too, all practically kowtowing to the headman of the Hidatsa. The young woman by the headman's side had stood up to usher the Cahokians away.

The four of them approached, Akecheta in the lead and Mahkah and Isleifur respectfully flanking the woman like an honor guard. Behind them the aging headman clambered laboriously to his feet and handed the pipe to another of his acolytes, who busily puffed at it to finish the tabaco. The headman bent and entered his lodge, and the doorskin fell back into place behind him.

"We will join the hunt," said Akecheta. "Today we

will purify ourselves and make ready. Tomorrow we leave at dawn."

"And that's all right with the Blackfoot?" Marcellinus asked, and the Hidatsa woman frowned and hissed at him.

"You will not speak again, Hotah," Mahkah said apologetically. "Not at all."

Startled, Marcellinus almost said "What?" but a sharp look from Isleifur silenced him.

"Nor you, of course," Mahkah said to Aelfric.

Aelfric frowned and gestured, *Hands, yes?*

"Yes, you may hand-talk," Isleifur said. "But no more sound from your mouths, no clapping of hands. No breaking of sticks. Try not to even fart where they can hear you."

Obviously Isleifur himself had not been silenced. Marcellinus hand-talked: *Why?*

"Because that is what the buffalo require of you."

This was not getting any easier to comprehend, and the Hidatsa woman was frowning at Marcellinus as if he were a moron. Mahkah glanced at her and leaned forward. "It is what you must do, Hotah, to be allowed to accompany us on the hunt."

Marcellinus's eyebrows shot up, and he looked at Sintikala, who seemed as surprised as he.

"You must wear the skin of the buffalo and never take it off until the hunt is over and you are back here by the Wemissori. You must be purified so that the wind and the sun, the wolf and the buffalo, do not know you. And you must do exactly as the buffalo caller or any of the Hidatsa say. You agree?"

With some difficulty, not having the appropriate hand-talk vocabulary, Marcellinus signed, *Buffalo talking who?*

Akecheta chuckled, and now it was his turn to earn a stern look from the young woman of the Hidatsa.

"She, here," Mahkah said. "This fine woman of medicine, this is Sooleawa, and she is the buffalo caller of the Hidatsa and much honored by the Blackfoot."

Marcellinus studied her more closely. Sooleawa's face was young, but she had deep creases by her eyes, perhaps because of the rigors of her life and the harshness of the elements. A rather shapeless elk-skin dress hung from her shoulders, and pendants of weasel skin from her ears. Across her brow was a headband of buffalo hide, and her hair was otherwise loose; Hidatsa women did not braid their hair as other Hesperians did. She wore no other adornments and looked much the same as any other woman in the winter camp.

Then again, her vaunted skills at buffalo calling—whatever that was—were probably just superstition anyway.

"Quickly, Gaius, Aelfric: smile and agree now or the chance will be lost."

"Not me," Aelfric said. "March into nowhere with winter coming in, and me not even able to complain?"

Although she could not understand his words, Sooleawa hissed in exasperation at Aelfric for speaking at all.

"After we went to all that effort?" Isleifur said. "Well, then, off you go, back to the ship immediately, and don't leave it until we're gone."

"Happy to. Have fun. See you when you get back."

As Aelfric walked away, Sooleawa and Mahkah looked at Marcellinus. "You?"

Marcellinus nodded and hand-talked. *Of course. I be silent. Hunt buffalo.* To the young woman of the Hidatsa he bowed and gestured, *I thank you.*

Sooleawa half bowed awkwardly in return and walked away past the headman's lodge to a smaller tipi beyond it.

"We will go with the Hidatsa," Akecheta said. "The fewer, the better, so just us. They will give us furs, but we must carry our own food and our bows, spears, and knives. And no Roman weapons, nothing of steel, only the weapons of our forefathers. Everything else stays behind. The rest of the crew stays here with the longship."

Marcellinus signed, *Black feet agree?* and Akecheta

nodded, remembering Marcellinus's earlier question. "Yes, of course. The Blackfoot and Hidatsa are not enemies. The Hidatsa here are just small villages and do not threaten Blackfoot territory. The Blackfoot trade with the Hidatsa for corn, beans, askutasquash. On the other side—" Akecheta waved westward, indicating a far distance. "—to the west, the Blackfoot do battle with the Shoshoni to keep them away."

"Here they're allied, particularly when it comes to buffalo," said Isleifur. "It doesn't hurt that the Hidatsa have a first-rate buffalo caller."

"But when we all meet up, try to stay away from them," Akecheta said. "The Blackfoot, I mean."

With their reputation, Marcellinus would be glad to.

He and Isleifur, Sintikala and Kimimela, Akecheta and Mahkah. Six of them, trekking off into the frozen grassland with the Hidatsa. Already he was cold, and this camp was in broken ground, relatively sheltered from the wind off the plains.

If he had been able to speak, he would have said, *Tahtay had better be worth all this.*

Sintikala read his expression. "Now you change your mind?"

Marcellinus shook his head, but another thought had occurred to him. The tipis must be heavy with their long lodge poles and their dressed buffalo-skin coverings, but without them, how could they ever survive the nights? He signed, *We take?* and pointed at the lodges. *How?*

"Do not worry," said Sintikala. "The Hidatsa will give them to the dogs."

"It is a great honor they give you," Mahkah said as they walked back to the longship to divest themselves of their steel and prepare for the journey.

Isleifur grunted. "Even I was surprised they went for it."

Marcellinus signed, *What price?*

"Kimimela's virginity," said Isleifur, and Kimimela laughed. "What? I'm joking, man. Good grief."

Marcellinus dropped his fists to his side and bit his tongue hard. Being forbidden to speak was already having its significant downsides.

He gritted his teeth and again signed, *What price?*

"The headman wants to see Cahokia before he dies."

"Really?" Kimimela said. "Cahokia?"

"Of course. The Great City, jewel of the Mizipi? The city of giant mounds and many thousands of lodges that he has heard tell of all his life but has never seen for himself?"

Akecheta nodded. "He wishes to come as an honored guest, to stand on the Great Mound and look out over the city. And he wants us to take him in the big canoe and bring him back safely afterward."

"Headman's holiday," Isleifur said. "Not now. Next summer or the one after, while his people are fat and lazy."

"And he wants to be blessed by Cahokia's greatest shaman," Mahkah said, and shook his head in some amusement.

Marcellinus was hand-talking, but nobody was looking and Kimimela beat him to the punch anyway. "Then you have not told them that we are banished? That the shamans . . . That we—"

"It seemed best to steer clear of politics," Isleifur said.

"Merda," said Kimimela. "You have balls, both of you."

Marcellinus winced. Isleifur and Akecheta grinned.

"Not me, though?" Mahkah asked, aggrieved.

"Yes, you have them, too."

"Seriously, though, you can't blame the old coot," Isleifur said. "I'm quite looking forward to seeing Cahokia myself one of these years."

Akecheta sighed, and Mahkah shook his head. "So are we," Kimimela said, suddenly mournful.

Everyone fell silent. The mention of Cahokia had knocked the wind out of their sails. Sintikala looked around them all and up at the sun. "We should rest.

Tonight will be long, and we will rise and walk before the dawn."

Marcellinus signed *Tonight, long?* but everyone else was lost in his or her thoughts, and his question went unanswered.

He shook his head and followed them.

CHAPTER 19

YEAR SIX, HUNTING MOON

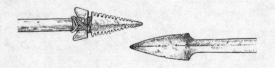

The trek to the hunt was brutal: six days of hell.

On the first morning the Hidatsa came to rouse them after what seemed like only two hours of sleep, and Marcellinus had great difficulty not groaning aloud. The night before had indeed been long: old men chanting and beating drums of buffalo rawhide with rattles, the younger men dressed in buffalo robes prancing and lowing and pretending to gore other braves dressed as hunters. Around them all, women drummed wooden poles on the ground to imitate the sound of buffalo hooves. And seated above them all on a wooden platform, Sooleawa smoking one of the long pipes of the Hidatsa people, the chill wind blowing the smoke away onto the plains in a straight line. They had shivered through prayers and incantations and incomprehensible jokes and mimes that made the Hidatsa and Cahokians roar, leaving Marcellinus smiling uncertainly.

Then had come the garbing of Sooleawa, in which she put aside her village skins to be clothed in a luxuriant buffalo-hide robe, its long winter hair inward. Richly decorated on the outer skin side with painted and dyed porcupine quills, the robe was the most splendid thing Marcellinus had yet seen in this back-country village. With bracelets and anklets of buffalo horn; a necklace made of buffalo teeth, herbs, and sweet-smelling roots;

and a crowning headband of calfskin and plaited buffalo hair, Sooleawa became regal in the flickering firelight, standing tall and calm above them all.

She had descended from her platform and walked among them, distributing morsels of dried buffalo tongue to the hunters from a parfleche. She had sung an interminable song, apparently a buffalo-charming anthem designed to appease the prey and persuade the wind to blow fair for the hunt. Marcellinus hoped she was also asking it to blow warmer.

Just as he had decided this must be over and they could all go to their beds, the dancing had begun again, with no sign of anyone wilting. Marcellinus had no idea how anyone would be able to walk the next day, let alone hunt.

Escape had been impossible. In Cahokia and Shappa Ta'atan, Marcellinus could beat a hasty retreat from the unfathomable Hesperian ceremonies. But as one of the hunt participants he needed to be as carefully blessed as the rest while being robbed even of the luxury of complaining aloud. He had been formally clothed in a buffalo robe of his own. Much less splendid than Sooleawa's and with no decoration, it was darkly odorous and must have weighed ten pounds but at least had the virtue of being warm.

Aelfric, of course, must have been even warmer under his blankets in the cozy tent of the longship's sail, rocked to sleep by the gentle Wemissori. No forced march across the prairies for the Briton. At that moment, Marcellinus hated him.

Then came morning, with the aroma of burning sweetgrass on the air as the Hidatsa again blessed their hunt. As early as it was, they obviously had been awoken at the last minute, because as soon as the six of them arrived blinking and yawning in the open area between the lodges, the dogs barked and they set off.

As he trudged into the chill of the dawn, a blanket masking most of his face from the icy wind, Marcellinus found himself in a ragged procession of around forty

Hidatsa hunters and twenty accompanying women, walking across the frost-crackled grass of the plains with their spears and bows slung across their backs. Several hundred yards ahead Sooleawa led the way into the wilderness; she strode alone in her splendid buffalo robe, her lilting croon audible even from that distance. Occasionally she would stop and take a few dance steps and bleat into the wind like a buffalo calf, and the small band of hunters would wait patiently and with respect. Then onward they would go, ever onward.

Beside them the dogs hauled the tipis, the crossed lodge poles tied together and resting across their shoulders, the pole ends dragging on the ground behind them. The buffalo skins that had made up the tipi walls had been folded and wrapped and tied to the cross-frames of the travois. Other dogs hauled firewood on similar frames. As each dog was dragging fifty pounds or more across the land, they limited the pace of the group. In addition, they were infinitely distractible: sometimes they would pick up a scent and try to skew away from their humans, sometimes they would bark frantically at nothing in particular, and sometimes they would just sit down hard and need to be coaxed back into movement. The marching line meandered and broke up, and sometimes even Sooleawa had to wait, arms folded and face expressionless.

It began to snow very lightly.

The first night they camped in a shallow depression, which was of some help in keeping the wind off them. They threw up the tipis and set a fire and ate their dried deer meat, then went to sleep in the dusk in some comfort, with Marcellinus, Akecheta, Mahkah, and Isleifur in one tipi and Kimimela, Sintikala, and two tough-looking Hidatsa women in the tipi next door. But the second afternoon there was no natural shelter to be had, and they wrestled the lodges up around them as a gale howled. They pitched only half the tipis before exhaustion and frostbite halted the effort. The chilly winds were so strong that they could not even light their fires and had to huddle in the cold and the dark, chewing buffalo pemmican and ashcakes. That night all six of the *Concordia* crew slept piled uncomfortably in a single tipi along with the two women none of them knew and two of the dogs, which even with their thick fur could not be left out in such bitter cold. Marcellinus lay wrapped around Sintikala and Kimimela as best he could, all of them fully clothed, with Mahkah's knee in his back, and slept barely a wink.

After that the days blurred, and even the men and women who were permitted to speak rarely conversed. Old Father Winter had come to the plains early indeed, and they were kicking their way onward through several inches of snow.

"It's not cold," Isleifur said unconvincingly. "The North Sea in winter, now that's cold. Vinlandia during the Long Night Moon, that's cold. This? Nothing." But at the end of the day, he was into their tipi just as quickly as anyone else.

As for Marcellinus, he was numbed mentally as well as physically. Conversation had grown sparse anyway, but as he could not participate, he almost stopped listening whenever anyone else said anything. The fur gloves made hand-talk essentially impossible. In principle he could cheat by whispering to the others in their lodge at night at times when none of the Hidatsa were around. In practice the Cahokians and Isleifur took the vow of silence as seriously as the Hidatsa did, their superstitious side out in full force. Even Kimimela would not allow him to speak to her, and besides, she collapsed exhausted at the end of every day's walk, buried in buffalo blankets and enfolded in Sintikala's arms for warmth.

The skies over the plains still hung heavy with cloud. If the clouds helped warm the land at all, it was hardly noticeable. Even the Hidatsa were looking upward nervously. If the snow got heavier, they could all die out there.

* * *

"Go left."

Marcellinus did not respond immediately, and Akecheta shoved gently on his right arm. "Wanageeska? We must go around them."

He looked up. Just a quarter mile in front of him, a herd of buffalo covered the plains as far as the eye could see. The sheer number of animals it must have contained beggared belief. Marcellinus's eyes widened and he began to pull off his gloves to sign, but Akecheta was ahead of him. "No, these are not the buffalo we will hunt. We must leave these in peace."

Marcellinus's feet were blistered from marching in the cold and the wet, and he and Akecheta were close to the rear of the Hidatsa column. In front of them the women steered the dogs far to the east in a much larger detour than the hunters were taking to avoid spooking the herd.

If there were gods in this world after all, they had played a terrible trick on the Hesperians; in place of sheep, goats, or honest cattle they had been cursed with the most ugly and ungainly creature on the earth. To Marcellinus, each of the buffalo looked like a hairy testudo with a bad temper, not only huge and stupid but also clumsy and dangerous. Any creature as tall as a man that surely weighed well over a thousand pounds, armed with horns more than six feet across, was definitely worth steering clear of.

Sooleawa, though, had walked into the herd and was slipping between the giant beasts, probably singing to them in her rather tuneless croon, even reaching out to touch them as she passed. The buffalo tolerated it, appearing to nod their great heads at her as steam billowed from their noses. Marcellinus wondered what it would mean for the hunt if one of the buffalo were to casually gore her or even knock her over by accident and step on her. It seemed entirely possible.

"Does your mouth water?" Mahkah had arrived on Marcellinus's other side but was talking past him to Akecheta.

"I hope their meat tastes better fresh than dried." Akecheta shook his head. "It is amazing that an arrow or spear can kill such a beast at all."

"It often takes many." Mahkah grinned. "If I cannot kill Iroqua, maybe killing a buffalo will make me feel like a man again."

Marcellinus tugged off his gloves. *You always a man, and good man.*

"Perhaps I would prefer to not be a good man."

Then again, perhaps the Hesperians' gods had been wise to put so much value into a single animal. The People of the Grass lived off the meat of the buffalo, of course, and used its skin to clothe their bodies and tipis, but Marcellinus already knew that they wasted almost no part of the ungainly creature. They used its rawhide for bags and clothes, shields, moccasins, and ropes, even for the hulls of their canoes. The muscles and sinew of the beast were used for bowstrings and bindings, the horns for cups and ladles, the hair for pillows and rope, clothing and ornaments. At the winter camp he had seen women using buffalo paunches to carry water, and the Hidatsa arrowheads and awls were all of buffalo bone. Aside from their use in rattles, buffalo hooves could be boiled to make a sticky resinous substance that could be used for glue. Buffalo skulls had been prominent at the prehunt ritual, and the brains that once had lived inside those skulls were used for tanning the hides. Even by Hesperian standards of practicality, the way the People of the Grass plundered every part of the buffalo was extraordinary.

Although it took more than two hours to skirt the perimeter of this herd, Marcellinus knew it to still be a relatively small grouping. In the summer, such herds might number millions of buffalo, even allowing for Hesperian exaggeration. Now the herds were fragmenting with the coming of winter as grass got scarcer.

As the women guiding the dog travois rejoined the line of hunters and they continued on their way, Sooleawa slipped out from the herd. Even as she jogged athletically past the Hidatsa and Cahokians to take her place at the head of the group, she smiled beatifically like a woman in a trance.

"I will kill ten buffalo!" Mahkah said. "I will show the Blackfoot what Cahokia can do!"

Akecheta grunted. "The Blackfoot or Sooleawa?"

"Everyone," Mahkah said with a smile.

Akecheta looked at the sky. "It seems warmer. Is it warmer? Or is it just Mahkah's rosy glow from Sooleawa?"

It did not feel warmer to Marcellinus, but in fact it was. At noon it began to rain, of all things, helping to melt the snow and turning the ground underfoot to mush. As the rain increased, lashing down in sheets, Sooleawa halted the caravan to erect the lodges in a circle and prepare the evening meal before dark. The mood among the Hidatsa had turned bleak. Even though no runners had come from the Blackfoot and Marcellinus had no idea how they might know, it appeared that after all they might arrive at the hunt too late.

"Nearly there," said Isleifur, arriving at Marcellinus's side as they struggled on into the wind. Beside him Akecheta trudged along, almost as miserable as he was. Only Mahkah was cheerful; hours earlier he had hurried forward to be in the vanguard of the group.

Hands wrapped in gloves, Marcellinus could only gesture vaguely.

"That's what the Hidatsa say, anyway. And Sooleawa has left us, run on ahead."

Marcellinus squinted into the distance. Sure enough, he saw no sign of the buffalo caller. His legs felt like they weighed a hundred pounds yet could snap at any moment. He shook his head in disbelief that anyone could run.

"I've been trying to find out what we're supposed to do. Not much, apparently. They don't want us to screw anything up."

Marcellinus could believe that.

"So we must stay clear, to the side, until after the jump. If we do something wrong and piss off the herd, they won't agree to die, and they will leave."

Marcellinus made a face and pulled off a glove to sign, *Jump?*

Isleifur shrugged. "All I know is that we must stay with the Dead Men."

Marcellinus looked at Akecheta, who shook his head. "I cannot help you, Wanageeska. The Hidatsa speak in their own way, like shamans of their medicine."

Marcellinus barely cared. He was beyond frustration at this point. He was thousands of miles from anywhere, on a fool's errand that seemed more foolish by the day, and it took a Norseman to translate one Hesperian language to the other Hesperians.

Marcellinus had given up any realistic hope of finding Tahtay. They were all fish out of water, completely at the mercy of the elements and of people who might kill them without a second thought. His only hope was that they might live through whatever was about to happen— all of them, but especially Kimimela and Sintikala—and manage to struggle back to the Wemissori.

When they finally arrived at the hunt site, Marcellinus did not realize it. He did not know why the Hidatsa women were pulling the dogs together and cutting the travois poles off them, did not know why the men were readying their spears or recognize the four warriors with red-painted faces who had appeared suddenly. He had lost track of Sintikala and Kimimela; when everyone wore the same buffalo cloaks and hoods and the hiking was so shambolic, he often ended the day's march among strangers. Then he blinked and saw even more men standing out ahead of him on the plains, solid thickset men spaced far apart and unmoving, staring at the skies, and in the distance he saw yet another herd of buffalo.

The Hidatsa men strode away. The poles and furs of the Hidatsa tipis were left where they lay, the dogs being hustled back the way they had all just come. Some of the Hidatsa hunters had cast aside their furs and run east, toward the sun. And still the row of tall men peered upward, unmoving.

Marcellinus wiped the tears from the wind away from his eyes and blinked again. Those still forms were not men. They were tall, narrow cairns of rock crowned with brush and draped with furs.

They were the Dead Men.

"Hotah?" Mahkah shoved back the hood of his cloak despite the chill and strode toward him. "You must come with us. You must run. You must stay absolutely silent. You understand? Any sound and the Blackfoot will kill you."

Marcellinus almost said "Blackfoot?" aloud. He swallowed. The walk had made him stupid. He pushed back his hood and gulped air.

"Have your spear ready. Come. Run low."

Marcellinus nodded. After days of trudging drudgery and little sleep, of his face being permanently chilled and his thoughts frozen, everything was happening too fast.

The tall piles of stones might not be human, but there were many more people around him now. Strong men and harsh, their faces smeared with vivid red war paint.

And on their feet, black moccasins. Marcellinus and Mahkah were running among braves of the Blackfoot tribe.

How had Aelfric described them? *A rough lot. Hard. Warlike. Tough as nails.*

Perhaps it was just as well Marcellinus was not permitted to speak. At least he could not say something stupid that would get him killed.

By Mahkah's side, Marcellinus jogged up a gentle slope toward the nearest of the Dead Men. Not far behind them Sintikala and Kimimela were also running. He had lost track of Isleifur and Akecheta, had no idea where they had gotten to.

The buffalo were coming. Inexplicably the herd was on the move, walking in their direction.

A warrior bounded in from their left, grabbing at their arms. He was much taller than Marcellinus and clothed in what looked like a wolf-skin tunic, and his face was smeared in a pattern of savage ocher that made him look angry. Or perhaps he *was* angry. He spoke urgently in yet another language that sounded closer to Algon-Quian than to Hidatsa or Cahokian. The Hidatsa hunter running next to them made a complicated hand-talk gesture in return and kept going.

It had not occurred to Marcellinus that the Hidatsa and Blackfoot would not speak the same language. Perhaps Mahkah was caught out, too. "What? We have come to hunt. Kill buffalo."

The Blackfoot warrior looked wary. "Hidatsa?" He shook his head, and his eyes narrowed. "Shoshoni?"

"Cahokia," Mahkah said quickly. "Mizipi. Cahokia. Mound builders."

The Blackfoot gaped at him, then looked more closely at Marcellinus. "Napikwan?"

Lost, Marcellinus pointed at himself and signed, *No speak.* He hoped that failing to answer a Blackfoot question was not in itself a capital offense.

But the Blackfoot warrior was nodding and shoving at them again, impatiently beckoning them to follow him. Marcellinus again broke into a run toward the line of Dead Men, panting, his spear in his hand.

Many of the Dead Men already had warriors or hunters behind them. The Blackfoot guided them to one that was as yet unspoken for. Marcellinus slipped in the mud and skidded and almost ran into the stone column. Now he saw another row of the columns several hundred feet away.

The Blackfoot glanced back at them and snarled a few words, gesturing. Mahkah said, "Hide, down, fall flat." Immediately and without thought, Marcellinus did so, landing on his face in the cold, muddy grass. Beside him was another Blackfoot, his face also painted red. Despite the cold, this warrior wore only a breechclout, an elk-skin hood, and a necklace of bear claws, revealing an impressively broad chest and arms of solid muscle. The new Blackfoot was humming quietly to himself, watching the buffalo approach from his right, but now he glanced back. Seeing Marcellinus bare-headed, he gestured and then reached out to touch his hair.

Marcellinus gritted his teeth and allowed it. At Cahokian markets, traders from out of town would sometimes touch his short Roman hair. Sometimes Marcellinus would even squat down so that Cahokian children could rub his head. But for an unknown warrior of a fierce and deadly tribe to reach out toward his hair—and the scalp it grew from—was another matter entirely.

The Blackfoot reached past his head and pulled the hood roughly over it. Then he looked back toward the approaching herd.

Marcellinus could smell them now, the giant rank smell of livestock, but richer and wilder. Of course, if they could smell the buffalo, the buffalo could not smell him and the other Hidatsa hunters and Blackfoot warriors who hid behind the Dead Men, prone on the frozen ground. Perhaps the buffalo caller's prayer to the winds had worked after all.

Out in front of the herd shambled a smaller buffalo with an odd limping, twisting gait, shoving itself upright, almost taking its weight on its hind legs and then dropping forward again. It was the most ungainly, warped creature Marcellinus had ever seen, not that any buffalo was exactly graceful to start with—

The malformed creature bleated, and Marcellinus knew it for Sooleawa. Half capering, half staggering, favoring her left leg to the point of swiveling as she hurried across the plain, Sooleawa squeezed out another of those awful high bleats.

A wounded calf. The buffalo caller was leading the herd onward by pretending to be a wounded calf. She looked bizarre to Marcellinus, an absurd caricature of a wild animal in pain. Even at the Hidatsa prehunt ceremony he had seen dancers who moved more like real buffalo than Sooleawa did now.

Yet it was working. Here came the buffalo in the thousands. From his prone position on the slope Marcellinus had no idea how many there might be, but he was looking at a sizable herd. The sea of animals had now passed the first of the Dead Men.

The logic of the Dead Men became clear. Two rows of cairns formed a narrowing channel three miles long, almost V-shaped. The buffalo instinctively stayed away from the Dead Men, preferring the middle of the drive lane.

Far behind the herd, out on the plains, living men were running now, trying to spook the buffalo into running faster, herding them into the drive channel.

Even as Marcellinus saw this, the buffalo herd broke into stampede, the ungainly beasts breaking from a trot into a full-force run. They panted, their breath puffing above them in clouds, but in moments they had reached a fearsome speed, perhaps even as fast as a galloping horse. As the buffalo passed them, Blackfoot hunters leaped out from hiding behind the Dead Men to wave and scream, driving the beasts on ever faster.

The rumble of the earth beneath Marcellinus's chest turned to thunder. The buffalo herd had become a swarm of black pounding fury.

Sooleawa had dropped her pretense and was running flat out up the slope of the hill, bent into a sprint. Her buffalo cloak streamed out behind her despite all its weight.

Marcellinus glanced to the left and right, measuring distances. The herd was almost upon them, the cows out in front and the heavier bulls dropping back, so close that he could see the clods of earth being kicked up into the air by their pounding hooves, their fur shaggy, their faces empty and bovine but somehow malevolent. And Sooleawa was slowing and looking behind her as she reached the crest of the hill. Marcellinus expected her to change course, dart left or right, take shelter behind one of the final Dead Men on the path before the jump.

She did not. Sooleawa bounced on the balls of her feet

a few times, her eyes narrowed, then turned her back on the lethal galloping herd and broke into a final sprint toward the escarpment.

The Hidatsa buffalo caller was sacrificing herself for the hunt.

"Merda!" Without realizing it, Marcellinus had pushed himself up onto all fours. He was at least two hundred feet from the woman and had no chance of catching her, and even now the buffalo were almost level with him, but he knew no one should have to do this, to give her life when it could be saved.

The first Blackfoot warrior's elbow smashed into his jaw, and Marcellinus spilled over onto his left side. His head rang with the pain. Through eyes that suddenly stung with tears he saw Sooleawa reach the peak of the hill and leap out into empty space, her legs together and her arms out. For a dazed moment Marcellinus almost expected her to sprout Hawk wings and soar away into the sky. She did not. Hair waving, buffalo cloak billowing, the woman arced downward and fell away from his sight in her long dive toward the ground.

But right by them the damage was done; the lead animals in the herd had caught Marcellinus's unexpected movement and veered away from the Roman toward the far row of Dead Men. For a moment the leading cows faltered in their headlong rush. Two cannoned into each other and fell onto their sides, skidding in the mud and snorting. The vanguard of the buffalo charge broke into chaos.

If it had happened farther down the hillside where the flaring V of the Dead Men was wider, the whole herd might have spilled into disarray, its momentum broken. As it was, there was no space; the sheer weight of numbers of the herd drove them on. More of the leading cows were bowled over by the animals behind them and rolled, scrabbling for purchase and goring one another. The rest of the herd tried to part around them but eventually pounded right over them. The herd continued its thundering rush.

Buffalo plunged blindly off the cliff edge in the hundreds, plummeting to their doom.

Now that the slaughter had begun, the Blackfoot were running out from behind all the Dead Men, calling and shrieking and raising a hullaballoo, driving on the panicked buffalo at the tail end of the mighty herd. Most of the animals ran on, following their fellows off the cliff into death. A few of the stragglers swerved, slowed, and turned their heads left and right, looking for another way out. Next to Marcellinus, the Blackfoot who had struck him raised his bow and sent an arrow into the closest buffalo just behind the last rib, then a second arrow above the hind leg. Enraged, the buffalo spun to face the threat, but more arrows flew and most struck their mark. Buffalo staggered, grunted, roared, and fell heavily onto their knees or crashed sideways. Mahkah raised himself up, cast his spear, then slid his bow off his back and nocked an arrow. From farther down the hill Blackfoot braves came running with stone-headed clubs and nimbly dodged between the buffalo to slam their weapons onto the stricken beasts' skulls.

Marcellinus sat up and spit blood. His head still throbbed and dizziness threatened to claim him, but he did not think his jaw was broken.

The Blackfoot warrior looked up and down the killing slope, a new arrow nocked, but all the nearby buffalo were down, dead or dying. Blackfoot and Hidatsa were running by, ululating in their bloodlust of joy, but the warrior's eyes were cold as he turned them on Marcellinus. He swung his bow around and pointed its arrow straight at Marcellinus's face.

Without apparent haste, Sintikala walked in front of Marcellinus. She did not speak but dropped to one knee, ducked her head, and waited.

Marcellinus held his breath. He did not know whether to apologize or beg for mercy or whether speaking further would guarantee that the arrow would fly into his eye or Sintikala's chest. Slowly he lifted his hands in an attitude of submission and surrender and, taking his cue from Sintikala, ducked his head.

The moments dragged out. From all around them came the joyful cries of the other warriors and hunters, elated at the success of the buffalo drive. The Blackfoot eased the tension on his bowstring and strode away from Marcellinus and Sintikala toward the crest of the hill.

Sintikala stood and reached down. "Stay silent, even now."

Marcellinus nodded dumbly and allowed her to pull him to his feet.

Together they walked to the cliff edge and looked down on a sea of death. At the base of the sixty-foot drop buffalo were piled on top of one another in a mass five or six beasts thick, thousands of them. The reek of blood and gore reached them there, even at the top of the escarpment.

Not all the buffalo were dead. Some still thrashed, their backs or legs broken, lowing piteously or in fury. Hunters ran among them, clubbing the beasts they could reach, shooting arrows or casting feathered spears into the mass of buffalo flesh where the dying creatures were beyond range of their clubs. As well as putting the sacred animals out of their misery, stopping them from thrashing would reduce further damage to their valuable skins.

Even used as he was to the carnage of battle, Marcellinus felt nausea welling in his throat. He raised his head for a gulp of cold air and scanned the periphery of the killing field.

He grabbed Sintikala's arm and pointed. Alive and well, Sooleawa stalked back and forth around the perimeter of the mass of beasts as if daring any of them to come back to life and flee the killing ground. She looked completely unharmed. Marcellinus shook his head, baffled.

Sintikala raised her eyebrows. "Perhaps they held out a buffalo blanket. Men were ready to catch her."

Such men would have had almost no time to react once Sooleawa dived off the cliff, then only moments to run clear before the massive herd came barreling off the cliff edge after her. And the drop was sixty feet or more. Was that even possible?

"Or she just has very good medicine." Sintikala grinned tautly.

Marcellinus tapped her arm again. The Blackfoot warrior who had struck him in the face and then aimed an arrow at him was approaching. Blood covered his legs and lips from the buffalo he had just slaughtered. Trying not to guess at what buffalo sweetmeat the warrior might have just popped into his mouth raw, Marcellinus stepped away from the cliff edge and adopted his pose of submission again.

"Cahokia?" said the warrior.

Sintikala stepped in front of Marcellinus and spoke in Algon-Quian and then Cahokian. "I am Sisika, daughter of chieftain in Cahokia. This man—"

But the warrior had already nodded and was walking away, beckoning them to follow him back down the slope.

Sintikala glanced at Marcellinus. "It seems we must go down."

From ground level the pile of dead buffalo was even more intimidating. Blackfoot and Hidatsa men and women were now there in the hundreds, dragging the beasts out and carving at them.

Again Marcellinus tried not to gag. The stench of blood and fresh death was almost unbearable. The base of the escarpment was a charnel house of buffalo death.

The Blackfoot brave escorted them under the cliff and stopped, clearly puzzled. Stepping up onto a buffalo corpse, he turned around in a complete circle, surveying the butchery.

The Blackfoot had thrown aside their furs and tunics to keep them from being spoiled by the blood of the buffalo. All around them were men and women dressed only in breechclouts, carefully cutting into buffalo hides, carving out buffalo guts, hacking out clean hunks of bloody meat and stacking them in an efficient operation.

"Mingan," said the brave. He jumped down and again led the way across the blood-soaked earth, around and through more buffalo corpses.

"Mingan." Marcellinus stopped, but the brave shoved him forward. "Mingan? Cahokia."

A Blackfoot brave looked around. His hair was shorn at the side, and like the others he had red war paint daubed across his cheeks, eerily matching the red that streaked his arms to the elbow from his butchery. Muscles bulged on his arms and legs. Unlike the other Blackfoot, he wore few war tattoos; like many of them, blood was smeared around his mouth.

Marcellinus blinked, and at his side Sintikala made an incoherent sound.

Kimimela caught up to them and stopped dead. Her mouth dropped open as she stared past them at the tall youth. *"Tahtay?"*

CHAPTER 20

YEAR SIX, HUNTING MOON

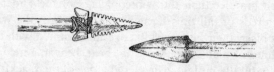

For a moment they all stood stock-still, and then Tahtay put his head on one side. He raised a bloody hand to rub his eyes.

Beside them, a buffalo lifted its head and mewled piteously. As Kimimela jumped aside, Tahtay snatched up his club and stepped forward to bring the weapon down on the beast's skull with a loud crack. The buffalo flopped back to the ground.

"Saved your life," Tahtay said sardonically.

Kimimela laughed at him. "The debt is the other way, idiot. We're bringing your life back to you."

Tahtay shrugged indifferently and glanced at the sky. "I am busy now. You should help if you can; we must cut all the meat so that my Blackfoot and your Hidatsa do not go hungry in the snows. After that, you will come back to my camp for the night."

"Your camp?"

"Ours. The camp of the Siksikauwa, the Blackfoot people." Tahtay grinned. "I am not being generous. Your Hidatsa will be coming there anyway for two nights while we cut up buffalo, before they return to the Wemissori. So unless you want to stay here for the night and help the men who will guard the carcasses against the wolves . . ."

Tahtay turned to Marcellinus. "I am surprised they let

you come. You are forbidden to talk? Yes? Well, take off your fine borrowed buffalo skin and pick up a stone blade and get your hands dirty, and then perhaps back at camp they will let you speak again."

The Blackfoot camp on the high plains was huge and much grander than the winter village of the Hidatsa. Hundreds of tall tipis formed a circle against the winter's blast, their buffalo-skin coverings painted with the outlines of many animals: wolf, bear, beaver, antelope, and naturally buffalo. The sacred lodge of the Blackfoot tribe was in the center of the circle. Offset from it was a bonfire twenty feet tall and blazing hot, but it was the press of people that seemed to generate the most warmth: Blackfoot warriors and hunters, women and children, as well as the hundreds of dogs that had hauled the lodges and the firewood so far and that eventually would help haul the thousands of pounds of buffalo meat, skins, horns, hooves, teeth, and tongues back to wherever the Blackfoot would spend the winter.

The Blackfoot were in a festive mood. The last great hunt of their season was over. Small bands might venture out onto the plains to supplement their food supply with fresh antelope if the weather allowed it or take a few buffalo in their full shaggy winter coats. But by and large their year was done, and now it was time to eat and be merry before settling in to rest with their families through the harshness of the northern winter.

As dusk crept across the camp, Marcellinus, Sintikala, and the others sat near the bonfire, trying to soak every drop of warmth into their bones that they could. All around them were tall, strong men, their faces painted red in the Blackfoot fashion, skins tattooed or scarified, each wearing a smile quite at odds with his reputation for ferocity and many wearing little more than a tunic and perhaps an animal-skin hat.

As for Tahtay, the shining hope of Cahokia and the reason they had come all this way, the youth had run on ahead into the Blackfoot camp, and they had not seen him since.

In the meantime, all the people in the camp were gorging themselves on fresh meat cooked on the giant bonfire or on one of the smaller fires outside the tipis that ringed it. The air was rich with the smells of roasting flesh, tabaco, and sweat.

"No beer," Mahkah said. "That is what makes this so different from Cahokia or Shappa."

"Huh," Kimimela said. "Otherwise exactly the same."

They had walked over two hours from the jump to get there. Marcellinus was exhausted and had no idea where they were going to sleep that night. The rest of the Hidatsa were somewhere in the camp, that was for sure, but finding them might be difficult. He signed, *Where hell is Tahtay?*

"He will not forget us, Wanageeska," Akecheta said.

"He's just making a point," Kimimela said darkly. "Showing he doesn't need us. When it suits him, he'll make his entrance."

"Who will?" came a voice behind her. She turned, and of course it was Tahtay.

Like many of the other Hesperians at the buffalo feast, Tahtay had managed to clean himself up. Not a trace of blood remained on his face and hands. He wore a buckskin shirt and leggings painted and quilled in horizontal bands, with a lighter buffalo-skin robe draped over it.

On his feet were moccasins so black that they looked charred. Most odd, he wore a sash of a red more vivid than any Marcellinus had seen since he had stood on the Iroqua stage at powwow. In Roma, such a red dye could have been made from vermilion or safflower. In Hesperia, Marcellinus did not know how such a bright color could be achieved.

"Ah," said Kimimela. "Can it be Mingan of the Blackfoot?"

Unexpectedly, Tahtay bowed. "Kimimela of the Hawk clan."

Robbed of her sarcasm, Kimimela blinked at him.

"Akecheta, centurion. Mahkah, mighty fighter. Sintikala, Hawk chief. And the Wanageeska, Gaius Marcellinus. You are welcome."

For some reason everyone looked at Marcellinus, who was the only person who could not reply.

"You may now speak, Hotah." Tahtay grinned mischievously. "In fact, you could have spoken as soon as the hunt was over. It just amused me to make you wait."

Marcellinus swallowed. "Thank you." His voice sounded strange to his own ears, and his throat felt as if it had a coating of buffalo hair on it. "You are looking very well, Tahtay. I am glad you live."

"I live. I thrive. I run like the wind."

"Do you?" Kimimela said.

Tahtay looked down at her coolly. "You doubt it?"

"No . . . I am glad."

He continued to stare at her. "You do not look glad."

In Latin, Kimimela said, "That's because you're scaring me. Tahtay? Are we still friends? Do you hate me?"

Tahtay glanced at Marcellinus, the only other person present who could easily understand what she had said, but Marcellinus did not react.

"Of course not," Tahtay said.

Kimimela shook her head. "Which question are you answering?"

But Tahtay had already turned to Sintikala. Reverting to Cahokian, he said: "Hawk chief, daughter of chieftain and friend of my father. Why are you here?"

"We have come for you, Tahtay. To take you home."

Tahtay said nothing, merely gestured around himself at the Blackfoot camp. His meaning was clear.

Sintikala met his gaze without blinking. "To take you to Cahokia, then."

"You take me to die?"

"No. We take you to lead. In your father's place."

Tahtay grinned, and all of a sudden—and briefly—he was once again the boy they all knew. "Then the cold has driven you mad. You are welcome here tonight and tomorrow night, and then the Blackfoot will go west and you will go north to the Wemissori and then east to Cahokia. Say hello to my Cahokian friends."

"Your father is dead," Sintikala said bluntly. "Come and help us avenge him."

"My father died without honor. I think instead I will stay and kill Shoshoni, and hunt buffalo, and look after my mother."

Sintikala's tone became brittle. "If you say that Great Sun Man died with no honor, then you are a fool."

"In your eyes. But in my eyes or the eyes of my people?"

"The Blackfoot aren't your people," Kimimela said.

"You say so?" Tahtay turned to Marcellinus. "You brought the *Concordia*? Who is with you?"

"All the crew from the trip downriver. The same."

Tahtay looked sad. "Not Enopay, then?"

"No. Enopay is still in Cahokia, building support for you."

"A pity. I would like to see Enopay again."

"Dustu is at the ship," Kimimela said. "And Hurit."

He shrugged. "When I was injured, you stayed with me. And the Wanageeska stayed with me. Hurit did not. I have nothing to say to Hurit."

"She . . ." Kimimela stopped.

"She could not bear to see you hurt," Sintikala said unexpectedly.

"I do not think that was the reason." Suddenly Tahtay took a step back and clasped his hands in front of him in greeting. "Sooleawa."

The buffalo caller strolled up to them almost jauntily, with none of the air of severity she had owned before the hunt. She now wore a tunic of buffalo calfskin and leggings like those the men wore, and her hair was loose. Unlike Tahtay, whose speech was guarded and painfully formal, Sooleawa looked calm and relaxed and happy, and younger than she had seemed at the village. Her big ordeal was over. Walking beside her and to the right was a Blackfoot girl younger than Kimimela. Sooleawa looked at Marcellinus and said something in Hidatsa.

The Blackfoot girl cleared her throat and spoke in Algon-Quian, which Sintikala translated into Cahokian. "Sooleawa says, 'So they let you live.'"

"Yes. Please tell her I am sorry."

"What did you do?" Tahtay asked him.

"I . . . started to run out to try to save her when I realized she was about to throw herself off the cliff."

Tahtay put his hand up to his head in disbelief. "You *are* mad."

Sintikala and the Blackfoot girl translated for Sooleawa. Now she laughed and spoke again at some length. Looking vaguely disapproving, the girl spoke in Algon-Quian, but this time nobody translated for Marcellinus. He looked at Kimimela, who shrugged: she could not follow Hidatsa or Algon-Quian any more than he could.

Now Sintikala looked at Sooleawa and grinned. In Cahokian and then Algon-Quian she said, "You fly well."

The girl translated. Sooleawa smiled, unabashedly joyful, and mimed wiping sweat from her face.

"Tell her that if she ever tires of charming buffalo, she may come to Cahokia to soar with the birds."

The Blackfoot girl did so. Sooleawa grinned again in wide amusement and stepped forward to clasp hands with the Hawk chief. Then, with nods to the others, she stepped away, almost skipping, to continue her rounds at the feast.

"What did she say?"

Sintikala followed the woman with her eyes as she walked away. "The sacred buffalo caller says you probably did save her life. She had not run fast enough and so displeased the buffalo, and had they followed her off the cliff so closely, they would have landed on her head and crushed her. As it was, the Wanageeska displeased the sacred buffalo more, and the moments you brought her allowed her to run clear."

"Oh," said Marcellinus.

"Also, she said that if the sacred buffalo had not given their lives by running over the cliff anyway, and if the sacred buffalo did not kill you, then the Blackfoot would have kept you alive for three moons."

If Marcellinus had ruined the hunt, he would have earned a long, excruciating death at the hands of a people even more bloodthirsty than the Iroqua.

All he could think of to say to that was, again, "Oh."

"I am glad I did not have to watch you die," Tahtay said politely. "And now I must find my mother. Perhaps I will bring her to talk to you if she wishes."

"Ask her about Cahokia," Sintikala said. "She may seek revenge more than you do."

"She may," said Tahtay, "but perhaps not enough to lose her son." He nodded to them and walked away into the night.

"Wow," Kimimela said.

After a brief pause Marcellinus said, "The red band Tahtay wears. What is it?"

Akecheta and Sintikala looked away, but Mahkah chimed in. "It is of the Fire Hearts. He will never run."

"I don't understand. He said he could run like the wind."

"I meant, never run *away*. When a Fire Heart faces an enemy, he stakes the long end of the sash into the ground. Then he will die before he will retreat."

"Juno," Marcellinus said, appalled. A year had been a long time in the life of his young friend.

"Many warrior societies do such. It is not just the Blackfoot."

Marcellinus looked at Kimimela, but her face was perfectly composed, as if she had heard nothing to surprise her.

A Blackfoot warrior stepped forward to throw more firewood and buffalo chips onto the blaze. The hunters and families nearby hooted as the flames shot up into the sky. Somewhere over on the other side of the camp the drumming started, but tonight of all nights, Marcellinus thought maybe he could sleep even through that.

"More buffalo?" Mahkah asked.

* * *

The next day was filled with work from dawn till dusk. The six from the *Concordia* could not rest easy while all the people around them were cutting buffalo meat, cleaning and scraping hides for the journey, collecting horns and hooves, and so on. The area under the cliff had become an abattoir, yet one that needed to be cleaned afterward. If the site smelled too strongly of death, the buffalo would not agree to return the next year.

The Blackfoot and Hidatsa preferred to dress the sacred meat themselves, and mostly the *Concordia* crew members were relegated to carrying and cleaning. Unusually, the sun shone and the wind had dropped, which only conspired to make the stink even worse. It was rough, greasy work, and Kimimela and Akecheta regularly turned a little green and had to walk away for a while.

Helping to carry bloody meat reminded Marcellinus of his first days in Cahokia, carrying dead Romans and Cahokians to their charnel pits. So although for the Blackfoot and Hidatsa this was a time of joy and fellowship, for Marcellinus it was yet another day for somber reflection on what he had lost.

And also for hopelessness. For he was convinced now that they had lost Tahtay. The youth had not returned to the fire with Nipekala later in the evening, and they did not see him all day. That evening Marcellinus walked all around the camp without finding him. He saw Blackfoot wearing the characteristic red sash of the Fire Hearts, but none were Tahtay.

"I don't think I'll ever eat buffalo again," Kimimela said as he returned to the small campfire outside the borrowed tipi they shared with the other Cahokians. Akecheta and Mahkah were lying flat on their backs, exhausted from hauling meat all day. Nearby the Hidatsa sat around their own campfires, talking and laughing.

"Where is Sintikala?"

"Where do you think?"

Marcellinus nodded. The Hawk chief was also out looking for Tahtay. He picked up a piece of cooked buffalo meat, stared at it, and put it down again. "And Isleifur?"

Kimimela pointed to where the Norseman was squatting by another campfire talking to a trio of elderly Blackfoot women. "Isleifur likes his girls wrinkly."

Marcellinus grinned. "When Isleifur is looking for information, he knows who to ask."

Kimimela did not smile back. "He won't come."

"Tahtay? Was he here?"

"No. And if he hasn't come yet, he won't."

"You don't know that."

She fed the fire with buffalo chips, and it glowed warmer, smelling faintly of flowers. "The merda of buffalo is the most pleasant thing about them."

Marcellinus picked up the meat again and took a bite. He would need strength for the long walk.

"Gaius, you've seen the Fire Hearts. Big haughty men, each acting like a chief, striding around, doing less work. They have pledged to give their lives to protect their brothers and families and to never retreat, and for that they are honored. Why would Tahtay throw that away to come to Cahokia?"

"If he can rise to become a Fire Heart in a single year . . ."

Kimimela shook her head. "I asked the woman I scraped skins with today. It is more about being strong and willing. Any strong man can be a Fire Heart if he can fight and will swear to die for his brothers."

Akecheta stirred. "Tahtay fights differently from the other Blackfoot, because we trained him. And he is the son of a chieftain of the Mizipi as well as of a woman of the Blackfoot. If he impressed them and was willing to pledge—"

"Here comes Isleifur."

The Norseman returned to their fire and sat. "They think it will not snow again for a week or two and that the river will not freeze for at least another moon. With the strength of the Wemissori current, we can be in Cahokia by then."

"What about Tahtay?"

Isleifur snorted. "Mingan of the Blackfoot is not in the camp. He is not standing guard at the cliff. Nipekala's friends have not seen her. And none of us have seen either of them today. We've wasted our time." He took off his moccasins and rubbed buffalo fat onto the blisters on his feet while Kimimela looked on in horror. "What? The women say it works."

Appearing between Isleifur and Kimimela with an abruptness that made them jump, Sintikala held her hands out to the fire. "We should sleep."

"So, nothing?" Marcellinus asked.

"We will just have to do this without him," she said bleakly.

"Can we?" Kimimela asked.

Sintikala blinked into the fire and did not answer.

The return trip took eight days, burdened as the Hidatsa party was with hundreds of pounds of meat, rolls of hides, and sacks of horns. The dogs groaned under the weight of the travois, and dogs and humans alike were so weary by midafternoon that they set up camp early.

On the last day the wind was from the north; it carried a bite, but they could smell the river and knew they were close.

"Warriors come, from behind us."

It was Mahkah who sounded the alarm. Everyone else was plodding along staring at the ground. Marcellinus turned, momentarily grateful not to be facing into the wind, as Sooleawa strode back through the party to squint back. She looked at the sky and gave some orders to the Hidatsa.

"She doesn't seem worried."

Marcellinus was. It would surely be easier for a rogue Blackfoot band to ambush them and take their meat than it would be to hunt for it in the first place.

He had no gladius or shield. Only a spear and a bow and arrows not his own.

"Only twelve men?" said Kimimela, who had keener eyes. "Running."

"Even so." Marcellinus had no doubt about the ability of twelve top-notch warriors to devastate this band of a few dozen Hidatsa hunters at the end of their strength.

Sintikala hurried to Sooleawa to confer, and the two hand-talked more quickly than he could follow.

Then Sintikala smiled.

An hour later the eleven warriors of the Fire Hearts and the woman who accompanied them caught up to the Hidatsa band. None were even out of breath, though presumably they had been running all day. Admittedly, they carried nothing more than their spears, a small blanket, and a rawhide provisions bag each.

Tahtay had not lied. Now he ran without a limp, although it was still visible when he walked.

"Do not think I am joining you on the river," he said. "I would see my friends one more time before they return. My mother would talk with Chumanee. And my brothers would see the big canoe. We will go ahead and await you."

"May I run with you?" Mahkah asked.

"Can you keep up?"

"We will see."

And off they went, eleven Blackfoot braves in buckskin tunics, leggings, and sashes of red; one older woman dressed the same except for the sash, much shorter yet seemingly having no difficulty with the pace; and Mahkah, who fell behind them within a mile yet doggedly kept going in their wake.

Marcellinus looked questioningly at Sintikala, but neither of them had the energy to discuss it.

"Fire Hearts do not help carry," Kimimela said dourly, and shouldered her load again.

They slogged on.

* * *

The Cahokians did not stop for long at the Hidatsa winter camp. Much of the meat they carried they left with the Hidatsa in thanks for being guided to the hunt, and in return they were gifted with the buffalo robes they had worn for the last weeks. The remainder of the meat they took to provide a feast for the crew of the *Concordia*. But by the time they arrived at the longship in the early evening, they found that Tahtay and his Blackfoot friends already had a fire going and were roasting haunches of buffalo, presumably acquired from the Hidatsa in passing. The party had begun without them and was cheerful to the point of being raucous.

Despite everything, Marcellinus found he had worked up quite an appetite. Even for buffalo.

Finally, Tahtay stood. "Ina. Hotah. Sintikala. Kimimela. Hurit. Come, I must talk with you."

Kimimela looked past him and shook her head. "What, out into the grass? At night?" As on most nights on the high plains, they could all hear the distant howls of the wolves.

Tahtay's eyes narrowed. "You would make me a chief in Cahokia yet you question everything I say?"

"No. Sorry." Kimimela stood and walked to the edge of the camp.

Marcellinus remembered the grizzled bears and the gray wolves but said nothing. He stood.

Tahtay pointed. "Him, too."

Aelfric looked alarmed. "Me? Leave me out. I don't know anything about this."

"That is why I want you. Come."

Tahtay walked into the grass. Sintikala stood and extended a hand to Nipekala. Together they strode after Tahtay.

"God help me," Aelfric said. "We all deserve to get eaten."

"I'll protect you," said Marcellinus, deadpan.

"That'll be the day." They hurried after the Hesperians, who were already a hundred yards out into the prairie.

"All right. Here."

Away from his new people, Tahtay had an edge of fear and nervousness to him. The Hunting Moon looked down on them. The winds waved the grass.

Tahtay looked at each of them in turn. "I swore I would kill them all. Avenaka, Wahchintonka, Matoshka, the men who killed my father and shamed me. Still I swear this. Is that what you want, Sintikala?"

"Wahchintonka . . ." Sintikala bowed her head and spoke more deferentially than Marcellinus had heard her talk to anyone but Tahtay's father. "Wahchintonka may yet be valuable to Cahokia. He—"

"Wahchintonka betrayed my father."

Sintikala looked around at the rest of them, but Marcellinus was not going to get sidetracked. He doubted the stalwart Wahchintonka had been a willing party to any plot against Great Sun Man, suspected that the Wolf Warrior lieutenant and many elders and clan chiefs had merely bent with the wind, willing to serve Cahokia just as Marcellinus had served Roma, under a broad range of rulers. "Go on, Tahtay."

"I swore this. But I am not ready. I am not yet strong enough."

Again everyone looked at Marcellinus. "And how long, Tahtay, before you are ready?"

"Three winters, I am thinking. And when I go, I will take my brothers of the Fire Hearts. Avenaka's wolves will learn to fear the Blackfoot fire."

Kimimela spoke up. "There will never be a better time than now, Tahtay, to become chief."

"Chief in Cahokia?" Tahtay laughed. "Ridiculous. I speak only of vengeance. I will have my revenge, make Avenaka grovel in the dirt before I slay him, and then I will return here. Cahokia will not make a boy their war chief."

"You are no longer a boy," Marcellinus said.

"My father was only twenty winters when he became war chief in Cahokia," said Sintikala.

"Yes, and twenty winters is not sixteen."

"Nonetheless, you must do it now," Kimimela said. "Later is too late. Do it now or stay here and hunt the stupid buffalo until one of them tramples you into the dirt like a dog."

"Kimimela . . ." Marcellinus began, but Sintikala's hand on his arm stilled him.

"You are going to fight me again, Kimi?" said Tahtay. "Try to break my balls? Here I know how the wind works. I know how to stalk, where the animals hide. I know many things I did not know when I was a child in the Great City."

Kimimela met his eye. "Enopay says we need you. He says you are the hope of Cahokia."

Tahtay's mouth dropped open. "Truly? Enopay says those words?"

"He does," Sintikala said.

"And you agree?"

"Yes. Avenaka will ruin our city and bring only war. You have friends in Cahokia. We must try this, Tahtay. Try to make you war chief."

"Must?" said Tahtay, and to Marcellinus's surprise, Sintikala lowered her eyes. "And what does Kimimela say?"

"Kimimela agrees with Enopay," said Kimimela. "Now is the time for this."

"Because that suits Kimimela. Not because it suits Tahtay."

Kimimela stepped forward. "You are strong enough, Tahtay. You can do this. I would not say it if I did not believe it. I would not risk your life."

"You will do what is in your own interests. Not mine."

"And I will be with you, Tahtay. At your side, whatever happens. Even if—"

"You will stand by me? A girl of thirteen winters? And

what will you do, badger Avenaka with insults till he begs for mercy?"

Marcellinus held his breath. He expected Kimimela to either fly in a rage and start battering Tahtay or storm away across the grass back to the camp. Kimimela did neither. She merely stared, upset.

"And what does Hurit say?"

Hurit wilted as he turned his gaze on her. Marcellinus had never seen the girl so afraid.

"Speak, Hurit," Tahtay said more gently.

"I do not want you to die," she said.

"And if I go to Cahokia, I will die?"

Hurit looked around. "Of all of you, Nipekala and I know Avenaka the best. Avenaka is a hard man. Harder than Great Sun Man, because he is more certain of himself. More cruel. If Avenaka decides you will die, then . . ." She stopped, swallowed, spoke again. "Avenaka says you are his enemy. If you walk into Cahokia, what do *you* think he will do?"

Tahtay nodded.

Hurit raised her chin. "But if you go, I will go and fight by your side, and if Avenaka kills you, then he will have to kill me as well."

"You are all fools," Nipekala said so quietly that it was almost inaudible.

Tahtay grinned and looked at his mother affectionately. "And that is what Ina says?"

"Yes. These people who say they are your friends? You think they will truly stand beside you when you pin your sash to the ground? No. They will stand behind you, far behind. And you? If they killed Mapiya, if they would have killed me, why will they not kill Tahtay?"

Sintikala said: "I will try not to let that happen."

Nipekala snorted. "You will try? That is very comforting, warrior."

"If Tahtay dies, I will die by his side. Not behind him. If they kill Tahtay, they kill me. This I swear."

Sintikala raised her knife to her arm, but Nipekala

reached out. "I will believe your words without blood, Hawk chief."

"But I swear to myself as well as to you." The blade went into her arm.

Marcellinus closed his eyes. Another vow. Now, to keep Sintikala alive, Marcellinus had to keep Tahtay alive as well.

"I, too, will stand with Tahtay," he said. "I swear it."

Tahtay regarded his mother. "And Ina, if I were to do as these people say and go to Cahokia, would you come with me and take your revenge on Huyana?"

"No," Nipekala said. "Never again will I walk among the people who killed my husband. Never again."

There was a long silence. Then Tahtay turned back to the Cahokians. "All this about standing by me, it is easy for you to say, for you are men and women with no tribe, no friends except your people on the big canoe. Outcasts. Your lives are already over."

"My life is not over," Sintikala said.

"But me, I have a tribe, and they have honor. I have a people, and it is not you."

"You are still the son of Great Sun Man. You are still the many-greats-son of Ituha."

"And what of that?" said Tahtay. "Am I not also my mother's son?"

Another long, brittle silence descended. Marcellinus shook his head. This was hopeless.

"Hey, *boy*," Aelfric said. "You've dragged me out here into the grass and bored me to death with your arrogance. I'm cold and I'm tired, and if you're not going to ask me what I think, I'm off back to the fire."

Everyone else grunted in shock, but Tahtay grinned. "Well said. What does Aelfric the Briton say?"

"I think you're right," Aelfric said. "You're not ready. You're too petty. Not mature enough. You may have that pretty red sash and all, but you're not even half ready to be a man."

Tahtay's grin evaporated. "You say so?"

Aelfric nodded. "I do, sonny. And I mean no offense.

I'm not your enemy. But you asked me out here to hear what I had to say. And me, I agree with you. You should stay here at least another two years, maybe three. Get strong. Grow up. And *then* raise some hell in Cahokia if you even care anymore."

Silence.

Marcellinus looked at Aelfric, who shrugged. "Your turn, Wanageeska."

"We don't have two years," Marcellinus said. "We don't even have one. Tahtay, your strength is not just in your arms and legs. Enopay and Sintikala are right. In two more years your father's memory will fade. Cahokia will forget you, perhaps even get comfortable under Avenaka."

"Then if they are comfortable—"

"I am still speaking," Marcellinus said.

After a pause, Tahtay nodded.

"I have two questions for you, Tahtay. Do you want to be the next Great Sun Man, paramount chief in Cahokia?"

"No," Tahtay said contemptuously.

"Very well. And who would make a better Great Sun Man than you? Who could do a better job? Who understands what must be done?"

"My father."

"Ah." Marcellinus bowed his head respectfully. "So now I finally hear you say that perhaps he was a man of honor after all."

Tahtay was silent.

Marcellinus went on. "Anyway, what I meant was, who among the living and breathing?"

Tahtay opened his mouth to speak and then closed it again.

"One more question and then I am finished. If your father could speak to you now, what would he tell you to do?"

Nipekala looked at Marcellinus sharply. Marcellinus kept his stare fixed on Tahtay. "Did I say two questions? I meant three."

Tahtay's fists balled. He took a step forward.

"Breathe," Kimimela said quietly to Tahtay.

Tahtay did not look at her but took a deep breath. "You think I do not know what my father wants of me?"

"I don't think anything. I'm asking *you*."

"And you think that I care what my father would say?"

"Yes, I do."

Tahtay nodded abruptly. "Go back to your camp. All of you."

Immediately Aelfric turned to walk away. "Come on, people. Tahtay has spoken."

"Kimimela can stay," Tahtay said. "The rest of you, go."

"Me?" said Kimimela, and glanced uncertainly at Nipekala and then Hurit. "Me, stay?"

Tahtay looked exasperated. "Always you must question me? Every single time?"

Kimimela shook her head, mute.

Side by side, Marcellinus and Aelfric walked away through the grass. Nipekala marched ahead of them, her back stiff and straight, with Sintikala hurrying after her and Hurit not far behind.

"Well, that was tactless," said Marcellinus.

Aelfric grinned. "Of Tahtay? A real man doesn't ask his mother what to do. He might ask a friend, though."

"I didn't mean Tahtay. I meant you. Too petty? Not half ready?" Marcellinus glanced over his shoulder to where Tahtay and Kimimela still stood three feet apart, looking out over the plains. "Nicely done, Aelfric."

Aelfric nodded. "Once, long ago, you asked me if I had daughters. You never asked if I had a son."

An hour later, when Kimimela walked shivering back into the camp by the longship, Marcellinus was waiting for her. "Where is Tahtay?"

"Where he was before. In the grass."

She made as if to walk by him, but Marcellinus touched her arm. "What did he say?"

"Nothing."

"What did he do, then?"

"Nothing."

"All this time?"

"We just stood quietly after you left us, and in the end he asked me to go, and I left him there."

Out on the high plains a wolf howled plaintively on the night air. Marcellinus shook his head. "I don't understand."

"It's true."

He examined her. "No, it isn't, Kimi."

"He . . ." Kimimela sighed. "Do you command me to tell you?"

Marcellinus thought about that. "No. I'm sorry. That's between the two of you. Come on, let's get you warmed up. The fire isn't completely dead."

He put his arm around her, but she did not move. "Wait."

Marcellinus waited. She looked up at the bright stars. "Tahtay no longer blames his father for seeking peace. But it hurts him to admit this, for he thinks it is . . . wrong of him."

"Well, he—"

Abruptly, Kimimela stepped away from him. "Wanageeska. We will not discuss it. I will tell you, but you will not speak."

Marcellinus had practiced being silent. He nodded. For Kimimela to call him Wanageeska, she must be deadly serious.

"Tahtay thinks it is not manly to seek peace. A warrior should destroy his enemies. Like the Blackfoot do, like Cahokia used to do. Yet his father . . ." She took a deep breath. "And so, part of him thinks we all betrayed him. You. Me. Cahokia."

Marcellinus nodded.

"And he wants to avenge his father. More than anything. For that, too, is what a warrior should do. But he is afraid."

Afraid? Marcellinus signed. If anything, he had grudgingly admired Tahtay's newfound strength and self-assurance.

"Yes. Tahtay is terrified."

Of course, Marcellinus also understood fear, and the tightrope a warrior had to walk between war and peace.

Kimimela turned to him. "I think Tahtay may come with us, Father. Back to Cahokia. But first he must ask the wolves."

"What?" Marcellinus could not stay silent.

"You will not understand. But Tahtay is also Mingan of the Blackfoot. Mingan means 'wolf.' On his walk north to the Blackfoot, many times the wolves stalked around his campfire in the night. Tahtay thought they would kill him. They did not. Instead, they talked to him. And when the Blackfoot first came to fetch Tahtay from the Hidatsa village, in their first words they asked him why he was skulking around like a wolf. And so that is his name here, and if he is to leave here, the wolves must tell him so. Father?"

Marcellinus had walked to the edge of the firelight, looking out onto the cold prairie.

"Tonight he will stay out there in the grass." She yawned hugely. "But me, I'm going to bed. Father? Leave Tahtay to the wolves."

"All night, without even a buffalo robe?"

"Father, come. You cannot go to him. I have spoken."

Marcellinus backed away from the wolves and the night, walked into the firelight, and reluctantly followed his daughter to the longship.

CHAPTER 21

YEAR SIX, FALLING LEAF MOON

They did not march into Cahokia en masse. They ambled into the city in peace and from all directions in ones and twos.

They had spent long hours debating the best strategy, for the right answer was far from obvious. If they marched on Cahokia as a single large party, they would be intercepted and probably attacked before they even arrived at the outskirts of the city. The Wolf Warriors would be watching for threats, whether from Iroqua war parties or from the gigantic Roman legions to the east, and Avenaka's spies surely would be abroad throughout the woodlands. But since the Night of Knives, Cahokia was also alert to the prospect of a hostile force creeping in in darkness. Arriving openly and individually in the early daylight seemed the best compromise, although Akecheta and Aelfric had worried that they would get picked off one by one and that few would survive to walk into the Great Plaza.

Aelfric was not coming, of course, and neither was Isleifur Bjarnason. This was not their fight, and the appearance of unknown non-Hesperian faces could only add a perhaps fatal complication to an already volatile situation. They would stay upriver, guarding the *Concordia*.

If Marcellinus had had his way, Kimimela and Chumanee would have stayed with them for safety, but after raising the idea once, he was so severely abraded by both that he held his tongue. It was their city and their decision, and he had to admit that the presence of obvious noncombatants would help them appear to be peaceful.

For above all else, they hoped that their invasion of Cahokia would be a peaceful one.

No one, least of all Sintikala or Marcellinus, expected this to happen. Tahtay and Marcellinus had been banished, and Sintikala had accepted banishment with them willingly. Their very presence in Cahokia would be a provocation that could not be ignored.

It was cold, crisp, and sunny, and the ground underfoot was dry. Marcellinus and Sintikala came in through the eastern bluffs, past the hill villages, the way least likely to be guarded by Avenaka's soldiers, but their hopes of remaining undetected were dashed quickly. They were noticed right away. Men and women going about their business saw Marcellinus's party of four strolling in and ran off to spread the news either to the Wolf Warriors at the Great Mound or to other parts of the city.

When they were still half a mile from the Great Plaza, Sintikala threw back her hood, and Tahtay did the same. After a brief hesitation Marcellinus followed suit. He had hoped for the dramatic effect of unveiling Tahtay in the Great Plaza, but so many people had recognized the young man already that further subterfuge was pointless.

On Sintikala's other side walked Kimimela, her face clear, her chin up, smiling. Of the four of them, she looked far and away the most relaxed.

And still nobody spoke to them and no one tried to block their way, merely watched them go by or hurried off.

As they approached the plaza, their small groups began to converge. Hanska and Mikasi were the first to join them, and then Akecheta and Mahkah; although he had not seen them, Marcellinus doubted they had ever let him and Tahtay out of their sight. Then all at once there were more, many of them people Marcellinus either did not know or only vaguely recognized. There were a few members of Sintikala's Hawk clan, paint around their eyes in the familiar falcon pattern. Sintikala nodded and smiled to each one. They were soon joined by a large group of men Marcellinus remembered from Ocatan. Against his intentions, a sizable crowd was forming. He gritted his teeth, waiting for it to go bad.

It did not, not yet. And they were within sight of the Great Plaza.

Wahchintonka awaited them on the path alone, a spear in his hand and a grim expression on his face. He ignored everyone but Akecheta, whom he greeted with a curt nod and stepped up to walk beside. Marcellinus glanced at Tahtay, but the youth kept walking and steadily ignored the presence of one of his sworn enemies.

"Wahchintonka, my brother," said Akecheta. "Do you join us, then?"

"You will not enter the Great Plaza. You will come with me."

Akecheta studied him. "We have fought the Iroqua side by side. We have laughed by the fire as brothers. Are we now enemies?"

Wahchintonka's eyes were pained. "I do not wish it so. But you must stop. Turn, walk away, and you may leave Cahokia with your lives."

"You would kill us, then? All of us and the son of Great Sun Man?"

"I would wish you alive, but for that you must turn around. Stay, and . . ."

"And? And, Wahchintonka, if we do not, then what? Say it to my eyes."

"That is up to Avenaka."

Akecheta nodded. "Ah, yes. Avenaka. How can you serve such a man?"

"He is war chief. How can I not?"

Wachiwi ran to them then, a little older but just as pretty, to walk with Hanska. Close behind was Takoda, with Kangee by his side. Marcellinus was astonished. If he had thought about it at all, he would have assumed that Kangee of all people would be against them. Had she liked Great Sun Man and Tahtay more than she had hated him personally? He looked back to see how large their group was becoming and noted that they had been joined by the brickworks gang, youths who had been mere children five years ago but were now on the verge of adulthood.

Enopay had done his job well.

Yet for all their numbers, they were tiny compared with the throng in the Great Plaza.

Marcellinus's breath caught in his throat. He had known the plan: people would begin accumulating in the plaza at dawn, again quietly and from all directions. He saw more warriors from Ocatan and several members of the First Cahokian who had not come on the voyage down the Mizipi, but it looked as if each person had brought ten more.

"Juno," he said. "We might win this."

It was the first words he had spoken for an hour. Sintikala glanced sideways at him with an expression he now knew to be dark amusement. "You think these are all friends to us?"

"Are they not?"

"No. They watch us, surround us."

Tahtay was growing agitated. Entering Cahokia, he had appeared to shrink. The imperiousness he had shown in the grass and for most of the journey down the Wemissori was evaporating.

Just the previous night, he had spoken to Sintikala, Kimimela, and Marcellinus almost formally to declare his strength for what was to come: "The mounds of Cahokia are the land. The grass is the land. I am my father's son, and I am of the land. In this I shall not fail."

He owned none of that sureness now. He was looking

around but avoiding people's eyes. Marcellinus could hear him breathing hard.

"Tahtay!" Sintikala said in an undertone. "Be calm."

Tahtay swallowed and coughed. "Futete. This is . . . we are dead."

"Trade," said Kimimela, and swapped places with her mother to walk by Tahtay. She seized his hand and squeezed it. Tahtay looked at her in surprise, and she met his eye. "Breathe deep. Be a leader. And stop being an idiot or I will smack your head again."

"Huh. Just try it," Tahtay said, but his breathing returned to normal and he raised his chin boldly.

"Better to die on the hunt," she prompted.

Tahtay nodded. "Better to die on the hunt, or in battle, than old or sick." It was a Blackfoot saying, words Tahtay had quoted to them many times on the journey south. "I shall not fail."

Marcellinus eyed the throng as they continued to walk. He saw frowns and scowls, smiles and simple expressions of interest. He could not tell who was for them and who against, but he was painfully aware that only the Wolf Warriors scattered among the crowd were carrying weapons.

Sintikala stopped. "Here."

Marcellinus came to a halt. Tahtay and Kimimela were to his left, Akecheta to his right, and Hanska, Mikasi, Mahkah, and Wachiwi not far behind. And surrounding them all was a huge and mostly silent crowd of Cahokians and Ocatani.

He had no idea what would happen next, but he was glad to be there. He had missed Cahokia's huge mounds, its grandeur, its people. And looking at Sintikala's steadfast face in the morning sunshine, he knew that she was happy and proud to be back in Cahokia as well.

The Longhouse of the Sun had grown even larger in their absence. The sides of the Great Mound and the other major mounds were more cleanly carved, their corners sharply delineated in dark clay. In that, they looked more like the mounds of Shappa Ta'atan than like the Cahokian mounds he had grown accustomed to. Marcellinus was all for neatness and had spent his professional life insisting on good order, but even to his eye this did not seem like an improvement. Avenaka's Cahokia was not as much to his taste.

The gates of the palisade around the Great Mound were closed tight. A double line of Wolf Warriors stood in front of it, and Wahchintonka had walked ahead to stand with them. Another new thing: warriors also stood along the top of the palisade. It now had a walkway inside it in the same style as Woshakee and Shappa Ta'atan. Cahokia had not needed such protections when Marcellinus had first arrived.

Until now they had seen no one atop the Great Mound. The space inside the palisade had seemed deserted. Now a man stepped out of the Longhouse of the Sun and walked to the plateau's edge, a muscular-looking man wearing a kilt and feather cape and carrying a chert mace in both hands, a man who looked so much like Great Sun Man that Marcellinus's breath caught in his throat.

"Shit," Kimimela whispered.

"I will kill him." Tahtay's voice was low, and he appeared on the verge of choking. "I *will* kill him. I shall not fail."

"Yes," said Sintikala. "But for now, hush."

As if they had heard, the buzz of the crowd stilled.

More people came out of the longhouse. Marcellinus recognized the elders Matoshka, Ogleesha, Kanuna, and Anapetu of the Raven clan, but most of the others were unknown to him. Two groups of warriors jogged around the building, each taking a place at a corner of the plateau. Two men walked down the cedar steps to the lower plateau and parted to stand on either side: the hand-talkers.

A speech, then. Avenaka had been alerted to their approach and had allowed them to pass through Cahokia to hear whatever he had to say.

Marcellinus scanned the faces of the Wolf Warriors

arrayed against them. He shifted his stance very slightly, now clasping his hands in front of him. From this position it would be easier to pull the cloak aside and grab his gladius. Sintikala did not look at him, but he knew she had registered the movement. Tahtay, carrying no weapon, glanced nervously back over his shoulder.

"Strength, Fire Heart," Kimimela whispered. "Stand tall. Show them all who you are."

Tahtay blinked, exhaled, and raised his head again.

"And so the wanderers return," said Avenaka.

Again Marcellinus noted that the new war chief's voice was deeper than Great Sun Man's but just as loud and sonorous.

"Yes," Tahtay said very loudly and without a tremor in his voice. "I would talk in council with Avenaka, the elders of Cahokia, and my clan chiefs."

Avenaka stared. A ripple of shock spread across the Great Plaza at his words. Nobody interrupted a war chief of Cahokia.

Nobody until today. The hand-talkers looked at each other and did not translate Tahtay's words into gesture, but the muttering of the crowd was surely enough to send news of the interruption back to those who had not heard it.

Smoothly, Avenaka recovered and continued. "Sintikala, Hawk chief and daughter of chieftain, and you brave warriors of Cahokia, you are welcome. I tell you again what I have said before: you are welcome in the Great City and may return to your families and friends with open arms if you pledge loyalty to Cahokia."

Sintikala lifted her chin and spoke. "I am Sintikala, Hawk chief, and always I am loyal to Cahokia. But to Avenaka? No, because Avenaka will lead Cahokia to destruction."

This, again, the hand-talkers of Avenaka did not translate for the assembled crowds.

Now Enopay appeared on the crest of the Great Mound and pointed to his left with both hands. The eyes of the crowd swiveled. On the Mound of the Sun to their left, clearly visible to most of them, stood another hand-talker, repeating Sintikala's words, pausing, and then repeating them again.

Avenaka glared across at Enopay. Marcellinus hoped the boy had not just signed his own death warrant.

Avenaka spoke. "Tahtay, son of a coward, son of a shamed chieftain: you I banished from Cahokia. But here you are before me. How can that be? Do you come to pledge allegiance to Cahokia? If so, despite the cold winters past, if you reject the father that betrayed us all, even you may be welcome."

A murmur rippled around the crowd.

Tahtay took a deep breath. "I do not pledge loyalty to Avenaka. I come to avenge my father Mapiya, Great Sun Man of Cahokia, loved by all his people, and I come to serve Cahokia, lead if Cahokia wills it, and help my people in their next great struggle, against the Romans."

Again Enopay's hand-talker relayed his words. The rustling of the unsettled crowd grew louder.

Avenaka laughed. "I do not need the help of a boy for that. Or of the Wanageeska." Avenaka regarded Marcellinus from the mound's platform, and despite himself, Marcellinus felt a chill. "You, a Roman whose life was spared by our mercy but who brought us death at the hands of the Iroqua and then helped the coward Mapiya rob us of our revenge. Yet Cahokia *will* have its revenge, after we have slaughtered the rest of your people."

Marcellinus grinned tightly and said nothing. The Great Plaza was not the place for him to speak, and he would not have risen to Avenaka's bait in any case.

"What shame can it be, I wonder, to stand here among the warriors who spilled the blood and took the scalps of your Roman soldiers as they wept and begged? To have watched them all die? And to know that these same warriors will destroy the next army of your people, will cut them down in droves? Me, I would die before I accepted such shame. But you? You we will keep alive, tied high on a frame to witness the slaughter. You, Wanageeska, will again be the last Roman we leave alive. And then we will keep you alive a little longer."

Kimimela edged forward in front of Marcellinus, her hand on the hilt of her dagger.

Out of the side of his mouth Marcellinus said to the others, "Wolf Warriors are moving through the crowd."

"Let them," Sintikala said.

"Soon we will be surrounded."

"No," said Sintikala. "The people will not allow it."

Marcellinus shook his head. She was wrong. So far Avenaka had sounded strong and reasonable, and he obviously had only gained in power and authority over the years. Enopay's idea of replacing Avenaka with Tahtay surely had to seem absurd to the Cahokians assembled here. And if warriors fell on them, it would be a brief and bloody fight with only one outcome.

Odd now to remember that just a few evenings earlier Tahtay had suggested that Avenaka might ignore them completely and then quietly kill them in the night.

Again, Avenaka was waiting.

Sintikala half grinned and raised her voice. "Then Avenaka will have to slay us all, and from the skies we will look down on Avenaka after death and watch how Avenaka fights the Romans without his Catanwakuwa, without his Wakinyan."

From the left came Demothi and the Hawk clan, forcing a path through the crowd. Men and women fell back out of their way so that they could take their place behind Sintikala.

From the right, and much more slowly, came the Thunderbird clan. They were led by Ojinjintka, who had seen so many winters that she was as wrinkled as old fruit. She walked with a stick and leaned on Luyu, who was Kimimela's age but was so skinny that she looked almost as frail as her grandmother.

Despite Sintikala's words, Marcellinus knew that this was barely half of the Hawks and a mere fraction of the Thunderbird clan. The aerial clans might have a better grasp of what was possible against a huge Roman army and what was not, but they were hardly united against Avenaka. This was a dangerous bluff. Avenaka would not be fooled, and indeed he was already laughing.

But this gambit was not aimed at him. Sintikala and Enopay hoped to win over the crowd.

"And so Avenaka is already defeated," Tahtay said boldly. "We will come forward now and claim the Great Mound."

Over on the Mound of the Sun, where Great Sun Man had lived, Avenaka's Wolf Warriors had gotten to Enopay's hand-talker and were dragging him away. Now Enopay himself stepped forward to translate Tahtay's words into hand-talk for the crowds below. A warrior detached himself from Avenaka's entourage and strode toward the boy.

Avenaka merely shook his head as if Tahtay were speaking gibberish, but Marcellinus could feel the rapid rise in the tension of the crowd behind him.

Marcellinus had seen riots before. He had quelled a few in huge cities deep in Asia. He knew that if conditions were dry enough, it took just one spark to turn a crowd into a mob. This crowd was ready; supporters and opponents of Avenaka were arguing openly, pushing and shoving all around him. The crowd was split, and now they were igniting like liquid flame. "Kimimela—"

The First Cahokian forced its way up to surround Tahtay and Marcellinus, Sintikala and Kimimela. It was not just the men and women who had accompanied them down the Mizipi but others who shoved through from the sides, unarmed yet ready for the fray. They and the Ocatani bunched around Marcellinus and the others and began to surge forward toward the gate.

The crowd did not stop them. The crowd had its own problems. Fights were breaking out all around them, and those not fighting were screaming, pushing, running to get away.

Marcellinus grabbed Kimimela, holding her close with one hand, with the other held out in front of them to prevent her from getting crushed. Sintikala and Akecheta stood shoulder to shoulder behind Tahtay, guarding his back. The five of them had become the epicenter of a giant brawling mob, some actively punching and kicking one another while others shouted and argued. And from beneath her cloak Sintikala had produced her ax.

Marcellinus risked a glance up. Avenaka was pointing now, gesturing left and right, and the Wolf Warriors were marshaling fast and taking control of the perimeter of the plaza as best they could. Exactly what Marcellinus would have tried to do in Avenaka's place.

The First Cahokian was propelling them forward so fast that Marcellinus was having trouble keeping his footing. He stumbled, and Tahtay grabbed his arm. "Steady, Hotah."

"Merda . . ."

On the top of the Great Mound a similar scene was playing out in miniature. Although he could not hear her he could see Anapetu shouting, her cotton Raven cloak billowing around her. A Wolf Warrior seized her arm and tried to pull her aside, but Anapetu and Kanuna fought him off.

Marcellinus had lost sight of Enopay. Where was the boy? Had Avenaka's Wolf Warrior gotten to him?

Amid it all Avenaka stood, calm as a beaker of water, ignoring the arguments to either side of him and looking down over the plaza. He gestured in broad movements that Marcellinus could not follow, the secret gestures of warrior sign.

If the Wolf Warriors prevailed and dispersed the squabbling crowd, Tahtay, the First Cahokian, and their more vociferous confederates among the crowd would be captured, swept away, and disposed of. It was they who had created the problem, they whom Avenaka would slay to restore the peace. And once they were gone, Avenaka could reestablish order quickly.

The First Cahokian had covered half the distance separating them from the gates when their momentum stalled. In front of the gates stood a double line of armed warriors under Wahchintonka's command. Although none of them looked thrilled at the prospect of fighting their own people, they obviously did not lack resolve.

Another movement from above caught Marcellinus's eye. At the corners of the Great Mound groups of bowmen were assembling. "Archers!"

Wahchintonka looked around in disbelief, then bellowed and signaled up the mound, fury in his every gesture, ordering the archers to stand down. They either did not hear or took no notice, nocking arrows and surveying the crowd, awaiting further orders.

As casually as if they had met by Cahokia Creek at the end of a quiet day, Akecheta said, "Let us through, Wahchintonka."

Wahchintonka barely spared him a glance.

Tahtay stepped up. "Wahchintonka, if you believe in Cahokia, if you ever loved my father at all, open the gates."

Wahchintonka shook his head helplessly. The men around him stood firm.

"This is the Cahokia you want? At war with itself?"

A high, terrifying sound cut through the furor. Enopay had reappeared and was running along the top of the Great Mound toward the archers, screaming at the top of his voice and waving at them in broad hand-talk, "No! No! No!"

As he drew close, the Wolf Warrior captaining the lefthand squad of archers stepped forward and kicked him, bowling him over. Enopay tumbled, slid on the grass, and went over the edge of the Great Mound. He rolled ten or twelve feet down the incline until he came to rest, curled up and clutching his stomach.

Tahtay howled and burst forward, away from Sintikala and Akecheta, crashing into the front line of Wolf Warriors. They recoiled, lifting their axes away to avoid harming him; Tahtay was young and held no weapon.

Their movement left a gap, and Sintikala lunged for it. One of Wahchintonka's men swung his ax, aiming a lethal blow. Sintikala swung to defend herself. The hafts of their axes met, and Sintikala's spun away into the air. Growling, she leaped forward and locked her hands around the warrior's throat.

Akecheta stepped up to shield Tahtay with his body as the rabble surged again with new vigor, the noise now deafening.

On the ground, Sintikala and the Wolf Warrior wrestled for the upper hand. Marcellinus shoved again, desperate to reach her. In front of him, Wahchintonka raised his club.

And at the same time shook his head and with his other hand gestured, *Hit me*.

Marcellinus clasped his hands and jumped, bringing his joined fists down on the warrior. The blow was all for show, for he pulled it at the last moment and his wrists bounced off Wahchintonka's shoulder. Wahchintonka made it look good: he spun in fake pain and dropped to the ground to the right of the palisade gate. He rolled and lay prone, his eyes darting to the left and right.

Sintikala snapped the neck of the warrior beneath her and leaped up. The braves on either side of her lowered their weapons and backed away.

"Step off, warriors!" Akecheta yelled against the din. "Let us through or die!"

And they did. Faced with the prospect of offering lethal force against Akecheta, Tahtay, and Sintikala, with their captain down and making no attempt to rise, the Wolf Warriors stepped back.

Tahtay pushed at the gate, Marcellinus at his side. The gates swung open. Hanska was to the left of Marcellinus and Akecheta to his right as the First Cahokian burst through.

Once again Marcellinus found himself pounding up the grassy slope of the Great Mound followed by a body of warriors, but this time they were Cahokian and Ocatani.

Above them, the archers loosed their shots. A wave of arrows flew by. Some barely skimmed the grass, and others flew over their heads. Were the warriors trying to get their range or deliberately aiming to miss? Marcellinus had no time to think about it. But when a Hawk craft soared over him, he ducked instinctively.

A second Hawk followed it into the air and then a third, obviously flying up off the launch rail behind the mound.

Akecheta and the other warriors of the First ran past Marcellinus now. Younger than he, angrier than he, they bellowed with rage.

Panting, Marcellinus looked up. A Hawk craft whirled by, and one of the archers on the mound's corner went over backward. With deadly accuracy, the Hawk pilot had hurled a rock with his sling.

More Cahokians surged through the gates, some trying to run up the mound and others trying to stop them. The massive brawl was extending onto the sacred surface of the Great Mound. Far off to his left on the mound slope Enopay was sitting up, gasping, his head lowered. But Sintikala had vanished, nor could Marcellinus see Demothi or the other Hawk pilots.

Now he heard the telltale ring of swords. The square below him might be mostly an unarmed brawl, but above the battle had turned deadly. Marcellinus's gladius still hung from his belt. He had promised Sintikala he would try to avoid spilling Cahokian blood, and so far he had kept his vow, but now . . .

Tahtay was above him and had acquired a sword. Still short of the mound top, he was engaged in a bitter duel with a warrior Marcellinus did not recognize, and this brave certainly was not pulling his blows. Akecheta and Hanska had engaged, too, and Mahkah and others were crashing into the fray. Marcellinus sucked air into his lungs and ran on.

Another Hawk flew up and unfurled, and Marcellinus recognized Demothi from his stocky frame. Larger than the average Hawk pilot, he was easy to spot. Apparently the archers hoped he would be just as easy to hit, because as he looped quickly around and down, a wave of arrows from the right-hand squad shot past him. Demothi in turn released a single fast arrow into their midst and hooked sharply upward.

Marcellinus had missed what had happened, but Akecheta and Tahtay now were running for the mound crest side by side. With a last desperate burst of speed Marcellinus drew his gladius and followed. As he achieved the crest of the mound, a warrior came barreling at him from his right. In the split second Marcellinus had to react, he recognized Ohanzee and raised his sword, but Ohanzee's club came down hard in a glancing blow, striking just below his shoulder.

Instantly, Marcellinus's arm went dead. His gladius dropped out of his hand and bounced on the grass.

Ducking to grab it would have been suicide. Instead Marcellinus leaned backward and away and drew his pugio with his left hand, but the Raven warrior's chest slammed into him and knocked him over.

Marcellinus rolled left, toward the edge of the mound, and Ohanzee's club thudded into the clay next to him. Ohanzee dropped to pin him, his knee on Marcellinus's good arm. Marcellinus kicked, and drove his knee into Ohanzee's ribs. Spittle flew from the warrior's mouth, but it was open only because Ohanzee was smiling. Snatching the pugio from Marcellinus's hand, Ohanzee stabbed it down into his chest, and bellowed.

The shout was one of pain, as Marcellinus was wearing his breastplate under his Cahokian tunic. Roman steel deflected Roman steel, and the pugio spun away.

Ohanzee punched Marcellinus viciously in the face. His other hand was coming in for Marcellinus's eyes. Marcellinus kicked again, but the warrior was impossible to dislodge. He thrashed as Ohanzee held his fist ready, waiting. The brave's next blow surely would break Marcellinus's nose and end the fight.

Another weight landed on Marcellinus's legs. Ohanzee's head jerked back, pulled by the hand that had just grabbed his hair. A blade flashed and sank deep into Ohanzee's neck. Marcellinus turned his head away to avoid the gush of blood and found himself looking up into Kimimela's eyes.

Her face contorted with fury, she pulled Ohanzee's spasming body off Marcellinus and hacked at his scalp inexpertly, jamming the pugio into the warrior's hairline again and again.

Marcellinus shook his head to fling away Ohanzee's blood. The fight still raged all around them, dozens of Cahokians slashing at one another, wounding, killing; Marcellinus could barely tell the two sides apart. He scooped up his gladius with his left hand and shoved himself awkwardly upright while at his feet his daughter took her unholy revenge on Ohanzee, who was still jerking in his death throes. "Kimi, stop! Stand up. Be ready . . ."

In front of them the tide of fighting bodies parted, and there was Avenaka, dressed in his kilt and tunic, swinging his chert mace against Akecheta, centurion of the First Cahokian. Akecheta parried the blow with his shield and swung with his ax, which the war chief knocked aside with contempt. Then another Wolf Warrior, fresh from a kill of his own, swung a club at Akecheta's legs, and he went down.

The sky above Marcellinus blinked as a Catanwakuwa flew over him so low that it almost grazed his head. It slammed into Avenaka and smashed him back into the wall of the Longhouse of the Sun. The Hawk exploded in a mess of spars, skin, and sinew, and Sintikala skidded and rolled and banged into the wall, still attached to the wreckage.

Avenaka shoved and spit, tangled up in the mess of the Hawk. Sintikala came upright, broken wood and wire hanging from her shoulders. She tried to pull an ax from its strap across her back, but it snagged in the remains of the wing.

"Sintikala!" Marcellinus threw his gladius to her. She knocked it aside out of the air and then saw what it was and picked it up.

Avenaka was on her now, his chert mace swinging.

She parried, but the stone club's greater weight knocked the gladius out of her hand, up and away.

But the mace was not an agile weapon, and it was still swinging in its arc as Sintikala ducked under Avenaka's arm, snatched the proffered ax from Akecheta's hand, and slammed it viciously into the war chief's chest.

Marcellinus ran forward in case others of Avenaka's men attacked her, but Tahtay was quicker, leaping in to slash his gladius across Avenaka's throat.

Tahtay swung again and a third time, and Avenaka's head came away from his body, rolling grotesquely across the clay of the mound top.

Already Wolf Warriors were backing away and tossing their weapons aside. Several dropped to their knees and held up their hands to protect their heads and show they were no longer armed.

Not Matoshka, though. The elder warrior thundered forward, ululating, his studded club held high. Marcellinus turned to face the threat. Mahkah was quicker, running in from the side to drag his gladius across Matoshka's gut. The warrior folded and fell.

Mahkah raised his sword, but Tahtay held up his hand. "Let the traitor bleed." Akecheta's arm was up, too. Mahkah backed off. Matoshka tried to pull himself to his feet, his face a snarl, and then swayed and crashed down again, clutching his stomach.

Sintikala ran to Kimimela and scooped her up to carry her away from Ohanzee's corpse, away from the other warriors. More than anything, Marcellinus wanted to follow and make sure Kimimela was all right, but there was work to be done here.

Mahkah helped Akecheta to his feet. Tahtay stood, gladius still held high, apparently dazed.

"What are your orders, sir?" Marcellinus said, and then, because this really could not wait: "Tahtay! We must stop the fighting below."

"Yes," said Tahtay, and looked toward Sintikala and Kimimela.

"You must tell them," Marcellinus said. "I cannot. Tahtay? It is not for me to give the orders. You must."

Tahtay blinked at him once, twice, and then reached down for Avenaka's head. Raising it high by the hair, he strode forward. "Stop fighting! The battle is won! Avenaka is destroyed!"

His words were almost lost in the noise, but from the mound's base came the boom of Wahchintonka's voice. "Everyone stand still! Avenaka is dead, and Tahtay is war chief of Cahokia!"

Akecheta took Tahtay's other hand and raised it. Behind them Mahkah and others were dragging Avenaka's bloody corpse forward, holding it up, too, for the people to see.

All across the plaza the riot was fizzling. Together, Wahchintonka's warriors and the braves from Ocatan, those of the First Cahokian who were still down in the square, and others were fanning out among the crowd and pulling the remaining brawlers apart.

Avenaka's reign had ended.

Not far away, Youtin and Kiche were flat on the ground, pinned by warriors of the First Cahokian. "Do not kill the shamans," Marcellinus said to Tahtay. "It will only inflame the people again. We need calm in Cahokia now. Be magnanimous in victory."

"As long as everyone swears fealty to me?" Tahtay shook his head as if still unable to believe what was happening around him.

Marcellinus frowned, uncertain whether the boy was joking. "No good leader demands fealty. He assumes it. Unite the warriors, and the people will follow." He gestured at the plaza. "Look, they are already working together."

"I can see that. I am not an idiot."

Marcellinus nodded.

Kanuna was by Matoshka's side, trying to staunch the bleeding from his gut. The elder warrior glared and grimaced with pain, but all the fight had left him. Hurit, sword in hand, had appeared and run to Anapetu, her clan chief, and Dustu stepped up to stand by Tahtay. Sintikala was still holding Kimimela, talking to her. Marcellinus ached to run to them.

Tahtay pulled himself together. "Hotah? Bring me my elders; bring me my clan chiefs. I must speak with them immediately. Akecheta? Put the Wolf Warriors to work taking away the dead and cleaning up. We must keep them busy, and blood must not stay on the soil of the Great Mound."

Akecheta nodded and turned away to give the orders. The First Cahokian began to escort Wolf Warriors off the top of the mound.

Hanska and Hurit were entering the Longhouse of the Sun with blades drawn, Anapetu in their wake. Marcellinus hesitated, wondering if he should go with them.

"Mahkah? When calm is restored, bring me Wahchintonka." He glanced at Marcellinus. "Yes, yes, I saw what he did. I will spare him, too. He is too useful to kill."

Marcellinus looked out over the city. The plaza was emptying, corpses being carried off, the injured and stunned being helped away. Chumanee was surely busy.

To his right were the Mound of the Sun and the Mound of the Smoke, and beyond them the giant red poles of the Circle of the Cedars. In front of him were the Mound of the Hawks and the Mound of the Chiefs. Dozens of smaller conical, platform, and ridge mounds dotted the landscape, and off in the distance was the brown ribbon of the eternal Mizipi. There were the steelworks and brickworks, and the Big Warm House, and the Mound of the Sky Lanterns. Late sunflowers still bloomed outside Cahokian huts.

It was hard to believe he was back in Cahokia. He had never expected to be here again. It definitely felt like coming home.

Behind him Hurit and Hanska reappeared at the door of the Longhouse of the Sun, dragging someone between them. By her clothing Marcellinus recognized Huyana, sister of Avenaka and past wife of Great Sun Man.

Huyana's nose was broken, her mouth full of blood, and she appeared too groggy to walk. Without ceremony, the warrior women dragged her to Tahtay.

Tahtay looked down at her as dispassionately as Huyana once had looked down on the dying body of her husband. "Huyana."

She blinked at him, dripping blood.

"See, here is your brother's head on a spear. Dead, as I swore." Tahtay squatted and looked into her eyes. "I should keep you alive for a very long time. Not for my sake but for my mother, who you would have killed if you had gotten to her before my friends did. But you are not worth the time. So we will kill you quickly and forget you, just as you would have killed and forgotten her. Huyana? Do you hear me?"

Huyana's lips moved. "I mourned when you fell in battle. I did all I could for you then. And the day Great Sun Man died, I urged Avenaka not to spill your blood."

"You supported Avenaka. Abandoned my father."

"Forgive me . . ."

"Beg my father for forgiveness. You will have none from me."

He nodded to Hurit.

Hurit slit Huyana's throat with the pugio, leaning in with all her strength to make it swift and sure.

Tahtay stood and turned away from her without another word. Hurit's eyes followed him, hurt, but Anapetu beckoned, guiding Hurit and Hanska off the mound, leaving Huyana's body lying in the grass.

Marcellinus felt sick. Had it come to this? Would Tahtay slaughter all his enemies one by one?

"Tahtay?" It was Kanuna, holding the wounded body of Matoshka upright on his knees. As Tahtay looked around, Matoshka ripped his necklace of bear claws aside, baring his breast in defiance. Tahtay walked slowly across the mound top toward him.

Marcellinus followed. Matoshka was panting. The deep gash in his stomach still wept blood.

"Ah, Matoshka, who supported Avenaka in killing my father."

Matoshka spit. "Avenaka was strong, and your father was weak. You know this."

Tahtay drew his pugio. "I swore I would kill you."

Matoshka smiled. "Then do it. Better to die in battle than live with cowards and bow to a boy."

"This is not battle," Tahtay said. "This is shame. And you, too, I should keep alive for a while longer, but you do not deserve that honor either. And nobody will eat your heart, for it is the heart of a coward and should be eaten by a dog."

"That is not true! I have the heart of a bear!"

"No, you do not, and you have failed Cahokia."

He reached down and grabbed Matoshka's hair, put his pugio to his throat, and then looked at Marcellinus.

In Latin, Tahtay said, "Should I kill him, Gaius?"

Marcellinus raised his eyebrows. "You are chief now. You decide."

"You once told me my first kill should not be a man in defeat on his knees. But it was. Should my second be also?"

"Avenaka was your first kill?"

"Yes. Is Matoshka still a danger to me?"

Matoshka squinted up at them, uncomprehending, but his head was drooping. Pain was winning out over bravado.

"Perhaps," Marcellinus said.

"If I spare him, will he think me weak like my father? Or can he help me be accepted by the Wolf Warriors and hard men in western Cahokia?"

"I don't know."

Tahtay looked exasperated. "Hotah, if you stood where I stand now, would you kill Matoshka?"

"No," Marcellinus said. "Enough have died already. And you are a bigger man than this."

"Huh," said Tahtay, taken aback.

Kanuna frowned. "Never mind. You have talked Matoshka to death . . . No, his heart still beats. He is just unconscious."

"Then perhaps when he awakens, it is worse to make him bow to a boy." Tahtay let go of Matoshka's hair, wiped his hand on his tunic, and walked away without looking back.

Kanuna looked up at Marcellinus. "Was that mercy, weakness, or prudence?"

"You're asking the wrong man," Marcellinus said. "Fetch Chumanee. Unless she's looking after someone more important."

Kanuna laid the unconscious Matoshka down and set off on his errand. Marcellinus flexed his right arm. The feeling was coming back into it. He walked to where Tahtay stood looking out over the plaza. "And where will you live now, war chief? Here on the Great Mound?"

Tahtay shuddered. "No. I will live on the Mound of the Sun, where I grew up." He looked at the longhouse. "This stupid golden hut has been here too long. My father should never have built it. I will tear it down as if it has never been."

"Good."

The plaza was now almost empty. Marcellinus cleared his throat. "Tahtay? Well done. You did not fail."

"You, too, Hotah," Tahtay said. "And now, please, my clan chiefs."

At afternoon's end, Tahtay addressed the people of Cahokia for the first time. Fortuitously, the clouds had rolled back and the sun shone across the plaza. The boy spoke well and clearly, giving the honor for the victory to Sintikala and Akecheta, who flanked him. To his left were the assembled elders, and to his right were the clan chiefs. Wahchintonka and Marcellinus stood together on the very edge of the group, with Kimimela and Enopay beside them.

Tahtay's speech dwelled on the iniquities of Avenaka and made no mention of the Cahokians who had supported him. The people in the plaza knew all too well which elders and chiefs and shamans those were and saw them now standing in unity with Tahtay.

It was the first time Marcellinus had stood on the Great Mound for a speech by a Cahokian leader since he had been hauled up there as a defeated Praetor. He had his doubts about standing there now, but Tahtay, Sintikala, and the elders had agreed that it was essential that all the important people in Cahokia be seen united. Marcellinus would be an essential part of any negotiations with Roma, and this was the time for the people of Cahokia to understand that.

Marcellinus had agreed on condition that he was not separated from Kimimela. His daughter was still in shock from the battle on this very mound just hours earlier, but as Tahtay spoke, Marcellinus felt her relax beside him and draw herself up to her full height. She would be a great leader, too, one day. Of that, Marcellinus had no doubt.

Tahtay finished by swearing to tear down the Longhouse of the Sun and to be the wisest chief he could with the help of the men and women around him, who *were* Cahokia and always would be. He promised to honor his father's memory and not to take the title of Great Sun Man for himself for another five summers, and then only if the elders and chiefs were in agreement.

As he raised his hands high and the audience in the plaza began to cheer, the sun set. In addition to a loud voice, Tahtay had inherited his father's sense of timing. It was an auspicious beginning.

CHAPTER 22

YEAR SIX, FALLING LEAF MOON

It was Tahtay's first night in the Mound of the Smoke, and he was late. Marcellinus arrived to find everyone present except their new war chief, a viciously hot fire blazing, and no one talking at all. Ogleesha and Matoshka sat side by side, glaring at Howahkan. Kanuna squatted as if at any moment he might make a leap for the door. The other elders sat motionless, including some Marcellinus did not recognize, presumably those introduced during the reign of Avenaka.

As he shuffled into the lodge and sat down by Howahkan, Matoshka turned his head to stare balefully at him. "Ah. The Roman."

Bandages wrapped the elder's midsection, and he moved with difficulty. Mahkah's slash obviously had not gone deep, but Marcellinus remembered the pain such wounds could bring. Marcellinus nodded. "Good evening, Matoshka."

The old warrior blinked. "Luck went with you, down the Mizipi. I had not thought you would still be alive."

Levelly, Marcellinus replied, "And you, too, are lucky to live and sit here among us."

Ogleesha opened his mouth to speak, then closed it and looked away.

Marcellinus glanced at Howahkan, read the warning in his old friend's eyes, and ignored it. "And so, Matoshka, and you, Ogleesha, tell me truly. You welcomed the death of Great Sun Man?"

There was a broad intake of breath from every elder present. Matoshka looked at him, not blinking. "You say so?"

"I merely ask."

Matoshka lowered his head. "I disagreed with Mapiya. I still do. The Iroqua cannot be trusted. We will not have peace until our enemy is dead and burned. And so I thought Great Sun Man was wrong. But I did not want him to die."

"Huh," said Howahkan.

Marcellinus persisted. "But once he was dead, you accepted Avenaka as leader."

"Of course. We are both Bear clan."

"And now that Avenaka is dead, you will accept Tahtay as leader." He did not phrase it as a question.

Matoshka eyed him. "For now, I do not see a better choice. And so again, yes."

"The people want Tahtay," Ogleesha said. "He is young and new, but his heart beats with the blood of Ituha. The people think they can make of him the leader they need. We will see if they are right."

"And why not Wahchintonka?" Marcellinus asked. "Wahchintonka is a great warrior. Wahchintonka defended Cahokia. He knows much of war."

Ogleesha shook his head. "You know why."

"Tell me."

"Because on the day the Iroqua entered Cahokia, Wahchintonka stayed behind the walls to defend the Great Mound while the Iroqua savages ran through the streets and slaughtered our people and broke open our sacred mounds."

"But those were his orders," Marcellinus said. "He was doing his duty."

"Orders?" Ogleesha snorted. "Those were his *people*."

"Those were his orders, and he was right to obey

them." Howahkan fed more sticks to the fire, and another great gout of smoke wafted up.

"Me, I agree," said Matoshka. "If we had lost the Great Mound, the city would have fallen forever. We know this, for we are wise in war. Wahchintonka knows this. But that is why he can never be war chief, because he knows *only* war, and the people remember what he did not do as much as what he did. More people blame him for the deaths in Cahokia than blame you."

Marcellinus shook his head.

"Yes. And that is another reason that I say luck goes with you, Wanageeska."

"There is no *luck*," Kanuna said. "For that day the Wanageeska also led an army of Cahokia against an Iroqua army. If he had not pushed back that army and forced it to rejoin the other army on the Mizipi, Cahokian blood would have fallen like rain, and yes, the city would have fallen forever. And so you are old and foolish if you talk of *luck*."

Matoshka sneered. "You know nothing of war."

Kanuna rocked on his heels and glared. "Oh, my friend, I know more than enough."

And then the doorskin was pulled back, and Tahtay crawled into the smoke lodge.

All eyes turned. Some of the elders looked at him with curiosity, for they barely knew him, and others eyed him with trepidation.

Tahtay nodded to them and, ignoring the empty place between Marcellinus and Howahkan, took a seat next to Matoshka. "I am glad to see you all. Thank you for coming."

Ogleesha and Matoshka looked at each other.

"You have been arguing," Tahtay said. "I see it in your eyes, and I smell it in the air. And perhaps you have been arguing about what to do about the armies of Roma that threaten us from two sides, and perhaps you have been arguing about me." He looked around. "Ah. Me, then. Well, I have one thing to say about that, and it is that none of you know me. Not a one of you."

Kanuna looked incredulous, but Marcellinus was inclined to agree: again and again, Tahtay was doing things he did not expect.

"You believe you know me either because you knew my father and think I am the same or because you knew me when I was a child. I am not that child, and if you do not see that now, you will learn it in the moons to come."

Tahtay met each man's eyes in turn. When he got to Matoshka, the grizzled old warrior said, "And what do you propose, boy?"

"I propose to defend Cahokia against Roma with my life and as many other lives as are necessary," Tahtay said steadily.

Now everyone looked at Marcellinus, who kept absolutely still and waited.

Tahtay continued. "And I will need your help. For I am young, and you are men of many winters and much wisdom. I will ask each of you what you think, here in the lodge and outside it, and I will respect what you say and weigh it when I make my decisions. I will also ask the clan chiefs and others of great knowledge, and respect what they say, and weigh it along with your words."

After a long pause, Kanuna said, "So we will fight?"

"If Cahokia must fight, then fight we will. Always we will fight if we must. Always we will defend ourselves. Always we will preserve our honor."

Kanuna and Matoshka's eyes locked.

"But," said Tahtay, and waited. The silence in the sweat lodge grew around him, and no man spoke. Tahtay nodded and continued. "But I will not shed Cahokian blood willingly or to no purpose. We must know more about the Roman armies that come to us. Avenaka would have led you into war blindly, in stupid confidence that we would win. I have no such confidence, and I am sure that no man here has any such confidence, either. I will go and look at the Roman armies, and with your help and the help of the Wanageeska, if we can find a path that will lead to peace with honor rather than war, then we will consider that path.

"I am no shaman who claims he can see tomorrow and the next day. I am just Tahtay, and I am young. But I am also Tahtay who was told he could never walk again, and now I am walking and running and fighting. More: I am Tahtay who ran a thousand miles alone to the Blackfoot, who met his spirit along the way and became a man among the Fire Hearts. And if you do not respect that, you are not wise, and worse, you are my enemy. I am Tahtay, and I have spoken."

Utter silence in the Mound of the Smoke except for the crackling of the fire. Again Tahtay looked every man in the eye in turn, including Marcellinus.

Eventually, Howahkan leaned forward and took a sip of water from his beaker and said almost conversationally: "Well, then, I follow Tahtay."

"I follow Tahtay," said Kanuna.

Matoshka smoothed his hair back. His fingers glistened with bear fat. His other hand still clutched at the wound in his stomach. "I, too, will follow Tahtay."

"I follow Tahtay," Ogleesha said.

One by one, the men moved and spoke.

Tahtay looked at Marcellinus.

Marcellinus had sworn an oath to never take Roman life. He would never face them in battle. But Tahtay knew that, and this was hardly a time for caveats, not when a young man of sixteen winters had just won over a hostile audience of elders with such aplomb.

If Marcellinus wanted to be trusted as an equal by these men, he really had no choice.

"I follow Tahtay," he said, and drank.

Tahtay nodded. He picked up the pipe, turned it over in his hands, and sniffed it. His face cracked in a wry smile. "And now I really have to smoke this thing?"

To everyone's surprise, winter arrived with the Romans having moved no closer. Perhaps they feared being caught in heavy snows while on the march, although this seemed unusually cautious. Marcellinus did not pretend to understand why they were waiting, but he, Tahtay, and everyone else were certainly glad of the stay of execution.

Meanwhile, an ever-growing and ever more proficient Cahokian army drilled daily in the Great Plaza under the command of Wahchintonka, Akecheta, and sometimes Tahtay himself. Everyone else tried to pretend life was normal despite the invading army just a few weeks' march away.

For Tahtay, this was an opportunity to consolidate his power in Cahokia. For Kimimela, it was her chance to be thrown into the air in her Hawk craft from the launching rail on the Great Mound for the first time, something Marcellinus steadfastly demanded not to be informed about. For Enopay, it was about counting grain and warriors.

As for Marcellinus, this was his sixth winter in Nova Hesperia but the first in which he worried that his toes and fingers might grow so brittle in the cold that they would snap clean off. Apparently overwintering in the south the previous year had destroyed his ability to endure the cold at Cahokian latitudes. Or, more likely, the buffalo hunt on the frigid plains had chilled him so deeply that he would never be warm again.

He would turn just forty-seven winters this year. Really, he should not have to run to the Big Warm House with the rest of the elders. In previous years he might have spent time in the steelworks, but these days the metalworkers were on a war footing. They were doing some things Marcellinus would rather not know about and other things he was actively forbidden to learn about, and there was frankly no space for him anyway.

And so, having been gifted a house that was much bigger than he needed, he had turned it into his workshop. And if he kept a brick furnace with a pipe leading indoors and stoked it a little hotter than most, that was no one's business but his own.

*   *   *

Hurit stomped into Marcellinus's house unannounced, snow tumbling from her boots onto his floor, her gladius banging against her thigh. "At last! You are hard to find. Juno, it's hot in here." She pulled off her fur-lined cloak and tossed it onto Marcellinus's workbench, on top of the wooden paddles and buckets there.

Marcellinus put down his hammer and wiped the sweat out of his eyes. "Hard to find in my own house with smoke coming out of the smoke hole?"

"I thought you'd be in the Longhouse of the Wings. Or with the ship. Or at the brickworks or the steelworks. Or with Wachiwi. Or with Takoda. Ah!" Spying the bearberry tea brewing on his hearth, she helped herself, splashing it into a beaker.

Marcellinus shook his head, amused at her presumption. This was the first time Hurit had ever been in his house, and he hadn't even seen her for weeks. "Make yourself at home. And 'Juno'?"

"Oh, I picked that up from you." Hurit paused. "Is it rude?"

"Juno is the queen of the Roman gods," Marcellinus said. "Also the goddess of marriage."

"Huh." Hurit picked up one of the flat boards he was working on. "This is for the *Concordia*?"

"No, it's for a waterwheel. Stand a stout wheel upright in the river with a series of these around the rim, or perhaps buckets, and the current will . . ." He stopped. She wasn't interested. "Tahtay still isn't speaking to you?"

"I ruined *everything*," she said, and flopped onto the bench with her head in her hands.

Marcellinus picked up a heavy file from his tool kit and began shaping the closest paddle, the only one he could reach without leaning across Hurit or moving her cloak.

"But you don't care," she said. "You're not going to help me. Why should you?"

"Tahtay is busy preparing to make war on my people. Him and his ten thousand warriors."

"There are not ten thousand of us, and it will not come to that. You will think of something."

Marcellinus shook his head. "What does Anapetu say?"

"About the war?"

"About Tahtay."

"That plenty of other good men in the city would happily sacrifice ten winters of their lives to marry me."

Hurit was one of the most striking young women in Cahokia and certainly the best-looking female warrior, although she was proficient enough with sword, spear, and ax to give any man pause. "Well, she's right, but it isn't worth marrying someone you don't love."

"You should know," she said nastily.

Marcellinus gave her a look and reached past her after all to pick up another paddle and compare its width with the one he was holding.

"I'm sorry," she said, suddenly contrite. "I didn't mean to be cruel."

Marcellinus was losing patience and trying not to show it. "What are you, Hurit, sixteen winters? There's no hurry."

"Of course there is no hurry to *marry*. But I want Tahtay!"

"Do you want him because he is Tahtay or because he is war chief of Cahokia?"

Hurit stared. "And now *you* are being cruel."

"You were less interested in Tahtay when he was wounded and limping."

"Only because he was being a constant pain in everybody's—"

"And Dustu seemed more to your taste."

She sighed dramatically. "Dustu sits at Tahtay's right hand. Tahtay trusts Dustu. He cannot look at Dustu and always see me. And I cannot marry Dustu but always be looking at Tahtay."

"And Dustu is boring?"

Hurit's face cracked in a sudden conspiratorial grin,

and despite himself, Marcellinus found he was smiling back at her. Really, Hurit was absurdly engaging.

"Yes, Dustu is boring . . . And Dustu is still my friend. But nothing more. And Dustu does not mind that, because he never expected to have me in the first place. And there are plenty of girls who would give ten winters of their lives to marry *Dustu*. Do you want some tea?"

He nodded in self-defense, still knocked off balance by her constant changes in mood.

Marcellinus had never played matchmaker in his life, but as Hurit knelt by his hearth to make fresh tea, he found himself thinking about it.

Tahtay was certainly busy, but he was also lonely. Because he was the new war chief of a large and complex city, there was a limit on who he could talk with candidly. He had Sintikala and the elders for advice but always had to be on his guard with them, building his reputation for dependability, preserving his outward face as a strong and reliable leader. Dustu was loyal and hardworking but unimaginative, and Marcellinus had no difficulty understanding why Hurit had lost interest in him. Kimimela and Enopay were Tahtay's friends and allies and could provide invaluable support, but Kimi was three years younger than Tahtay and Enopay was maybe six years younger.

Tahtay had spent a year as a member of a Blackfoot warrior society, a brotherhood of young men much like himself. Marcellinus and Sintikala had ripped him away from that brotherhood. Tahtay had no Cahokian family left: Great Sun Man was dead, Nipekala was with the Blackfoot, and Great Sun Man's mother and younger half brother had fled after he was killed.

Tahtay had few people to confide in, and nowhere he truly belonged.

"Gaius?" Hurit peered up at him from the floor, worried.

Marcellinus had been lost in his thoughts. "Sorry. I was remembering long ago, when I was the chief of the first Roman legion that came to Cahokia." He waited for a caustic comment, but Hurit just handed him a beaker of tea. "It can be lonely being a chief. And dangerous. One of my friendships was nearly the death of me, and I was only barely saved by the other."

"Aelfric. He told me the story."

Marcellinus nodded.

Hurit leaned forward. "I would be there for Tahtay. It's what I want. To be by his side. And I would . . . protect him. If he needed it. Die for him if I had to."

She was staring deep into his eyes as she said this, and for all her tendency toward drama, Marcellinus utterly believed her. He did not doubt her courage.

Hurit shook her head. "But he no longer even notices me."

Tahtay might be lonely but could also be maddeningly touchy and obstinate. And proud. Especially having been rejected by Hurit once already.

But perhaps that could be mended. And if so, Marcellinus had no fear that Hurit would ever tire of Tahtay or he of her. For all her inflated opinion of herself, Hurit would be a sparkling and intelligent match for Tahtay and loyal to the death. She was fast with numbers and could read and write almost as well as Enopay. And she could wield a gladius like no one else her age.

Marcellinus nodded. "I will talk to Tahtay when next I see him."

Hurit's jaw dropped almost comically. "You will?"

"Yes, I will. But you will have to do something for me in return."

Her eyes narrowed. "Does it involve sewing?"

"No. It involves gears." Marcellinus had a moment of inspiration. "Tahtay is very interested in my waterwheel, you know."

Again she looked startled. "He is?"

"Yes. It's at his urging that I started working on it again. With a waterwheel you can grind corn much more quickly, between two round flat stones." Marcellinus mimed the way the stones ground together. "You can power bellows without needing people to constantly pump. If you have fast water, you can even make a saw-mill and cut wood more easily."

He had lost her already, and no wonder. "So what do you need from me?"

"Gears." He held up his hands at right angles and interlocked his fingers. "Two wheels that connect like this. Turn one wheel, and it makes the other turn."

Hurit shook her head. "If I can barely thread a needle, I certainly cannot fashion wood. I can bake bricks, fight, and collect buffalo chips. That's about all. And this looks much harder than bricks."

"Sometimes the hardest things to achieve are those which are the most worth doing."

"Are they?"

He grinned. "Help me talk to the woodturners. Help me put together a group of them to do nothing but this until we get it right. My novelty value in Cahokia is over. They will do it for you long before they do it for me."

She gave him an arch look, and he pointed at her face. "Exactly, Hurit. That expression is what I need. And if you can do this, Tahtay will be pleased."

Hurit wagged her finger at him. "You think you are big clever, but I know what you are doing."

He smiled back. "Is it working?"

"Yes. I will talk to the woodturners. You will talk to Tahtay. But Gaius, you should really come to Ocatan with Anapetu and me."

Now it was Marcellinus's turn to be confused. "What?"

"Ocatan. They are the real workers of wood. You have seen their palisade? It is much better work than the palisade here in Cahokia even though some of their men came to help us. And their bowls and canoes are better. The *Concordia*'s oars were made in Ocatan. The men who came south with us and patched the ship and did the woodwork we needed? Many were originally Ocatani."

"Hmm." Marcellinus vaguely recalled that now. He

also knew that Anapetu, their Raven clan chief, regularly went to Ocatan to spend time with her sisters and daughter and their families. Hurit and Dustu sometimes went with her; they had friends among the brickworkers and presumably among the woodworkers as well, since the Big Warm House required a great deal of wood as well as brick.

But still. At this time of year they could not go by river, and it would be a long hike, a hundred fifty miles or more. Despite the heat in his hut, Marcellinus shivered involuntarily.

"Cold already?" Hurit said, her natural impertinence returning.

"Yes."

"Well, sometimes the hardest things are the ones most worth doing." She stuck out her tongue. He made a face at her.

Hurit sobered. "Also, I think it may be good for you to get out of Cahokia for a while. There is less talk of the war in Ocatan. Let them prepare here in Cahokia without you, since you are not helping anyway. After you have talked to Tahtay about how wonderfully forgivable I am, of course."

Marcellinus laughed.

"Treaty?" she said.

"Treaty," Marcellinus replied, and clasped her forearm in the Roman style.

As Marcellinus walked through the streets of Cahokia, he tried to see it through Roman eyes. Behind him and to the left a Sky Lantern was suspended from the mound adjacent to the brickworks, ably piloted by Chogan himself. A few small wheeled carts traveled along the edge of the Great Plaza, pulled by men; the Cahokians had developed the carts themselves, using Marcellinus's wheelbarrows and the carts of the Romans as inspiration. Over to the northeast the steel foundry belched its smoke into the air, the harbinger of Cahokian industry.

Despite being the greatest city in Nova Hesperia, despite all Marcellinus's work and improvements, perhaps it would still look very muddy and provincial to them.

He was looking for Kimimela but found Aelfric, who was leaning against a brand-new red cedar post on the eastern edge of the Great Plaza while the Cahokian army did charge-and-retreat drills, looking for all the world like a man watching a chariot race or an athletic contest.

"They're not bad, these boys," the Briton said. "They'll do you proud when they go up against the legions."

Marcellinus grunted. Akecheta was drilling the First Cahokian to the north of the plaza while Wahchintonka was bellowing orders to about six hundred Cahokian warriors who stood in a credibly straight formation, five ranks deep, with frequent breaks in it.

Aelfric pointed. "They've already figured out to leave spaces for the horses to charge in between if they want to. And then they can pick 'em off at leisure. And all this before they've even seen cavalry in action. You didn't tell them to do that?"

"No."

Aelfric pointed again. "And reserves. I haven't asked, but it looks like Akecheta is keeping men in reserve so they're not all fighting at once even though Wahchintonka's lot outnumbers them. Fresh men."

"I did tell them that," Marcellinus admitted. "But that was when they were fighting Iroqua."

"Well, I'm sure that'll be all right with Roma, then."

"Have you seen Kimimela?"

"Nope."

Marcellinus squinted upward, then looked down at the ground at the pole's base. "How long has this pole been here?"

"They winched it up yesterday morning. Only took five of them. Usually takes dozens."

Whenever war was coming, the Cahokians erected more cedar poles. Even now Marcellinus didn't know why.

"You know they use that winch to pull throwing engines up onto their mounds right quick?" Aelfric said quietly. "You gave them this stuff for the best reasons, but—"

"I know. At least I can't see them fighting Hadrianus with a waterwheel."

"I wouldn't put it past Tahtay."

In front of them on the plaza, Akecheta's men had repulsed another charge by the Wolf Warriors. "So when do you and Chumanee leave?"

"First thaw. Maybe. I'm having trouble persuading her to go."

"Oh?"

"Here comes your child prodigy."

Enopay had just walked out of the Great Mound's side gate. Spotting Marcellinus and Aelfric, he made a beeline straight across the Great Plaza, ignoring the military maneuvers going on all around him.

The last Marcellinus had heard, Chumanee would be guiding Aelfric off into the upland villages as soon as the Romans came within a week's march. And as far as was necessary. They weren't the only ones making plans to leave in the spring, Marcellinus knew. "Chumanee doesn't want to go, now?"

"Loyalty to Tahtay and Cahokia." Aelfric shrugged and grinned. "Ridiculous."

"Of course. What about Isleifur?"

"He can come if he likes. He hasn't asked."

Enopay reached them. "You have changed your mind about helping us fight? Or you are memorizing our battle tactics so you can tell Roma?"

Marcellinus was not completely sure Enopay was joking. "Neither. Is Tahtay busy? Have you seen Kimi?"

"Tahtay is on the sun." Enopay gestured, meaning the Mound of the Sun, where Tahtay lived. "No one else is with him at the moment. I think he is eating. You will teach him more Latin?"

"Perhaps. And Kimimela?"

"I just saw Kimimela walking up the Master Mound to the Longhouse of the Wings."

"Hmm." Marcellinus glanced at both mounds and regretfully decided that Tahtay was the higher priority. "I will be going to Ocatan soon, Enopay. Do you want to come?"

Enopay shook his head, dismissing the question. "We are your people now, Eyanosa. Not the Romans. If you cannot bring us peace with them, then you should help us with war."

"Oh, I think the Eyanosa has helped you quite a bit already," Aelfric said. "In *all directions*."

"That's what you'd do?" Marcellinus demanded of Enopay. "If the Iroqua had captured you, and you had made friends there, and then Cahokia attacked? You would fight Cahokians?"

"No, because I would never make friends with the Iroqua in the first place."

Marcellinus felt his nerves fraying. "Do you wish I had never come here, then?"

Enopay was quiet, looking out across the plaza. "I have always been glad I met you. And even now we have more hope with you here than without you. But you should ask me that question again in six moons if any of us are still alive."

"I will," Marcellinus said.

"And now I have a message for the rope makers, and so I must go." Enopay walked off.

"What a little ray of sunshine," said Aelfric.

Marcellinus followed the boy with his eyes. The Romans were not there yet, and already he felt he was losing all his friends. "He's not wrong. Anyway. I have to talk to Tahtay."

Marcellinus and the Raven clan group hiked wearily back into Cahokia's Great Plaza a month later to find an Eagle craft being launched off the mound, crewed by Sintikala, Kimimela, and a Hawk clan boy of a similar age. Immediately the blood began rushing around Marcellinus's body much more quickly. "Juno," he said.

"Do not worry," Hurit advised him. "Kimimela has such a hard head that even if she lands on it, she won't do herself any harm."

"Hurit," Anapetu said warningly. Hurit had been tormenting Marcellinus all day, and even Anapetu was wearying of it.

The three-person Eagle was banking left and then right. The turns looked a little shaky, and the craft was losing height quickly in the cold of the day even with the heat from the Cahokian fires to provide something of an updraft.

Hurit yawned. "I would wrestle a bear for a beaker of sarsaparilla tea. Whose fire can we steal?"

"I'll see you later," Marcellinus said, and remembered to bow to his clan chief. "That was an excellent trip, Anapetu. Thank you for allowing me to accompany you."

The Raven chief nodded. "You are always welcome, Gaius Wanageeska."

For a heart-stopping moment Marcellinus thought the Eagle had gone into a death spiral, but apparently Sintikala was doing it deliberately. The Eagle continued its tight corkscrew down to the plaza, where its three pilots ran it to a halt.

The sand of the Great Plaza looked chewed up and slushy. As he walked over to the Eagle, Marcellinus wondered what kind of military maneuvers he had missed on his trip south to the confluence town. By the time he arrived at their side, the three of them had unstrapped and four men of the Hawk clan had arrived to take the craft from them and run it back to the Great Mound. "Sintikala. Kimimela."

Sintikala smiled at him with a warmth that made his heart skip a beat, but then turned to the boy copilot to lecture him about the line of his body in the air. The boy was already pale and shaking, and Marcellinus pitied him a little.

"You had a good time in Ocatan?" Kimimela asked.

"Very successful. But very cold." Marcellinus pulled two cogwheels each a foot across from his buffalo-skin pouch. "See? This is how the teeth fit together. A pole through each wheel, and a horizontal torque can be converted to a vertical one and magnified. The woodworkers of Ocatan are making much bigger cogs, and frames for the waterwheels. I'll be going back again soon, after I have taught Tahtay more Latin for negotiating with Roma . . . Kimimela, I am very happy to see you again."

She hugged him. "I am glad you came back. I was getting bored here with nobody to tease."

Sintikala clapped her hands. "Enough. Kimimela, we must fly again before the wind drops. Gaius, I would talk with you later."

"Yes. I would like that."

Sintikala nodded and smiled again and turned to jog back to the Great Mound.

Kimimela bounced on the balls of her feet. "Oh, and Father?"

"Yes?"

"Go to the baths first."

And with a wicked wink that almost managed to be solemn, Kimimela sprinted after her mother.

"Gaius?"

Marcellinus turned at the top of his mound to see Sintikala striding up the cedar steps. He expected to see the Hawk paint still around her eyes and the leather tunic she had worn in the air, but her hair was down and her skin clear and glistening. "We may speak?"

"Yes, if I may sit." It had been a long day. He led the way to the bench outside his door. By now he had almost grown accustomed to the way the Great Mound loomed over it.

"Perhaps inside." She walked past him through the doorskin and stepped down into his hut.

He followed her in and found her looking at his lares in their shrine, with the golden Shappan birdman amulet resting next to them and a bark fragment with "Kimi thank Gaius" written on it in looped charcoal finger-talk on the other side.

"You have been gone so long, yet you go back to Oca-tan again soon?" she said.

"Once more. One final trip before . . ." He grimaced.

"Before we leave for Roma."

"In a way. Where is Kimimela?"

"She talks to Tahtay and Enopay. Tahtay relies on her just as he relies on his elders."

Marcellinus nodded. "And on Enopay. Sometimes when Tahtay speaks with such assurance, I hear Enopay's words in what he says . . . Hmm."

"What?"

It had just occurred to Marcellinus that perhaps one of the most beneficial consequences of his coming to Ca-hokia was the closeness between Tahtay, Kimimela, and Enopay. "I was wondering if those three would be friends if I had not come."

Sintikala shook her head. "So much would have been different if Great Sun Man had killed you as I sug-gested."

His hut, which once had seemed so large to him, now seemed intimately small. Suddenly he did not know what to do with his hands and feet. "Sometimes you are disconcertingly honest."

"I am?" She picked up the birdman amulet and exam-ined it thoughtfully. "Lately . . . I have had bad dreams."

Well, so had Marcellinus. "Dreams are just dreams."

"Blood and fighting. Romans in steel. Thunder and lightning." She put the amulet back and turned away from the lares. "You are sure that the Romans will not kill us as soon as we enter their camp? You they may murder immediately, for losing your men and living with us. And I walked into a Roman camp once before and was lucky to walk out again."

"That was not luck," he said.

"Yes, it was."

He shook his head again.

"Neither do I," she said, just as if he had answered *No, I do not know whether the Romans will kill us.* "Gaius . . ."

She walked over to him and looked up into his eyes. He felt himself reacting to her stare, to her stern beauty and her strength, and did not know what to say.

"Have you chosen your death song?" she said, and smiled.

He grinned back, recovering his composure. "Romans do not torture. Usually."

"That is comforting."

"They do execute, though."

"How?" she said with genuine interest. "For you, if they did, how? Sword? Rope? Knife?"

Bizarre how Sintikala could be so matter-of-fact. "For me it would be a sword."

"How?" She raised her hand, palm up. "If it would take your confidence, we need not speak of it."

"They would probably have me kneel and drive the gladius downward by my neck, through my shoulder, into my heart." He gestured, showing the vertical path the sword would take. "Or they would tell me to do it myself, to fall on my sword and cut open my own stomach. Or perhaps they'd take me back to Roma and the senators could hold a lottery to see who gets the honor of cleaving the head from my shoulders."

He had meant the last as a dark joke, but now Sintikala was looking at him very seriously. Their eyes locked, and for the first time it was he who read the message in hers. His heart leaped. "Sisika?"

Finally she said, "Gaius, if I ask you to do one thing, will you do that one thing and no more?"

"Yes, I will."

She opened her arms, and he drew her in. She clung to him, her face against his chest. His arms enfolded her.

His lips rested against her hair, unmoving. He breathed her in, concentrating on the feel of her in his arms, her lean, muscular body now quiet and relaxed and gentle. Sometimes so dangerous and brutal but now in repose.

"Gaius, Gaius," she said.

"What?"

"With Wanageeska always there is change." He felt her smile. It was what she had said on the night they had exchanged blood.

"And with Sisika, apparently."

She looked up at him again, her lips just inches from his, her eyes even more serious and searching.

Marcellinus leaned away. He had, after all, made her a promise: one thing and no more. She smiled again at that, and again his heart threatened to stop. "Sisika . . ."

For a moment she seemed on the verge of saying something. Then she looked into his eyes and just nodded, and put her hand behind his head, and pulled him to her, and they kissed.

At first they were tentative, as if it had been so long for either of them that they had forgotten what to do. He kissed her lips and then paused to look in her eyes again, and she kissed his lips and his cheek and said, "Wait."

Again he made as if to pull away, but she did not allow it. Now his lips were against her forehead, and her face was turned downward, eyes closed. She appeared to be in deep thought or even praying. He held her, still marveling that she was in his arms.

Then she said, "All right."

He stroked her hair, her shoulder. "What is all right?"

"I was saying good-bye."

Marcellinus understood, but she clarified anyway: "Saying good-bye to my husband, who died over ten winters ago."

She raised her head and looked into his eyes again, and her lips found his once more, and this time there was nothing tentative. She kissed him gently, then her lips parted, and with a shock that was almost like lightning their tongues met for the first time. Overwhelmed, Marcellinus pulled her in and kissed her fiercely: insistent, demanding.

It seemed like an hour yet was just an instant before

Sisika broke the kiss, breathing heavily. Her fingers were in his hair, her eyes wide. He stroked her cheek, her neck, her shoulders.

She leaned back. "If we do not stop now, we never will."

His fingertips caressed her cheeks again. "Not stopping is fine with me."

"But you might be dead by next moon. Gaius, what?"

He was laughing. The likelihood of his being dead within a month, a week, or a day had been a constant for as long as he had been in the land, indeed, for as long as he could remember. She smiled back, a little mystified, and swatted him on the shoulder. "Gaius, serious?"

"All right. Sisika, I promise I will try to live as long as I can."

He tried to pull her in again but stopped when she resisted. "Gaius, I cannot . . . We must not do more, you and I. Not if you may soon be dead. You understand?"

He thought about it and then nodded. "Let me hold you a little longer, though."

"For warmth, like warriors?" she said, faintly mocking.

"Yes, of course, like warriors."

She sighed. "I did not want us to walk in there, into Roma, without you knowing . . ." She held his hand, and their fingers twined. "You understand? About this at least, I wanted to be honest."

"I think so. I hope so." Marcellinus raised her hand and placed it over his heart and then said, " 'About this at least'?"

She looked at him somberly. "Until recently, Gaius, always I was honest with you."

He squeezed her hand. "You mean about this? About us?"

"No," she said, and her fingers slipped out of his. "When you flew to the Haudenosaunee, you made sure that you did not know our plan, when our war parties would march, which route they would take. So that the Iroqua could not cut the information out of you."

Marcellinus nodded.

"Soon we will go to the Romans, and *we* have made sure you do not know things. Tahtay and I and the elders, we all are agreed. If you are going to them, you must not know all that we know. And so in fact I am no longer honest with you."

"You have plans you are not telling me?"

"Of course."

In an instant the mood had changed. Two legions stood between them now. "Always there will be something," he said, trying to make light of it.

"Roma is a big something."

"It's all right," he said. "In your shoes, I might keep secrets, too."

"In my shoes?"

She glanced down at her moccasins, baffled now, and he laughed. "Yes, secrets in your shoes . . . Sisika, please. Smile for me again."

Sisika looked up into his eyes and smiled. Marcellinus squeezed her. "Perhaps I should not go to Ocatan again. Perhaps I should stay."

"You must go. And I must fly to look and make sure that the Romans are still held in camp by the spring mud."

"But I could look at you forever."

She mimed drawing a line. "All right. Kiss me one more time, and then I am going away, to sleep." She poked him. "Yes, Gaius, I am going away. Be ready."

"I will be ready," he said, and pulled her close again, and they lost themselves in each other for a little longer.

PART 4

ROMA

CHAPTER 23

YEAR SEVEN, GRASS MOON

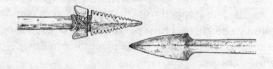

Cogs engaged, and wheels began to turn. In the open air of the Ocatani South Plaza, eight woodturners and Hurit sweated in the springtime sun.

Then Hurit muttered a snarky challenge to the woodturners, her eyes glinting. They really put their shoulders to the wheel, and the mechanism spun.

The woodturners held a long handle connected to a large vertical wheel. Broad wooden cogs reinforced with thin steel plates linked this wheel to a second horizontal wheel, which was mounted on a pole anchored firmly in the soil of the plaza. This second wheel then drove a much smaller vertical third wheel, which spun so quickly that it was soon a blur.

Marcellinus took a step back. The wooden structure the wheels were attached to was rocking alarmingly, and there seemed a good chance the third wheel would fly off into the air. He had a brief, dark, but rather satisfying vision of its steel-lined cogs slicing off someone's head. Even ten feet away he could feel the breeze off the wheel.

Well, that certainly would grind some corn.

Marcellinus grinned. It was a waterwheel—no river would ever drive it this fast even in spate—but it was hard to fault Hurit's enthusiasm.

He glanced around, wishing Anapetu were there to

see it, but his Raven clan chief was outside the walls of Ocatan, washing clothes in the blue Oyo with her sisters and grandchildren and enjoying the spring day. Anapetu had taken a leading role with the Sky Lanterns but was baffled by the waterwheel; it was clear she thought it was a waste of time and effort.

"All right," Hurit said, and the woodturners released the handle and stepped smartly back before it could spin around to hit them. Hurit peered at the cogs linking the second and third wheels as the machine ran down, looking for damage.

Marcellinus wondered what else they might use it for. Perhaps the gears could be linked to bellows to help circulate air into the Big Warm Houses more easily and into the Sky Lanterns at launching. Perhaps—

He shook his head. The gears were beautiful, but for the life of him he could think of few other practical uses for them.

Suddenly there was a snapping, braying sound, and Marcellinus instinctively reached for Hurit, assuming that the mechanism was breaking.

It wasn't. The snapping became an arrhythmic drumming, and from the ramparts of the Temple Mound behind them came the clash of rocks on copper sheets.

The braying from the south sounded for all the world like a Roman trumpet. Marcellinus had not seen or heard one since his days with the 33rd, even at the Market of the Mud, had not known that any had survived the battle.

He *did* know that the combination of sounds was quite unpleasant.

The wheels spun slowly to a halt. Even in his distraction, Marcellinus noted how frictionless the bearings were, how well the lubrication of the sunflower oil kept the wheels going.

All across the plaza the Ocatani had stopped dead in their tracks and turned toward the Temple Mound. Now they broke and ran in different directions. Parents grabbed their children. Warriors darted into their huts to emerge clutching either spears and axes or pila and Roman shields, or donning the wooden matting armor of the Mizipians. Men raced for the town walls.

Marcellinus looked around him, astonished at the sudden change in the atmosphere and the speed of the Ocatani response.

Then that absurd braying sounded again, and with a jarring shock Marcellinus finally recognized it as a Roman cornicen calling troops to arms. Over the Ocatani alarm drums he now heard a steady, deep drumbeat.

Iniwa, war chief of Ocatan, and a squad of thirty elite warriors burst out of the Longhouse of the Temple Mound and ran full tilt down its slopes.

Slowly, slowly, the gates of Ocatan began to swing closed.

But Anapetu and her family were still outside the walls, down by the Oyo, along with hundreds of other Ocatani.

Marcellinus turned in sudden fear and realization. "Hurit—"

She was already grabbing his arm. "Come. Swords."

They ran up the wooden steps on the inside of the palisade to one of the firing platforms. Ocatani braves with bows and arrows stood aside, allowing Marcellinus to see past them.

As he took his first look, there was an astonishingly loud blast of Roman trumpets, almost as if they were saluting him.

This was his fourth visit to Ocatan, and by now he was familiar with the terrain. To his right was the Mizipi, to his left the broad sweep of the Oyo as it curved in from the northeast to converge with the Mizipi and form a single river heading south. Both rivers were still swollen from the spring thaw.

Speeding up the Mizipi against the current came seven Roman quinqueremes, giant triple-decked warships, in a V formation. Each flew the same legionary standard, a golden thunderbolt against a red background.

The quinqueremes were immense. The *Concordia* was close to a hundred feet long. The lead quinquereme was almost twice that length and much broader. Its top deck was a good fifteen feet above the waterline, and fore and aft it carried a fighting tower an extra twenty feet taller, painted to look like stone. Even more intimidating was the vessel's huge curved prow that concealed its steel-tipped ram, an armored beak twelve feet long.

A solid bulwark surrounded the deck. That bulwark and the upper deck levels were painted a bright red, changing to a dark green at the third rank of oars near the waterline. As the warship neared, Marcellinus saw the traditional large eye painted on its bow to ward off bad luck. Today the bad luck lay solely with the Ocatani.

The Roman warships came astonishingly fast, propelled by hundreds of oarsmen in three enclosed tiers. Their decks were crammed with legionaries in red-plumed helmets, red and white tunics, and steel armor. Around the centuries ran sailors in gray tunics and blue cloaks and caps, responding to the shouted commands of their captains.

Marcellinus reeled, still not quite believing his eyes.

Then his practiced eye made out the white plume of a Praetor standing in the high stern of the leading vessel, and it became all too real.

Roma was attacking. The two legions in the east might still be trapped by the spring mud, but Ocatan was under assault from the Legio VI Ferrata from the south.

And with Hesperian help, for behind the Roman galleys came a fleet of native war canoes, paddling hard. They were Mizipian craft, as if Cahokia itself were attacking its own satellite city, but of course that was not so.

"Bastard. Verpa. I should have killed him."

Hurit shook her head impatiently. "What, who?"

"Son of the Sun. The Shappa Ta'atani have allied with the Romans just as he threatened."

Hurit spit over the ramparts. "Then we will make sure he dies slowly."

"Seven quinqueremes," he said. "Three hundred oarsmen and two hundred marines on each. All legionaries ready to fight. And perhaps five hundred warriors of Shappa Ta'atan."

Hurit shook her head.

Even in the terror of the moment, Enopay would have blurted out the answer. Marcellinus swallowed his impatience. "Three and a half thousand Roman troops in all, plus Son of the Sun's men. As many soldiers as there are *people* in Ocatan."

Marcellinus looked back. The First Ocatani was forming up into three straight ranks in the plaza, with shields, pila, and gladii. Perhaps five hundred warriors, they looked pitifully small compared with the forces of Roma storming down on them outside.

A Sky Lantern rose into the air beside the Ocatani Big Warm House, crewed by eight braves armed with bows and arrows. It wobbled and dipped, but two warriors lobbed pots of liquid flame into the jar at the same time, and the Lantern lurched upward. As it did so, the first Ocatani Catanwakuwa flew into the air from the rail behind the Temple Mound. A ball of wood and skin, it spread its wings and locked open, banking away from the Sky Lantern. A second Hawk followed it and then a third.

That was all very well, but one Lantern and a few Hawks were not going to deter the Sixth Ironclads.

With the Mizipi in flood, its waters stopped barely two hundred feet from the Ocatani palisade. And the galleys were only a thousand yards distant. Soon, the Romans would be within bow range.

The Ocatani guards had half closed the gates, and there they stopped. The nearer, faster townsfolk were already running into the town, but there were still far too many people outside.

The swift appearance of the Roman warships had caught the people outside the walls by surprise. They had been spread up and down both riverbanks, enjoying the spring day. Some were swimming with their children or out in canoes. Others had been washing clothes farther up the Oyo, where the river water was clearer, not yet merged with the sediment-laden waters of the Mizipi. Many ran back toward the palisade now; others walked more slowly, weighed down by their infants or possessions or helping their elderly relatives and friends. Some milled around in terror or merely stood and gaped foolishly, as if the warships were objects too unbelievable to be feared.

"Anapetu, Anapetu, Anapetu." Hurit stamped her foot, as if trying to conjure their clan chief into view.

"There." Marcellinus pointed.

She ran down the bank of the Oyo like the wind, almost flying, her big raven-feather cloak billowing out behind her. On either side ran her sisters Dowanhowee and Leotie and her daughter Nashota, their heads down and panting. In front of them were Anapetu's grandchildren, four in all.

Then they split up. Dowanhowee, Nashota, and the children ran back toward the gates. Anapetu and Leotie headed not toward the walls of Ocatan but out to the riverbank to help the others, carry infants, and support the elderly.

"Futete!" Hurit swore, and ran.

"Hurit!"

She dashed down the stairs ahead of him. Marcellinus hurried after her, but Hurit had jumped to the ground and sped to Ocatan's gate before he even made it to the foot of the uneven stairs. He followed her between the tall gates and out of the palisade.

They were not alone. Even as the ordinary folk ran in, Ocatani warriors spilled out of the gates, leaving the safety of their town walls to defend their people. Only a handful of braves even wore the reed or wooden mats that the Hesperians used as armor. None carried a scutum. Once the Romans landed, the carnage would be immense.

Marcellinus had sworn he would never lead a Hesperian army against Romans. But this? Stand by and do nothing while innocents faced a massive Roman surprise attack?

Marcellinus had once been a soldier of Roma. Now he was a member of the Raven clan of Cahokia, and his chief and his friends were trying to save helpless people from fully armed and armored Romans.

Oaths or no oaths, Marcellinus could not simply stand idle and watch the Ocatani be slaughtered in droves.

Marcellinus wore no armor and no helmet and carried only a gladius. He had a pugio in his belt but chose to keep his left hand free rather than draw it.

The leading quinquereme was now a scant four hundred feet from the bank. Marcellinus could hear the barked orders in Latin even over the beat of the drums and the piping of the martial flutes that gave the time to the three ranks of oarsmen.

The first flight of arrows came then. One of the galleys had turned broadside to the shore and was holding position. An arrow whizzed over Marcellinus's head. Around him Ocatani screamed and fell; the Romans were picking their targets with care.

Running like a rabble for the gates was not the answer. The Ocatani had to retreat in an orderly fashion from the Romans as a shielded group or they were all dead.

"Come together!" Marcellinus bellowed in Cahokian. "All of you, come here to me, group up! If you panic and run alone, you die! Warriors, form a line! Women, children, you others: get behind them!"

He ducked back inside the gate. "First Ocatani! Come out now, on the double! First Ocatani!"

Anapetu began shouting, too, shooing the children and the elderly and the other women toward Marcellinus. The warriors jogged around him and formed a stout line, the younger, fitter men and women joining them in defense.

Anapetu came to his side. His Raven chief was narrow-eyed, breathing heavily but alert, not panicking, thinking clearly. Good. "Get them in," Marcellinus said. "Through the gates and behind the walls. Hurry."

"Can you stop them, Gaius Wanageeska?"

"The Romans? No."

"Talk to them, hold them, give us time?"

Aside from Marcellinus's short hair and lack of tattoos, little differentiated him from the mass of Hesperians behind him. "They won't stop to talk. They'd cut me down and walk over my corpse."

Another shouted Roman command from just off-shore, another flight of arrows.

One of the first arrows caught Anapetu in the right shoulder, shot with such force that its sharp steel point passed through her to reappear close to her armpit. Anapetu glanced down at it with a mixture of surprise and irritation before the pain hit her. Her eyes widened, and she stumbled. Hurit seized her and shoved her upright, pulling her back.

On Marcellinus's other side Leotie crashed down, an arrow in her thigh and another in the center of her back. Even as Marcellinus bent over her, he knew it was hopeless; Leotie would never make it back to her feet, and they could not carry her. Leotie knew it, too: mute, face racked with pain, she shook her head, waving him on.

The First Ocatani came at last, at a steady march, and Jove be thanked, they all bore honest-to-gods Roman steel shields of the 33rd Hesperian. Marcellinus struggled to remember the name of their Ocatani centurion, a tall slender warrior carrying a Roman gladius, with bright but hastily applied war paint smeared across his cheeks. "Centurion! . . . Coosan! Line them up, raise shields, defend the people, be ready for an organized retreat."

Marcellinus ran right and left, helping people get into the formation, sending the elders and children ahead where he could. He had lost sight of Hurit and Anapetu but knew they would be doing the same thing.

The first quinquereme rammed the muddy bank, riding up high on the shore. At the same time the marines dropped the corvus, a wide gangplank at the bow that anchored itself into the bank with a heavy metal spike. Legionaries were jogging onshore with a jangle of heavy armor before the warship had stopped moving.

To either side the second and third quinqueremes also beached and began to disgorge soldiers. Behind them in the water the fourth and fifth warships rowed past, heading upstream into the mouth of the Oyo, and their drumbeats slowed as the captain commanded his oarsmen to hold position against the current.

"Throwing engines!" Marcellinus shouted as Hurit ran up to his side. "Look out!"

The leftmost warship rocked in the water as the first onager loosed its missile, an irregularly shaped iron ball that tumbled lazily end over end in the air before smacking into the palisade just a hundred feet north of Marcellinus and Hurit. The wall shivered. Splinters flew.

The townsfolk were retreating as fast as they were able under cover of the First Ocatani's shields. From behind them came a smattering of arrows from Ocatan's palisade. The legionaries of the Sixth Ferrata raised their own scuta. They were swiftly forming ranks, arraying along the bank in a solid line. The auxiliaries put their bows over their shoulders and stepped back, their job done for the time being; the troops in the first rank locked together in close order, shields up, pila at the ready.

Behind them legionaries continued to pour off the three beached galleys. Marcellinus had lost sight of the Praetor, but he knew the Sixth Ferrata was only moments from its first charge.

Out on the river the fourth and fifth warships again swayed as they fired their onagers. One ball slammed into the stockade. The other flew over the wall into the town. Marcellinus had no doubt that the missile would do its work of spreading terror even if by sheer luck no one was hit.

The last two quinqueremes had split off. The sixth was rowing at full speed across the Oyo toward the much smaller Ocatani fort on the other bank, and the seventh pulled in to land on the riverbank a few hundred yards northeast of the rest of the Roman force.

Marcellinus had backed up almost as far as the gates now. The civilians were almost all inside, the First Ocatani retreating steadily. "Halt!" Coosan cried.

Marcellinus turned. Anapetu stood close by him, leaning on Hurit's shoulder. A dozen other Ocatani and Cahokians were waiting to enter the town.

They had stopped to let Iniwa's warriors stream out of the fort, armored in reed and wooden mats and armed with the usual motley collection of weapons from swords to axes to rocks and carrying only the occasional wooden shield, ready to do battle with the Romans, with the war chief Iniwa himself in the lead.

Marcellinus swore. This was craziness. Out in the open field of war the Romans would utterly destroy them.

A Catanwakuwa flew over his head, its pilot hurling pots of liquid flame down onto the Romans. The pots exploded, showering the front line of the legion with the searing incendiary. A second Hawk pilot came in from the right, dealing her own pots of flame into the massed Romans. A grenade of liquid flame exploded onto the deck of the first galley, and the crew scattered away from it. But the largest pot a Hawk pilot could carry was the size of a man's head. These were not the giant sacks of flaming death that Cahokia had unleashed on the 33rd Hesperian Legion all those years before. Here the attacks from above were at worst a minor annoyance.

With another blare of cornicens and a loud clanking, the Romans started their advance. Not an energy-wasting full-out charge but a strong walk behind a line of red Roman shields bearing the golden thunderbolt of the Sixth.

Roaring their battle cries, the warriors of Iniwa ran forward to engage them.

Marcellinus didn't hear the order, but the legionaries in the central third of the Roman line hurled their pila as one. A stout wave of spears slammed into the Ocatani war line. The sheer force of the heavy spears knocked warriors off their feet, spun them around, and in some cases pierced straight through their chests.

Marcellinus turned. "Inside! All of you! Move!"

Another iron ball smashed into the palisade to his right, its impact so loud that he dropped into a squat and covered his head as shards of wood and clods of earth rained down on them. He stood to find the warrior centurion Coosan in front of him. "The First Ocatani, inside? You say so?"

It was a fair question. The last of the townsfolk were disappearing within the gates of Ocatan. The firing platforms and palisade above were lined with archers who were holding fire so that they would not hit their own warriors in the back. Down by the river the Sixth Ferrata still advanced, hacking its way through Iniwa's men. The warriors fought valiantly but were hopelessly outnumbered and outequipped.

"In, in!" said Marcellinus. "Hold the town. Let the Romans lay siege to us."

"Siege?"

Marcellinus resisted the urge to punch him. "You will not throw away your men's lives out here. Fall back! I have spoken!"

Coosan tried to mask his relief with little success. "Inside!" he commanded. "Man the walls! From the right, double time!"

The far end of the line turned and jog trotted back into Ocatan, retreating to safety.

"Back!" came a yell from just a hundred feet away. "Back!"

Iniwa was calling the retreat as well, but it had come much too late for most of his men. Over a thousand warriors had run forward from the walls to fight the

Romans. Fewer than a third of that number were running, walking, or limping back.

With another blare of trumpets the center of the Roman line broke into a run, surging forward. Marcellinus could see the whites of their eyes, their faces blank under their helmets. Their pila cast, they were charging with shields up and gladii held out in front of them.

It was a terrifying sight.

The First Ocatani was in, with Iniwa and most of his warriors on their heels. Marcellinus checked left and right; Ocatani were down and bleeding in front of him and all around him, but he could not help them, not if he wanted to keep his own head on his shoulders.

He ran through the heavy gates of Ocatan, and they swung shut behind him. Wooden cross-braces fell into place. "Fire! Shoot!" Marcellinus shouted, because nobody else was doing it, and above him on the palisade the archers sent a hail of arrows into the Roman lines.

Iniwa and his men were climbing the steps to the palisade. Some looked dumbstruck, others terrified. Some stumbled and fell, dazed or wounded. Again Coosan was looking at Marcellinus, almost beseeching him.

Marcellinus glanced up at the palisade. "Coosan, keep the First Ocatani together down here. Order your men back, hold ranks. If the wall . . . when the wall falls, have your men ready to step into the breach. Try to hold the Romans back. Or if the Romans concentrate on the gate, be ready in ranks thirty feet back to attack the legion as soon as it starts coming through."

"Shit," said Coosan.

Marcellinus clapped him on the shoulder. "Strength, centurion. The people of Ocatan need you."

An iron ball flew over them and thudded into the Temple Mound two hundred feet behind them. At the same moment the Ocatani launched another Hawk in the opposite direction. The warriors in the Sky Lantern were shooting arrows over the wall at the Romans. Marcellinus could only hope that it was Ocatan's best archers up there and that they were aiming for centurions, perhaps tribunes—

He caught himself, rocking on his heels. Now he was wishing Roman officers killed?

Marcellinus pulled himself together. His one duty here was to protect the innocent, save whoever he could. As he looked all around him at the Ocatani townsfolk milling in confusion in the streets, he realized that the clamor of the Roman forces from the other side of the stout wall had dimmed.

Where had Hurit taken Anapetu?

"Wanageeska!"

Iniwa was calling to him from the top of the palisade. Marcellinus ran up the steps two at a time. "What is it?"

"Your silver men. They are leaving?"

The legionaries had broken formation and moved back fifty feet, some almost strolling. Several had walked back across the gangplanks onto their ships. They seemed dismissive of the Ocatani arrows that landed around them and with fair reason, considering the weight of steel that armored them.

Iniwa peered at Marcellinus, irritated at his silence. "They are raising their masts to sail away?"

"No. Those are not masts, and they are not raising them. Those are battering rams, Iniwa. They will bring them up to the gates of Ocatan and smash them down."

Iniwa scowled. "They will not. We will drop stones upon their heads, throw liquid flame, boiling water. Shoot them from above. They will not smash the walls of Ocatan."

"They will." Marcellinus felt momentarily weary. "See, now: those stout sheds they are carrying off the ships, each like the roof and side walls of a hut, but with no ends? They will hold those in sections over the soldiers and the battering ram, making . . . a longhouse that will cover them and keep them safe." He squinted. "The sheds are wooden but covered in hides. See them wetting down the hides with river water? Those will not burn. They will be hard to break, and if you do break one, they will just replace that section with a fresh section. The battering ram will be protected. Ocatan's gates will fall."

"They will not. I have spoken."

Marcellinus nodded. "As you say. But your people should flee anyway, great Iniwa. We should get the townsfolk out of the northern gates and into the grass, the woods, to hide until it is over. Is it not so?"

Hurit jogged to the base of the palisade and clattered up the steps to his side. "The Romans are leaving?"

"No. How is Anapetu?"

"Angry and bleeding. Will we fight?"

"No, we will run, escape. Is Anapetu still lucid? Can she run?"

Iniwa stared, open contempt in his eyes. "The great Wanageeska will run like a child? We will not flee. We will go to the gods first."

"You think there are gods?" Marcellinus said. "Look around you. There are none. Your people—"

Marcellinus recoiled, his face burning. The Ocatani chieftain had slapped him. "Those are *your* people who attack us! Your silver men. You will go out and stop them, tell them they must leave or face the wrath of Ocatan!"

Hurit shoved at the war chief's chest. "You will not hit the Wanageeska again. Do not touch him!"

Iniwa raised his fist. Marcellinus stepped forward. "These are not my Romans, great Iniwa. They will not listen to me, you, or anyone here."

"They are your brothers. At least make them pause. No?"

"If I walk out of here now, they'll slay me without hesitating or drag me away as a prisoner."

Iniwa's lip curled. "You fear them."

Any sane man would fear the Sixth Ironclads. Marcellinus opened his mouth to respond, but the Ocatani war chief was speaking again. "Then we will fight."

"No, no. Iniwa, hear me. You have to run. Get the hell out of here. Escape out of the northern gate before the

Romans surround Ocatan. Some of us must stay here and fight a rearguard action."

But Iniwa had walked away, not even deigning to respond.

"Damn it," said Marcellinus. "Then you, Hurit. We'll marshal them, and you'll lead them north, away from here. To Cahokia if you can."

"While you stay here?"

He swallowed, glancing again at the Sixth Ferrata's methodical preparations as they brought the battering ram forward with the sheds in position over it. They were wasting precious minutes. "Yes."

"No."

How to make her understand? Marcellinus grabbed her arm, walked her down the steps, tried to hustle her toward the north gate, but she pushed back. "Hurit, listen. The Romans will destroy Ocatan. Today. Soon. There is no doubt, no hope of resisting them. And if you are still here and still alive, then . . . their soldiers will hurt you. Use you." He took a deep breath. "Hurit, you are young and beautiful, and they will keep you alive a long time and hurt you horribly . . . viciously. I have seen what Roman legions do to . . . girls like you. You *have* to get away from here and take with you Anapetu and Dowanhowee and Nashota and every other woman or girl who can run."

She stared at him, mouth open.

"Hurit, go. Please. Run."

Tears sprang into her eyes. She blinked them back. "You think I am a coward? That I fear those verpa, that I would let them . . . ?"

Marcellinus changed tack. "No, Hurit. I think you have to protect the others, the younger ones who cannot fight the way you can. Get the young girls out of here and keep them safe. Please."

Hurit's eyes widened. "Futete."

Because above them on the palisade a new hubbub had broken out, and Iniwa was striding toward them, his face hot with fear and anger. "Four-legs!" he shouted. "Romans with four legs! Beasts in armor!"

"Beasts?" Hurit said.

But now Marcellinus could hear for himself the thunder of galloping hooves on the other side of the palisade walls. "Holy Jove . . ."

Once again he ran up the nearest steps, with Hurit close behind. As they came up to the level of the walkway, he put his hand on her head to shove her down. She immediately understood, and they approached the parapet at a crouch and peered carefully over.

Roman cavalry wheeled outside the town. The seventh quinquereme, the warship that had beached at some little distance from the first three, was still disgorging a steady stream of horsemen, their hooves clattering on the gangplank.

They wore short-sleeved mail shirts over wool tunics, braccae, and iron helmets, and each man bore a long spatha sword and a flat oval shield with a signum of laurels and moons. Light cavalry, and under a standard that Marcellinus knew, at least by reputation: the Cohors IV Gallorum Equitata.

He turned back. "Fourth Gallic Cohort. Specialized cavalrymen."

Hurit's face was ashen. "They are . . ." She lowered her voice to a whisper. "Monsters? One thing or two?"

About to snap at her, Marcellinus suddenly recalled his shock at first seeing the Iroqua flying machines in the mountains of the Appalachia. How even the battle-hardened Corbulo had been terrified and confused by the vision of the Iroqua Hawks wheeling overhead. There was no shame in Hurit fearing horses.

"They are two things, Hurit. Men, just ordinary men, astride beasts of burden."

"Huh." She squinted at them.

Marcellinus saw only one standard, that of the Fourth Gallorum. Therefore, there would be just 128 horsemen in total, four turmae of thirty cavalry, with each turma led by two officers: a decurion and a duplicarius. Surely a single quinquereme could not hold more than that, anyway.

En masse, though, weaving within the infantry to take their supporting positions, it certainly looked like more.

"I hate them," Hurit said suddenly. "The four-legs. They are horrible, not ... *right*. Get me away from them."

The first and second battering rams were ready, on the bank under their protective sheds. Foot soldiers were lined up to carry them. In a few minutes they would be marching forward to smash Ocatan's gates.

The horsemen were forming up in loose groups. Once the walls came down, the cavalry would wreak havoc in Ocatan.

Iniwa strode along the palisade walkway shouting orders. The Ocatani were preparing rocks, amassing pots of liquid flame. The Roman onagers had ceased firing, perhaps to conserve the iron balls. The battering rams would do the job much more efficiently.

Legionaries were falling into ranks again, ready for the next assault. Again the terrible trumpets sounded.

Only about half the Roman force was rallying: the cohorts who had rested on the flanks the last time. The remainder was being held in reserve. The Praetor leading this assault was supremely confident, and his confidence was justified. As Marcellinus had predicted years before on his first visit to Ocatan, the silver men of Roma would take Ocatan with ease and within the hour.

Marcellinus would probably die here. But with luck, Hurit and hundreds of other Hesperians would not.

The land north of Ocatan was largely flat and grassy; the Ocatani had cleared the trees away from their walls, leaving a wide empty perimeter so that Iroqua and other ancient enemies could not use them for cover. The nearest forest cover was several miles to the northwest. The Mizipi passed Ocatan to the west and then curved left and right in two giant oxbows before heading north. The trail to Cahokia followed the Mizipi for three miles, then continued straight when the river turned—

"Hurit, lead them into the bottomlands. The mud where the Mizipi has burst its banks."

She looked at him as if he were mad. Marcellinus was getting a little tired of that look today.

"The horses can't follow you there. If the soldiers pursue you, swim. Jump into the river, let the current take you. The Romans will not take off their armor to follow you into the water. Swim hard, come ashore on the west bank, walk north to Cahokia-across-the-water."

"With the four-legs, the Romans will get to Cahokia before we do."

"No. This is their strategic goal. They'll stop and fortify here."

Hurit shook her head. "How can you know that?"

"The Sixth can't take Cahokia by themselves. They want Ocatan, where the rivers meet. They will wait here at the confluence to join up with the legions from the east and the rest of the Sixth Ferrata from the south. This confluence is their strategic target for today. Whoever rules the rivers rules Nova Hesperia."

"The Mizipi is our river."

"Not anymore. Hurit, it's the territory they want. This position. Slaughter is not their primary goal, though they'll do it if they have to. Which is why you all need to scatter into the countryside, and quickly."

"And you will not come?"

"No. I will stay here."

Trumpets sounded. The legionaries roared, and with a mighty crash the battering ram struck the gates.

Hurit put her hands up to her ears. Marcellinus saw panic moving behind her eyes, shock beginning to creep in. He had to get her moving.

Hating himself, he shoved her. "Hurit! Are you a coward or a warrior? Snap out of it. Now. Come *on*."

They hurried past the Temple Mound, north through the streets of the town. The word was spreading, and Ocatan was organizing. On their right Dowanhowee and four other women were gathering people from outside their houses and chivvying them north. Anapetu walked twenty feet to their left doing the same thing, the arrow shaft still protruding obscenely from her shoulder. No time now to pull it out and dress the wound.

The north gate was ajar. Some men, women, and families were already escaping. Fleeing the town was hardly an original idea. But too many people still stood around confused or in shock, waiting for friends or family, waiting to be told what to do, or just terrified of leaving the protection of the palisade.

That protection was illusory. Even here on the far side of the small town they could hear the battering rams slamming against the gates. It was a testament to the Ocatani skill with wood that the gates still stood, but they could last only a matter of minutes.

"Go, Hurit. Lead those who will follow. Those who won't, leave them behind. Save who you can."

"Shit, Gaius . . . shit . . ."

Marcellinus put his hand on her shoulder and looked calmly into her eyes. "Hush, Hurit. You can do this. I trust you. Go."

Hurit nodded, smiled weakly, then turned away and raised her voice to a shout. "Come, all of you! We have to go, run toward Cahokia. By the river, near the mud. Follow me! Come!"

She hurried out of the gate. People followed. Marcellinus and Anapetu shooed others after her: families, women, elders. Dowanhowee gathered her children, pushing them on, nodded briefly at Marcellinus, and disappeared out the gate.

Marcellinus looked at Anapetu. "You too, clan chief."

Anapetu eyed him tautly. "Not while I breathe."

He almost laughed. "You'll flee once you're dead?"

A huge splintering crash. A roar. The tumult of steel against steel. The Romans were through the gates of Ocatan.

Anapetu put her head on one side, still birdlike. The

scar on her cheek pulsed. "I do not see you running either, Gaius Wanageeska."

"No . . ." Marcellinus gave it up. "Come on, then."

As they came back around the Temple Mound, they entered Hades.

The mighty gates of Ocatan were broken off their hinges and flat on the ground, along with the left firing platform and the complete fifty-foot section of wall between that and the next platform. The section of palisade on the right side of the gate was in flames, smoke billowing west toward the Mizipi.

The First Ocatani stood firm, still in triple formation, fighting two cohorts of the Sixth Ferrata with swords and axes. In some places the warring armies were pressed together, the shields of the 33rd in Ocatani hands locked firm against the shields of the Sixth. Men pushed and shoved and had fallen on both sides, soldiers of the Sixth as well as warriors of Ocatan. Elsewhere in the lines there was some separation, with the freedom to swing weapons.

It was the only struggle in the plaza that looked even, and it couldn't last long. Everywhere else was melee, legionary against Hesperian warrior, steel against stone and wood and iron, and above them all two dozen circling Hawks of Ocatan picking out their targets.

If nothing else, Ocatan was not making it easy for Roma.

"Help the wounded onto the Temple Mound," Marcellinus said, and looked down at Anapetu. "The other wounded. Don't take risks."

"No risks?" she said wryly, and was gone from his side, running to the left. Again her cloak billowed.

With a scream, a man hurtled out of the sky to smash into the ground almost at Marcellinus's feet, instantly silenced by his harsh communion with terra firma. Marcellinus looked up. Only four warriors remained alive on the Sky Lantern, and one of them was no longer shooting arrows; he clutched his neck with one hand and hung grimly to the steel frame with the other.

Iniwa and his men were in the main fray. Off to the left on the Mound of the Cedars, a squad of Ocatani archers stood methodically loosing arrows, many of which were finding their mark. For a fleeting moment Marcellinus thought that perhaps the Ocatani could hold the Romans back, that this battle was not a foregone conclusion, after all, and then two things happened almost simultaneously.

Soldiers of Roma had secured the area around the gate. Now in came the Cohors Equitate, the horsemen of the Fourth Gallorum. They rode in a paired formation, two by two, their swords held in front of them, ready to cut down barbarians from the saddle. Once through the gate, they wheeled to the left as one. Some of the braver Ocatani ran at the horsemen howling their war cries, only to be mercilessly slashed down. The cavalry came on, curving in an arc to the right through the plaza, and Marcellinus saw that they would soon flank the First Ocatani and attack them from the rear.

Just moments later the Shappa Ta'atani came over the broken stockade to the left of the gates. To Marcellinus's experienced eye the Shappans looked completely different from the Ocatani in their clothing as well as the harsh tattoos and jagged scarifications that marked their faces, in contrast to the more subtle markings and quickly applied war paint of the more northerly Mizipians. However, to ensure that the Romans did not inadvertently slay their allies in the heat of battle, the Shappans also—bizarrely—wore lengths of red ribbon twisted into their hair roaches or the shoulders of their tunics.

The Shappa Ta'atani forces parted in the middle. The leftmost column made a beeline for the Mound of the Cedars, cutting down all the Ocatani in their way, while the warriors on the right attempted to hack a clear path toward the Temple Mound. Son of the Sun obviously

had been given his orders: neutralize the archers of Ocatan, take and hold the high ground.

Even now, Marcellinus balked at fighting Romans.
But he would happily shed Shappan blood.

As he ran for the Mound of the Cedars, he passed two
Ocatani hacking scalps from Roman heads. "Leave that
now!" he shouted. "Come with me!"

Marcellinus was about to snatch up a discarded
Roman helmet when two legionaries burst out of the
fray and rushed toward him. He glimpsed a gladius in
midswing and jerked up his wooden shield instinctively.
The gladius hacked right through the cedar wood, sending the top third of the shield spinning away through the
air. Rather than fall back, Marcellinus lunged forward
and thrust the remains of the splintered shield into the
legionary's face. The man parried it and stabbed forward again, but Marcellinus slashed at the soldier's
thigh just above his leg greave. The wound gushed blood,
the legionary went down, and Marcellinus jumped over
him. Meanwhile, one of the two Ocatani buried his ax
in the neck of the second soldier and yanked it free as
the man fell.

Marcellinus had just spilled Roman blood. Perhaps
not a killing stroke, but—

He shoved the thought out of his mind. He would
probably be dead in moments, anyway.

He ran on, two dozen more Ocatani braves pounding
in his wake. Shouting "Ocatan!" they ran up onto the
Mound of the Cedars.

The Shappa Ta'atani whirled to meet them. Marcellinus swung, ducked, and slashed again, and a warrior
with spiral whorls etched into both cheeks and a red
ribbon at his throat went down with blood spilling from
his gut. Marcellinus grabbed the brave's shield and
jammed it into the face of another warrior of Shappa
Ta'atan.

The bloodlust was filling him now, the warrior fury
that he needed. It had been a long time since the battle
rage had consumed him with such force, and he bel-

lowed with a kind of crazed laughter. Two Shappan warriors jumped at him; he dodged the stone mace of the first and drove his shoulder into the man's chest, thrust upward with the gladius right through the reed armor, swung the shield at another ribboned enemy.

More Ocatan warriors were coming to him now, many from the First Ocatani. In his brief glances at the battlefield Marcellinus could see that Ocatan was losing the fight badly. These were the survivors of the combat, fleeing the horses, falling back to the high ground. He saw no sign of Coosan. The Ocatani centurion must have fallen.

Even as more came, Marcellinus and the Ocatani warriors around him pushed the Shappans back, slaying them right and left. The men of Ocatan were on their home turf, and their battle spirit was greater than that of the southern braves.

Always Marcellinus looked for Son of the Sun. The Caddoan war chief must be there, surely. He was a huge man who had made his reputation from war, and so it was unthinkable that he would not be leading his men, but Marcellinus could not see him.

Once more, his Hesperian shield was smashed to splinters. He dropped it and grabbed an ax with his left hand, slamming it into the head of a strong Shappan woman who had just cut an Ocatani to the ground in front of him. She went down, still jabbing at his legs; he kicked her, and another brave of the First Ocatani thrust a gladius into her kidney before she could get up again. Marcellinus hamstrung yet another warrior with his blade, parried, and dropped a red-ribboned and insanely grimacing warrior who had appeared from nowhere above him on the slope of the mound, then swung again, panting.

There were no more. The few remaining Shappans were running down the mound. Arrows whizzed past Marcellinus's head. The Ocatani archers at the mound's crest were still doing their deadly work.

Marcellinus achieved the plateau and took stock. He

was covered in blood and felt the dull ache of bruises and the sharp bite of cuts from half a score of places on his body, but he had all his limbs and—a mercy—nobody had landed a blow on his unprotected head.

He was surrounded by sixty or seventy men and women of Ocatan, the vast majority of them warriors with weapons.

The plaza was strewn with dead Mizipians and a much smaller number of dead Romans, many of whom were already being carried out of the town and back to their legionary medici on the ships.

Elsewhere, the fighting had paused. The crest of the Temple Mound was held by several hundred Ocatani. A third of the way between the Temple Mound and the gates, a mob of Shappa Ta'atani stood waiting. The few dozen warriors of the First Ocatani who were not either dead or on one of the mounds had been herded together by a century of the Sixth Ferrata to stand against the still-sound palisade wall on the western side of the town, along with the few women and children who had not escaped or climbed the Temple Mound or perhaps remained hidden in their huts. The Roman legionaries had withdrawn to the town's edge to rest before the final push; safely beyond bow range, they sauntered around and chatted like men at the baths or a public park.

No Hawks flew now. Marcellinus could not see the rear of the Temple Mound, where Ocatan's Longhouse of the Hawks sat at the mound's base, but it was obviously in Roman hands by then. Similarly, the Sky Lantern no longer floated above him; he hoped the surviving warriors had pulled the bolts to free themselves and let the winds blow them to safety.

From the height of the Mound of the Cedars and with the gates demolished and a large section of the palisade smashed or burned, Marcellinus could see clear down to the river. All seven of the Roman quinqueremes were now beached. Rolled-up tents and sacks of grain were being unloaded onto the shore.

The mopping up was yet to be completed, but as far

as the Romans were concerned, the battle was already won.

The cavalry was gone. Sometime during Marcellinus's fight to rescue the Ocatani archers from the treacherous Shappa Ta'atani, the Cohors IV Gallorum Equitata had finished its work of annihilating the First Ocatani and had left the town. Marcellinus felt cold.

Then Son of the Sun walked out from the mass of Shappa Ta'atani in the plaza and stared up at them, his legs apart and his hands on his hips. He was not wearing the regalia of a Mizipi chieftain, of course, but his size and stance were unmistakable.

Marcellinus's blood boiled again.

His survey of the battleground had taken only moments. The braves around him were beginning to slump, staring bleakly out at the smoking remains of their town, their battle ardor draining. "Up, up!" he said. "Is that all you have? Are you all-done?"

Two of them raised their axes instinctively, and a third stepped forward, his fists clenched.

Marcellinus met his eye, not blinking. "Warriors, hear me. If we do not get ourselves to the Temple Mound, we will die here in minutes. Those Shappa bastards will attack in force. So let's go. Up, up!"

The Shappa Ta'atani outnumbered them five to one. Better to unite with the much larger group of Ocatani on the Temple Mound.

The warriors measured the distance with their eyes. "We will just die there instead of here," said the brave who had confronted Marcellinus. "Perhaps before we even—"

"Then we will sell our lives dearly."

They looked blank. The individual words were right, but the phrase made no sense in Cahokian. Marcellinus tried again. "Why wait here for death? Let us die well, shoulder to shoulder with our friends, on the sacred mound."

He hoped Anapetu had survived long enough to make

it to the Temple Mound. He tried not to think about Hurit.

Or about Sintikala and Kimimela and all the others he would never see again.

Suddenly he remembered the thunder and lightning of Sintikala's dream. The blood and the steel.

And the feel of her strong body, warm in his arms. Probably the last time he would ever hold her close . . .

He gritted his teeth. "Choose, Ocatani. Come with me to the Temple Mound or die here like dogs."

He bent forward at the waist and sprinted down the Mound of the Cedars.

The Temple Mound was perhaps two hundred feet away. The Shappa Ta'atani were three hundred feet to the side, but they reacted immediately, leaping up and nocking arrows. Marcellinus saw Son of the Sun turn, imagined the man's contemptuous glare.

Son of the Sun would have to wait. First Marcellinus had to get to the Temple Mound.

The Ocatani braves pounded along behind him, whooping. At least Marcellinus would not die alone.

An arrow flew past him. And then Son of the Sun raised his hand in command, and no more arrows came.

Many of the Ocatani, younger and fitter than Marcellinus, passed him on the level ground. They ran ten feet up the Temple Mound and slowed and turned, waiting for their brothers.

"Now!" came the shouted command of Son of the Sun, and the arrows flew.

Marcellinus saw them for an instant, the wave of death looming in his vision. He tried to react, to hit the ground, but there was no time.

An arrow struck him in the thigh, spinning him. Instants later another ripped a gobbet of flesh out of his upper arm.

Around him, Ocatani stumbled and fell. Marcellinus took the weight on his uninjured leg, the left leg, and tried to hold up one of the other men. He failed, and they both collapsed together.

Son of the Sun's arm was up again. The Shappans stopped shooting and watched them with interest.

At least ten of the Ocatani around Marcellinus were dead, pierced with arrows. Six more were down and screaming and would not be moving much farther in this life. Marcellinus could do nothing for them. He stood, tested his leg, and began to hobble up the Temple Mound as best he could, waiting for the arrow in the back that would end it.

The Temple Mound was only two-thirds as high as the Great Mound of Cahokia, but it looked infinite to him in that moment.

He heard a new bubbling scream beneath him and looked down. The Shappa Ta'atani had shot the rearmost Ocatani brave, the man lowest on the mound. He clearly heard Son of the Sun say, "The next," and half a dozen arrows slammed into the next warrior up. That man toppled and died without a sound.

Marcellinus understood.

So did all the men around him. Their nerves cracked, and it became a deadly race, men scrambling up the steep slope of the platform mound, Marcellinus only just managing to stay ahead of the last of them. Blood was pouring from his leg now.

Two more men died, arrows appearing to bloom from their bodies. Again it was the men lowest on the mound, the men losing the race.

Laughter, cruel laughter from below them in the plaza.

Iniwa's voice boomed from way above Marcellinus, and a wave of arrows flew in the opposite direction. Covering fire . . . The Shappa Ta'atani were forced back, farther from the mound's base.

Arrows thudded into the mound around Marcellinus now but barely pricked the soil. Some even slid in the grass. He was high enough, out of range.

His breath painful in his chest, his leg on fire, Marcellinus achieved the crest of the Temple Mound, the last to arrive of perhaps thirty surviving men he had brought across from the Mound of the Cedars. His vision clouded, and he slumped to the ground.

Somebody poked him. "Gaius Wanageeska," came an urgent voice he knew. "You must see this. Can you walk? Come."

Anapetu had pulled the arrow from her shoulder. She held a dirty cloth over the wound at the front; at the back, she let it bleed freely.

As for Marcellinus, the wound in his thigh was closing around the shaft of the Shappan arrow, but the much shallower gash on his arm was still dribbling blood. A woman of Ocatan, perhaps a healer, tried to staunch and bind it while he hobbled painfully the remaining fifty feet to the western edge of the Temple Mound. From this height they could see past the burning houses and over the palisade to the north and west, out toward the Mizipi.

Off in the distance he saw men and women running up the riverbank.

Following them, closing the distance rapidly, were two turmae of the IV Gallorum Equitata.

Marcellinus had been wrong. There would be no escape from Ocatan after all, even for the defenseless.

"Can you see Hurit?" he said.

"From here? No."

They needed Mahkah or Dustu, whose eyes never faltered however great the distance. But now Marcellinus saw one of the tiny running figures stop and turn to face the horsemen, standing still while the others continued to run. And as she braced herself, sword held out, he recognized her fighting stance.

"Get in the river," he said, willing her to move. "Get into the Mizipi. Go. Go."

The horses were walking now; obviously, the ground beneath them was treacherous. And indeed some of the other Ocatani were diving into the Mizipi now, wading in as best they could and then throwing themselves bodily into the waters.

And still the lone figure stood between the fleeing people of Ocatan and the relentless horsemen of Roma.

"Jove, Hurit. Please, damn you, you've done enough."

The first horseman was upon her. The decurion of the leading turma lifted himself in the saddle and swung his spatha in a blur of movement. Hurit parried, jumped back, darted left, slashed again.

The horse stopped, backed up, moved forward. The decurion hacked at her. Hurit lunged and again danced out of range, trying to move around the horse to attack the decurion from his left side.

The horse reared. Hurit jumped back. The decurion leaned forward and thrust his sword down.

"Shit," Marcellinus said.

The other riders were past the decurion now, running down the rest of the Ocatani. The decurion's horse was back at a canter as he hurried after them, leaning forward in the saddle, clutching at himself.

Was he injured? Behind him, was that a body in the mud?

"I can't see her," Marcellinus said. "Can you see? Is she dead? Anapetu?"

Anapetu had walked away to the north, still clutching her injured shoulder, looking not toward the Mizipi but up into the sky, saying words Marcellinus could not hear.

He did not need her to tell him. The decurion was alive, although perhaps wounded. And Marcellinus couldn't see a swimmer in the water near where Hurit had been.

Hurit was dead.

His heart felt leaden. His vision swam. He could no longer even see the Mizipi.

Pulling his pugio from his belt, brushing at his eyes, Marcellinus leaned forward and studied the arrow in his thigh.

At least Roman steel arrowheads went through cleanly.

*　*　*

They had the healing white salve in the Longhouse of the Temple Mound and plenty of weapons. And a Roman pilum worked well as a crutch.

Iniwa lived on top of his Temple Mound, and his longhouse was sturdy and lined with ramparts. A surprising number of Ocatani had survived; Marcellinus and Anapetu shared the mound top with perhaps two hundred other warriors and citizens.

Unfortunately, they had almost no food and very little water.

Summoned at last, Marcellinus hobbled into the longhouse, a single great hall with walls lined with chert figures, bare earth floors, and ladders leading up to the battlements above. In the hall's center stood Iniwa, now wearing the full regalia of his office, his face covered with a complicated pattern of war paint in red and blue and black. The war chief of Ocatan had dressed up to die.

"What happens outside, Wanageeska?"

"The Romans are unloading supplies. Digging in their defenses, building up an earthen rampart and ditch beyond the walls. Some are going house to house, looking for people hiding. I hope they don't know to check the grain stores under the floor. Those they find, they have ..." Marcellinus swallowed. "They are already forcing your people, captured Ocatani, to rebuild the areas of the palisade that were smashed or burned. The women they have kept aside in a separate pen for ... later on."

"Slaves," Iniwa said. "My people are slaves."

"The Romans need to secure Ocatan by nightfall," Marcellinus said. "They have enough men to make the town theirs and defend it against any counterattack."

"But we are still here."

"Not for long."

Iniwa stared at him balefully. "How will your people come for us?"

"They may storm the Temple Mound in the late afternoon. March up its slopes with Roman steel, keeping formation, shields up. An overwhelming number of legionaries, fully armored, would march right over us and kill us all. Or they may surround the mound and wait for you to come out and die in battle, or to starve and die, or kill yourselves. It depends on the whim of their Praetor." Marcellinus took a deep breath. "For now, we are guarded by the traitors of the Shappa Ta'atani. If we attack now, we may take some of them to hell with us, but the end result would be the same. Death. Unless."

"Unless what? Speak."

"Unless you surrender," Marcellinus said.

Iniwa stared at him, not blinking. "You say so?"

"Yes. Surrender, Iniwa. Yield the field. Lay down your weapons. No one could have done more than you, but it is over now. Enough Ocatani have already died. Your people up here have fought well, and they deserve to live."

"Leave our weapons on the sacred mound? Walk down and kneel to be butchered?"

"Yield freely and they will not slaughter you," Marcellinus said.

"And then all will be well?" Iniwa said sarcastically.

"Of course not, mighty chief. They will enslave you. If you are fortunate, you may be able to bargain to fight for Roma instead of against them, especially if you bring strong warriors they can use. Such things do happen. We can try to find out."

Iniwa still had not blinked as far as Marcellinus could see. He wondered if the chief was in some kind of fugue state or merely thinking intensely.

"Find out?"

"I can walk down under a white flag of parley, either alone or with you by my side, and we can talk with Roma."

Iniwa stood slowly, his face less than a foot from Marcellinus's. "You would parley now? When you refused before?"

"Then, the assault had begun. Their Praetor would

not have stopped it to talk to me. Now the town is theirs. They—"

The chief kicked away the pilum that Marcellinus was leaning on. Marcellinus fell hard onto the earthen floor, clutching his thigh and trying not to cry out. Iniwa grabbed the Roman spear up and whirled it around.

Marcellinus found himself flat on his back with the steel point of the pilum jabbing painfully into his abdomen. He forced himself to relax, lowering his injured leg to the ground. "Iniwa, mighty chief—"

"We will not grovel to Roma! We are strong! We are Ocatan!"

"You are defeated," Marcellinus said. "It is over."

Iniwa shoved the spear forward an inch. Marcellinus cried out, sucking in his stomach. "Iniwa, wait."

"You speak of the treachery of Shappa Ta'atan. What of the treachery of the Wanageeska?"

"I am no—"

"Twice a traitor! Once to your own people and now to me. You seek to buy the gratitude of Roma by giving me and my people to them?"

"No," said Marcellinus. "You, the Romans may spare. Me, they will likely kill as soon as the day is done."

Iniwa bent over and stared into Marcellinus's eyes. Now it was Marcellinus who forced himself not to blink.

"You lie," said the chief.

"No. I am sure of it."

Iniwa stood, spun the pilum again in his hands, and thrust its blunt haft into Marcellinus's stomach, driving the wind out of him. Marcellinus doubled up and rolled, retching. The chief tossed the spear aside. "It does not matter. Ocatan will not beg. Ocatan will die well. We will kill Romans and Shappa Ta'atani until we are called to the gods, in honor. You?" Iniwa looked down at him contemptuously. "You will do anything to live, say anything. I am all-done with you."

The war chief of Ocatan strode from the room without another word.

By the time Marcellinus had regained his breath, fetched his pilum crutch from the corner of the room, and staggered back out into the fresh air, the Ocatani were massing for their last charge with Iniwa at their head. Down in the plaza the Shappa Ta'atani had risen to their feet, weapons at the ready. Again Son of the Sun stood in front of his men with his hands on his hips and stared up at them.

Farther back, Roman legionaries stepped away from their labors and wiped sweat from their brows. Some picked up their swords; others merely folded their arms and watched with interest as if they were at the gladiatorial games.

In a way, they were. This would be a last battle of Hesperian against Hesperian, the remains of the once-proud Ocatani warriors against five times that number of Shappa Ta'atani. The outcome was not in doubt.

The Ocatani braves went over the edge of the mound roaring, with their spears and axes and maces and swords held high. None carried shields. They knew they would not live to see the sunset.

It was hard to watch, but Marcellinus forced himself, sinking down onto the grass with his head in his hands.

They fought valiantly, the last warriors of Ocatan. Iniwa met Son of the Sun head-on at the bottom of the mound, trading blow for blow for what seemed like half an hour before Son of the Sun cut him down, hacked his head from his shoulders, and mounted it on his spear.

Most of Iniwa's warriors were dead by that time. The Shappa Ta'atani lost maybe two dozen men.

The Romans watched cheerfully as the Shappa Ta'atani scalped the warriors of Ocatan and collected the best of their weapons, and then two centuries of the First Cohort of the Sixth Ferrata began to assemble in the plaza.

"It ends," said Anapetu. Sometime during the battle the Raven clan chief had come to sit by his side.

Marcellinus could not meet her eye. "If they had surrendered . . ."

"There is no surrender for us."

Marcellinus glanced around the mound top. Maybe twenty men and women remained with them. Six were warriors too wounded to fight, the rest ordinary townspeople, beaten, shocked, defeated. "We should save the Romans the trouble. Go down and surrender."

"No, Gaius Wanageeska." Anapetu drew her pugio.

"What? No!" Marcellinus reached out to grab her wrist.

She met his eye calmly. "My sisters are already dead. Leotie, Dowanhowee, perhaps the children, too. And what do you think will happen to me when the Romans take me? You see the pen they have put the women in. Why would I want to live for that?"

"Anapetu, you cannot."

Marcellinus still had her right hand imprisoned. She passed the pugio into her left hand and held it out to him, hilt first. "Then you must."

Aghast, he said: "I will not kill you, Anapetu. I can't."

"I would prefer it." Anapetu looked deep into his soul. "Gaius. Please?"

He sat, frozen.

Down in the plaza the Roman centuries had fallen into formation, two squares each ten ranks deep. Marcellinus heard the barked command, and the troops of Roma marched toward the base of the Temple Mound.

"Please, my friend," she said. "Honor me. For your Romans will not."

Marcellinus took the pugio and stared again into her face.

"You cannot disobey me," Anapetu said almost lightly. "I am your clan chief."

"Don't look at Roma," he said. "Look out at the river, the great Mizipi. Turn toward the sun. Feel it on your face."

As she turned into the light, he placed his hand on her cheek and kissed her forehead.

Marcellinus barely heard the legionaries arrive on the mound top. By that time he was one of only eight alive on the Temple Mound, the others having taken their own lives rather than be captured. He looked up only when he felt heat on his back; the Romans had set the longhouse on fire and were watching the blaze carefully in case warriors burst out of it. None did. All the warriors were dead or enslaved.

Anapetu lay in his lap. Marcellinus had covered her face with her raven cloak. Occasionally it billowed, almost as if her spirit were trying to fly away. Her blood soaked his legs.

The point of a gladius jabbed him in the ribs. He looked up to see a Roman legionary, shiny in steel, his helmet red-plumed. He looked a second time and saw a boy hardly older than Tahtay, clear-faced and clean-shaven but wearing a look of contempt and disgust so profound that the sneer was almost etched into his cheeks.

"Up, redskin," said the soldier. "Drop your filthy squaw."

Behind him they were rounding up the three living women at gladius point, taking them away separately. Marcellinus's gorge rose.

If he threw himself on the soldiers, they would kill him in an instant. Half of Marcellinus wanted that: to take them to hell and for all this to be over.

But he had sworn oaths. To do all in his power to prevent war even though he was in the middle of one. To protect Tahtay. And not to kill Romans, especially in cold blood.

He could not help Cahokia once he was dead.

And these were just boys Tahtay's age, trying to be men.

In Latin, Marcellinus said: "This was a great woman. She died well, just as the other dead men and women of

Ocatan you see before you died well. You will treat them with respect and let their people bury them with honor."

The legionary's mouth dropped open.

Marcellinus laid Anapetu's body down and struggled to push himself up onto his feet. He did not reach out for the spear to support himself. This boy would cut him down the moment he touched a weapon.

Nausea still wreathed him, but he felt as if he were a hundred miles away from his body.

"Lads?" The legionary beckoned. Three more soldiers hurried over.

Marcellinus looked at each in turn. Had he ever been as young as these men? Had his armor ever gleamed so brightly?

"I am Gaius Publius Marcellinus, late of the 33rd Hesperian Legion. I will see your commanding officer, and I will see him now."

They knew his name. The first soldier took a step back, stunned.

Marcellinus swayed on his injured leg, looked down at Anapetu again, swallowed. "I am Gaius Publius—"

The second soldier smashed him in the mouth with the butt of his gladius. Marcellinus fell across Anapetu and tried to push himself off her to show her some respect in death.

Then the legionaries started kicking him.

It took him much too long to lose consciousness.

CHAPTER 24

YEAR SEVEN, PLANTING MOON

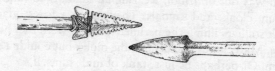

Racked with pain, he awoke several times to a blood-red haze and a deathly pounding in his head, as if he were still being beaten. The first time, Marcellinus threw up and disappeared back into the blackness without even knowing where he was. Later, he opened his eyes to find himself lying out in the sun in his own filth. Pain was everywhere, in his legs and arms and chest and head, above him and below him and stretching out into the distance.

Perhaps he should have gone with Anapetu. Maybe he would have found Hurit there.

He blinked painfully, and it was dark, nighttime, and he was rocking back and forth very slowly. On a boat?

He blinked again, found himself in the act of eating some kind of gruel, and coughed.

The next time he awoke, he was bent over a mule, arms and legs tied, or perhaps just broken so extensively that he was incapable of moving them. He could not tell, did not really think about it, just inhaled the stink of the mule and tried to straighten his neck. His ribs hurt.

Water, dashed into his face. Kimimela must be awakening him petulantly for another long day pulling the *Concordia* up the Mizipi.

Consciousness returned, along with anger. He flexed his fingers, found himself unbound, hard ground beneath him.

Marcellinus rolled over and sat up.

A soldier was inspecting him, a man perhaps ten years older than the four who had beaten him senseless. The man was out of armor, wearing an unadorned tunic, a sagum cloak, and sandals. They sat in a forest glade, with soldiers lining the perimeter. There were two bonfires. Marcellinus could smell the mules but couldn't see them. Or perhaps he just stank of mule himself.

Marcellinus glanced down. He still wore his Cahokian tunic, which was now ragged, sweat-stained, and blood-soiled.

"Who are you?" he said.

"I?" The soldier took a drink from his water skin and examined him more closely. "Ah. Fully lucid this time, I see. The earlier times you raved terribly. I am Lucius Agrippa."

The man's patrician attitude shone through every pore, and Marcellinus caught the scents of wine and rose water. Not a common soldier, then, despite his youth and clothing.

Marcellinus's head ached, but at least there was no nausea this time. His thigh burned like hell, and he was bruised everywhere, but no limbs seemed broken.

He looked up to find a soldier sitting before him in an unadorned tunic. Marcellinus blinked. "I'm sorry. Again?"

"Lucius Agrippa. And you are Gaius Marcellinus."

"Yes."

Agrippa's lip curled. "Turned native, I see."

Marcellinus saw a water skin lying next to him. He picked it up and put it to his lips, half expecting Agrippa to knock it out of his hands. It didn't happen. He tasted water and swallowed carefully.

"Marcellinus, who lost the 33rd."

"The same."

"Who stood with the Ocatani against us."

"Trying to prevent a massacre."

"Well, so much for that. And I hear you also stand with Cahokia."

Marcellinus looked around again. "Where are we?"

"On our way to the 27th."

"The 27th Legion?"

"No, man, the 27th of Maius. For Jupiter's sake, try to get your wits about you."

"Sorry."

"And so . . . ?"

"What?"

"You stand with Cahokia," Agrippa said with exaggerated patience. "You are a traitor to Roma."

"I was trying . . ." Trying to raise Cahokia to become a suitable province for Roma? Seeking peace? Creating a series of alliances up and down the great rivers of the land to give the Hesperians bargaining power with the Roman Imperium? Marcellinus shook his head. However honorable the path he thought himself on, however true he thought the words, they would sound ridiculous coming out of his mouth to this young fop of a, what, tribune?

Marcellinus met Agrippa's eye bleakly. "I have no interest in your opinion. Take me to your commanding officer immediately."

He expected a blow. Instead, Agrippa smiled. "You expect my commanding officer to take a brighter view of this than I?"

In an almost leisurely way, Agrippa reached out and took hold of Marcellinus's hair. Marcellinus's reactions were so slow that he did not even raise a hand to try to prevent it.

Agrippa tugged, tilting Marcellinus's head back. Again came the dissonant smell of rose water. With his other hand, Agrippa drew a line across Marcellinus's throat with his thumbnail. "You do not give me orders, traitor. You are a disgrace to Roma and to the Praetorship you once held. Think yourself lucky I *have* a commanding officer in the field, for if I did not, I would kill you this moment and enjoy it."

He let go of Marcellinus's hair. Marcellinus put his hand to his throat and said nothing.

Agrippa leaned back and propped himself up on his elbow as if he were on a couch at a fine banquet. "And so, to my commanding officer you will go. D'you think he will show you mercy?"

Carefully, Marcellinus shook his head. "I do not."

"Well, then," said Agrippa. "You shan't be disappointed."

The soldiers fed him, lashed his wrists together with sinew and steel wire, and then slept around the fire. Marcellinus was awake for half the night but after that slept and did not awaken until they threw him over the back of a mule the next morning.

Off they went again, following the line of the Oyo northeast. Sometimes the muddy trail took them along the riverbank and at other times through the spring-green forest; the trail was straighter than the river. Marcellinus's vantage point on the mule gave him little opportunity for sightseeing, but eventually he noticed that the Roman centuries were being guided by Hesperians, perhaps Cherokee by the sounds of their voices.

Agrippa and his centurions rode horses. The common soldiers did not march in formation but walked at their ease. The mules carried the food and the shields and armor. The Romans were obviously confident that the territory around them had been tamed.

Two days later Marcellinus was begging to walk with them, his wounded leg notwithstanding. Traveling thrown across a mule's back was ignominious and nauseating. To his surprise Agrippa readily agreed to let him try it under his own power and even ordered a soldier to fashion him a crutch. Now Marcellinus hobbled along the path at the back of the group with a rope tied about his waist, presumably to save the legionaries the inconvenience of strolling after him if he should attempt to make a snail's-pace break for it.

From time to time the centurions spoke to him to order him to hurry up or stand aside, eat or take a latrine break. The rank and file treated him with contempt and refused to respond to his questions. Agrippa, on his horse at the front of the party, was too far away to talk to.

As for Marcellinus, his thoughts were dominated by images of Anapetu's face as she lay bleeding to death in his arms.

Ocatan had fallen. What would happen now to Sintikala, Kimimela, Tahtay, Enopay . . . to Cahokia?

He might never find out the answers.

His leg grew stronger and his bruises retreated gradually, but in the midafternoon when the pain in his limbs became unbearable, he would find his lips moving and realize that under his breath he was singing his death song.

They were coming upon the legionary camps from the west, and the wind was out of the east. The aromas of wood smoke and latrines, horses and leather were already in the air. The combination of smells was almost unbearably nostalgic to Marcellinus even amid the grimness of his thoughts.

The blue Oyo was to his right; he occasionally saw it sparkle through the trees in the sunlight. They were reaching the forest's edge. The damp, fetid smell of the Roman camp grew even stronger.

Briefly Marcellinus dropped to one knee, his hand against a tree. His breath was becoming short, and he felt very alone. This was worse than walking into the Iroqua powwow.

His captors jerked the rope around his waist, almost pulling him over. Marcellinus pushed himself upright on his crutch and hurried on.

He looked up into the trees. This was a type of terrain he was familiar with from his long trek with the 33rd.

And in the next few moments he would look upon a castra again, filled with Romans he did not know.

Nova Hesperia had been invaded once more. Marcellinus could almost smell the sharpness of Roman steel on the air.

All of a sudden, they were out of the forest.

This was not a natural clearing. Until recently this hill had been wooded. Now the trees were gone, excised near the ground so that even their stumps would provide little cover for a skulking Hesperian. The clearing reeked of their sap.

Their wood had been used to build one of the biggest fortresses Marcellinus had ever seen, down the gently sloping meadow and up the other side from where he stood, with a long view across the Oyo.

The fortress was much larger and more permanent-looking than he had anticipated. He was so stunned that it took him a full minute to notice the second, identical fortress a mile beyond it on the next hill.

Identical, that is, aside from a tall red and blue banner, etched in black with a stylized face, that hung from a high pole mounted in the center of the camp.

That banner accompanied the Imperator and was never flown unless he was present.

His heart began to race, hammering like a manic blacksmith. His breath came short. "Holy Jove. Futete . . . Gods help us all . . ."

Marcellinus had stopped in his tracks. Agrippa was walking his horse back, looking down his nose at him with an expression of patrician amusement. "Welcome to Roma, Gaius Marcellinus."

"The imago of the Imperator," said Marcellinus.

"Just so," Agrippa said.

"His banner. The Imperator is *here*."

Hadrianus III was personally leading the invasion of Nova Hesperia.

One more surprise like this and Marcellinus might lose his mind completely. "Why?" he asked. And then, suspiciously: "Who are you?"

Agrippa smiled at Marcellinus's discomfiture. "Me? I am Lucius Flavius Agrippa, Praetor of the Legio XXVII Augusta Martia Victrix." He leaned forward in the saddle. "Still keen to speak to my commanding officer, traitor?"

Marcellinus shook his head, still in shock.

"Come," said Agrippa, and, mechanically, Marcellinus started walking again, down through the logged meadow toward the Roman fortresses.

Around and between the fortresses a mixed unit of Roman infantry and cavalry was exercising. The combined cohortes equitate of Marcellinus's experience had consisted of six centuries of ground troops along with four turmae of thirty-two cavalrymen each, and it looked very much as if two such cohorts were drilling in mock battle against each other.

It was, Marcellinus knew, even more important to keep horsemen trained and drilled than it was for infantry; cavalry lost its edge more quickly. He wondered how many horses Hadrianus had brought with him. The Imperator certainly would have brought some dedicated cavalry units along with these.

The far hillside and the valley beyond were dotted with grazing animals. They were four-legged, but from the size of their heads and the length of their ears, Marcellinus knew them for mules.

To protect himself, the Imperator would have brought the strongest, most professional fighting legions he had available. Hard. Efficient. Used to winning against all odds.

Marcellinus cleared his throat. "Lucius Agrippa?"

Agrippa's horse was a fine white Arabian, a beast of a quality Marcellinus had not seen for ten years. From high on its back, Agrippa eyed him. "Gaius Marcellinus?"

"Which is the second legion?"

Agrippa made a negligent gesture toward the nearer of the two fortresses. "The Legio III Parthica. Glory days long past if you ask me, but a competent enough bunch for all that."

"Very good." Marcellinus nodded calmly. "Very good indeed."

Inside, his thoughts were turbulent.

The Third Parthica had been raised by Septimius Severus in A.D. 197 for his Parthian campaign and then led by his son Geta in the civil war in which he had defeated and eventually killed his violent and unstable brother, Caracalla. The Third Parthians had gone from one victory to the next in the thousand years that followed and most recently had been one of the key legions on Hadrianus's eastern front.

If the Third could be spared from Asia—and the Imperator, too!—at least the war against the Mongol Khan must be going well.

"And if you would: remind me about the 27th."

Agrippa looked irritated. "The Augustan. Gemina, as was."

"Ah, of course, from the Middle East. My apologies, Praetor. My memory is rusty."

The Legio XXVII Augusta Martia Victrix had been formed much more recently, during Marcellinus's lifetime. Two legions decimated in the wars against the Khwarezmian Sultanate and other Islamic powers had been merged into one by Titus Augustus, the first Imperator Marcellinus had served. They had been known initially as the Legio XXVII Gemina to mark their rebirth and two-legion heritage, but Titus Augustus had rededicated them after they had earned their laurels in their second successful campaign.

Another extremely professional legion, hardened in battle on unforgiving terrain.

Marcellinus blew out a long breath. The Third Parthian and the 27th Augustan? Could it be any worse? "Nova Hesperia isn't going to know what hit it."

"Quite," Agrippa said.

"I liked Titus Augustus."

Agrippa's mouth crinkled. "Didn't know him personally."

"Your loss."

"None of the men serving now knew him, either." Agrippa smirked. "They're too young."

"Thanks a lot." Some of the seasoned centurions probably did. The aquiliferi honor guard. Marcellinus wasn't *that* old. He let it drop.

"And Gaius Marcellinus?"

"Lucius Agrippa?"

"Don't try to befriend me. You're still a traitor."

Marcellinus raised his eyebrows. "So noted, sir."

Two turmae of horse wheeled around their centuries at full gallop, lances up and maintaining perfect formation. Too far away to be sure, but those men looked like auxiliaries from central Europa or western Asia, Roma's provinces with a strong equestrian tradition. Marcellinus could not help but wonder how Hesperian warriors—even well-trained squads such as the First Cahokian—would fare against the dazzling proficiency of elite horse units like this in a military action on an open field.

Soldiers emerged from the Westgate of the nearer fortress, marching in step. A full cohort of the Third Parthian, also drilling; once they were all on open ground, they quickly broke out into a battle line facing the mixed cohorts and began an advance-and-retreat exercise as the cohortes equitate hurriedly merged to defend against them with the infantry in the center and the cavalry flanking it.

The shouted orders of the centurions wafted on the breeze to Marcellinus and the others. Hadrianus kept his men sharp. From the rear fortress yet more men were coming forth in formation, a single century of what looked like Praetorian Guard from their height, impeccable bearing, and ornate oval shields. They were led by officers on four matched Persian horses and marched in a direct line toward Marcellinus and Agrippa.

Their centurion barked a single command. The Praetorians split neatly into two columns and parted to flow around Agrippa, Marcellinus, and the rest of the party.

Their escort turned and began its way back through the shallow valley to the second Roman fortress.

Entering the fortress of the XXVII Augusta Martia Victrix felt like being consumed. Marcellinus walked into the Southgate beneath the legionary signum of a rampant scarlet lion, through walls ten feet thick, and past immaculately dressed Roman sentries who watched them, expressionless.

The intervallum of the fortress was a flurry of activity. Centuries marched, loaded carts rumbled, individuals hurried right and left. Among the Romans Marcellinus spotted the occasional Hesperian: a Cherokee scout here, a Piscataway brave there.

Every Roman soldier not marching in drill stopped to stare as they passed. The news of Marcellinus's capture had preceded him; these soldiers knew who he was and despised him. They understood how he had failed his men. Their antipathy made that abundantly clear.

Shaken, his soul heavy, Marcellinus looked around at the buildings and tried to distract himself.

All Roman fortresses had the same plan, and even after all these years he knew the layout of the streets around him better than he knew the map of Cahokia. Having entered through the Porta Praetoria, or Southgate, they were now walking up the Cardo with barrack blocks to their left and right. Soon they would pass the weapons workshops and stable buildings and come to the cross street that was always named the Via Principalis. Then the granaries would be to his left, the Praetorium to his right, and the Principia, or legionary headquarters building, directly ahead.

From the size and stature of the buildings this looked like a fortress that had stood for years. Yet it was all new, and the wood still smelled fresh.

At another order from their centurion most of the Praetorians wheeled aside. Just six men now flanked the

Cahokian deputation, with Praetor Agrippa walking alongside.

They swung right and entered the Praetorium building.

"Lucius Flavius Agrippa, Gaius Publius Marcellinus: enter the presence of Imperator Hadrianus III," said the Praetorian centurion with professionally repressed distaste toward Marcellinus's name.

Marcellinus tried to take a deep breath, but his ribs were still painful from the punishment he had received on the top of Ocatan's Temple Mound. He was to be given no time to prepare; apparently he would enter the Imperial presence just as he was, dirty, rank, and unshaven from the long journey from Ocatan.

The doors opened. Marcellinus limped forward into a large wooden hall with a plank floor and high windows, with Lucius Agrippa by his side and the Praetorian Guards dogging his heels.

The Imperator of the Roman world was a well-built man with curly hair wearing the armor and uniform of a Praetor with a purple sash in addition to denote his office. He had changed very little in the ten years since Marcellinus had seen him last. Accustomed to soldiers and now to braves who were outdoors in all weathers, Marcellinus thought that Hadrianus seemed baby-faced and pampered, slightly effete.

It was an illusion. Marcellinus knew that Hadrianus had a keen political brain and an iron will and was an excellent judge of character. He was a ruthless strategist in the corridors of Roma and on the fields of war. Underestimating him could be a fatal error.

"Hail, Caesar." Agrippa saluted. "The navy of Calidius Verus did its job well. Ocatan is taken, the confluence secured. The cream of Ocatan's warriors slain, the remainder enslaved. Minimal casualties to the Sixth. The Shappa Ta'atani fought well for us. Oh, and we captured Gaius Marcellinus."

"Hail, Caesar," Marcellinus said, and bowed.

"Ah, our rogue Praetor," said the Imperator, and waited.

Marcellinus cleared his throat. "Six years ago, the 33rd Hesperian Legion fell in battle. I alone bear full responsibility for the loss of the men under my command."

Above them the wind whistled in the eaves. Marcellinus heard terse commands out in the street and the regular tromp of marching feet. From somewhere in the distance came the clatter of hammering.

"Perhaps you come to deliver to me the Eagle of your fallen legion?" the Imperator prompted.

"The Aquila of the 33rd is in Cahokia in safekeeping." Marcellinus hesitated. "Perhaps I can bring it to you in due course."

"Or perhaps I will go and fetch it myself," Hadrianus said.

Agrippa grinned unpleasantly. Marcellinus kept his eyes lowered. "Just so, Caesar."

The air around him felt brittle. Marcellinus waited.

"And so here we find you at last, Gaius Marcellinus, carving out your own private Imperium in Nova Hesperia. Building a little empire among the red men."

Marcellinus stared at him, shocked beyond words. "What?"

Two Praetorians grabbed him, knocking his feet out from beneath him. Marcellinus fell forward onto his hands and knees and roared at the sudden blaze of pain through his injured leg.

"Sit up, man," Agrippa said.

Marcellinus pushed himself back onto his knees as best he could, hands clamped around his thigh. He hoped the wound had not reopened.

"Well?" said the Imperator.

Marcellinus gritted his teeth. "No, Caesar. Building an empire for myself was the farthest thing from my thoughts. Never once did I consider it. Never."

Hadrianus walked around him slowly, maintaining a distance of some six feet. Marcellinus was reminded of

Avenaka's predatory circling on Sintikala's mound, taking his measure. "Really? Not even the glimmer of such an ambition?"

"Quite sure, Caesar."

"Well, that seems beyond belief," Agrippa said.

Marcellinus glowered up at him. "Because you'd have attempted it, in my place? You would have failed spectacularly."

The Imperator completed his circuit and appeared in front of him again. "Now, now, Lucius. That matches what they said of him back in Roma. Praetor Gaius Marcellinus, a solid soldier and a good commander. Reliable. Loyal. Always the Imperator's man."

It had not occurred to Marcellinus that his record and reputation might count for anything. "Thank you, sir."

Agrippa smiled lazily. "Gaius Marcellinus. Strong on tactics. Weak on strategy. Not a general of . . . long-term vision."

This, Marcellinus did not honor with a reply.

"And that is one of the reasons I selected him for Nova Hesperia in the first place," said the Imperator.

"Because he was dispensable?" Agrippa asked.

"Oh, tut, tut, Lucius Agrippa. That was not my meaning at all." Hadrianus squatted down by Marcellinus and stared into his eyes, his expression icy. "None of my soldiers is dispensable."

Marcellinus swallowed. Clashing images warred in his mind: the men of the 33rd Hesperian falling under the liquid flame from Cahokian Thunderbirds, Ocatani warriors and ordinary townsfolk slain by the pila and gladii of the Sixth Ferrata.

Pollius Scapax. Yahto. Hurit. Anapetu.

"Your opinion, Gaius Marcellinus?"

"I agree, Caesar. No one is dispensable."

"Although I must say that when I ordered you to deploy to Nova Hesperia, I did not expect you to take to the place with such . . . enthusiasm."

Marcellinus lowered his head.

Hadrianus stood. "A long and somewhat distinguished life of service to the Imperium. You would say so?"

"Yes, Caesar."

"And what services to the Imperium can you show me for your past six years on my behalf?"

This was it. Marcellinus took a deep breath.

Beyond anything else, he wished he did not have to give this speech on his knees.

"I led the 33rd Hesperian against Cahokia and was defeated largely because of their use of Greek fire, delivered against my legion from the air. We had no way of defending ourselves from such an attack. I then led a final assault on the Great Mound of Cahokia, which was repulsed. I was captured and found myself stranded in Cahokia."

" 'Found yourself'?" Agrippa murmured.

Marcellinus ignored him. "I alone was spared by the Cahokian paramount chief, to teach them my language. In time I also introduced various innovations, certain civilizing improvements to the city: a bathhouse and other structures of brick, wheelbarrows and wagons, progress with metals, a design for a waterwheel, and so forth. My motivation for doing this was to make Cahokia a worthy province for Roma."

Agrippa's eyes narrowed. "A worthy province with a longship, Roman weaponry, siege engines?"

All Marcellinus could do was brazen it out. "Yes. I have commanded Cahokian warriors in battle against their ancient enemy, the Five Tribes of the Iroqua. I have also helped them make a treaty of peace with those tribes, a treaty that currently holds. The Iroqua captured a longship from Roma, and Cahokia took it in battle. I used this ship to travel down the Mizipi to the southern sea a thousand miles distant and back again, and also up another river to the plains in the north and west."

The Imperator and Agrippa exchanged a quick glance, and Marcellinus realized that for the first time he had told them something they did not already know.

"The plains," Hadrianus said.

"Quite the exciting life you have led," Agrippa added.

"And all in service of Roma," said the Imperator somewhat ironically.

"In original intent." Marcellinus took a deep breath. "Although . . ."

"Yes?"

"Last year, far down the Mizipi, my longship was attacked by an expeditionary force from the Sixth Ironclads. We did not even know they were there until they attacked us. We defended ourselves. And although I myself did not draw Roman blood—"

"Of course not." Agrippa smirked.

"You may consult their centurion, Manius Ifer, on that point. Nonetheless, blood was spilled. And after we defeated them, we let the survivors go free . . . But you knew of this."

Hadrianus was smiling tautly. "I know everything."

"Then you also know that had we been captured by the Sixth, it is probable that the Yokot'an Maya would have come to our aid. It appears that Calidius Verus has antagonized them."

"Verus can be a little ham-fisted at times." Hadrianus cocked an eye at Marcellinus. "Anyway, yes, dispatches do eventually crawl up the coast to the Chesapica and then along the trail to me."

Marcellinus nodded. "Then you also read my letter? I prepared letters and sent them to the leaders of the Powhatani and Nanticoke people of the eastern shores."

"I received four copies. They are the sole reason you still live. Any other Imperator might have thrown you in chains already, or pulled your tongue out through the back of your head, or some other such unpleasantness."

Marcellinus nodded, temporarily lost for words.

Agrippa stepped in. "However, the fact remains that you squandered your legion and then kept yourself alive at all costs. Raising a province for Roma, you say? Preposterous."

Marcellinus gave him a long look but addressed his words to the Imperator. "Cahokia—the whole of Nova

Hesperia—can make a good trading partner for Roma. My legion is lost, but—"

"Much worse than *lost*," Agrippa said.

Marcellinus glanced at him, suddenly fearful. "Worse?"

"Oh, has no one told you yet? You and your legion have suffered the Damnatio Memoriae."

Marcellinus froze. Even his lips felt numb. "My legion? Damned?"

The Damnatio wiped his legion from the lists, its name and number expunged as if it had never existed. If the name of the 33rd had been engraved on any monuments, it would have been chiseled out, and Marcellinus's own name likewise, blacked out of any historical scroll or military record that once had contained it.

Gaius Publius Marcellinus and the Legio XXXIII Hesperia had been removed from history.

He might have expected such ignominy for himself. But his whole legion? Aelfric and the loyal tribunes, Scapax and the career centurions, the veterans of the aquiliferi, the thousands of good men under his command, all disgraced in death, their families robbed of their honor, military pensions, and perhaps even their property?

"You're lying," Marcellinus said hoarsely.

"Am I, now? The scrapings of the Imperial army, swept together into a legion of misfits and cowards who could not even survive the feeble peckings of these redskin savages—"

Marcellinus hurled himself forward. His hands were fettered, but his shoulder crashed into Agrippa's chest before the Praetor could even raise his hands in defense. Agrippa sprawled back across the floor. Marcellinus brought his head down, aiming for Agrippa's nose, but the younger man jerked away and Marcellinus's forehead smacked painfully into his collarbone. Both men shouted in pain.

Marcellinus whipped his head up and caught Agrippa on the chin, snapping his teeth together onto his tongue. Blood spilled from Agrippa's mouth, and he kicked upward, catching Marcellinus's thigh wound.

The Praetorian Guards seized Marcellinus and dragged him away. Agrippa got in a kick to his gut before they took him out of range, and then two more of the Imperator's guards grasped Agrippa's shoulders to pull him back.

Marcellinus curled up and went limp. Hot anger still surged through him, but he hardly needed another beating.

A boot went into his ribs, and another met his chest, and he howled in mixed rage and pain.

"Enough!" The Imperator's voice cut the air like a blade. "Desist."

Marcellinus turned his head and was gratified to see Agrippa still down, gasping for breath and staring at him with an expression of unblinking hatred.

Hadrianus, in contrast, was smiling broadly. "Really, gentlemen. Guards, please lift my generals to their feet. Place them on couches ten feet apart. Stand over them to keep them there."

Clearly the Imperator was heartily amused. Marcellinus blew out a long breath as the Praetorians half dragged, half carried him to a couch and plunked him on it without ceremony.

His ribs were not broken. It would have hurt more. Agrippa still had blood pouring from his mouth, and thank the gods, Marcellinus had done enough damage to his tongue to stop him from talking.

"Caesar," Marcellinus said once he had enough breath. "Repeal the Damnatio, I beg you. Not for me. I accept all blame for the loss of the Fighting 33rd. I take their shame entirely onto my own head. But I beseech you to lift the Damnatio from the souls and memories of my men."

Hadrianus shook his head. "And this is the matter that concerns you most at this precise instant?"

"Yes, Caesar."

Hadrianus stared, no longer smiling. The moment extended. Agrippa wiped his mouth on a napkin brought by one of the Praetorians and glared.

The Imperator said: "Gaius Marcellinus, under some circumstances you might have died a hero. Since you inexplicably survived when your entire legion perished, there are serious charges leveled against you. You do understand this, yes?"

"Yes, Caesar."

"Then tell me why I should not have you killed."

Marcellinus paused. "Because I have information. And because I might be able to make some helpful suggestions."

"Information?"

"Not everyone in my legion perished," Marcellinus said. "I heard that some four dozen survivors set out for Vinlandia. I do not know whether they made it. It appears a handful more may still live far up the Wemissori River to the west." He chose not to mention Aelfric and Bjarnason. Let them make their own decisions.

He waited. "Did they make it to Vinlandia?"

"Never heard of them," Hadrianus said.

Agrippa was frowning. "And why did you not also try to make your way to Vinlandia?"

"I judged my place was in Cahokia," Marcellinus said levelly.

"In the city where your legion was destroyed?"

"Exactly so."

Agrippa spit into the napkin. "You are a dead man, Gaius Marcellinus."

"Only once I say so." Hadrianus considered it. "You are extremely dirty, Gaius Marcellinus."

"I was not permitted the luxury of preparing myself," Marcellinus said. "Caesar? The Damnatio?"

"Good grief, man; mention that once more and I'll kill you myself." Hadrianus snapped his fingers, and the tallest of the Praetorians stepped forward. "Get this terrible specimen washed up. He stinks like a redskin. Bring a medicus to look at his leg. And for gods' sakes, dress him like a Roman again even if it's just for show."

* * *

Escorted back to the Praetorium building two hours later wearing a simple Roman tunic, Marcellinus was ushered into a peristylium area, a small courtyard open to the sky surrounded by a portico of rough wooden columns. Hesperian sunflowers in pots marked the four corners of the square.

At a table in the rear of the peristylium Hadrianus poured wine into a beaker and added water. He had thrown aside his purple sash of office and now unbuckled his breastplate one-handed as he drank. Beneath it he wore a tunic of fine Egyptian linen, a thin purple stripe on either side from shoulder to hem the only indication of his rank.

Agrippa was not there. Marcellinus was alone with his Imperator. Just as he had never imagined he would address the assembled Haudenosaunee nation, he had hardly foreseen a private audience with the master of the Roman world. Once again he found himself in a situation for which he was ill prepared.

The Imperator tossed his breastplate onto one of the low couches and stepped into the sunlight in the middle of the peristylium. "Thank the gods it's getting a little warmer. The cold and damp of Martius and Aprilis here were quite unbearable."

None of the Imperator's Praetorians were in evidence, not even a slave. In principle, if Marcellinus wished, he could leap on Hadrianus and attempt to strangle him.

If the Imperator did not kill him first, that was. Hadrianus was a good seven years younger than Marcellinus and looked fit and healthy.

But murder was not Marcellinus's style or intent, and he was willing to bet that Praetorians stood hidden just a quick call away. He picked up the proffered beaker and swirled the watered wine.

"It isn't poisoned," the Imperator said. "Please, sit."

Marcellinus took a sip. It was good wine.

"So, no gold in this godsforsaken land?"

Marcellinus unhooked the pouch at his belt and handed Hadrianus the golden birdman amulet. "This is the only piece I've laid my hands on the whole time I've been here, Caesar. The city of Shappa Ta'atan has a little, the traders at the Market of the Mud a little more. I think most of it comes up from the People of the Sun, the Yokot'an Maya, on the southern side of the gulf beyond the market, down where the Sixth Ironclads were stationed before they . . . came north."

Hadrianus grimaced and handed it back. "Hmmm. We'll keep looking."

Marcellinus nodded and massaged the side of his neck. The tension of the day was beginning to make his head ache.

"Agrippa insists that I kill you," the Imperator said. "He believes you a dangerous complication to what is otherwise a rather simple military engagement."

He appeared to be awaiting Marcellinus's reaction, but Marcellinus was tiring of games. "And yet I am not dead."

"I am hoping you are not entirely lost to us. That you might have some usefulness that would justify me keeping you alive. A man still passionate about the honor of his war dead . . . Well. Stirring stuff."

Marcellinus waited.

"Also, I believe you may have amassed some influence in Cahokia despite your protestations of innocence."

"I am innocent of empire building," Marcellinus said.

Hadrianus tasted his wine again and nodded. "I am a pragmatic soul, Gaius Marcellinus. I don't plan to spend the rest of my life in this abject wilderness, and so I need to do as expediency dictates and cut a corner now and then. You understand?"

"Perhaps," Marcellinus said, and then shook his head. "Actually, Caesar, I'm not sure that I do."

"I need Cahokia," the Imperator said bluntly. "Can you deliver it to me?"

Marcellinus blinked. "No, Caesar."

"I need grain, and I need gold. And then I will need flight. Cahokia has all of these things."

"Gold, I cannot promise you. Grain . . . well, there may be some scope for negotiation."

"So you do have some pull with these people?"

Marcellinus breathed deeply. "Caesar, I believe Cahokia—perhaps the entirety of Nova Hesperia—should govern itself as an ally and trading partner to Roma. I believe this would be in the best interests of Roma as well as the Mizipian people. And I am prepared to justify that statement at whatever length you have time for."

Hadrianus stared. "You think I should pay for my grain like a merchant? That I have crossed the Atlanticus for commerce?"

"No, Caesar. Just that—"

The Imperator raised his hand. "I require Cahokia's complete submission, and I require it immediately. If they lay down arms and surrender their city and their grain, I am prepared to be lenient. If they resist . . . well, by now the lesson of Ocatan should have sunk home.

"Gaius Marcellinus, I believe you may be able to persuade them of the futility of opposing Roma. If not, you are of no further use to me. Well? Will Cahokia surrender?"

"No, Caesar."

"Even if the alternative is their complete eradication?" Hadrianus said, and Marcellinus had to stifle a shiver at how casually the Imperator said the words.

"Well," he said. "Naturally, that's hard to answer."

"Answer it," the Imperator said.

Marcellinus frowned and took an extended sip of his wine.

The Imperator Hadrianus III was a cunning man and a good reader of other men. For all his apparent collegiality, he obviously was talking to Marcellinus only in the hope that he could be of use.

In a moment of clarity, Marcellinus realized two things. The first was that attempting to pull the wool over this man's eyes would be suicide. If he attempted to lie, the Imperator was smart enough to detect it; he had been surrounded for over a decade by the best dissemblers in Roma and beyond. Marcellinus needed to take this man very seriously.

Second, there had to be much more to this than met the eye. Yes, all Imperators—all leaders—were obsessed with money, food, territory, and control. When Marcellinus was the Praetor of a legion marching across Nova Hesperia, most of his waking thoughts had been about gold, supplies, and discipline. But Marcellinus had been ordered to come here. Hadrianus had come entirely of his own accord despite having competent generals he could have sent instead.

Hesperia—perhaps even Cahokia—was critically important to Hadrianus. And Marcellinus had no idea why.

"And hurry," said the Imperator, "because your friends are on their way."

"My friends, Caesar?"

"It appears that the locals travel faster than Lucius Agrippa and his mules."

Marcellinus struggled to bite back his impatience. "Who is coming?"

Hadrianus stared, his eyes bleak once more. Marcellinus hurriedly dropped his gaze. "My apologies for my tone, Caesar. I was . . . startled. You say that envoys are coming from Cahokia?"

"Yes, indeed. Two days ago a lone savage showed up at the gates under a white flag with an epistle written on deerskin parchment by Tahtay of Cahokia. A chieftain there?"

Marcellinus's heart surged. "Yes, Caesar, the paramount chief of Cahokia."

"The letter informed me that Tahtay wished to come and talk with me, with some of his village elders in tow, if I would guarantee his safety. Of course, I assured the messenger that I would."

"And when do they arrive, Caesar?"

The Imperator smiled thinly. "Today, Gaius Marcellinus. Today."

"Great Juno," Marcellinus said.

"And that is why I thought it advisable to give you a bath. I would not want you to stink worse than they do and embarrass me."

"No, Caesar."

"And so you will assist me in this little conversation to ensure that Cahokia surrenders. Yes?"

Dry-mouthed, Marcellinus said, "Yes, Caesar. I will." His forehead creased. What on earth *was* he going to do?

"Good." The Imperator led the way to the edge of the courtyard and then stopped and turned. "And Gaius Marcellinus?"

"Caesar?"

"Leaders like you and I, we are men of cool blood. We see things as they truly are. But the rank and file bear grudges. Your legion was destroyed, and my troops are keen to avenge it. Soldiers are soldiers. And if men such as these were to be unleashed in Cahokia, that city would suffer, believe me. The slaughter and pillage would be unspeakable." Hadrianus smiled thinly. "You know how soldiers are. They need their rewards, just as senators do. And they have been here a *long* time."

Marcellinus swallowed. A threat, and not so thinly veiled. Suddenly they were back on the ground he had expected when he had walked into this fortress. After all, back in what now seemed a very distant past, Marcellinus himself had given his legionaries free rein in taking their revenge on a bunch of Iroqua captives.

"Yes, Caesar," he said.

"Help me talk to Cahokia, Gaius Marcellinus. Help them understand what is at stake. Bravado is admirable, but the consequences of resisting Roma are not in doubt. One way or another, I will feed my legions with Cahokian corn."

CHAPTER 25

YEAR SEVEN, PLANTING MOON

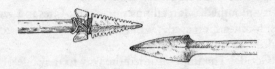

"There."

The Praetorian pointed as the Cahokian delegation walked out of the trees, but Marcellinus had seen them already. He had almost sensed them approaching even before they broke cover.

In the lead came Tahtay, bearing the golden Aquila of the 33rd Legion in his arms. Behind him walked Sintikala and Kimimela side by side, with Kimimela holding high the white flag of parley. And in the rear came Kanuna and . . . Wahchintonka.

"Well," Marcellinus said. Wahchintonka had not been included in any of their winter discussions.

Agrippa was watching his reaction with interest. "Not expecting Cahokia to send women and children to beg for mercy, Gaius Marcellinus?"

Marcellinus guarded his expression. "They are not children, Lucius Agrippa. Far from it. And I doubt that you will see any begging from them."

Marcellinus and the others were standing on the watchtower by the Westgate. Now that gate opened, and a turma of heavy cavalry swept out, fully armed and armored. In formation, the horsemen galloped across the clearing toward the Cahokians.

Marcellinus remembered Hurit's reaction to the monstrous four-legs. "Intimidation, Caesar?" he murmured.

The Cahokians had stopped dead when they saw thirty-two horsemen pounding toward them. Now they started walking again, Kimimela perhaps holding the white flag a little higher and walking a little closer to her mother.

The turma broke into two lines and slowed to a walk surrounding them. The Imperator smiled. "Merely an escort, Gaius Marcellinus. We must honor our guests with all due pageantry, must we not?"

The Cahokians marched into the Praetorium building with calm faces and raised chins. It was clear to Marcellinus that Tahtay and Kimimela were daunted but trying not to show it. They all looked dusty and tired, and he wondered how far they'd had to walk this day.

Kimimela surveyed Marcellinus quickly from top to toe, taking in the wound to his leg, the way he leaned on his stick, the bruises to his face and legs. Registering no visible emotion, she looked away. Tahtay nodded to him. Wahchintonka frowned. Sintikala and Kanuna did not acknowledge his presence.

Probably they had not even known Marcellinus still lived. Yet here he was, considerably battered and beaten but sharing the company of the Imperator. Hadrianus smiled, apparently pleased with the effect he had created.

The Cahokians ducked their heads in respect to the Imperator, and after a moment's hesitation, Tahtay came forward and handed the Eagle of the 33rd to Marcellinus.

It felt heavy in his hands, as if it held the weight of a thousand men. It had always been the plan for Marcellinus to bring it here to present it to Hadrianus. He had not known the Cahokians would bring it anyway.

"Praetor?" said the Imperator.

Marcellinus coughed but could not dislodge the lump in his throat. No words seemed appropriate. "Imperator Hadrianus III of Roma, I return to you the Eagle of the

33rd Hesperian Legion," he said simply, and raised it up before him.

With a clatter of boots the Praetorians all stood to attention. Kimimela jumped at the sudden sound, and even Sintikala looked around with eyes narrowed.

The Imperator bowed solemnly to the Aquila and stepped forward. "If I may?"

Now the moment had come, Marcellinus was oddly reluctant to release it. He turned the standard in his hands and looked long and hard at the eagle rampant, its gold plate chipped but still resplendent. The plaques beneath bore the "S.P.Q.R." of the Imperium and the "XXXIII Hesperia" of the Legion. His legion. His last command. His life's great disaster.

Marcellinus held it out.

The Imperator took the Aquila. He carried it to the doorway, where he handed it to the Praetorian centurion and muttered instructions into his ear.

Two other guards fell in on either side of the centurion. With great solemnity and a clatter of steel the trio saluted, wheeled, and marched out of the Praetorium building.

Rather forlornly, Marcellinus watched the Eagle of the 33rd depart from his life. He wished he had time to sit with closed eyes and absorb the moment.

Imperator Hadrianus returned. "Praetor Marcellinus. Perhaps you would care to make the introductions."

"Certainly, Caesar." Marcellinus stepped aside and half turned. "I present to you Tahtay, paramount chief of the Great City of Cahokia on the Mizipi, son of a chieftain and also a Fire Heart of the Blackfoot tribe. I present to you Sintikala, leader of the Hawk clan, chieftain and daughter of a chieftain. I present to you Kanuna, respected elder of the city. Finally, I present to you Wahchintonka, mighty warrior lieutenant, and Kimimela, who will help translate."

Hadrianus studied each in turn as they were introduced, staring into each face. Marcellinus had the impression he was cataloging the Cahokians, taking detailed mental notes.

Tahtay looked at Marcellinus. Marcellinus looked at the Imperator.

Hadrianus said, "Tahtay, Sintikala, Kanuna, Wahchintonka, Kimimela: you represent Cahokia?"

"We do, Caesar," Tahtay said in courteous Latin.

"Then I demand your complete and unconditional surrender. The city of Cahokia must bow to Roma immediately. It must provision us with supplies to maintain us through the winter and keep the Iroqua in check to prevent them from further harassing our legions. It must provide us with auxiliary troops for our armies. And it must provide aerial resources for the guidance and protection of our legions."

Tahtay glanced again at Marcellinus, who stared back at him impassively. Kimimela cleared her throat, and Tahtay swiveled his head back to meet the Imperator's eye.

"Well?" the Imperator asked Marcellinus. "They understand? You told me you had instructed them in Latin."

"I understand perfectly," Tahtay said. "And I regret to inform you that Cahokia cannot comply with your demands."

Hadrianus regarded him coolly. "Oh?"

Tahtay drew himself up to his full height, which was barely an inch shorter than the Imperator's. "I bring the greetings of the Great City of Cahokia on the Mizipi to the Imperator Hadrianus from across the sea. If your soldiers are hungry and seek our mercy, be assured we will not let them starve, for we are a kindly people and wish you no harm. However, Cahokia will not surrender, nor will we give you our corn. Although they are now allied with us, we cannot speak for the Five Tribes of the Haudenosaunee; those you must speak with separately. And our Hawks and Thunderbirds will not fly at your command. I am Tahtay of Cahokia, and I have spoken."

Marcellinus breathed a huge inward sigh of relief. For many weeks over the winter he and Aelfric had trained Tahtay for this, teaching him the formal language he might hear from a Roman general and coaching him in some phrases he could use in response. Enopay, Sinti-kala, and Kimimela had provided valuable extra help. But now that it had come to the crunch, Tahtay had exceeded Marcellinus's expectations and had looked calm and composed while doing so.

"That is unfortunate," Hadrianus said. "No doubt you comprehend the size of the forces that surround you. You can see the steel weapons they hold. Outside you will have admired our cavalry. We have thousands more. Your new friend Gaius Marcellinus has no doubt ad-vised you of the strength and discipline of a well-trained Roman legion, despite the inadequacies of his own. And I have two such legions here, and most of a third just a few days south of Cahokia. You will have heard from the remains of the Ocatani how effortlessly we destroyed their defenses and took their town from them. If Ca-hokia opposes us, its destruction is inevitable. And then we will take what we need from you and much more besides."

Silence fell while Tahtay regarded the Imperator with his serious brown eyes. Hadrianus had used several dif-ficult phrases, but Marcellinus thought Tahtay could probably deduce their meaning. Kimimela also had suf-ficient Latin to follow along. Sintikala and Kanuna, less fluent, were standing straight and calm and waiting to see what would happen next. Wahchintonka could have understood none of it, but his eyes moved from face to face, and even he would have felt the tension in the room.

Tahtay smiled. "Caesar, you are quite welcome to try."

They stared at each other, the Imperator of the Roman world and the boy from the Mizipian city.

Until that point Marcellinus had been surprised at nothing. Demanding Cahokia's surrender was the Imperator's obvious opening gambit. No sane commander fought a war if he could intimidate his opponent into submission.

But at this stage in the conversation both Marcellinus and Enopay had counseled Tahtay to compliment the Roman leader fulsomely and attempt to begin a negotiation.

Instead Tahtay had stood his ground. But looking at Hadrianus's face, Marcellinus thought the young war chief had made the wise call. Tahtay's simple resistance had thrown the ball back into the Imperator's court.

Unsmiling, the Imperator said, "Your city will burn. Your people will be crushed. Your women will suffer terrible indignities. And for what?"

"We have destroyed a Roman legion before. Perhaps you have not heard."

Marcellinus blanched. This was way off the script.

Now Hadrianus did smile, and it was not pleasant. "I have heard. But it will not happen again. Come, boy; you have Roman steel to the south of you, Roman steel to your east, and the river at your back. I already know how to mitigate the threat of your flying machines. I suggest you seek terms, and quickly."

Tahtay looked at Marcellinus. "Now I need to understand. 'Mitigate'? 'Terms'?"

Marcellinus spoke in Latin so that nothing would be hidden from Hadrianus. "By 'mitigate' Caesar means he believes he can minimize the danger to his troops from Cahokia's Hawks and Thunderbirds. 'Terms' would be the details of Cahokia's surrender."

Tahtay nodded and to the Imperator said, "What do you really want? How many deaths would please you?"

Kimimela closed her eyes briefly.

"Surrender and there need be no killing. Then Cahokia would become Roma's friend. My troops need food for the winter, and in the spring they will go on, confident in your friendship and support." The Imperator's voice had become sardonic. "Surrender and you, Tahtay, may remain as the chief of your people and become an honored vassal. Surrender and we will be merciful.

"Resist and all this will be impossible. Thousands of Cahokians will die, and I guarantee that you, Tahtay, will be among them."

Tahtay eyed him shrewdly. "It is not just Cahokia you would rule, but all of Hesperia?"

Hadrianus did not blink. "Yes."

"The whole of the land is a lot for one man to chew and swallow. Even a Caesar of Roma."

The Imperator regarded them keenly. "Tahtay, here is my offer, repeated clearly so there can be no mistake. If Cahokia yields its granaries, no Cahokian need die. Cahokia will remain a city, and my legions will go on. I will require your Hawk craft and pilots to fly them. They will be as well treated as any men in my army. Other Cahokian warriors who join Roma will enter my armies as auxiliaries and will also be treated well. Your friend Gaius Marcellinus can explain this to you in more detail, as necessary.

"Cahokia has corn, and I must feed my men. If there is gold in this country, it is Roma's and not Cahokia's." He eyed Marcellinus. "They know what gold is, yes?"

"Only because I have shown it to them."

"Nonetheless." The Imperator addressed Tahtay again. "Most important of all, if Cahokia makes peace, Roma will seek no revenge on you for destroying the legion commanded by Gaius Marcellinus. Evidently he has forgiven you. My forgiveness is harder to come by, but you may earn it if you lay down your spears and clubs and rocks immediately and agree to become a province of Roma.

"Agree and there need be no Mourning War between Roma and Cahokia. You understand, yes? Just as Cahokia relinquished its revenge on the Haudenosaunee, Roma would relinquish its vengeance on Cahokia. Do you see?"

Marcellinus raised his eyebrows. The Imperator was *very* well informed.

Hadrianus continued. "This is a good offer, Tahtay of Cahokia. It is the best that you will hear. The alternative is that Roma will march on you with steel and weapons and horses and siege engines. We will crush you and rip Cahokia apart. We will take all your corn and slay all your deer, and your men and women will serve Roma by force as we spread our dominion through Nova Hesperia to the west."

Again he turned to Marcellinus. "I trust they know what 'slaves' are?"

The breath caught in Marcellinus's throat. He vividly remembered giving a speech similar to this to Sisika the day he first met her, and it made him feel sick to his stomach.

With some difficulty he turned to face the Cahokian party. Sintikala's face was stony. Kimimela's lips had parted, and she was frowning as if lost in thought. Tahtay, for all his studied attempts to be statesmanlike, was glaring at the Imperator. The conversation had left Kanuna behind long before, but he had picked up on the change in mood and was looking back and forth from the Imperator's eyes to Tahtay's. Only Wahchintonka stood stoically.

The Imperator nodded. "I see that they do. And so, Tahtay, your answer?"

Tahtay cleared his throat. "I would talk more with you, great Caesar. Cahokia has much to trade. Your needs are many, and we—"

"No trade." The Imperator spared Marcellinus an irritated glance. "If this man has told you Roma seeks trade, he has misled you. You will surrender unconditionally or there will be war. There is no third way. Do you understand?"

Tahtay's face was red, and his eyes narrowed. His fists opened and closed.

"Breathe," Kimimela whispered almost imperceptibly.

"You will be sorry," Tahtay said thickly. "Imperator Hadrianus, if you make war, we will make you sorry.

We will slay your men, and we will burn them in a pit, and we will keep you alive for a very long time."

"At least we are in agreement that I will live a long life." The Imperator waved his hand. "Stay. Talk to one another. Discuss my offer. Think upon the death and destruction of everything you know. We will talk again later."

Tahtay shook his head slowly.

The Imperator snapped his fingers. "Agrippa, Marcellinus. Come."

Marcellinus glanced at the Cahokians. "May I—"

"Come." Hadrianus gestured to his Praetorian Guard, nodded in a perfunctory way to Tahtay, and strolled out of the room without another word.

The Cahokians looked at Marcellinus and past him. "Is the Imperator coming back?" Kimimela asked.

"Hotah?" Tahtay said uncertainly.

"Stay here," Marcellinus said in Cahokian. "Let me see what I can do."

Two Praetorians came to Marcellinus's side. The other guards closed the door from the street the Cahokians had walked in through just a few minutes before and took up position on either side of it. Sintikala glanced around the room with narrowed eyes, her fingers flexing. Tahtay looked to Kimimela, who still stood staring past him.

"Do nothing rash," Marcellinus said over his shoulder as he was hustled off in Hadrianus's wake.

The Imperator and Agrippa awaited Marcellinus in the peristylium. "You have trained him well," Hadrianus said.

"Trained?"

"His confidence is impressive for one so young. Come now, do you deny you coached Tahtay for this little confrontation?"

"Tahtay is a remarkable youth," Marcellinus said. "He has already survived more than many men twice his age. He was recently established as the paramount chief of Cahokia with almost no help from me. He requires little coaching."

"Do not take me for a fool," the Imperator said quietly.

Marcellinus saw the vicious amusement in Agrippa's eyes and the anger in Hadrianus's and quickly bowed his head. "My apologies, Caesar. Yes, I did my best to prepare Tahtay to talk with you. Hesperians negotiate differently. Often in a low sweat lodge over a pipe of tabaco. Others helped Tahtay also: Kanuna and Sintikala, whom you saw today, and a, uh, wise man of Cahokia named Enopay."

"Yes, yes. So the boy Tahtay is not your puppet, I see. Cannot be relied on to do as you say, though it is clear you know him well."

"Tahtay is nobody's puppet."

"But he is your friend? You have taught him our language, after all."

Marcellinus saw little advantage in risking being caught out in an obvious lie. "Tahtay is one of the first friends I made in Cahokia. He was assigned to learn my language by his father, the previous war chief of Cahokia. The young learn more quickly than the old. But Tahtay cannot be relied on to follow my advice."

"And the woman and the girl, they, too, are your friends?"

"Certainly, and Kanuna, too," Marcellinus said as casually as he dared.

The Imperator nodded. "I quite understand how one can grow fond of such people. I myself largely grew up in Aegyptus and Germania. Two more different peoples you couldn't hope to meet, and they each have their rough appeal."

"Just so," Marcellinus said.

"Can you persuade them to see reason?"

Agrippa laughed shortly. "Of course he cannot. They are too proud to realize they are already beaten."

"Gaius Marcellinus?"

"Truly, they will die first. Caesar, I beg you—"

The Imperator's hand was already raised. Marcellinus backed off. "I will talk to them."

Hadrianus nodded. "Go. Speak to your barbarian friends. Persuade Cahokia to surrender and you have saved your worthless life. Fail and I will put your head on a pole myself." The Imperator turned to Agrippa. "In the meantime, perhaps we might send for some lunch."

Leaning heavily on his stick, Marcellinus limped out to meet the Cahokian delegation.

The five Cahokians stood exactly where he had left them. Around the walls the Praetorians, too, stood in the same places. The Praetorian centurion had returned from taking the Aquila to safety and now stood ramrod-straight just to the right of the door, the vine stick of his office clamped under his arm.

Tahtay looked past Marcellinus for the Imperator. His face clouded with irritation once he saw that Marcellinus was coming alone.

For the first time Marcellinus realized how incongruous the Cahokians looked with their Hesperian tunics and tattoos in a Roman Praetorium while soldiers in gleaming steel lined the walls, ignoring them.

Tahtay frowned. "Hadrianus has sent you to persuade us to surrender?"

"Yes," Marcellinus said.

"Is he bluffing?"

"No."

"Gaius, are you all right?" Kimimela asked.

"Yes," he said.

"You were in Ocatan when . . . ?"

He nodded.

Kimimela glanced at Tahtay, who still stood tight-lipped and angry. "And what of Hurit?"

Marcellinus felt the pain of it almost as another wound. "Hurit is dead."

"You saw it?"

"Yes. She was north of the walls, leading townsfolk to

safety. She died bravely and well, defending Ocatani from Roman cavalry."

Tahtay looked desolate, but at the same time his fists closed. Kimimela glanced sideways at him in alarm.

"Anapetu is dead, too. She died in my arms."

"Merda," Kimimela muttered, and, suddenly bereft, Kanuna turned away and squatted down on the floor, hands up to his face.

"Hurit dead, Anapetu dead, but *you* alive," Tahtay said venomously. "Here in the heart of Roma, the Wanageeska lives on. Am I surprised? I am not. Why would that surprise any of us?"

"I'm sorry about Hurit, Tahtay. She—"

Tahtay cut him off with an abrupt and abusive hand-talk gesture. "Shut up! Go back to your Romans and die with them when we fall upon them and drown them in their own blood!"

Kimimela was still staring at Marcellinus. "Tahtay, Gaius is doing his best."

Tahtay snorted. "You still defend him?"

Kanuna looked up. "Wanageeska, if we give your Romans all they want, we might as well be dead."

For the first time Wahchintonka spoke. "This is simple. We die with honor or we die without."

Sintikala had been staring at Marcellinus since he had reentered the room. Now she said, "There is something you are not telling us. What is it?"

Marcellinus dropped his gaze. "I cannot say."

Her tone became brittle. "You have sworn another oath?"

Marcellinus shook his head.

There was no more he could say. Someone would be watching, listening. Hadrianus had never asked Marcellinus for his assistance in translating, and the Imperator must surely have other word slaves, collaborators from the native population.

Indeed, Marcellinus had seen Cherokee and other Hesperians walking the streets of the fortress. One of those men surely would be eavesdropping from behind the Praetorium walls.

Besides, it would take too long to explain the dark, creeping suspicions that lurked in Marcellinus's mind.

"And now you are Roman again," Wahchintonka said. "I always knew it, and many others knew it, too."

Marcellinus shook his head and looked at Tahtay. "War chief, might you consider some concessions? Corn is what the Imperator desires most to ease the strain on his supply chain. If you were to offer—"

Tahtay met his eyes. "Praetor, I will not surrender to Roma, nor will I starve my own people."

Sintikala nodded gravely. "If you cannot persuade your Roman chieftain to make trade, we must fight. Cahokia will not bow to Roma. Tahtay has spoken."

"I understand," said Marcellinus. "But—"

"Be careful," Kimimela said suddenly. "Be safe, Gaius. I do not want to lose another . . . friend."

She nodded very slightly. Marcellinus stared, helpless, and then returned the nod.

It would take more than care to keep Marcellinus alive now. Once the Cahokian delegation left, Marcellinus would be of no further use to the Romans. Clearly, Kimimela did not realize this.

Tahtay raised his eyes to the ceiling of the Praetorium, obviously swallowing his disgust, and then turned and strode toward the door. He looked up at the Praetorians and in Latin said, "Open it, please."

"Tahtay . . ." Marcellinus took a step forward. "Stay. Talk again with the Imperator. Consider—"

"No. We will go. If these men will allow it."

Sintikala looked at the Praetorians and at Marcellinus. "Let us go, Gaius," she said softly.

Their eyes met. For an instant he saw the sorrow in her heart. Kimimela might not understand, but Sisika certainly did. In the moment of an eye blink she was saying good-bye.

The Praetorian centurion looked stolidly at Marcellinus, who eventually turned with reluctance and said,

"Officer, what are your orders? Did the Imperator instruct you to detain the Cahokians?"

The centurion came to attention. "The redskins are here under a flag of truce. They are free to go if they want to. And if you say they can. Sir."

"Then open the door, centurion. Give them safe conduct to the gate. Let them leave in peace."

"Yes, sir."

"Come with us, Gaius," Kimimela pleaded.

"No," the centurion said in Cahokian. "Wanageeska stay here."

Everyone's head turned. Kimimela's jaw dropped.

"You speak Cahokian?" Kanuna asked.

Tahtay nodded as if he'd known all along. The officer grinned nastily and said in Cahokian: "Go now. Hurry. Before Imperator changes his mind."

At his nod, the Praetorians swung open the heavy wooden door.

They walked away from Marcellinus then, Tahtay and Kimimela, Sintikala, Kanuna, and Wahchintonka, out of the Praetorium building and into the streets of the Roman fortress with their Praetorian escort, and only Kimimela looked back.

Four Praetorians took Marcellinus back to the peristylium area. The Imperator looked up from his plate. "And?"

"The Cahokians will not capitulate to Roma. They will not gift their corn and leave their own people to starve. They have left."

Agrippa grinned tightly and said to the Imperator, "As I predicted, he has proved to be quite useless, and so we will have war."

Marcellinus nodded. "I feel fortunate I will not live to see it. I did not expect to change their minds, Caesar. Their resolve was clear. I just wanted to talk with them one last time before Lucius Agrippa demands that you put a blade to my throat."

Hadrianus eyed him. "Defiance in the face of death, Gaius Marcellinus?"

"Yes, Caesar. If I may?" Marcellinus hobbled to the table and, without being invited, poured himself some wine and water.

The Imperator shook his head. "Guards, seize him. Lucius?"

Two Praetorians stepped forward to seize Marcellinus's arms. Knocked from his grasp, the beaker spun across the wooden floor, spraying wine.

Marcellinus would not be chained up and taken back to Roma or made an example of in front of the massed legions. All he warranted was a quick death in the lunchroom.

Marcellinus gritted his teeth. Even with his time so short, he could not appear to be begging for his life. He must show calm, confidence. Dignitas.

Lucius Agrippa stood. "Put the traitor on his knees and hand me a sword."

Marcellinus rocked back as best he could as two Praetorians thrust him down, but still the impact of his kneecaps against the floor sent twin stabs of pain up his legs and into his pelvis.

The third Praetorian stepped forward, gladius in hand, its point reversed. Agrippa seized the hilt, looked at the blade, slashed it experimentally in the air.

Marcellinus said: "You will at least be gratified to learn that I did not tell the Cahokians my suspicions about the real reason you are in Nova Hesperia."

"By all the gods, traitor, accept your death in silence," Agrippa said.

Marcellinus laughed shortly. "I do not take orders from you, Lucius Agrippa. Although I might have served Roma better had you not both kept me in the dark."

Agrippa raised the gladius.

But Hadrianus raised his hand. "Hold."

"It scarcely matters what a traitor thinks he knows," Agrippa protested.

Ignoring the blade over his head, Marcellinus held the

Imperator's gaze. "I have made many mistakes in my life. The worst were when I killed men who might have been of use to me. Even the Hesperians don't make that error. How goes the war in Asia, Caesar?"

Hadrianus looked simultaneously irritated and intrigued, Agrippa merely exasperated.

Marcellinus continued. "When I discovered you had come to Nova Hesperia in person, I was convinced you must have defeated the Mongol Khan, that he was no longer a threat. How else would you have the leisure to lead an invasion on the other side of the world? Now I think otherwise. And although your original entry into the continent was slow and methodical, now you appear to be in quite a hurry."

"The Imperator only arrived in country a few weeks ago," Agrippa said dourly. "His legions were preparing the way for him. Now he leads us into battle."

Hadrianus sat forward. "Go on. Please step back, Lucius, I would not want you to slip and accidentally slay Gaius Marcellinus before he has run out of ways to entertain me."

"Yes, Caesar." The young Praetor lowered the gladius, turned on his heel, and went to the table, sloshing wine into a wooden beaker with bad grace.

Once again Marcellinus wished he was not on his knees. It was hard to radiate confidence in such a submissive, painful position. He spoke bluntly. "Caesar, you have come to Nova Hesperia with two of the best legions in the world. You originally sent me here for gold, yet you seem to have little interest in it; the People of the Sun have it in abundance in the south, yet your thrust is westward. My mention of having knowledge of the plains intrigued you both, and after grain your principal interest in Cahokia is its air power."

"Oh, I have a considerable interest in gold, Gaius Marcellinus. This adventure is far from cheap."

Marcellinus inclined his head. "Just so, sir. But you are clearly playing a much bigger game than that."

"Haven't you heard?" Hadrianus said lightly. "I would

leave as my legacy a world where the sun never sets on the Roman Imperium. It is my most oft-quoted epigram."

"Caesar, I respectfully request a private audience. And to get up off my knees."

Agrippa drained his cup. "Caesar—"

The Imperator gestured for silence. Marcellinus waited. Eventually Hadrianus said: "Are you merely stalling, or do you propose to be of some service to Roma at last?"

"Caesar, if my suspicions are correct, I do believe I can help you."

Hadrianus smiled. "At last."

Agrippa looked from one man to the other. "I should go and meet with my tribunes soon, Caesar, if you will permit it."

The Imperator sat back and began eating again. "By all means, Lucius Agrippa, by all means. And Marcellinus, *now* you may drink. Your throat seems a little parched."

"I take it you realize that I keep you alive largely to annoy Lucius Agrippa?"

With this Imperator, that might be flippant or it might not. Standing at the table, still trying to rub the feeling back into his legs, Marcellinus nodded casually. "Then I shall be sure to keep irritating him. It should be easy enough. May I . . . be seated?"

"By all means," said Hadrianus. "I grow tired of your head being higher than mine."

Marcellinus blinked and sat hurriedly. Hadrianus laughed uproariously, rocking back on his couch and breaking the tension of the moment. "That was a joke, Gaius Marcellinus. From my youth in Aegyptus. I'm an Imperator, not an old-time pharaoh."

"Of course," said Marcellinus. He sipped at his beaker of wine and water and waited.

Still chewing, the Imperator studied him anew. Marcellinus endured it patiently. After all, he had trained for this. The scrutiny of the master of the Roman world was not more terrifying than having Sintikala stare through his eyes and read his soul.

"Very well," Hadrianus said at last. "Why, pray, am I in Nova Hesperia? I am quite dying to know."

Marcellinus nodded. "You did not come around the world merely to acquire territory. That, in Agrippa's words, would be preposterous. You have already stated that you are too pragmatic a man to be driven by revenge at the loss of a single legion, so you are not here to claim the glory of rubbing the Cahokians' noses in their own defeat. An 'abject wilderness' hardly requires your personal attention."

Hadrianus looked at him coolly. "I believe that is for me to decide. And I believe you may have forgotten whom you are addressing."

"Perhaps," Marcellinus said. "If so, Caesar, I apologize. May I continue?"

Hadrianus gestured.

"So, if not for territory, then what? You did not bring legions for annexation. You brought legions for combat, elite cavalry as well as infantry. Thus, here in Nova Hesperia there must be an opponent worthy of them." Marcellinus slowed to choose his words carefully. "I confess that I do not know how such a thing could have happened. I have been out of the world for many years. They must have made great strides or acquired great allies. But somehow . . ."

"Yes?"

"Somehow your greatest enemy is here in Nova Hesperia. And so you have come to face him. And that is why you need Cahokian corn and Cahokian air power and why, if possible, you would seek to add Cahokian auxiliaries to your already extensive legionary force."

The Imperator looked at him thoughtfully and then appeared to make up his mind. "Gaius Marcellinus?"

"Yes?"

"We clearly approach the moment when we must speak of things your Cahokian friends have no knowledge of. Obviously, you have been in a difficult position these past years. Trying to do your duty to Roma the best you can without being cooked and eaten by these savages."

"The Cahokians are not cannibals," said Marcellinus, taken aback.

"Some tribes on this continent most assuredly are. No matter. I have an Imperium to run and a war to win, and I have given up the comforts of Roma to be here in this muddy field talking to you, so you may be sure that this is of the utmost importance."

"Very well," Marcellinus said.

"And so . . . I need to know where you stand."

"I stand before my Imperator," Marcellinus said. "I am a Roman, and I can be nothing else. However, I believe—"

"Yes, yes. Stop there. So what if I were to confide in you a great strategic secret and command you to never share it with your barbarian friends, in the unlikely event that you were ever again permitted to speak with them? If you were to give me your word, could I trust you to keep it?"

Marcellinus's mind whirled. He had not dared to imagine that there might come a situation in which he could speak to Tahtay and the others again.

"The oath you would make to me to keep these matters confidential would override any other oaths you may have taken. Especially recently."

This Imperator was a very shrewd man.

"I will answer your last question first," Marcellinus said. "If I swear an oath, I keep it absolutely."

"Once you swore an oath to serve Roma."

Marcellinus did not even blink. "And serve Roma I have."

"So such an oath would not be hard for you? Then do you wish to swear it?" Hadrianus's lips twitched. "You claim to have served the Imperium your whole life. This should be an easy question."

Marcellinus took a deep breath. "It is. I will swear the oath."

The Imperator stared at him intently. "And why?"

"Because I need to know what is going on."

To be taken into the Imperator's confidence was far more than Marcellinus could have hoped. It surely could only be in Cahokia's interest as well as Roma's.

If he was to be the master of privileged information that he could not tell the Cahokians, that was the price he would have to pay.

"Then so swear and shake my hand."

Marcellinus got to his feet and looked around the room. Still he was alone with the Imperator Hadrianus III and was about to enter into a compact that might pull him away from Sintikala, Kimimela, Tahtay.

Was he betraying them? He did not know yet.

"I swear that any . . . strategic information you may entrust to me, I will not divulge to any other person, unless and until you give me leave to do so."

"That I or any of my generals may entrust to you," Hadrianus corrected him.

"Very well. I will share no information you or your Praetors may reveal to me."

The Imperator reached out and grasped his hand.

Suddenly the voice echoing in his mind was Sintikala's, from their conversation on the Oyo after returning from powwow: *And you still believe you can march with Roma and dance with Cahokia?*

Marcellinus had answered *Yes*. And now his confident declaration was about to be put to the test. He braced himself, ready for the ground to open and swallow him.

"Very good," Hadrianus said. "And so we will talk again tomorrow."

"What?"

"Tomorrow, you and I and Agrippa, with Decinius Sabinus of the Legio III Parthica. I require Sabinus in this conversation, and he is currently out—" The Imperator waved his hand. "—marching his men around. I think you may find Sabinus a useful foil for Agrippa, and I will be curious to hear his opinion of you."

All Marcellinus could do was nod. "Yes, sir."

"Besides, I have had quite enough of you for one day, and there are other matters I must attend to. In the meantime, I daresay we will have to find quarters for you."

CHAPTER 26

YEAR SEVEN, PLANTING MOON

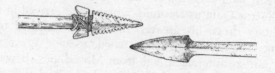

"We must talk of the Mongol War," said Imperator Hadrianus III. By his side Praetor Flavius Agrippa smiled, an almost predatory expression.

"By all means," Marcellinus said.

He was back in the peristylium of Hadrianus's Praetorium building on a cool and breezy morning. Lucius Flavius Agrippa of the 27th Augustan lolled on a couch wearing his usual unadorned tunic, sagum cloak, leggings, and sandals like any common soldier. He and Marcellinus had been ordered to be civil to each other; thus commanded, Agrippa had immediately begun to behave as if the fights and other acrimony between them had never occurred. While they waited for Sabinus, the two of them had even exchanged some rather stilted small talk about their careers and Asian commands.

Agrippa was in his late twenties and by his speech and demeanor a member of the senatorial class. It turned out that he was a young general of the smart set who had been the Imperator's right-hand man in planning and executing the campaigns against the Mongol Khan.

Marcellinus had never come across him in the east. While Agrippa had been making his name repelling the Mongol Horde in Kara Khitai, Marcellinus had been a couple of thousand miles away on the other side of the Himalaya. There, having secured the Delhi Sultanates, he had received orders to pack up and prepare for deployment in the far west with a brand-new legion specifically formed and named for the task. Ironically, back then Marcellinus had not had a clear idea of where Nova Hesperia was and at first had thought the Imperator was inexplicably relegating him to Hispania.

"Ah, Sabinus. Good of you to join us."

Praetor Quintus Decinius Sabinus had arrived in full military dress, his greaves and helmet polished to a shine. The Praetor looked starched, a senior career officer not so different in age from Marcellinus. It was a long time indeed since Marcellinus had talked with such a man.

Presumably Sabinus had walked across from the fortress on the opposite hill occupied by the Third Parthica. He doffed his helmet as he entered the courtyard, of course, and set it on the table, where it glinted accusingly. Marcellinus felt distinctly rumpled by comparison.

He assessed Marcellinus. "Good day, sir."

"Good day, Praetor Sabinus."

The Imperator waved his hand. "Agrippa, if you would describe matters on our eastern front."

Agrippa scratched and sat back. "Very well. To cut a long tale short, the Mongols ran ragged across the southern steppes clear across to Samarkand till three years ago, and there I stopped 'em. Jochi has made his attempts to break out and ride farther west into the Imperium, but we've shut him down every time. Must be a tad embarrassing when he has to tell his dad. Don't worry, Marcellinus: we still hold the Delhis and other sultanates that you fought so hard for, but we're getting push from the other brothers in the lowlands."

Marcellinus shook his head, already lost.

"Lord's sake, take pity on the poor man," said Sabinus, perching stiffly on one of the other couches. "He's been trapped out here in the sticks for over half a decade."

Hadrianus paced, hands behind his back. "Yes, yes.

Marcellinus, the Mongol Khan has many sons, and each leads an army. His most important sons are Jochi, Chagatai, Ogodei, and . . ." Hadrianus thought for a moment. "Tolui. He also has daughters, who serve as administrators and wield considerable power in their own right."

Marcellinus struggled to remember. "The Mongol Khan must be getting on in years by now."

"We've heard several reported birth dates for Chinggis Khan, Temujinus as was. The most reasonable one makes him sixty-two this year. Early sixties, anyway, but still strong as an ox. Vital enough to rule his sons, and that's saying something. Still leading armies in the field."

Fifteen years older than Marcellinus and still leading campaigns. Marcellinus nodded.

"Jochi, his eldest, is the one I have bottled up in Samarkand," said Agrippa. "At least, that's how I left him. I don't doubt they could get around us by heading in a big loop to the north if they felt like it, but it's a long haul without much plunder on the way. Meanwhile—"

"Meanwhile," said Hadrianus, "since they couldn't break out farther west, they headed east."

Marcellinus nodded. "The Khan already held the Jin Empire clear down to Kaifeng when I left the field. He'd set up one of his sons in the capital?"

"Yes, Ogodei, in Zhongdu," said Sabinus.

"And so now he has the whole of the Southern Song Empire to go with it?"

"Led the campaign himself," Hadrianus said. "Chinggis Khan, with Chagatai Khan by his side, and Subutei, his greatest general. Swept down like a dose of salts through one of the mightiest nations of the east. What d'you think of that? Gives you pause, doesn't it?"

"It certainly does." If the Mongol Khan had added the Song Empire to his takings, he now controlled territories equivalent in area to the entire Roman Imperium. Marcellinus supposed it might be tactless to point this out.

"And they've allied with the Khmers and others clear

across to Pagan, which is why they're knocking on our eastern door there."

"Bengal?" Marcellinus asked, momentarily chilled.

"Just so," Sabinus said. "But we'll hold them back, never fear. It's a narrow enough strip of land between the Bay of Bengal and the Himalaya to keep the beggars cordoned off."

"Except that they now own the entire Song navy," Marcellinus said.

Hadrianus and Sabinus looked at each other. "Not a complete yokel, then," said Agrippa, and smiled to take the sting out of his words. Marcellinus forced himself to smile back.

"Yes, indeed," Hadrianus said. "The Song navy."

"The Mongols swept down the coast," Sabinus told him. "While you were marching the 33rd into Nova Hesperia, Chinggis Khan was storming along the Yangtze and down through the Song. They besieged Hangzhou for half a year, but once those walls fell to the Mongol trebuchets and the Ningzong Imperial family fled, the rest caved quickly. Quanzhou, Guangzhou. All the great seaports, all the ships, all the shipyards."

The Song had been a significant maritime nation, plying its trade along the coast as far as Arabia. Marcellinus knew little of ships, but clearly those of the Song were substantial.

They were waiting to see what he would say next. "Well, how exciting for you all."

"Counting on your fingers, Gaius Marcellinus?" Agrippa asked.

"Counting years."

Marcellinus had arrived in Nova Hesperia in A.D. 1218, but the plans for his invasion had been put in motion over two years earlier. Plenty of time for the Mongol Khan to have gotten wind of it. Even during wartime the Silk Road was still a two-way street, carrying information as well as spices.

Marcellinus nodded slowly. His suspicions had been correct.

"Yes," Hadrianus said. "Was Chinggis Khan going to sit quietly while I took the riches of Nova Hesperia? No, he was not. And so Nova Hesperia has become the newest front in the war with the Mongol Khan."

After a long pause to let this sink in, Marcellinus shook his head. "Well, if there were any riches here in the first place . . ."

"Oh, there's gold here," said Agrippa. "Or silver. Or gems. Or something. We just haven't found it yet. It's not possible for a land this vast to have nothing worth taking, even if it's only the people."

Marcellinus was momentarily stunned. Hadrianus stepped into the frosty silence. "The first Mongol ships sailed from Hangzhou three years ago. More from Guangzhou a little later. At first we expected they might sail west to attack the Imperium. They did not. We waited. And then our spies brought the word, and our captives, and all said the same. The ships went east, Gaius Marcellinus. And they were *huge* ships."

Marcellinus nodded. "And that is why you brought three legions and excellent cavalry, why you are here in person, Caesar, why you're consolidating every step, why you're sending out small expeditionary forces in the south seeking information rather than attacking the People of the Sun for their gold."

"And that is why I simply do not have time to mess around. I do not wish to share another continent with Chinggis Khan. Cahokia must surrender and feed our legions. It must keep the Iroqua in check and stop them from harassing our supply lines. It must provide us men for our armies. And it must provide us with flight."

"The Mongols are great horsemen," Agrippa said. "In truth, their cavalry runs rings around ours. It is only our infantry that keeps us solid. But Cahokia has the air."

Hadrianus stood crisply, hands behind his back. "We have two choices before us. Cahokia can capitulate, the lands east of the Mizipi will become a Roman province forthwith, and we will continue westward with their support, annexing territory as we go. Or I will march right over the city and lay waste to it with fire and the sword, and the shackled survivors will grow corn and fly their wings for us anyway. Hesperians will become either our warriors or our slaves."

"Gods," said Marcellinus, appalled.

"Gaius Marcellinus, your precious Cahokians need us. They just don't know it yet. What do you suppose will happen when the Mongol Horde sweeps across the plains? Will *you* hold them back? Will Tahtay? What happens to your darling Mizipian backwater then? And after that, when the Mongols steal the secret of flight and take it home to Asia? Can the Imperium resist a Mongol army of horsemen *and* birdmen?"

"Maybe. The Cahokians make flight look easy, but it isn't. The Mongols aren't going to be able to churn out flying craft and pilots by the hundreds."

"And you're quite sure of that?"

Marcellinus was mute.

The Imperator paced. "It has taken me five years and fifteen legions to hold off the Mongols in Europa and Asia—no, no, one-*quarter* of the Mongols, commanded by Chinggis's sons Jochi and Ogodei. The new ships of the Mongols are big five-masted freighters that dwarf even our troop carriers. And they whipped up a fleet of them and got all set to sail for the west coast of Nova Hesperia in next to no time. You underestimate the Mongols at your peril."

"Fifteen legions?" Marcellinus said. "And here you have just three?"

"I have a fourth and a fifth preparing in Tarraco. If I could spare more, I would have brought them. I cannot. If I show weakness in Europa, then Chinggis's other sons will break out and attack me there.

"These are desperate times, Gaius Marcellinus. The inhabitants of Nova Hesperia are primitive, but the size of the land is on their side . . . for now. But I need their support. I believe this is something you can achieve for me. So please do so. Deliver me Cahokia and deliver it now."

Sabinus cleared his throat. "Perhaps it would be even more persuasive if we raised the topic of . . . fire?"

Hadrianus looked at each of the three Praetors in turn, considering it. Finally he said, "Very well."

Sabinus nodded. "Unfortunately, as a result of the Mongols' invasion of the Jin and Song, the sophistication of their warfare is accelerating in leaps and bounds. You are already aware of Song ships and naval power. Perhaps you have also heard of Jin salt?"

"Salt? No."

"It is an incendiary, an explosive. It comes as a black powder. The Song and Jin empires have used it against each other for a hundred years in their endless duel for territory."

"Bombs, baskets, and buffalo," Agrippa said.

Marcellinus shook his head. "Sorry?"

Sabinus ignored Agrippa, which made Marcellinus like him all the more. "First is the thunderclap bomb: Jin salt and smashed porcelain, all wrapped in stiff parchment. Sometimes with lime added to make a fog that will burn the eyes of men and horses. Worse is the thunder crash bomb, similar but encased in iron, which explodes into even more lethal fragments. With these the Song tried to resist Mongol sieges of their cities, but to no avail. Sometimes they launched the exploding salt in baskets, and yes, Lucius, the Song even attached Jin salt bombs to armored oxen, on a long fuse, and then drove the poor animals against their enemies. That, at least, is a trick the Mongols have not yet acquired."

Marcellinus shook his head, trying to remove the bizarre mental image. "How is Jin salt made? What does it smell like?"

"Saltpeter, charcoal, sulfur. The best charcoal is made from alder or willow, and the best saltpeter from dung heaps and privies—"

The Imperator leaned forward, cutting him off. "It does not smell of privies. It smells bitter. What is it, Gaius Marcellinus?"

"Could it be delivered using an iron tube, perhaps six feet long?"

Suddenly he had their rapt attention. Agrippa swung his legs off the couch. "And where could you have seen such a thing?"

"At the Market of the Mud. The smell was distinctive, and the scorch marks. And it was on sale alongside a complex bow of some considerable—"

The Imperator slapped the table with his palm, making them jump, then leaped to his feet and paced again. "I should just have Calidius Verus flogged and have done with it!"

"You did not purchase them?" Sabinus asked Marcellinus.

"The tube, yes. It is in Cahokia. What is it?"

"A fire lance," Hadrianus exclaimed. "Damn them!"

Decinius Sabinus gestured in the air, defining a long tube and then gripping his fist at the near end of it. "A large packet of Jin salt at the near end, ignited from a tinderbox. Concentrated flame shoots out the tip as far as ten or fifteen paces for ten minutes or more." He glanced at Hadrianus. "Our troops fear them quite considerably at close quarters. And they are most effective at breaking up infantry formations."

"It seems Chinggis Khan has so many that he's already losing them," the Imperator said vindictively. "And I have to hear this from *you* rather than the legion I specifically sent south to look for signs of the Mongol Horde?"

Marcellinus thought Sabinus gave him a small conspiratorial nod, but it was so brief that it might have been his imagination. "It could have arrived at the market from anywhere but probably came with a merchant down a river from the western—"

Hadrianus raised his hand. "And, Gaius Marcellinus, that is why we must also gain the Hesperian Greek fire. So that we can, quite literally, fight fire with fire. With luck, Greek fire from above can trump this Mongol black powder from trebuchets and fire lances on the battlefield."

"Great Juno," Marcellinus said, overwhelmed.

Agrippa put his feet back up on the couch. "I do believe our cunning deserter is finally beginning to understand the stakes."

The Imperator calmed himself and sat. "And so, Marcellinus, you will now tell us everything you know about Hesperian liquid flame."

It wasn't much. Marcellinus described its composition and oily, gelatinous appearance before being detonated, its methods of delivery, and the gruesome details of its effects. He told them the Cahokians made it in a far-away village for reasons of safety and secrecy but not that this village was somewhere to the south and east of Cahokia.

The last thing he could have borne on his conscience was for the legions to acquire Greek fire and use it against the Mizipians.

As Sintikala had predicted so long ago, it was hard to both march with Roma and dance with Cahokia.

Once he had ground to a halt, shaking his head at the magnitude of what he had learned, the Imperator fixed him with a bleak gaze and said: "Gaius Marcellinus, you will agree to do all in your power to help us against Cahokia and the Mongol Horde or we will declare this meeting adjourned."

And there it was. The choice was stark. Marcellinus could help Hadrianus bring Cahokia to heel or he could refuse.

If he refused, he was worse than useless to Hadrianus. Marcellinus was under no illusion about what "adjourned" meant. He could hardly expect to be kept alive out of kindness.

Besides, the Mongol threat to Nova Hesperia was massive and very real.

"Surely we must tell the Cahokians about the Mongol incursions. If Chinggis Khan has already landed an army on the western coast of Nova Hesperia and is spreading out into the continent, that changes everything. To the Mongols, the vast grasslands of the Hesperian plains will be much like home."

"Of course not," Agrippa said. "We simply cannot risk it. What if the Mizipians were to decide to align with the Mongols against us? What if they do not believe us about the Mongols anyway? Telling them of the Khan considerably weakens our position."

"Agrippa is right." Hadrianus spoke definitively. "The Mizipians and Haudenosaunee must be convinced of the overwhelming strength of Roma. They cannot know that another enemy of equal stature may face us across the plains. You must surely see that, Gaius Marcellinus."

Marcellinus found himself nodding. From a Roman perspective, the logic was unassailable. "I do."

Unfortunately, Cahokia did not take its orders from Marcellinus. Getting Cahokia to submit willingly to Roma was quite simply beyond Marcellinus's capabilities. Even if he somehow could persuade Tahtay to capitulate and yield Cahokia's unique military resources, another war chief would rise from within to depose him. The warriors of Cahokia had already murdered one war chief who would not stand up to the Iroqua; what price Tahtay if he did not stand up to Roma?

Marcellinus nodded. "I see the problem. It is not a simple matter. I must think on it."

"Think quickly, Gaius Marcellinus," the Imperator said. "Think quickly."

CHAPTER 27

YEAR SEVEN, PLANTING MOON

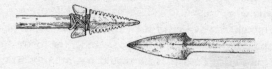

The sun had set two hours earlier, but the soldiers of the 27th Augustan still thronged the streets of the fortress. Even in their casual dress—belted tunics and sagum cloaks against the evening breeze, leggings and caligae sandals—each man was smartly turned out and walked with his head held high. From their features and accents Marcellinus guessed these troops had been recruited from Italia, Macedonia, and Syria. However, it was in their demeanor that they were a different breed from the soldiers of the Legio XXXIII Hesperia. To a man the 27th were clear-eyed and respectful, well organized and efficient. Lucius Agrippa might be arrogant and sarcastic, but he was obviously doing things right when it came to instilling dignitas and discipline in his legionaries.

From what Hadrianus had mentioned privately and perhaps jocularly to Marcellinus, the troops of Legio III Parthica over on the next hill were even better.

Marcellinus was strolling the streets largely unregarded. His escort, a Praetorian called Cassius, was shadowing him closely but had been directed not to engage him in conversation, which suited Marcellinus admirably. The fresh clothing that Agrippa's quartermaster—another Visigoth, by coincidence, just like Leogild of the 33rd—had provided Marcellinus with was similar to that worn by the men around him. Thus dressed as a common soldier, clean and tidy, Marcellinus was no longer immediately recognizable and excited no comment.

Even more unusually, none of the Cherokee or Algon-Quian braves gave him a second glance either. After all this time in Nova Hesperia, Marcellinus was unaccustomed to fading into the background so completely. Despite the oppressive weight on his mind, part of him was enjoying it.

One galling aspect of the experience was that he had been permitted such freedom to wander the fortress only on his sworn oath that he would not attempt to elude Cassius and depart from it and that he must shortly report back for dinner with Hadrianus, Agrippa, and Sabinus in the Praetorium. Polite dinner conversation was not Marcellinus's strength at the best of times, and he would have much preferred to dine under the sky by a legionary campfire or a Cahokian hearth than to lie on a couch being waited on by slaves. Indeed, he felt lucky to have survived his dinners with previous Imperators at all, speaking both gastronomically and socially.

But it could not be helped. In the circumstances, difficult dinner conversation was the least of his worries. And he had enjoyed the look on Agrippa's face when the Imperator had granted him this largely symbolic freedom to wander.

By this point Marcellinus had admired the strength of the gates and the well-crafted wooden walls, chatted to the veterans of the first sentry watch, and been thrown out of the blacksmith's forge for being a nuisance and was beginning to wend his way back toward the heart of the castra, with Cassius five paces behind. So it was that he was out in the open on the Via Principalis with the low, solid granary buildings to his left and the stable block to his right when the first Thunderbird roared over his head.

He heard it before he saw it. First came the odd thrum of the wind in its spars and sinews, a sound so chillingly familiar from his nightmares that it stopped Marcellinus in his tracks even before it cut through the quiet bustle of men in the streets. Next, the mules and horses caught wind of the intruder and started to whinny and stamp in their stalls. Then Marcellinus heard two orders called in calm Cahokian from directly above him at almost the same time but in two different voices, male and female: "Swing left!" and "Fire!"

And now, again almost overlapping, came the horns of Roman sentries belatedly sounding the alarm and the hiss of arrows being loosed.

Marcellinus dropped to one knee and raised his arm over his head, instinctively holding up a shield that he was not carrying, and looked up into the maw of a dragon.

The Thunderbird was dazzling, its huge wing outlined in fire. Bright lanterns swung at its prow, along its leading edge, and at its wingtips. The shadowy shapes of twelve warriors of the Wakinyan clan hung beneath it, some focused on steering the behemoth while others nocked arrows and selected their targets with care.

Around Marcellinus the soldiers of the 27th shouted and scattered. On the edge of panic, Marcellinus braced himself for a deluge of burning pain; even after all these years he dreaded the Cahokian liquid fire. But the agony did not come. The dragon roared by, shot its second round of arrows, and banked left, disappearing from his sight behind the granary.

Marcellinus had never seen a Thunderbird launched by night. Hawks, yes, but Thunderbirds? It seemed unspeakably dangerous. But beyond that, he could not imagine how they had launched the craft at all. This was a countryside of low rolling hills; the two Roman fortresses were atop the highest hills around, and there were no mounds or other suitable launch sites nearby. The torsion equipment, counterweights, and launching rail could hardly be packed up and carried a hundred miles across the countryside. How on earth had the Cahokians done it?

Tahtay and Sintikala had indeed been keeping secrets from him.

The hairs inside his nose prickled. Marcellinus's flesh might not be burning, but something was. Down the street ahead of him, above the legionary headquarters of the 27th Augustan, the imago of the Imperator was aflame. The giant banner smoked and rippled.

A second Wakinyan flew in from the south, a little higher. It was lit by lamps just as the first had been, and as it passed over the fortress walls, its pilots pulled in their rudder bars and rocked the Thunderbird into a dive so steep that some of its lamps flickered and went out.

The Thunderbird lurched upward as it dropped its load. In the lamplight from the streets and the Wakinyan itself and the firelight from the burning banner, Marcellinus saw the lazy arc of a cloud of liquid spread and spatter across the roofs of the troop quarters, the stable blocks, and then directly across the street where he stood.

"Merda . . . Cassius! Get down!"

As the liquid hit them, he cried out, spun, and dropped to the street, anticipating that intense burning, the stink of naphtha and his own bubbling flesh . . . Again it did not come.

Stunned almost into insensibility, Marcellinus looked down at the splash of liquid in the mud of the street. It glistened back at him in the firelight.

Cassius was by his side now, his hand on Marcellinus's shoulder, speaking to him regardless of his orders. "Oil, sir. Just oil."

Yet another Thunderbird was approaching, this time from the north, accompanied by a clatter of flaming arrows.

"Incendiaries!" Marcellinus shook off Cassius's hand and strode down the street, bellowing. "Fire is coming! Fire! Get indoors, under cover, on the double!"

Some men looked at him as if he were insane, but a centurion of the 27th hurried down the Via Principalis repeating the order. All around them soldiers ran for the nearest door. In Marcellinus's case that was the stable block, and he threw himself toward it, sliding on the slick oil. Out of the corner of his eye he saw the blue and red banner of the Imperator fluttering down. The Thunderbird's fire had burned through the cord that had held it high on its pole, and the imago slowly crumpled, still aflame.

Two more Wakinyan were coming in from the southeast, the second one flying above and to the right of the first, and above both there was a pair of Catanwakuwa. As Marcellinus watched, those Thunderbirds tilted forward into a shallow dive. It was a maneuver Marcellinus recognized, one that would forever haunt his nightmares. "Holy Jove . . . Shit . . ."

A torrent of fire fell from the first Wakinyan. A sound like a thunderclap came from behind Marcellinus, and the terrifyingly familiar red-white flames climbed into the sky, dazzling against the night.

The leading Thunderbird had disgorged its load of Greek fire—Cahokian liquid flame—right onto the main barracks blocks of the 27th Augustan. Marcellinus heard the screaming of men in pain, the bark of orders. Roman trumpets sounded the retreat even though the soldiers were already in camp. Their message was clear. *Back. Back. Defense, not attack.*

A blaze was spreading across the tops of both barracks. The stink of smoke blew over the camp. In the stables beside Marcellinus the braver cavalrymen were grabbing their horses' heads, talking to their mounts and trying to calm them. Other horses, terrified and enraged beyond control, pounded their wooden stalls with their rear hooves. The whole stable block shook.

The trailing Wakinyan had separated from the first and was drawing a direct line along the Via Principalis, the widest lane of the fortress, which was still thronged with Roman legionaries. It began to spray fire, not in a stream like the leading Wakinyan but in a fine rain. This was liquid flame meant to maim, to burn as many men as possible.

Far behind Marcellinus there was a splintering crash as a roof gave way.

The first flight of Thunderbirds had felled the imago and spread the oil. Now the real assault had begun.

The horses kicked at their stalls with an unholy thumping. Men were panicking, already blocking all the doors, fighting one another to get under cover.

"Squat *down*!" Marcellinus bellowed at the men around him. "Defenses *up*! Cover your skin; make yourself a smaller target!" He strode down the Principalis and turned at the Via Praetoria. "Move against the walls of the buildings! *Don't look up!*"

Even as Cassius grabbed his arm, the deadly thrum of the Wakinyan came again, and instinctively Marcellinus disobeyed his own command. He lifted his head, his hand raised in front of it, and saw the Thunderbird soar over just a couple of hundred feet above him, its pilots feathered and bird masked.

"Down! Down!" He threw himself onto the muddy ground at the base of the workshop wall and curled into a ball as the fiery spray came down on him, searing his bare legs and neck. He bellowed and rolled. The liquid flame burned through his tunic and lacerated his back as well. He jerked upright, then fell and rolled again in the mud. Beside him Cassius wailed and slammed into the wall beside him. All around them legionaries writhed in agony.

A legionary ran toward Marcellinus, a bucket of water in hand. "No!" Marcellinus kicked out and toppled sideways again, avoiding the water that would have spread the Greek fire even farther across his skin. The legionary tried to quench the flames on another of his comrades instead, and a harrowing shriek greeted his mistake.

Marcellinus lay on his back, panting. The pain was ebbing now, but the backs of his legs still felt as if they had been stung by a thousand bees. The stench of burned meat hung over the lane. Gouts of flame shot skyward from the burning buildings to Marcellinus's left.

"Cassius?"

The guard was down, unconscious, his skin still burned and bubbling. Either the shock or the collision with the wall had knocked his wits from him. "Merda."

Once again he heard men calling for water.

He struggled to his feet. One mercy of being peppered with liquid flame was that he had briefly forgotten the chronic ache in his thigh. He looked down at himself in the flickering firelight but was too besmirched with mud to be able to tell how bad his injuries were.

He could not run; that was for sure. Alone, he took off at a fast half-limping trot down the Via Principia toward the Southgate.

Legionary efficiency had taken over. Centurions from the barracks nearest the Southgate had rallied their men. From beyond the walls Marcellinus heard the thudding of hooves; some turmae at least had mobilized to protect the path to the Oyo. A bucket brigade had already begun.

And in another moment of uncanny instinct, Marcellinus stepped out and looked up into the sky.

A shadowy Hawk craft, unlit by any lamp, sailed over the fortress. As it passed overhead, its wing waggled in victory.

Maybe it was ridiculous, but Marcellinus couldn't help thinking Sintikala knew exactly where he was. And with that feeling came a moment of loneliness and heartsickness that threatened to overwhelm him.

The attack was over. Cahokia had sent its message. The fortress burned.

The Roman fortresses were a combination of large wooden buildings. They did not have the wagons and pumps for firefighting that the vigiles had in Roma and other great cities of the Imperium. The Oyo was their only source of water, and they were not close enough to it to adequately deal with an emergency like this.

Marcellinus did not see anyone he could identify as a tribune. He hurried to the centurion at the gate who appeared to be leading the effort, perhaps the primus

pilus—the lead centurion of the 27th. "Centurion, instruct your men: don't throw water on the flames. It will
just spread the liquid fire, spread the burning. The tim-
bers already aflame are gone anyway. Instead, soak the
buildings that have *not* yet caught fire, the dry wood.
You understand? Pass the word."

The centurion looked Marcellinus up and down,
noted his tone of command, and did not question him.
"Yes, sir." He turned to pass the order.

Marcellinus headed east along the intervallum area
between the buildings and the high wooden wall, trying
not to be bowled over by the legionaries who ran efficiently back and forth. Some areas of the barracks were
still ablaze, others subsiding. The outer walls looked
relatively unscathed; the few burning areas from the beginning of the Thunderbirds' strafing run were being
isolated efficiently. Foot soldiers were putting up ladders, carpenters working to make sure the walls held.

Marcellinus repeated his admonition against water to
the men at the wall. Then he turned north at the camp's
corner and found himself face-to-face with four Hesperians he did not recognize.

Instinctively he dropped his hand to his belt, but of
course he was not wearing a gladius.

Their leader peered at his wounded leg, then up at his
face. In Cahokian, the man said, "You are the Wanageeska?"

Marcellinus glanced behind him. "Who asks me?"

"You seek to escape Roma?"

Two looked like Cherokee from their dress and tattoos. The others were indistinct in the shadows. Marcellinus sighed and leaned against the wall. "No. I swore
not to leave the fortress, damn it. I'm just trying to stop
people from dying."

"A message, then? For the Cahokians outside?"

Marcellinus's mind blanked. Again came his immense
loneliness. What could he possibly tell Tahtay, Sintikala,
Kimimela in a short message that would mean anything
to them? He shook his head. "None. Thank you."

The Cherokee nodded, and in the next moment his whole bearing changed. "Chief Agrippa has summoned you. Come with us."

"A hundred eighty deaths reported so far from fire, arrows, rocks from slings. Twenty-four men crushed when their roof fell in on them. Nineteen cavalrymen trampled by their own horses, nine trampled by their bunk mates."

The First Centurion of the 27th was a wiry veteran with close-cropped hair, his tunic and parade armor so impeccable that they looked freshly minted, vine stick tucked under his arm. He was barely keeping his rage in check at the loss of so many men as he gave his report to his Praetor in the legionary headquarters building.

Agrippa nodded grimly. "Injuries?"

"Hundreds. Major burns. Broken skulls and arms and legs. Twisted ankles from slipping in the oil. Cavalrymen booted up the ass by their mounts. It'll be dawn before we get a full accounting."

"Fire damage?"

"A diagonal line of heavy burning across the eastern barrack blocks. Minor damage to the Southgate and Eastgate and to this legionary headquarters and the Praetorium, sir. Arrows through some of the cohorts' standards. The imago burned. Slippery mess everywhere in the streets."

"Your barbarians are fine shots." Hadrianus strode into the room, tossing his cloak onto a table by the entrance. "The three Roman arrows they shot into the door of the legionary bathhouse were a nice touch."

Agrippa turned to glare at Marcellinus, who was standing by the wall flanked by the four Cherokee. "I do not like to be threatened, sir."

"Does anybody?" Marcellinus turned to the Imperator. "That was only a taste of what they're capable of."

"Where did you find him?" Agrippa demanded.

The Cherokee pointed. "Corner, south and east. Walking."

"And when you offered to help him escape?"

"He refused. Said that he swore to stay."

Agrippa almost growled with frustration. "Messages to his friends?"

"He gave no messages."

On receiving Cassius's shamefaced report that he had lost Marcellinus, Agrippa had sent the Cherokee to try to trap him into revealing his treachery. If the situation had not been so grim, Marcellinus might have smiled at the man's discomfiture.

The First Centurion cleared his throat. "Permission to speak, sir?"

Agrippa waved a yes, still looking narrow-eyed at Marcellinus.

"The prisoner told us how to fight the fire, sir. How to hold it in check, best prevent it spreading. And he was right."

"I do not break my oaths, Caesar," Marcellinus said.

"Yes, yes." Hadrianus strode forward. "This redskin attack, Gaius Marcellinus. Your interpretation?"

Marcellinus still felt as if he were inhaling smoke. "A threefold attack, well planned and coordinated. The first target was your imago, to show their accuracy and damage Roman pride. Chosen to make their intent clear. Then the oil as an additional incendiary."

He paused. The use of oil was a new trick that would work well against large buildings like these and conserve the liquid flame. Marcellinus detected the mind of Enopay behind the idea. "Their second target was the buildings, to demonstrate the destructive capabilities of their Thunderbirds. Their third objective was to injure soldiers, drive them indoors. Prevent them from fighting the fires. Damage morale. Show Roma what they are dealing with."

"An effective assault indeed," Agrippa said acidly. "Perhaps you helped them design it."

Marcellinus shook his head. "I don't even know how they launched the Thunderbirds. You should have been safe from them here."

The Imperator frowned. "Lucius Agrippa, I think we have learned by now that Marcellinus does not lie even when any other sane man would do so."

"That does not make him any less dangerous," Agrippa said.

Marcellinus snorted. "You think I am dangerous? Look to Cahokia."

"Orders, sir?" Agrippa's First Centurion was growing restive.

"Double the sentries on the gates and corner towers," Agrippa said. "Assign a century of archers from the auxiliaries to stand ready on the ramparts, each side, all night, three watches. The next time anything larger than a buzzard flies over my camp, I want it on the ground riddled with arrows. Have the tribunes spread the word to their centurions to get the men bandaged, fed and watered, and bedded down. Don't let them sit up fretting into their wine and water."

"Sir." The First Centurion saluted crisply and marched out of the Principia. From the jangle of metal, Marcellinus could tell he had broken into a trot as soon as he was out of sight of his commanding officers.

"Well?" Hadrianus looked again at Marcellinus.

"This was a highly visible display of power. The Cahokians want respect. They want you to take them seriously. Know what they're capable of."

"I'll *respect* those savages all right," said Agrippa, pacing. "Burn my legionaries? Set fire to the Imperator's imago? The 27th Augustan has some *respect* we can show them in return."

"The Cahokians are not a people you will find easy to cow into submission, Lucius Agrippa."

"Perhaps you did not try hard enough."

"And perhaps you do not have time to fight a war you could avoid."

Agrippa shook his head and looked at his Imperator. "I must go and be seen around the camp, sir. In the meantime, can we clap this man in irons yet?"

"Certainly," Hadrianus said.

Marcellinus recoiled. "What?"

The Imperator studied him. "Come, Gaius Marcellinus, you must surely see how this changes things. Your people just attacked us." Agrippa made a signal, and four of his soldiers came forward.

"Is this necessary, sir?" Marcellinus said to the Imperator. "I can—"

Hadrianus held up his hand. "For now, Gaius Marcellinus, we need you under lock and key." He looked wry. "Think of it as being for your own protection."

Another centurion hurried into the room. He saluted Hadrianus and then Agrippa. "Redskins massing outside the camp, sir. In the thousands."

Agrippa froze. "You're joking."

"Preparing to attack?" Hadrianus asked.

"Not yet, Caesar. Grouping all around the clearing."

The soldier stood to attention, staring into the middle distance over Hadrianus's shoulder. With no time to change into armor, he wore the usual off-duty garb of tunic and cloak, and despite the coolness of the night the sweat was pouring off him.

Agrippa strode forward. "Cahokians or Iroqua, soldier?"

"Uh, we don't know, sir."

"Cahokians, probably," Marcellinus said. "Maybe a mix, but those were Cahokian Thunderbirds. Take me to look and I'll tell you."

"Will they attack us tonight?" Agrippa demanded.

"I don't know," Marcellinus said.

"And how *did* they launch those birds?" The Imperator stared at him through slitted eyes. "They have no higher ground, no mound with a rail."

Marcellinus shook his head. "I don't know, Caesar."

"Remind me why I keep you alive, Gaius Marcellinus."

Marcellinus caught himself about to say I *don't know* again. Instead he said: "In case I may be of assistance tomorrow, Caesar."

"They'll wait till dawn before they attack?"

"I think so. But—"

"But you don't know. Yes, yes, I understand that."

The Imperator paced, and Marcellinus fell silent.

"They won't get through my walls tonight or over them," said Agrippa. "I don't care how many barbarians pop out of the woods, it can't be done. Not with ladders, not with Greek fire, not with weight of numbers. Not against my 27th or even the bloody Third Parthian."

"I agree," said Marcellinus.

Hadrianus looked at him. "They have siege engines?"

"They may have brought their onagers and ballistas. They can be broken down into pieces for easy transport. But the Cahokians will expect you to come out and fight ... or come out and talk. They know Romans don't hide behind walls. I'm guessing they won't lay siege tonight."

"You guess a lot," Hadrianus said.

"That is because Tahtay did not tell me his war plan," Marcellinus said. "If war is what he truly intends."

Agrippa was fidgeting. "I must go to my men, sir."

"Of course." Hadrianus strode to the table at the corner of the room, threw his cloak over his shoulders, and fastened it at the breast with a silver brooch. "Come, Gaius Marcellinus; let's get some shackles on you and take a look at your barbarian horde, eh?"

Trailing in the Imperator's wake, flanked by two Praetorian Guards, Marcellinus climbed the low wooden watchtower on the southwest corner of the fortress and looked out over the clearing.

The night was deceptively calm. The low winds had died away, and the air was crisp. The clouds had rolled back, and the light of an almost full moon shone down on the Cahokian army spread out over the valley and the hills opposite.

Most were building campfires or already sitting around them. Some prowled back and forth, spears in hand, presumably looking back toward Marcellinus and the others in the twin fortresses of the XXVII Augusta Martia Victrix and the Third Parthica.

"Cahokians, then?" Hadrianus had gone ahead to talk to the soldiers of the watch but now returned to Marcellinus. "This is all of them, the entire Cahokian force?"

"Hard to say." Marcellinus peered to the farthest reaches of the clearing. Just by counting a sample of campfires and doing simple arithmetic, he could see that there had to be several thousand warriors out there. "They'll want to be warm around their fires. I can't imagine anyone wanting to hide in the trees instead."

"Insolence, Marcellinus?" the Imperator murmured, and Marcellinus stood up a little straighter. His tone was perhaps getting a little casual. Then again, it was hard to stand on ceremony with his wrists chained together. "Well, come on, man. You trained these savages. How will they fight?"

Hadrianus was right. It was time to start viewing the landscape in front of them as the battlefield it would probably become when the sun rose. "One moment, please, Caesar." Marcellinus did a slow scan around.

A mile to his southwest was the fortress of the Third Parthica. Lamps glowed in its streets and all along its wooden battlements. Fires smoldered there, too; the Third had suffered its own Wakinyan assault. The distant dark shapes of Sabinus's soldiers lined the walls.

A hundred yards to Marcellinus's south and east flowed the Oyo River, fifteen hundred feet wide at this point, with low hills and copses faintly visible beyond.

He turned back. The massive war party of Cahokia was spread out over the rolling land to his north and west, with the closest campfires four hundred yards away, safely out of bow range.

The Romans had clear-cut the area when building their fortresses, both to use the wood and to denude the area of cover. The nearest forests were at least two miles distant. Although the fortresses sat on the highest points, the slopes and inclines were all gradual and the lowest part of the shallow valley was only a couple of hundred feet below the short tower where Marcellinus stood. The Romans' high ground would give them little advantage in a battle.

Although there were no Cahokian warriors directly between the two Roman fortresses, they were still too close for comfort. The two legions were cut off from each other for the night and would have to resort to signaling back and forth with lanterns.

There would be no question of the Roman cohorts going out to engage the Hesperians tonight. Night battles were rare in the Roman world at the best of times, and clearly neither side was expecting trouble until the sun rose.

"Tahtay will permit your cohorts to march out and form up. When my own legion arrived in Cahokia, his father, Great Sun Man, allowed us to form a battle line before his forces charged." The Cahokians had also waited for Marcellinus to defeat his mutinous First Tribune in single combat, and in a sudden moment of insight Marcellinus realized one of the reasons why he disliked Flavius Agrippa: the Praetor reminded him of Corbulo.

He continued. "It was part of Great Sun Man's strategy to allow my legionaries to establish themselves in large blocks that would be vulnerable to Greek fire from his Thunderbirds. Tahtay, Wahchintonka, and Akecheta will do the same."

"They will attack us in formations? Roman formations?"

It had to be admitted. "Yes, sir. Most will not fight individually. They will form ranks. They may cast pila, shoot waves of arrows, and march through ranks to keep up a rapid pace of fire, just as your troops will do. And they are familiar with basic Roman tactical movements: the testudo, orbis, cuneus, and so forth."

"We will destroy them anyway," said the Imperator. "And then march on a Cahokia stripped of its best warriors."

Marcellinus nodded. Hadrianus looked at him sideways. "You agree? That we will win?"

"Eventually," Marcellinus said.

"Both of these legions have faced the armies of the Mongol Khan on the steppes of Asia. They have little to fear from redskins in a field. Even redskins trained by a rogue Praetor."

"Just so," Marcellinus said.

"And the Thunderbirds? Where will they come from?"

Marcellinus still did not know how the Cahokians had launched the Wakinyan, but it hardly mattered. "The first two overflew us from the east and the south. I suspect they were launched from the far side of the Oyo. But the third came from the north, so they must have another launching site somewhere beyond the trees that border the clearing."

He did not feel that he was betraying his Cahokian friends in speaking so freely. Such conclusions were obvious to anyone, and indeed, the Imperator was already nodding. "The Third Parthian has ballistas and will have them set up by morning. I have heard that ballista bolts do a fine job of downing Thunderbirds."

Marcellinus grinned, trying to hide his chagrin. "Caesar, it appears I can tell you little you do not already know."

"Then perhaps we should adjourn for the evening." Hadrianus took one more look across the battlefield and then nodded to Marcellinus's guards. "Don't worry. I'll have you woken bright and early for the slaughter."

Shackled, locked into a barracks room small enough to be a cell, Marcellinus lay on his back and stared upward, gripped by despair.

Tahtay was a proud youth, and Sintikala was easily his match in obstinacy and confrontation. Tahtay had made his speech to the Imperator and been rebuffed, and Sintikala had gazed into the dead eyes of Roma once again. Hadrianus had utterly rejected their overtures. And so they had withdrawn, flown their Wakinyan, and unleashed the Army of Ten Thousand.

They had expected it. This Cahokian army had set out long before Tahtay had even met Hadrianus for the first time. Wahchintonka, Akecheta, and the others had known their orders long in advance: bring the army and withdraw only if peace was achieved after all.

This had been Tahtay's plan all along. This was the secret that Sintikala could not tell Marcellinus in Cahokia: that Tahtay and the elders were far more ready to wage war than they had allowed him to believe. They had given Marcellinus his chance to hold back the tide, and he had failed them.

Was it a risk to bring such a substantial Cahokian force eastward with the Sixth Ironclads just a few days south at Ocatan? Perhaps Tahtay had left enough troops to defend Cahokia, or perhaps it had been clear enough to all of them that Verus would wait for the other two legions before launching an assault on Cahokia.

As for the Wakinyan . . .

"The waterwheel," he said aloud, and, if his hands had been free, would have used one of them to smack himself in the head.

I can't see us fighting Hadrianus with a waterwheel.
I wouldn't put it past Tahtay.

On the Wemissori, Marcellinus had towed Kimimela into the air like a kite. In Cahokia, he had given Tahtay the winch. The young Cahokians had joined the dots, and now they were winching Thunderbirds into the air from level ground. That was why the wheels made in Cahokia and Ocatan had been so wide: to accommodate substantial lengths of the steel-cored hempen rope.

While Marcellinus had been giving the Ocatani their direction, Hurit had been talking with them privately to ensure that Tahtay got the type of cogged wheel he really needed. They obviously had experimented with the earlier versions of the equipment to practice the technique while Marcellinus had been away on his many trips south. That explained why the normally impeccable surface of the Great Plaza had been so torn up on Marcellinus's return.

That was why Tahtay had been so interested in the waterwheel and the winches even with Cahokia on the edge of war with Roma. That was why Hurit had come to Marcellinus's house in the first place: to add to the encouragement, to persuade him to go to Ocatan.

Marcellinus had been played. Countless Cahokians had been in on the plot, including many of his most trusted friends, and he hadn't had the slightest suspicion it was happening.

He was oddly proud of them.

But war was still coming. As Marcellinus turned awkwardly onto his side on the rough straw bedding, pulled the rough blanket to his chin, and tried to close his eyes for a few hours, he was in no doubt that the dawn would bring war between Cahokia and Roma, the very war he had spent so many years trying to avert.

"Up," said Pollius Scapax.

Marcellinus came awake all at once. He tried to roll up onto his feet, but the weight of the shackles held him down and left him floundering and blinking stupidly.

"Come," said Scapax. "Time for battle."

As the man yanked his blanket away, Marcellinus realized his mistake. This was not Scapax, the trusted First Centurion who had been slain on the Great Mound of Cahokia six years before, but an anonymous centurion of the 27th.

Marcellinus awkwardly pushed himself upright and raised his hands.

"I don't have the keys to those," said the centurion. "You're to come to the wall with me."

"What's happening?"

"The sun is rising, and we're about to mow down your stinking savages in the thousands."

It was cold outside and overcast again. Marcellinus wondered how the First Cahokian and the other warriors of the Great City had fared overnight out in the open.

"Look sharp, man," the centurion said, but Marcellinus's wounded leg was stiff and he was walking as quickly as he could.

It was amazing that Marcellinus had slept at all, let alone been dead to the world for so long. If the centurion had not been sent to fetch him, might he have slept through the whole war?

Arriving on the south tower at dawn, he found Lucius Agrippa and Imperator Hadrianus with their heads together, pointing and having a discussion in low tones. Marcellinus stepped up to the ramparts and looked out over the battlefield.

A thousand bonfires still smoldered in the meadow, but now they lay unattended. The Cahokians had backed up and even now were forming a line a mile long, from southwest to northeast, about three-quarters of a mile distant. The ends of the line were reinforced twenty men deep, presumably to guard against being outflanked by cavalry. They also had left several gaps in the formation, just as they had when practicing in the Great Plaza. Marcellinus suspected that any cavalryman who galloped into one of those gaps would meet a speedy death either from a hail of arrows or by being dragged from his horse and clubbed.

The Imperator noted his arrival. "I see pila, Marcellinus. I see gladii and scuta. I see helmets and breastplates. I see onagers and ballistas. Everywhere I look, I see Roman equipment in Hesperian hands. You have outfitted and trained an army against me."

"That was never my intent."

Hadrianus looked away. "Perhaps you even believe that."

As for the Romans, the infantry of the Third Parthica were taking the field already, their shields bearing the blue bull crest of their legion. They were deploying from all four gates at once and marching around to form ranks on the western side of the fortress.

They did not form a triple line. Instead they formed up in shallow ranks, by cohorts, with the double-strength First Cohort forming a much larger block at the northern end. Marcellinus spied Praetor Decinius Sabinus standing in front of the First Cohort chatting with his tribunes and First Centurion.

They were leaving plenty of space to move should Thunderbirds overfly them. And on the flat roofs of the Third Parthica's barrack blocks and stable buildings Marcellinus counted six ballistas and four onagers, each crewed by three contubernia.

As for the fortress of XXVII Augusta Martia Victrix where he stood, the streets behind him were abustle with centuries on the march, but the two gates Marcellinus could see—the Southgate and Westgate—remained locked and barred, the hillside around the fortress empty of troops. Parts of the barracks still smoldered and smoked and there was a queasy smell of burned flesh, hair, and grease in the air, but the soldiers he saw looked organized and determined and not even a tiny bit cowed.

In the center of the camp a new imago fluttered from a tall pole set on the Principia's roof. The Imperator apparently traveled with a spare banner.

Beyond the fortress to Marcellinus's left, a heavily armored cohort of the 27th marched to the Oyo to hold the riverbank. The Romans would not be taken unawares by a surprise flanking attack from the river.

As Marcellinus turned back, he felt a stabbing pain in his forehead and temples so vicious that he raised his chained hands up in front of his face. The pain dwindled and then pulsed back in full force. For the first time in several years, the headache he had gotten regularly after the sack of Cahokia had returned. He breathed deeply, trying to dispel it.

"They're moving."

"Hawk ho!"

Agrippa and the Imperator suddenly stood erect. The

Cahokian war party was walking forward, not marching in step. A Hawk craft had appeared above the Cahokian army, flying north along the line and then flipping around to fly back in the opposite direction, as if tacking in place over the force. Behind it, nosing above the tree line a hundred yards apart, came two Sky Lanterns, still tethered but rapidly gaining height. The breeze blew from the northwest; if they dropped the tethers, the wind would carry the Lanterns over the assembled Roman armies.

"Aha." The Imperator smiled.

A trumpet sounded, and the ten cohorts of the Third Parthica all came to attention in a single precise movement.

The pain in Marcellinus's head momentarily blurred his vision. He pushed water out of his eyes with his thumbs, and when he looked again, the First Cahokian had emerged in the exact center of the Cahokian line, six hundred warriors coming forward in close order, pila held up in front of them like a forest of steel. At their left edge Akecheta marched with gladius drawn and chin high.

It looked very much as if Marcellinus's own Cahokian Cohort would be the first into action against the cohorts of the Third Parthica, one of the oldest and most experienced legions in the Imperium.

Agrippa glanced back over his shoulder. "Nice job, Gaius Marcellinus. Don't you wish you were over there with them right now?"

Marcellinus did not respond. He was too busy trying not to fold and retch with the pain in his head. But as the Cahokian Army of Ten Thousand continued to walk forward, his eyes were drawn to two patches of color close together in the line to the north of the First Cahokian. The first was a figure only two-thirds of the size of the soldiers around him, dressed in a pale color approaching white. And from right next to this figure came a sudden flash of red.

Enopay was walking in the front line of the Cahokian

army, and by his side Tahtay, war chief of Cahokia, had pulled aside his cloak to reveal the vivid red sash of the Fire Hearts.

Marcellinus forced himself to breathe. The slim figure walking on Tahtay's other side had to be Kimimela, a bow in her hand. "Shit. Shit."

The Sky Lanterns were continuing to rise and were now several hundred feet up, safely out of range of either archers or siege engines. Sintikala had lost height and disappeared behind the trees. Now she appeared again above the Cahokian line. Tossed into the air by a throwing engine, she was next to invisible until her wing unfurled. Again the Hawk chief began her sweeps back and forth, occasionally darting forward to look down at the formations of the Third Parthica.

The Army of Ten Thousand had covered about a third of the distance separating it from the Third Parthica. Now, as if the reappearance of Sintikala had been a sign, the massive army stopped. The First Cahokian marched on fifty yards ahead of the others and halted, too, grounding the butts of their pila in the grass.

Enopay and Kimimela stayed in the Cahokian line, but Tahtay kept coming, walking clear of his forces.

Around Marcellinus the fortress of the XXVII Augusta exploded into action. With a loud bang the gates were thrown wide. A column of heavy auxiliary cavalry galloped from the Westgate. A second column of light cavalry appeared from behind the fortress, obviously having exited from the Eastgate and formed a block fifteen horses wide and fifty deep. This second and much larger group swept on behind the fortress of the Third Parthica and came to a smooth halt to the left of the infantry.

From the Southgate the soldiers of the 27th emerged on the double, century by century, spreading out over the slopes.

Undaunted, not even breaking stride, Tahtay continued his lone walk toward the military might of Roma.

"Gods' sakes . . ." Marcellinus stepped forward.

The Imperator Hadrianus III smiled. "Something to say, Praetor?"

Behind the Cahokians, men spilled from the trees. Hundreds, perhaps thousands of warriors in groups of six broke cover and jogged toward the rear of the Cahokian army.

"Iroqua," Marcellinus said.

"Really?" Now Hadrianus was frowning.

A lump came to Marcellinus's throat. The Iroqua were joining the Cahokians, thickening the line, standing side by side and shoulder to shoulder with Tahtay's warriors from the Great City. Their numbers swelled the size of the Hesperian army across the valley by almost a half again.

"You said there wouldn't be any more in the trees," Hadrianus said sardonically. "Wrong again, Gaius Marcellinus. It's as if you're doing it deliberately."

"Good, good," Agrippa said. "We can put paid to all of them at once. We can finish this today."

Now it truly was an Army of Ten Thousand. Numerically, at least, the Romans and Hesperians were close to equally matched.

Marcellinus coughed, trying to clear the lump in his throat, and his head stabbed with pain again. "Mostly Iroqua. By the headdresses, the style of the tunics, and the breeches I'd guess Caiuga and Onondaga, with some Tuscarora from the east. Plus a few hundred of the Blackfoot tribe of the plains. The Haudenosaunee and the People of the Grass have joined the Cahokians against you, Caesar. You're facing—" He stopped, blinked, nodded as the realization sunk home, and spoke more boldly. "Imperator Hadrianus, you face a mighty alliance. A confederation of Hesperian nations stands against you."

"'Against you'?" Hadrianus said. "Your words betray your sympathies."

Marcellinus lifted his shackled arms. "I am not a combatant."

"You'd like to march out with us? Kill a few Cahokians at last?" Agrippa taunted.

"No, what I'd *like* is for you not to slay the war chief of Cahokia, who is walking alone across the field of war to parley with you."

"Is that what he's doing? I thought perhaps he was committing suicide."

Marcellinus surged forward dangerously, and his guards grabbed his arms. "Lucius Agrippa, I'd like to see you have the balls to walk alone across a valley toward an enemy army."

His eyes bleak, Agrippa let his hand drop to the hilt of his gladius.

Hadrianus raised his hand. "Marcellinus, Agrippa: do shut up."

"Caesar, I will not be silent until you agree to hear what Tahtay has to say." Marcellinus steeled himself. "If you're going to let him die unheard, you'll have to kill me, too."

"That should not pose a problem," Agrippa said.

In the skies above the Cahokian line, Sintikala continued to swoop back and forth. Marcellinus could almost feel her agitation as she looked down on the lone figure of Tahtay. The war chief had reached the lowest point of the gently sloping valley and was strolling up the other side, directly toward Praetor Decinius Sabinus and the massed cohorts of the Third Parthica.

"I made a vow." As Marcellinus said the words, the pain in his head dwindled. Now his voice came more strongly. He looked again at Sintikala in the sky and Tahtay walking through the grass. He raised his shackled hands. "Along the Wemissori River, I swore that I'd do everything in my power to keep that boy alive. Other Hesperians were the threat then, not Romans. But I brought Tahtay to this, and an oath is an oath. Free me and let me stand with him as he dies. Or come with me and find out what he has to say. Or strike me down, and Hades take you all."

Agrippa laughed derisively. Hadrianus stared at Marcellinus as if he were a new type of creature never beheld before.

"Caesar, let me go," Marcellinus said. "If you will not attempt to make peace with these people, I'm of no use to you anyway. I will not lift a gladius against Roma. But if I'm to die, let me die out there with Tahtay."

Hadrianus raised his hand. "Hush."

Somewhere in the far distance, a wolf was howling.

Tahtay heard it, too. His head came up, and he halted a hundred yards in front of the First Cohort of the Third Parthica. He looked right and left as if he expected the beast to appear, although it was obviously many miles distant.

Tahtay nodded, raised one hand high above his head in salute, and then lowered it.

"That was peculiar," the Imperator said. "Explain."

"I don't believe I can," Marcellinus said.

Agrippa's irritation was growing. "Should I kill him now, Caesar? Or should we march him onto the battlefield and cut him down in front of his redskin friends?"

Marcellinus grinned without humor. He had been here before, faced by a Hesperian army, with a senior officer of Roma close by threatening to kill him. Both armies fully deployed and waiting for orders.

But today Marcellinus was a captive rather than a general, with no tribunes, no officers, no soldiers. His closest friends were on the other side of the battlefield, preparing to charge to their deaths.

Perhaps he had lived long enough.

"Talk to Tahtay," Marcellinus said. "Just once more, Caesar, I beg of you."

Hadrianus looked around. The trumpeters stood awaiting his command. The Third and the 27th were fully deployed. The First Cahokian stood, a solid block of steel in front of a mile-wide array of Hesperians.

Tahtay pulled a small stake out of his belt and began to unravel his red sash. It was longer than Marcellinus would have guessed, perhaps ten feet in length. One end was securely anchored to his waist. Tahtay took the stake and drove it into the ground through the other end of the sash.

Then he lowered himself and sat cross-legged a hundred yards from the Third Parthica. From the front of his legion Decinius Sabinus turned and looked up toward Marcellinus and the Imperator, nonplussed.

"Tahtay has pinned his sash," Marcellinus said, his heart heavy.

"Meaning?"

"In addition to being the paramount chief of Cahokia, Tahtay is a member of the Fire Hearts, a Blackfoot warrior society. He will stand and fight where he is. He will not retreat from that position."

"Well, that will make him easier to kill," Agrippa said.

Marcellinus ignored him. To Hadrianus he said: "Tahtay is giving you one last chance. A chance for peace. A chance to go and talk to him. If you don't take it and Tahtay dies there, his warriors will fight to the last man." He looked out at where Kimimela stood in the front line and up in the air at Sintikala. Hanska would be somewhere out there, too, bouncing on the balls of her feet, ready to cleave Roman scalps with her ax.

Not Hurit, though. Marcellinus swallowed. "To the last man and woman, the last Cahokian or Iroqua or Blackfoot. Caesar, do not mistake Tahtay for a barbarian. He is not. He is an honorable man."

With a metallic ring, Agrippa unsheathed his gladius. "I believe we have heard enough, Gaius Marcellinus."

Marcellinus stepped forward to face him, hands up before him, unblinking.

Agrippa raised the sword. "On your knees, traitor."

Marcellinus stood where he was. "Before you, verpa? Never again."

Agrippa nodded, held the gladius high, and looked at his Imperator.

In the skies, Sintikala's Catanwakuwa jerked in the air and slewed left. On the ground before them, Tahtay suddenly had risen to his feet.

Marcellinus hoped with all his heart that Kimimela, at least, was still too far distant to see this.

He braced himself, his chained fists raised in defense. "Imperator Hadrianus," he said. "Caesar, by all the gods: please talk to Tahtay, but above all else, please tell me I do not have to fight this moron yet again in order to make my point to you."

Hadrianus stared, flabbergasted. The guards and Lucius Agrippa all looked to him for orders. Marcellinus kept his eyes fixed on Agrippa, ready to throw himself forward as soon as the Praetor moved against him.

Marcellinus had been prepared to die quietly on many other days in Nova Hesperia, but not today. Not today.

"Oh, Great Jove above." Hadrianus shook his head. "Send the signal to hold the legions. Agrippa, lower your sword and order my horse to be brought to the gate. Gaius Marcellinus, your Cahokians have one last chance to come to their senses before we annihilate them. One."

Chapter 28

Year Seven, Planting Moon

The Imperator rode a fine high-stepping chestnut Nisaean with its forelock braided into a poll knot and its harness decorated with silver disks. On either side of the horse walked the Praetors Decinius Sabinus and Flavius Agrippa in full-dress uniform and armor. Marcellinus, still wearing the tunic he had slept in, walked to Agrippa's left and a little behind him, escorted and guarded by a common foot soldier of the Fourth Cohort, 27th Augustan.

In front of them stood Tahtay, alone. He had eschewed the regalia of a war chief of Cahokia; he wore a fine buckskin and the red sash of the Fire Hearts that anchored him, but wide copper armbands and ankle bands were the only other indications of his rank. It was a good choice. The Romans would have found the full kilt, cloak, headdress, and mace of a Cahokian paramount chief barbaric rather than magnificent.

The two unequal parties met on the hill in the middle of what soon might become a bloody battlefield.

Tahtay frowned up at the Imperator. "You have brought several men with you. I would bring up three chiefs of Cahokia to stand behind me and hear our words. It is permitted?"

"Certainly," Hadrianus said. "If they are unarmed and keep their distance."

Tahtay nodded. "One of them is . . ." He pointed upward. "She will come down now. Do not fear her."

Agrippa snorted.

Tahtay tilted his head back and made hand-talk with large gestures: *Land in peace.* Then he turned, pointed to the Cahokian line, and signaled some more.

The Romans stiffened. Tahtay had turned his back on the Imperator. "He means no offense," Marcellinus said quickly.

Tahtay faced them again. "Offense?"

"We allow it," Hadrianus said even as Agrippa shook his head and grimaced.

Tahtay looked at Marcellinus, who said, "Never mind, Tahtay. Carry on."

Two men and a girl detached themselves from the Cahokian line. The girl was Kimimela, and one man had to be Kanuna, but Marcellinus could not immediately identify the other. It was not Wahchintonka.

Then the man put his hand to his belly, and Marcellinus knew him. Marcellinus blinked and squinted, but the elder's rolling walk was very distinctive, that and the way he still held his hand protectively over his stomach, as if he expected the wound he had suffered after the toppling of Avenaka to open up again at any moment.

"Yes?" Hadrianus said. "Speak."

"The man on the left is Kanuna, whom you met before, walking with the translator, Kimimela. On the right is Matoshka, another elder of Cahokia, much more experienced in war."

He deliberately had spoken loudly enough for Tahtay to hear and used words the war chief would understand.

"Yes, of course," Tahtay said. "If it happens that Cahokia must march its army away, it must be Matoshka who takes the word back to Wahchintonka and his Wolf Warriors. Otherwise, why else would they agree to spare you, having come so far?" He looked up at Hadrianus and spoke almost apologetically. "Lately they have been robbed of many wars, and thirst for battle. They know they can take many Roman scalps. I am sure you have men among your army that wish to fight today, too, who you must also . . ." He glanced at Marcellinus and gestured.

"Appease," Marcellinus said. "Placate."

Hadrianus nodded. "Certainly."

By his side Agrippa smiled tautly, and Tahtay picked up on the movement and gave him an ironic half bow.

Sintikala had looped around to the west. Now a white ribbon unfurled behind her wing, and she came in fast and low behind Tahtay. Hadrianus's horse raised its head and blew air out of its nostrils with a harrumph. Sintikala landed running and unbuckled her wing.

The two groups faced each other. On one side was the Imperator Hadrianus, flanked by Sabinus and Agrippa, with Marcellinus beside them; on the other, Tahtay, Sintikala, Kimimela, Kanuna, and Matoshka. They sized one another up for a long moment. Kimimela glanced at the shackles on Marcellinus's wrists, her face bleak. None of the other Cahokians spared him a second glance. The wind blew cool over the meadow.

Tahtay nodded and spoke. "Caesar. Before, in your castra, we spoke with you at your pleasure, at your time. You did not treat us with respect. We were not happy."

He fixed the Imperator with a sharp stare, and Marcellinus cringed a little. Even with Tahtay's speaking skills, this was veering dangerously close to pantomime.

Then again, Marcellinus knew Tahtay well. The Imperator and the two Praetors did not, and they appeared to be taking him completely seriously.

"Perhaps you look at me and see a boy. But look behind me, Caesar. There stand the finest warriors of Cahokia, the greatest city on the Mizipi and in all the land. I have the best warriors from the plains, the Fire Hearts of the Blackfoot. I have the best warriors of the Haudenosaunee, the Five Tribes from the Great Lakes. And these men all came for me and against you. You will not defeat us, Imperator Hadrianus. You cannot."

"And yet here you are, talking to me."

"Yes. Because I do not want to see thousands of your

men and mine slain for no good reason, when you can just say a few words and make a treaty for peace and all will be well.

"You are a man of pride, Imperator Hadrianus. You are proud, and so you should be. Your army is fine and strong, and their armor shines. But perhaps you can also be proud of not fighting. Perhaps you can be proud of winning without needing to fight."

And in that moment, and whatever happened next, Marcellinus knew that Tahtay was truly a worthy heir to Great Sun Man.

Hadrianus raised an eyebrow. "You are prideful, too, Tahtay of Cahokia. And you can say just two words and we will not fight. The words are 'We surrender.' Order your savages to lay down their weapons on the grass and disperse, and give us Cahokia."

Tahtay shook his head. "I think not. I choose to negotiate from strength rather than weakness. Here are Cahokia's terms. Take them or leave them."

This was not how one spoke to an Imperator. Marcellinus could almost see the thoughts buzzing in Hadrianus's brain. "Tahtay . . ."

Tahtay turned his acid gaze on Marcellinus and said, "You will not speak unless commanded."

Marcellinus bowed.

To the Imperator, Tahtay said, "Take my terms or leave them, Caesar. They are not bad terms, for we are a fair people. Please, I ask you to listen."

Hadrianus looked at Marcellinus. "And you say you did not coach him?"

Tahtay frowned in irritation. "Or you may not find them agreeable, and if so, we will fight. Today. Our young men have been restless since we declared peace with the Iroqua. How to prove themselves other than by taking scalps? And today we have an even bigger war party, because the Haudenosaunee have sent warriors to fight alongside us. Because we have a bigger enemy than each other, and that is you."

Easy, Tahtay, Marcellinus wanted to say. The Imperator regarded the young war chief impassively. "Yes, yes. Go on."

"Cahokia will not be a Roman province, defeated. Cahokia will be what it is now: a city, independent.

"Your legions will not come into Cahokia. You will not approach except at our invitation, and if we invite you, Caesar, or any of your men in ones and twos, you will leave our city before nightfall. Your legions will pass Cahokia on a trail we will provide, well to the south of the city. Also, we will help your legions cross the great Mizipi.

"Until recently we had another city on the other side of the Great River called Cahokia-across-the-water. Few live in it now, for the Iroqua did a great killing there, but we have mended the city. This is where you can make castra. We will provide wood for you if you wish for a walled castra like these."

The Imperator regarded Tahtay thoughtfully. "You realize that the wood and the passage across the water are not the items of greatest concern to me."

Tahtay nodded. "You want to feed your soldiers. I have two answers for you. First, the buffalo. Perhaps you have already seen them, for some herds live east of the Mizipi. But on the west side, near and far, there are many more. A thousand-thousand."

The Imperator looked at Marcellinus. "How many?"

"Tahtay means massive herds, hundreds of thousands of animals. You could feed your legions from the buffalo indefinitely and still not dent their numbers."

"Second, we will give you corn," Tahtay said.

"How much corn?" Hadrianus asked.

"Half of all in our granaries. Half of what we harvest once we bring it in from the fields. It is a good offer."

"We will decide if it is a good offer," Agrippa said, but Hadrianus silenced him with a gesture.

"Half," said Tahtay. "No more, for we have a city to feed, but it will be an honest half. We have a friend who counts everything and makes marks in a book. We keep good records in Cahokia now thanks to this man here, whom you were good enough to send us."

Tahtay had allowed a note of sarcasm to enter his voice. Marcellinus was relieved to see the ghost of a smile on the Imperator's face.

"Also, we will allow your . . . train?" Tahtay looked at Marcellinus and made the hand-talk for *Speak*.

"Supply train," Marcellinus said.

"We will allow your supply train to pass through, along that same road to the south of Cahokia."

Hadrianus nodded. "What else?"

"Else?" Tahtay shook his head. "There is no 'else.' Already we are more than generous. Take our offer and avoid the shedding of much blood."

Taking his time, the Imperator surveyed the Hesperian war party. "Tahtay, Tahtay. Do you honestly think I fear your band of barbarians? That they would stand any chance against my wall of Roman steel?"

"Huh," said Tahtay. "Do you believe I fear *you* up on your big horse? I do not. Listen, Imperator: a few years ago Cahokia fell to the Iroqua, and it nearly destroyed us. You understand? Cahokia will not fall again. If we fell to you, we would die as a people, but we will not die.

"Cahokia is united. We are one city, all agreed. Matoshka and Howahkan, Ogleesha and Kanuna, every elder of Cahokia. Every clan chief, including Sintikala, Ojinjintka, and Anapetu when she lived. Also Wahchintonka, who leads the great army you see in front of you, and Akecheta, a warrior chief who has fought by the Wanageeska's side."

"Yes, yes," said Hadrianus, impatient with the litany of names.

"You do not know all these people, but the Wanageeska does. He can tell you that they are all the important people in Cahokia, every great chief and elder, and none would say a thing they did not mean.

"Cahokia is united, and more: it is allied with the Iroqua. And so Cahokia and the Iroqua will defeat you, and if it happens that we do not, we will give you a bloody fight you will never forget.

"Come now, Caesar. You do not want *us*. You do not care about one city on one river. You do not care about revenge. I see it in your face. You want food and to go on into the west. And we, too, want you to go on. Can we not agree on that?"

As if bored, Hadrianus surveyed the battlefield, taking in the Hesperian army, siege engines, and Sky Lanterns. Tahtay waited, standing perfectly still.

Eventually, the Imperator looked down. "Perhaps. If we were to go on with your help."

Agrippa frowned. Marcellinus's breath caught in his throat. Tahtay scrutinized the Imperator even more closely. "And what help is that?"

"Guides. Men who know the lands and rivers ahead of us, who know the conditions we will face. Men who can talk to the other tribes we will meet."

Tahtay nodded slowly. "We may have such men and women who may be willing to come with you."

"But in addition to food and guides, I will need gold."

Tahtay shrugged. "We have none."

"So you say, and I believe you. But I think you know where gold comes from, Tahtay of Cahokia."

Their eyes met.

"Yes," Tahtay said. "Gold comes from rivers and streams to the north and west and sometimes from mountains, in addition to coming from the People of the Sun."

"Futete!" said Marcellinus. "Holy fucking Jove . . . Tahtay, what?"

The Imperator glanced at Marcellinus accusingly. "Rivers and streams, Gaius Marcellinus?"

Out of words, Marcellinus shook his head and gestured as best he could with his hands chained in front of him.

"The Wanageeska, your captive, does not know this," Tahtay said. "My father thought it safer not to tell him, and all agreed. But in the north and west, along the

Wemissori where my Blackfoot brothers live, there are riverbeds where gold can be gathered in chunks and as dust. There are mountains where it can be found in a band in the rock. And I know people who may show you where such riverbeds and mountains are."

"You will do more than that, Tahtay," Hadrianus said. "You will help us gather and mine it."

"Perhaps we will. But not as slaves, never as slaves."

The naked greed on Hadrianus's face was easy to read. "Your blackfooted people will help us find the gold, and when they do, it is ours and not yours."

"If we cared for gold, we would have pulled it from the water and the earth ourselves. Take it if that is your price for leaving us in peace."

Hadrianus had fallen into a brief trance. Now the alert look returned to his eyes. "Good, good. But also, Tahtay? There may be other enemies ahead of us whom you can help us with."

Tahtay frowned. "You wish us to fight other tribes for you? We will not do that."

"Not Hesperian tribes," the Imperator said.

Tahtay looked at Marcellinus. "You may speak to help me understand."

Marcellinus had sworn an oath, and the Imperator's eyes were upon him. "I cannot explain, Tahtay."

"Then I cannot help you with things I do not understand," Tahtay said. "But if you want food, and to be guided through the land, and if the gold is to be yours and not ours, it will cost you one more thing, Caesar, and that is Ocatan. Cahokia cannot help you while your soldiers live in our city and our brothers and sisters are forced away from their land and work for Roma as slaves. You must rebuild Ocatan and give it back to its people. Build a new castra somewhere up the Oyo if you must, but the city and the land of our people must be returned. All the slaves you have taken must be freed. All. All."

The Imperator nodded slowly. "Perhaps. But if *that* is to be done, it will cost *you* one more thing, Tahtay of

Cahokia." And he pointed above the heads of the Cahokian contingent. The Sky Lanterns.

For a moment, Tahtay appeared lost in contemplation. Then he nodded. "The Lanterns we will give you. The Hawks and Thunderbirds must be a question for another day, once trust has grown between our peoples. But for today? Yes, Caesar; we will instruct you in the use of our Sky Lanterns."

Agrippa smiled. Marcellinus looked at Sabinus and Hadrianus and saw the same change in them, but more subtle.

Tahtay owned the same calmness, and he did not look at Marcellinus.

Marcellinus kept his face calm, but a vast sense of relief flooded him.

Tahtay had played his hand perfectly.

These were the deal makers: Cahokia's assistance in helping the Romans spearhead their advance through the continent, Cahokia's help in finding gold, and Cahokia's flying craft. These were the things of most value to Hadrianus, much harder to obtain than provisions.

From Hadrianus's viewpoint, he had gained huge advantages in exchange for almost nothing. Tahtay's offer included most of what Roma had come for.

And Tahtay had extracted his price for it. The conquering of Ocatan had been a sharp blow to the Cahokians, Hadrianus's object lesson; he had smashed Ocatan to put pressure on Cahokia. In reality, the Romans had no need to leave a legion there indefinitely. A free Ocatan was a concession the Imperator could make easily.

Tahtay—or perhaps Enopay—had guessed as much. Marcellinus was quite sure of that. But by presenting it as a high price in the negotiations, Tahtay could go back to Wahchintonka and the Wolf Warriors and ease the sting of depriving them of another battle by saying, "See, I have kept the Romans out of Cahokia, and see, I have forced them to rebuild Ocatan and return it to our people." Matoshka, once his deadliest opponent, had witnessed the negotiation and was nodding as Kimimela translated quietly for him and Kanuna.

To Roman eyes, Hadrianus had gotten everything he had asked for. To Cahokian eyes, Tahtay had forced the Romans to back down and had gotten everything *he* had asked for.

Each man could present this as a victory. It had been a virtuoso performance.

"One last thing, so there is no mistake," Tahtay said. "If this treaty were to fail or be breached, and if one day you march into Cahokia after all, you will find no corn. We will burn our granaries. We will burn our fields. If the treaty falls, we will destroy every ear and every grain before we feed a Roman. I have given the order already. Men and women stand ready in Cahokia even now to make it so. I have spoken."

"One moment, please, Tahtay of Cahokia," Hadrianus said. "We will discuss your proposal."

The Roman party backed up, Marcellinus among them.

"Comments, gentlemen?" the Imperator murmured.

"We should take the offer, sir," Sabinus said. "We had planned to face Cahokia with three legions, an overwhelming force. Here we have only two. Best to accept the alliance and not suffer the casualties."

Agrippa shook his head. "Two legions is enough. You understand that this is largely a bluff? That we can destroy them handily?"

"But it is a competent, well-thought-out bluff," Sabinus pointed out. "Can you imagine any other Hesperians we've yet encountered being this well organized? Which may make them good allies."

Hadrianus looked thoughtfully at Marcellinus. "It is you who raised them to this. Before you, they would not be so bold."

"Perhaps," Marcellinus said.

Agrippa shook his head. "They are fools. They have given away their hand. We now know where the gold is and which tribe can lead us to it. We don't need the Cahokians at all."

"Much easier with the Cahokians than without them," Marcellinus said. "Tahtay himself knows the key Blackfoot people you should talk with."

"We cannot trust them," Agrippa insisted. "And we can't trust *him*, either. Listen: once the Cahokians have us on the western side of the Mizipi, they can close the door and cut us off. That is not a tenable situation.

"Instead, we can make this simple. Let us fight. Or if not, by all means let us smile at them now and avoid battle today, while they are prepared. Once they are quiet and calm back in their city, we can march in quickly and mow them down before they have time to torch the granaries. Take what we need and be done with it."

"Treachery?" Marcellinus said, appalled. "Make a treaty only to break it? You would have Caesar swear to the nations of Nova Hesperia in bad faith?"

Agrippa looked at him with some satisfaction. "And so Marcellinus reveals his true colors. D'you see, Sabinus? We keep this man in chains because it is obvious which side *he* is on."

"Agrippa raises a point," Hadrianus said almost lazily. "What if the Cahokians merely bluff now and wait till they have us at their mercy?"

"The Cahokians can be trusted to the ends of the earth and beyond. Can you?" Marcellinus nodded toward Agrippa. "Can *he*?"

Agrippa gritted his teeth, and his hand went to his pugio.

"Not on my watch," Sabinus said, laying a muscled hand on Agrippa's arm. "Great gods, gold and corn and our legions intact and whole to fight the Mongol Khan? What more do you want, Agrippa, gems raining from the skies?"

"Look at this." Marcellinus swept his bound hands in front of him. "The forces of Nova Hesperia. Massive and proud and all allied as ... as a single Hesperian

League. You want this with you, Caesar, when you go up against Chinggis Khan."

"But can you control them, Gaius Marcellinus? Perhaps even lead them for me?"

Marcellinus met his eye. "If they agree to fight the Khan, I will do my very best."

"Enough." Hadrianus studied each of the three men in turn. "Very well. We will make this treaty."

"And?" Marcellinus demanded.

The Imperator looked irritated. "And if the Cahokians stay in line, I will honor it. We will have plenty of time to measure their helpfulness. Obviously, they must keep every part of their pledge. If they do not, then we are bound by none of it."

Marcellinus opened his mouth again, but Sabinus shot him a look and he desisted.

"Any other words of wisdom, gentlemen?" Hadrianus said drily.

The three Praetors looked at one another. One by one they shook their heads.

At last, the Imperator dismounted from his Nisaean and walked forward. "Tahtay, I accept the terms we have discussed here and pledge peace with you and Cahokia."

Tahtay nodded and drew his dagger. Hadrianus jumped back, and Agrippa sprang forward to protect his Imperator. Sintikala, too, stepped forward with her hand on her own dagger.

Tahtay looked surprised. He glanced at Marcellinus. "What?"

Marcellinus's heart still pounded. "Caesar, Tahtay expects you to join with him in swearing an oath. In blood."

"You must be joking."

"I'm afraid that's what this is going to take, sir."

Tahtay was looking back and forth between them. "Are you an honorable man, Caesar?"

"I am." Hadrianus smiled faintly.

"Then perhaps we do not need to spill blood."

The Imperator surveyed the Cahokian army still patiently lined up before him. "But to gain your trust?"

"And to prove your sincerity," Marcellinus said quietly.

Hadrianus grinned. "It won't be the first time I've bled for the Imperium. And it probably won't be the last. But Tahtay, I can hardly be seen performing a barbarian ritual in front of my men. Can we do this privately at another time?"

Tahtay returned the dagger to his belt and bowed. "I understand. Can we bury the ax instead? And later smoke a pipe?"

"Yes, yes, let it be done."

"Then bring forward a Roman ax, and we will bring one, too. Matoshka?"

The elder turned and made broad gestures in handtalk. Mahkah stepped forward from the battle line, placed his bow and quiver of arrows on the ground, and unslung his ax from the strap over his shoulder. Dangling it loosely at arm's length, he jogged across the meadow.

Marcellinus cleared his throat. "Perhaps a sword from Roma? In the legions hatchets are tools, not weapons."

Sabinus turned and signaled to one of his centurions. Shortly afterward, a soldier trotted out from the fortress of the Third Parthica bearing a sword and a mattock for the digging.

Tahtay looked at the manacles around Marcellinus's wrists. "We would suggest one thing more. Not as part of the treaty. This Roman is yours, and you will do with him as you wish. But if possible, we ask that he continue to help us in our talking. He knows both Cahokia and Roma and may help us avoid misunderstanding each other." Tahtay half grinned. "If we have learned anything, it is that good translators are hard to find."

"I will consider it," the Imperator said.

With great solemnity the unnamed soldier of the Third and Mahkah of Cahokia dug a shallow hole, placed the gladius and the ax in it, and covered them. Tahtay and Hadrianus stamped the dirt into place over the weapons.

Tahtay nodded in satisfaction. "And now we must persuade our warriors to walk away and not fight you. May we go and do so? And you will do the same with your soldiers?"

"Let it be done," the Imperator said gravely.

The two sides in the parley withdrew from each other, with Hadrianus leading his horse by its leather bridle.

"The kid is growing on me." Hadrianus grinned at Marcellinus. "I like him more than I like you, truth be told."

Marcellinus bowed. "It is more important for you to like him, Caesar. But when will you tell them about the Mongols?"

"I wouldn't wish to complicate things." The Imperator eyed him. "You counsel that we should tell them now, after all? Before we even know for sure where the Mongols are? You see an advantage to that?"

All Marcellinus's instincts rebelled at keeping so great a secret from Tahtay, but now he was forced to consider the question strategically.

"No," he said.

"And why?"

"Because we will need to negotiate with Cahokia for auxiliary troops and assistance. And the use of their liquid flame in battle. And before that negotiation we'll need to know more about what we're dealing with. The Mongol numbers and location. How much help we need and of what kind."

Hadrianus nodded. "I see you are not entirely lost to us."

In speaking of Roma, Marcellinus had used the word "we." He blinked. He might not be lost to Roma, perhaps, but he was temporarily lost for words.

Regaining his composure, he said, "When you do tell them, you should address a full council of the elders and chiefs of Cahokia. They should hear it directly from you, not Tahtay."

The Imperator barely glanced at him. "Perhaps. If we're still at peace by then."

The ghost of a smile flitted across Agrippa's face. Marcellinus paused, then nodded.

So there it was. The minutes-old agreement between Roma and Cahokia was the most fragile of treaties. One that Hadrianus clearly would not hesitate to break the first moment it was in Roma's interests to do so.

The Romans were the wolf at the door, and for better or worse, Cahokia had invited them in.

EPILOGUE

YEAR SEVEN, FLOWER MOON

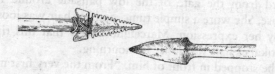

"May I come up?"

In Roman armor, Marcellinus stood at the base of Sintikala's mound. He knew she was there. He had seen her hearth fire from the first plateau of the Great Mound, where he had just been talking with Tahtay and Enopay.

Perhaps she had not heard him. He looked uncertainly at the cedar steps.

"Gaius?" Kimimela appeared at the mound's edge.

"Kimimela?"

"Sintikala says you may come up, but not as a Roman. Leave your shiny armor behind." Kimimela shook her head. "I do not like it either."

"I cannot," Marcellinus said.

"Cannot?"

"Sabinus and Agrippa are in the city. And Aelfric, with another tribune and the quartermaster of the Third Parthica, talking with Tahtay and Enopay about grain. I am not completely trusted, and I must not be seen putting aside my Roman armor for Cahokian clothing."

"Aelfric is a Roman again, too?"

"He is on probation with Decinius Sabinus." Marcellinus did not mention that Sabinus hoped to use the Briton one day to command Cahokian auxiliaries.

Kimimela swallowed. "Come, then."

Marcellinus ascended the stairs slowly, aware of the

clink of steel at his shoulders and hips, the gladius that hung from his belt, the weight of the helmet on his head. That, at least, he could forgo. He undid the straps and pulled it off, then thrust it under his arm.

"Come no farther, Praetor."

He halted at the mound's edge. Sintikala walked forward from the gate of the low palisade around her house. She wore a simple tunic, and her hair was loose.

By her expression, Marcellinus knew that this time Sintikala's hair was loose in mourning.

She stopped in front of him. "From the very first moment of the very first day, I knew that if we spared you, you would one day go back to Roma and stand against us."

"I do not stand against you," he said. "And I have not gone back to Roma."

"But you stand with Hadrianus."

Carefully, he said, "Cahokia must help Roma in this or there can be no peace between us."

"And you?"

"I best serve Hesperia by serving Roma. If this is to work at all, I have to stand with them."

"They are forcing him to do this," Kimimela said to Sintikala. "Aren't they, Gaius?"

Sintikala raised her eyebrows.

"They do not force me," Marcellinus said slowly.

"Then why?"

Marcellinus had sworn an oath. And it was only by his keeping that oath that Roma could hold its tenuous peace with Cahokia.

All their fates hung on a knife edge. Any wrong step imperiled him, imperiled Cahokia. Imperiled Sintikala and Kimimela.

Imperiled his family.

"I have no choice, Kimimela. I cannot tell you why."

Sintikala regarded him. "Cannot or will not?"

"Cannot."

Kimimela shook her head. "I do not understand you."

"One day, you will."

She gazed at him for a long, bleak minute. "And maybe one day you will understand what you have done."

"I know already."

"I do not think you do," Kimimela said. "I cannot have a Roman father."

A yawning emptiness opened up beneath him. His voice caught. "Kimi, I was always Roman."

"Not like this."

He swallowed.

"And so you are no longer my father." Her back straight, she turned and strode away.

"Kimimela!" He surged after her, but Sintikala stepped into his path with her hand raised. "Hold," she said, and Marcellinus backed away and lowered his head.

Sintikala gestured after her daughter as she walked down the north side of the mound and disappeared. "See? Another thing broken."

Marcellinus had come prepared for Sintikala's venom. He had not expected her sorrow.

"Not everything is broken. I still keep my oaths."

"Do you? Do you even remember them?"

"Sintikala, the oath I swore to you, I will never break. But I have sworn an oath to Roma, and I must keep that, too."

Her gaze burned him, and his heart weakened and melted. "I'm sorry," he said. "I can't explain, not completely, but this is very important. If it were not—"

She reached up and placed her fingers on his lips, stilling him. "Gaius, I believe you."

He kissed her fingertips. Her eyes widened, and she lifted her hand away.

"You see it in my eyes?" he said.

"In your eyes I see only what I already know."

As so often happened, Marcellinus was lost in her presence. His thoughts stumbled. "How?"

"Gaius, by now I know what you are capable of and what you are not. And if that were not enough, I would have seen it in your face as you watched your daughter walk away."

Kimimela. The hand of despair still clutched at his heart. "Can you explain it to her? Help her understand?"

"I do not think so. Kimimela is her father's daughter."

"Her Iroqua father?"

"Her new father."

Tears pricked him, and he looked away. "I should go."

"Stay," she said softly.

The entreaty in her voice almost broke him. He shook his head. "I must leave Cahokia before dark."

"Why?"

"All the Imperator's men must be gone by then."

"But you—" She stopped and nodded. "You are a Roman again, forever, now?"

"For as long as Roma behaves honorably toward Cahokia."

She looked up at him. "And so now I do not know what to wish for."

Her hands came up, and she reached for him.

Marcellinus leaned away. "We may be being watched."

"I do not care what they see," Sintikala said, and the next moment they were in each other's arms.

She filled his senses and his soul. Her strong beauty overwhelmed him.

"I love you, Sisika. And I love Kimimela."

She slumped against him, and he felt her shaking her head against his chest. "And now you tell me this? Now?"

"You knew before. That, too, you have known for a long time."

Gently she pushed him back. Now she would not meet his eye but closed a fist and knocked lightly on the breastplate over his heart. "Go and serve Roma, Praetor. Roma . . . and the land."

"I will." Marcellinus thought about it, looked down at her again, and said it more emphatically. "I will."

"And remember . . ."

"What?"

"That Cahokian blood beats in you, too." She lifted her arm, and he raised his, and they pressed their skin together where she had cut into them both and mingled their blood.

"I have never forgotten," he said. "I never will."

Sintikala looked up at the Great Mound and to the left toward the city and seemed to come to a decision.

"I love you," she said very slowly and seriously. "I love you, Gaius Marcellinus."

The world stopped around him. A great warmth filled him. His forearm began to shake where it touched hers, and he put his other hand up to her cheek. "Thank you. And thank the gods."

She smiled. "Which ones?"

"Any. All. Sisika—"

Once again she put her fingers on his lips.

Once again he kissed them.

Their forearms slid apart. She glanced up at the mound again, and her lips quirked. "And in the end . . . you got your Hesperian League."

"I did," he said ironically. "Exactly as I intended."

"And sunset is coming."

"Yes."

"I . . ." Sintikala hesitated, then looked up at him, deep into his eyes and into his soul. "Gaius, we have lived through so much, and I wish you could stay here. Tonight. With me."

Suddenly Marcellinus was having difficulty breathing. "I wish that, too. One day . . . perhaps I can."

And then he added, because he had to: "On a day when there are no longer any secrets between us."

Because now this was much bigger than all of them.

To the east and south were the Romans. But far off in the west of Nova Hesperia the Mongol Horde was gathering under Chinggis Khan.

And that was something Marcellinus could tell no one in Cahokia. Not even Sisika.

"Well, then," she said. "I hope that day will come soon."

Marcellinus nodded. "And . . . Sintikala?"

She noted his change of tone. "Yes, Wanageeska?"

He took another breath and lowered his voice still further. "Do not let the Romans have the Cahokian liquid flame. Guard it well. Hide the villages where it is made. Protect the secret."

She nodded. "I understand. And Wanageeska? Do not tell the Romans where the Blackfoot buffalo jump is."

He blinked, surprised. They frowned at each other, and both exhaled at the same moment.

Marcellinus steeled himself and stepped back. "I understand. And so good night, Sintikala, Hawk chief, daughter of chieftain."

She smiled sadly. "Good night, Gaius, Praetor of Roma."

One last time he looked deeply into her eyes and she into his. Then Marcellinus turned and walked away, down the cedar steps of the mound, through the Great Plaza, past the Mound of the Chiefs where Great Sun Man lay in death, and south out of the Great City toward the Roman castra beyond.

ACKNOWLEDGMENTS

The last couple of years have been quite the voyage of discovery, and I'm lucky to have been steered through them by a host of true professionals.

Once again I'd like to extend my thanks and gratitude to my intrepid agent, Caitlin Blasdell of Liza Dawson Associates, and my enthusiastic and extremely sharp editor, Mike Braff at Del Rey/Penguin Random House. *Eagle in Exile* benefited a great deal from their insights, and thanks to their steady guidance and cheerfulness I am a lot closer to being *compos mentis* than I might otherwise have been. Sincere thanks and high fives also go to Alexandra Coumbis and Greg Kubie, media and publicity experts at Penguin Random House, and Miranda Jewess, my editor at Titan Books UK. I'm also grateful to designer and illustrator Simon M. Sullivan for working patiently with me to create the literally fabulous map of Nova Hesperia.

Backing up a few decades, I owe profound thanks to my parents, Peter and Jill Smale, who taught me to read early and thus ensured that I would blow through books rather quickly in my childhood. They later encouraged my faltering steps into my own fictional universes, and even preserved the results. In my writing life and otherwise, they have always been helpful and supportive.

I sincerely appreciate the efforts of my valiant beta readers—Karen Smale, Chris Cevasco, Peter Charron, and Fiona Lehn—who gave generously of their time and smarts to wade through the manuscript and alert me to problems, inconsistencies, and oddities. Each approached the text from a different perspective and provided feedback about different areas, which is just what you want from beta readers. Great stuff.

I'd like to give a general shout-out to the SF writing community, which I've found to be incredibly supportive. Writers near and far, some good personal friends and others distant online acquaintances, have helped me with advice, reassurance, and good sense at various points, sometimes without even knowing they were doing it.

Finally, I'm indebted to my wife, Karen, for encouragement and joy through this entire process. Thanks for taking this journey with me.

APPENDIXES

APPENDIX I:
CAHOKIA AND
THE MISSISSIPPIAN CULTURE

Many people are familiar with the Aztecs and the Maya and the other great civilizations of Mesoamerica. Far fewer seem to know of the thriving and extensive cultures of North America in the centuries before the arrival of European ships.

For over five hundred years the Mississippian civilization dominated the river valleys of eastern North America, building thousands of towns and villages along the Mississippi, the Ohio, and many other rivers. Like the Adena and Hopewell cultures before them, they built mounds by the tens of thousands: conical mounds, ridge mounds, and the distinctive square-sided, flat-topped platform mounds. In all likelihood the founding events of Mississippian culture took place in Cahokia and then radiated out across the continent.

In its heyday Cahokia was a huge city covering over five square miles, occupied by about 20,000 people and containing at least 120 mounds of packed earth and silty clay, many of them colossal. In the twelfth and early thirteenth centuries Cahokia was larger than London, and no city in northern America would be larger until the 1800s. Cahokia's skyline was dominated by the gigantic mound known today as Monks Mound, a thousand feet square at the base and a hundred feet high. Monks Mound had four terraces, and archeological data reveal that it was topped with a large wooden structure 105 feet long and 48 feet wide. This great earthwork and longhouse overlooked a Grand Plaza nearly fifty acres in area, meticulously positioned and leveled with sandy loam fill a foot deep. Cahokia's central 205 acres were protected by a bastioned palisade two miles long and constructed of some 20,000 logs, enclosing the Great Mound and Great Plaza and eighteen other mounds. The downtown area was surrounded by perhaps a dozen residential neighborhoods, some of which had their own plazas. Cahokia was bounded several miles to the west by the Mississippi and to the east by river bluffs of limestone and sandstone, and was surrounded by the floodplains of the American Bottom that allowed the cultivation of maize in vast fields to feed its population.

Much of Cahokia was built in a flurry of dedicated activity around A.D. 1050, but to this day nobody knows why or by whom. The city and its immense mounds are not claimed by any existing tribe or tradition, and no tales about the city's foundation or dissolution have been passed down through oral history. The Illini who lived in the area when white settlers arrived appeared to know little about the mounds and did not claim them or show much interest in them. However, archeologists and ethnographers are reasonably confident that the ancient Cahokians were Siouan-speaking, and I have gone along with that assumption in the Clash of Eagles Trilogy.

We can, however, be certain that the original residents of the Great City did not call it Cahokia. "Cahokia" is actually the name of an Algonquian-speaking tribe that probably did not come to the area until several hundred years after the fall of the city. Nor did the Iroquois call themselves by that name. "Iroquois" is probably a French transliteration of an insulting Huron word for the Haudenosaunee. However, in this case and some others I have used familiar terms to avoid needless obscurity. For the river names, I may be on firmer ground (so to speak). The Mississippi and Missouri rivers are named from the French renderings of the original Algonquian or Siouan words, and the Ohio River was indeed "Oyo" to the Iroquois. "Chesapeake" and "Appalachia" have their roots in Algonquian words.

Even for names that are unambiguously Native American, it is sometimes not clear when those names started to be used. The individual names of the Five Nations of the Iroquois may not have been in wide use before A.D. 1500, although the ancestral Iroquois certainly had a strong cultural tradition by the 1200s and were building longhouses long before that. I also may have anticipated the foundation of the Haudenosaunee League by a few hundred years. Other aspects of the longhouse culture, along with their clothing and weaponry styles, are taken from the historical and archeological record. As far as the "hand-talk" is concerned, the Plains Sign Language did indeed become something of a lingua franca, though perhaps not as early or universally as I have postulated.

Otherwise, in writing the Clash of Eagles series I have tried my best to remain accurate to geographical and archeological ground truth. The size and layout of Cahokia are accurate for the period to such an extent that the geography of the city and its environs has often not so subtly driven the plot. Every mound featured in the book exists, and I placed the Big Warm House and the brickworks and steelworks in open areas where there were no known mounds or buildings. The Circle of the Cedars corresponds to a monumental circle of up to sixty tall cedar marker posts designed as an early calendar, based on seasonal celestial alignments. The established large-scale agriculture and fishing, available natural resources, food types and weaponry, pottery and basketry, and so forth, are as accurate as I can make them. Granaries, houses, hearths, storage pits, and so on, all match current archeological findings. Chunkey was a real game. The clothing depicted is true to the times, including details of Great Sun Man's regalia and his copper ear spools of the Long-Nosed God; much of what later would become stereotypical Native American clothing, including large feather war bonnets and extensive beadwork, probably originated centuries after Cahokia.

We have much less detailed knowledge of the social structure of ancient Cahokia, and extrapolation can be dangerous. Although Hernando de Soto found strongly hierarchical chiefdoms with a complex caste system in his 1539–1543 expedition to southeastern areas at the tail end of the Mississippian era, it does not follow that those social systems were universal. In fact, in Cahokia's case the evidence may point the other way—to a heterarchy of diverse organizations within the city. I have assumed a pragmatic, rather nonhierarchical structure for Cahokia rather than the superstitious and ritual-bound structures that some postulate for such societies.

Clearly, I have given the Hesperians credit for a few additional technological achievements. Native flying machines are unsupported by the archeological record, although because they are made of sticks, skins, and sinew and wrecked Catanwakuwa and Wakinyan are ceremonially dismantled and often burned, we might not find their remains even if they had existed. However, birds and flying were highly revered in the cultures of the Americas before the European invasion. Hawks, falcons, and thunderbirds were venerated and are central motifs observed throughout ancient American cultures. There is evidence for a falcon warrior ideology in Cahokia and also strong suggestions that the birdman cult originated in Cahokia before spreading across the Mississippian world. Feathered capes, birdmen, and falconoid symbolism abounded. Bird eyes, wings, and tails are extremely common iconography on pots, chunkey stones, and other items. In many Native American traditional stories, key figures are able to fly.

Catanwakuwa and Wakinyan may be a stretch, but oddly, I may be on slightly safer ground with the Sky Lanterns. Although this is speculative, it has been suggested that balloons may have been feasible for peoples of a Mississippian technology level. Julian Nott, a prominent figure in the modern ballooning movement, has pointed out that the people who created the Nazca lines in pre-Inca Peru had all the necessary technologies and materials to create balloons. To prove his point he has constructed and flown a hot air balloon with a bag consisting of 600 pounds of cotton fabric made in the pre-Columbian style, launched and powered by burning logs, with a gondola constructed of wood and reeds. For the Cahokians, the cotton would have been the key. Cotton grows only weakly in Illinois north of the Ohio River and can be wiped out easily by frost, so realistically their cotton would have to be imported from the south. But since the Cahokian trading network extended to the Gulf of Mexico, this would have been at least possible.

The Mourning War is an authentic idea, with many historical examples of long-standing feuds and territorial disputes between native peoples of North America. Although there is no direct evidence of such a large-scale and pervasive feud between the Mississippian and Haudenosaunee nations, there is archeological support for an increase in the palisading of towns and villages from A.D. 1200 on in those cultures and also in Algonquian territory. Clearly, these peoples were not establishing such vigorous defenses just for fun. And although people nowadays tend to associate the practice of scalping with the colonial wars, it was in fact a form of violence frequently perpetrated long before the arrival of Europeans.

The Iroquois were noted for their competence in the lethal arts. However, there are no grounds for believing them responsible for the deaths of the Cahokian women buried in Mound 72 (the Mound of the Women), as Great Sun Man tells Marcellinus. In our world, those women probably perished as part of a home-grown ritualized killing. In reality the women may not even have been from Cahokia; their teeth and bones are more typical of people originating from the satellite towns and eating poorer diets.

Just in case there is any doubt, the People of the Hand include the ancestral Pueblo peoples at the tail end of the Great House culture centered in Chaco Canyon, and the People of the Sun are the postclassic Mayan culture.

Many of Cahokia's mounds still remain, and walking among them inspires awe. The Cahokia Mounds State Historic Site is just across the Mississippi from modern St. Louis, Missouri. It is well worth a visit and, failing that, can be investigated on the Web at www.cahokia mounds.org.

APPENDIX II:
THE CAHOKIAN YEAR

The approximate correspondence between the Julian calendar and the Cahokian moons and festivals is as follows:

JANUARIUS	Snow Moon
FEBRUARIUS	Hunger Moon
MARTIUS	Crow Moon
LIBERALIA	Spring Planting Festival
APRILIS	Grass Moon
MAIUS	Planting Moon
JUNIUS	Flower Moon
VESTALIA	Midsummer Feast
JULIUS	Heat Moon
AUGUSTUS	Thunder Moon
SEPTEMBER	Hunting Moon
SOL SISTERE	Harvest Festival
OCTOBER	Falling Leaf Moon
NOVEMBER	Beaver Moon
DECEMBER	Long Night Moon
BRUMA	Midwinter Feast

In Cahokia, the exact dates of spring, midsummer, harvest, and midwinter are determined by the position of the sun on the horizon at sunrise and sunset, as measured from the Circle of the Cedars.

In order to maintain the alignment of the lunar cycles with the annual solar cycle, a thirteenth month is added into the Cahokian calendar every three years. This is the *Dancing Moon*. As its name implies, the Dancing Moon can be inserted into the Cahokian calendar at the most convenient time, as chosen by the shamans.

Other ceremonies and celebrations occur during the Cahokian year but are scheduled when the signs, time, and weather are right, at times that may appear arbitrary to the uninitiated.

APPENDIX III:
NOTES ON THE MILITARY OF THE
ROMAN IMPERIUM IN A.D. 1218

After the death of Septimius Severus in A.D. 211, the bloody civil war between his sons Caracalla and Geta nearly destroyed the Imperium. No one then alive could have foreseen that that decadelong firestorm would forge a new, stronger Roma that would last another thousand years.

Once the turbulence subsided and the rebuilding began, Roma's new Imperator and Senate did their utmost to prevent such a calamity from ever happening again. A thoughtful and intelligent Imperator, Geta proposed a number of civil reforms designed to limit his own powers and those of his successors, and having lived in terror of the vicious and predatory Caracalla for the previous ten years, the Senate was only too happy to pass those reforms into law. By and large Geta succeeded in stabilizing the Imperium and returning it to its former greatness, but further military reforms were needed in the centuries that followed to prevent the Roman army from growing too strong and again playing a political role. Key to the successful preservation of the Pax Romana was deterring individual legions from aligning themselves with pretenders to the Imperial throne. This had the useful secondary effect of strengthening Roma's borders against the threats of barbarian invasion.

And so by A.D. 1218 the army has been re-formed and streamlined while maintaining those elements which enabled Roma to establish a mighty Imperium in the first place. The legionary structure is largely intact, but mobility between ranks and the assignation of commanding officers is now almost entirely merit-based, reducing the opportunities for ambitious young consuls or governors to seize control of their local legions and mount a bid for the Imperial purple. Rather than being kept separate, legionaries and auxiliaries are combined within their cohorts and considered equal members of their units, reducing the risk of mutiny. Finally, officers and soldiers are now permitted to marry and to take leave between campaigns, and they receive sizable bonuses in money and land upon honorable retirement from the army.

APPENDIX IV:
GLOSSARY OF MILITARY TERMS FROM THE ROMAN IMPERIUM

A glossary of Roman terms, Latin translations, and military terminology appears below. Many aspects of Roman warfare have remained unchanged since classical times, but language does evolve, and in a few cases the meanings of words have migrated from their original usage in the Republic and the early Empire.

Ala: Cavalry unit or "wing." An ala quingenaria consists of 512 troopers in sixteen turmae; an ala milliaria consists of 768 troopers in twenty-four turmae (plural: alae).

Aquila: The Eagle, the standard of a Roman legion. Often golden or gilded and carried proudly into battle; the loss of an Eagle is one of the greatest shames that can befall a legion.

Aquilifer: Eagle bearer; the legionary tasked with carrying the legion's standard into battle (plural: aquiliferi).

Auxiliaries: Noncitizen troops in the Roman army, drawn from peoples in the provinces of the Imperium. Career soldiers trained to the same standards as legionaries, they can expect to receive citizenship at the end of their twenty-five-year service. Originally kept in their own separate units, auxiliary infantrymen have now been integrated into the regular legionary cohorts.

Ballista: Siege engine; a tension- or spring-powered catapult that fires bolts, arrows, or other pointy missiles of wood and metal. Resembles a giant crossbow and often is mounted in a wooden frame or carried in a cart.

Braccae: Celtic woolen trousers, held up with a drawstring.

Caligae: Heavy-soled military marching boots with an open sandal-like design.

Cardo: Colloquial term for the wide main street oriented north-south in Roman cities, military fortresses, and marching camps (more formally known as the Via Praetoria for the southern part and the Via Decumana for the northern part).

Castra: Military marching camp; temporary accommodation for a legion, often rebuilt each night on the march.

Centurion: Professional army officer in command of a century.

Century: Army company, ideally eighty to a hundred men.

Close order: Infantry formation, with men massed at a separation often as small as eighteen inches, making a phalanx or another close formation difficult to penetrate or break up.

Cohort: Tactical unit of a Roman legion; each cohort consists of six centuries. Sometimes the First Cohort in a legion is double-strength.

Cohortes equitate: Mixed units of cavalry and infantry that train together, generally consisting of either six centuries and four turmae or ten centuries and eight turmae or some other combination with a similar ratio of foot soldiers to cavalrymen.

Contubernium: Squad of eight legionaries who serve together, bunk together in a single tent (in a castra) or building (in a fortress barracks), and often are disciplined together for infractions (plural: contubernia).

Cornicen: Junior Roman officer who signals orders to centuries and legions by using a trumpet or cornet.

Corvus: Literally, "crow"; wide gangplank or rotating bridge that anchors a Roman warship to the bank with a heavy metal spike or can be embedded into the deck of an enemy vessel so it can be boarded.

Cuneus: Literally, "wedge" or "pig's head"; dense military formation used to smash through an enemy's battle line or break through a gap.

Decurion: Professional army officer in command of a turma of cavalrymen. Roughly equivalent in rank to a centurion.

Dignitas: Dignity.

Duplicarius: A decurion's deputy, second in command of a turma.

Forum: Public square or plaza, often a marketplace.

Gladius: Roman sword (plural: gladii).

Greek fire: Liquid incendiary, probably based on naphtha and/or sulfur, although the recipe was lost in Europa and is a closely guarded secret in Nova Hesperia.

Imago: Image, copy, ancestral likeness. The image of the current Imperator displayed on a standard or banner.

Imperator: Emperor; Roman commander in chief.

Imperium: Empire; executive power, the sovereignty of the state.

Intervallum: Walkway or area just inside the exterior fortifications of a castra; in other words, the space between the ramparts and the blocks of tents or barracks.

Lares: Roman household gods, domestic deities, guardians of the hearth.

Legate: Senior commander of a legion, more completely known as legatus legionis. By the thirteenth century, "legate" and "Praetor" are synonymous.

Legion: Army unit of several thousand men consisting of ten cohorts, each of six centuries.

Legionary: Professional soldier in the Roman army. A Roman citizen, highly trained, who serves for twenty-five years.

Medicus: Military doctor, field surgeon, or orderly (plural: medici).

Onager: Siege engine; torsion-powered, single-armed catapult that launches rocks or other nonpointy missiles. Literally translates to "wild ass" because of its bucking motion when fired. Often mounted in a square wooden frame.

Open order: Infantry formation, with soldiers in battle lines separated by up to six feet and often staggered, providing room to maneuver, shoot arrows, throw pila or swing gladii, and switch or change ranks.

Orbis: Literally, "circle"; a defensive military formation in the shape of a circle or square, adopted when under attack from a numerically superior force.

Patrician: Aristocratic, upper-class or ruling-class Roman citizen.

Peristylium: Within a Roman building, a courtyard open to the sky, often surrounded by a portico with columns or pillars.

Pilum: Roman heavy spear or javelin (plural: pila).

Porta Praetoria: South gate of a legionary fortress or castra, leading onto the Via Praetoria (or Cardo).

Praetor: Roman general, commander of a legion or of an entire army. In the Republic and early Empire the term was also used for some senior magistrates and consuls; the latter usage has died out by the time of Hadrianus III, and only legionary commanders are referred to as Praetors.

Praetorium: Praetor's tent within a castra or residence within a legionary fortress, situated at the center of the encampment.

Principia: Legionary headquarters building, situated at or near the center of a legionary fortress.

Pugio: Dagger carried by legionaries; Roman stabbing weapon.

Roma: The city of Roma, capital of the Roman Imperium, although often used as shorthand to mean the Imperium as a whole.

Sagum: Military cloak made of a rectangular piece of heavy wool and fastened with a clasp at the shoulder.

Scutum: Roman legionary shield (plural: scuta).

Senior Centurion: Also known as the primus pilus. The most experienced and highly valued centurion in the legion, he commands the first century within the First Cohort.

Signum: A century's standard, usually consisting of a number of metal disks and other insignia mounted on a pole (plural: signa).

Spatha: Roman long sword, often used by cavalry (plural: spathae).

Subura: Notorious slum and red-light district within the Urbs Roma.

Testudo: Literally, "tortoise"; Roman infantry formation in which soldiers in close order protect themselves by holding shields over their heads and around them, enclosing them within a protective roof and wall of metal.

Tribune: Roman officer, midway in rank between the legion commander and his centurions. Originally a more generalized military staff officer; by A.D. 1218 the tribunes have administrative and operational responsibilities for specific cohorts within their legion.

Triplex acies: Three-line battle formation.

Turma: Squadron of cavalry, subunit of an ala. One turma consists of thirty troopers and two officers (a decurion and a duplicarius) (plural: turmae).

Urbs: City.

Via Decumana: Northern part of the Cardo; wide north-south main street of a legionary fortress extending from the Principia to the north gate.

Via Praetoria: Southern part of the Cardo; wide north-south main street of a legionary fortress extending from the south gate to the Principia.

Via Principalis: Wide lateral street of a legionary fortress, extending from the west gate to the east gate and passing in front of the Principia and Praetorium.

Vigiles: Literally "watchmen"; firefighters and police of Rome and other large cities.

APPENDIX V:
FURTHER READING

In addition to the books listed in the Further Reading section of *Clash of Eagles*, I found the following useful in researching and writing *Eagle in Exile*:

Stephen Ambrose, *Undaunted Courage: Meriwether Lewis, Thomas Jefferson, and the Opening of the American West*, 1997.

Nancy Marie Brown, *The Far Traveler: Voyages of a Viking Woman*, 1988.

Duncan B. Campbell and Brian Delf, *Roman Legionary Fortresses, 27 BC–AD 378*, 2006.

Ross Cowan and Angus McBride, *Imperial Roman Legionary AD 161–284*, 2003.

Ross Cowan and Angus McBride, *Roman Legionary 58 BC–AD 69*, 2003.

Raffaele D'Amato and Giuseppe Rava, *Roman Centurions 31 BC–AD 500: The Classical and Late Empire*, 2012.

Dayton Duncan and Ken Burns, *Lewis & Clark: The Journey of the Corps of Discovery*, 1997.

John C. Ewers, *The Blackfeet: Raiders on the Northwestern Plains*, 1983.

Nic Fields, Donato Spedaliere, and S. Sulemsohn Spedaliere, *Hadrian's Wall AD 122–410*, 2003.

Tim Flannery, *The Eternal Frontier: An Ecological History of North America and Its Peoples*, 2002.

Lynn V. Foster, *Handbook to Life in the Ancient Maya World*, 2005.

George Franklin, *Cannibalism, Headhunting and Human Sacrifice in North America: A History Forgotten*, 2008.

Horatio Hale, *The Iroquois Book of Rites*, 1883.

Jason Hook and Richard Hook, *The American Plains Indians*, 1985.

Elias Johnson, *Traditions and Laws of the Iroquois*, 1881.

Michael Johnson and Richard Hook, *American Indians of the Southeast*, 1995.

Michael Johnson and Jonathan Smith, *Tribes of the Iroquois Confederacy*, 2003.

Michael Johnson and Jonathan Smith, *North American Indian Tribes of the Great Lakes*, 2011.

George E. Lankford, *Reachable Stars: Patterns in the Ethnoastronomy of Eastern North America*, 2007.

Charles Godfrey Leland, *Algonquin Legends of New England*, 1898.

Meriwether Lewis and William Clarke, *The Journals of Lewis and Clarke*, undated.

James Bovell Mackenzie, *A Treatise on the Six-Nation Indians*, undated.

Castle McLaughlin, *Arts of Diplomacy: Lewis and Clarke's Indian Collection*, 2003.

Lee Sandlin, *Wicked River: The Mississippi When It Last Ran Wild*, 2011.

Paul Schneider, *Old Man River: The Mississippi River in North American History*, 2013.

Quinta Scott, *The Mississippi: A Visual Biography*, 2009.

Mark Twain, *Life on the Mississippi*, 1863.

Jack Weatherford, *Indian Givers*, 1989.

Gaius's adventures in Nova Hesperia continue in

EAGLE AND EMPIRE

Read on for an exclusive first look
at the third volume of Alan Smale's thrilling
Clash of Eagles Trilogy

Coming in 2017 from Del Rey Books!

CHAPTER 3

YEAR EIGHT, THUNDER MOON

As the *Concordia* pulled in at the Longhouse of the Ship, Napayshni stepped out with the rope to moor the drekar. He still limped from the wound he had received fighting the Panther clan of the Shappa Ta'atani years before. The rowers shipped their oars and stood to stretch their weary arms and shoulders.

A lone brave was racing down the rearward slope of the Great Mound. From his fleetness of foot and his red sash, Marcellinus knew him for Tahtay. As soon as they caught sight of him the Blackfoot warriors whooped and vaulted out of the longship to sprint toward him. They moved astonishingly fast, despite the cloying humidity of high summer.

Now Marcellinus could see two Blackfoot elders sitting more sedately in the stern, and alongside them the stooped figure of the headman of the Hidatsa, the chieftain who two years before had permitted them to go on the Plains buffalo hunt that had led them to Tahtay. The headman's price for this assistance had been to see the Great City before he died, and Cahokia paid its debts. Beside him stood Sooleawa, buffalo-caller of the Hidatsa, in her elkskin dress and hairband of buffalo hide, her loose black hair blowing freely in the Hidatsa style.

Now they stepped ashore, moving their heads back and forth almost comically. They resembled nothing so much as Roman farmers from the sticks stepping into the marbled Forum for the first time.

Tahtay and the Blackfoot warriors met halfway between the foot of the Mound and Cahokia Creek, and an involuntary dance of glee broke out. Marcellinus smiled. Tahtay had grown so serious since the Romans arrived. Even with Taianita and Dustu often by his side he had so few friends, so few opportunities for release, that it was a joy to see him with his Fire Heart brothers.

However, when Tahtay summoned Marcellinus just after the evening meal, his face was stony enough to grind corn. Marcellinus walked into the war chief's house on the flat top of the Mound of the Sun to find Tahtay sitting with Enopay, Taianita, Dustu, and the Blackfoot warriors and elders around a mess of bowls of corn, fish bones, hazelnut cakes, and tea. The Blackfoot warriors studied Marcellinus intently, their elders ignored him, Taianita lolled back frowning, and Enopay wouldn't meet his eye at all.

Marcellinus was wearing a Cahokian tunic. Tahtay shook his head. "Dress in your Roman clothes. We go to Hadrianus."

"Now, Tahtay? Why?"

Tahtay stared at him with dead eyes. "There is trouble in the west. Fetch your Roman tunic and cloak, and come back."

Marcellinus drew himself up and saluted. "Yes, sir."

Something was very wrong. The Blackfoot had brought news, and it was not good.

Romans ate later in the evening than Cahokians, and the Imperator and Praetors dined even later than their men, and so Marcellinus and the others arrived at the Praetorium building of the Third Parthica to find Hadrianus still at table. Tahtay requested entry courteously enough, his face now more sad than angry.

They were just three: Tahtay, Taianita, and Marcellinus. A fourth, a Blackfoot friend of Tahtay's, had helped paddle the canoe the half mile across the Mizipi, but he had stayed with the boat. Neither of the Cahokians had spoken to Marcellinus during the journey, and he felt very much at a disadvantage as they were ushered into the Imperial presence by a Praetorian in full armor. He was surprised that Tahtay had brought Taianita, and discomfited that the war chief had not included Sintikala, Chenoa, or Kanuna, Cahokians with far more gravitas.

Hadrianus looked just as surprised to see them. Decinius Sabinus was there, along with two tribunes Marcellinus did not know. He breathed a quiet sigh of relief that Agrippa was apparently dining in his own castra. Whatever was going on, it would surely be easier to resolve without the Praetor of the 27th in attendance.

"Tahtay and Taianita, welcome," said the Imperator. "An unexpected pleasure. And Gaius Marcellinus."

"Caesar." Marcellinus bowed.

Decinius Sabinus got to his feet and bowed to Taianita, who smiled coyly back at him. Marcellinus blinked. Both men knew her?

Hadrianus waved at the table behind him. "You will take wine?"

"I will," Tahtay said to Marcellinus's surprise, and moved to the table himself to pour. Equally unexpectedly, Taianita strolled over to the Imperator's couch and perched on the end of it. Neither Hadrianus, Sabinus, nor his two tribunes reacted to this overfamiliarity, and with a moment of shock Marcellinus realized that the Tahtay and Taianita were now more frequent visitors to the Imperator's table than he might have supposed.

Tahtay brought wine-and-water to Marcellinus, handed a beaker to Taianita, then turned to the Imperator. "And so, Hadrianus, my friend, once again you have lied to me."

The Imperator's face was slightly red. It was not the drink, but the blazing Hesperian sun of high summer. His sunburn and quizzical smile made him look a little comical. "Never before have I met a man who owned as little trust as you, Tahtay of Cahokia."

Tahtay gave a short sharp laugh. "Trust? You say so? Futete!"

"Certainly." Hadrianus raised his cup in toast. "As best I recall, I have not broken a promise to you this entire moon."

"Huh." Tahtay sipped his wine, and for a moment seemed lost in thought. Then he nodded and spoke. "I am much saddened, Caesar. Truly, my heart grieves. Despite all the pain and violence between our peoples, over recent months I had begun to have hope. I had thought perhaps we were finally coming to an understanding, you and I. That this might not all end in bloodshed and ruin between your Romans and my people. But that is not so, is it?"

Sabinus looked wary. Hadrianus's smile faded. "Tahtay, you will need to stop speaking in riddles if you expect me to answer."

"There are many more Romans than you have told us of," said Tahtay. "Many, many more. You have tried to delude me into believing your army will one day march away into the Grass, but they have shown few signs of doing so. And today I know why. It is because other Roman legions have already arrived, far to the west past the great rocky mountains, and there they have slain thousands upon thousands of Hesperians and enslaved the rest. The rivers are running with blood, Caesar. The Land itself is weeping."

Tahtay stood upright, his face calm and his body controlled, but Marcellinus knew he must be surging with strong emotions to be using such words.

Taianita drained her wine with a single swallow and held out her beaker impertinently to the Praetorian guardsman who stood by the wall. After a moment Decinius nodded, and the soldier stepped forward to refill it.

Meanwhile, Hadrianus and his Praetor and tribunes sat so still that they might have been carved in stone. Tahtay nodded. "From your eyes I see that I am right."

Now the Imperator leaned forward, his expression intent. "Where are they, these new armies you speak of? How do you know of them?"

"I am a savage," Tahtay said brutally. "I am a barbarian. I am a redskin. So you call me, and perhaps I am. But I am not a fool, Caesar. Far from it. I can see that you have long known of this, and that confirmation is all I needed." He drained his beaker and tossed it aside, and it clattered across the floor. "I must go and summon the clan chiefs and elders and decide what must be done. Because if Roma has already taken the west, you have lied to me from the very start. You have no need to leave Cahokia. Ever. And that, Cahokia cannot tolerate."

Taianita finished her second beaker and stood, swaying slightly. In Latin made broken by wine she said, "Good night, Caesar. I hope you happy with what done. For this will end bad. Bad." In hand-talk, she gestured *Many deaths.* "Tahtay is spoken."

"Wait, Tahtay, Taianita." Hadrianus swung his legs off the couch. "I beg of you: Tell me what you know. I am in earnest. Please answer me."

Tahtay's brow furrowed. He said nothing.

"You may tell him, Gaius Marcellinus."

Marcellinus looked carefully at his Imperator. "You release me from the oath I swore to you, before Roma and Cahokia buried the ax?"

"Yes, yes, Marcellinus; you may speak candidly to Tahtay of Cahokia about the threat we face. Perhaps he will believe it more readily from you."

Still Marcellinus hesitated. "Perhaps we should call a council of the elders. All should—"

Tahtay spun and fixed him with a glare. "*Merda,* Hotah! Tell me *now!*"

"They are not Romans," Marcellinus said. "The armies that have landed on Hesperia's western shores are Roma's implacable enemy, and will soon become enemies of Cahokia as they sweep across the Land destroying all in their path."

Tahtay eyed him unblinking. Marcellinus went on. "They are called Mongols, and they are utterly ruthless.

They come from a continent we call Asia, far across the ocean to the west. In Asia the Mongols have already defeated many nations—great kingdoms, territories of mighty chiefs, in all as broad in extent as the Land from the Mizipi to the Atlanticus."

Decinius Sabinus nodded, but everyone else in the room still stood or sat as if frozen. Marcellinus continued. "Caesar and his armies have fought long wars with the Mongols in Asia, trying to hold their armies in check and prevent them from sweeping over Europa and sacking its cities. Tahtay, I swear the truth of this to you. The Mongols are great warriors. They fight on horses, the same four-legs the Romans use. Their war chief, Chinggis Khan, is here to command his armies in person, just as Caesar commands the armies of Roma. And if the Mongols have already taken the whole western coast of Hesperia, and if the Blackfoot know of them now, it cannot be long before they break out beyond the mountains and come flooding across the prairie to attack us here."

"*Merda* . . ." Taianita frowned into his eyes, a little blearily. "Speak true?"

Marcellinus held her gaze and hand-talked *I speak true. Wanageeska swears.*

Tahtay's eyes were wide. "Hotah, you too have fought these Mongols?"

"No." Marcellinus had faced the armies of Kara Khitai, who were steppe warriors of a similar vein to the Mongols, and he had partnered with the Chernye Klobuki and Polovtsians of southern Rus in his battles with some of the principalities of Kiev, Galicia, and Volhynia. He was familiar enough with the horsemen of Asia, but he had never seen the armies of the Great Khan in battle. "But about the Mongols you may believe these men of Roma, and what they say."

"Asia is a *huge* land," said Decinius Sabinus. "Marcellinus may be too cautious on this score. The sum of the Mongol homelands, added to their conquests of the Jin and Song Empires, may well be larger in extent than *all* of Nova Hesperia. And when the Mongols swept over the Asian lands, before we beat them back, they must have slain twenty million people. That is twenty thousand-thousand." He looked at Hadrianus. "More, you think?"

The Imperator shrugged. "Who's to say? Millions upon millions of the Song alone."

"Why? Why?" Tahtay shook his head. "It makes no sense. What would such men want? We do not know them. Why would they attack us?"

"Because that is what the Mongols do, Tahtay. They kill and destroy, and they take. They conquer."

Marcellinus shook his head and addressed his remarks to Tahtay again. "War chief, we must hold a council. The Imperator and his Praetors, and myself, and you and your elders and clan chiefs. We must prepare for the Mongols. All of us together, as one."

Wei, NXei, Lleeqhez. And when the Mongols form
over the Asian lands, before we are aware, they
numbers slain twenty million people, that is, why
thousand thousand. He looked at tradition, saying
was that?"

The Emperor stopped. "Who is to say? Millions
on millions. Choose anhuu..."

"So? Who?" said the emperor, his brow. "It makes no
sense. What would such impudence? We are those
them. We would not attack us."

Syseng... that is what the Nestudu... somewhere. Unless they
did the caring and the... rate." They conquer.

Marcellius smiled as he read and addressed his remarks
to Tanley again, "When he gave this, both reconciled
the Emperor and the Pacifico, and myself, and you
and vanquished individuals. We have made peace in the
Mongol. All of us together as one.